THE DAUGHTER OF ADOPTION

broadview editions
series editor: L.W. Conolly

For Ilse Thompson

THE DAUGHTER OF ADOPTION

A TALE OF MODERN TIMES

John Thelwall

edited by
Michael Scrivener, Yasmin Solomonescu, and Judith Thompson

broadview editions

Library and Archives Canada Cataloguing in Publication

Thelwall, John, 1764-1834
     The daughter of adoption : a tale of modern times / John Thelwall ; edited by Michael Scrivener, Yasmin Solomonescu, and Judith Thompson.

First published in 1801 under pseudonym John Beaufort.
Includes bibliographical references.
ISBN 978-1-55481-063-5

     I. Scrivener, Michael Henry, 1948- II. Solomonescu, Yasmin
III. Thompson, Judith Asta, 1957- IV. Title.

PR3729.T4D38 2013   823'.6   C2012-908231-7

Broadview Editions
The Broadview Editions series represents the ever-changing canon of literature in English by bringing together texts long regarded as classics with valuable lesser-known works.

Advisory editor for this volume: Michel W. Pharand

Broadview Press is an independent, international publishing house, incorporated in 1985.

We welcome comments and suggestions regarding any aspect of our publications—please feel free to contact us at the addresses below or at broadview@broadviewpress.com.

North America
Post Office Box 1243, Peterborough, Ontario, Canada K9J 7H5
2215 Kenmore Avenue, Buffalo, NY, USA 14207
Tel: (705) 743-8990; Fax: (705) 743-8353
email: customerservice@broadviewpress.com

UK, Europe, Central Asia, Middle East, Africa, India, and Southeast Asia
Eurospan Group, 3 Henrietta St., London WC2E 8LU, United Kingdom
Tel: 44 (0) 1767 604972; Fax: 44 (0) 1767 601640
email: eurospan@turpin-distribution.com

Australia and New Zealand
NewSouth Books
c/o TL Distribution, 15-23 Helles Ave., Moorebank, NSW, Australia 2170
Tel: (02) 8778 9999; Fax: (02) 8778 9944
email: orders@tldistribution.com.au

www.broadviewpress.com

Broadview Press acknowledges the financial support of the Government of Canada through the Canada Book Fund for our publishing activities.

This book is printed on paper containing 50% post-consumer fibre.

Typesetting and assembly: True to Type Inc., Claremont, Canada.

PRINTED IN CANADA

Contents

Acknowledgements • 7
Introduction • 9
John Thelwall and His World: A Brief Chronology • 35
A Note on the Text • 37

The Daughter of Adoption; A Tale of Modern Times • 43

Appendix A: Biographical Documents • 483
  1. From John Thelwall, "Prefatory Memoir," *Poems, Chiefly Written in Retirement* (1801) • 483
  2. From John Thelwall to Susan Thelwall (18 July 1797) • 486
  3. From John Thelwall to Dr. Peter Crompton (3 March 1798) • 486
  4. From John Thelwall, *A Letter to Francis Jeffray* [sic], *Esq.* (1804) • 487
  5. From Samuel Taylor Coleridge, *Specimens of the Table Talk of the Late Samuel Taylor Coleridge* (1835) • 488
  6. From William Wordsworth to Henrietta Cecil Thelwall (16 November 1838) • 488
  7. From William Wordsworth, Notes Dictated to Isabella Fenwick, first published as Notes in the *Poetical Works* (1857) • 489

Appendix B: Contextual Documents • 491
  1. Literature and Education • 491
    a. From Henry Fielding, *The History of Tom Jones, a Foundling* (1749) • 491
    b. From Thomas Day, *The History of Sandford and Merton* (1783-89) • 494
    c. From John Thelwall, *The Peripatetic* (1793) • 499
    d. From Richard and Maria Edgeworth, *Practical Education* (1801) • 502
    e. From John Thelwall, *Introductory Discourse on the Nature and Objects of Elocutionary Science* (1805) • 506
    f. From John Thelwall, "The Historical and Oratorical Society," *A Letter to Henry Cline* (1810) • 508
  2. The West Indies and the Abolition Debate • 510
    a. From John Thelwall, "The Connection between the Calamities of the Present Reign, and the System of Borough-Mongering Corruption," *The Tribune* (1795-96) • 510
    b. From John Thelwall, *Rights of Nature, against the Usurpations of Establishments* (1796) • 511
    c. From Baron de Wimpffen, *A Voyage to Saint Domingo, in the Years 1788, 1789, and 1790* (1797) • 514
    d. From Bryan Edwards, *An Historical Survey of the French Colony in the Island of St. Domingo* (1798) • 516
    e. From John Thelwall, "The Negro's Prayer," *Monthly Magazine* (April 1807) • 521

3. The Revolution Debate • 522
   a. From Mary Wollstonecraft, *A Vindication of the Rights of Woman* (1792) • 522
   b. From William Godwin, *An Enquiry Concerning Political Justice, and Its Influence on Morals and Happiness* (1798) • 527

Appendix C: Reviews of *The Daughter of Adoption* • 533
   1. *Critical Review* (February 1801) • 533
   2. *Monthly Magazine* (20 July 1801) • 534
   3. *Monthly Review* (August 1801) • 534
   4. *Annals of Philosophy* (1801) • 535
   5. Thelwall's Reply to the Reviews, from "Prefatory Memoir," *Poems, Chiefly Written in Retirement* (1801) • 535

Works Cited and Recommended Reading • 537

Acknowledgements

We wish to thank the British Library for its copy of the London edition (BL 1154.i.2), and the Harvard Houghton Library for its copy of the Dublin edition (Houghton Harvard Depository 19462.24.75 v.1 & 2). We are profoundly grateful to Ilse Thompson for transcribing the novel.

Introduction

Combining astute sociopolitical analysis with psychological insight, maudlin melodrama, and flat-out farce, John Thelwall's *The Daughter of Adoption; A Tale of Modern Times* takes readers on a panoramic journey of political and personal adventure and critique in which popular narrative conventions of the eighteenth century confront the revolutionary ideas and forms of the Romantic period. Published pseudonymously in 1801, at a transitional moment in his own and England's history, it is the only full-scale novel by a notorious radical writer and orator at the peak of his powers and the nadir of his public reputation.

Virtually forgotten for well over a century except as a footnote to Coleridge, Thelwall was rediscovered by E. P. Thompson in his *The Making of the English Working Class* (1963) and subsequent works, and then by other historians and literary scholars. Now there is at least a generation's worth of articles, dissertation chapters, modern editions, collections of essays, and monographs on one of the most remarkable figures of the Romantic era. This passionate speaker and prolific writer of fiction, drama, poetry, journalism, and various kinds of prose—political, medical, and pedagogical—is done a great disservice by the concept of "literature" as a separate category of writing that is divorced from speech and performance, and considered more "creative" and less tainted by historical contingencies than other print genres. For the duration of Thelwall's life, "literature" still signified writing in general, everything from sonnets to sermons and political speeches to lyrical dramas, and it was integrally connected to a lively culture of conversation and public performance. At a time of increasing intellectual specialization, Thelwall was a man of letters and a man of action, with great intellectual range. The son of a London silk mercer, the lower-middle-class Thelwall did not attend university, but he acquired another kind of education as an apprentice, journalist, radical orator, and speech therapist. Accordingly, he brought to the role of man of letters social experiences that inevitably shaped literary expression.

Few contributed more than Thelwall to the democratic reform movement from the 1780s to the 1830s. In the 1790s he was the most important radical lecturer in England, the London Corresponding Society's most popular orator, the third defendant acquitted in the treason trials of 1794, a member of intersecting political and literary circles that included Coleridge and Wordsworth, Godwin and Opie, Hays and Hazlitt, and a victim of relentless political repression that drove him in 1798 to seek a retreat in Llyswen, Wales, where he settled with his family at a small farm and composed *The Daughter of Adoption*. The retreat was not absolute, for he engaged in an energetic correspondence with fellow writers, reformers, and radicals; he was suspected of political agitation even in Wales, and thought it wise to publish his novel under the pseudonym John Beaufort (adopting the name of the nerve centre of London radicalism, the Beaufort Buildings from which he had delivered his political lectures).[1] Shortly after finishing his novel, Thelwall founded the profession in which he is no less important though lesser known, returning to public practice and, eventually, to prosperity and prominence, as a healer of speech impediments, a lecturer on elocution, and proprietor of a Institute for oratory in London's fashionable Lincoln's Inn Fields. He subsequently published three more volumes of poetry, two weekly periodicals, and several works of elocutionary theory. Always outspoken, he once again faced prosecution and persecution in 1820, and once again fell into obscurity, but remained active in local politics and various literary endeavours, and was honoured at the Great Reform Banquet of 1832. He died of "some affection of the heart"[2] on a lecture tour in Bath, on 17 February 1834.

Origins

What we know of the origins of *The Daughter of Adoption* comes chiefly from an appendix to the "Prefatory Memoir" in Thelwall's *Poems, Chiefly Written in Retirement*, also published in 1801 (Appendix A1), which suggests that he began the novel relatively early in his three-year "retirement" in Wales (1798 to 1800), intending to supplement his income from farming in a year of bad harvests. In this he succeeded, receiving an advance from Richard Phillips, publisher of the *Monthly Magazine,* on the strength of its vivid and suspenseful first chapter. The novel was not completed, however, until two years later, "upwards of two thirds" of it having been "hurried through" under the lengthening shadow of despair cast by the "deceitful harvest of the year 1800" (Appendix A1). That bitter harvest included the failure not only of his farming venture, but of the entire reform movement of the 1790s, as well as the resumption of the political persecution he had hoped to escape in Wales, and the apostasy and betrayal of friends including Wordsworth and Coleridge. The coup de grace came at the very end of the decade, with the sudden death of the child in whom he had invested what remained of his hope for the future, his six-year-old daughter, Maria. Whatever his original intentions, *The Daughter of Adoption* was completed as a tribute to her; much like the "Paternal Tears" elegies he was writing at the same time, it was an epitaphic expression of grief and a form of therapy, an act of compensation and a symbolic resuscitation. Maria's loss compounded, and was folded into, the death of Mary Wollstonecraft, whose *Memoir* (written by Thelwall's friend William Godwin) and unfinished novel *The Wrongs of Woman;*

---

1 The pseudonym was fairly transparent; as Southey pointed out in a letter to a friend, "The novel you mention is by John Thelwall, and in the assumed name of Beaufort you may trace the Lecturer in Beaufort Buildings." *New Letters of Robert Southey*, ed. Kenneth Curry, 2 vols (New York: Columbia UP, 1965), 1: 256.
2 From Thelwall's obituary in the *Gentleman's Magazine* ns 2 (1834): 549-50.

or *Maria* he also read at this time. These Mary/Marias shaped his imagined *Daughter* and are combined in its title character and moral centre, Seraphina, whose late entry in Book IV of the novel may be a sign of the disjointed and hurried composition of which he speaks in his "Prefatory Memoir." In spite of this, however, his novel is remarkably coherent and carefully plotted. Its four volumes are divided into an epic twelve books (he was also writing his epic *The Hope of Albion* at this time); each volume contains three books, each three chapters long, and they are interconnected through a network of coincidences, secrets, and sudden revelations that owe as much to Thelwall's passion for the theatre as to his fondness for Fielding's "comic epic poem in prose," *Tom Jones*. Occasional inconsistencies of structure and style are signs of Thelwall's deliberate and hallmark hybridity, and contribute to an underlying ethical-aesthetic pattern that is essential to the novel's therapeutic and reformist aims, for himself and for the nation.

For all its cosmopolitan and melodramatic sweep, Thelwall's *Daughter* reflects the confinement of Thelwall's exile at Llyswen, in which pastoral idyll, political repression, and personal betrayal are inextricably intertwined. From the fatal secrecy and forced silence of its opening pages to the "telescope of espionage" (277) that oversees the complicated conspiracies of its climax and denouement, its plot (in the fullest sense of the word) is informed by the anti-Jacobin persecution and paranoia that forced Thelwall's flight to Wales, and followed him there; it dramatizes the "system of spies and informers" he had diagnosed in his lectures and revisits a central question of those lectures: how to foster and maintain moral agency in the face of secret agency. The picture of Thelwall's life at Llyswen is sharply focussed in Books III and IV with the introduction of the title character and her "recluse and eccentric family [...] of philosophical hermits" in a "country whose beautiful and romantic scenery is an inexhaustible source of contemplation and delights" but whose society leaves them intellectually isolated, as "month sometimes succeeds to month without our having conversed with a single soul beyond our own family" (139, 149). Parkinson's efforts to "unite the useful and the delightful—the picturesque with agricultural improvement" (147) by diverting a stream to build a waterfall near his secluded cottage precisely match Thelwall's "hobbyhorsical industry" in constructing "a cascade of 8 or 9 feet height" and near it, a "rude hermitage" for himself (Appendix A3). The site of Thelwall's cottage itself, on a steep bank overlooking a treacherous double-hairpin bend in the Wye river, is likewise accurately depicted in the eddying pools and furious rapids in which Amanda and Parkinson are swept away while Seraphina and Morton are thrown upon a "romantic ridge" that "frown[s] triumphant over the revolutions of elements that have raged for generations around them" (204). In this allegorical landscape, as in the shipwreck scene of *The Hope of Albion*, Thelwall captures his spiritual state at Llyswen, "pent up in desperate and insulated security!—walled and imprisoned by that hideous torrent which had overwhelmed all that, as yet, was dear to my afflicted soul" (204). The death of his beloved Maria is addressed explicitly in the story of Parkinson's daughter, "cut off—suddenly cut off in the very bloom of heath and cheerfulness. Within a few short days bounding before me in sprightly vigour, all smiles, and grace, and loveliness, and stretched in expiring anguish upon this arm" (154-55). In Parkinson's adoption of Seraphina as not simply a replacement for but "the resurrection of his child" (155), Thelwall merges figurative and literal, fiction and autobiography in an act of complex compensation, displacement, or surrogacy that is announced in his title, exemplified in the secret that initiates the plot (but is not revealed until its end), and articulated most fully in the final scene of revelations and resurrections: "he lives!—he lives again!—my child revives! [...] in thee he is again restored!" (364). The same logic of surrogacy governs another autobiographical scene in Book IX, when Seraphina retreats to a cottage on the outskirts of London that is given the same address, Walcot Place, as the Thelwall family home in Lambeth. Her "lame and aged" hostess, the "Old Lady of the Garden," is based on Thelwall's mother, whose absent son (away on one of his frequent "eccentric" jaunts to mark the "varieties of men and manners") is obviously Thelwall himself (355, 364), who at the time this scene is set, 1792, had set off on one of the "eccentric excursions" that make up his 1793 work *The Peripatetic*. He draws on another personal experience (also alluded to in *The Peripatetic*) in the melodramatic scene in which Henry is waylaid and attacked in the lane to Walcot Place. By having Edmunds disarm and rescue Henry from the ruffian, Thelwall engages in another act of retrospective revisionary therapy, rewriting his life to make himself his own saviour.

Talking Treason

Of the numerous surrogates through whom Thelwall rewrites and redeems his own experience, Edmunds is in some ways the most important, since in his character and friendship with Henry, Thelwall revisits one of the most immediate inspirations for his novel, his galvanizing yet troubled relationship with and visit to Wordsworth and Coleridge in Somerset, which occurred shortly before his retreat to Wales. Critics have long recognized that the philosophical discussion between Henry and Edmunds in the dell at Limbé, in which Edmunds remarks that nature is enough "to make one forget that treason was ever necessary in the world" (142), is Thelwall's version of a well-known conversation also recorded by Coleridge and Wordsworth (Appendix A5-7), that took place during that ten-day visit in July 1797. The description of the "luxuriantly wooded glen" (140) and their meandering approach to it mirrors the landscapes through which he, Coleridge, and Wordsworth walked and talked in the Quantocks (though rendered tropical, thereby anticipating Aldous

Huxley's famous insight into Wordsworthian nature.[1]) But this is only one of several dialogues and debates in a novel that is deeply informed by, and responsive to, Thewall's visit to Alfoxden (and the return visit of Coleridge and Wordsworth to Llyswen a year later), as well as the works of the *annus mirabilis* which it inspired (which include the *Lyrical Ballads* and Coleridge's conversation poems). These debates provide the moral underpinning of a novel that both commemorates and attempts to revive the "literary and political triumvirate" whose shifting positions are variously personified in all the novel's characters.[2]

In the relationship between Henry and Edmunds in particular, Thelwall plays out the homoerotic drama of brotherhood and betrayal in his conflicted friendship with Coleridge, whose "Ode to the Departing Year" is conspicuously quoted at the climax of Book V, followed by a poignant reference to meeting "old friends" with "new faces" at the beginning of Book VI. If Edmunds is a surrogate for Thelwall, then chapter two of that book, in which Edmunds expresses his unrequited love for Seraphina, but seems content to subordinate his desires to the success of an undeserving Henry, may reflect Thelwall's reluctant acceptance of his own marginalization within what would soon become the Wordsworth circle. Like Tristram to Arthur in *The Fairy of the Lake*, he is always the sidekick, never the hero; but he remains loyal to his muse, and the "noble principles" they once shared: "I would labour night and day, with my head and with my hands [...] I would write your history, madam, under some fictitious name, and call it a novel [...] and the only reward that I would ever wish should be the [...] consciousness of having discharged, with fidelity, the functions of an humble friendship" (249).

Thelwall's novel also grows out of, and contributes to, the discussions that would issue in Wordsworth's "Preface" to *Lyrical Ballads*; for example, when the emotions of Amelia and Nerissa "mused themselves into something like tranquillity" (60) or when the effusions of Morton and Seraphina are retraced like Wordsworth's "subtle windings" of "maternal passion" through "the labyrinth of the human heart" (335).

---

1   In his classic, post-Darwinian 1929 essay "Wordsworth in the Tropics," Aldous Huxley famously asserted that Wordsworthian nature worship was impossible in the tropics, where nature was essentially "foreign, appalling, fundamentally and utterly inimical to intruding man [...] always alien and inhuman, and occasionally diabolic." See Huxley, *Do What You Will* (London: Chatto and Windus, 1929), 114. Thelwall's view of nature is closer to that of Erasmus than Charles Darwin, but the shocking collision between pastoral idealism and savage brutality in his portrayal of the tropics is strikingly prescient.

2   For a similar but more developed analysis of the work of the Llyswen period as informed and inspired by Thelwall's "silenced partnership" with Wordsworth and Coleridge, see Judith Thompson, *John Thelwall in the Wordsworth Circle: The Silenced Partner* (New York: Palgrave Macmillan, 2012), to which some of the following is indebted.

But Thelwall's most sustained and important engagement with Wordsworth's poetic theory is in his use of "the real language of men" to explore the "laws of our nature." Farmer Wilson's down-to-earth dignity teaches Henry "what energy there is in simple passion" and "that uneducated nature could be so eloquently moved" (90). Thelwall enters just as deeply as Wordsworth into the feelings of nature, but also lets his common man speak for himself more fully, more philosophically, and often more realistically than in *Lyrical Ballads*, as he develops the Wordsworthian encounter between gentleman and rustic into a sustained meditation upon class, reason, and language that harmonizes with his political and elocutionary lectures.

As much as Wordsworth's poems, Thelwall's novel reflects the experience and theories of a "man speaking to men" who, even as he wrote the novel, was laying the foundations for his new profession based on the same principles that underlay his political writings and lectures: the primacy of "DISCOURSE the sole discriminating attribute of Man—'Destitute of this Power, Reason would be a Solitary and ... unavailing principle'" (Appendix B1e). As a result, his style is an essential part of his message. For all its machinations and conspiracies, the plot of *The Daughter* is based more on speech than on action, shaped and driven by dialogue, much of which is presented dramatically, as in a script. Imitations, appropriations, abuses, and ventriloquism of written and oral style are crucial to the plot, much of which hinges upon forged, duplicated, misdirected, or mixed-up messages; at one point the narrator laments that if Seraphina had only read a letter aloud her ear would have recognized the forgery missed by her fond and hasty eye (368). Falsehoods, verbal facades, and exaggerations are analysed and exploited for comic and satiric effect in the speeches of Nerissa, Melinda, and Moroon, and, like the punning games of crambo played by Henry's "Confederates" in "Dissipation," (291) they reflect the commodification of language and identity in a corrupt society. Plot and character develop through a remarkable variation in speech acts and styles, from the vivid realism of Henry's childhood exchange with his mother, to Nerissa's pretentiously superficial multilingualism, to the simple dignity of rustic and nautical dialect spoken respectively by Farmer Wilson and "honest sailor" Ben, to the "incomparable, incomprehensible, super-anglicized style" of Moroon's hilarious courtship and seduction scenes (332). Even the stereotype pidgin English of Mozambo is varied and dignified by his natural eloquence, as he employs the same oratorical parallelism as Parkinson; and while he and the other slaves roll their eyes, and display other conventional forms of body language, so do Henry and the other European characters. Thelwall's attention to body language, an important feature of his elocutionary theory, is also evident in his attention to breath and gesture in the dialogues of Montfort and Pengarron. Here, as in *The Peripatetic*, he demolishes stereotypes and conventions of language and character not by appealing to a transcendent norm of nature, but by highlighting and complicating them, forcing his readers to become aware and enquire into the relativities and ills of language, as Henry does in response to Farmer Wilson's lecture.

The adjective used repeatedly for Henry's character, "motley," describes the style, structure, and philosophy of *The Daughter*, which grows out of his experience and experiments with the miscellany form, and anticipates the modern concept of "creolization" in its validation of cultural, social, and racial mixture, inclusiveness and equality in place of rigid hierarchies and "purity" of blood, behaviour, and identity. It also shares the elusive allusiveness of "seditious allegory," a technique that Thelwall developed in resistance to the "Gagging Acts" of 1795,[1] allowing him to "talk treason" (and write it) while sidestepping prosecution by authorities unable to pin down his meaning.[2] In *The Daughter* as in all his work, this elusive mobility takes the form of complex wordplay, especially on names and identities, which shift and multiply at a dizzying pace, from Farmer Wilson's insistence that Henry identify himself ("Tell me who and what you are" [89]) to the narrator's interrogation of "our hero" ("Hero! shall we call him?—No: Renegade and Apostate be his title from hence forward" [300]), to the revisionary pronouns of Henry and Seraphina's engagement (when "*I* and *you* and *your* and *my*" are lost in "our" [411-12]), to the final joyous renamings of the individual in reciprocal relation ("Call me friend—call me patron—call me Henry Montfort"; "Woodville is Montfort—and Montfort is Woodville—But Henry is not Montfort" [473, 477]).

The Daughter in the English Novel Tradition

Hybridity also marks the genre of *The Daughter*, whose transatlantic crossings of culture, class, race, and gender take place at a transitional moment in the history of the British novel. Published eight years after Thelwall's "quasi-novel" *The Peripatetic*, *The Daughter of Adoption* shares some of its "intergeneric conversation," based in the eighteenth-century periodical tradition, as seen in the digression on Staunton in Book I, for example, or the anecdotes of Nerissa and Melinda, both of whom are modelled upon Beatissa, the "Platonic Fair" of *The Peripatetic*. But whereas the narrative thread of *The Peripatetic* was buried in such miscellaneous eccentricities, *The Daughter of Adoption* has a strong narrative thrust, and all characters and incidents are carefully interwoven and essential to the central plot. While it remains episodic and didactic, and shares the type characters and conventions of popular literature, it also stands firmly in the central tradi-

---

1 In November 1795, Pitt's government passed the Two Acts against Seditious Meetings and Treason, targeting Thelwall and other reformers; they were popularly known as the Gagging Acts.

2 On seditious allegory as a political and literary technique, see Michael Scrivener, *Seditious Allegories: John Thelwall and Jacobin Writing* (University Park: Penn State UP, 2001), 11-27 and 168-78.

tion of the English novel, and particularly the picaresque and sentimental novels of Henry Fielding, Tobias Smollett, and Frances Burney.

Thelwall's debt to the picaresque tradition, which follows a rogueish but good-natured male protagonist on a series of adventures, is evident in his chapter titles (reproduced in the Note on the Text), reminiscent of Fielding's 1749 *Tom Jones*, as well as the brief prose arguments that follow them, summarizing the content of each chapter after the manner of Smollett's 1748 *Roderick Random*. Like these classic English picaros, Thelwall's Henry is adventurous but generous; both his reckless encounter with Farmer Wilson, and the rueful bookselling scheme by which he attempts to extricate and redeem himself, look back to Tom Jones's famous trespasses (Appendix B1a), including his selling of his Bible. Every picaresque hero has his Sancho-Panza sidekick and foil, and for Henry it is Edmunds. Their voyages in love and war, at home and abroad, recall those of Smollett's Rory and his companion Strap, whose nautical adventures (including in the West Indies) were based on Smollett's experience as a naval surgeon (like Thelwall's grandfather). Thelwall also borrows much of Smollett's comical dialect, not only for Ben, the "honest sailor" of St. Domingue, but for Dr. Pengarron, who is based in part on Smollett's Welsh Dr. Morgan. Yet in the case of all these characters, as with the picaresque plot in general, Thelwall goes into greater depth, by making them more philosophical, using type characters to enquire into social conditions and circumstances, which are also shown forming their characters, thus individualizing them; this is easily seen in both Edmunds and Pengarron, who rise above comic stereotypes to become surrogate heroes, authors, and authority figures.

He does the same with the sentimental novel of female development, typified by Burney's 1778 *Evelina*, whose famous coach scene is alluded to in his Book VIII, and whose central plot and themes (indicated by Burney's subtitle "The History of a Young Lady's Entrance into the World") are reflected in Thelwall's title and his prefatory reference to the "debut" of his *Daughter*, whose "history and adventures" focus on similar questions of paternity/maternity and legitimacy. But Thelwall's approach to and conclusions upon these themes are not only more philosophical but also more subversive, as is shown in *his* coach scene (which precisely reverses Burney's, as his male hero is kidnapped by a predatory woman) as well as in the very name of his heroine, in whom the moral dignity and strength of a quasi-divine "Seraph" take the place of the weaker vessel "Eve." Seraphina's command of language contrasts with Evelina's stuttering silence, and in *her* kidnap scene, her assailant is chastened and palsied by the "conscious dignity of virtue" that seems to have "elevated her to some higher sphere" (374). Yet Seraphina remains a sentimental heroine: no sooner does Moroon retreat than she collapses, although she remains powerfully eloquent even in her emotional excess, and it is this that saves her, as her voice (and body language) literally open the door of her prison. In much the same way, Thelwall breaks out of the prison of eighteenth-century fiction, employing but subverting their plots and characters to enable a more thoroughgoing reform of society in place of the status quo that Smollett, Fielding, and Burney question but ultimately reinforce.

In his modifications and subversions of eighteenth-century precursors, Thelwall takes his place among other revolutionary novelists of the 1790s, many of whom were members of his circle in London. He creates out of the Jacobin novel of Thomas Holcroft and William Godwin a cosmopolitan version of the didactic "novel of purpose," intervenes forcefully in the debates characteristic of abolitionist literature, "out-monks Monk Lewis" and the Gothic novel, and develops new areas of the feminist novel as practiced by Mary Wollstonecraft and Eliza Fenwick. His variations and innovations upon these genres and their themes of education, slavery, (anti)gothic, and feminism are detailed under appropriate subheadings below. But he also stands out among his contemporaries in three important ways. First, Thelwall was alone among the Jacobin novelists an orator, and this gives his novel an unprecedented depth of theoretical analysis and practical insight into the politics of language. Second, like Holcroft and Lewis, Thelwall was a playwright as well as a novelist; his immersion in the world of the theatre is reflected in numerous quotations from both Shakespeare and contemporary dramatists, as well as in the melodramatic theatricality and physical comedy of climactic scenes like the "haunted house" of Book IX. Finally, whereas most Jacobin novels end tragically, *The Daughter of Adoption* is comic, not only in its happy ending but in its vivid and eccentric characterization and its stubborn faith in the goodness of man and the triumph of reason in the face of terror and despair. Thelwall had more reason than most to descend into misanthropy; that he was able to rise above it is a testament to his resilience and the enduring appeal and relevance of his vision and his voice.

In its outspoken, theatrical humour and vitality, Thelwall's *Daughter of Adoption* provides a missing link in the history of the novel, between the great eighteenth-century comic tradition and the well-known social reformers and satirists of the Victorian period. Thelwall anticipates Thackeray in the sophistication of his self-conscious satire, while his comic characterization (especially of Dr. Pengarron, with his memorable verbal tics) might indeed be labelled proto-Dickensian. When Pengarron inveighs and schemes against the "parcel of hungry legacy hunters," "the whole rascally legion of second and third cousins that have been gaping open-mouthed, like so many carrion crows, for my death" (411), he points the way not only to the greedy Pocket family in Charles Dickens's *Great Expectations* (1860-61), but also towards Featherstone's legacy and the fate of Stone Court in George Eliot's *Middlemarch* (1870-71). Although little has yet been done to trace the circulation and influence of Thelwall's novel, it is not impossible that his *Daughter* "built up a family" among a later generation of radical writers and activists.[1]

Education and/as Health

Judging from the account in his "Prefatory Memoir," as well as its first and earliest written chapters, *The Daughter of Adoption* probably began as an enquiry into the growth and development of a modern hero.[2] Although the bildungsroman is soon superseded by the love plot, with all its feminist, cosmopolitan, abolitionist philosophical complications, education remains a central theme in the novel; in some measure it is a structuring device, as each volume focuses on Henry's (and the readers') (re)education under the mentorship of different teachers, circumstances, and settings, that share, but illustrate different faces and phases of, the same essential moral philosophy, most simply articulated in the final scenes of the novel: "They build a family indeed, good doctor, who bring them up in social equality and reciprocal love" (474). Volume I offers "several particulars of the early education of our hero" (61) under the kindly and rational tutelage of Amelia, farmer Wilson, and Parkinson, whose benign influence is counteracted by the vain and irrational self-interest of Montfort (and his partner St. Valance in St. Domingue) to produce the instability that marks Henry's character and becomes the greatest obstacle to his happiness. Volumes II and III follow Henry's sentimental education from nature (shaken by revolutionary chaos) to culture (complicated by conspiracy) under the passionate mentorship of Seraphina, ably assisted by Edmunds and obstructed by Lewson and Melinda. That so many of Seraphina's lessons occur on Henry's sickbed prepares for the mergence of themes and metaphors of health and education in the final volume, in which Dr. Pengarron takes on the role of mentor-father, presiding over the moral reformation and recovery not only of Henry but also of old Montfort, and through them, of the reader.

For each of these stages in Henry's education, Thelwall draws on rich sources to develop his own approach to "one of the most hotly contested and frequently discussed topics" of the Romantic era.[3] Among "the little

---

1   This is especially possible in the case of Dickens, whose background and theatrical personality were very similar to Thelwall's, and who shared a common friend in Thomas Noon Talfourd (whom Thelwall mentored, and who mentored Dickens in turn).

2   The origins of *The Daughter* coincide with similar enquiries into, and revisions of, the heroic in *The Hope of Albion* and *The Fairy of the Lake*, as well as poems on the growth and development of mind by himself ("Proem to Poems Chiefly Suggested by the Scenery of Nature") and Wordsworth (*The Prelude*). See Thompson, *Silenced Partner*, esp. 187-218.

3   Alan Richardson, *Literature, Education and Romanticism: Reading as Social Practice 1780-1832* (Cambridge: Cambridge UP, 1994), 2. See also Thomas Pfau and

sensible publications" (67) with which Amelia stocks young Henry's library are the moral tales and lessons of Anna Barbauld, with which Thelwall had already experimented in his "Digression for Parents and Preceptors" in *The Peripatetic* (Appendix B1c). Amelia's philosophy of childraising is also consistent with the rational moralism of Maria Edgeworth, whose 1798 *Practical Education* likewise encourages parents to foster reason in children (both male and female) through experience, consistency, choice, open discussion, understandable rules, and dispassionate punishments (Appendix B1d). In her West Indian examples (drawn from some of the same sources used by Thelwall), Edgeworth makes a similar point about the corrupting influence of slave ownership upon intellectual and moral development, as does Thomas Day in his hugely popular tales of *Sandford and Merton* (1783-89), which influenced Thelwall's episode of Famer Wilson (Appendix B1b). Torn between his mother's sensible English upbringing and his father's West Indian depravity, Henry's motley character combines the down-to-earth warmth of Sandford, the sturdy son of a simple farmer, with the vanity and weakness of Merton, the spoiled son of a West Indian planter.

The dawn of Henry's sexual consciousness in his encounter with the farmer's daughter Mary, based in part on Thelwall's own experience (Appendix B1c), sets the stage for the next phase of his sentimental education, in the West Indies. His affair with Marian, the seductive slave-mistress who supplants the bashful farm-girl in his affections (and whose similar name and age point the contrast between them) prepares for the introduction of Seraphina (also aged sixteen), who articulates and dramatizes the Wollstonecraftian theories of education that shape these books, and much of the novel (Appendix B3a). Like Fenwick and other female Jacobin novelists (including Wollstonecraft herself in *The Wrongs of Woman*), Thelwall not only expounds feminist principles through Seraphina's dialogues with Morton, Edmunds, and Henry, but expands the many illustrative sketches or exempla in *Vindication* into full-blown narrative form: Amelia and Morton, for example, build upon Wollstonecraft's vignettes of sensible and foolish mothers, while Nerissa illustrates the evils of dependence and Melinda develops "the prevailing opinions of a Sexual Character."

While Thelwall draws on a wide variety of progressive contemporary sources, his novel also reveals the roots of his unique pedagogical system, based on his own experience, including his medical training. His novel, like the best part of his (self-) education, is built upon friendly conversation, reciprocal exchange, and those Socratic methods that he had idealized as early as the *Peripatetic*'s "The Tutor" (Appendix B1c), and which he would formalize in the Historical and Oratorical Society that would

Robert Gleckner, eds., *Lessons of Romanticism* (Durham, NC: Duke UP, 1998) and, more recently, Carolyn Weber, ed., *Romanticism and Parenting: Image, Instruction and Ideology* (Newcastle upon Tyne: Scholars P, 2007).

become a central feature of his Institute (Appendix B1f). Both the structure and the philosophy of his novel dramatize the expansive principle of virtue that would be the cornerstone of his elocutionary lectures (as it was of his political ones), proceeding from individual feeling, through comparison and generalization, to relative affection and universal sympathy: "But I suppose this is the new philosophy too; and the universe is to be *our* family" (475). Like his lectures, his novel alternates didactic discourse, illustrations, and spontaneous effusions; like the curriculum of his Institute, it demonstrates the "formation of the mental character" through history, moral philosophy, and poetry. Finally, his novel, like his Institute, harmonizes education and therapy, and champions the reciprocal powers of mental, moral, and physical health, to triumph over superstition, suspicion, tyranny, and oppression. Like Pengarron—the sarcastic, sceptical, humane, tolerant, earthy, teacher-doctor who succeeds Seraphina as the central authority figure—Thelwall triumphs by talking his readers, like his patients and pupils, "into a good humour with others" (414), and into social equality.

Ami des Noirs: St. Domingue, Slavery, and Insurrection[1]

The most important episode in Henry's education, and surely the most engaging for a modern reader, is his visit to St. Domingue[2] in Books III and IV, where he not only meets Seraphina but is caught up in one of the most dramatic events of the revolutionary era, the Haitian slave rebellion of 1791-1804. Although Thelwall never visited the West Indies or witnessed slavery, as a young man he was acquainted with West Indians in London where he came to dislike the "Creolean character," with its "effeminate, or rather childish vivacity, that unfeeling and tyrannical vehemence, and that sort of hoggish voluptuousness" (Appendix A1). The issue of slavery became a nationally celebrated cause in the 1780s precisely when he was acquiring a mature political identity by speaking in debates on slavery at Coachmaker's Hall. "The discussions on the subject of the Slave Trade, into which he entered with an almost diseased enthusiasm, led the way to very considerable changes in his political sentiments," as he became a radical reformer (Appendix A1).

Just as British slavery was central to Thelwall's politics, so the West Indies was anything but marginal in the 1790s for the British economy

---

1 Parts of the following paragraphs on St. Domingue have been reworked from Scrivener, *Seditious Allegories*, 240-44 and *The Cosmopolitan Ideal in the Age of Revolution and Reaction, 1776-1832* (London: Pickering and Chatto, 2007), 126-45.

2 We have adopted the name used for the French part of the island of Hispaniola, where the novel takes place; Thelwall combines its Spanish and French names in calling the island St. Domingo. It is now divided into two nations, the larger Dominican Republic and smaller Haiti, whose languages and customs are derived from the original colonial settlements.

and the military struggle against revolutionary France. Although costly in treasure and manpower, Britain sought to retain control of its own sugar islands (Jamaica), suppress slave rebellions (St. Domingue), and steal colonies from the French (Martinique). Between 1793 and 1798 when Britain withdrew, military action in St. Domingue entailed expenditures of over £4,000,000 and soldiers' deaths over 80,000, mostly from tropical diseases, according to C.L.R. James's classic history of the Haitian Revolution, *The Black Jacobins* (James 200). Yet if the British and French experienced heavy losses, they hardly matched the fatalities of the St. Domingue blacks, who in the ten years between 1791 and 1801 saw a third of their people die in the revolution.[1] James's history emphasizes not just the hideous level of violence but the political significance of the Haitian Revolution for modernity and transatlantic political history as the first successful slave rebellion against the European powers—an anti-colonial, anti-imperialistic insurrection. That Thelwall makes St. Domingue central in his novel suggests that he understood the world-historical significance of the Haitian Revolution when other writers did not.[2]

The novel's represented slave rebellion has only a few comparable parallels in Romantic-era literature: John Gabriel Stedman's *Narrative of a Five Years Expedition against the Revolted Negroes of Surinam* (1796), William Earle's *Obi; or, The History of Three-Fingered Jack* (1800), and Leonora Sansay's *Secret History; or, The Horrors of St. Domingo* (1808) are the most obvious. Stedman's account of the military campaign against the maroons of Surinam in the 1770s does not seem to have shaped Thelwall's novel, except to reinforce the sexual stereotypes of enslaved women—stereotypes available from many sources at the time. Earle's *Obi*, on the other hand, by representing sympathetically a rebellious slave in Jamaica, could have reminded Thelwall that British political culture was not uniformly hostile to movements of self-emancipation, even when they used violence. In his *Incle and Yarico* (1787), Thelwall had already constructed a radically counter-factual account of Native Americans triumphing over Europeans who sought to enslave them, and in another play, *The Incas* (1792), he rewrote the sixteenth-century Spanish Conquest of the Inca Empire with a victory of the Natives over the Spanish, thus allegorically rewriting the more recent defeat of the Native American uprising led by Tupac Amaru (1780-82) in the Andes. Although Thelwall does not romanticize political violence and counsels against revenge, he provides an explanatory narrative for it. As he states in *The Rights of Nature* (1796): "Had the Maroons and negroes never been most wickedly enslaved, their masters had never been murdered" (Appendix B2b).

---

1   C.L.R. James, *The Black Jacobins: Toussaint L'Ouverture and the San Domingo Revolution*, 1938, 2nd ed. (New York: Vintage, 1963), 242.

2   For the Haitian Revolution's world-historical significance, see Susan Buck-Morss, *Hegel, Haiti, and Universal History* (Pittsburgh: U of Pittsburgh P, 2009)—which makes no mention of Thelwall's novel.

Sansay's *Secret History*, which tells the St. Domingue story in 1802-04 as General Jean-Jacques Dessalines (1758-1806) takes over from Toussaint Louverture (c. 1743-1803), reproduces uncritically the sexual stereotypes of Creoles and enslaved people, and leaves the reader with haunting images of violence, much of it black on white; compared with Sansay's novel, Thelwall's is far more analytical and reflective. Thelwall approvingly imagined the violent self-emancipation of slaves, according to Raphael Hörmann in a recent essay on the Haitian Revolution. Thelwall's novel and other writings, which are similar to the much later ones of the Marxist C.L.R. James, affirm the "right of the Afro-Caribbean slaves to destroy the colonial system of exploitation and the right of the European lower classes to overthrow their socially and politically repressive regimes."[1] In another recent essay Peter J. Kitson takes a more unfavourable view of Thelwall's novel for its ideological shortcomings: focusing on the Haitian Revolution's most violent beginnings rather than the heroic career of Toussaint Louverture, the novel reproduces the stereotypes of black sexuality, from seductive mulattas to black male rapists of white women, and finally, the narrative is unable "to fashion an appropriate textual iconography for the suffering of the slaves."[2] Although Kitson's criticisms are arguably persuasive, his essay cannot point to any other writing in the early nineteenth century that achieves an ideological lucidity superior to Thelwall's representations of the Haitian Revolution. Perhaps, as Arnold A. Markley argues, Thelwall was forced to use conventions in which he did not believe in order to get published.[3]

Thelwall's novel also relies on stereotypical images and biased information because all the representations of the St. Domingue conflict were written by whites.[4] His two principal textual sources, *A Voyage to Saint Domingo* (1797) of Baron de Wimpffen, and the influential *Historical Survey of the French Colony in the Island of St. Domingo* (1797) of Bryan Edwards, which contains an account of the actual rebellion, were written by white planters from Jamaica and St. Domingue. But Thelwall's moral and political analysis diverges greatly from theirs. At the time of the novel's publication in 1801, the British were worried about rebellions in Jamaica, their largest West Indian sugar colony that had experienced an

---

1   Raphael Hörmann, "Thinking the 'Unthinkable'? Representations of the Haitian Revolution in British Discourse, 1791 to 1805," in *Human Bondage in the Cultural Contact Zone: Transdisciplinary Perspectives on Slavery and Its Discourses*, ed. Raphael Hörmann and Gesa Mackenthun (Münster: Waxmann, 2010), 159.

2   Kitson, "John Thelwall in Saint Domingue: Race, Slavery, and Revolution in *The Daughter of Adoption: A Tale of Modern Times* (1801)," *Romanticism* 16.2 (2010): 120-38.

3   Markley, *Conversion and Reform in the British Novel in the 1790s* (New York: Palgrave Macmillan, 2009), 112.

4   Jeremy D. Popkin, *A Concise History of the Haitian Revolution* (Malden: Wiley-Blackwell, 2012), 8.

uprising of the Trelawney Maroons in 1795-96. By making the St. Domingue rebellion begin in 1795 (159), four years later than was the historical case, the novel blurs St. Domingue and Jamaica, French and British slavery, although the incorrect date was probably just a printer's error.[1] For the British reading public in early 1801 "St. Domingue" would signify a violent slave rebellion, the failed intervention of British troops, and the remarkable rise to power of Toussaint Louverture, a former slave who expelled the British in 1798, invaded Spanish Santo Domingo and freed its slaves (1800-01). Although the heroic Toussaint was eventually captured by Napoleon, in whose prison he died in 1803, the trajectory of independence was inexorable.

Despite concentrating on the French colony, the novel does not permit the reader to forget about British colonialism, as when Edmunds exclaims to Henry, after they had witnessed the French whites torturing the rebels: "O Jamaica! Jamaica! Thou island of abominations and horrors! What inconceivable cruelties are there with which those who insult our national virtue by calling themselves English planters have not polluted thee!" (170). Edmunds then recalls Tacky's Revolt of 1760 and the subsequent punishments of the rebels, including hanging two of them alive in chains "for nine whole days" (171). The *Analytical Review*, a liberal journal published by Joseph Johnson and probably read by Thelwall, attended closely to the Maroon rebellion in Jamaica (1795-96), protesting the brutality of the whites and the numerous injustices to the blacks.[2] The notorious aftermath of these rebellions—the Trelawney Maroons were transported en masse to Nova Scotia, whose climate could not have been more unlike that of Jamaica—anticipated the ethnic cleansings of the twentieth and twenty-first centuries.[3]

A principal villain of the novel, Lucius Moroon, a young planter-smuggler and one of the wealthiest Creoles in Barbados, aggressively pursues Seraphina, and his name suggests "maroon"—the name for African slaves who had run away and achieved de facto emancipation. His very presence in the novel, including the first time the reader learns of the character when his name is spelled "Maroon," would remind readers of the Trelawney Maroon Rebellion and its suppression. His character is not designed to favour the historical maroons; rather, his villainy shows Thelwall's overall hostility to the planters and the Creole enterprise of extracting profits from enslaved labour. One political inference from the character Moroon is that

---

1   The date may also be another sign of the hasty composition of the novel; however, other dates corroborate the idea that Thelwall is deliberately blurring times and events: in Book IX, after Seraphina is rescued from the haunted house, she sends a letter dated February 1795. But this is approximately two years after their departure from St. Domingue.

2   *Analytical Review* 25 (March 1797): 266-69.

3   Michael Craton, *Testing the Chains: Resistance to Slavery in the British West Indies* (Ithaca, NY: Cornell UP, 1982), 125-39, 211-22.

the white Creoles mirror the negative stereotypes they have constructed of the enslaved blacks.

The novel's two main characters and principal romantic couple, Henry Montfort and Seraphina Parkinson, have their first meeting during the slave rebellion of St. Domingue, precisely when Seraphina is about to be raped by a slave. This melodramatic and iconically racist moment, which reinforces the contrast of white morality and black savagery, is contrapuntally contextualized by the planters' sexual exploitation of enslaved women and the planters' torturing of their captives. Planter savagery and immorality are strongly present as a set of conditions for slave atrocities. Nevertheless the *Critical Review* insists that the story of black violence is sufficient to refute the novel's abolitionist ideals (Appendix C1). The Haitian Revolution was indeed violent and cruel, but Thelwall had no access to unbiased information, which might have inspired more resistance to the melodramatic representations of white victimhood. In fact, black victims far outnumbered white, as most of the 30,000 Creoles escaped to safety during the Haitian Revolution, while 100,000 blacks were killed.[1] General Dessalines's notorious slaughter in 1804 of the whites who remained in St. Domingue cemented the savage image of the Haitian Revolution in the eyes of Europeans for much of the nineteenth century.[2] The inflammatory rape image along with sexually alluring images of the mulatta also distort the picture of plantation sexuality, which included active hostility to black families, which goes largely unrecorded in the white representations.

Henry Montfort, torn between his planter father and his liberal mother, is possibly modelled after London Corresponding Society martyr Joseph Gerrald (1763-96), who was the rebellious son of a wealthy West Indian planter and who received a liberal education from Samuel Parr (1747-1825).[3] Seraphina, modelled after Mary Wollstonecraft, accesses the Creole symbolism in a different way, as the "nature" to the "culture" of Cap Français and London, perhaps following Jacques-Henri Bernardin de Saint-Pierre's Rousseauvian *Paul et Virginie* (1787), an idyllic love story set in beautiful Mauritius. Seraphina's surname, Parkinson, resonates for Thelwall because one of the Jamaican Maroon leaders in the Trelawney uprising of 1795-96 was named Leonard Parkinson; like Thelwall he was a wanted man, in his case with a bounty of £100 on his head.[4] One of Thelwall's colleagues in the London Corresponding Society had the same surname: James Parkinson (1755-1824) was one of many politically radical doctors in Thelwall's circle, and his name would live on in the nerve disorder that he first diagnosed.

---

1 Popkin, *Concise History*, 140.
2 Ibid., 137.
3 Michael T. Davis, et al., Introduction, *London Corresponding Society, 1792-1799*, ed. M.T. Davis et al., 6 vols (London: Pickering & Chatto, 2002), 1:xxxiii.
4 *Analytical Review* 25 (March 1797): 268.

The turning-point in Henry Montfort's moral education is the best-known episode in the novel—already discussed earlier—in the mountainous wilderness near the sea at the Glen of Limbé, where he and Edmunds allow themselves to connect emotionally with the sublime and beautiful natural scenery (140-43). For Edmunds the beauty of nature makes one forget politics, but for Henry the beauty also points to the ruins of Spanish mines worked by Indian slaves. An example of the cosmopolitan imagination at work, this episode uses an experience of the picturesque and romantic not only to describe aesthetically pleasurable impressions of the landscape, but also to lay a moral foundation from which to contest the legitimacy of the enslaving imperialists. Henry becomes ever more "enthusiastic," a term used in the late eighteenth century to describe an emotionally compelling experience that destroyed older structures of feeling and allowed new ones to emerge.[1]

The slave rebellion constitutes another set of lessons in the education of Henry in this innovative bildungsroman. The dialogue between Edmunds and Parkinson on the wisdom of violent resistance to slavery, which rehearses the debate between Thelwall and Godwin in 1795 over political associations and public meetings,[2] tilts in Edmunds's direction when Mozambo defends violence against the planters. The Godwinian position taken by Parkinson—that slavery would be best abolished gradually as it has in other parts of the world—receives several rebuttals: while Edmunds cannot imagine the planters voluntarily giving up something from which they acquire so much benefit, Mozambo, one of the rebel slaves, defends the violence as a way to end their suffering immediately and not eventually (162). That Thelwall gives a voice to an imagined slave who is rational rather than simply emotional subverts the racial stereotype. Through Mozambo, Thelwall is contesting the biased images of black violence in Edwards's and other white accounts, which emphasize the ruthlessness of the rebels. Explaining why he is saving the lives of the Parkinson family, Mozambo distinguishes between innocent and guilty whites (162), another line of argument counter to the dominant story of indiscriminate black violence. When the novel describes slaughtered women and children, Parkinson calls the rebels "mere ignorant savages" (164), and Edmunds and Henry join a group of white planters who attack "a body of negroes" (165). However, after they later witness numerous cruelties inflicted by the whites on the rebels, they regret having sided temporarily with their fellow Europeans, whom they consider infected with "cannibal ferocity" in their retaliation against the blacks (168). Like Olaudah Equiano's *Interesting Narrative*, the novel turns the charge of cannibalism against the Europeans.[3]

---

1 On enthusiasm, see Jon Mee, *Romanticism, Enthusiasm, and Regulation: Poetics and the Policing of Culture in the Romantic Period* (Oxford: Oxford UP, 2005).

2 See Scrivener, *Seditious Allegories*, 59-60.

3 *The Interesting Narrative of the Life of Olaudah Equiano*, ed. Angelo Costanzo (Peterborough, ON: Broadview P, 2001), 70-76.

Even after witnessing much violence by the rebels, Seraphina—who was almost raped—defends the justice of Mozambo's rebellion. "The atrocities of revolted slaves, can never reconcile me to the tyranny that made them so atrocious" (202). By representing slave atrocities—what Kitson has aptly called a "worst case scenario"[1]—Thelwall hopes to strengthen the power of his abolitionist argument because he has provided a rational context by which the violence can be understood.

Thelwall took Mozambo's name from one of his planter sources, Baron de Wimpffen, and the outlines of the story from another planter source, Bryan Edwards (Appendix B2c-d), but he fashioned these materials to undermine Wimpffen's counter-revolutionary ideas and Edwards's defense of the planters. The character St. Valance, Montfort's business partner, articulates an argument of Edwards's *Historical Survey*, that the "friends of the blacks" ("Amis des Noirs") assisted the rebellion by their ideas. Henry, however, defends being a friend of "the whole human race" (168). Edwards, who depicts the slaves as both the puppets of European abolitionists and savages who deserve to be enslaved (Appendix B2d), makes a Burkean argument by attributing to reformers the power to motivate the rebellious slaves, just as Burke's *Reflections on the Revolution in France* (1790) constructed a chain of causation from Rousseau and the philosophes to English Dissenting liberals such as Richard Price to Parisian *sans-culottes*.[2] Like Burke in his sensational scene of the near rape of Marie Antoinette,[3] Edwards accents the violation of the domestic sphere, focusing on individual families murdered and sexually violated (Appendix B2d) and using these scenes of atrocity and inflammatory rhetoric to incite retribution. Thelwall's novel in contrast contextualizes the racial and political dynamics of the spectacular violence in order to promote rational understanding. He reworks his sources to write precisely the kind of abolitionist text that Edwards thought was responsible for the slave rebellion.

The Daughter as Anti-Gothic Novel

The rhetorical and aesthetic effects of the atrocity narratives partake of Gothic horror; in countering such narratives Thelwall employs the anti-Gothic mode that had been part of his political writings of the mid-1790s, which repudiate as restraints on individual rationality and political justice the "old Germanic, or gothic custumary" of feudal social and political institutions famously championed by Burke. "Mr. B's *Nature* and mine are widely different," Thelwall remarked in *Rights of Nature* (1796); "With him everything is natural that had the hoar of ancient prejudice upon it;

---

1 Kitson, "John Thelwall in Saint Domingue," 124.
2 Burke, *The Writings and Speeches of Edmund Burke*, gen. ed. Paul Langford, 9 vols (Oxford: Clarendon, 1981-96), 8:61-66. Hereafter cited as *WS*.
3 Burke, *WS* 8:126-28.

and novelty is the test of crime. In my humble estimate, nothing is natural, but what is fit and true, and can endure the test of reason" (see Appendix B2b). Referring to Burke's alarmist analogies between French Jacobins and rebel slaves as cannibals in *Letters on a Regicide Peace* (1796), Thelwall observes that, "Mr. B. is a *romance writer* of the German school: If he can but excite horror, no matter how incredible the tale, [he will]" (Appendix B2b).

Thelwall's anti-Gothic is not limited to the St. Domingue books of the novel. The spectre of racial miscegenation, the deepest taboo of a slave-owning society, is not addressed directly in the West Indian books, but it is displaced to form one of the most persistent themes in the novel: incest. Surfacing on four occasions, culminating in the mistaken revelation that Henry and Seraphina share the same father, the incest threat—specifically its repeated deflation—exposes the hollowness of contemporary objections to equality, rational choice, and universal relative affection as alternatives to patriarchy and primogeniture.[1] Such objections found frequent expression in the anti-Jacobin novels of the day. The heroine of Elizabeth Hamilton's *Memoirs of Modern Philosophers* (1800) speaks for the wider opposition to the New Philosophy when she asks, "what shall we say to this sort of philosophy, which builds the fabrick of morals on a direliction [*sic*] of all the principles of natural affection, which cuts the ties of gratitude, and pretends to extend our benevolence by annihilating the sweet bonds of domestic attachment?"[2] In *The Daughter*, this fear of social and sexual anarchy nearly drives Montfort mad:

> "And I——shall see all Nature's abominations thickening round me!—a sea and chaos of unnatural lusts—All orders mingled—all connections jarred—all ties, and all affinities confounded—with uncle fathers, and with sister wives.
>
> "I hear the universal shout of hell peel out my crime!— [...]
>
> "Would that it were distemper!—The thought of madness, and not madness from the thought!—Would that it were phrenzy indeed—the dream of bewildering passion!—that Montfort were not Woodville, nor Woodville Montfort!" (458)

Woodville is the name that Montfort assumed in the West Indies, and under which he seduced Morton. And Morton, it turns out, is really Anna

---

1 The attentions of Seraphina's natural father, her adoptive father, her lover (briefly thought to be her brother), and her suitor (who turns out to be her brother) are successively cast into doubt. For a reading of incest threats in the eighteenth-century novel in terms of the middle-class challenge to aristocratic or landed ideology, see Ellen Pollak, *Incest and the English Novel, 1684-1814* (Baltimore, MD: Johns Hopkins UP, 2003).

2 Hamilton, *Memoirs of Modern Philosophers*, 1800, ed. Claire Grogan (Peterborough, ON: Broadview P, 2000) 271.

Newcomb, who called herself "Morton" when posing as Seraphina's nurse. The implication is that if anyone is to blame for social disintegration, it is parents who have cast off their responsibilities and their names as parents. Montfort's ravings recall the famous passage in the *Reflections on the Revolution in France* in which Burke argues that that no individual or corporation is entitled to dissolve the social contract, for

> if that which is only submission to necessity should be made the object of choice, the law is broken, nature is disobeyed, and the rebellious are outlawed, cast forth, and exiled, from this world of reason, and order, and peace, and virtue, and fruitful penitence, into the antagonist world of madness, discord, vice, confusion, and unavailing sorrow.[1]

As noted above, Burke had employed the rhetoric of panic to consolidate opposition to the French Revolution, likening the revolutionaries to rebel slaves and cannibals. Much like Thelwall's political writings of the mid-1790s,[2] *The Daughter* appropriates this rhetoric to dismiss paranoid fears that "Murder and rape!—Incest and fratricide!" are the inevitable consequences of equality (395). *The Daughter* demonstrates that, as in St. Domingue, the responsibility for social degeneration would rest squarely with those who upheld the corrupt older order.

Another way in which Thelwall debunks Burkean values in *The Daughter* is by exposing the sensational, supernatural artifice of contemporary Gothic fictions—the supernatural "trash" that Montfort incautiously allows Henry to read as a child (68). This occurs chiefly in Books IX and X when, by means of a forged letter, Moroon conveys Seraphina and Morton to a ruined mansion on the Sussex coast and urges Seraphina to accept his proposals of marriage. Left to weigh these options, Seraphina sets to grappling with the locked door of the storeroom where she and Morton are confined. As if by supernatural agency, the wall begins to shake and rumble, and a panel slides away to reveal a chasm that descends into darkness. Seraphina rushes in, and the panel shuts behind her (377). While rumours spread of "yawning earth, and claps of thunder, and ghosts in winding sheets flying away with ravished virgins" (387), a local magistrate investigates the site of the disappearance and discovers "the whole arcana" behind the moveable panel, including a "bolt, with its internal and external spring" and a "chain of intricate cellars, or excavations, [… that] communicate with the warehouse […]" (388), and eventually discovers the missing women at the tunnel's seaside exit. Conscious of the "horrid uses"

---

1 Burke, *WS* 8:147.
2 On Thelwall's bold appropriation of the Burkean rhetoric of panic in *Rights of Nature* to warn against the dangers of continued oppression in Britain and the colonies, see Marcus Wood, "William Cobbett, John Thelwall, Radicalism, Racism and Slavery: A Study in Burkean Parodics," *Romanticism on the Net* 15 (August 1999). 23 May 2007 <http://www.erudit.org/revue/ron/1999/v/n15/005873ar.html>.

to which the mansion—a former smuggler's hideaway—might be converted, the magistrate decides to demolish it. But nature does the job instead, causing the cliff that supports the mansion to collapse (388-89). The destruction of the Gothic ruin under the effects of nature provides a fictional counterpart to Thelwall's rhetorical assault on the corrupt social and political institutions of the "Gothic custumary" in the name of nature.

Against the superstitious credulity exemplified in this episode, *The Daughter* champions the virtues of openness and rational enquiry that get to the root of the mystery. For the inquiring magistrate Sir Elmsley, "testimony of any kind against the evidence of his senses was no testimony at all" (395). The primacy of such evidence is also asserted when the doctor Pengarron begins to view Seraphina and Henry's connection in a more favourable light after taking the opportunity of "seeing with his own eyes" (399), and again when Montfort asks his duplicitous agent Woodhouse whether he has witnessed Henry's alleged misdemeanours "'with [his] own eyes'" (417). Woodhouse's reply is telling: "'Was it consistent with [...] the sacredness of my holy character, [...] that I should participate in these profane orgies and abominations?'" (417). "Participation" is synonymous here with the first-hand knowledge that Montfort has failed to acquire by hiring Woodhouse as his spy, the only kind that can effectively promote the sorts of individual moral reforms that the novel dramatizes, the "adoption" of new ways of seeing.

Building Up a Family: Marriage, Adoption, and the Triumph of Relative Affection

Slavery presented eighteenth-century novelists with a potent metaphor for reflecting on the topic of inequality, particularly as it related to marriage.[1] In legal terms, at least, the analogy was justified. According to William Blackstone's *Commentaries on the Laws of England* (1765-69), at marriage a woman's legal existence was incorporated with that of her husband, and her rights were severely circumscribed. She could not enter into contracts or legal suits on her own behalf, and she ceded her entitlement to any property she brought into the marriage.[2] One of the most vocal critics of

---

1 Peter J. Kitson points out, moreover, that anti-slavery discourse was one of the few forms of opposition to Pitt's government possible after the passage of the Two Acts in 1795. See "Romanticism and Colonialism: Races, Places, People, 1785-1800," in *Romanticism and Colonialism: Writing and Empire, 1780-1830*, eds. Peter J. Kitson and Tim Fulford (Cambridge: Cambridge UP, 1998), 13-34.

2 Blackstone, *Commentaries on the Laws of England, in Four Books*, 1765, 12th ed., vol. 1 (London, 1793), 441-45. On the rhetorical conjunction of slavery and marriage in the period, see, for instance, Markman Ellis, *The Politics of Sensibility: Race, Gender and Commerce in the Sentimental Novel* (Cambridge: Cambridge UP, 1996), 109-14, and Stephen Wolfe, "Are Such Things Done on Albion's Shore? The Discourses of Slavery in the Rhetoric of English Jacobin Writers," *Nordlit* 6 (1999): 161-73.

this system of female dependency was Mary Wollstonecraft, who argued in *A Vindication of the Rights of Woman* (1792) that only once women were treated and educated as the rational equals of men could they properly fulfill their duties as wives and mothers, and thereby contribute to social harmony and the progress of virtue (see Appendix B3a). The following year William Godwin proposed the abolition of marriage on grounds that it compromised the exercise of individual rationality (see Appendix B3b).

Taking its forceful parallels among women's oppression, marriage, and slavery from the pages of Wollstonecraft and Godwin, *The Daughter* presents gender relations in Britain as continuations of master-slave relations in the West Indies. It applies a feminist critique to women's inequality, masculine culture, and slavery itself in order to make the case that women are enslaved by a system that degrades not only blacks but also white men who are figuratively enslaved by false ideals. Abolishing the slave trade provides an opportunity for society to free itself not just of racial slavery, but of racial, class, and gender hierarchies that have had debilitating effects on men and women. Henry's mother explains that she has allowed Montfort to treat her like a puppet, a child, and a slave because "'my mind had not yet soared to the equality of the sexes; nor had I acquired the firmness of character to repel oppression, and assert my rights'" (56). It is a different story with Seraphina, who proves herself to be a true daughter of the New Philosophy when she describes marriages of interest as "legalised prostitution" (217)—echoing Wollstonecraft's phrase "legal prostitution"[1]—and refuses to play the part of Henry's mistress while he pursues another woman. "'Shall I be bought like a slave—shall I be hired like a courtezan?'" Seraphina demands of Morton, who has encouraged her to show more guile (252).

In terms of the conventions of the British novel, Seraphina upsets the norms at least as much Wollstonecraft's Maria in the *Wrongs of Woman*. First, Seraphina does not conceal her sexual attraction to Henry, and she affirms her sexuality, refusing equally to repress it as recommended by the conduct books and to make instrumental use of it, as the women around her so often do. Second, neither her premarital sexual experience nor her pregnancy shames her. That earlier sentimental heroines like Clarissa took refuge in death after the "dishonour" of being raped indicates the extraordinary power of the culture's virginity fetish, to which Seraphina is utterly indifferent. Third, the poor Creole orphan establishes the terms of her marriage to which Henry and Henry's father finally agree; these terms redeem the educational program of Amelia and the "petticoat philosophers" that her husband scorns (66). By refusing to make any concessions that would have violated her ethical norms, Seraphina is the unmoved mover of a series of actions that effect the moral reformation of both the

---

1   Wollstonecraft, *A Vindication of the Rights of Men* [1790] *and A Vindication of the Rights of Woman* [1792], ed. D.L. Macdonald and Kathleen Scherf (Peterborough, ON: Broadview P, 1997), 286.

gambling, whoring, and heavy-drinking son Henry and his slave-owning father Percival. Finally, the novel carries out under Seraphina's leadership a triumphant feminisation of values based on a feminist critique of masculine culture. The novel reinforces the sexual equality of Henry and Seraphina by having each one in turn take care of the other when they are ill and helpless. Delegitimated male activities such as duelling and gambling parallel the most harshly delegitimated male activity of all, racial slavery. According to *The Daughter of Adoption*, the moral insensitivity of slavery is symptomatic of the overall moral obtuseness found in normative social practices and beliefs.

Like the heroines of contemporary Jacobin fictions by women, Seraphina attempts to live in defiance of patriarchal norms. Considering herself to be Henry's de facto wife by virtue of their emotional and sexual connection, she is happy to dispense with the formality of marriage and its "gingle of mystic phrases" provided Henry reciprocates her affection (253).[1] But Henry is "the slave of forms and ceremonies" (253), and cannot immediately bring himself to view marriage in Seraphina's radical way, as an "entire and absolute union of soul" that "annihilates individuality" and "considers the blended stock of both [...] as the common property of each" (409). Henry has already been complicit in the exploitative sexual economy of St. Domingue in dalliances with "the beautiful negress Nannane" and the mulatto dancer Marian (129, 135-36). On his return to Britain he discovers that the sexual mores of the new world are perfectly compatible with prevailing practices in the old. Morton speaks for the old orthodoxy when she remarks of marriage settlements, "What are they but deeds of bargain and sale?—the commodity in general having been regularly, and wisely, knocked down to the highest bidder?" (252). As for female chastity, Morton deems it "a bubble of bubbles—a commodity in which she would have trafficked, at any time, wholesale or retail, with as little remorse as though she had been a West-Indian by birth, and all womankind had been negroes" (230).

In one sense, then, *The Daughter* is the story of Henry's moral reformation, his "adoption" of the New Philosophy over the prejudices of birth and gender that he has inherited from his father. But although Seraphina's view of marriage ultimately prevails, her high-minded principles also undergo a necessary transformation. At first, Seraphina is determined to live according to her principles whatever others might think. When Morton warns her that the world will surely disapprove of her attentions to Henry as long as they remain unmarried, Seraphina declares herself

---

1 Having read *The Rights of Nature*, Coleridge remarked to Thelwall in a letter of February 1797 that marriage remained "the best conceivable means (in the present state of Soc. [Society] at least:) of ensuring nurture & systematic education to infants & children" (*Collected Letters* 1:306). Thelwall echoed this opinion when he responded to reviews of *The Daughter* in the "Prefatory Memoir" of his *Poems, Chiefly Written in Retirement* (Appendix C5).

"not one of the world's family." Referring to the island off the coast of St. Domingue where she and Henry first meet, she insists, "The heart of my Henry and the bower of Margot are universe enough for me" (215). When Henry's heart proves fickle, and on several subsequent occasions, Seraphina resolves to live in seclusion, confident of thereby "insulat[ing]" herself from the "contamination" of the world (264). She lives in Somers Town, the area of London where Wollstonecraft lived with Godwin from their marriage until her death in 1797, and gives birth to a child who dies almost immediately. But, like the "new Recluse" of Llyswen farm,[1] Seraphina begins to feel a renewed "desire of social intercourse" (275). Only then does she begin to understand that "that the censure of the world is something—even when the judgment revolts from the principles upon which that censure is founded" (274). At last, when all hope of Henry's reformation seems lost, Seraphina comes to the painful realization that her education by Parkinson has been faulty:

> With a system of action deeply engraved upon her heart, that con-
> sulted only the happiness of others, she had not considered how
> essential to the permanency of our exertions for that happiness, it is
> to provide for the security of our own; and, with feelings alive to
> every generous sympathy and emotion, she had never considered that
> generosity may become bankrupt from too inconsiderate a profusion;
> and that, when the heart has not wherewithal to support its tranquil-
> lity, its benevolence to others must expire in a wish and a sigh. (301)

Situated at the mid-point of the novel, this pivotal moment dramatizes the heroine's awakening to the fundamental flaw of Godwinian philosophy: its failure to weigh the influence of relative affection and public opinion in the balance with rationalism and benevolence. Seraphina realizes that she must reconcile the ideal of individual rational judgment with the reality of life in a community.[2] Her discovery that no woman is an island—symbolized by her rescue from a coastal shoal where she is trapped at high tide (384-85)— is part of the novel's case for a more pragmatic version of political justice.[3]

---

1 Thelwall, *Poems, Chiefly Written in Retirement*, 1801 (Oxford: Woodstock Books, 1989), xxxviii.

2 Seraphina shares this insight with Thelwall, who in 1795 had responded to Godwin's attack on his practice of political lecturing by remarking that the attack was "proof how great and how dangerous a tendency the life of domestic solitude led by this singular man, and his scrupulous avoidance of all popular intercourse has to deaden the best sympathies of nature, and encourage a selfish and personal vanity, which the recluse philosopher first mistakes for principle, and then sacrifices it to every feeling of private, and sometimes public justice [...]." See *The Tribune, a Periodical Publication, Consisting Chiefly of the Political Lectures of J. Thelwall*, 3 vols (London, 1795-96), 2: xv.

3 By contrast, Beverly Sprague Allen finds *The Daughter* to be in perfect consensus with Godwinism, including in its concessions to received opinion. See "William Godwin's Influence upon John Thelwall," *PMLA* 37 (1922): 679-81.

Pragmatism is a defining feature of the vision of "social equality and reciprocal love" celebrated at the end of the novel. Responding to Pengarron's jibe that, "I suppose this is the new philosophy [...]; and the whole universe is to be *our* family," Seraphina remarks that such a "height of abstraction" could never be attained in practice, and serves only as an ideal. In the meantime, she adds, "we will not forget what duties we have to perform, on the smooth lawn of friendship, and the lowly vale of relative attachment" (475).[1] On the importance of "relative attachment," at least, *The Daughter*'s New Philosophy converges with the old: it does not propose the abolition of the family, as Pengarron fears, but defends its status as the basic unit of society—with certain caveats.

The first is the abolition of primogeniture, or the exclusive descent of property to the first-born. Henry and Seraphina's rejection of "the Gothic savagery" of this custom picks up on similar denunciations in the Jacobin fiction of the 1790s (474), and echoes Thelwall's own declamations against the "barbarous" law which maintained wealth in the hands of a minority (see Appendix B2b). *The Daughter*'s radical social vision is also premised on the legitimacy of children born outside of wedlock and the parity of relationships based on consanguinity and those based on choice and mutual affection. These last two tenets of the novel's social philosophy—the legitimacy of bastards and the parity of "natural" and adoptive relationships—are literally embodied in the characters of Henry and Seraphina, whose identities as legitimate and illegitimate, natural and adopted, bleed together with each new twist of the plot, as the illegitimate daughter is revealed to be legitimate, and the natural son turns out to have been adopted. In all, the novel features no fewer than five formal adoptions and four guardianships, several of which are also described as adoptions. This web of relationships help make the case for the extended definition of family. As Parkinson explains to Henry and Edmunds, although Seraphina is not his daughter by birth, their relationship is "as indissoluble [...] as that of nature" (151).

The acts, bonds, and vows of reciprocal love and social equality in the final chapters of Thelwall's *The Daughter of Adoption* not only build up a family, but also build suspense and set up a formidable dénouement in which fatal secrets are revealed, original sins are redeemed, generations are reconciled, tyrants are dethroned, hypocrites are defrocked, taboos are defanged, and the dead come back to life, all in a rush of earthbound enlightenment, reciprocal affection and good cheer. Seraphina's ecstatic "He lives!—He lives!—He lives!—He lives!—He lives!" is a cry of triumph that rings across oceans, nations, cultures and ages, as a resounding testament to Thelwall's lively and enduring achievement.

---

1 For an analysis of attempts by French writers, artists, and philosophers to re-imagine social relations on the model of universal brotherhood, rather than on the older model of patriarchy, see Lynn Hunt, *The Family Romance of the French Revolution* (London: Routledge, 1992).

John Thelwall and His World: A Brief Chronology

1764	27 July: John Thelwall (JT) born to London silk mercer.
1787	*Incle and Yarico* (comedy); *Poems on Various Subjects* (JT). Society for the Abolition of the Slave Trade established.
1789	14 July: Storming of Bastille; French Revolution begins.
1790	8 March: French decree granting political rights to propertied men of colour. October: Vincent Ogé starts rebellion of mulattos in St. Domingue.
1791	9 March: Ogé and Jean-Baptiste Chavannes executed, St. Domingue. 22-23 August: St. Domingue slave uprising begins. 21 September: French Republic inaugurated.
1792	*The Incas* (JT opera libretto). Mary Wollstonecraft, *Vindication of the Rights of Woman*.
1793	January/February: War between France and Britain begins. *The Peripatetic*; *An Essay towards a Definition of Animal Vitality* (JT). 20 September: British invasion of St. Domingue begins.
1794	4 February: France abolishes slavery. May: JT arrested for treason; acquitted in November.
1795	December: Maroons surrender, concluding the Second Maroon War in Jamaica. *The Tribune* (JT). December: "Gagging Acts" passed.
1796	*The Rights of Nature* (JT). JT lectures outside London.
1797	17-27 July: JT visits Nether Stowey; October: JT settles in Llyswen, Wales; August-October: writes "conversation poems" to Coleridge, including "Lines Written at Bridgewater," "On Leaving the Bottoms of Gloucestershire," "To the Infant Hampden," "Maria: A Fragment." 10 September: Death of Mary Wollstonecraft.
1798	January: Godwin's *Memoir of the Author of the Vindication of the Rights of Woman* and Wollstonecraft's *The Wrongs of Woman; or, Maria*. October: British military leaves St. Domingue. JT begins *The Fairy of the Lake*, *The Daughter of Adoption*, *The Hope of Albion*.
1799	9 November: Napoleon takes power. 28 December: Death of Frances Maria Thelwall (JT's daughter).

1801	*Poems, Chiefly Written in Retirement*; *Daughter of Adoption*; *Pedestrian Excursion* (JT).
	November: JT gives first elocutionary lecture in Sheffield.
1802-05	JT lectures on elocution throughout northern England and Scotland.
1803	JT settles in Kendal; visits Wordsworth and Coleridge.
1804	January: Republic of Haiti declared.
	January: *A Letter to Francis Jeffray*; March: *Mr. Thelwall's Reply* (JT).
	JT begins to publish on elocution in *Monthly Magazine*.
	August: JT addresses "Pegasus O'erladen," "The First Gray Hair," and other poems to Wordsworth and Coleridge.
1805-06	*Selections and Original Articles, for Mr. Thelwall's Lectures on the Science and Practice of Elocution*; *Poems, Chiefly Suggested by the Scenery of Nature* (unpublished) (JT).
	November-December: Oration on the death of Nelson and *The Trident of Albion* (JT).
1806	April: JT opens first Institute, Bedford Place, London.
1807	March: Parliament passes bill for Abolition of the Slave Trade; JT publishes "The Negro's Prayer" in *Monthly Magazine*.
1807-18	JT gives regular lectures on Poetry, History, Elocution, Oratory, Milton, Shakespeare (JT).
1808	"Ode Addressed to the Energies of Britain on Behalf of the Spanish Patriots" (JT).
1810	*The Vestibule of Eloquence*; *A Letter to Henry Cline* (JT).
1814	JT's first visit to France.
1815	Autumn: JT's Institute moves to Lincoln's Inn Fields.
1816	Autumn: Death of Susannah Vellam Thelwall (JT's first wife).
1817	May: Marriage of JT to Henrietta Cecil Boyle; July-August: Irish tour: JT lectures in Dublin, Cork, Belfast.
1818	August: French tour: JT lectures in Paris, Brussels; December: JT purchases the *Champion* newspaper.
1819-20	*The Champion* (JT).
1820	May: JT indicted and arrested for seditious libel; December: JT abandons *Champion*, sells Institute, settles in Brixton.
1824	December: JT settles at Pall Mall East.
1824-25	JT edits the *Monthly Magazine*.
1826	January-June: *The Panoramic Miscellany* (JT).
1832	June: passage of Great Reform Bill; July: JT attends Great Reform Banquet; October: death of political reformer Thomas Hardy; JT gives funeral oration.
1834	17 February: death of JT, on lecture tour, in Bath.

A Note on the Text

The copy text is the London edition published by Richard Phillips in four volumes in early 1801. According to the "Prefatory Memoir" of *Poems, Chiefly Written in Retirement* (1801), after the disastrous harvest of 1799 Thelwall walked from his Welsh farm with a single chapter in his pocket, with which he was able to get an advance for the novel from one of the main radical publishers in England (xlv-xlvi). Phillips, a vegetarian who had been imprisoned in Leicester Gaol for eighteen months (1792-93) for selling Thomas Paine's *Rights of Man*, published a biographical sketch of Thelwall (*Public Characters of 1800-1801*, pp. 177-93), and had established in 1796 the important liberal journal, the *Monthly Magazine*, in which Thelwall published numerous essays. If Thelwall had an extended relationship with fellow radical Phillips, there is no evidence that has come to light on his relationship with Nicholas Kelly, who published the novel in two volumes later in 1801 in Dublin apparently for commercial rather than ideological reasons. It appears that the Dublin edition was printed from the published London edition. (A list of major textual variants follows.) The Dublin edition would have been among the first Irish-printed works to fall under the provisions of the Copyright Act, which took effect in Ireland in 1801 following the Act of Union of 1800. Before 1801, Dublin had been the centre of a thriving offshore trade in reprints of London publications that were cheaper than the originals, but could not legally be imported into Britain.[1] Kelly, who was a Dublin printer, bookseller, and haberdasher between 1764 and 1828, was known for "the great variety of novels and children's books" that he published.[2]

We have silently corrected obvious typographical errors but have retained the spellings that were acceptable in Thelwall's own period. We have kept as well what would violate contemporary norms of consistency where different spellings in Thelwall's time were acceptable (*phrensy, phrenzy*). We have retained the London edition's punctuation, except in those few instances of an obvious error.

We have retained all of Thelwall's own footnotes, and we have added our own numbered footnotes for explanatory purposes: identifying quotations, allusions, and words unfamiliar to many twenty-first-century readers; calling attention to some important historical events; and bringing in some contextual information on Thelwall's writing and career.

---

1 William St. Clair, *The Reading Nation in the Romantic Period* (Cambridge: Cambridge UP, 2004), 104, and Vincent Kinane, *A Brief History of Publishing in Ireland* (Dublin: National Print Museum, 2002), 13-24.

2 Mary Pollard, *A Dictionary of Members of the Dublin Book Trade, 1550-1800: Based on the Records of the St. Luke the Evangelist, Dublin* (London: Bibliographic Society, 2000), 336-37.

The following list of chapter titles may help the reader navigate *The Daughter*. On the novel's structure, see the Introduction.

Chapter Titles

Volume I

Book I

Chap. I. Containing an imperfect, but necessary Retrospect of some Circumstances that took Place before the Birth of our Hero.

Chap. II. Containing several Particulars of the early Education of our Hero.

Chap. III. Containing several Circumstances relative to the Conduct and Connections of Montfort in the West Indies, and the Influence of Events upon his Character.

Book II

Chap. I. Containing some Account of the Conduct of Henry at Eton; with the first Part of an Adventure disgraceful in its Commencement, but interesting in its Progress.

Chap. II. Continuation of the preceding Adventure, and its Consequences.

Chap. III. In which our Hero attains the Age of Manhood.

Book III

Chap. I. Containing a Voyage to the Island of St. Domingo, and the Adventures of our Hero at Port-au-Prince.

Chap. II. Containing the History of a short residence at La Soufriere.

Chap. III. The History of Seraphina.

Volume II

Book IV

Chap. I. Containing the military Exploits of our Hero during the Insurrection of the Negroes.

Chap. II. The Adventures of a Coasting Voyage from Cape François to the little Island of Margot.

Chap. III. The Conclusion of the Adventures in the Island of Margot.

Book V

Chap. I. The Hero and Heroine proceed on their Voyage towards England.

Chap. II. In which the Adventures and the Voyage are continued till the Arrival of the Ship at the Madeiras.

Chap. III. Adventures in the Bay of Fonchiale.

Book VI

Chap. I. Containing, among other Matters, the Arrival of the Lovers in England; the Renewal of the dissipated Career of Henry; and the fruitless Researches of Edmunds after Parkinson's Will.

Chap. II. Containing a Dialogue between Seraphina and Morton; and another between Henry and young Edmunds.

Chap. III. The Reconciliation of the Lovers, and the Death of Amelia.

Volume III

Book VII

Chap. I. Containing the Space of somewhat less than a Year, from the Death of Amelia, to the Arrival of Intelligence of the Death of Montfort in the West-Indies.

Chap. II. Containing only a short space of time; in which, however, the Hero will make considerable progress in regaining the good opinion of the reader.

Chap. III. Plans of Lewson and his Confederates to recall Henry to the career of Dissipation.

Book VIII

Chap. I. The Amour between Henry and Melinda; comprising, in point of time, only the distance of a few weeks beyond the preceding Chapter.

Chap. II. The Progress of the Conspiracy between Lewson and Melinda—the Time of Action—Part of a Night of Dissipation, and a Portion of the ensuing Day.

Chap. III. A long Chapter, embracing, exclusive of Retrospects, only the short Space of a few Hours; but in the course of which the Reasons of a very mysterious Attachment will be explained.

Book IX

Chap. I. Containing the Space of a few Weeks from the Return of old Montfort, to the double Conspiracy against the Fortune and Life of Henry.

Chap. II. The Conspiracy of Moroon for the Assassination of Henry, and the Rape of Seraphina.

Chap. III. Further Particulars of the desperate Attempt of Moroon upon the Person of Seraphina.

Volume IV

Book X

Chap. I. Containing the Conclusion of the Adventures of the Haunted House.

Chap. II. The return of Seraphina to the cottage; and her conduct under the new circumstances in which she finds herself to be placed.

Chap. III. The Recovery of Henry; and the Eclaircissement with Seraphina.

Book XI

Chap. I. Schemes of Dr. Pengarron to reconcile Old Montfort to Henry, and the purposed Marriage.

Chap. II. The Visit of Seraphina to Old Montfort.

Chap. III. Containing the Space of about three Months; from the fatal discovery to the death of Morton.

Book XII

Chap. I. In which our History advances only a few Days, in point of Time, from the Death of Newcomb to the Disclosure of a Private Marriage.

Chap. II. The Amour of Woodhouse and Nerissa; an essential Episode.

Chapter the Last. Containing in the Space of a few Weeks, a Funeral, a Resurrection, and a Wedding; equally conducing to the happy Catastrophe of our Drama.

Major Textual Variants

The notes that follow indicate major variants between the four-volume London edition of *The Daughter of Adoption* and the two-volume Dublin edition (D), both published in 1801. The chapter synopses are completely absent in the Dublin edition.

Book III, Chapter 1
p. 71:   the natural sloth and inactivity of the rascally negroes, ...] the natural sloth and inexhaustible themes of animadversion. (D)

III.2
p. 84:   "What a scene, and what an hour, Edmunds," said he, bantering, "to hatch treason in!"] [This sentence is missing from D.]

IV.1
p. 110: black lubbers] lubbers (D)

V.2
p. 158: for she abhorred a rope] for she abhorred a rape (D)

VI.1
p. 167: so ample an extent] so simple an extent
p. 173: could it be supposed, madam! for a single moment, madam!— as sure it cannot, madam!—] [The last phrase, "as sure it cannot, madam!," is missing in the Dublin edition.]

VI.2
p. 175: those foolish books] those books (D)

VII.1
p. 192: the mystic jargon of their schools."] the magic jargon of their schools." (D)

VII.3
p. 207: together with your general habits of body and way of living,] together with your body and way of living, (D)
p. 217: But it was not ... terrors of his tongue.] [This paragraph is missing in the Dublin edition.]

VIII.1

p. 223: was now thought] was not thought (D)

p. 226: to receive private intimation of her intention, in a circuitous
way:] private intimation, in a circuitous way: (D)

VIII.3

p. 243: I yet can pardon that.] I yet cannot pardon that. (D)

IX.1

p. 247: By this notable exploit he made no doubt of securing to himself
the inheritance of, at least, a considerable portion of the alienated property.] By this notable exploit he made no doubt of
securing to himself the inheritance of the alienated property.
(D)

p. 255: Baker-street] Brewer-street (D)

IX.3

p. 275: disjointed indeed and marred] jointed and marred (D)

X.3

p. 300: an inherent property] an inheritance (D)

XI.2

p. 318: obdurate and unfeeling] unfeeling (D)

THE

DAUGHTER

OF

A D O PT I O N;

A TALE OF MODERN TIMES.

IN FOUR VOLUMES.

BY JOHN BEAUFORT, LL.D.

****

VOL. I.

****

LONDON:

PRINTED FOR R. PHILLIPS, ST. PAUL'S CHURCH-YARD;

SOLD BY T. HURST, J. WALLIS, AND WEST

AND HUGHES, PATERNOSTER-ROW.

****

1801.

[*T. Davison, White-Friar's.*]

ADVERTISEMENT.

========

NOTHING can be more impertinent than apologies for the defects of literary composition. The book that is not worth reading (under whatever circumstances it may have been written), it is an insult to print: and the public, who pay for *entertainment* and *instruction*, have but one thing to consider—whether the purchase be worth the price. If it be not so, what are the excuses of the author, but acknowledgments that he was conscious of the fraud?

The present work, therefore, is ushered into the world without any of the accustomed supplications, or appeals to candour, which the circumstances under which it has been composed, might well supply; and its merits and its defects (whatever they may respectively be) are alike submitted to the ordeal of impartial criticism.

If, thus abstracted, "THE DAUGHTER OF ADOPTION" should happen to excite an interest that may entitle her to more ceremonious introduction, her second *debut* may be marked with some details that will shew her history and adventures to be *no coinages of a heart at ease*.[1]

---

1 *Romeo and Juliet* 4.5.103-05 and *Hamlet* 3.4.139. Thelwall alludes to a second edition, which never materialized.

THE
DAUGHTER
OF
ADOPTION.

=============

BOOK I.

CHAP. I.

Containing an imperfect, but necessary Retrospect of some Circumstances that took Place before the Birth of our Hero.

Maternal Feelings—Infant Emotions.—Nerissa; Sketches of Boarding-School Accomplishments, and decayed Gentlemen;—Relatives! And Friends!—Hints and unintelligible Obscurities—The Narrative; Parental Prudence—Husband à la Mode—Consolations of Friendship—The Libertine by Contagion—Romantic Attachments—The Fatal Relapse—A melancholy Catastrophe.—Interruptions and Disappointments.[1]

IT was about the latter end of September, 1776, when Amelia Montfort, after a long silence, received a letter from her husband, informing her of his arrival from the West Indies.

A thousand emotions, arising from the peculiar circumstances of their separation, rushed immediately on her mind, and almost overpowered her reason.

Montfort had been absent for upwards of six years; and it had been doubtful whether he could ever return to his native land: for an affair of, what the profligate world calls *honour*, had compelled him to take refuge in precipitate banishment; the relations of the deceased had made it a point of principle to be steady in the pursuit of revenge; and there were circumstances, in the history of the transaction, which would necessarily be regarded as aggravations by an upright jury.

But public justice slumbered at length over the forgotten crime: and in a country where the worst and the best emotions of the soul are alike put up to auction, where slandered reputation may be compensated by a fine, and the anguish of an injured husband appeased by an action of damages, it is not surprising that a man of Montfort's unbounded wealth should silence, at length, the private clamours of relative indignation.

Amelia's attachment for her husband had never been distinguished by that romantic ardour

"Which in the breast of Fancy's children glows."

---

1 This chapter synopsis and all subsequent ones in the book are wholly omitted in the Dublin edition.

All she had ever felt, or ever professed, amounted to no more than that
"Decent affection and complacent kindness,"[1]
which, in well-disposed natures, the mere sense of relative duties may inspire, independently of the preferences of the heart. Neither the circumstances that occasioned his flight, nor his conduct during his exile, were calculated to strengthen this attachment: for it was no secret, that the fatal quarrel originated about a woman of loose character, with whom the fugitive and his antagonist had been in company at Vauxhall: and so far was Montfort from atoning for his infidelity by contrition or conjugal solicitude, that his correspondence was languid and precarious; and the few letters which he deigned to write, were melancholy proofs that his mind was embittered, not softened; and that to the pride, licentiousness, and caprice of his early character, he had added the sourness of misanthropy, and the gloom of superstition.

In short, Montfort was a man of strong passions and blunt sympathies; and Amelia would have been a bad calculator if she had expected any increase of happiness from his return. But the wife and the mother rushed upon her soul; and these emotions were mingled with others of a wilder nature. The mangled body of the unfortunate Bowbridge—the death-bed agonies of her dear Louisa—all the past, and all the probable future, floated in her imagination. But above all, her mind was agitated with doubts and anxieties for her little Henry, on whom she doated with more than a mother's fondness.

She had no child but him; nor was ever likely to have. Of all she had ever loved—of every hope, and every sweet affection of her youth, he was the sole memorial: the only wreck spared by the storm that had swallowed up her happiness. From the time of his birth he had been the constant companion of her widowed hours, and the object of her fond solicitude. Her cares for him had stood in the place of the amusements and pleasures usual to persons of her condition; and the hours had seemed short, because busied in the promotion of his welfare.

But the dominion of her love was now, perhaps, to be supplanted by the tyranny of moroseness and caprice. He was to be introduced to one who would assume the authority of a father without his feelings: who would be conscious, perhaps, of no paternal emotions: who had read, it is true, in her letters, many a fond tale of his infantile graces and prattling innocence; but whose affections had been roused by none of those endearments which entwined him to her heart; and who might regard him as an alien and a stranger.

Such, among others of a still more embarrassing nature, were the reflections that agitated the mind of Amelia, on the receipt of her husband's letter. To conceal, or rather to indulge the emotions which these reflections inspired, she withdrew to the solitude of her study: a retired apartment, where she had a valuable collection of well selected books, her

---

1 John Home, *Douglas* (1756), 1.1.90-91.

daily companions and instructors. There her meditations were uninter-rupted till the close of evening; when Henry, accompanied by Nerissa[1] and the maid, came running into the room, to exchange the farewell kiss, and receive, as usual, the brief lesson of maternal solicitude on the conduct and events of the day.

But the mind of Amelia was ill prepared for the calmness of moral instruction. She seized him, with eager agitation, in her arms—she printed a thousand kisses on his lips, his cheek, his neck—and gazing upon him with an ardour of passion,

"Thou shalt not go, my child!" she exclaimed—"thou shalt not go yet—thou shalt stay and see thy fa—"

The word faultered on her tongue. She sunk into a deep reverie. She flung herself upon a sopha, seated the child upon her knee, and rivetting her eyes upon his face—

"His father!!!" she repeated, with great emphasis, and burst into a flood of tears.

"Father! Father!" exclaimed the child, with great eagerness, "—Is he coming?

"Why do you cry, mamma? Papa won't send me away from you; will he? I have not been naughty—have I?—like the poor boy there, in the story book, that was sent abroad, and cast away in the ship."

The thought had daggers in it. She clasped him in an agony to her breast.

"No—no, my child! nothing but death shall part us. I will be a mother to thee still, though thou should'st find no father."

She set him down on the sopha; walked two or three times across the room; and then pausing and calming her agitation—

"Thou shalt go to bed, my child—

"I will introduce him in the morning," continued she, musing. "My soul will be more tranquillised.—

"I am not prepared to-night."

"Shall I not have a papa to-night, then?" said the child, almost in tears at his disappointment. "I should be very glad to have a papa and mamma too. I never had a papa in all my life."

"True—true! my babe!" exclaimed Amelia, with a fresh burst of anguish—"thou never hadst!—thou never hadst!!!"

"But don't cry, mamma!" continued the little orator. "I shall have one now, you know. Oh! I shall so like to have such a papa as master Norton,[2] to buy me real right earnest horses, and make me kites, and trundle hoops, and take me a walking with him, and teach me all about the names of flowers and things that grow in the fields, and among the great tall trees!"

---

1 Nerissa is Portia's waiting-woman in *The Merchant of Venice*.

2 Mary-Ann Kilner, *The Happy Family, Or, Memoirs of Mr. and Mrs. Norton: Intended to Shew the Delightful Effects of Filial Obedience* (1785), an example of children's lit-erature with which Thelwall was familiar.

"Will HE be *such* a father?" said Amelia, with unvoluntary emphasis, still pacing about the room.—"Will he be *such* a father?"

"Do let me have my papa to-night," continued the child, a little more confidently.

Amelia stood musing in silence.

Henry's countenance brightened—his eyes sparkled—his cheeks were flushed with expectation; and every animated feature beamed with hope.

"I shall have a papa to-night—shan't I, mamma?" exclaimed he, running to her, and clinging to her knees.

Amelia waked from her reverie. She smiled through her tears, as she felt the pressure of his little arms; and delight and anguish wrestled in her heart.

She would fain have yielded to his importunities: but her spirits were shattered, and her mind disturbed: and as the first impression appeared to her a matter of infinite importance, she was anxious to have every faculty at command, that she might be able to watch the emotions that arose in the mind of Montfort, and give them a favourable direction.

"Not till to-morrow, my child!" said she, embracing him. "I dare not to-night—indeed I dare not."

"Dare not!" repeated the child—terrified at her unusual wildness—"Is papa angry to-night, as he was when he killed that poor gentleman?"

"Killed that poor gentleman!" echoed Amelia, almost petrefied. "Who told thee that story, child? As thou would'st be loved by me—by every body, never let those dreadful words come from thy lips again.

"*Killed that poor gentleman!*" repeated she, inwardly, as she paced about the room, fixing her eyes on Henry, with great agitation—"*Killed that poor gentleman!!*"—And thou, sweet babe! must call him father!—must climb his knees, and hang about his neck, and lisp the words of love to him.

"Yes thou must love him—and, in a thousand little fond endearing ways, wind into his rugged heart, or we are wretched."

The tongue gave no utterance to this exclamation. It was a mute soliloquy; in which the mind communed only with itself: but every accent was felt at the heart so audibly, that, starting from her reverie, she suspected that she had talked aloud.

She seized the child once more in her arms—kissed him with convulsive fondness—bade him good night, and delivered him to the maid: while poor Henry, overpowered by her emotions, sobbed, and retired in silence.

In the preceding scene, a young lady was introduced by the name of Nerissa. The mind was then too much occupied to attend to ceremonials; and we therefore passed her by for the moment, as though she had been a person of no importance. But as this will appear in the sequel to be very far from the real state of the case, it may not be improper to seize the present opportunity of imparting some information concerning the family and education of one whose adventures are to occupy some eventful pages of our history.

Nerissa was an unfortunate young lady, about eighteen years of age; of a person and mind *truly feminine*; and who had acquired all the feminine graces and accomplishments of a boarding-school education. She could dance in the most fashionable style; sing the most fashionable airs; write long letters without the unfashionable aid of pronouns, prepositions, or conjunctions; work silk pictures, *vastly like copper-plate*; and make fillagree[1] like nothing but itself. She could draw both flowers and landscapes an immense deal finer than any thing that was ever seen in nature; could run her fingers over the keys of a harpsichord with astonishing velocity, and had acquired such skill and erudition in the English, French, and Italian languages, that she could mingle them altogether in a single sentence, so as to make it equally unintelligible to the native of either of the respective countries.

With all these shining attainments, she blended, however, the less conspicuous advantages of a heart unconscious of one malignant feeling, and a kindliness of manners which had its origin, at least, in pure and unadulterated good-nature.

She was the orphan daughter of a *decayed gentleman*: or, in other words, of one of those dupes of parade and vanity, who having aspired to follies and vices that *surpassed* his *fortune*, dragged out the latter years of his life in the bitterness of dependence; and who, sinking from melancholy to desperation, was believed to have appealed from charity to the dice-box, and from the dice-box to the chymist, for relief.

However this may be, Nerissa, in her sixteenth year, was thrown upon the world an unprotected orphan, with a small annuity of about fifty pounds, which was all that could be preserved from the general wreck.

From her wealthy *relations* (for she was of *a good family*) she received but little countenance; but her youth and innocence, her good dispositions, and her insinuating manners, made her some *friends*, with whom her time was alternately consumed, in a sort of easy dependence, which sometimes indeed wounded her feelings, and destroyed the little consistency or energy of character she might otherwise have attained, but which tempered her mind to a sort of uniform and soothing melancholy, perhaps not unpleasing to herself, and assuredly very interesting to others.

In short, Nerissa was seldom regarded with indifference: and among the many families in which she was partly domesticated, there was scarcely a matron who was not desirous of seeing her well settled; or a wife, a sister, or a daughter, who was not ready to rely on her sympathy in all the tenderness of unlimited confidence.

This latter disposition, in particular, Nerissa never neglected any opportunity to improve. Experience soon convinced her, that the friend who had once unbosomed herself without reserve, had given the surest bond of continued friendship. When she was once in possession of an important secret, the value of her acquaintance was enhanced; and its continuance depended rather upon necessity than caprice.

---

1 Or usually filigree; delicate, intricate design on ornamental object.

Nerissa's solicitude to be acquainted with all the concerns and interests of her friends, was therefore of a character very different from what is usually termed *female curiosity*. It had its origin, perhaps, in her natural disposition to sympathy and compassion; but it was cherished and expanded by a sense of interest growing out of the habits of her situation. Accordingly, her eagerness to be in possession of any secret, was not followed by the vanity of displaying the confidence that was reposed in her; nor among all the families into whose mysteries she had been initiated, had she ever, by tattling loquacity, been the cause of a single pang.

Among the kindest of Nerissa's friends was Amelia Montfort. She did not love her, indeed, with that ardour she had formerly felt for her departed Louisa: but she had a soul made up of the kindliest sympathies; and her feelings never swelled so high as when pity threw open the floodgates of affection. The situation of Nerissa had deeply interested her; and that interest was much increased by her deportment: for the poor girl really reverenced her, and approached her with the air of one who was at once soliciting protection and information: so that a sort of attachment subsisted between them, not unlike what is sometimes entertained by two sisters whose ages are so dissimilar, that one might have been the parent of the other.

In certain respects also she enjoyed the fullest confidence. Amelia had the most ample reliance on her prudence and integrity; and, whenever she was under the roof, the house and family were consigned entirely to her management. She was *vice-commander in chief*, for the time being, of all the castles, sideboards, redoubts, and corner cupboards of the garrison.

Before such a person as Nerissa, the scene that has been described was not likely to pass without interest or observation. She was indeed extremely agitated: for, in addition to her habitual sympathy, she had an affection for little Henry, inferior only to what was felt by Amelia herself. She continued, however, to weep in silence, for some time after Henry and the maid had retired.

Amelia walked three or four times across the room. Her serenity returned; but she continued meditating and absent. She paused, almost unconsciously, near the settee on which Nerissa reclined. Nerissa clasped her hand and pressed it to her bosom.

"You are strangely *derangé, ma chère* Mrs. Montfort," said she, gazing with tearful tenderness in her eyes. "*Mi trafigge il cuore!*[1] Would I were worthy to be the confident of your sorrows!"

A. "In the name of Heaven, Nerissa, who can have been so malicious—or so indiscreet, as to tell the child that fatal story?

"Killed the poor gentleman!!!

"I tremble to think what might be the consequence if, on his first introduction, or before the habitudes of affection have roused into activity

---

1 "Upset" (*derangé*), "my dear" (*ma chère*) (French); "I am heart-stricken" (*Mi trafigge il cuore*) (Italian).

what are called the parental feelings, his childish simplicity should repeat these words.

"It is frightfully unlucky, Nerissa: but it is not surprising. The servants, the neighbourhood, all the world are acquainted with the cause of Mr. Montfort's exile."

N. "And yet, my dear Mrs. Montfort, to your *povero devotissimo,*[1] at least, the *particulars* of that melancholy adventure are, as yet, unknown.

"You have frequently flattered me with the promise of your confidence; but still are you *envelopé*[2] and mysterious: and often when you have been gazing on your dear little cherub till your eyes were suffused with tears, or when your bosom has been swoln and agitated, as if it laboured with the tempest of some hidden sorrow, you have talked of awful secrets and begun your narrative; but, alas! confidence has evaporated in the first tide of passion; and retiring into yourself, you have consigned me to painful and mortified expectation."

A. "It is a sad tale, Nerissa, and an awful one. The peace of my returning husband and myself, of my beloved Henry, and the hovering shade of my ever to be lamented martyred friend, are all involved in it.

"It were better," continued she, laying her hand upon her heart, "that it should sleep and perish here."

N. "Have you destroyed the letter then, concerning which, during your late illness, you gave me such emphatic instructions?"

A. "No, Nerissa, no: it is still in my bureau, together with the affecting testament of my dying Louisa. The whole mystery of my sorrows is chronicled in those papers.

"A time may come when it will be important, perhaps, that their contents should be known. Circumstances may arise to make it necessary to conceal them for ever. While I live, indeed, it is in my power to regulate myself by those circumstances, whatever they may be. But what foresight can properly determine the provision I ought to make against the incalculable events that may take place when I am no more?

"Painful, awful perplexity!

"If Montfort survives me, these papers may prove a sad and forcible appeal to his justice. They may furnish him with pretences for the most capricious cruelty.

"But he returns, and we must endeavour to rivet his affections by some stronger hold.

"I talk in riddles to thee, Nerissa—I talk in riddles—and why should I do so?

"I had once a friend to whom I could unbosom every woe; and then my woes were light. It is a sad thing to keep a sorrow cankering in the heart, and never give it utterance!

---

1 Poor, very devoted friend (Italian).
2 *Enveloppé* means enveloped, wrapped, or veiled (French).

"Come, my poor girl! I will confide in thee, I always meant to do so, and the hour is arrived when it must be done or never.

"Draw yourself a chair nearer to the fire, and I will beguile the hours till the arrival of Mr. Montfort, by relating the sad history of former years."

Nerissa seated herself close by the side of her friend; who, pressing her hand in hers, after some hesitation, began as follows.

"My father, Nerissa, was a man of more ambition than discernment, and more parade than affluence. The great passion of his soul was *to see his daughter well settled.* His imagination dwelt on nothing but matrimonial bargains; and he valued every grace and every accomplishment only as it might be likely to advance my price; or, as he himself more delicately expressed it, might elevate me to rank and fortune.

"In one part of his conduct, however (an essential part), he seems to have looked beyond these narrow views, and made some provision for my permanent and independent happiness.

"The fact is, he had himself some taste for literature; and being, partly from circumstances, and partly from inclination, a man of very domesticated habits, he had experienced the inconvenience of having a partner and companion who could neither participate in his pleasures, nor be interested in his favourite topics of conversation. What was deficient in a wife, therefore, he was desirous of supplying in a daughter; and he gave me, accordingly, something more than an ordinary female education; to the accomplishments of fashion adding several of the most interesting branches of useful knowledge.

"My own propensities accorded very well with this particular humour of my father; and there was even some danger that the fine lady should have been prematurely spoiled by what my mother was pleased to consider as the lumber of college pedantry.

"Attached to books and retirement, and regarding my occasional intercourse with the giddy circles of parade and dissipation as sacrifices of obedience to parental authority, I was little impressed by the attentions with which the frequenters of those circles occasionally distinguished me; so that I preserved my heart in perfect freedom and tranquillity till I had completed my twentieth year.

"At this time Mr. Montfort singled me out as the object of his indefatigable addresses.

"I will not pretend that he inspired me with any affection. That glow of passion, those hopes, those fears, that trembling sensibility which poets, and your darling novelists, so pathetically describe, it was never my destiny to feel. Not that I was incapable of such emotions. The ardour of friendship with which I glowed for my Louisa, and the more than maternal fondness that swells my heart for my little Henry, convince me how romantically I should have loved, if the scenes I moved in could have presented any object for such a passion.

"But if *my* affections were not rivetted, those of my parents were. They were solicitous, even to diseased anxiety, that I should not lose the opportunity of such an offer; and as Mr. Montfort's age was not very dispro-portionate, for he was little more than thirty; as his person was not unpleasing, and his manners were insinuating and agreeable, I yielded to the wishes of those to whom obedience was a settled habit, and was sacrificed, without a murmur, at the shrine of prudence.

"Ah, Nerissa! it was a sacrifice indeed!

"In entering into the matrimonial state, I had inflated my imagination with no intoxicating anticipations of beatitude and elysium. My expectations were humble, very humble. I hoped to be just no unhappier than I was before. Yet was it not my destiny to escape the bitterness of disappointment.

"Mr. Montfort was not a man with whom even this negative happiness could be enjoyed. The polish of his manners and the conciliation of his deportment were occasional embellishments, not constituent parts of his character; and though the drawing room or the assembly could not be visited without them, they were discarded at home for the coarse habits of austerity and pride. Add to this, I had soon the mortification of discovering that I was far from enjoying his undivided affections.

"His conduct was a problem which my youth and inexperience knew not how to solve. It was impossible, I imagined, to attribute his attachment to any other motive than love; and love I had been taught to consider as a passion that could not be divided; and yet we had been married but a few months, which it was evident that he had the same sort of attachment to some ten or a dozen more; and, in all probability, if they had been approachable in no other way, and the laws of the country had permitted, he would have married them all, in due succession, just for the same reason as he married me.

"This was a mortifying discovery: for if I was not violently in love I was tolerably vain; and, with all my thirst for knowledge, I was somewhat unwilling to discover how limited a meaning is affixed to the word *eternal* in the vocabulary of vows and courtship.

"I could have endured all this, however, with less regret, if his devotion to others had been accompanied with nothing worse than indifference to me. But the same vicious habits that rendered his heart a mere brothel house of prodigal licenciousness, had generated a hard insensibility and contempt for our whole sex; which, together with his enormous pride and bigotted notions of masculine superiority, rendered his very society a heart-rending persecution.

"In short, his whole conduct, from the first hour of our union, was calculated to produce, in a mind like mine, nothing but vicissitudes of disgust. His fondness, while it lasted, reduced me to the level of a puppet or a child, and when this had subsided, his contemptuous tyranny hurled me to the distance of a slave.

"I bore every thing, however, with silent resignation: for I was superior to the abjectness of complaint; and though I was conscious of being entitled to a different rank in the scale of being from that which he assigned me, my mind had not yet soared to the equality of the sexes; nor had I acquired the firmness of character to repel oppression, and assert my rights. But the sense of injury festered in my heart; and if my affections had found no other resting place, I should have been, indeed, most wretched.

"The happiness denied me in a husband, however, it pleased Heaven to confer upon me in a friend.

"Louisa Benfield had been the favourite playmate of my girlish days, the companion of my little pleasures, the depositary of all my secrets, my hopes, my disappointments, and my fears. She was three or four years younger than myself; but she had a quickness of sensibility, and a premature acuteness of understanding, that counterbalanced my experience, and brought us to that sort of level of intellectual equality essential, perhaps, to genuine friendship.

"While our attachment was yet maturing, we were unfortunately separated by one of those accidents of family arrangement, of which it is the lot of our sex to be the incessant sport.

"This separation was an object of reciprocal regret; and we endeavoured to supply by letters the defect of personal intercourse.

About three years after my marriage with Mr. Montfort, Louisa was also sacrificed, by the provident affection of her parents, to the arms of a man whom she could never love. She did not yield, indeed, as I had done without a struggle; for though her lover was as wealthy as the plunder of the east could make him, he was old and ugly, and his constitution and temper were alike infected by the diseases of the climate in which his property had been amassed.[1]

"Poor Louisa, however, at length was overpowered by that parental kindness

Which hospitals and bedlams would explore,

To find the rich, and only dreads the poor.[2]

"But her bondage was not of long duration. Mr. Winfred died in less than a twelvemonth after their marriage, leaving her a life interest in the whole of his immense property, *upon condition that she should never marry again.*

"Louisa was now her own mistress; and the first use she made of her liberty was to fly to me, take an adjoining house, and devote herself, in her own words, 'a vestal to the shrine of friendship.'

"From this time our attachment grew to the most excessive height of tenderness. We had much to communicate, much to sympathise upon, and for more than a year neither of us had any object to divide our affections.

---

1 Louisa's husband, a stereotypical "Nabob," got his wealth from India.
2 James Hammond (1710-42), "An Elegy to a Young Lady" ["Elegy XV"] (1733, 1743), ll. 90-91.

"It was remarkable that after this delightful intercourse had subsisted for some time, Mr. Montfort became somewhat more attentive to me. The attractions of Louisa occasioned him to spend more of his time at home than had hitherto been usual. At the same time the elevation of her character restrained his unhallowed thoughts, and the vivacity of her imagination, the variety of her knowledge, and the acuteness of her remarks, compelled him to feel that she was an intellectual being. Meanwhile the share I had an opportunity of taking in conversations better suited to my taste and education than any thing which the polite world ever thinks of introducing in the company of women, led him to a discovery, of which he had never dreamed, that I was myself something more than a mantua-maker's[1] doll to hang fashions upon.

"I began to be almost respected; and, perhaps, it had some share in increasing my attachment to Louisa, that she had been the cause of the change.

"But about this time a circumstance happened, which, though it promised to increase, eventually destroyed all the prospects of our growing felicity.

"Among the dissipated youths who had abused the name of friendship in the licencious groups of the university, was one, to whom Mr. Montfort had been particularly attached, of the name of Bowbridge; who, by the advice of a powerful relation, had renounced his academic pursuits for the *profession of the sword*; and who had spent some time in foreign service, that he might *learn his trade*.

"Captain Bowbridge, if not the handsomest, was one of the most elegant young men I ever saw. He was, indeed, in point of person, the maturity of all that my Henry promises to be. The fruit, and this the flower!

"He had also some singular traits of an exalted mind: qualities both of the head and of the heart, which, but for the blighting mildews of the college and the camp, would have rendered him an ornament to his country. He had natural good temper, and well-cultivated sense; and the urbanity of his manners was, accordingly, not a frail and superficial varnish, but a lustre emanating from the gem itself.

"Such was the man who, returning from his foreign campaign, became the guest and constant companion of Mr. Montfort.

"In our house, of course, he could not reside without being frequently in company with Louisa; nor was it long before we perceived that it was equally impossible for two such persons, and two such minds, to associate much together without feeling something more than the sympathies of friendship, or the reciprocations of esteem, and admiration. They felt the genuine fire of nature, equally removed from the smoke of epicurianism

---

1 Dressmaker.

and the phosphoric mockery of platonic illusions.[1] It was a due mixture of the finest elements; the light was ardent and the warmth was bright. In short, in the course of a few months, they became most deeply and mutually enamoured.

"All obstacles vanished before the enthusiasm of their attachment. The romantic ardour of Bowbridge was only inflamed by the tenure upon which Louisa held the whole of her property; and though he had himself no other provision than his commission and an inconsiderable annuity, he pressed, and Louisa consented to an immediate marriage.

"I own I was enthusiastic enough to enter into all their feelings; and, convinced as I was of the folly of grandeur and the vanity of wealth, I applauded the wisdom of a choice that preferred affection to opulence, and the fine feelings of the heart to the sordid pursuits of a rapacious world.

"It seemed, also, as if in every respect my happiness was to be connected with that of Louisa. Montfort appeared infected with the social contagion. He became affectionate and domesticated; and for some time continued to display a degree of fondness much more rational, and scarcely less ardent, than the first raptures of his unsatiated desire.

"But this second passion was as short lived as the first. He had neither sentiment nor understanding enough to be permanently reclaimed. The tide of his wanton passions rushed again upon his heart; and not satisfied with yielding himself to the current of profligate dissipation, he exalted in dragging back the irresolute Bowbridge into the same destroying vortex.

"Unfortunately this was but too easy a task; for though the dispositions of Bowbridge were much better than those of Montfort, his habits were equally profligate, and almost equally confirmed; and though he really continued to love his Louisa with something like a chivalrous ardour, such was the vitiated taste which a long-continued course of depraved indulgence had produced, that his senses seemed always athirst for variety; and though in the private circle he was a benevolent sentimentalist, and in retirement almost a philosopher, in the throng of dissipation and the hour of Bacchanalian hilarity, he was nearly as licentious, though not as unprincipled, as Montfort himself.

"There were some traits of distinction, indeed—generous traits!

No virgin's easy faith he e'er betray'd,
His tongue ne'er boasted of a feign'd embrace![2]

"In short, with all his irregularities, he had much feeling, and some reflection; and, though a soldier and a debauchee, the man of principle was not entirely lost in the man of pleasure, or even in the man of honour.

---

1   Here Epicureanism and Platonism have little to do with the actual philosophers Epicurus (341-270 BCE) and Plato (424-348 BCE), and signify instead unrestrained sensualism—"free love"—and sexless intimacy dominated by repressed and sublimated sexual desire.
2   James Hammond, "Elegy IV" (1743), ll. 9-10.

"Poor Louisa! how many a tear did she shed over his weaknesses and follies! she would scarcely acknowledge them to be vices. How many a plan did we devise for his reformation! How fondly did we exult in the consolation of our mutual friendship, and dwell upon every circumstance that assimilated our hapless destinies!

"There was one coincidence, in particular, of a very interesting nature, which tended, at once, to increase and to alleviate the calamities that were to follow. We were both, for the first time, with child; and both in the same stage of our pregnancy: and often, in those lonely conversations in which the strongest sympathies of the heart were excited, did we look forward with a thousand cheering hopes and trembling anxieties to that period when we should know what it was to be mothers.

"On Bowbridge, in particular, we fondly expected that this circumstance would have a powerful operation. He had a mind likely to be roused by a sense of paternal duties, and a heart that could not but be impressed by the endearments of infantile innocence.

"But, alas! vain were our hopes!—delusive were our expectations! and what we hailed as the dawn of returning felicity proved the last twilight of returning comfort. Even while we were calculating our happiness, our misery was sealed. While we anticipated the fruit, the very bud was blasted.

"Oh! Nerissa! Nerissa! how shall I unfold to thee the tale of horrors?—how paint the chilling anguish that congealed my blood, or the phrenzy that shattered my poor Louisa's brain?

"Our time was fast approaching—According to our calculations, neither of us had many days to go. We were sitting together in my chamber—cheering each other's spirits, and colouring the anxious prospect with the tints of hope.

"Pleasing—transient illusion! We had our anxieties indeed—our aweful terrors for the untried approaching situation: but in spite of these we were happy, Nerissa!—truly happy!—for we had dwelt on pictures of felicity till imagination had realised them all: and, for the moment, at least, not a thought or an emotion existed in our minds that was not allied to tenderness and hope.

"Ah! happy moment!—the last we could ever call so!—for while we were thus indulging ourselves in visionary delights, pale—breathless—and frantic, a servant of Louisa's rushed into the room, whose very countenance was a title-page of horrors.

"Articulate she could not—but the mystery was too quickly fathomed—

"Captain Bowbridge was brought home dead—

"Killed in a duel!—

"Shot by my husband's hand!"

Amelia was too much agitated to proceed. Painful remembrance absorbed all the faculties of her soul, and tears and sobs choaked up the powers of utterance.

Nerissa was not less affected than herself. Curiosity was suspended by an agony of sympathy. Pale, trembling, and bathed in tears, she sat motionless by her side, indulging the anguish of her heart in silence, and not venturing even to look in the face of her friend while their mutual agitation continued.

These violent emotions having spent themselves in tears, and both the relater and the hearer having mused themselves into something like tranquillity, Amelia resumed her narrative.

"From that time, Nerissa, I have never seen Mr. Montfort. He did not venture to return to his own house; for the whole town rung with clamours against him; and the powerful family of Bowbridge breathed nothing but insatiable revenge.

"He concealed himself in some obscure corner, I know not where, till he had an opportunity of getting on board a West-Indiaman, then preparing to sail. By this conveyance he escaped into the Island of Jamaica, where he assumed a fictitious name; and believing himself beyond the reach of justice, he buried his remorse in new scenes of riot and profligacy, indulged without control in his wonted licentiousness, and hardened his heart, by familiarity with those tyrannic cruelties which necessarily spring out of the distinctions of master and slave.

"He entered, also, into the hideous traffic of the country, and pursued it with the most unfeeling avidity. In short, rapacity and dissipation went hand in hand; and, in every point of view, he became a very West-Indian.

"But the fate and character of Montfort were the least interesting of all the considerations that pressed upon my heart. Esteem had long since given place to indifference, and indifference in its turn was supplanted by horror.

"Bowbridge seduced—and murdered by his seducer!—Louisa widowed in the pangs of childbirth!—and her unhappy infant orphaned in the womb!—These were the reflections that rendered Mr. Montfort as much an exile from my heart as from his country: and to the former, at least, he took no sort of pains to be restored.

"But if he had, my heart was too full to give him entertainment. Grief rushed upon grief, affliction upon affliction, till all the warm emotions of my breast were chilled and frozen.

"But the consummation of horror was yet to come. Fate hastened it forward. He struck the ruthless blow; and every hope, and every consolation (one, only one excepted!) was dead within me.

"A broken heart conspired with the usual pangs of nature; and Louisa died in child-birth—died in a stranger's arms. I had been delivered only the day before. I could not be present to hold her to my heart, and catch her parting breath."

"And the child?"—said Nerissa, eagerly.

"Ah Nerissa! Nerissa!" replied Amelia (drying up her tears on a sudden, as if grief had yielded to some stronger passion), "this is the most awful part of the story; and my soul is shaken with terror as I relate it.

"That child, Nerissa—that child!" repeated she, looking round the room with wild anxiety—

"I will tell thee all, my girl!" continued she, rising from her seat, and pressing Nerissa's hand with great emotion—"I will tell thee all."

Her eye beamed with tender confidence; and poor Nerissa was all ear; when the conversation was suddenly broken off, by a loud knocking at the street door, which proclaimed the arrival of Montfort.

CHAP. II.

Containing several Particulars of the early Education of our Hero.

Mysterious Agitations.—First Emotions of a Father.—Seeds of Paternal Jealousy.—Maternal Tuition; Discipline of the new School—Paternal Authority; Vindication of the old School.—Demonstrations of the Superiority of discordant Systems.—Conjugal Toleration.—Indications of Character.—Human Consistencies.

NEVER was interruption more unseasonable; at least in the estimation of poor Nerissa; whose hopes of possessing an important secret (so often promised, and so anxiously expected) were once more disappointed at the very moment when sympathy and curiosity were mutually excited to the very climax of agitation.

The heart of Amelia vibrated to the sound of the knocker. It vibrated with delirious agitation. She awakened as from the midst of some troubled dream: and her spirits were as flurried, and her thoughts as disarranged, as though the resounding of the door had been the first warning of the approaching interview.

She stared at first around her with vacant wildness; then suddenly let fall the hand of Nerissa, flew with feverish impatience from room to room, as if she knew not what she was about, or were desirous of shunning, rather than meeting, her returning husband.

The sound of his footstep on the stairs, however, seemed to recall her consciousness, and remind her of the line of conduct she ought to pursue. Collecting, therefore, what little resolution she was mistress of, she rushed forwards, with flattering congratulations, to receive him.

Montfort returned her greetings with morose indifference; a deportment, however, that wounded not her sensibility: it being, in reality, no other than she expected: besides, her mind was occupied with very different emotions.

The ardour and impatience, therefore, with which he enquired for "his Henry! his son! his boy!" more than compensated for his want of apparent affection, almost of civility, towards herself.

With a hasty step and palpitating heart, she conducted him to the bedside of her little cherub, and drawing back the curtains, with mute and motionless anxiety waited the issue of the first important impression.

The innocent was fast asleep: but he smiled amidst his slumbers. His little head rested upon his right arm, while the other was stretched carelessly over the bed-clothes, and his dark and glossy ringlets, wantonly straying over his glowing cheek, his arching eyebrows, and long thick eyelashes, gave character and animation to a picture, which nature could alone delineate, and can only be shadowed by the retentive feelings of parental admiration.

Hard must have been the heart of that man, defective even in one of the strongest passions of corrupted minds, who did not feel a swelling gratification in contemplating himself as the father of so promising a little being!

Montfort indeed was not over-gifted in the more tender sympathies; but, in the passion alluded to, he was by no means wanting, as the reader must already have concluded. Every thing to which the pronoun *my* could be attached had considerable importance in his eyes. From this rule we must not even except his wife; with respect to whom, though he scrupled not to aggravate neglect by insults and moroseness; and though he came, at last, almost to hate her for the evident superiority of her understanding, yet was he as sensible as the fondest husband in the universe, of the personal consequence he derived from being *Lord and Master* of a woman who attracted admiration from the whole circle in which she moved.

It is hardly necessary, therefore, to inform the reader what was the effect of the portrait thus exhibited. The heart of the rugged Montfort swelled with exultation. Parental pride, parental tenderness, all the gentle and the ardent feelings that constitute the better part of the family of self-love thronged around his heart, relaxed his features, and melted in his eyes.

"My Henry! My fine boy! My child! my lovely child!" he exclaimed with great fervour.

Even Amelia was no longer regarded with indifference. From the infant to the mother was a transition of tenderness almost inevitable; and his eye rolled from one to the other with a complacency that seemed to be replete with propitious omen to the former, and made the heart bound in the bosom of the latter. Her felicity was too great to be restrained. Every vice and every injury was forgotten in the man who felt as a father to her little Henry; and, overcome with delight and gratitude, she fell upon his neck, and watered it with a shower of tears.

But the very fondness of Montfort was rugged and precipitate. The dread of jarring, with too sudden conflict, the irritable nerves of slumbering infancy, entered not into his calculation of moral evils; and, disentangling himself from the embraces of a wife, he snatched our little hero eagerly and hastily to his bosom, and awaked him with a frantic kiss.

Poor little Henry had never been familiarised to such ungentle fondness. He was accordingly bewildered with terror; and finding himself in the strong grasp of a stranger, whose harsh features and sun-burnt countenance were ill calculated to soothe the apprehensions of childhood, he began to shriek and struggle for emancipation, and stretch forth his imploring hands to Amelia for protection; nor would he, at any rate, be pacified, till, reluctantly resigned to her arms, he sunk in conscious security on that bosom, where he had been accustomed to be sustained and cherished.

Natural as this trifling incident may appear, it awakened in the breast of Montfort some of those malignant feelings, whose mischievous tendency, in the formation of the mind of our little hero, the reader will hereafter have sufficient occasion to observe.

So inconsistent is the self-love of the morose and envious—so confounding to the understanding are those ill-grounded, confused, and superstitious notions, too generally entertained, of parental rights and filial reverence, that he seemed to challenge the fond compliance of a *child* before he had even avowed the aweful relationship of a father, and (absolute stranger as he was) felt as though he were injured in the preference given to one whose care and indulgent fondness had been familiar from the earliest dawn of infantile remembrance.

These emotions escaped not the observation of Amelia: for, to do him justice, Montfort was no hypocrite: and, though his tongue was not very communicative, he had neither the inclination nor the power to conceal the passions that so frequently agitated his soul. Amelia beheld them, in the present instance, with peculiar anxiety, and endeavoured to counteract the unfavourable impression.

"Wilt thou not go to thy papa, my dear?" said she to Henry. "Art though frightened at thy dear papa, whom thou hast so often talked about, so often wished to see?"

The question operated as she desired. He sprung upright in her arms, turned himself half round to Montfort, and clapping his little hands together, "Papa!" exclaimed he, eagerly. "And have I got a papa to-night?"

Amelia looked in the face of Montfort. His features were softened. The demon was quelled; and the father was again triumphant.

"Thou hast, my babe! thou hast," replied she, emphatically; "thank heaven thou hast! Go to him, my dear babe! Kiss him, and make him love thee, as I do."

Henry's cheeks were flushed with the deepest crimson. He twined his little arms around the paternal neck, and testified his delight by a thousand caresses, and infantile endearments. All that was human in the breast of Montfort was again awakened; and Amelia for a while was happy.

Thus were the apprehensions of Amelia effectually removed by the event of the first interview between Montfort and her little Henry: nor did his affection abate with his experience of the endearing manners and promising intellect of the little hero. The vanity of the father seemed almost to swallow up every other passion, and "*my* clever little Henry! *my* fine boy! and *my* brave lad!" were the constant themes of arrogant exultation.

But it was not long before Amelia had reason to reflect that the paternal affection she had been so anxious to inspire in behalf of her little cherub, was, in reality, more to be deprecated than all the neglect and moroseness to which she had looked forward with so much terror.

Had the animated countenance and affectionate deportment of Henry taken no possession of the heart of Montfort, he would have been resigned, of course, with few and transient interruptions, to her management, and to that rational system of education, upon which she had hitherto acted with such flattering appearances of success. But, as it was, the caprices of paternal fondness broke in upon all her plans; baffled every effort towards the formation of a benignant, persevering, and consistent mind; and counter-acted all those theoretical and practical lessons with which it was her constant labour to nerve the intellect and ameliorate the heart.

Before the return of Montfort, Henry had never felt the weight of a blow. He was acquainted with pain only as one of the accidents of the constitution of nature, or of the necessities, or involuntary consequences of thoughtless indiscretion.

What is commonly called punishment (that is to say, the *revenge* of the strong against the disobedience of the weak) was not even known to him in any of its modifications: nor was the sweetness of his temper ever ruffled by capricious restraints, or the refusal of any reasonable indulgence.

When it was necessary to refuse, however, it was done with a prudent mixture of mildness and inflexibility; and the true reason of the restriction was invariably assigned in terms the best accommodated to his childish understanding. Neither did he ever know what it was to obtain any gratification, even in itself the most innocent, by perverseness or ill humour.

He never was caressed because he was fretful; nor appeased with sugar plumbs when impatient under inevitable disappointments: nor were his ingenuity or his virtues rewarded by sensual ministration to his pride or appetites: by buns and sweetmeats, toys and gaudy apparel.

Whatever was proper in this way, flowed as a general consequence of the love of those around him, not as the price of any particular good action. But every trait he exhibited of sympathy, of generosity, or good nature, was sure to be succeeded by those endearments, those looks and expressions of attachment which his little heart soon began to consider the best rewards, or rather as the invaluable *consequences* of benignant conduct.

He had also his circle of exercise and amusement; a little world, as it were, of his own; within the bounds of which, at proper intervals, sometimes alone, and sometimes with companions of his own years, he enjoyed what some would consider as a sort of savage liberty, which strengthened his limbs, expanded his lungs, and gave vigour and independency to his mind.

There was besides another apartment in a remote part of the premises (but not a dark hole, or a chamber invested with any dungeon-like terrors), to which, when the frowardness of childhood made its appearance in tears or gusts of passion, he was calmly conducted, without any marks of vehemence or anger, and left by himself, with some toys and playthings around him, merely secluded from the society of those to whom his ill humour was troublesome, till he returned to his wonted cheerfulness or tranquillity.

To these regulations Amelia attributed a considerable proportion of that amiable tenderness of disposition, that general cheerfulness, that promptitude and energy of mind, which made her little darling the love and admiration of all who knew him.

But this system was too refined, and favoured too much of innovation for the gross conceptions, and rooted prejudices of Montfort: even if caprice and sullen moroseness had suffered him to be systematic in any thing.

He had also another very powerful objection to this new mode of tuition. It was his wife's invention; and therefore a sort of infringement of his intellectual prerogative: an outrage against the natural superiority of his masculine understanding.

A counter-revolution was therefore presently attempted: and the new order of things attacked with all the vehemence of paternal indignation.

In this respect, however, Amelia (so prudently passive on every other point) maintained her ground with the most steady perseverance, and upheld her system unaltered in every thing that respected not only her own deportment towards the child, but the deportment, also, of the generality of the household.

But it was impossible to prevent Montfort himself from acting upon the old principles of lawless might and established anarchy; and he

"(imperious lord of pleasure and of pain)"[1]

proceeded, accordingly, in the capricious distribution of blows and caresses, unreasonable indulgence and unprovoked austerity, and all the wantonness of inconsistent tyranny.

The consequences of this discord were soon perceptible in the mind of little Henry. Reason loses much of its force in proportion as other motives are habitually appealed to, because the mind in reality is thereby rendered less rational; and the sullen insensibility produced by capricious punishment, makes the ear of childhood deaf to the else-powerful charm of affectionate remonstrance. Accordingly, Henry became less docile to the instructions and admonitions of his mother; and that consistency of character, that amiable tenderness, that confident serenity, and almost uniform cheerfulness which had formerly distinguished him, gradually gave way to capricious fretfulness, wanton acts of petulance and tyranny; and, in short, to occasional sallies of almost all those evil dispositions that mark the ravages of inconsistent mode of education.

Amelia beheld these ravages with the deepest affliction, and though she had little confidence in the power of reason over such a mind as Mont-

---

1 Lady Mary Montagu (1687-1762), "On the Death of Mrs. Bowes" (1724), ll. 8-9.

fort's, she determined to try the experiment; and, taking the opportunity when he was in one of his best humours, she began to lament, in terms the most mild and inoffensive, the change that had taken place in the mind of Henry, since he had been subjected to the occasional influence of blows and unreasonable indulgences.

"Madam!" replied Montfort sternly, "none of your newfangled notions for me. I am not to have my brains turned topsy-turvy with the doctrines of your petticoat philosophers.[1] I shall have my boy educated like other boys."

Am. "Then you must be contented, Mr. Montfort, that he should be like other boys; that he should be petulent, revengeful, and untractable. That he should be vehement on the one hand, or sullen on the other. That he should be at once outrageous and timid, sly and improvident, ignorant and assuming: that (except in the little circle of those who are attached to him by the vanity of self-love), he should neither love nor be beloved: and should know no other distinction between right and wrong than the punishment he dreads, and the gratifications he desires."

Mont. "It is not my intention, madam, to chop logic with petticoat orators! nor shall I be persuaded by *you* to make grave speeches and talk a parcel of rigmaroll about reason and duty, to boys of seven years old. The reason and duty of a child is to obey his father; and, if he does not do it without, he must be thwacked[2] into it, or the father must expect to be despised."

Am. "And yet, Mr. Montfort (with all your blows and your severities), you are always complaining that I (who appeal to no such expedients) have more influence over the child than you have."

Mont. "Aye, that's because you humour and spoil him with your d—d foolish effeminate nonsense."

Am. "Nay, prithee, Mr. Montfort, have the candour to recollect, that you yourself are continually complaining (with too much justice) that the boy is not half so good as he used to be; that is, when he had nothing but this effeminate nonsense to influence him.

"Now, what is this but admitting, that he did better without this thwacking, as you call it, than he does with it? and that, the less he is reasoned with, and the more he is beaten and pampered, terrified and humoured, the more all that was once so amiable and interesting is perverted and obliterated from his mind?"

"No, madam; no; I say no!" replied Montfort, elevating his voice more and more at every repetition of the conclusive negative. "I tell you no!

---

1   Women educational writers include Anna Laetitia (Aikin) Barbauld (1743-1825) and Mary Wollstonecraft (1759-97), both published by Joseph Johnson, a prominent source of liberal educational works.

2   In Henry Fielding's *The History of Tom Jones* (1749), Rev. Thwackum, Tom Jones's teacher, relies on corporal punishment.

"The boy indeed does grow worse and worse every day, in spite of all I can do to reform him. But you spoil him for the purpose; and teach him to despise and hate me, with your foolish jargon and mock morality."

Am. "I spoil him for the purpose, Mr. Montfort! I teach him to hate you! Is it not very evident, that it is the principal object of my anxiety to teach him to love you, and endear himself to your affections?"

Mont. "No, madam, I say no. That's your d—d hypocrisy to make him hate me so much the more. But mark me, madam," continued he, rising from his chair, and lifting his voice to the very height of fury and indignation, "by G— he shall either love me, or I will take care he shall not love you long.

"Chew upon that, madam! Chew upon that, and remember, that as I have a right to be obeyed, so, also, I have the power to enforce obedience."

What he meant by this threat, or whether he had any defined or specific meaning in his head, we pretend not to determine: for the tongue of malice frequently outstrips its invention; and the vehemency of threats is almost an indication of the impotence of performance.

Be this as it may, as he uttered these words, he turned suddenly round, with a look expressive of some meditated vengeance, and rushing out of the room, left the poor terrified Amelia to ponder at leisure over his mysterious denunciations; convinced, by this experiment, not only of the inutility, but the danger of all further remonstrance.

As the deportment of Montfort, with respect to little Henry, was far from being improved by the preceding dialogue, the ill consequences to the temper and disposition of the child became daily more apparent; while, at the same time, there was too much reason to apprehend that his understanding might be as fatally undermined as his morals and his happiness.

Hitherto the books he was to read in had been selected with the most scrupulous attention, both to the style and subjects. The little sensible publications of Mrs. Barbauld,[1] and others who have trod in the same paths of instruction, were the first articles of his library; and before even these were put into his hand, they were carefully perused by Amelia herself, who expunged every passage that appeared to be inconsistent with her own particular plan of education. She cultivated, also, herself the art of copying the printed character; and, by that means, was enabled to embrace every opportunity of impressing the moral arising from temporary circumstances on the mind of her pupil; making him, from time to time, little appropriate lessons, in the form of dialogues and short pathetic tales, applicable to the incidents of the day; and which on that account, made the more lasting impression on his mind.

At the same time, all those silly, or those mysterious books that are calculated to impress erroneous or disputable notions of the general system

---

1 Anna Laetitia (Aikin) Barbauld (1743-1825), prominent poet and educational writer, came from a liberal Dissenting background. Her *Lessons for Children* (1778-79) was especially influential.

of things, to inculcate false systems of morality, and the idle terrors of superstition, were carefully kept out of his way; till a proper foundation of facts and realities should be laid, from which he might soar, without danger, into the regions of fancy and opinion.

But these precautions were rendered abortive by the mischievous fondness of Montfort for old wives' tales, and narrations of the terrible and the marvellous.

His principal delight was to teach the boy to recite all the antiquated jargon of the nursery; and to see him shuddering at some tale of nautical superstition, which he would frequently enforce with all the fantastic gestures and distortions of countenance which his perverted humour could suggest.

In vain were little Red Riding Hood, the Seven Champions, and Jack the Giant-killer[1] excluded from the nursery: they found admission in the parlour: nor would this perverse and capricious being ever permit the child to read any thing between his knees but tales of devils, witches, and hobgoblins, with which he generally filled his pockets every time he passed by the stalls where trash of this description is exposed to sale.

These attempts of an inconsiderate father to corrupt the understanding of his child, were but too successful. Henry soon contracted a passion for these marvellous absurdities: and learned, as a natural consequence, to shake with idle terrors in the dark, and to stand in awe of all the bugbears conjured up by the disordered imagination of ignorant credulity.

In the mean time, Montfort was not forgetful of his own gratifications. Time and circumstances had deepened the shadows, rather than altered the lines of his character. He was surrounded by the same dissipated connexions (as far, at least, as the mutations of morality will permit) in which he had formerly delighted. And he plunged, if not with equal delight, with increased avidity into the same, or still more sordid pursuits of voluptuousness and profusion.

This circumstance, however, gave little anxiety to Amelia. All things considered, it will not be thought surprising that she, who had long regarded the depravity of her husband as perfectly incorrigible, and the first object of whose anxiety was the moral and intellectual prosperity of her darling child, should regard with complacency every event that detained her husband from his home.

She had formerly suffered sufficiently from his shameless profligacy: nothing was now so formidable as his domestication. She took care, therefore, to throw no impediments in the way of his irregular pursuits; and was even not displeased at the visits of his loosest and most prodigal companions, because they were most likely to draw him away on parties or excursions of pleasure: and she esteemed any injury he might do to his

---

1 Popular chapbooks for children. The educational debate in the novel reflects the actual debate between rational moralists, who advocated educating the understanding, and Rousseauvian advocates of nature and imagination.

fortune, while abroad, as of trifling consequence, in comparison with those mischiefs he was sure to be heaping, while at home, upon the mind of Henry.

The consequences of this deportment were even more favourable than she expected; for Montfort, finding that he was never thwarted in any thing that related to his own appetites, began to have less pleasure in counteracting her plans of education; and, though he had not understanding enough to alter his own conduct towards Henry, yet, as he could not be quite blind to the progress he made under her management, in every thing that did not interfere with his own parental authority, he left him without further contention, to her disposal.

In this manner glided away between four and five important, and in some respects, decisive years; while Henry rapidly advancing in stature and youthful grace, began to exhibit, in a very striking manner, that diversity and inconsistency of character which were the inevitable consequences of his discordant education.

The mother's part, indeed, predominated in his disposition; but the father's was too conspicuous. Hers were his sentiments, his principles, his generous emulation, and, in many essential particulars, his manners also. Her rational and endearing management had expanded his mind, cultivated his intellect, and awakened in his breast all the strong and corrective feelings of sympathy and benevolence: but, on the other hand, the capricious flux and reflux of tyranny and indulgence he had experienced from his father had broken and enfeebled his spirit, had deformed his better qualities, and given a dash of pride and petulance to his disposition, very inconsistent with that general philanthropy which Amelia had inculcated as the most amiable characteristic of human nature.

Equally inconsistent with that fortitude and independence of mind which she regarded as the essential guardians of every other virtue, was that timidity which had been produced by the threats and blows of Montfort; while the voluptuous propensities which had been fostered by an idle indulgence of his appetites, and still more to be the baneful influence of paternal example, had destroyed in some degree, that correctness of taste and simplicity of manners so essential to happiness and conspicuous virtue.

One principle, however, had been inspired by Montfort, which, though somewhat of an ambiguous character, might rather have a tendency to counteract the evil influence of some of the preceding traits. Both the ridiculous books he had purchased for the boy, and his own hyperbolical tales of marvellous sights and adventures, had encouraged a romantic thirst of enterprize and a desire to be distinguished by extraordinary exploits.

Neither did that nautical roughness and hardihood of manners which Montfort had acquired during his residence abroad, and which were cherished by the moroseness of his temper, render him a whit the less desirous of giving his son every accomplishment and exterior advantage of educa-

tion consistent with his rank in life and that ample fortune he might hereafter expect to inherit.

He was, indeed, careful to imbue his mind with notions of the superiority and consequence that belonged to these advantages: and, perhaps,
nothing would have gratified his vanity so completely as that Henry
Montfort should be considered as the most accomplished young gentleman of his age.

In this feeling, though under the regulation of much better principles,
Amelia entirely sympathised. She considered exterior accomplishments as
the proper embellishments of wisdom and virtue; and she was ever ready
to maintain that persons of rank and fortune owe it to society, in remuneration for those advantages they enjoy under its institutions, that they
should, both by their patronage and example, contribute to every species
of refinement that may soften the asperities of human passions, and exalt
the character of nations and of man.

Neither cost nor attention were, therefore, spared in this respect; and
the two parents, who could agree in nothing else, seemed to vie with each
other in promoting the avidity of our hero in the pursuit of every elegant
accomplishment.

The progress he made was correspondent to their cares and their
wishes; and, before the completion of his eleventh year, he began to attract
the admiration of all who were acquainted with the family, by the liveliness of his fancy, and the fascination of his deportment and conversation.
Nor was he less distinguished over his youthful companions by the attainments in the learned languages and other more valuable departments of
education.

Still, however, a degree of untractable impetuosity became daily more
and more conspicuous in his deportment; and the frequent sallies of
youthful irregularity, which maternal admonitions could not always
restrain, were occasions of almost continual irritation on the part of
Montfort, and of mournful anxiety in the affectionate bosom of Amelia.
Nor will it appear at all surprising to those who are acquainted with the
inconsistent movements of that proud and irritable organ the human
heart, that the former of these should be the more intolerant to these
irregularities, from the recollection that they were precisely what had been
predicted as the inevitable consequences of his own deportment.

The vices of the son were irrefragable proofs of the superior discernment of the mother, and were, therefore, not to be endured by the lordly
intellect of the father.

By a trick of mind not uncommon in the juggling of human intellect,
he contrived, however, to exculpate the real criminal, by criminating the
monitor who would have prevented the crime; as though in the predic-
tions of reason, as has been sometimes the case, perhaps, with those of
pretended prophecy, the person who had foretold was to be regarded as
the aggressor who had produced the deprecated catastrophe. But the

ingenuity of self-deception had been exerted to little purpose, if no practical inference had been adducible from its subtile theorems. Montfort's
logic was not of so inert a quality. Having advanced so syllogistically in the
first instance, he proceeded to his inferences with equal accuracy; and
very deliberately persuaded himself that the boy would correct his errors
if he were but removed from the influence of the only person who had any
sort of power in restraining them. This logical conclusion being once
established, he determined to act upon it without delay, and send him to
Eton college for the laudable purpose of correcting his irregularities and
improving his morals.

Though Amelia was by no means convinced of the ameliorating tendency of the examples that would there surround him, she was far from
being dissatisfied with this resolution.

It was, indeed, the very thing she wished; conceiving that a youth of
Henry's ample expectations ought to have more early opportunities of
becoming acquainted with the world, and of forming extensive connections, than could be furnished by a private education, how liberal soever
might be the principles on which it was conducted.

She shuddered also at the reflection that he was rapidly advancing
towards an age when the profligacy of his father's morals would not fail to
be observed and comprehended in the full extent; and when, of course,
she would be reduced to the distressing alternative of either yielding up
his youthful mind, unwarned, to the influence of so fatal and powerful an
example, or of weakening the bonds of filial reverence and affection, by
painting, in all their proper hues and lines of deformity, the ruinous and
disgraceful vices in which her infatuated husband was so deeply plunged.

Under these alarming apprehensions she had fixed her eyes upon a
public school as the only asylum of her hopes; and had only forborne to
give utterance to her wishes, lest the very circumstances of her suggesting
them, should be the means of their disappointment. Indeed she had little
doubt that, if the capricious mind of Montfort was left to its own direction, the pride of having his son educated in the usual seminaries of the
great, or the malignant desire of depriving her of the beloved society of her
Henry, would, sooner or later, lead him to the adoption of the measure.

The event justified her calculations. The resolution was suddenly taken
and as suddenly executed; and our hero was sent to Eton at the conclusion of his eleventh year, where we shall leave him, for awhile, to his tutors
and his playmates, while we trace the progress of some of those changes
in the mind of Montfort, which have been already alluded to in the conversation between Amelia and Nerissa, and which, in the estimation of
many of our readers, may not render him either the more respectable or
more beloved.

CHAP. III.

Containing several Circumstances relative to the Conduct and Connections of Montfort in the West Indies, and the Influence of Events upon his Character.

West-Indian Morality.—As Adventurer from Rotten-row.—A Friend in Need.—Mortgager and Mortgagee—The Courtezan—Progress of Accumulation.—Indication of a troubled Conscience.—Progress of a depraved intellect.

MONTFORT's six years' residence in the West Indies had not been a mere blank in his existence. On the contrary, it had been one of the busiest and most eventful periods of his life.

The passions and vices of the climate, or, to speak more correctly, the habits of the order, or *disorder*, of society there established, had seized, with irresistible violence, on a mind already predisposed to their influence. He had his amours, his intrigues, his sensual revelries; he had also his avaricious projects, his rapacious pursuits, and usurious speculations.

In short, while on the one hand he became voluptuous beyond the measure of European habitude, on the other, inordinate rapacity entwined itself with the propensities of excessive indulgence, and more than kept pace with his growing profusion.

He did not, indeed, in the first instance, become himself a planter. This was rather eventually the result of the use he made of his capital and consequent influence, than the immediate object of his speculations. But those who have observed the facility with which, even in our own hemisphere, the transition is made from the character of mortgagee to that of proprietor, will not be at all surprised that in a country so frequently resorted to by half-bankrupted adventurers, from the vain hopes of rapid accumulation, and where a mortgage is far from being as marketable a commodity as among us, a similar sort of transition should occasionally occur; and that borrowing should end in sale, and loan be converted into purchase.

Such was the case with respect to a transaction in which Montfort was engaged shortly after his arrival in Jamaica.

A young man of the name of Staunton having run through an estate of several thousands a year in England, had been induced, by the vulgar idea of the case and rapidity with which property is to be accumulated in the West Indies, to turn his eyes upon that quarter of the world, with a view to dispose of the few thousands he was able to preserve from the general ruin, in the purchase of a sugar plantation; by means of which he had no doubt of returning, in the course of a few years, to his native country, with more than original splendour.

Full of this idea, with no other preparation than a mere letter of introduction to a notorious proctor,[1] he repaired to the island of Jamaica; where

---

1 Person hired to manage someone else's business affairs.

he arrived much about the same time with Montfort, accompanied by a young female of more personal attractions than either character or accomplishments; and whose licentious vivacity was, perhaps, even a more powerful attraction than her beauty. Upon her he had wasted, in England, no inconsiderable proportion of his substance, and to her, in the ruin she had contributed to hasten, he continued to be attached with an infatuation not likely to be abated by the cheerfulness with which she consented to share his fortunes in the new and distant scenes of his speculations.

It will not appear surprising that the man who had never been in the habit of calculating what he could afford to spend, should not have thought it necessary to make an estimate of what he could afford to buy; or even to enquire, before he undertook so long and hazardous a voyage, the extent or nature of the establishment necessary to realise his views.

What had his superior genius to do with calculations?

He had sold his estates, his plate, his furniture, his studd,[1] his equipage, his every thing. He had paid what he could not avoid paying. He had converted the residue into bank notes. He had embarked with them, sink or swim, in his portmanteau from the port of London, and arrived, safe and sound, body and baggage, wind and limb, at Kingston in Jamaica. What more had he to do? Fortune would come flowing in upon him of her own accord.

"Whip them up, Mr. Negro-driver! damme make the black cattle work, that the sugar may dance across the herring pond, and the shiners[2] come rolling in; then, heighho for England and Rotten-row[3] again; with my phoenix of Arabia by my side, and my six barbaries[4] in hand, and Hyde-park shall be all in a blaze, my boys."

But hold, master Phaeton![5] not so fast, if you please. The horses are not properly harnessed, your chariot of the sun has a rotten axle-tree, and you may chance to get a broken neck before you arrive at the goal.

On applying to his proctor, our dashing adventurer was presently informed that a plantation of at least 1000 acres of good productive land was absolutely and indispensably necessary to his views. At the same time an estate of that extent, then under sale, was recommended at the moderate price of 12,000l.[6]

The very mention of this sum, as it exceeded the totality of his portmanteau, threw the degraded hero of Rotten-row into a most profound state of melancholy and depression; for as for credit, he had already used that too freely in those parts of the world where he was known, to be able

---

1 Stable of horses.
2 Coins.
3 A fashionable riding-track and meeting-place in Hyde Park, London.
4 Barbary horses.
5 A light, four-wheeled, open carrriage. Phaeton was the reckless driver of Zeus's solar chariot in classical mythology.
6 The final "l" signifies pounds sterling.

to build on any resources of that description; and in Jamaica—he was utterly a stranger.

Fortune, however, seemed to favour him beyond his expectations; for the proctor perceiving from the whole deportment and conversation of his client, that he was one of those characters who seldom fail to be profitable commodities in the hands of an agent who understands his business, and, having satisfied himself that what properly he did possess would be immediately forth-coming, thought it a great pity that so promising a transaction should slip through his fingers.

To make short of a long story, our worthy proctor happened to be acquainted with the worthy planter who was the host, and sole friend and confident, of the exiled Montfort; and by the logic of these two worthy go-betweens, he was influenced to advance to young Staunton, in the first instance, the money that was requisite to complete the purchase; and, after that, at successive times, still more considerable sums for the purchase of mules, and negroes, and other cattle, the clearing and planting of due proportions of land, and the erection of mills, boiling-houses, curing-houses, distilleries, trashes[1] and shingles,[2] hospitals and stables, and all those innumerable et cetera essential to such an establishment: but the very tythe of whose enormous amount had never entered into the imagination of the inconsiderate adventurer.

Still, however, he went on from step to step for upwards of two years, borrowing and speculating, and feeding his imagination with a prospect of distant riches; while the expenditure, as must always be the case in the forming of a new plantation, immeasurably exceeding the returns, plunged him still deeper and deeper into inextricable embarrassment. At the same time, his crops being of necessity disposed of, without competition, to the agent of his creditor, fell infinitely short of his expectations in the revenue they returned, and his prodigal expenses were constantly regulated, not by his present means, but by his distant hopes.

It is scarcely necessary to add, as the sequel of this adventure, that the ruin began at the faro bank of the great house in Pall Mall,[3] was rapidly completed on the plantation in Jamaica; and that, Staunton being importunate for fresh loans while Montfort was strenuously insisting on the repayment of what was already advanced, law and authority siding with the latter, he obtained complete possession of the whole property upon terms dictated by himself, or rather by the same worthy proctor by whose advice he had, in the first instance, entered upon the speculation.

Staunton returned to England upon the brief and final settlement of his affairs, with only a few hundred pounds in his pocket; with which he determined, however, to make a dash upon his arrival, just to get himself

---

1 Place where refuse from sugar cane processing was deposited.
2 Shingled buildings.
3 Faro, a card game, and Pall Mall, known for its fashionable London clubs, where gambling was not uncommon.

into credit again; and from thenceforward to be a rook[1] at those very gaming tables where he had formerly been so frequently pigeoned:[2] a resolution in which he found abundant consolation for every loss he had sustained, that of his mistress only excepted; who no sooner perceived that his fortunes were absolutely irretrievable, than she began to discover that her attachment was not quite so ardent as in the season of his prosperity she had so frequently professed:—

> Did I but purpose to embark with thee
> On the smooth surface of a summer's sea![3]

This woman, whose biography may not, perhaps, be entirely uninteresting, was the daughter of a laundress at the fashionable end of the town; and though she had considerable attractions, a pair of very fine eyes, a clear and glowing complection, a tempting lip, and a premature voluptuousness of form, she had continued to carry home shirts and cravats till she entered upon her nineteenth year, to many of the first gentlemen of the ton,[4] husbands, bachelors, and widowers, without any blemish upon her reputation.

At the critical period, however, that sly young gentleman master Cupid, veiling himself, like his grandpapa of old, in a shower of gold, prevailed over the self-denial of Miss Danae;[5] at a time when, perhaps, the danger of discovery was thought to be entirely out of the question, from the circumstance of her intended nuptials with a young shop-keeper of the neighbourhood; which, according to agreement, were to have taken place at the distance only of a few weeks from the period of this two-fold temptation.

But the death of a near relation, and the customs of the world, which, in spite of a handsome legacy, compelled the intended bridegroom to be dismally sorry for the six succeeding months, unfortunately deferred the happy day, till certain indications began to render it conspicuous that the happiness he expected had been anticipated from some other quarter.

The consequence may be readily suggested; and though the fruit of the unfortunate amour came silent into the world, the reputation of our young laundress was gone, and her hopes of an eligible establishment, in the matrimonial way, being effectually destroyed, she began, from the very same motives that for a time had induced her to preserve her chastity, to consider how she might thenceforward dispose of it to the most permanent advantage.

With this view she gradually renounced the servile occupation of her mother, and began to assume the appearance, confidence, and manners

---

1 Swindler.
2 Swindled.
3 Matthew Prior (1664-1721), *Henry and Emma* (1709), ll. 4-5, 15-16.
4 Fashionable world.
5 A Greek mythological daughter, imprisoned in a tower; Zeus came to her in a shower of gold and impregnated her.

of that rank of life which she had hitherto contemplated at humble distance. In the mean time she threw out her lures and glances at suitors of fortune and fashion, and by the dexterity with which she played her part, had soon a train of lovers at her feet, whose devotion she imagined would enable her to look rather with satisfaction than regret on the disappointment of those hopes which had been inspired by the attachment of the young mercer;[1] an expectation in which she had the more reason to confide, as she had command enough over herself to yield her favours only upon long and earnest solicitation, and to make the conquest a matter of importance to the vanity as well as the desires of her lovers.

The liveliness of her manners, and the charm of her conversation (which, though neither very refined nor particularly intelligent, was exceedingly insinuating), gave a sort of permanency to the influence of her personal attractions; and Staunton had not prevailed upon her *to put herself entirely under his protection*, without entering the lists with several powerful competitors, who contended for the same honour with a degree of chivalrous ardour, that might have gratified the vanity of the most immaculate heroine of romance. It is even possible (notwithstanding the height of his curricle,[2] and the splendor of his liveries) that he was, at last, indebted for the preference that was given him, to his having actually inspired her with all the partiality of which her temperament and character were susceptible.

But although this partiality had been strong enough to influence her to cross the Atlantic, and to enter into all his hopes and speculations of retrieving his shattered fortune, it was not sufficiently permanent to induce her to return again with an actually ruined bankrupt, whose only prospect of subsistence was the faro table.

In short, new scenes were opened to her, and new projects were formed. She beheld with a discerning eye, those attractive artifices by which the mulatto women, in defiance of all the disadvantages of complexion, and the opprobrium of "relations on the coast,"[3] eclipsed at once the more delicate charms and boasted accomplishments both of the European ladies, and the native whites. She beheld it at first, indeed, with surprise and indignation; but soon discerning the cause, with a spirit not very unlike that boasted virtue of patriotism, which has prompted so many noble and so many detestable actions, she determined to vindicate the honour of white and red, against the triumphant voluptuousness of the olive complexion and tawney-coloured votaries of the West-Indian Venus.

Accordingly she soon learned to practise all the seducing blandish-

---

1 Thelwall's father was a silk mercer.
2 Light, two-wheeled carriage.
3 According to Baron de Wimpffen (1797), this was the expression by which the French expressed their contempt for those they suspected of having even a drop of African blood (41-42; see Appendix B2c).

ments of that lascivious race; to dance the chicca[1] with all the vivacity, the grace, the enticing wantonness of her instructors, to rival them in that alluring negligence of dress, which rather shades than conceals the beauties of a voluptuous form, and, more than all the profusion of elaborate ornament, gives fuel to the impetuosity of desire. Nay, she even learned to bind the handkerchief round the head with a surprising grace; adopting only the form of that ornament, and judiciously selecting such colours for its embellishment, as might best accord, not with the complexions of those whom she imitated, but with her own.

Her attention to these minutiae was not bestowed in vain. She had not only the satisfaction of preserving the undivided affections of Staunton, but of becoming the only European woman whose conversation was not abjured by the gayer part of our sex for the more insinuating caresses of the woman of colour.

Charmed with these flattering appearances, she conceived the ambitious project of becoming the Aspasia or the Laiis[2] of Jamaica; and perceiving how things were going with her old gallant, she had transferred her affections, or, in other words, yielded the clandestine possession of her person, some time before his departure, to a new and more powerful lover, under whose protection we shall take the liberty of leaving her for the present, while we return to other subjects more obviously connected with our history.

The final catastrophe of Staunton's hair-brained adventure, having put his mortgagee into absolute possession of a large and flourishing plantation, the new proprietor was by no means indifferent as to the means of turning it to the best advantage. He saw very plainly that, by a resident planter, at least, who had an unembarrassed capital, there were some sweets to be collected from 1000 acres[3] of sugar-canes: and as he seemed to want some employment to fill up the pauses of sensuality (the islands not presenting the *diversity* of amusements he had been used to in the capital of his native country), he determined to retain what he had thus acquired in his own hands.

Thus did the exiled Montfort, the once heedless haughty devotee of fashionable dissipation in the metropolis of Britain, become a planter of sugar-canes in the West Indies. And as he had obtained an extensive possession (by a very easy purchase), the larger part of which was already brought into a high state of cultivation and order; and as he possessed an

---

1 Snycopated dance of African origin, described by Wimpffen as strongly erotic (111-13). "Chicca," a fermented drink from maize, might suggest *chicca*'s association with intoxication and uninhibited expression. (See Appendix B2c.)

2 Aspasia and Lais of Corinth were fifth-century BCE hetaera—courtesans—linked with famous men, Pericles the politician with Aspasia and Aristippus the philosopher with Lais.

3 Not above 600 perhaps would be in canes; but what has our history to do with these minutia? We write of the heart, not the pocket. [Thelwall's note]

independent property, which enabled him to keep clear of all compulsory engagements with merchants or their agents, and consequently to dispose of his produce at the best market, he soon began to taste so much the advantages of this sort of connexion, as inspired an irresistible desire of extending his profitable concerns.

"The miser's passion rushed upon his soul!"[1]

He accordingly visited several of the islands; purchased estates in more than one of them; trafficked, without remorse, in the blood of his sable brethren, by whom those estates were to be cultivated; and entered into the various commercial arrangements consequent upon the possession of such property.

With the extent of these arrangements Amelia was not properly acquainted till a considerable time after his arrival in England. Indeed, it was an affair with which she did not concern herself: for, though she had a sort of notion that a wife had a right to know the actual circumstances of a family whose affairs she was to superintend, and whose expenses, in a considerable degree, at least, must necessarily be regulated by her, yet as she was perfectly aware that she had to deal with a being with whom not the rights of others, but his own power, should be made the question of expediency; and as he was always disposed to give even a greater latitude to expense than her habits disposed her to indulge, she neither disturbed his mind by enquiries, nor her own by any conjectures upon a subject in which, comparatively, she felt but little interested.

These arrangements, however, occupied (occasionally, at least) a considerable proportion of the attention of Montfort; and the desire of accumulation growing upon him with his years (for he was verging towards that period of life when such passions are very apt to preponderate), he began to feel that his heart was in reality enchained to that part of the world where his property was principally improving; and to consider his residence in his native country as a sort of banishment from that, which is indeed the only country of an avaricious mind, the theatre of its lucrative operations.

While Henry remained at home, these feelings made but little progress. Notwithstanding his continual complaints, his castigations, and his tyrannies, he was in fact devoted to the boy with all the pride of paternal egotism; and, while he was in sight, his heart had scarcely room for any other object. But memory and imagination are but languid principles in the selfish mind. It is in bosoms only of a more generous temperament (in which the gentle and social passions are nurtured by sentiment and reflection) that they glow with that ardent solicitude which makes the absent object of affection even dearer than the present.

In short, how powerfully soever the presence of Henry might excite the vanity of Montfort, interest was the only affection that could strongly stimulate his mind any longer than its object was immediately before him.

---

1 Richard Cumberland, *The Wheel of Fortune* (1795), Act 1.

Such, then, were the palpable causes of that gloom and discontent that pervaded the mind of Montfort, and of that anxious solicitude with which his thoughts were incessantly travelling to the western hemisphere. Amelia, however, had too much penetration not to discover that they were seconded in their operation by some other and more mysterious feelings, the causes of which it was neither in her power nor her inclination to fathom; though, knowing, as she did, his character and dispositions, she imagined it not very probable that she should be entirely mistaken in the nature of their origin.

That his mind was racked by apprehensions, and harassed by remorse, was indeed sufficiently evident: nor was it less conspicuous that the remembrance of the fatal affair with Bowbridge was not the source of this perturbation. That disastrous occurrence seemed to be entirely forgotten: and, indeed, as he killed his friend according to the rules of honour, it is very probable that his conscience scarcely reproached him with the murder.

Some soreness indeed there might remain upon this subject: for he never so much as mentioned the name of Louisa, who had been always an object of his particular admiration, nor enquired after the fate of that offspring with which he knew her to be pregnant at the time of the fatal accident. But a variety of little circumstances that presented themselves, unsought for, to the observation of Amelia, convinced her that this wound by which he was lascerated was of a more recent date; and some broken exclamations (of "Anna!—my babe!—my babe!") which she once accidentally overheard, seemed to place it beyond a doubt that the perturbation of his mind had reference, in some shape or other, to some more recent amour.

These conjectures rather passed through her mind than were entertained there. She sought not to unravel the mystery of his conduct. It was long since he had enjoyed any share either of her affections or esteem: and she was not of a temperament (however common) to be jealous where she could not love.

All her desires were concentrated in two objects: the promotion of the welfare and happiness of her dear Henry, and the enjoyment of a sort of literary tranquillity, which she employed in the researches of history, and in elevating communion with the moralists and the poets of ancient and modern times. With respect to every thing that was not connected with the one or the other of these, she had brought herself to a kind of philosophical indifference, which she was little disposed to interrupt by prying into the secrets of a husband between whom and herself the reciprocations of confidence never had existed.

In the mean time, his anxiety and dissatisfaction appeared almost daily to increase. His mind became more irritable; the packets from the West Indies were expected with increased agitation; and the effect (far beyond the value of the circumstances) which some ill news from one of the plantations had upon his mind, plainly shewed the alarming progress of one part of the intellectual disease under which he laboured: while, the gloom of dissatisfaction still gathering on his brow, little of his early character, except his pride and his vehemence, remained.

Even his prodigalities and his pleasures seemed to lose their relish. The gloom of superstition succeeded to the impetuosity of lycentiousness. A mind too much disturbed to find enjoyment in its wonted pursuits, and too depraved for genuine reformation, vibrated between two opposite extravagancies; and the conventicle became the rival of the brothel-house.

But neither the one nor the other had any tendency to soften the asperities of his character. His dissipation did not polish, nor his devotion humanise; and he appealed to fanaticism, as the Turks do to opium, rather to stupify the feelings than to socialise the heart.

At length some further intelligence concerning a plantation he was connected with, in the French part of the island of St. Domingo, determined him to return to the West Indies; or at least furnished the pretence for that determination.

He accordingly quitted his native country once more; about nine years after he had returned from his former banishment: a circumstance which Amelia was far from considering as unfortunate, since, as Henry would thereby be resigned once more to her sole direction (as far as youth at a public school can be under the direction of a parent), she flattered herself that she should yet be able to eradicate from his mind those seeds of vicious irregularity which had been scattered there by the misconduct of Montfort; and which seemed to have taken root to an extent that was truly alarming.

BOOK II.
=========
CHAP. I.

Containing some Account of the Conduct of Henry at Eton;
with the first Part of an Adventure disgraceful in its Commencement,
but interesting in its Progress.

Juvenile Confederacies, and collegiate Morals—Favourable Indications.—The Frolic.—The Mastiff.—Rustic Morality.—Solitary Reflections.—Ghosts and Goblins.—Rustic Sympathy.—Admonitions and
pathetic Remonstrances.—Dissertations on Honour.—The Portrait.—
Emotions of a generous Heart.—Pastoral Sorrows unnoticed by Virgil
or Theocritus.—Stewards and Lawyers.—Intrigues of a Monopolist.—
Ardours of Benevolence.

IF, by his removal to Eton, Henry had been rescued from the mismanagement and evil example of Montfort, he was released, on the other
hand, from the restraints which his love and veneration for Amelia had, in
some degree, imposed on his irregular propensities. Left, therefore, in a
considerable degree, to the direction of his own eccentric humours, his
motley character soon began to display itself in still more forcible colours.

Among the unruly lads, destitute alike of reflection or principle, who
are always to be found in such seminaries, he was, of course, but too much
exposed to the danger of meeting with associates who would countenance
and enflame every mischievous and extravagant propensity. Such, indeed,
were almost his only companions; and, seconded by their co-operation,
and stimulated by their applause, Henry was soon distinguished as the
ringleader of every mischievous frolic, and every violation of scholastic
regulation and decorum.

As the passions unfolded with the progress of time, new temptations
presented themselves. The vices of youth began to allure him in new forms
of attraction; and, prompted by a forward and vigorous constitution, he
became prematurely conspicuous in profusion of expence, the wantonness of appetite, and a dissolute love of pleasure.

The gaming table and the brothel-house will be considered as strange
places of resort for a school-boy; but they are ill acquainted with the state
of morals, even in those public seminaries that are to be met with in some
of our smaller and remote provincial towns, who would feel any astonishment at meeting with a youth in his thirteenth or fourteenth year, in either
of those scenes of ruinous folly and debauchery.

With respect to the latter, however, Henry had as yet preserved himself
untainted. Very fortunately, his taste was somewhat more correct than his
morality; and he turned away with disgust from that low and sordid
species of sensuality in which he frequently beheld boys of his own age
plunge with a degree of avidity that modesty forbears to dwell upon.

But, if the stews had no attractions for him, it will be seen hereafter, that he was not without his early propensities to the fashionable accomplishment of a more refined, though more unjustifiable, species of intrigue.

It was impossible that his parents should be long unacquainted with these habits of dissipation. In fact, they were assailed with complaints from various quarters: and from some, perhaps, with exaggeration.

These complaints made a deep impression on the mind of Montfort. As his temper became more morose, and his spirit more perturbed by gnawing reflections, he, of course, became more and more intolerant to the failings of youth; and the bias his mind had received from superstition aggravated the vehemence of parental tyranny.

Amelia trembled for the consequences.

She, also, was deeply affected: but affected in a different way. Her regrets had nothing of asperity. Her censures were without resentment. She bewailed the fatal ravages of youthful indiscretion; but her love for the object was not diminished. Nor was it a small consolation to her mind that, together with these reprehensible traits of character, her dear Henry still continued to exhibit many others of a more promising and amiable description; that his understanding was not retrograde, nor his sympathy destroyed.

The progress of his attainments was as rapid as the fondness of parental wishes could have anticipated; and every complaint reiterated by his tutors, was qualified by admissions of the aptitude with which he acquired all the solid advantages of the scholar, and the polite accomplishments of the gentleman. At the same time it was repeatedly apparent, that his generosity was as active as his passions: that if he was proud and petulant, he was liberal and humane: that the wantonness of mischievous aggression was frequently lost in the grace and nobleness of his atonements; and that his unconscionable expences were not more the results of his prodigality than his unbounded benevolence.

A single instance that occurred not long after the departure of Montfort to the West Indies, may place this matter in a proper point of view: and it may not be amiss to dwell upon the adventure somewhat at large; not on account of its consequences, but because it will present, in more striking colours than a thousand laboured descriptions, the incongruities of the youthful character of our hero; and will shew, at once, how much there was frequently to admire in what it was necessary to condemn, and how much to reprobate in what it was impossible not to applaud.

It was at the beginning of the harvest season of the year eighty-five, a season as delightful to the eye of taste and sentiment, as gratifying to the heart of the farmer; when Henry, who had just completed his fifteenth year, and who had an eye for all the charms of rural scenery, and a heart that could animate the pleasures of vision with the soul of sentiment, had been spending the afternoon in an excursion on the banks of the Thames.

His companions were such as the seminary afforded. Some of them had intellect; but all had prodigality. The majority were of a taste to relish more the tumults of sensuality than the calm of meditation. And indeed, no troop of satyrs ever startled the woodland echoes of Arcadia with more wild and obstreperous revelry, than that in which our youthful excursionists occasionally indulged.

But such innocent pastime as the sylvan scene might furnish, would not alone suffice. As the day began to close, a drinking bout was suggested: or, in the undisguised language of the proposer, *a debauch*. The proposer was seconded with much vociferation, and a tea-house in the neighbourhood of Windsor was resorted to as the scene of action. An expensive supper was ordered; wines of the best *description* were set before *their honours* in abundance; and the usual excesses ensued. Glasses were smashed; empty bottles were hurled through the windows; the waiter's head was broken with the dislocated leg of a chair, and well healed again with a golden plaster. In few words, the boys (from fourteen years old to seventeen) were all most gloriously drunk.

At such a season, of course, no proposal could be too extravagant to have its immediate abettors; and Henry (who, though he was rarely the first proposer of any flagrant breach of morality, was established generalissimo in all excursions of hazard and enterprize) was persuaded to undertake the conduct of an expedition of no less honour and importance than robbing the henroost of a neighbouring farmer, to furnish the table for *another jollification*.

The resolution was no sooner taken than the plan of operation was hastily devised; and, with our hero at their head, forth issued the battalion on their destined forage, and reeled to the scene of action; animating each other, on their way, with bets, and boasts of hardihood, and glorying in their policy and their might.

The attack was in the first instance successful. Henry proved himself worthy of command, by being the first to encounter the danger: "vaulting the trench like Perseus on his steed";[1] or rather, like Ulysses in the Trojan camp passing the slumbering centinel;[2] he penetrated to the pavillions of the enemy, and began the work of death. A chosen companion followed the example, whilst the rest kept watch without, to give notice of approaching danger.

And now, glorying in their triumphs, and gorgeous in their plumy spoils, the champions were preparing to return, when the enemy, starting from his ambush, arrested them at the sortie of the plundered citadel, and overwhelmed them with consternation and terror.

In plain, unsophisticated English, they were suddenly assailed by a great mastiff dog, who had been walking his watchful rounds at the time of their entrance, and had arrived again within the hearing of the hen-

---

1 Richard Cumberland, *The Battle of Hastings: A Tragedy* (1778), 1.1.68.
2 *Iliad* 10.

roost, just time enough to alarm the family with his furious howlings, and oppose his formidable jaws to their retreat.

The boys who were keeping guard without consulted their safety, as may be expected, by making the best use they could of their heels; and the companion of the perilous enterprize had the presence of mind, by repeated feints of stooping for a stone, to keep his formidable adversary at a distance, till he arrived at the fence, which he cleared with a vigorous leap. But Henry, whose valour was not of the cool prudential kind, and who was rather rash than courageous, no sooner found himself assailed by the mastiff, than all reason and reflection were lost in the apprehension of being devoured or torn to pieces by his tremendous jaws. Accordingly, insensible to every other danger, he sprung back into the outhouse, which had been the scene of depredation, fastened the door behind him, and ascending from the henroost to the hayloft, buried himself under the hay, and abandoned himself to the most bitter reflections on the danger and the disgrace that awaited him.

The old farmer and his man, alarmed by the incessant barking of the dog, jumped out of their beds, and seizing such rustic weapons as lay in their way, hurried to the scene of action. The headless ducks and gasping pullets explained the cause of the uproar; and the faithful dog, by indications sufficiently intelligible, pointed out the lurking place of the aggressor.

The lanthorn accordingly was fetched: the hay-loft was searched; and poor Henry was dragged from his retreat, half dead with terror and confusion.

"What ha' we here?" said the man, thrusting his lanthorn in his face, with one hand, whilst he hauled him forward, a little roughly, with the other. "What ha' we here? Why a be a devillish young one seemly, master. Hast learned thee trade by times, lad; ha slim and slight i' faith. But thee'lt fetch thee weight in time, no fear on't.

"Mortal fine too!—a seems, mortal fine!

"There turn about, Mr. Henrooster; turn about, and let's ha' a look at thee," continued the fellow, moving his lanthorn up and down, and examining his dress very attentively. "Faith this here hen roosting must be a mortatious[1] good trade to sport all this. Why 'It make a figure at the gallows with these fine shining stockings, and huge buckles, and all this fine geer."

"For heaven's sake, good husbandman!" exclaimed Henry, falling on his knees, "let me go. I am no thief; indeed I am not. I am a gentleman. I'll give you a guinea; I'll give you two, and pay for all the mischief that has been done into the bargain, if you'll forgive me, and let me go."

The mention of guineas softened the fellow's heart instantaneously. His eyes looked less ferocious; his hand relaxed its hold; and his palm was expanding, almost as instinctively as a courtier's; but recollecting that his

---

1   Mortally.

master was present, and would claim of course the reward of mercy, if mercy was to be shewn, a fresh revolution took place in his mind, as suddenly as the former, and his bosom burned as fiercely as ever with the sacred love of justice.

"Guinea!" exclaimed he, with a thundering voice, "thee and thee guinea be d—d! Gemman indeed! I say gemman! A gentleman hen-rooster, and no thief! But I warrant gemmen thinks they may do what they please now-a-days, and go scot-free wi' their gentility; while a poor countryman is to be hanged like a dog.

"Gemman indeed! If I were master, thee shouldst hang so much the higher for genteryship. 'Tis high time, trow, to begin wi' these gentleman thieves; for poor folk ha' been hanged long enough, and starved too, I think, o' my conscience. Gemman, indeed!!!"

With what sort of sensations Henry listened to this harangue, it is not difficult to conjecture. Happily, however, the master had not the same rancorous aversion for gentility as the servant. Gentleman was to him an awful name: and from long settled habit, he paid it a sort of trembling obeisance.

Add to which, he was a man of subdued passions; and if the mild spirit of contentment was not within him (disasters, alas! had banished that), he was rather despondent than revengeful, and less forward to retaliate than to repine.

The youth and appearance of Henry interested him in his behalf; and without suffering him to be tormented any longer with the boisterous insults of the unpitying hind, he took him by the arm, and ordering the servant to return to his bed, conducted the trembling culprit into the house.

"Young gentleman," said he, "I cannot talk with you at present. The night is chilly, and I am an old man, and but half dressed. You must be content with a homely sort of lodging for once at least, while I lay my head upon the pillow, and think what is to be done with you in the morning."

So saying, he locked him in a little room, through the small casement of which, not much larger than the doorway of a common dog-kennel, and half overgrown with ivy, the mournful moon-beam (never before so truly mournful in the eyes of poor Henry) shed an ambiguous light, on the antiquated furniture of the apartment.

To the proud, though dejected mind of our hero, this little lodging room was itself a dungeon, and assisted him to anticipate all the horrors for which he thought himself perhaps reserved.

Perhaps the first thing his gaoler would do in the morning would be to go in quest of the officers of justice, to conduct him to a gaol indeed.

Perhaps he was to be disgraced as a common pilferer in the eyes of all the world; his family dishonoured; the noble mind of an affectionate mother overwhelmed with anguish, and himself exposed to some ignominious punishment: and all for a drunken frolic.

"A drunken frolic!" continued he, "and what had I to do with drunken frolics?

"Is profligate vice—is premature licentiousness the best apology for my dishonour?

"Drunkenness! midnight robbery! a dungeon! a public trial among housebreakers and foot-pads!—[1]

"Is this the progress of an Eton scholar? Are these the gradations by which I am to rise to those honours and distinctions, with the prospect of which my dear unhappy mother so frequently excited me to a more honourable ambition?

"That mother too! How will she support it? How shall I support myself?"

Overwhelmed with these poignant reflections, he sat himself disconsolately on the bed, and with folded hands, and low-drooping head, sighed for the return of morning, which he yet dreaded to behold; and groaned in melancholy response to the vibrations of a wooden clock, whose hoarse clickings, in an adjoining room, alone interrupted the silence of his prison-house.

While Henry was thus yielding up his mind to reflections that made him almost lothe his very existence, he imagined he heard the padding of a foot in the long entry of the antiquated mansion. He was not mistaken: the padding of a foot did sound in the long entry; and a gleaming light was seen through the crevices of the door.

His ear, his eyes, all his senses were directed towards the place from whence it proceeded; and his heart was agitated with new alarms.

Ghosts, goblins, murdered travellers, clanking chains and demons of the night—all the horrible absurdities with which Montfort's favourite tales and story-books had stuffed his remembrance, recurred to his mind; and his whole frame was bedewed with the chilly sweat of terror.

Not that Henry was, in reality, a believer in apparitions. His judgment, immature as it was, already rejected the phantastic creed of the nursery; and, in disputation at least, he could, as it were mathematically, demonstrate the absurdity of such ideas; and ridicule, with pointed sarcasm, the ignorance of our forefathers, who swallowed, with such eagerness, the fables of blind credulity.

But his childish fancy had been harassed by such bugbears, and his memory was imprest; and even in minds much more matured than that of Henry, the operations of reason and imagination are frequently so distinct, and even opposite, that one can hardly be surprised at the opinions of those ancient philosophers who compounded man, in their theories, of several essences; and assigned to each its various powers and functions, its classes of sensations, and capacity of separate existence.

In fact, the case of Henry was no uncommon one. He *trembled without believing*; and shrunk from imaginary bugbears which his understanding

---

1 Burglars and thieves.

at the same time exploded.

In the present instance, in particular the surrounding objects (to him so perfectly novel)—the little detached chamber, the long entry through which he had been conducted to it, the half-ruined antiquated mansion in which the few apartments of the farm had been rudely fitted up, with painted pannels half blurred by time, and fragments of rude gothic carved-work—together with the depressed state of his mind, and that drowsiness which seldom fails to visit the eyelids of youth, even under the most unfavourable circumstances, all alike conspired to favour those ambiguous impressions; and fancy triumphed over reason.

Pad—pad—pad, went the foot slowly along the passage; and you might have heard the response of poor Henry's heart, as audibly as the echo in some hollow cavern.

These mysterious impressions were but of short duration. The door presently opened and revealed, not the fresh-streaming wounds of the murdered traveller, nor the saucer eyes of old Incubus,[1] but the well-remembered countenance of the injured farmer.

The old man had indeed laid his head upon his pillow; but sleep (though a rustic deity) attended not to steep his temples with the poppy of forgetfulness. To the thorns of care which had been planted there by misfortune, another was now superadded by the adventures of the night.

His busy mind (sagacious though rude, and though irritated benevolent) roved through the discriminations of turpitude with an inclination always towards the favourable side.

"It is but a trick of youth," said he, "and young gentlemen will have their frolics.

"But is it right that the poor should suffer for their wantonness? that the little property of industry should be the sport of the dissipation of the rich?

"But I am doomed to be always unfortunate; always suffering injury upon injury, and loss upon loss! Landlords and schoolboys, stewards, lawyers, and highway robbers, all join to oppress and ruin me; and no one has compassion on my misfortunes.

"Compassion!" repeated he; and the benevolent countenance of Henry presented itself to his mind.—

"Alas! he is not acquainted with my misery.—Perhaps *he* would compassionate me, if he was."

What little asperity had lurked in the mind of the good old rustic, softened at the suggestion; and pity supplanted revenge. He arose; put on his clothes; and, with a candle in his hand, proceeded, as we have seen, to the little chamber.

Henry was overwhelmed with two-fold confusion. Abashed by the recollection of his disgraceful situation; abashed by the remembrance of those

---

1 Male demon who preys, usually sexually, on women who are asleep. The female demon who preys on men was called a succubus.

ridiculous impressions to which he had so weakly yielded up his imagination, he scarcely ventured to look the honest farmer in the face; but, bending his head upon his bosom, sunk again into his despondent attitude.

The old man sat himself down on a chair. He threw himself back; rested his elbows on the half-worn-out arms; and clasping his hands before him, began to examine very attentively the appearance and deportment of the culprit.

At length, after a considerable pause, "Well, young gentleman," said he, with a voice much less formidable than Henry had expected, "what have you to say for yourself?"

"Nothing," said Henry, with a deep sigh, without even lifting up his head.

F. "Nothing, young gentleman?"

H. "Nothing—nothing—only that I am the most unfortunate boy in the world."

F. "Unfortunate! young gentleman—unfortunate! because you could not rob a poor old farmer's hen-roost, and kill all his ducks and pullets without being caught in the fact?

"But there is a different language for the rich and the poor. Mayhap if you were speaking of some poor boy who had done half so much from mere hunger and necessity as you have done in drunken wantonness, while mayhap your pocket is full of money, he would have been a wicked wretch, and a vagabond, and a thief, mayhap, that deserved hanging.

"Nay, if my own poor boy had been living—God rest his soul! he used to sleep upon that very bed, where you are now sitting—if it had pleased God to have spared him to comfort my grey hairs," continued the farmer, wiping away a tear, "he would have been about your age.

"Ah, young gentleman! if it had so happened, and he had killed a hare or a pheasant on your father's estate; or over his garden wall, and pleased his boyish appetite with a little fruit or so, he might have his leg snapt off with an iron trap; or been hanged, or transported—I think they call it—to be sold among the blacks; or ha' been sent to wheel ballast at Woolwich,[1] there, with a fetter upon his leg, to the last day of his life.

"And yet, young gentleman, what is all the fruit in a rich man's garden? He has money and can buy more.—Or what is all the money and furniture in his house? He has great estates and riches in other places.—What are they all, young gentleman, in comparison with the ducks and pullets you have robbed me of, who am but a poor, friendless, hopeless old man?

"But so it is, young gentleman! as a poor cottager said hard by here, when the common was closed—If the poor rob the rich, there is a great cry about justice; but nobody says any thing about justice when the rich rob the poor!"

---

1   Woolwich on the Thames in southeast London was a major naval centre and
    dockyard; a common form of prison labour was to move iron and other heavy
    objects used as ship ballast, in wheelbarrows.

H. "Oh! it is true—it is true. But I did not think."—

F. "No, no, young gentleman, the rich do not think; but the poor are obliged to feel!"

H. "Poor!—poor again! Oh wretch that I am! and have I robbed the poor?

"But, thank heaven! it is yet in my power to make compensation.

"I will pay for all the mischief. I will pay you three-fold," continued he, thrusting his hand into his pocket; and venturing for the first time to look the farmer in the face.

"Hold! hold! young gentleman!" said the farmer; "we will talk of that by and by. But, in the first place, who are you? What is your name?"

Henry sunk again into his former attitude.

The farmer repeated his question.

"Oh! do not ask me. Do not ask me that," said Henry with a groan, throwing himself at his length upon the bed.

"Oh! I shall die!"

"Die!" repeated the farmer, somewhat affected by his agitation: "no, no, young gentleman, you shall not die this time, even if it were out of clergy. But look ye, young gentleman, I must know who you are. Your parents must be informed what courses you are running, that they may take better care of you in future."

H. "Oh, my mother! my mother! It will break her heart!—It will break her heart!"

F. "You have a mother, then, to instruct and cherish you; and yet you can do such things! My poor girl has had no mother since she was three years old: and what instruction could I give her?

"Alas! I was working in the field all day; and I can but just read and write myself.

"And yet my poor girl would not rob a neighbour of a pin—rich or poor. She would not pluck a gooseberry from a neighbour's hedge, till he had bid her twenty times.

"But she works hard; and labour keeps her honest: while you, young gentleman, have nothing to do, but to get fine learning at the great school, perhaps, and drink fine wines that make great people mad and wicked; and be clothed in fine garments by the labour of your poor tenants.

"But look you, young gentleman, I must know who you are; and I will. So you may take your choice; either tell me by ourselves, or tell me before his worship, to-morrow morning."

"His worship!" exclaimed Henry, throwing himself upon his knees— "O! for God's sake, do not take me before a magistrate: do not expose me. Have compassion on my youth—have compassion on my family. I will give you any thing—any thing you can ask—all that I have."

"Young gentleman," replied the farmer, indignantly, "I am not mercenary, what though I be poor and unfortunate. But if you expect me to favour you, tell me who and what you are."

H. "I am Henry Montfort, an Eton scholar. My father, Percival Mont-fort, esq. a man of family and fortune, is now on his voyage to the West Indies; and my mother—oh my poor mother!—but do not tell her—do not break her heart—my mother resides in London—in Grosvenor Square."

F. "And who were your companions, young gentleman, in this pretty business?"

H. "Com-pan-panions?—I—I—I had no companions."

F. "Nay, nay, young gentleman, you did not come to rob my hen-roost alone. Besides, I heard them scampering away; and one of them jumped over the gate, just as I opened the window. So come, young gentleman, you must tell me all; or, as I told you before, you must tell his honour, the justice, to-morrow morning."

"I shall tell neither of you," replied Henry, with great firmness, "what-ever be the consequence. Though, in the hour of intoxication, I have been hurried into a disgraceful frolic, there is no power on earth shall terrify Henry Montfort into the dishonour of betraying his companions."

"Dishonour! dishonour!" repeated the farmer, shaking his head. "Ah! honour, to be sure, is a fine thing among gentlemen: like your *burglary* wines, and such like, only fit to be used among one or other. We poor hard-working men may hear the name now and then; but are never suf-fered to have a taste of it. You enter into combinations to oppress and rob us; and then it is honour to stand by one another in your wickedness, and prevent us from having justice.

"But we ha'n't flesh and blood like your fine folks.

"There is no honour towards us, because we ha'n't fine clothes, and don't understand fine words.

"A poor old man, whose back is almost broken by the oppression of landlords and tax-gatherers, by bilking stewards and roguish lawyers—who, after forty years' labour and carefulness, finds himself bowed down by misfortune, and at the very door of a jail—he may be robbed and plun-dered for mere frolick sake, forsooth; and the robber, detected in the fact, because his father is a man of family and fortune, thinks himself a gentle-man of true honour, if so be he refuses to impeach his fellow thieves.

"The common footpads, who robbed and half murdered me, a few weeks ago in point of honour, young sir, perhaps are as good gentlemen as yourself."

If Henry was abashed and confounded by the sharpness of this reproof, the circumstances with which it was interwoven, and the emotion with which it was delivered, still more powerfully awakened his better feelings. He knew not before what energy there is in simple passion; or that uned-ucated nature could be so eloquently moved.

In short, his very consciousness of his own situation was almost sus-pended; and, impressed with a sort of mingled feelings, of pity and vener-ation, he lifted up his head, and attentively examined the features and appearance of the old rustic.

It was an interesting picture.

Benevolence and affliction had traced their mingled lines on every feature. The eye, rather bedimmed by sorrows than by age, had yet a glimpse of its former ardour. The cheek was seered and sunken. Labour had swollen the veins and given a rigidness to the muscles; and in the wrinkles of the brow sat care, half shrouded by the silver locks that calamity as yet had spared. The drapery was in harmony with the figure. It was homely, and bore the evident marks of long service; yet it was in *thorough repair*. The linen, though coarse, was clean; as was also the silk handkerchief round the neck; and the knitted hose, darned all over, with patient perseverance, displayed the laudable efforts of economy, to reconcile necessity with neatness.

Henry beheld him for a while, if I may so express myself, with a sort of classical veneration. He recollected what he had read of the patient poverty of some ancient heroes, and believed that Fabius and Cincinnatus[1] might have made, perhaps, no better appearance. Wealth, birth, and distinctions lost, for a while, their lustre in his eyes; and his heart expanded to the family of the human race.

"Father! father!" said Henry, clasping the hard hand of the rustic, with great emotion, "you have been bowed by many sorrows. Imperfectly as I understand your story, enough is conspicuous in those broken hints, to convince me that you are one of those whom Fortune and her minions have made it their sport to frown upon.

"And have I, then, rioting in licentious abundance, invaded the scanty leavings of your misfortunes?—broken into the fold, to steal an only lamb, while my herds were bleating through every valley, and browsing upon every hill? Have I conspired with disaster, and leagued myself with oppression, to bruise the reed already broken?[2]—to aggravate the ruin that villains have too well completed?

"Yet, perhaps there is a way——

"No—no"—he exclaimed, chasing about the room in great agitation—"it will look as if I only wanted to purchase exemption from the punishment and infamy I have merited.—

"And suppose it should?" continued he, stopping short, and placing his hand over his chin, in an attitude of self-recollection——"Suppose it should? What signifies what it looks like?

"Has benevolence no charms?"——He erected his chest as he put this question to himself; and renewed his motion, but with an altered pace——"Has benevolence no charms but in the trappings of exterior admiration? Is one never to do a good action but when one's name may be emblazoned on the walls of churches and of hospitals?

"This poor man is on the brink of ruin; and I, perhaps, may save him.

---

1 Roman political leaders, Fabius in the third century BCE, Cincinnatus 520-430 BCE, the latter an icon of simplicity and political restraint.
2 Matthew 12:20.

"It would be making a noble atonement. It would be beginning reformation with a good grace: and the recollection would be a rock upon which, for the future, my resolutions of amendment might rest with confidence."

Such were the reflections with which Henry, in a sort of reverie, midway between soliloquy and articulation, soothed his feelings, and stimulated his virtues; while the quickness of his pace, and the earnestness of his action filled the gaping farmer with an astonishment, which his broken sentences and half-stifled ejaculations were by no means calculated to remove. At length—

"Father! father! venerable old man!" exclaimed he, aloud, with great agitation, seizing him again by the hand and pressing it between both his own—"did you not say you were on the brink of ruin?—in danger of a jail?—that cheats and oppressors, lawyers and night-robbers had plundered you of all that forty years of frugal industry had scraped together?—that you were hopeless and undone?"

The poor farmer was silent with astonishment. That quick electric sympathy—that fervour of enthusiasm which goaded and agitated the expanded mind of young Henry, "his fate forbade";[1] nor could he comprehend the object or tendency of such vehement enquiry.

"But you will not unbosom yourself to me," continued Henry. "You cannot make allowance for the follies of an inebriated youth? You cannot confide in a midnight robber; and your honest simplicity disdains the friendship of a headlong profligate who has broken through all the fences of morals and of honesty.

"Yet do not reject my proffered assistance; nor make me consider myself in so despicable a point of view, as if I were unworthy the opportunity of doing a generous action.

"Tell me your story, that I may know whether it is in my power to serve you."

"My story, young gentleman?" replied the farmer; "I do not understand you."

H. "The story of your misfortunes I mean. The oppressions and calamities that have robbed you of all your little savings."

F. "Why as for savings, young gentleman, I never have been able to save: for I have been unfortunate all my life time. Lands are dear and taxes are high, and times are often bad; and those that are under us, God knows! are often as dishonest as those above us. He need have eyes on all sides that would avoid being cheated in these days.

"Then I married while I was very young; and I began the world with little; and my farm is small; and sickness and lyings-in are sore draw-backs upon a poor man.—

"But the heaviest expences of all, young gentleman—the heaviest to the heart of man, are burials, young gentleman!—and they, God knows have gone full often from my door.

---

1 Pope's *Iliad* 21:600.

"Two in particular I shall never forget.—

"My wife—ah, young gentleman! it is now eleven years since I have read her name upon the footstone night and morning every sabbath day, as I have gone to church.

"And then my boy!—One poor boy I had—ah, it was so good a youth—so dutiful!—The others, God rest their souls! died while they were children—but he lived till he was fourteen; and I hoped that it would have pleased God to spare him, to be a prop and a comfort to me in my old age. But he died also; and all my consolation was to read the verse, which our school-master wrote, upon his footstone, telling people how good he was.

"Well, well: we must all of us die," continued he, wiping his eyes.

"As for this world's matter, all that I could ever hope was just to pay my way honestly and make both ends meet; and with the blessing of God, I have always been able to do that, till the unfortunate affair of the robbery: and that has ruined me for ever."

"Cheerily! cheerily!" said Henry, sobbing: "there is hope, man, even yet. How much did you lose?"

"Five-and-thirty pounds," rejoined the farmer, "in bank bills; and a guinea and nine shillings in a little bag; and my silver watch, that I bought while I was courting my poor dear wife that was.

"I have counted the minutes upon it many's the time, when she had promised to meet me.

"To be sure it had seen its best days; like myself. It was not worth much. But I loved it; because it reminded me of many things that are past and gone.

"Well, they took it; and they took all I had.

"It was down in that there ugly lane, as you turn out of the Uxbridge road.

"Five-and-thirty pounds in bank notes!

"I had taken them that very day for some corn—all I had to dispose of.

"I had sold it at a bad market. But my rent was due; and I had no choice.

"I had drank a little freely, to be sure—God forgive me! But when a poor man leads a hard life, and all other pleasures are out of his reach, he is apt to do so sometimes, to forget his cares.

"Well; they rushed upon me, with their great sticks, out of the thicket; and, as I was a little heady, as I said, young gentleman, I was easily thrown off my old mare: and they gave me a blow on the head that stunned me: and after that they robbed me, and threw me into a ditch.

"But it did not please God that I should die. So I crawled home in the morning all over blood and dirt—my money gone, and my barn empty!—No means of paying my landlord!—Obliged to run a bill with the doctor for journies,[1] and surgery, and medicines.

---

1 Individual doctor visits or consultations.

"In short, I was completely ruined."

H. "But your landlord, perhaps, was a rich man?"

F. "Aye, rich enough, for matter o'that. Seven thousand a year, they say's; besides no end of money before hand."

H. "That, at least, was in your favour: for as he could not want it, he, of course, would not trouble you about his rent, after such an accident.— At any rate; not till you had time to turn yourself about."

F. "Do gentlemen never take any thing from the poor but when they are in want of it?

"Ah, young gentleman!—want or not want—crop or not crop—robbed or not robbed—alive or dead, the king and the landlord will have their due. When the steward or the tax-gatherer is at the door, with a receipt in one hand, and a distress in the other, it is of no use to make long faces, and tell sorrowful tales."

H. "And did they distrain[1] under such circumstances?—Shame upon the halter that shall hang the highwayman, while these worse than robbers are unpunished!"

F. "Why not quite so, neither, young gentleman. But, for matter o'that, it might have been better if they had.

"But the steward pretended to compassionate me. 'So look ye,' said he, 'Mr. Wilson, to be sure my lord is a very punctuous[2] man; and he will have every thing to a day, willy nilly. But as your farm is well stocked,' said he, 'and in very good order, and matters will be sure to come round in time, suppose I vaunce[3] the money out of my own pocket. But then,' said he, 'I must have something for risk, you know; that is but reasonable; and something for the use of my money. Let me see,' said he, 'you shall give me that little poney, you know. It will do nicely for my little boy to ride upon. And then as for interest,' said he, rubbing his forehead, 'let me see—twenty per cent. One may make of one's money in trade. Twenty per cent. It is a poor trade, Mr. Wilson, that will not bring twenty per cent. However you are an unfortunate man,' said he, 'and I would not wish to be hard upon you; I will only take ten, as it is from you. Let me see,' said he, putting his hand before his eyes, 'let me see—ten per cent. upon forty pounds, for three years, is twelve pounds; and you will be sure to bring matters about in three years. Twelve and forty is fifty-two—fifty-two—fifty-two,' said he, 'but come,' said he, 'as you are an unfortunate man and have always been punctuous, Mr. Wilson, I will make you a present of the odd two pounds; so you shall only give me a bond and judgment for the fifty; just as a sort of security, you see, against deaths or other accidents; and I'll give you a receipt for the half year's rent, and five guineas to pay your doctor's bill, and set all things square again.'

---

1 Seize property.

2 Punctual.

3 Advance.

"In short, young gentleman, since you wish to know my story, and (what though you have played me this wicked trick) as you seems to have a pitiful heart, I must tell you, that I did not know how to help myself; so I struck the bargain with the steward, and thought he had done me a great kindness.[1]

"So he brought a lawyer, with a paper, and a deal of fine writing in it, which I didn't understand; only that it was about fifty pounds, and giving security in a hundred. But both the steward and the lawyer told me it was all right; and so I signed my name, and put my thumb upon a bit of wax, and said something about its being my act and deed; and the lawyer witnessed it, and I got a receipt, and the five guineas; and thought that all was well for three years, at any rate, if I could not pay before.

"But, by and by comes the lawyer again, with a long bill of three-and-four-pences and six-and-eight-pences, and I know not what all, only that it came to a matter o' five pounds; and when I thought it too much, and talked of shewing it to another lawyer, he told me, 'As if I murred[2] about it, he should 'vise his friend, the steward, to put the judgment in execution, and take me, body and goods, immediately, for the fifty pounds.'

"Then it was that I first found my mistake. But there was no help. So I was obliged to make up the money, by hook or by crook, and pay the lawyer his bill.

"It went hard with me. But I comforted myself that I had put off the evil day, at least; and, in the mean time, who knew what Providence might do for me.

"But, alas! young gentleman, the worst part of the business was yet to come. My rich neighbour, the great 'nopolist,[3] who rents a matter o' seven or eight hundred a year in these parts, besides freeholds—He has, all along, *been adding field to field, and farm to farm*, notwithstanding what scripture says;[4] and has brought many a poor family to ruin. Yet he goes to church, and says his prayers, and has his name upon a board for five pounds to charity; and calls himself a christian, for all he has no bowels, as a christian ought to have.

"Well, he had long had an evil eye upon my little spot; because it lays so 'tiguous to his farm. So finding that I was in arrears, he goes to the

---

1 The tale of Wilson's economic oppression is a kind of narrative found throughout Thelwall's oeuvre, including *The Rights of Nature* (1796) and the *Pedestrian Excursion* (1798-1801). Tyrrel's oppression of the Hawkins family in William Godwin's *Things As They Are; or, The Adventures of Caleb Williams* (1794) is comparable and may have influenced Thelwall here.

2 Demurred, that is, "objected."

3 Monopolist.

4 Allusion to Leviticus 25, the fifty-year "Jubilee" when debts are cancelled and property returns to the original owners. The land reformers Thomas Spence (1750-1814) and his radical movement based their political radicalism on this scriptural passage.

steward and offers him a good round sum if he could get me out, so that he might have the lease.

"So what does the steward do but he comes to me in a great hurry: 'Wilson,' says he, 'I have some good news for you, my old boy!' and slaps me on the back so friendly. 'What will you say if I put you in a way to pay off that fifty pounds you owe me; and set your old heart at ease, without the loss of a shilling?'

"'Why to be sure, Mr. Talbot,' says I, 'I should be mortally obliged to you; but how is it to be done?'

"'Look ye,' said he, very gravely, 'I want the money, Mr. Wilson, directly; and the money I must have. But what o' that; there's your neighbour Walcot,' says he, 'he has always money enough. He will stand your friend. Do you make over the lease to him (I'll answer for my lord's consent to the 'signment),[1] and he will give you the full market-price for every thing: by which you will save all expences of lawyers and sheriffs' officers, and all the loss and discredit of a public auction. And look you,' added he, in a sort of whisper, though, Lord help me! there was nobody by but ourselves, 'between you and I, as he has left every thing of that sort to my 'betration,[2] fix your own price now, in the lump; and if you come within ten or fifteen pounds of the mark, he sha'n't boggle[3] with you, but down with it upon the nail.'

"'And what am I to do then, Mr. Talbot?' said I; 'Will what is left stock me another farm, even if I knew where to get one?'

"'O, as for that,' says he, 'Walcot shall take care of you. You shall have a good salary, drive your own team, and live in the house here, as usual. Mr. Walcot, you know, is a man of generosity; and never boggles about trifles, in these cases.'

"'Mr. Talbot,' says I, 'Mr. Talbot' (for my heart was almost broken), 'I have been master now these five-and-thirty years; and though I have had hard times of it, and many misfortunes and losses, and sometimes found it difficult enough to do, God knows! yet master is master still, and I cannot go to service at this time of life.'

"'O, very well, Mr. Wilson,' says he, 'very well. You may consult your proud stomach about that, if you please. But look ye,' says he, with a loud voice, 'my money I must have; and I will. I give you ten days to settle with Mr. Walcot; or the sheriffs' officers will settle with you on the eleventh':— and so he bounced away."

"And when do these ten days expire?" said Henry, with great eagerness.

"Eight are already past," replied the farmer, with a heavy groan.

"And have you no part of the money ready?"

"About ten pounds, young gentleman. Perhaps, by one means or other, I might raise eight or ten more. But if it were forty, out of the fifty, it would

---

1 Consignment, that is, signing over property to another but retaining ownership.
2 Arbitration.
3 Raise scruples; hesitate.

be no use. Mr. Walcot wants my farm; the steward wants his bribe; and the money is only demanded because they know it's impossible for me to pay it."

"But it shall be paid," said Henry, with great vehemence. "By him who made me, it shall be paid! Here—here," continued he, rummaging all his pockets, "I have three guineas and a little silver about me; take that. I have a little more in my trunk, at the college; that you shall have also; and if there is money in Eton, and Henry Montfort has not lost his credit, to-morrow, or next day at furthest, you shall be able to set this jew of a steward, and this vulture of a monopolist, at defiance.

"But, I forget I am your prisoner; and you will, perhaps, consider this as the mere rant of a school-boy, who, finding himself under the rod, is willing to *promise* any thing, to escape from punishment."

"Young gentleman," replied the farmer, after a pause, looking alternately at the gift and the giver, "as I am a living man and a christian, I know not what to think. I thank you for this, howsondever. If I never see you again, nobody shall ever hear of any thing that has past, but your generosity.

"But, perhaps, I ought not to take this. All I ought to expect is, that you should pay for the mischief you have done. What remains, however, may perhaps be useful; and, if ever I am able, I will pay it you again."

So saying, he conducted our hero out of the premises; who, renewing his assurances of assistance, shook the old farmer affectionately by the hand; and they parted with reciprocal acknowledgments.

CHAP. II.

Continuation of the preceding Adventure, and its Consequences.

Arithmetic of Enthusiasm.—Liberality of Prodigals!!!—The Jockey.—Mortifications of Enthusiasm.—The Grub.—Triumphs of Enthusiasm.—Little Mary, or the Child of Nature.—Tender Insinuations.—Affecting Remembrances.—Effusions of Gratitude.—Perils of Gratitude.—Seasonable Interruption.—Projects of Seduction.

HENRY was now in the element for which maternal instruction had fashioned him. Ardent, active, and sympathising, he was, in reality, never so completely happy as when engaged in some pursuit of generosity and benevolence; and he had now an adventure of this sort upon his hands, that challenged all the exertions of diligence, and all the resources of his mind.

To raise forty or fifty pounds in eight-and-forty hours, was an undertaking in which no school-boy who had not the zeal and enthusiasm of our hero, would have ventured to embark. But, before the ardours of youthful imagination all difficulties vanish. He made no sort of doubt that his companions and instigators in the frolic would contribute as liberally as himself (and the reader, perhaps, may be of opinion, that they owed thus much, at least, to the disinterested perseverance of Henry, in concealing the part they had acted in that affair). When their purses were exhausted, he supposed he should find other resources for any trifling deficiency that might remain.

But Henry had fallen into the mistake so common with benevolent enthusiasts. Judging of all mankind by himself, he had proceeded upon the erroneous calculation of multiplying the sum total of his own virtue and activity by the given number of those with whom he was to act; and, confiding in such arithmetic, had looked forward to extravagant results.

Alas! he was much too inexperienced to have discovered how large a proportion of his species are mere cyphers; who, in any honourable enter-prize, are too apt to get shuffled on the wrong side of the numerals, where they fill out the line indeed, but add nothing, in reality, to the account.

His companions listened, it is true, to his adventure with eager curios-ity. All were forward in declaring that he was a brave lad, for not deliver-ing up their names; neither, when he detailed, with pathetic earnestness, the story of the old farmer, were they less unanimous in subscribing— their whole stock of curses and execrations, against those d—d old rascals, the steward and the lawyer. But, when he came to wind up the whole with his proposal for relieving honest Wilson from his embarrassments, their countenances were instantly altered.

One considered it as "a d—d good fetch[1] of Henry's to get himself out of limbo"; but thought "he had posted rather more poundage than was necessary." Another dubbed him "the Don Quixote of Eton"; and swore "it was a better quiz for a burlesque novel than any thing to be found in Cervantes"; and almost the whole group joined in a horse-laugh at his eccentricity; and took it for granted, "that together with his liberty he had recovered his senses."[2]

One of them, indeed, threw down his guinea "for the old cock"; and a second (the son and heir of a most puissant and illustrious horse-jockey), in the true spirit of the turf, pulled out his whole stock upon the table, and staked it, heads or tails, on a single throw, whether it should go to the old farmer or to a w———. Unfortunately, tails came uppermost; and, in the balance of the blind deity, the scale of benevolence was found wanting.

The gamester, however, as he held the stakes himself, determined to mitigate the decree: for, dividing the prize into two equal portions, and

---

1   Contrivance, dodge, stratagem, trick.
2   Don Quixote, the eponymous hero of the novel by Miguel de Cervantes (1547-
    1616), became a byword for unrealistic idealism and chivalry produced by reading
    too many romance narratives. In the eighteenth century, *Don Quixote* (1605,
    1615) was cited often as an antithesis to a sober, pragmatic, reasonable outlook
    on life. Charlotte Lennox's *The Female Quixote* (1752) is a good example of a cau-
    tionary narrative against reading-induced idealism.

assigning one to the necessities of poor Wilson, he swore that the wenches must be contented with the other, till he could obtain a fresh supply.

This generosity had some effect upon the rest; and at last they unanimously agreed to contribute their crowns a-piece; and *talked* of proposing a subscription to the *whole form*.

It was with no small degree of indignation that Henry discovered these traits of selfishness in his prodigal companions; and his spirits sunk into the most painful dejection, when he saw the evening closing upon him, with only fifteen guineas in his hands, out of the forty he had proposed to raise: though, even of this small portion, between four and five had come out of the purse of a frugal, pensive, wayward youth, who was neither a child of riot nor a minion of fortune; with whom Henry had little fellowship, and to whom he had applied only on the score of that reputation for sympathy which had obtained him many queer, but honourable, nicknames among his more opolent,[1] but less respectable, school-mates.

Night succeeded to the evening, and brought the head of our hero to the pillow; but brought no slumber to his eyes. The disastrous lot of the poor farmer, the sacred obligation of his promise—honour and sympathy, and the disdain of being baffled in an enterprize in which he had embarked with so much confident enthusiasm, all conspired to torment him, and lengthened out the sleepless hours.

At last, however, an expedient was thought upon that gave him some ease.

Though there are some particular traits that are almost general to youth, and mark the features of its moral as of its physical physiognomy, in contradistinction to those of the more advanced stages of life; yet has it also, as well as age, its discriminations of individual character; and a great school is, perhaps, a much more accurate picture of the state of society and morals in the universe, than is generally supposed. Gamesters, rakes, and prodigals, we have already seen, in the group that has been exhibited: but Eton had, also, its money-broker; its penurious usurer; who, though liberally supplied by his parents, was parsimonious, to the last excess, in all his own pleasures and expences; and made a regular traffic of the prodigalities of his school-fellows; by supplying, in their exigences, with small sums of money, for which he never failed to exact the most extravagant interest.

This boy, by name Walter Marlow (a phenomenon, undoubtedly, at his time of life), was known throughout the whole college by the nick-name of "The Grub": to which, indeed, both his habits and his appearance equally entitled him: for his person was mean, his deportment sullen and suspicious, and his pleasures (if he had any beyond that of accumulating what he had no disposition to enjoy) were taken in dirty holes and corners, in darkness and in solitude, without witness or participation.

With this being Henry (from an inculcated abhorrence of all that is mean and sordid) had, hitherto, avoided all intercourse, even in his worst necessities; and he had submitted to many mortifications, and rushed into

---

1 Opulent.

many hazardous expedients, rather than countenance a disposition he so much abhorred.

But the best and strongest passions of our hero's soul were now too deeply engaged to be counteracted by such considerations. His honour must be preserved—the necessities of poor Wilson must be relieved; and the steward and the monopolist must be disappointed of their prey, from whatever quarter he sought for the supply.

In short, he determined to apply to *The Grub*, for the loan of five-and-twenty pounds; and to be the bubble of an usurer, rather than fail in his benevolent undertaking.

This resolution was no sooner taken, than watchfulness fled from his wearied eyelids; and he fell into that sweet slumber, to which virtuous feelings can alone administer.

His sleep, though sweet, was not protracted. He arose, gay and vigorous, while the rising sun was dispersing the vapours, and the matin bird carolled his first strain of gratitude over the teeming meadows.

The bargain was soon struck. Henry was too little of a hypocrite to conceal his eagerness; and Marlow already too well acquainted with his trade, not to make his advantage of this circumstance. The terms were as extravagant as the amount of the loan was unusual. Yet Henry, after engaging his honour, in a written obligation, to repay both the principal and the premium, on his return from the next vacation, hugged the sordid reptile in a transport of gratitude; and vowed, in his heart, that even an usurer is a more useful member of society than a prodigal without benevolence.

The money was no sooner in the pocket of our hero, than he burned with impatience for the hour that should release him from scholastic regulations, and leave him at liberty to hasten to the fulfilment of his promise. But time was too tardy for his enthusiasm; and he determined, at the hazard of castigation, to break his way through

"The fix'd and stated rules
"Of vice and virtue in the schools."[1]

In short, he shewed his *jailors*, as he called them, a light pair of heels; and in a most propitious-unpropitious hour, arrived at the place of his destination.

The old farmer was not at home. Business had called him away; or, perhaps, the torturing spirit of melancholy had urged him to take a last survey of those fields of grain which himself had cultivated, and which were now waving their orient heads, ripe for some stranger's sickle.

The lips, however, that announced this intelligence, prevented it from being unwelcome.

It was little Mary, the only child—the only comfort of poor Wilson, that

---

1 Ardens [Thelwall, probably], "On Enthusiasm of Character," *Universal Magazine* 90 (March 1792): 205; 204-07.

met him, with an anxious countenance, at the door; and, with mingled eagerness and timidity, invited him into the little parlour.[1]

Henry accepted the invitation; and followed his bashful guide with no unobservant eye. He gazed! He wondered! He admired! He believed he had at last met with one of those pastoral nymphs, or rural deities, so frequently celebrated in his favourite classics.

Mary was, indeed, a damsel that might have excited interest in feelings less enthusiastic and poetical than those of Henry.

She was in her sixteenth year; an age which, even abstracted from any particular advantages of form or feature, is seldom without its attractions. Mary, however, possessed these advantages in a considerable degree; and to the novel charm of uncorrupted simplicity, added a symmetry and a softness, a glow of health and modesty, and a countenance at once beautiful and animated.

Our hero's heart throbbed with something more than its accustomed ardour. He felt a sort of sensation he did not remember to have felt before; and as Eton is not precisely the most favourable place for the encouragement of those retired and bashful habits which sometimes occasion the passion to be deeply rooted before the seed is suspected to have been sown, he immediately asked himself *if it was not love?*—a question which many a young gentleman of fifteen, who has been in the habit of reading plays and novels, and aping the man, with an unbristled chin, may perhaps have asked himself upon much slighter foundations.

Little Mary, on the contrary, was far from imagining herself in any danger either of imbibing or inspiring such a passion. She had neither studied Pamela, nor the Fortunate Country Maid;[2] and her brain was intoxicated with no vain ideas of farmers' daughters making their fortunes by captivating young gentlemen at first sight.

"Pray, sir, be seated," said she, in a great flurry, wiping a chair with her apron, lest there should happen to be a little dust upon it. "Pray, sir, do sit down; though it is but a mean place for such a gentleman as you to sit in. But since you are so condescending"—

H. "Embellished by your beauty, my pretty maiden; it is a palace for a king; and, since you reside here, if I can add any thing to its happiness, I am a king indeed!"

M. "O dear, sir, you gentlemen talk so fine. My life on't, sir, you are the young gentleman that was here the other night."

H. "I am the wicked reprobate that robbed your father's hen-roost; and, I am afraid, disturbed your slumber into the bargain. But I hope Miss Wilson will forgive me."

---

1 The Mary Wilson episode is similar to others Thelwall narrated, both autobiographical and fictional (see Scrivener, *Seditious Allegories*, 272-75).

2 Both Samuel Richardson's *Pamela; or, Virtue Rewarded* (1740) and Charles de Fieux Mouhy's *The Fortunate Country Maid* (1758) tell stories of the rise of girls of humble origins to high social status by virtuous behaviour.

M. "Forgive you!—O, sir, I will pray for you night and morning. You were so good! You are so good to come again now. Oh! dear! dear! that my father should be out of the way.

"Ah, sir! he said he should never see you any more. But I told him not to despair; for to be sure you would be as good as your word."

"You were right! you were right!" said Henry, pulling out the money, and throwing it into her apron. "There, there, sweet girl! Your father shall be happy; and you shall be happy; and I will be happy too—most happy! if *you* will make me so."

The emphasis of the concluding part of this sentence was lost upon poor Mary. She was overcome with this rush of favourable fortune; and throwing herself upon a chair, she looked first upon the money, and then in the face of Henry; and then turned round to the window, as if looking for her father, till her agitated feelings found vent in a shower of tears.

Henry pulled out his handkerchief to wipe her eyes; but his own wanted wiping also.

H. "I will mingle my tears with your's, sweet rustic! O that I could mingle my soul!"

M. "Ah, this will make my father so happy! But he would never believe that you would come. And when I told him that to be sure you must be a good young gentleman, or you never would have given him that other money, 'Yes, yes, Mary,' said he, 'that is very true: but it is too much, Mary—it is too much. But I am sure he is a good young gentleman, notwithstanding. I shall always love him. He spoke so pitifully; it did my heart good. Yes, I will always love him.' 'Aye, father,' said I 'and so will I too.'"

"And will you keep your word?" said Henry, seizing her hand and pressing it to his heart.

Mary was embarrassed.

"Yes—yes—sir. I will love you as I loved my poor brother."

The voluble—the overflowing heart, dictated the comparison:—the heart, which, like the grave, knows no distinctions; and, in the moment of strong excitement, overleaps the yawning chasms by which rank and fortune are insulated from the great continent of man.

But the abyss was no sooner past than Mary looked back and trembled. She blushed; she faltered; she was confounded at her own presumption.

"If I may venture to compare such a gentleman with a poor boy like him," added she, endeavouring to recall her words.

"But I will love you, sir, in a very different way; with humility and reverence; as we love those things we must only look upon at a distance:—or, as we love the holy man that teaches us to be good on a Sunday. And I will pray to God, sir, every time I go to church, that you may live a great long time, to do many such good deeds as this, and to have the reward of them."

"But suppose I cannot live?" said Henry with impressive tenderness. "Suppose there should be something the matter here"—pressing her hand to his left side—

"God forbid! sir," answered Mary with great simplicity—"It was that our poor William died of. And he did so gasp—and fetch his breath so short!

"Ah, poor dear boy! he was so affectionate, sir, to the very last!—He thought nothing brought him any ease unless Mary gave it him."

H. "And nothing will bring *me* any ease, delightful maiden, unless Mary will give it *me!*"

M. "Ah, sir, you are only joking now. Thank God you are well, sir; and you have better and dearer friends than a poor simple girl like me, to nurse you and take care of you."

H. "But suppose I should not be well. Supposing I should be dying with this malady here," pressing her hand still closer to his side, "and nobody else could do me any good, would Mary give me ease, if it were in her power?"

M. "Oh, sir, I would watch you all night long. I would do all that I was bid, and all that I could think of. And if you must die, and had no sister of your own to close your eyes, as I did my poor William's, I would pay you my poor services to the last. And when I could no longer be afraid that my sorrow should appear presumptuous, I would throw myself in an agony upon your breast, as I did upon his, and wash your pale, sweet countenance with my tears."

Henry's heart was melted. The mounting blood fell back to a purer channel. He felt a holy horror creeping round his heart; and cursed himself for the unhallowed thoughts he had been entertaining.

The tender tete-a-tete was now interrupted by the arrival of Wilson; and—

Mary no sooner beheld him at the gate of the fold, than she ran out to meet him in a transport of grateful rapture; to shew him the money that Henry had poured into her lap, and conducted him to his youthful benefactor.

The countenance of the old man brightened the instant he beheld her. Her whole physiognomy was prophetic. Her eyes, her haste, her attitudes, that buoyancy of soul that urges on the frame, almost, in appearance, like the ethereal creatures of the poet's brain—

"Smooth gliding without step"—[1]

all spoke for her, before she had breath enough for utterance; and the happy father knew the whole of her tale, while the first accent was yet quivering on her lips.

He seized her in his arms, and interrupted her with an embrace of almost convulsive fondness; while a mutual shower of tears gave vent to their reciprocal feelings.

Henry beheld the scene through the little casement. His eyes, also, were full, and his heart danced within him. He felt the pure delights of a

---

1 Pope's *Iliad* 20:375.

rational being, born for benevolence, and sympathising in the joys and sufferings of all around him.

Wilson rushed into the room. His heart was big with exultation and gratitude:

"You have saved me! you have saved me!" he exclaimed—"You have saved my little girl. We were ruined: but Providence sent you to our relief and we are preserved and happy."

In short, our hero was overwhelmed with a profusion of thanks and blessings, which were not the less gratifying to his heart, for being echoed by the melodious voice of the fascinating little Mary.

Henry found the gratitude of this little damsel far too delightful not to be desirous of enjoying it again. He accordingly revisited the farm-house, a few days after; not without some lurking hopes that he might again find the farmer from home.

In this he was not disappointed. The weather was fine. The corn was ripe, and Wilson was busy in preparation for gathering in the harvest.

Mary was sitting at the door, singing a love ditty to her wheel; and, in the estimation of Henry, at least, looked even more beautiful than when he first beheld her.

It was before, the beauty of the sun breaking through an April shower; splendid indeed, and joyous, but with a watery beam, and a brow yet clouded by the half scattered vapours. Now it was the cheerful serenity of May; when the unruffled azure smiles over the fragrant blossoms as they unfold, and listens to the chorus of the groves.

Such were the poetical similitudes with which Henry indulged his partial fancy.

Mary rose from her seat the instant she saw him approaching. Her wheel was suffered to stand still; while, with rustic courtesy, she invited him again into the little parlour. Henry was better pleased with the porch,

"For talking age, and whisper lover made."[1]

The woodbine that mantled it emitted a cheerful fragrance. The cock, gallanting, with his gilded plumes, among the feathered seraglio; the pigeons cooing and fluttering around the dove cot on the right; the gay insects sporting among the flowrets in the little garden on the left; the little birds chirping and sporting among the branches of the apple-tree—in short, every thing was in harmony with his feelings.

He pressed the hand of little Mary; drew her gently down upon the seat again; placed himself by her side,

"And sigh'd and look'd, sigh'd and look'd,
Sigh'd and look'd, and sigh'd again."[2]

The damsel blushed, and looked she knew not how. She turned her wheel round with unusual rapidity; broke the thread half a dozen times in the space of two or three minutes; and, to increase her confusion, lost the end.

---

1   Oliver Goldsmith, *Deserted Village* (1770), l. 14.
2   John Dryden, *Alexander's Feast* (1697), ll. 112-13.

Henry was charmed with her agitation. Embarrassment never looked half so lovely.

"I spoil your industry, I am afraid, Mary?" said he tenderly.

M. "Dear! I cannot think what makes me so aukward."

H. "It is a graceful aukwardness, Mary. Am I cause of this pretty embarrassment?"

M. "Indeed, sir, I am not used to sit by such a gentleman.—And such a good gentleman!"

She would have risen from her seat.

H. "Nay, Mary! Mary! my pretty Mary! you would not leave me, I hope."

M. "O sir! you are such a gentleman! So kind! So condescending!"

H. "Mention it not my sweet girl! mention it not. If I have contributed to your happiness, Mary"—

M. "O sir! you have made me the happiest creature in the world. God knows, sir, I never lie down o'nights but I think of you. I even see you in my dreams."

H. "Dear Mary! How we sympathise! I see you in mine perpetually."

M. "You have made my father so happy, sir. He went that very night and paid the wicked steward; and when our rich neighbour, Mr. Walcot, came the next morning, and thought himself sure of his bargain, my father shewed him the receipt.

"'No, Mr. Walcot,' says he, 'you do not have my farm, this time, I assure you. To be sure I was a ruined man: ruined and hopeless; and you would have taken advantage of my distress, Mr. Walcot, notwithstanding what is said in scripture about *trampling the bruised reed.*[1] But it pleased God to raise me up a friend in my time of need—a kind sweet young gentleman! Mr. Walcot; and, thank God! my lease is not expired.'

"And so Mr. Walcot looked so black and frowned, and blustered, and looked as if he could have killed us."

H. "And did he frown at thee, Mary? Is it possible!"

M. "Ah, dear sir—he does not look at me as you do. But he glouts[2] at me always, with such nasty ugly looks: and yet I don't know why—only that he has a daughter, about my age, who wears a parcel of fine silks, and earrings, and necklaces, and makes such a bustle, as she goes up the aisle of the church every Sunday, to her pew, just before the parson begins to read the service; and so some of our foolish neighbours have given it out that *for all her finery, I am handsomer than she.*"

H. "And I will be sworn that it is true, Mary—be she as fine as she will."

M. "O dear, sir, if Mr. Walcot knew that you said so, he would hate me worse than ever.

"But I don't know how it is, sir, your kind looks put me out of countenance, as much as his nasty ugly frowns do. And yet I am not frighted at you, sir, as I am at him. But my heart does so beat! and my breath—

---

1 Matthew 12:20.

2 Frowns, scowls.

"I hope I am not going to be as my poor brother was!—But indeed, sir,—I—I can't tell what's the matter with me."

H. "Beat! Mary. Does thy heart beat? Pretty little heart! Let me quiet it, and thou shalt quiet mine."

He laid his hand upon her heart.

It was an electric touch. His whole frame sympathised to the vibration. He bent towards the blooming maiden. He clasped her in his arms. He snatched an unmeditated—unresisted kiss.

Mary's heart beat quicker than ever. Her bosom heaved with an emotion never before experienced. Her cheek out-blushed the rose. Her head reclined in fearful bashfulness; but her humid eyes still lingered on the graceful form of Henry.

The moment was critical.

Mary was at that time of life when the passions are awakened, but suspicion still slumbers. She knew not the nature or tendency of her own sensations; and no maternal monitor had ever warned her inexperienced youth against their stealing influence.

Desire crept into her heart in the insinuating form of gratitude; and resistance might have been impossible, before she knew she had any thing to resist.

Henry, on the other hand, was bold and ardent. Among the licentious groupes of Eton he had lost the timidity natural to his years. He perceived, though she did not, what was passing in the heart of Mary, and he neglected no art or blandishment that might inflame the desires he had kindled.

In short he repeated his caresses, with increasing ardour. He pressed the glowing bosom of the struggling, fainting virgin. He even ventured to approach it with his lips.

His presumption was but faintly resisted: and, emboldened by the success of these first advances, he clasped her in his arms, and lifted her from her seat, with intention of carrying her into the house and gratifying his triumphant passion.

At this moment of delirium, when all was presumption on one side, and embarrassment on the other, they were suddenly aroused from the intoxication of passion by the voice of old Wilson.

It was doubly fortunate that, as he was giving instruction to his man, who was at work in another field, he was heard before he was in sight: so that Mary had time to run into the house; and Henry to compose himself, with two or three turns in the garden, previous to their re-encounter.

That Henry should be desirous of knowing the catastrophe of the business with the steward and Walcot was so in unison with his former conduct, that his visit awakened no suspicion in the breast of the honest farmer.

Mary was, however, for the future, more upon her guard. She looked back with terror upon the precipice from which she had escaped; and although the person and manners of Henry—the flattering things he had looked and whispered, and even the familiar blandishments in which he had indulged his passion, had, altogether, conspired to awaken feelings in her mind that rendered her but little disposed to avoid his society; yet she received him, ever after, with a degree of timidity and virgin coyness, which, while it increased his desires, restrained his presumptuous ardour.

But Henry was not to be so repulsed. The very precautions of little Mary betrayed her passion; and her eyes (untrained in the school of hypocritical formality) told him all that he could desire to know.

In short, he persevered in his addresses; and as it was evident that the frequent repetition of his visits must awaken the suspicions of the father, he prevailed upon the infatuated maiden to give him occasional meetings in the retirements of neighbouring groves, and listen to his treacherous vows and seductive insinuations in many a twilight walk.

Yes, too credulous—too unguarded maiden! thou didst listen!—thou didst imbibe the sweet—sweet poison of youthful tenderness, and yield up thy unsophisticated heart to the emotions of sympathy, which Nature, thy only guide had emplanted there! Neither was thy simplicity initiated in those laws of prudence which the opinions and customs of the world have made paramount to Nature; nor thy affections regulated by those institutions of society which have superseded her benign dominion, have separated into ranks and factions the distracted family of mankind, and perverted the finest sympathies of the uncorrupted soul into fruitful sources of misery and of vice.

This was thy crime; and bitter was the penalty of tears in which thy simplicity was amerced.[1] But still more bitter that penalty might have been, had not accident interfered where precaution failed—had not timely separation given a breathing space to passion, ere the last barriers of yielding chastity were overwhelmed by the increasing torrent.

In short, the season of vacation arrived, before Henry could find a convenient opportunity of consummating his amour: and our hero was, for a while, compelled to relinquish the neighbourhood at once of the muses and the loves, for the superintendence and solicitude of maternal affection.

CHAP. III.

In which our Hero attains the Age of Manhood.

Disgraceful Expedients.—The partial Eclaircissement.[2]—The Love-letter.—Supernatural Agency.—Final Explanation.—A Glance at the University.

HENRY was now, once more, the domesticated companion of his best and earliest tutor: and never was a time when her admonitions were so necessary, or required so completely all the auxiliary force that might be derived from filial affection and veneration. Amelia, therefore, redoubled

---

1 Legal punishment by a fine.
2 Explanation (French).

her attentions; and neglected no opportunity of working upon his affections, before she began the more unpleasant task of animadversion.[1]

The mind of Henry, in the mean time, was busily employed in devising expedients to satisfy the demands of Marlow.

What was to be done?

All that, in the ordinary course of things, could be expected from his mother and his friends, would scarcely discharge the debts he had contracted, independently of that affair. It was necessary, therefore, to appeal to other projects.

Had Henry possessed the frankness of mind and moral fortitude which the early management of Amelia (unthwarted by the example and interference of Montfort) could not have failed to produce, the character of that amiable woman would at once have suggested a project equally honourable and simple: namely, a full disclosure of the amount, and the causes of his embarrassment. But, a principle of false shame, arising from the circumstances in which the adventure originated, and a still more powerful passion with which that adventure had now become associated in his mind, restrained him from this proceeding, and put him upon a thousand disgraceful expedients for his extrication—or, more properly, for deferring the evil day.

Having privately disposed of every portable article he could properly call his own, the facility with which he found a market for one description of these commodities, in particular, suggested the desperate expedient of buying other commodities of the like description, upon credit, and selling them again for whatever he could get.

In short, he had met with a dealer in second-hand books, who was ready enough (provided the article was left to his own valuation) to purchase, without impertinent questions, whatever might be brought to him, by whatever hand. At this shop, valets de chambre and house-maids trafficked in the classics; and writers on the belles-lettres were recommended to temporary accommodation, by critical commentators who had found their way from the chimnies to the shelves of elegant libraries.

Thus provided with so friendly a co-operator, Henry repaired to a capital bookseller, at the west end of the town, with whom his mother was in the habit of dealing; and, on promise of early payment, procured first one valuable book and then another, which he readily took to the repository in question, and as readily disposed of for about a third part of its value.

But the frequency of his visits soon alarmed the cautious prudence of the bookseller; who thought requisite to inform him (in the gentlest terms and genteelest manner he could devise) that he could not permit him to have any thing further in this way, without the knowledge and approbation of Mrs. Montfort.

This was a terrible stroke. His word was pledged—his reputation was at stake. Without the money, it was impossible to return to Eton.

---

1 Critical reflection.

What was to be done now?

The same evil spirit (the spirit of secrecy and false shame) that had suggested the first expedient, suggested a second still more disgraceful. This was no other than to write a letter to the bookseller, in his mother's name, testifying her knowledge and approbation of his proceedings.

Every impediment now appeared to be removed: and Henry having made considerable advances towards raising the necessary supplies, began to glory in his stratagems; to devise new schemes of pleasure and expence; and even to look upon this project of buying and selling books, as one of the ways and means by which his future expences might be supplied.

But from this dream of culpable folly he was presently awakened. The suspicions and precautions of the bookseller were, indeed, at an end: but accident effected a discovery that penetration overlooked.

Amelia (with whom the library of Henry had become an object of serious consideration) happened, about this time, to call upon the bookseller, to purchase several articles with which she meant to present him on his return to Eton; and it so happened, also, that several of the articles in the list she presented to the bookseller were the same as Henry had already procured.

"Already!" repeated Amelia, with some surprise. "Well, well! I am happy to hear that Henry has money to spare for such purposes, and wisdom enough to dispose of it in such a way."

"O! as for that, madam," replied the bookseller, "after the letter you was pleased to honour me with, I could, of course, have no anxiety about the money."

A. "Letter! Mr. Probart! I do not understand you."

B. "The letter, madam, I received from you the other morning, desiring me to let master Henry have whatever books he wanted."

Amelia was astonished and confounded. But, collecting all the self-command she was mistress of—"Aye—aye—that letter"—continued she—"It is very well, Mr. Probart: but, be kind enough to let me look at it. Perhaps I may have expressed myself more unreservedly than I intended."

The bookseller bowed; pulled out his pocket-book; and presented it with another bow.

Amelia turned aside to conceal her emotions.

"Upon second thoughts, Mr. Probart," said she, "I believe it will be better that I should order the articles myself. Be kind enough to make out your bill; and I will pay you now, as I am here."

The bookseller bowed, and thanked, and obeyed; and took his money; and thanked and bowed again, with right tradesman-like courtesy: and Amelia stepped back into her carriage, with the letter in her pocket, and with a heavy heart.

Amelia was now convinced that her purposed admonitions must be no longer delayed—that the mind of Henry must either be instantaneously aroused to a juster sense of honour, and of virtue, or be hurried, by rapid gradations, along the downward path of vice, below the character and estimation not only of the moralist but the gentleman.

As soon, therefore, as she returned home, she sent for him into her study (the apartment in which he was first introduced to the acquaintance of the reader), and addressed him in the following manner.

"Henry!—My dear Henry! hast thou forgotten that happy season of innocence and unbounded confidence, when, at the close of every tranquil day, thou wert wont to rush, with eager transport in thy looks—with an eye all openness, and an ear that was all attention, into this little apartment, to receive my evening instructions—my monitory warnings, or more grateful commendations? And when the closing kiss of maternal fondness used to imprint upon thy infant remembrance the lessons that I hoped would have been indelible?"

(Henry knew not what to make of this address. He was abashed and silent.)

"Hast thou forgotten, my child, those days of blessedness, when all was confidence, and all was joy?—when Henry never once thought of disguise or subterfuge; for his heart had no vices—and the errors of childhood were sure to be regarded with indulgence, to be reproved without harshness, and corrected not with severity, but by reason?

"Ah! Henry! Henry! had that confidence remained, you had never been betrayed into a mean, a dishonourable—Oh! that I must add, a dishonest action!"

[The embarrassment of Henry increased. The affair of the hen-roost, and the still more disgraceful affair of the books, rushed together into his mind. Though Amelia paused for some time, he did not dare to speak; but waited, in silent confusion, for the developement.][1]

"See here, Henry," resumed the agitated monitresss, producing the letter—"See here the witness of a depravity that disgraces you to a level with the swindler and the felon:—obtaining goods under false pretences, and supporting fraud by forgery!

"And what have you done with the books so dishonestly procured?

"Your trunk would not contain them. In your room they are not to be seen.

"The circumstances speak for themselves. Like the common swindler, you have defrauded the honest tradesman of articles for which you had no demand, and carried them to some of those receptacles for stolen goods, where they might be converted into ready money.

"And this is Henry Montfort!—the accomplished! the polite! the high-spirited Henry Montfort! whose polished manners fascinate the circles of fashion; whose scholastic attainments render him conspicuous over the youth of his acquaintance; whose pride endures no equal, and is frequently so injuriously painful to those beneath him!

"Oh, what chaos of inconsistencies!

---

1 Brackets in the original.

"But what scenes of vice and prodigality—what career of debauchery and dissipation, can have exposed you to the necessity of such an action?

"But tell me not, Henry—tell me not, even now. I will not put your remaining virtue to the blush. I will not harden your front so much in vice as to call upon you for the disgusting picture of licentious dissipations. I will not ask you in what detested brothel—in what abominable gaming-house you have plunged yourself in those embarrassments, from which such an expedient could seem necessary for your redemption.

"Let the remembrance of the past live no-where but in your own bosom; and there, as a needful warning, let it ever live. I well shew you, even in this extremity, that, however low you may have sunk in vice, you need not sink still lower, from the dread of making me your confident.

"Say only that you have been vicious, and have plunged yourself in embarrassments: nay shelter yourself, if you will, behind some gentler phrase.—Call it imprudence; tell me the amount, however frightful, of your necessities, and let me but see the ingenuous blush of penitence upon your cheek, I will trust, even yet, to the reaction of those good principles I have taken so much pains to inculcate.—I will subdue your prodigality by indulgence and generosity—if yet it is possible to subdue it. It shall be once more in your power to be virtuous and respectable; to begin a new, a better career than you have of late been running; and to realise those prospects you were once so eager to indulge.

"One thing I will say to you, Henry, and only one, to induce you to serious reformation. Present, or absent, do not forget me, my dear Henry, nor the solicitude with which I have endeavoured to promote your happiness.

"Do not forget that in this frail and perishable world (in which I am not likely to be a very long sojourner) there is no happiness for me—no, not one ray—no joy, no consolation, but what must be derived from the project of seeing you advance in those courses of wisdom and virtue that may conduct you to the goal of honourable manhood; happy in yourself, and useful in your exertions to promote the happiness of others.

"When I am no more, Henry—when those eyes can no longer weep over your failings, nor these lips admonish you, then will you know, my Henry! that you have greater obligations to me than at present you can possibly conceive—that I have stronger claims to your gratitude than Nature herself can give.

"Suffer me not, then, my dear Henry! my more than child!—suffer me not to sink into the grave without the comfortable reflection, in my latest hour, that I leave one behind me, dearer than life itself, who will owe his happiness to my solicitude, and may enjoy the felicity that has been denied to me."

The heart of Henry was ready, almost, to burst.

"My mother! my mother!" he exclaimed, throwing his arms round her neck, while the tears rushed in torrents from his eyes—"Oh! my mother! I have been to blame—much to blame—perhaps I have been criminal. But I have not been so vicious as you suspect.

"Though I have been guilty of many follies, my present embarrassment does not proceed either from my prodigality or my licentiousness. It has originated in those principles you have yourself inculcated—in sympathy towards my fellow-creatures—in the exercise of what, from your precept and your example, I have learnt to consider as the noblest qualities of our nature.

"To snatch a poor farmer and his family from distress and ruin—from bankruptcy—from beggary—from a gaol, I have contracted a heavy debt, and my crime, my only crime is the means by which I have attempted to discharge it."

"Oh! make but that appear," resumed Amelia, with an ardour of expectation, "make but that appear, and dearer shall you be to my heart from this failing, than all the formal virtues of prudent wordlings ever could have rendered you."

The heart of Henry overflowed with generous emotion. He was about to unbosom himself without disguise. But the disgraceful circumstance of the hen-roost, rose to his remembrance, and overwhelmed him with confusion. He could not bring himself so immediately to the disclosure of that part of the adventure; but, after some hesitation and recollection, related, without introductory circumstance, the story of poor Wilson's disaster; the difficulties he had met with in fulfilling his promise; and the engagement into which he had entered.

Amelia listened with powerful emotions. The painful feelings of her heart subsided. Pity, joy, admiration divided her bosom; and, as soon as the tale was concluded—

"Thank God! thank God!" exclaimed she, clasping him in her arms— "thank God thou hadst the heart to do this deed!

"But why was I thought unworthy to be the confidant of such an adventure? How could Henry doubt for a single moment, the alacrity with which I should discharge a debt so contracted?

"But come, let us settle this business without delay; and then we will talk, as friend should talk with friend, of those errors and irregularities, which it is so necessary to our mutual happiness that you should correct.

"What shame, my Henry, that the soil that can produce such fruit, should be overgrown with nettles and nightshade!"

To those who are acquainted with the maternal heart, it will appear natural enough that, in the eyes of Amelia, Henry, after this eclaircissement, should appear more amiable than ever.

Time, that had matured her judgment, had not abated her admiration of those sublimer traits of romantic enthusiasm, which are the proper characteristics of youth. She knew how to discriminate, and to value, the materials of which superior virtue and superior intellect are composed; and for one generous action, irregularly great, could pardon a thousand of those little extravagancies and eccentricities which make the

—"Slaves of business, bodies without soul,
"Important blanks in nature's mighty whole"—[1]
shake their grave heads, and give up a young man for lost. The remembrance of all that was censurable in this affair was, therefore, presently lost in admiration of the generosity of the leading incident.

Still, however, she could not but wonder at his concealing such an adventure from her knowledge. The story also seemed to want a commencement and consistency. The embarrassment and hesitation with which he began, had not entirely escaped her notice; and she was at times almost induced to suspect, that there was still a lurking something behind that was not entirely right.

This suspicion, indeed, was rational enough, and might, by logical induction, have led to further enquiry. But Amelia's heart, though regulated by somewhat more than an ordinary share of philosophy, was not a mere thing of abstractions, that always reasons and that never feels; and she was much too happy in the sensations produced by so much of the adventure as had been divulged, to search, with an over-jealous curiosity, for minuter circumstances that might have a tendency to diminish its lustre.

The conscience of Henry, however, was not quite so complaisant. It boldly accused him of the want of that degree of candour and confidence to which the liberality of his mother was so peculiarly entitled: and the applauses and caresses of Amelia rather seconded than silenced the appeal.

In short, these self-reproaches became so importunate, that he at last determined to silence them, by a full disclosure of the adventure he had so disingenuously concealed.

While Henry was yet meditating this ingenuous acknowledgment, another disaster befel him, that, in the event, produced a more ample disclosure than that which even now he meditated.

His departure from Eton had not broken off his connection with little Mary. On the contrary, his fervour seemed to be increased (and perhaps the infatuation also of that simple maiden) by this temporary separation. He accordingly continued to carry on his seductive courtship, by letters,
"The moving messengers of love."[2]
And as the fluency of his language was equal to the ardour of his desires, the manner in which he conducted this correspondence, the images with which it teemed, and the sentiments it breathed, were perhaps more formidable to the virtue of the object assailed, than even his direct conversation.

One of those glowing epistles (in which he had announced his approaching return to Eton, and requested the little rustic to meet him at

---

1 Charles Churchill, *An Epistle to Robert Lloyd* (1761), ll. 7-8.
2 James Thomson, *Spring* (1728), l. 1042.

a stated time) Henry had entrusted to the care of a servant who, among other errands, was going to the post-office with some letters from Amelia.

It so happened, however, that the fellow (who was an Irishman, and loved a drop of the creature[1] to his heart), meeting with a countryman and old acquaintance, was induced to step aside into a public-house, that they might just renew their friendship over a sober pot, and make an enquiry or two about their different adventures.

As the devil would have it, this old companion had been a great traveler since their last meeting—had seen many strange countries, dressed his master's hair in many strange fashions, and heard many learned conversations in languages of which he did not comprehend a single word. He had, therefore, many wonderful things to relate; and as our knight of the brush was no less curious, than *he* was communicative, tale succeeded to tale, and tankard to tankard, till the object of his errand was forgotten, and honest Teague rolled merrily home with the letters safe in his pocket.

This was not the first time that Teague had mistaken the tippling-house for the post-office; and so long as there were neither animosities nor heart-burnings among his fellow servants, all this was very well;—the matter was hushed up; and the letters took the next opportunity of proceeding on their journey.

But that deformed and malignant little demon whom Don Cleofas Leandro Perez Zambullo[2] let out of the astrologer's bottle, being in one of his mischievous humours, and determining to play our hero a sort of dog's trick, had, for that purpose, so dispensed his influence as to inspire a deadly spirit of jealousy and hatred between the said Teague and one Taffy ap Williams a rival brother of the brush.

The prince of leeks, therefore, took the present opportunity of revenging himself on the nursling of potatoes and butter-milk;[3] and the letters were carried up stairs, together with an exact account of the state in which Teague had returned with them from the tippling-house.

Amelia had none of that jealous spirit of domination that prompts to inquisition—or that would regulate the morals of youth by suspicious meanness. She was not, therefore, in the habit of opening the letters that Henry might either send or receive; and observing, in the present instance, a letter more than she had delivered, the direction of which was in his hand-writing, she laid it conspicuously apart, upon a little shelf in the study, that he might have it again when he returned home.

---

1 Whiskey, in Hibernian English.
2 Main character in Alain-René Lesage's (1668-1747) picaresque novel, *Le diable boiteux* [The Lame Devil], 1707, which was translated into English in 1708. The English versions, which included theatrical adaptations, went by the title *The Devil Upon Two Sticks*, a text Thelwall alludes to in his early writing, including *The Peripatetic* (1793).
3 The Welshman Williams is associated with the national symbol, the leek, and the Irishman Teague stereotypically with the potato.

But in doing this, her eye fell accidentally upon the name of Wilson.

"Wilson! Wilson! What particular association should there be with that name that makes me recoil upon myself?

"It is the name of the poor farmer.

"Miss Mary Wilson, Ditton, near Windsor, to the care of Mrs. Fell, fruiterer.—*The care of Mrs. Fell!*

"But who should this Mary Wilson be?—

"A daughter, perhaps!

"But Henry mentioned no daughter.

"Good God! if all this apparent benevolence should have originated in such motives!—if this should be the reason why the commencement of his acquaintance with the old man was so mysteriously concealed? And if not, why does he correspond with her?—Why was her name omitted?—Why direct to the care of this convenient fruiterer?"

The suspicion was insupportable. The situation in which she stood was irksome. What was she to do? Nothing less than an unlimited disclosure could still the agitation of her mind: and how was this to be obtained?—

"Should she make use of the clandestine means that accident had thrown in her way?"

There was a littleness in this, repugnant to all the feelings and habits of her mind.

"Should she deliver the letter, unopened, into the hands of Henry, and trust to his report for the contents?

"This was trusting to a broken reed. If her suspicions were well-founded (and, from all appearances, it was difficult to hope any other), the mind capable of duplicity under the circumstances of the former explanation, could have little difficulty in resorting to subterfuge to elude the present enquiry."

In short, general principles yielded to particular expediency. The letter was opened; and the contents seemed to confirm her apprehensions, in the fullest extent. Every line exhibited her darling Henry not only in the odious light of a seducer of innocence, but of one who had been capable of converting the misfortunes of the father into the means of seduction against the daughter—who had relieved the distresses of the former as the price of the innocence of the latter; and then, arrogated to himself the merit of benevolence, when prodigal licentiousness was his only motive.

"So early, too, Henry!" exclaimed she—"so early! Can you practise, in your very boyhood, the vices of him I was so anxious you should call your father?

"Thou *hast* called him so. Thou hast imbibed the poison of his instructions: and this is the result.

"O Montfort! Montfort! where will the ravages of thy evil dispositions end?

"Bowbridge!—Louisa!

"Hast thou murdered too the mind of this only relic? Is Henry also the victim of thy licentious vices?"

While Amelia was giving way to these painful reflections, Henry returned home. He hastened immediately to the study where she was sitting. But he had no sooner opened the door than her disconsolate attitude filled him with apprehensions. Nor was the impression, though varied, less afflicting, when, withdrawing her hand from before her eyes, with a severe and scrutinising glance, she checked the impatience with which he was running towards her.

Never before had Amelia regarded him with such a look! Her tone—her language, were equally unwonted.

"Young man!" said she, "for the language of endearment must now be laid aside: the follies of youth—nay some even of the vices of that season, may challenge indulgence; and are better chastened, perhaps, by the admonitions of the friend, than the severity of the judge; but when absolute depravity is arraigned before us, distinctions of age are done away, and so should be the feelings of affection. The crime—the unpalliated crime should be considered in the abstract; and reason should alone decide."

Henry was thunder-struck.

He stood silent for a few seconds.

At length; "My mother! my mother!" he exclaimed; and throwing himself at her feet, with a burst of agony, endeavoured to seize her hand. But she drew it suddenly away; and covering her face, to conceal her emotions—

"Young man!" continued she, "forbear your supplications. I am not the injured party, but the judge; and were it otherwise, it is not by abject submissions that I would be appeased.

"Hear me then, young man!"—

"O my mother! my mother!" exclaimed Henry, interrupting her, "whatever may be my offence, kill me not with that cold expression.

"I had once a name, my mother!—I had once a name!"

A. "You had—a dear one!—A name that never vibrated upon this tongue but with rapture!—A name by which I never shall endure to distinguish a detected hypocrite—an unprincipled profligate who aspires to the reputation of generosity, when he is only prodigal in his licentiousness; and to whom Charity herself, the fairest child of heaven, is only estimable when she can be made subservient to his lascivious appetites."

H. "And am I that hypocrite—that profligate?"

A. "Yourself shall answer that question. Old Wilson!—poor old Wilson! Is there nothing connected with that story which you have thought it necessary to conceal?

"I will assist your memory, young man," continued she, taking the letter from her pocket. "Look upon this—the fatal evidence your own pen has furnished of the premature depravity of your heart.

"Is it not enough that virgin innocence must be made the prey of your unruly passions? Is it not enough that a poor helpless maiden, who has no fortune but her virtue—no means of subsistence but by her rep-

utation, must be stripped of every hope and consolation by your seductive artifices—that the powers of your mind, and the advantages of your
education, must be basely prostituted to poison the credulous mind of
a simple uneducated rustic—to varnish vice and veil destruction; but
must you add to all this, the cruelty—the superlative baseness, of
making the miseries of a poor family the means of your selfish gratifications?—bargaining, perhaps, with a distracted father for the indulgence of your wanton appetites; and undermining his repugnant virtue
by the cruel alternative of the prostitution of his daughter, or the
horrors of a gaol?

"This couldst thou do? And then, with unblushing profligacy, impose
on my maternal fondness with a role of pretended benevolence and heroic
generosity?"

"Oh! accuse me not, my mother! accuse me not," said Henry with great
emotion, "beyond the measure of my crime.

"Guilty as I am, I am not the profligate you suppose.

"I have been hurried away by passion. I have disgraced, by one part of
my conduct, the disinterestedness of another. I have been guilty of concealing what the generosity of your deportment ought to have induced me
to acknowledge. But I have assumed the merit of no motive but that by
which alone I was actuated.

"When I relieved the distresses of the father, I had never seen the
daughter:—I scarcely knew that he had a daughter in existence."

"Henry! Henry!" said Amelia, in a somewhat altered tone—

The very name was like the voice of redemption.

He seized her hand, and bathed it with a shower of tears.

"Nay," continued she, stifling her emotions, "I know not whether I
must yet resume that name.

"If your fable be true, how did your acquaintance with poor Wilson
begin? And why was that part of the story suppressed?"

Henry replied by relating the adventure of the hen-roost, and making
a candid confession of the origin and progress of the amour.

Amelia's heart was considerably relieved by this explanation; and
though she did not fail to express her reprobation, in the strongest terms,
of all that related to the connection with little Mary, and to paint in the
most forcible colours the cruelty of taking advantage of those feelings of
gratitude which the artless maiden had so naturally, but so dangerously
indulged, yet as the seduction was not completed, she consented to
restore Henry to her favour, upon his solemn engagement never to see
again the object of his illicit attachment.

She was aware, however, that such promises were not very much to be
depended upon: and she felt herself deeply interested in the behalf both
of Mary and of old Wilson. That she might better provide, therefore, for
the innocence of the one, and the future comfort of both, she persuaded
the father to remove, without delay, to a larger and better farm, at that
time vacant in another part of the country; and, by her liberality, obviated

the impediments that might have prevented him from embarking in such an enlarged concern.

The admonitions that resulted from the preceding disclosure, and the serious, but endearing exhortation with which Henry was, for the last time, dismissed to Eton, were not without their weight: for he felt, in reality, for his maternal monitress all the affection which such a parent can alone inspire; and though (seduced by the contagion of ill example; impelled by the force of habitual connexion, and influenced by the false shame that blushes as often at reformation as degeneracy), he occasionally relapsed into his former irregularities, the words, the image, the affectionate anxiety of a beloved mother were perpetually recurring to his remembrance, and checking him in his dissipated career.

But the nerve of steady and consistent resolution was, unfortunately, destroyed; and the period soon arrived at which he was to be placed in circles of increased temptation; more remote from the observation and influence of his benignant tutoress, and more resigned, of course, to the guidance of his own headstrong passions.

In short, Henry was removed from Eton to Oxford; where, though he did not actually plunge into the very vortex of that dissipation which swallows up the intellect and destroys the morals of so large a proportion of the pretended students, he was too frequently hurried away by the stream of evil example, and even distinguished by the profusion of his extravagance, and the occasional levity and irregularity of his conduct.

On the scenes of profligacy and disgusting licentiousness, so frequently exhibited on this great theatre, it is not our intention to dwell. Respect for a venerable institution which has produced so many brilliant characters, induces us to draw a veil over its abuses and defects, and to consign to oblivion the concomitant process of that noviciate through which our teachers of morality and religion, and, for the most part, the framers of our laws and institutions, are initiated into the mysteries of divinity and legislation. Suffice it to observe, that all the seeds, whose characteristic germinations we have already observed (all the good and all the censurable), continued to unfold, to blossom, to fructify, in the mind of our hero; and to exhibit much (very much) that was to be wished, more (perhaps) that was to be regretted, and all that was to be expected, from the early culture and management of the soil.

Let the reader, then, consider young Henry, with all his imperfections on his head, as having completed his twentieth year; with a mind enlarged, but not philosophical; a temper susceptible and affectionate, but capricious, impetuous, and unstable; with noble principles, but unsupported by self-denial or consistent resolution; and with an unbounded benevolence, which, however, too frequently "lost the name of action,"[1] from the total want of that economy which is equally necessary to affluence and to mediocrity.

---

1 *Hamlet* 3.1.88.

Let him add to these incongruities, passions the most ardent, and the most insatiable love of pleasure, and the portrait will be entire; exhibiting, altogether, rather a mass of splendid foibles than an instance of rational intellect and organised virtue.

Such was Henry Montfort, when he was first called into the arduous scene of adventurous action; his conduct in which—his errors, his efforts, and his disasters, it will be the business of the ensuing books to describe.

BOOK III.

=========

CHAP. I.

Containing a Voyage to the Island of St. Domingo;
and the Adventures of our Hero at Port-au-Prince.

Paternal Alienation.—The clerical Reporter.—Pangs of Separation.—
The Voyage and the Voyagers.—The Parisian Creole.—Port-au-Prince.—
The Supper and the Society.—A morning Concert in the West-Indian
Style.—The Negress.—Noon-tide Recreations for those who are too
busy to read.—The Chicca.—Mariano.

TO those who are acquainted with the inconsistencies of human character, it will not be very surprising that, while Amelia, who had laboured to
prevent the seeds of depravity from being sown in the mind of Henry,
bewailed the irregularities that had sprung from them, with affectionate
sorrow, Montfort, to whose perverseness the evil was entirely to be attributed, was inflamed with an indignation that almost changed parental
regard into animosity. But such is the common progress of malevolent dispositions. We are ever foremost to condemn the mischiefs we have ourselves occasioned; and man is seldom so completely out of humour with
others, as when he feels a sort of latent conviction that he has reason to
be out of humour with himself.

Neither will it be thought more astonishing, when the indefatigable
diligence of malicious rumour is taken into consideration, that the distance which separated the father from the son, and the seas that rolled
between them, were inadequate to prevent the former from becoming
acquainted with those scenes of youthful prodigality which it was so much
the interest of the latter to conceal.

In short, in a matter of so much importance, Montfort had not chosen
to depend upon what he called "the infatuated partiality of a mother." He
had, accordingly, been informed of all the irregularities of Henry, by a
confidential agent: a distant relation, who, being a Bachelor of Arts, a
preceptor, and a resident of one of the colleges, had ample opportunities
of becoming acquainted with those "passages of life," an account of
which he supposed it his peculiar duty to transmit to his patron and
employer.

This reverend gentleman, whose name was Emanuel Woodhouse, was
a being originally of a cynical and envious turn of mind, which had not
been a little soured by the disappointment of his clerical ambition, and
which, perhaps, on the present occasion, was somewhat spurred and irritated by the prospect, that the less devotedly Montfort might feel himself
attached to an only son, the larger portion of his increasing affluence
might be divided in legacies among such of his relations as had the good
fortune to live in his remembrance.

It is scarcely necessary to add, that by such an artist the harsher lines of the picture would seldom be softened down by any of those delicate touches of apology or modification, which might render the features less offensive. On the contrary, the likenesses, if so they might be called, of this saturnine limner, were distinguished rather by their force than their accuracy; and partook more of the nature of caricature than embellished portrait.

The conduct of Henry could ill afford to be regarded through such a medium. It is not, therefore, surprising that the mind of Montfort should become alienated more and more with the contents of every packet: and as, in his consequent letters to Henry, he had repeatedly *commanded him, in the most authoritative style*, to alter the whole tenor of his conduct; and had enforced his mandates with all the logic of anger, and all the eloquence of threats and denunciations, he considered the small degree of attention that was paid to these *personal admonitions*, as a sort of rebellion against the *divine right of fathers*, which called for little less than the capital punishment of final disherision[1] and reprobation.

One expedient, however, he determined to try, before he proceeded to such extremities. This was no other than to remove him, at once, from the scene of his studies and his dissipations, and place him under the care of the French planter in St. Domingo, with whom it has been already observed that Montfort had a connexion of co-partnership.

To this resolution it is possible he was moved by more considerations than one. We have already noticed the progress of avarice in his mind, or, more properly speaking, of rapacity (for neither age nor superstition abated his voluptuous dissipation), and, as the Domingo estate was very extensive, and there were circumstances in the situation of the French planter that rendered it probable the whole might come into the hands of our calculator, he imagined, perhaps, that his interest might be considerably promoted by having his son upon the spot, while he himself resided on his Jamaica plantations. Neither is it impossible, considering the deepening gloom of dissatisfaction, and consequent malevolence, that was gathering over his mind, but that he might feel a sort of ambiguous satisfaction in depriving Amelia of the happiness she derived from the occasional society of Henry: for, in minds of a certain temperament, there is a soreness, the very inverse of sympathy, which occasions the happiness of others to be felt as a sort of aggravation of affliction.

Be that as it may, the only pretence assigned in the letter that communicated his orders was, "the necessity of checking a headstrong reprobate in the ruinous career of profligate dissipation."

This was an afflicting stroke to poor Amelia. To have her dear Henry not only torn from her arms, but exposed to all the dangers of a long and perilous voyage, and the ravages of all those diseases so frequently fatal to Europeans, was itself sufficient to drive her almost to distraction.

---

1 Disinheritance.

But this was not all. She regarded the state and organization of society in the West-Indies even with more abhorrence than the climate. The very conditions of master and of slave, and all those distinctions which measure respectability by the gradations of complexion, were equally repugnant to her principles and her feelings; and in her opinion, more fatal to the best virtues of humanity than even that unbounded licentiousness of morals which seem, almost universally, to characterise the tropical regions.

She was, also, perfectly aware, that the only restraints that at present kept the irregular passions of Henry within any bounds, originated in her admonitions, and his anxiety for her peace and happiness. What, then, might be his conduct when those restraints should be removed by the distance which was about to separate them? And when every passion should be inflamed and aggravated by the example of a state of society in which voluptuousness is order, and licentiousness is law?

Strongly, however, as she was impressed by these reflections, she would not venture to delay her compliance with the imperious mandate.

She had long been sensible that Henry had some lurking enemy, who injured him in the mind of Montfort; and that some storm was hovering over his head, which any opposition to the present proposal might occasion at once to burst, and overwhelm him in irreparable ruin.

As for Henry himself, his romantic imagination was delighted with the prospect of a voyage that promised to gratify his curiosity with an infinitude of new and interesting objects—new countries, a new world of vegetation, new characters, new customs, and new associations—in short, a new creation. His fancy luxuriated with all the enthusiasm of a poet, in the anticipation of those curiosities, and those adventures, with which he supposed himself certain of being perpetually gratified.

These enthusiastic feelings, however, were frequently interrupted by the more tender emotions of filial affection; and, in spite of that ardent desire with which he panted to engage in the busy world of enterprise, there were times when he thought of separation from so affectionate and so excellent a mother appeared like the stroke of death; and he almost resolved to disobey the mandate of his father, rather than encounter so sharp a trial.

However gratifying these feelings might be to Amelia, she was very far from encouraging them. On the contrary, convinced of the necessity of his compliance, she summoned up all the heroine in her mind, and fortified his staggering resolution with her superior philosophy.

The hour of his departure at length arrived; and, after a most heart-rending separation, and a thousand promises of writing by every opportunity, and informing her of every circumstance that might occur, Henry took leave of his mother and embarked for France, where a vessel bound to St. Domingo was ready to receive him, and conduct him to the place of his destination.

Henry pursued his voyage with some degree of mortification and disappointment. From the time of his quitting the British coast, nothing like an adventure had occurred.

Even France, fruitful as it was of political events, and interesting to the speculative observer, presented to his animadversion nothing more than a transient survey of the bustle of a sea-port, and the turbulence of nautical preparation.

He landed from one vessel only to pass through the forms of official examination, and then embarked on board another, which, under a favourable gale, soon lost sight of that vast theatre, on which twenty millions of men were exhibited poised, as it were, on the revolutionary balance, and vibrating between anarchy and despotism.

The passage was most insipidly prosperous; and Henry soon became impatient of its duration.

The manners and characters of the crew, although, from their professional peculiarities, they, of course, had something novel in them, were but food for the observation of a day or two. The captain was little better than one of those blocks of hard and knotted wood, out of which the laborious hand of application, working only to a single object, sometimes contrives to fashion a sort of rough but useful machine; capable, indeed, of performing its destined part with some degree of effect; but of little value in any other point of view: exhibiting as little to the gaze of curiosity as of taste.

The passengers were of a description scarcely more interesting. They consisted of a young Creolean master and miss, who had been qualifying themselves (one at a celebrated monastery, and the other in the coffee-houses of Paris) to vaunt their superiority over the other colonists, among whom they were to reside; and two or three planters, who had been spending, in a few months of ostentatious parade, all that the rapacity of six or eight years had scourged out of the limbs of their miserable negroes.

From such a group, little of that information or intellect was to be expected, without which perpetual conversation is worse than the silence of solitude.

The boundless prospect of seas and skies, indeed, and the phenomena of the evening and the morning, under such original associations, at first delighted the imagination of our adventurer. But these, upon repetition, lost their charm; and so perverse were the elements, that they refused to gratify him even with so much as a serious squall, to variegate the tame monotony, and excite that agitation of passions so necessary to the enjoyments of dispositions of a certain class.

One person, indeed, there was on board the vessel—one wayward youth, in whom Henry could not but feel himself considerably interested: but he—was a menial—a lad whom fortune had thrown into so abject a station, that under any other circumstances, our hero, perhaps, would scarcely have condescended to hold any other intercourse with him than that which usually exists between two widely-separated classes, one of whom considers it as a prerogative to command, and the other as its destiny to obey. But when the opportunity of selection is precluded, the natural appetite for communication is very apt to level the pride of artificial distinctions: and this, like other necessities, is sometimes conducive to valuable discoveries.

Such was particularly the case in the present instance. The lad in question was, indeed, a servant—

"But yet poor *Edwin* was no vulgar boy":[1]
Edmunds I should have said, if harmony would have permitted so slight an alteration of the verse: for Edmunds was, in reality, his name.[2]

This youth (to whom Henry was somewhat the more readily attached from the circumstance of his being an Englishman) was, at this time, only in his eighteenth year. He had been an enthusiast from his cradle; and though, in the composition of his character, there was, perhaps, a dash too much of turbulence, he had a disinterestedness of soul, and a nobleness of principle, much above his condition and circumstances of life.

These circumstances, indeed, were much more humiliating than he once had reason to expect: for he had received the rudiments of a classical education, at a public school; and the facility with which he advanced in every branch of study, and the talents he displayed, were promising recommendations to notice and patronage; and he was, on many other accounts, considerably respected and beloved by those of better fortune than himself.

But the audacity with which he not only displayed but gloried in some peculiarities of opinion, particularly offensive to the governors of the institution, and the firmness with which he refused to retract those opinions, occasioned him to be prematurely dismissed from the seminary, and all his budding hopes were entirely blasted.

The same disposition had exposed him, afterwards, to many disasters; had driven him, a sort of exile, from his native land, and destined him to lead a vagrant life in search of a precarious subsistence.

After having rambled over several of the provinces of France, necessity partly, and partly a roving disposition, and a desire to see and to observe, had induced this lad to accept the offer of visiting St. Domingo, in the capacity of servant to the captain of the vessel: a connection not very accordant to the disposition of young Edmunds, who, prone to be equally fervid in his attachments and his aversions, soon began to consider every thing he did for this imperious tyrant as an insufferable burthen.

For Henry, he, very evidently, cherished a directly opposite feeling. He was zealous, and even officious, in his voluntary services to him; and threw out some very strong insinuations of the satisfaction he should feel (if servitude must continue to be his lot) in changing his present master, for one of so much more generous and amiable a disposition.

To these suggestions, it is probable that Henry the more readily listened from certain arrogant feelings of nationality, for which few of our

---

1   James Beattie, *The Minstrel* (1771), Bk. I, xvi.
2   Edmunds shares Thelwall's own social background.

readers, we suspect, will be very angry with him—feelings, that made him revolt, as it were, from the idea of a Frenchman having a *free-born Briton* for his servant. In the mean time he could not resist the temptation of entering into frequent conversations with the youth, on terms somewhat more familiar than accorded with the kind of connection that was about to subsist between them.

In short, Edmunds became a sort of humble companion to our hero; and, in the course of the voyage, so much endeared himself by his good qualities, as to become almost habitually necessary to him: and he accordingly prevailed (with no great difficulty) upon the Captain to consent to the transfer Edmunds so much desired.

The vessel had scarcely dropt its anchor in harbour of Port au Prince, when the planter, St. Valance, came on board. His desire to pay every attention to the son of his partner, had induced him to make a journey from the plantation at La Soufriere, to that town; the more especially as he had a particular friend there, at whose house (or casa) he was sure of a welcome reception, during the time that he might have to wait for his arrival, and by whose means he hoped to introduce the young stranger into such a circle of society, as could not fail to reconcile him at once to this new region.

After the customary salutations and introductions, Henry was accordingly conducted to the shore, by his intended guardian, and their temporary host, Morency; who did not neglect this early opportunity of displaying the advantages of his Paris education, by affecting all the vivacity and politesse of that gay metropolis, and still more by interlarding every part of his discourse, of which he was by no means sparing, with digressions of what he had seen, and whom he had associated with, during the time he sojourned there.

As for St. Valance himself he was a native Creole, had been educated in the island, and resided upon it all his life-time; and accordingly, though far from deficient in the vivacity and sensibility essential to the climate, he shrunk, as it were, before the assumed superiority of his more travelled and more experienced friend. The conversation accordingly lay entirely between Morency and our hero; or more properly speaking Morency was sole conversor, and Henry sole conversee; while St. Valance, if the transition from *law* to *grammar* be not too bold an incongruity of metaphor, appeared throughout a mere third person singular; occasionally spoken of, but neither addressing nor addressed.

But the boat had no sooner touched the shore than Morency had the mortification to observe, that even his fluency, with all the advantages of gallic politeness and parisian education, had no longer the power of fixing the attention of our hero; who, eager to become acquainted with the wonders of the new world, began to turn his inquisitive glances on every side, in quest of expected novelty.

The first specimen, however, was far from answering his expectations.

He had formed (like most Europeans) extravagant notions of the opulence and magnificence of West-India planters; and he was now in the capital of the principal colony of the gayest and most ostentatious nation of Europe—the nation of genius, of science, of elegant refinement!

What could he expect but taste and splendor? the superb and the grand?

But instead of these, in the buildings of this metropolis, he discovered a rude chaos of wooden houses, or casas, as they are called, with barracks and public edifices of the same material, interspersed with miserable huts that the peasantry of many parts of Europe would scarcely consider as habitable.

One solitary mansion of stone, indeed, the residence of the governor, in the modern style of European magnificence, lifted its head over this jumble and confusion of ill-contracted, and ill-ordered buildings; but this only served to shame the meanness of the rest, and to disgust, rather than relieve the eye, by the abruptness and violence of the translation.

"Ah, my friend!" exclaimed Morency, "I perceive that our state of building is not to your taste. Port au Prince, in these respects, indeed, is not Paris. The mansion of our governor, alone, aspires, as you see, to gallic magnificence, or reminds the observing traveller, that the planters of St. Domingo are descended from the most polished nation in the universe."

St. Valance bit his lips. *Pot au Pince*[1] was to him the centre of all that was grand and delightful—the depot of elegance and pleasure; and it was somewhat like treason, according to the fashion of philosophising, for a planter of the island to give vent to such disadvantageous comparisons.

"The haughty mansion that engages your admiration," said he, breaking his silence, with some asperity, "will not long continue to insult our more accommodating dwellings. The first hurricane or earthquake will throw those doric and corinthian pillars into a new *order* and give us a fresh lesson of the folly and wasteful extravagance of those European fopperies."

"Why, as for that," replied Morency, "it is built at the expence of government; and so it does not signify. It is only a few additional *millions* to the account of incidental expences, happen when it will; and the expenditure will create a fresh patronage, so necessary to support the executive power in this season of agitations and popular encroachment."

Henry was not in a humour for political discussion; and the reflection passed unanswered.

His attention was diverted to other objects.

If his eyes were little gratified by the buildings of Port au Prince, they were powerfully attracted by the novel effect of the motley population. Whites, Blacks, and people of colour, in all the infinitudes of shade—planters, in garments of callico, lounging in lazy lordliness, and negroes, male and female, in a state of nudity, bending under their loads, or leaning

---

1   Creole pronunciation of Port au Prince (Wimpffen 207).

on their pitchers, and mixing in noisy gabble, at the brink of the aqueduct, were fruitful sources of amusing—and of painful meditation.

These latter groups seemed far from being destitute of vivacity. Noise and laughter, resounded from almost every quarter; and the levity of many a manual joke, illustrated their else unintelligible jargon.

"It is thus that man dances in his chains," said Henry, musing—"or rather it is thus that he dances when their weight is for a few moments taken off.—But sophisticated reasoners, observing only the short season of recess, would persuade us that the burthen of oppression is not felt."

These objects, and these reflections, occupied the senses and filled the heart of Henry: and notwithstanding the repeated remonstrances of St. Valance and Morency, he continued to ramble from place to place gratifying his curiosity with observing the features, the deportment, the manners of the motley throng, heedless of the fatigues of his voyage, or the calls of refreshment, till the sudden close of night put a period to his melancholy musings.

The interior structure of the casas, did not appear to Henry much more ingenious or artificial than their exterior. But if the buildings of St. Domingo were defective in the luxuries of embellishment, this was by no means the case with respect to the accommodations of the table.

Here voluptuousness poured out all her stores—every thing that could stimulate, or could gratify the appetite.

"Edible creation deck'd the board";[1]
and hospitality degenerated to prodigal excess.

In short, Henry soon perceived, that we must not in the West-Indies, as in the great cities of Europe, estimate the opulence or the luxury of the inhabitants by the appearance and construction of their dwellings. The modes of luxury are as infinitely diversified as those of dress. Every sense has its appetites, which circumstances render more or less imperious; and what is wanted in particular states of society (of what is called polished society, at least) to the gratification of one, is generally made up by abundant sacrifices to another. If Domingo has few of those artists that cater for the eye, the intellect, or the imagination, of those whose talents are devoted to *taste*, in the pure, derivative, and unsophisticated acceptation of the word, there could be no difficulty of forming there a Royal Academy.

Henry, though far from indifferent to these indulgencies, would gladly have exchanged a part, at least, of the cayennes and capsicums,[2] the ardent spirits, the costly wines, and candied spices of the banquet, for the simple seasoning of a little true attic salt.[3]

But of this there was but scanty dole. Morency, indeed, had some smartness, and a vein of pleasantry and humour; and from the specimen

---

1 Matthew Prior, *Solomon on the Vanity of the World* (1718), 2:668.
2 Tropical spices.
3 Refined, delicate, poignant wit.

of the party assembled, the general character of the Creoles seemed far from deficient in conversational *capabilities*. But their topics were neither the most diversified, nor the most interesting. The price of sugar, and of slaves; the flavour, and the age of rum; and the natural sloth and inactivity of the rascally negroes, were inexhaustible themes of animadversion.

To some of these subjects the inquisitive mind of Henry would not have been indifferent; but unfortunately they were about to become matters of business with him; and he imagined he should both hear and see quite enough concerning them when he arrived at La Soufriere.

But the less interesting the conversation the more brisk the circulation of the glass. Bumper succeeded to bumper—the vintage of the Madeiras to that of France, and the fragrant spirit of rice to that of the sugar cane, till every character was developed, and every passion afloat.

Pride, ferocity, and effeminate licentiousness alternately predominated; the voice became loud, the language unrestrained; and in that chaos of intemperate conversation which raged on every side, the recent insurrections of the mulatto men were every now and then introduced with expressions of infuriated rancour that formed a curious contrast to the voluptuous admiration and infatuated devotion with which they talked of their mulatto women.

But among the pleasures that were dwelt upon in the most rapturous strains of enthusiasm, nothing seemed to be regarded as equally delightful with the *Gragement* and the *Chicca*.[1]

At first our European novice could not properly comprehend the meaning of these words. Upon enquiry, however, he was presently informed that these were the names of the most celebrated dances of the people of colour, and which the lordly whites regard as one of the finest spectacles ever exhibited by the votaries of the paphian goddess.[2]

In short, the young Englishman had seen nothing till he had seen the pretty Mulatto girls dance the Chicca: and it was resolved that he should be accompanied, the next evening, by the whole party then present, to an exhibition of that description.

This agreement was ratified by a half-pint bumper, all around, of arrack punch,[3] in which water was the only article that was deficient. Another and another still succeeded, till the prostration of part of the company warned the rest to reel, as well as they could, to their respective homes and apartments: and thus concluded our hero's first evening in St. Domingo.

The aching head of Henry, the consequence of his nocturnal debauch, was not suffered to be composed by the protracted slumbers of the

---

1   Syncopated dances of African origin, described by Wimpffen as strongly erotic (111-13). "Chicha," a fermented drink from maize, might suggest *chicca*'s association with intoxication and uninhibited expression.

2   Paphos, site of Aphrodite worship; associated with illicit sexuality.

3   West Indian liquour from fermented molasses.

morning. On the contrary, he was awakened, at day-break, by sounds so new and so terrible as to bereave him almost of his very senses.

A confused and hideous noise of groans and cries and shrieks and resounding stripes came rushing on his unaccustomed ear:—a medley of horrid discords, such as his senses had never before recognized, nor the most gloomy imagination could have conceived.

Such a peal would, at any time, have torn the sensitive nerves of Henry; but now that his imagination was distempered with the fumes of inebriety and indigestion, when his pulse was already throbbing, and his brain was all on fire, the horror became ten times more horrible.

Every nerve shook with trepidation. He believed himself suddenly transported to the regions of the damned; and springing half out of bed, he began to bellow, almost as loud as those with whom he sympathised, and look around for the agents and instruments of torture; nor was his consternation diminished, when he found himself presently drawn back again by the familiar gripe of a pair of hands and arms, that, in colour, at least, did not ill accord with this coinage of his distempered imagination.

"Fiend! Fiend!" exclaimed he, in a tone of frantic desperation—"whither do you drag me?"

He turned fearfully around, and beheld—not, indeed, a demon of torture, but the exuberant symmetry and sable softness of the beautiful negress Nannane: one of the African Hebes[1] who had handed round the cup at the banquet. The finely harmonised form and alluring blandishments of this sable nymph had soon attracted the particular notice of our hero, and compelled him, tacitly at least, to acknowledge that *beauty is of no standard, in tint any more than in stature.*

Nannane had not been insensible of the impression she had made, or desirous of weakening its force. Her charms, not much incumbered with the superfluities of dress, had courted rather than shrunk from those ardent glances with which the inebriated youth had regarded her, as she waited upon him with officious service.

Neither the morality nor the decorums of the West Indies, presented any obstacles to the indulgence of this transient passion: for here, where every thing else is enslaved, love, at least, is permitted to riot in unbounded freedom. The incontinence of the slave is reckoned among the sources of emolument by the master. Even ladies, of *unblemished virtue,* make no sort of scruple of trafficking in this species of prostitution; and of all the civilities the hospitable planter displays towards his guests, there is none that he offers with less reluctance than the range of his sable seraglio.

The candle had accordingly been entrusted to Nannane, to light the youthful stranger to his chamber; and in that chamber, as we have seen, she was found on the succeeding morning.

A gleam of imperfect recollection shot across the mind of Henry, the

---

1 Greek goddess of youth, female attendant of Aphrodite, goddess of love.

instant he beheld her. He blushed at his superstitious terrors. But the groans and stripes still continued to ring in his ears.

"Good God!" exclaimed he, "what can be the meaning of all this?"

"Meaning, massa?" repeated Nannane—"What meaning?"

"These groans—these shrieks—these stripes?" resumed Henry.

"Mean dat, massa!" replied Nannane, laughing; "oh! negro-drive whip negro—dat all."

"All! all!" exclaimed Henry, his blood curdling at her insensibility; and hurrying on his night-gown and slippers, he rushed out of the casa, like one bewildered, and ran, without stopping, to the nearest of the wretched buildings from whence the noise proceeded.

Mansion of wretchedness, indeed! It was one of those hovels built for the habitation of slaves. A negro-driver was rousing them from their slumber, by the accustomed salutation of the *arceau*,[1] and reiterating his stripes in proportion to the tardiness of the poor sufferers, or his own capricious aversion.

"Monster!" said Henry, seizing him by the hand, "what is it you are about?"

"'Bout, massa!" replied the driver, for he was himself a negro; "what me bout! Not you see, massa, me call up negro man, go work?"

H. "Call! Is this your way of calling? barbarian! Have you not voice enough to make them hear, that you stripe them in this unmerciful manner?"

D. "Hear, massa! Ha! ha! Me like very well see driver make negro work by hear. No, no, massa! Arceau hab best voice make negro do him duty."

So saying, he began to repeat his blows with more vehemence.

"Monster!" said Henry, with a voice still more loud and indignant, placing himself at the same time, between the driver and the victim— "have you no sympathy for our own countrymen?"

D. "Simthy, massa! what simthy? When me slave, driver whip me. Him no simthy."

H. "Have you, then, been a slave yourself? And have you already forgotten what you suffered in slavery?"

D. "Forget, massa! no, me no forget. Me remember well me suffer so."

As he repeated these words, he turned suddenly round to the other side of the hovel, and began to lay about him with his arceau, still more unmercifully than ever; and Henry, perceiving that all his remonstrances only irritated the fury of the tyrant, and aggravated the sufferings he meant to relieve, returned to his chamber, full of painful and desponding thoughts,

---

1   "Hoop" is the ordinary meaning, but in West Indian usage it means "whip." A "short-handled whip," according to Wimpffen (98-99). The usual word for whip, "le fuet" (or "fouet"), is replaced by the cruel euphemism, presumably because a whip can be twisted to look like a hoop, and the mock innocence of the word conceals a violent aggression.

and execrating the state of society in which it appeared to be his future destiny to reside.

"And such," said he to himself, "are the secondary consequences of the systems of oppression! How much more horrible than the oppression itself! Thus is all sympathy exterminated by the excess of sufferance! Man ceases to feel for man, and brother for brother; and human nature is degraded below the brute!"

Full of these reflections, he seated himself by the side of a bed.

Nannane sighed, and blandished, and rolled her fine eyes, and shewed her ivory teeth, in vain. She had lost her fascination. He gazed upon her, indeed, occasionally; but it was the deep-musing insensibility, the penetrating inquisitiveness, with which the naturalist regards some curious and enigmatical monster; not the dissolving tenderness with which the lover languishes on the object of his desire.

In short, an impression of the deepest melancholy had taken possession of the mind of Henry, and rendered him insensible to every other emotion: and Nannane retired, indignant and disgusted; entertaining, from this specimen of the gallantry of her English lover, no very exalted idea of our national character.

The breakfast hour arrived; and the table once more exhibited the profusion of West-Indian luxury. But nothing could arouse the attention, or the appetite, of Henry.

"What is the matter, young Englishman?" said Morency, observing the settled gloom upon his countenance. "Would not Nannane suffer you to sleep away your head-ache? or did our morning concert disturb you somewhat too early?"

"Concert!" repeated Henry, shuddering.

"Ha! ha! ha!" resumed Morency—"Monsieur Anglois is troubled with the qualms, I perceive. But these d—d European women, with their slip-slop morality, and their sentimental trash, ruin all the lads that are entrusted to them.

"I'll warrant now, mamma has told some very pretty tales, about the innocence, and the docility, and the simplicity, and I know not what all, of these lazy, hulking, rascally negroes; and my young gentleman, as in duty bound, has swallowed every word, with true catholic credulity, till tickling the sable scoundrels into a sense of their duty appears to be a crime against nature."

"Good God!" exclaimed Henry, "and is it possible that a gentleman and a christian can treat with such levity the horrible cruelties perpetrated by this driver?"

"Cruelties! What cruelties?" said Morency, somewhat alarmed. "I hope nothing of that kind has happened among my scoundrels. I do not allow any cruelties to be perpetrated upon my plantations, I assure you."

"No, I dare say not," continued Henry, a little encouraged; "you are too much of a gentleman, and a man of honour. Humanity is the concomitant of politeness: and I verily believe, that if it were possible the poor slave should be always under the immediate eye of his master, these horrors would, in general, be avoided."

M. "Horrors—good God! what horrors?—What do you mean, sir?—What has this scoundrel of a driver been doing?"

H. "Doing what I have scarcely language to describe: waking the miserable negroes with an inhuman whip; whose lash is still resounding in my ears; while the blood, that followed at every stripe, still streams before my eyes!"

M. "The whip?—ha! ha! ha! was it only the whip? Faith I was afraid, by the grave face you put upon it, that the sulky rascals might have provoked him to cripple half a dozen of them; so that I might not only have lost their labour for a month or two, but have had the devil and all of expence with them at the hospital."

Every nerve of Henry seemed to coil within him. He did not sigh—he did not groan. He had not breath enough for either; but, in the silent anguish of his soul, "Is this human nature," said he to himself; while he gazed upon Morency, with an expressive mixture of indignation and astonishment.

"Ha! ha! ha!" said St. Valance, "our young planter does not understand these things as yet. But we shall soon subdue these prejudices, when we get him to La Soufriere."

"God forbid!" ejaculated Henry, with great fervour—"God forbid that I should ever regard without horror the torture of my fellow-creatures!"

Breakfast being concluded, a turn or two in the galleries of the casa soothed, in some degree, the agitation of Henry's mind; and, after amusing himself with a thousand benevolent projects for ameliorating the condition of the slaves at La Soufriere, the thirst of curiosity succeeded to the pains of sympathy; and he returned, in quest of St. Valance and Morency, to propose a walk through such parts of the town and neighbourhood as had not yet fallen under his observation.

His search was not difficult. He found them stretched upon settees, in the same apartment where he had left them, in a posture somewhat between lying and lolloping,[1] and with eyes rather open than awake.

His proposal, however, was far from meeting with as ready an assent. "Nobody could think of stirring abroad in the middle of the day. The shade of the casa was essential to habituate him, by degrees, to the fervour of a new climate; and rest was absolutely necessary after the fatigue of a long voyage—especially as the engagements of the evening would again prevent them from being very early in bed."

Henry yielded to these arguments, or rather to the unconquerable *vis-inertia*[2] of those who should have been the guides and companions of his ramble. He accordingly sat himself contentedly down, to pass away an hour or two in such conversation as might probably render the objects

---

1 Lounging.
2 Inactivity.

that should afterwards pass in review before him, the more intelligible and interesting. But a yawning duetto dashed his hopes again—

"Heigho!" said Morency.

"Heigho!" replied St. Valance.

Henry was stricken mute: for there is an electricity (if I may so express myself) in dulness; and the most lively imagination will frequently be chilled in an instant, by the vicinity of this torpedo.

Henry felt and dreaded its benumbing influence; for nothing was so hateful to him as the inanity with which he was threatened. One resource, however, still presented itself to his mind. He was in the mansion of opulence; and inartificial as was the construction of the building, the furniture was sufficiently costly:—a library, of course, there must be—studious or not studious, literary or ignorant, this is an article with which, on the score of parade and embellishment, the man of fashion and ostentation cannot dispense.

Alas! our European was now in the West-Indies; where, as no man was studious of any thing but his interest, and the indulgence of his appetites, no one thought it necessary to affect to be so; and where, the number of slaves being once calculated upon his estate, nothing could be added to the reputation or respectability of the proprietor, by all the morocco and gilded calf-skin that could be heaped upon his shelves.

Books, he was given to understand, were articles that could not be preserved in the West-Indies—"we are so infested by moths and insects."[1]

"Besides," continued St. Valance, yawning, and composing himself for his mid-day nap, "we planters are men of business, and have no time to read."

"True," rejoined Morency, with a responsive yawn, covering his face with a handkerchief, to keep away the mosquittoes. "Besides, young Englishman, you may take my word for it, there is no doing without a nap in the middle of the day in this climate.—None—I assure you—no—o—ne."

"Umph!" said Henry, after a pause, "how do the poor negroes manage it?—

"Alas! the vertical sun and the lash of the inhuman driver, are, at this very instant, writing the answer upon their backs."

Neither Morency nor St. Valance made any reply. They were better employed than in settling accounts between reason and conscience. The drowzy god had seized, with his accustomed facility, upon their senses. They were *dreaming* of cargoes of sugar, and freights of black cattle; the revels of Cytherea,[2] and the orgies of Bacchus.[3]

Henry left them to their busy occupations, while he retired to his chamber, and vented his feelings in an affectionate epistle to his mother. Before this was completed he was rescued from the danger of any new

---

1 From Wimpffen 110.

2 Aphrodite (Greek) or Venus (Roman), goddesses of love.

3 Roman God of wine.

attack of West-Indian ennui by the arrival of Edmunds, who had been left behind to take care of the baggage of his new master, and settle his accounts with his old one.

If the inanity of the day had led our hero to consider the Creoles as a sort of lethargic race, whom the promethian[1] torch had scarcely touched, the diversions of the evening exhibited them in a very different light. Nothing now could equal their vivacity—their animation—their ardour. The elasticity of their limbs—the expression of their countenances—their gestures altogether, and the very tones of their voice, all seemed to characterise them as a distinct race of men from those who had lounged and slumbered away the day in the galleries and apartments of their casas.

The dances of the people of colour were not forgotten. The sun was no sooner set than the whole party hied to the place of rendezvous and an obsequious mulatto did himself the honour to conduct them to the spot, where the dancers were already assembled and the sports begun. Males and females, all ages and all complexions, one only excepted, were mingled in rapid and intricate motion—mulatto and free negro, Griff, Quarteron, Tierceron, Metis and Mamelouc,[2] all writhed, and whirled, and footed, and languished, and spread their lures, with equal enthusiasm. Even the musicians themselves were not less active than the dancers: and it would have been no small amusement, of itself, to behold the animation, the sympathy, the eagerness, with which they riggled, or rather leaped about upon their seats—the heavy part of man keeping time and tune in its motions with as much exactness as the more nimble joints of the feet and hands.

The spectacle was as curious as it was new. But the attention of Henry was rivetted by the grace and dexterity of other performers. His brain had no sooner recovered from the first giddy emotions of surprise and delight, than general admiration yielded to more particular impressions, he began to single with his eyes the most seducing of those families whose "rapid and fugitive graces"[3] were at once developed, and concealed by the volubility of their motions.

All was excitement—all was ensnaring voluptuousness—all fascination. The shafts of desire were never scattered about with so much rapidity or effect in any other circle of dissipated amusement.

Henry wondered no longer at the enthusiasm with which his new friends had spoken of their olive-complexioned mistresses.—He conceived, at once, how easy it was for men of voluptuous habits and pampered appetites to slight, for the vivid animation and amorous sensibility of these, all the charms even of European beauty—its carnations and its lilies—its coral lips and blush of ingenuous modesty.

---

1 Prometheus, the Titan who stole fire for humanity; associated with knowledge.
2 French words designating mixed-race people.
3 Wimpffen 111.

In short, he presently began to feel that he was not himself of a temperament to escape individual impression in this blaze of voluptuous attraction.

Among the votaries of the American Venus most distinguished by their graceful activity in these rites, was a pretty mulatto, then only in her fifteenth year, whose luxuriant form and transcendent powers of fascination were not displayed in vain to the frequent gaze of the young stranger. Henry was presently ensnared. His eyes followed her from group to group, through all her evolutions; and his hands, his looks, his voice, all joined in testifying his admiration, whenever, in "the mystic mazes of the dance,"[1] she happened to glide near the place where he stood.

Marian, also, had eyes; and the person of our hero had, also, its attractions. She perceived the impression she had made, and determined to complete her conquest. She disappeared for awhile; but it was only to return with additional lustre. The bandeau was laid aside, and another handkerchief, of still more fresh and variegated colours, half bound her wanton tresses, and gave animation to a complexion, which the most critical artist must have admitted to be her only defect; and which was now even exalted into a perfection in the estimation of the infatuated lover.

Her garments, of the purest white, flowed with a more graceful negligence—her neck was decorated with more costly ornaments, and her taper wrists sparkled with jems and bracelets.

Thus adorned, she floated again before the ardent gaze of our hero, rolled the dark, expressive eye, with ineffable seducement, heaved the half-obvious bosom, as she glided by him, with a neck curving in sweet languishment; and breathed, through teeth of ivory, sighs sweeter than the most costly perfumes of Arabia.

The infatuation of Henry knew no bounds. He would have sprung forward from the group of spectators, and mingled in the dance, had he not been prevented by Morency and St. Valance. Not that it was any part of their system of morality to throw impediment in the way of an amour of this description. "No: it was very proper that the young gentleman should have a companion, for the amusement of his leisure hours; and he was fortunate that a young female of such accomplishments and so unblemished a character, should so soon have thrown herself in his way. But the dignity and honour of the European complexion must not be so degraded.

"What reduce himself to a level with people of colour! and disgrace himself in the eyes of the whole island, by publicly mingling in their sports and pastimes!

"Good God! could he so far forget himself? Or was he so uninformed of the state of society in the islands!

"Did he not know that no white man who had the least sense of

---

1 Thomas Chatterton, "Narva and Mored; an African Eclogue" (1770), l. 5.

decency, or regard for his character and reputation, would even condescend to sit at the same table with a man of colour?"

In short, Henry (though he did not enter very heartily into the spirit of these distinctions) was prevailed upon to keep himself within the bounds of *West-Indian decorum*: and Morency, on his part, undertook to procure him a more eligible opportunity of making such overtures as his passion and a due regard for prudence might render proper.

With such facility did the unguarded and irresolute heart of Henry slide into the voluptuous vices of this baneful soil.

Morency was as good as his word. Henry was gratified with the desired interview; and, as Marian had hitherto preserved her reputation, and cultivated the attractive graces of deportment, only for the purpose of qualifying herself for such a connexion, she yielded, with little hesitation, to the flattering addresses and liberal offers of Henry; and, not many days after, accompanied her protector and planter St. Valance, to La Soufriere.

Edmunds attended his new master, more as a friend than a servant:—for the wide distinctions of freeman and slave—of white, and man of colour, swallow up and obliterate, as it were, the less important gradations; and correspondence in the two essential attributes, brings the dependent and the employer to a sort of comparative equality, which the established prejudices make it a sort of point of morality to support: and Henry (whose pride might, under other circumstances, have kept him in some degree aloof from an unfortuned youth, whom his better judgment could not but hold in considerable respect) very readily fell into a sentiment, which left him at liberty to pursue the unsophisticated emotions of his nature.

CHAP. II.

Containing the History of a short residence at La Soufriere.

Sketches of the Picturesque and Sentimental.—Symptoms of Ennui.—
Marian—Creolean Females.—The Exception—Prospects of eccentric
Association.—Traits of melancholy Enthusiasm.—The Glen of Limbé—
The Descent.—Trophical Phenomena.—Meditations and Traits of
Character.—The Cataract.—Terrors of Imagination.—The Recluse—
A promising Encounter.—Disappointments and mortifying Recollections.—Agriculture and the Picturesque.—The History of Parkinson—
Persecution for Opinion.—Emigration and Seclusion.—Comments and
Conjectures—The Insinuation repelled.

THE whole country from Port au Prince to La Soufriere appeared to Henry a constant succession of wonders and delights—an ever varying series of the picturesque and the sublime, the luxuriant and the romantic. Nor was the plantation itself without its charms.

The hour of their arrival was propitious to the enjoyments of those who delight in the phenomena of nature. It was towards the close of day; and the splendour of a cloudless sky, reflected in the rapid but transparent streams—the luxuriancy of a vegetation unbounded in the novel varieties of tint and form—and all the rich diversities of hill and dale, with their broad shadows and masses of vivid light, conspired to awaken a thousand enthusiastic feelings in his mind: but with these were presently associated the more painful impressions of the horrors and reciprocal barbarities which had been lately perpetrated, during the insurrection of the people of colour; and which had formed the principal topic of conversation, on the part of St. Valance, during the whole of their journey.

Full of these varied impressions, the busy sense of Henry roved and expatiated over the whole expansive scenery, from the cultivated fore-grounds to the blue distant mountains; or where, in another direction, the fascinated eye dwelt on the glittering splendours of an apparently unruf-fled sea. He gazed; he glowed with admiration; and marvelled with himself, how in the midst of such scenes, where beauty triumphs in all her gorgeous majesty, and plenty seems to pour out all her treasures from a double horn, any thing like wretchedness, or the turbulent and malignant passions could ever have found a residence.

"But what is there," exclaims he, "of fair and beautiful in this magnif-icent structure of the universe that commercial rapacity will not deform? Where is the elysian scene that vice and misery will not pervade, when oppression bears sway in the land? when impious man, trampling the sacred rights of nature in the dust, erects the arbitrary distinctions of races and of colours; and makes the vulgar accidents of climate—the tints and traits of feature imparted by a too fervid sun, the shallow pretexts for traf-ficking in human gore, and bending the necks of a large proportion of the human race under the iron yoke of slavery?"

This ejaculation, uttered with no small degree of emphasis, filled the planter St. Valance with astonishment and horror. He had already, from a variety of circumstances, formed a very unfavourable idea of Henry's principles. His suspicions were now confirmed in the fullest extent.

"Mon dieu!" exclaimed he, "has my friend the Englishman sent me an *ami des noirs* to assist me in the management of our plantation. I am afraid we shall find, before we are much older, that we have too many of the agents of that infamous society among us already."

Marian and Edmunds, however, listened to the rhapsody with emo-tions of a very different kind. The former, sympathised, at least, with the wrongs and sufferings of her own class, and dropped a tear to the memo-ries of Chavane and Ogé;[1] and, as for the latter—he was really and liter-

---

1 Jean-Baptiste Chavannes (c. 1748-91) and Vincent Ogé (c. 1755-91) were St. Domingue mulatto leaders of an unsuccessful rebellion; both were tortured to death by the planters.

ally an *ami des noirs*.[1] He had declaimed, young as he was, in the debating societies of London in favour of negro emancipation; and he had been an agent of the society of the Friends of the Blacks in Paris, and disseminated (with active enthusiasm) many thousands of the placards and little pamphlets by which they endeavoured to call the national attention to that interesting subject.

With such a character, the sentiments that excited so much indignation in the mind of St. Valance, was of course an additional passport to respect and veneration. He treasured, however, his admiration in silence; while Henry, who was too much absorbed by the pleasures of vision and imagination to be at leisure for the gravity of dispute, turned a deaf ear to the animadversions of his creolean friend;—the more especially as he had already had too many specimens of his self-willed and opinionated obstinacy, to expect to make any impression upon him by the appeals of humanity, or the inductions of argument.

The residence of our hero at La Soufriere, of course, introduced him to a new circle of society. Generally speaking, however, it was in names and faces alone that this novelty consisted. In other respects it was only a repetition, on a smaller scale, of that with which he had already been pretty well satiated at Port au Prince:—The same sensuality—the same luxury and inebriation—the same paucity of topics—the same ebulitions of childish flippancy—the same barrenness of idea, and superabundance of verbiage, characterised them both. The only essential difference was the sort of rusticity that distinguished the ostentation of the village from that of the provincial capital.

The reader, who has properly appreciated the character of Henry, will readily believe that his whole time and attention were not divided between the concerns of the plantations, and the conversation and amusements of such a circle. The former, even independent of those circumstances, that revolted the best and strongest feelings of his nature, was an object much too sordid for the bent of his genius; and the debaucheries of the latter were too gross, and too unvaried, not to pall and disgust a youth familiarised to the dissipations of a more refined and more intelligent circle; and who, in the utmost career of prodigality, had always mingled the luxuries of intellect with those of sense, and had been allured into the paths of intemperance more by the blandishments of Fancy and the invitations of Wit, than the rank steam of sensuality, or the impulse of a depraved and vitiated appetite.

Even the dominion of the fascinating Marian was but of short duration. The voluptuous sensibility that characterises the females of this cast, and the exquisite symmetry that distinguished the form and features of this young female in particular, rendered him for awhile, it is true, insensible to every defect. But possession cooled, by degrees, the fervours of desire; and though the unsuspected fidelity of Marian, and her undissem-

---

1 Société des Amis des Noirs (1788-93) [Society of the Friends of the Blacks] was an important French abolitionist society.

bled attachment to her patron had claims upon his gratitude, to which he was not of a temper to be insensible; yet to inspire in the heart of Henry that more permanent and delicate passion, which is dignified by the name of Love, required the co-operation of qualities which were looked for in vain in the character of our young Mulatto.

Person, indeed, was something in the estimation of our hero. It was so much, that, in the ardour of first impressions, where this was perceived, he was ready to give credit for all the rest; but where fancy, intellect, sentiment, and information, were wanting, beauty soon came to be regarded as a lifeless mass—a piece of statuary to gaze upon, not a companion to interest the finer sympathies of the soul.

If the fondness of Marian, however, did not meet with an adequate return, her jealousy was without an object. She had, properly speaking, no rival: the defects of Marian were the evident defects of all the creolian females (whites as well as mulattoes) whom Henry had ever seen. The former, indeed, appeared to our gallant as little better than masses of inanimate affectation. Listless and indolent, because industry was the virtue of a slave; and ignorant, because education had no privileges, and arts and literature no admirers. Recluse from pride, and modest from neglect, their constitutions seemed to be enfeebled from the inanity of their lives; and their whole care and ingenuity to be confined to preserving the sickly delicacy of their complexions, and repelling, by masks and gloves, by curtains and umbrellas, the dreadful influence of the tropical sun.

Of one female, indeed, and only one, who was an exception to this rule, our hero had heard occasional mention. But he had never seen her. She was rarely seen. She was a native of another island; was supposed to be of English parentage; and the recluse and eccentric family, "a group of English oddities," under whose protection she resided, mingled neither in the business nor in the pleasures of the colonists.

The privacy, however, which they courted, had not prevented the fame of Seraphina from being spread throughout the neighbouring country. She was talked of as one of the wonders of St. Domingo; as a female historian, a philosopher, and a poet: names indeed to which the generality of those who repeated them could affix no very accurate idea; and which some, perhaps, would have regarded with almost as superstitious an abhorrence as those of witch, or necromancer, or hopgoblin, if it had not been the universal acknowledgment of her uncommon beauty softened, in some degree, the prejudices and bigotted asperity, of one sex at least, and converted their abhorrence into pity.

Henry, for his part, neither pitied nor abhorred. He listened, on the contrary, with an insatiable curiosity to all the marvellous things (some of which were as true as they were credible) that were said of his fair recluse; and, though he was not romantic enough to fall over head and ears in love with a female he had never seen, curiosity was enflamed to an uneasy excess; and he would have considered almost any accident that might introduce him to her acquaintance, among the fortunate events of his life.

In short, the want of intellectual society left a void in the heart of Henry, which the lascivious prodigality of West Indian dissipation was by no means capable of filling up.

To supply this deficiency, he appealed (as will be seen) to pleasures of a more pensive and a more eccentric kind.

We have heretofore given the reader sufficiently to understand, that our hero was capable of looking on nature with a painter's and a poet's eye; and it may be naturally concluded, from the sketch already given, that the neighbourhood of La Soufriere was not without its advantages for the gratification of a taste of this description.

Henry indulged himself, accordingly, in many an evening, and many a midnight ramble, among rocks and woods and tumbling torrents, through trackless dingles or on mountain tops; inhaling the cooling breeze, or indulging the effusions of fancy.

Sometimes he would

"—Brush with hasty steps the dews away,

"To meet the sun upon the upland lawn";[1]

and sometimes, beneath the ample shade of the banana, he would stretch himself at length, protected from the intolerable fervours of noon, and give reins to his luxuriant imagination; soothed by the dash of waters, whose white foam glittered in the vertical beam, or whose eddies were darkened by the overhanging rocks.

In these rambles he was sometimes accompanied by young Edmunds, whose character, as it developed itself, more and more endeared him to our hero; and whose taste for these pensive pleasures, and the frequent pertinancy of his remarks, heightened the enjoyments, without destroying the tranquillity, of seclusion.

One afternoon, in particular, as they strayed together to a considerable distance from the plantation, enjoying the extensive prospects from the summits of the mountains that approach the sea shore, they arrived on the brink of a deep luxuriantly wooden glen, from the bottom of which the dashing murmur of the stream arose in reverberating echoes, while the winding path that was but just discernable among the bushes, invited them, with irresistible fascination, to descend.

They yielded to the impulse; and they were amply rewarded.

Every step they descended, the scene was constantly improving upon them. Here as the little track meandered to the right, an occasional glympse was caught of the neighbouring sea, whose glittering expanse, seen through the yawning boundary of the chine,[2] melted at immeasurable distance into the clear horizon. There again, as they wound in an opposite direction, the contracting dingle[3] stretched its sinuous length in

---

1 Thomas Gray, *Elegy Written in a Country Church-Yard* (1751), ll. 99-100.
2 Fissure.
3 Deep cleft between hills; shaded dell.

many a fantastic curve, descried only at a distance, by the towering eminences of rocks and wooded promontories; sometimes abrupt, and sometimes more gradually sloping towards the bed of the torrent.

Meantime the torrent itself, dark from the shadows of approaching banks, except where diversified by spray and foam, eddying among fragments of rock, and dashing down the rapids, and among the roots and tangles of a luxuriant underwood, hurried, with impatient brawlings, from its obscurity:—"Like youthful emulation," said Henry, "bursting from humble privacies of domestic life, to dissipate its happiness, and lose its purer virtues in the treacherous tide and brackish ocean of popularity!"

A few meanderings more, and sea and distant eminences were alike concealed. The eye was bounded by some approximating curve, or rested with solemn transport on the grandeur and sublimity of the opposing bank: some wooded amphitheatre, whose trees, of gigantic growth, corresponded with its awful wildness; some luxuriant coppice, whose sloping acclivity flamed by the superior splendour of its foliage, the cultivated gardens of our more parsimonious hemisphere; or some enormous rock, whose naked and abrupt escarpment formed a striking contrast to the richness of the neighbouring scenes.[1]

Meantime the birds of gaudy plume winged their slow flight towards their aëries in the clifts of rocks, and tops of the hanging woods; and the descending sun, tipping with transcient fire the summits of the several screenes, heightened the effect of the whole, and gave a more impressive solemnity to the thickening gloom below.

In these regions, where the descent of the sun is almost perpendicular, the twilight, of course, is but of short duration. Evening and morning, properly speaking, are almost unknown; at least they are little other than mere points of time: and night treads immediately upon the heels of day. It is night, however, without any of its Arctic horrors. The luminaries of heaven shine with a more unclouded splendour; the planets, like secondary suns, reflect a more discriminating ray, and the moon, when at full, and in her zenith, sheds a light over the tropical landscape, differing more in softness than indistinctness from that of the great regent of the day.

Such was the night that now overtook our wanderers, still unsatiated with the beauties of nature, and which, by its less garish tints and shades of more sombre melancholy, variegated, rather than interrupted, the pleasures of their ramble.

They continued to descend by a regular and easy course; the path, by this time, having forsaken its serpentine direction, and meeting the descent of the dingle, with a gradual sweep, till it conducted to the very brink of the torrent.

---

1 The setting of the dell and waterfall, and their approach to it, descending from the hills with glimpses of the sea shore, precisely reproduces the scene of Thelwall's rambles through the Quantocks in 1797, which inspired him to reproduce the scenery at his new home in Wales.

A fragment of mossy stone, projecting from the base of the declivity, and contracting the enraged flood, offered an inviting seat to the pensive Henry. He threw himself carelessly upon it, and leaning his head upon his hand, with vacant eye gazed on the eddying foam, and moralized on the scenes and the attachments of his youth.

Contemplation, that began at home, gradually extended itself to more distant objects. The physical and moral universe expanded before him—the Chronicles of Time, and the world of Fiction.

Thought followed thought, and subject succeeded to subject, without apparent connection, and with a rapidity that precluded utterance, till at last the mind, weary of exertion, began to relax itself; and loquacious flippancy succeeded to the profundity of meditation.

"What a scene, and what an hour, Edmunds," said he, bantering, "to hatch treason in!"

"What a scene, and what an hour, sir," replied Edmunds, with the most undisturbed composure, "to make one forget that treason was ever necessary in the world!"[1]

The sentiment was unexpected, but it revealed more than volumes of apologies could have done, the genuine feelings of the speaker.

"True Edmunds," rejoined our hero, "if the facts of history could be forgotten also. But, alas! if I mistake not the hand of Tyranny has engraved even here the indelible memorials of her cruelties and oppressions.

"Look at yon cavern, half way up the rock. The faint appearances of a long neglected road will conduct your eye to the spot. That opening, which is now more than half obscured by the luxuriancy of the surrounding foliage, was once, perhaps, the entrance of one of those mines, in the cruel drudgery of which, the barbarous Spaniards consumed the whole aboriginal population of this ill-fated island.[2]

"Could time tread back its steps again, Edmunds, and could you and I become Indians, possessing the souls and faculties we do, and did we meet, by design or accident, on this spot, I suspect that our minds would be occupied by other ideas than those of the picturesque and the romantic—that these rocks, these pendant forests—this deep solitude, with the foaming eddies beneath, and all those splendid luminaries above, might only embolden us, by a sense of security, to question the authority of our oppressors, and to demonstrate that against the ravages of foreign usurpation, at least, it is at all times lawful both to conspire and to act."

"True, sir," said Edmunds, with the same quiescence of tone and gesture, "but the things are not. And lacking these preliminaries, I own I

---

1   This dialogue, which is wholly omitted in the Dublin edition, repeats almost verbatim S.T. Coleridge's account in *Table Talk* (27 July 1830) of a conversation among himself, Thelwall, and Wordsworth at Nether Stowey, 1797 (see Appendix A5).

2   Hispaniola's native people, the Taino, were driven out and killed by Europeans.

am a little surprised that a gentleman of your taste and turn of mind—a philosopher and a poet, can, in the fulness of such a scene, find room for such a reflection.

"For my own part, sir, I know you consider me as a sort of headstrong turbulent boy; and when an enthusiastic youth has the audacity to speak his thoughts freely upon all occasions, and at all hazards, and presumes, moreover, to maintain, that one ought not to lick the dust at the bidding of every prosperous knave whose bags are full of plunder: I am aware that mankind in general are apt enough to suppose that he is capable of entertaining no other ideas than those of daggers and insurrections; and that, if he seeks the shade of solitude, it is only to brood over plots and treasons: yet I assure you, sir, such is the complete possession that these scenes take of my imagination, and such is their influence upon the whole system of my mind, that, when thus surrounded, I find it almost difficult to persuade myself that there are such things as passions and contentions in the world.

"Rocks, woods, and cataracts are to me a sort of divinities. *The world's mad business*[1] is suspended by their aweful presence; and all that a religious man would call *the fleshly lusts and vanities of the world*,[2] fall prostrate before them.

"Oh! how grand is every object of vision that surrounds us! How unspeakably magnificent! How impressively sublime!

"How tranquillising the murmur of these waters! How inspiring the mingled fragrance of these innumerable aromatics! What sense is there that is not gratified! How, above all, the inward sense! the comparing and reflecting powers of our nature! the fountain of sentiment and imagination!

"These, sir, are the scenes—these are the hours of my life, in which, and which alone, I find it impossible to doubt whether existence be in reality a blessing."

"Edmunds! Edmunds!" said Henry, after a pause, seizing his hand, with the most hearty familiarity, "thou art my servant no longer! Thine is *no serving mind*! Hence-forward be my confident, and my friend.

"In other situations, perhaps, I might have been insensible to your worth. The proud distinction of master and servant might have deprived me of the instructive pleasure of your conversation. But here the want of equals in my own rank of society, has enabled me to discover one in the class beneath me. And, though I feel that I am by no means destitute of the pride of family and fortune, I shall endeavour not to be so much a slave to the opinions of society, as to rebel against the more sacred order of nature.

"But come; let us pursue our way. The upward course of the dingle is promising; and, if I mistake not, I hear, from no very great distance the

1   Jonathan Swift, "Day of Judgment" (c. 1731), l. 19.
2   1 Peter 2:11.

rush of some headlong cataract which may perhaps not be unworthy of terminating the ramble of the night."

Henry was not mistaken. They had not proceeded far before the white spray began to be distinctly marked, spattering beyond the blue foliage of a luxuriantly mantled precipice, glittering like a moving galaxy in the reflected beams of the moon, and spreading its misty veil over the surrounding objects.

Our wanderers hastened with eager curiosity to the spot, and beheld, with equal wonder and delight, a considerable stream of water gushing, at a single leap, from a fissure in the rock, down a precipice of several hundred yards.

While they were contemplating this grand and interesting object, and examining the component parts of the scene, they observed that a few paces below the cataract, the path by which they had been conducted, crossed to the opposite side of the dingle, over some huge fragments of rock, which, having been torn in some convulsion from the overhanging cliffs, and being too large to be received in the narrow bed of the waters below, had rested their craggy sides against the approaching banks, and formed a sort of natural bridge; whose massive rudeness harmonized with the wild sublimity of the surrounding objects.

But where should this path conduct? For awhile, indeed, it was seen winding its spiral line up the cliff, and guarded by a rude rail that seemed to bespeak the providence and the neighbourhood of man. But, after a variety of convulsions, it appeared to be lost in the cataract, while another track, at no considerable distance above, seemed to make its appearance on the opposite side, and point its waving course to the summit.

This was a phenomenon too extraordinary not to excite the curiosity of Henry and his companion. They determined, therefore, to unravel the mystery; and, crossing the rocky bridge, ascended by secure, but slow and laborious steps, to the point where the lower path appeared to terminate. And here (if fear had been a more powerful ingredient in their composition than curiosity) their excursion would have terminated also: for their onward way conducted between the tumbling torrent and the rock; a natural excavation in which had been improved into a secure, but tremendous-looking walk, from whence the tumbling stream was seen, in all its majesty of horrors, rushing to the deep-worn pool beneath; while the deafning roar, echoing and rebellowing from side to side, like accumulated thunders, seemed to shake the very foundations of the rock, till imagination could scarcely resist the appalling idea of universal earthquake and approaching chaos.

"It was either some very powerful necessity," said Edmunds, as they entered this awful cavern, "that turned this path in this direction, or it must lead to the habitation of some eccentric recluse. Collins might have borrowed from this spot additional imagery for his sublime *Ode to Fear*. What, in comparison with the uproar and downward view from this subcataractorian cave, is his ridgy steep of the loose hanging rock, on which his imaginary being throws himself to sleep!"[1]

Henry could not reply. The deafning roar confounded all hearing and articulation. His head turned giddy, and his breath grew short with horror.

At length, "Thank God!" said he, as they issued again into the open path, "we behold once more the beauteous face of heaven. The darkness, visible and hedious[2] uproar of this cavern have almost overpowered my reason.

"What difficulty to persuade oneself that this whole scene is a mere illusive vision of enchantment? or this cavern here the residence of some demon? from every yawning chasm of which, as we passed along, my blood almost curdled with the expectation that he should rush upon us, and, with infuriated malice, dash us into the horrid pool below."

"Hush! hush!" said Edmunds, "if your imagination, sir, delight in excursions of this description, you may now, if you please, suppose yourself under the influence of demons of a more benignant character. For, hark you now! what sweet and pensive melody steals on the night breeze from the summit to which we are ascending.

"For my own part, sir, you know I am not overdone with superstition. I believe the greatest quarrel you have with me, is my running, as you conceive, a little too far into the opposite extreme; but I assure you I shall acknowledge as little less than guardian angels any beings we may encounter that will administer a little to certain vulgar necessities, from which even the most romantic enthusiasts are not exempt: though, in the ardour of our favourite pursuits, we sometimes forget to make due provision for the satisfying of them.

"I know not how the matter may stand with you, sir, but I confess, that, independent of muscular fatigue, I begin to have some internal feelings that diminish, in no small degree, my enjoyment of this romantic scene!"

"Faith, Edmunds! and so do I," replied Henry, "now you mention it.

"In truth, we have been very imprudent; strangers as we are in this wild country. How the devil shall we get back to La Soufriere?"

"I trust in yon music," answered Edmunds, "as you, sir, ought to do in Providence, that we shall have no occasion to think of that till we have satisfied the importunities of hunger."

Our wanderers had now an additional motive for pursuing their way with alacrity; and as the mellow tones of the flute were heard with more and more distinctness, in proportion as they were further removed above the dash and uproar of the cataract, Henry entered very readily into the hopes and expectations of Edmunds. Nor were they disappointed: for the path winding into the chasm, a little above the place where the water discharged itself, con-

---

1 Edmunds alludes to William Collins's *Ode to Fear* (1746), ll. 14-15.
2 Hideous.

ducted them immediately into a valley, or amphitheatrical dell, which was at once adorned and fertilized by the stream whose precipitous fall had been the source of so many awful and so many delightful impressions.

The music, indeed, had ceased; but the cottage of the minstrel was descried at the farther extremity of this little sequestered spot. The taper was burning in the window;[1] and the minstrel himself was walking, with the instrument in his hand, in silent composure, before the door; a venerable form, whose courteous demeanour and locks, white with the frost of age, gave additional interest to the scene.

Henry accosted him in French; and was proceeding, in that language, to make known their situation and their wants. But what was their mutual satisfaction, when the stranger, recognizing, in his imperfect pronunciation, the accents of his native tongue, invited him as an Englishman to the participation of English hospitality.

"A recluse, and an Englishman!!" said Henry to himself, as he entered the house; "my life upon it, the abode of Seraphina!!!"

Expectation was on the tip-toe. But it was doomed to have a fall.

"Sit down, gentlemen, sit down I pray you," said the host, bustling. "You must be content with bachelor's entertainment: for the women of my family, by a sort of ill-timed miracle, are all from home. They are gone to pay a visit in the neighbourhood of La Soufriere, to meet a countryman of ours; somewhat of an extraordinary young man who has lately arrived here. I was to have been of the party myself: but I have a sick negro in the house, who would have had nobody to attend to him, and so I was obliged to defer the pleasure I had promised myself, till another opportunity. My disappointment, however, proves to be fortunate; and my forbearance you see is rewarded."

"A sick negro!" exclaimed Edmunds with a mixture of surprise and admiration.

"Aye!" replied the venerable philanthropist. "I have but two of them; and it was necessary the other should go to drive the mules. If I, also, had gone, who, in this lonely situation, should have taken care of the poor fellow that has so often taken care of me?

"We have indeed a white servant; a sort of nurse: an Englishwoman also. But she, tho' apparently attached to us, from some principle or other which I cannot comprehend, relishes not our solitude; and is frequently away from us; as she has now, been, for three or four days together.

"But let me see what my pantry can afford for your entertainment."

"Excellent old man!" said Edmunds, following him with his eyes. "Thy own good heart be thy recompence!"

Henry heard not a word of all this.

"In the neighbourhood of La Soufriere!" repeated he, striking his forehead; as if crossed by some vexatious recollection.

---

1 Thelwall identified his own cottage in Wales as the minstrel's cottage, and the taper in the window symbolizes the torch of liberty.

"In the neighbourhood of La Soufriere!!! This then was what Rabeau so enigmatically alluded to when he talked of *treating me with a dish that would suit my English palate.*

"May I perish, Edmunds, if I ever recollected, till this instant, the engagement I was under for this evening!"

"My life upon it, sir," resumed he, as the cheerful host was returning, "your name is Parkinson?"

P. "Even so, sir, at your service."

H. "And your lady, and her fair friend, are, at this time, visiting the planter Rabeau?"

P. "Exactly so, sir," replied the host, with astonishment; "by what necromancy soever you may have discovered it."

"Curses confound my forgetfulness! and I am here"—said Henry, chaffing.

P. "Here?—You!—Why—sure—are you"—

H. "The Englishman who was to have met them there. But I was not apprised of the honour intended me; or I should never have forgotten the engagement: For I assure you, Mr. Parkinson, your fame has not failed to reach my ears; even from this obscure retirement."

P. "The fame of Seraphina; I suppose you mean. But sit down and compose yourself, Mr. Montfort. I am happy (from what I have heard of you) that our acquaintance has commenced. And as for the rest, though your conduct will appear a little ungallant, and the ladies will not be a little disappointed, you shall tarry where you are till to-morrow, and see what apology you can make to them at their return."

The countenance of Henry brightened at this proposition.

"But by what accident, or what eccentricity of taste, came you to approach our little mansion in this direction; you are the first persons, I believe, except Seraphina, my Amanda, and myself, who have ventured to pursue that path, since the waters were turned in that direction."

"Turned," said Henry, with astonishment—"Is it possible that the cataract we have beheld has been produced by art?"

P. "Even so I assure you: and of art labouring, in the first instance, for the vulgar purposes of utility. The waters were collected by draining an extensive marsh; a part of the concession of Mons. Rabeau: and, as the works were carried on under my direction (the attempt indeed having been suggested by myself), I determined to unite the useful and the delightful—the picturesque with agricultural improvement.

"I had already fixed upon this little dell as the place of my retreat: and observing that nature had, in a manner, scooped out a channel, through which the torrent might easily be directed, I caused the drains to be all collected to a single focus; and, having made a breach in the face of the rock, by the assistance of gunpowder, I opened all my sluices, and trusted the issue to the influence of the simple laws of gravitation.

"The consequences are, that Mons. Rabeau has brought several hundred acres of waste land into a state of successful cultivation, and I have embellished my retreat with one of the finest waterfalls[1] in St. Domingo."

"I am afraid, sir," said Edmunds, "there is another consequence, which you have not taken into the account."

P. "I understand you, young man:—the negroes who cultivate that waste. I own, indeed, with some confusion, that, in my zeal for agricultural improvement, I did not consider that circumstance till it was too late."

H. "It seems then, if you had considered, it would have had some influence on your conduct. In this, sir, as in every other part of your character, you seem to be the very reverse of a West-Indian.

"It must have been some very extraordinary concurrence of events that could have brought a man of your tastes and feelings to fix upon this island for the place of his retreat."

P. "Faith, not so either. It was the will of my father that I should have a call to preach the gospel; and it happened that he had an opportunity of making what is called a comfortable provision for me, in that way, in the island of Jamaica! But it so happened, that, in the course of those very enquiries which I undertook to qualify myself for the conscientious discharge of the duties of my function, I stumbled upon certain opinions that no more accorded with the profession of the ministry, than my general principles did with the state of West-Indian morality.

"While my father lived, however, I had no alternative: at least none that I had disinterested resolution enough to take. If I had thrown up my living, my father might have disinherited me of his little estate; and what then was I to have done?

'I could not dig; and to beg I was ashamed.'[2]

"His death, however, no sooner released me from these apprehensions, than I relinquished, at once, the profession and the emoluments of religion; changed my black coat for a brown one, and determined, thenceforward, to live on my scanty means, with a quiet conscience.

"But whatever quiet I might have from within, it did not please my quondam friends that I should have much from without. What I considered as honourable consciousness, they, on the contrary, regarded as an enormous crime.

"I had dishonoured the established religion, it seems, by refusing to receive seven or eight hundred a year from its funds; and my throwing off my black coat was a profligate and insolent avowal of atheism.

"If the loss of their society had been all I had to suffer, I should not have much regarded their resentment; for I had certainly as much abhorrence of their morality as they could possibly have of my opinions; with which, by the way, I was never so much of a zealot as to trouble them.

"But though I had no objection to be secluded from society, I had no inclination to be persecuted by it. I was not ambitious of the honours of

---

1   Thelwall constructed a small waterfall (still extant) in Llyswen, Wales.
2   Luke 16:3.

martyrdom: especially as I had no very settled opinion that society could be benefited by the promulgation of my sentiments.

"I determined, therefore, to quit the island. But I had no inclination to change the climate. It agreed with me, and I was not at a time of life to be trying experiments upon the constitution. Add to which, I had been thirty years out of England, and had no friendships or attachments there to compensate for the capriciousness of its foggy atmosphere.

"I turned my eyes upon St. Domingo, which, from mere rambling curiosity, I had visited in my early days; and where my acquaintance with Mons. Rabeau, and the impression which this then neglected spot had left upon my remembrance, emboldened me to expect, with confidence, a quiet and pleasant hermitage.

"For St. Domingo, accordingly, I embarked, with my wife, my adopted daughter, and our nurse (as we call her): a woman whom, upon the main, we hold in but little estimation, but whose attachment to our family, and whose tears and entreaties to be permitted to accompany us, in whatever part of the world we might determine to settle, so far overcame our objections, that we had not resolution enough to leave her behind.

"Here, accordingly, we settled: and here, for almost six years we have continued to reside—a family of philosophical hermits! with a small income regularly transmitted, a select, though not very extensive library, and a country whose beautiful and romantic scenery is an inexhaustible source of contemplation and delights.

"Happily our tastes are somewhat similar: my wife, Seraphina, and myself, are a sort of picturesque voluptuaries; and when, in pursuit of pleasures of this description, we are disposed to travel further than our feet will conveniently bear us, we have an old tub of a coach and a pair of mules to drag us from place to place.

"As for what is called society in this island, it squares a little with our circumstances as our taste; and we accordingly dispense with it so completely, that month sometimes succeeds to month without our having conversed with a single soul beyond our own family.

"Madame Rabeau, indeed, sometimes makes a half hour's visit to our English dairy,[1] as she calls it; and Rabeau himself, when the news arrives of any extraordinary movement in Paris, is very eager to hear my speculations upon the subject; but though repeatedly invited, we have never visited them above two or three times, and our inducement to comply with this last invitation was principally, and even exclusively, the account that Madame Rabeau had given of what she called your English eccentricities, but which we regarded as the evidences of your moral and intellectual attainments.

"But I must go and see how it fares with my poor negro. A few hours before you arrived, I laid him to sleep, with an opiate; after which I ven-

---

1   As in *The Peripatetic* (1793) and *Pedestrian Excursion* (1798-1801), access to and consumption of milk is a measure of healthy, modest, and virtuous living.

tured to amuse myself with a soothing strain or two upon my flute. He was sleeping when I was last out of the room: you will excuse me while I look again."

"Well, Edmunds," said Henry, "and what do you think of our host?"

E. "What do I *not* think of him, sir! And pray what think you of the island that can furnish no society for such a man? or of that which would not even suffer him to exist upon it in peace and quietness?"

H. "Name them not, Edmunds—the islands nor the islanders! They cannot sink lower in my estimation than they have sunk already!

"You may rail as you will against courts and large communities; but give me the vices of nobility rather than those of merchants and planters! the polished licentiousness of a gay European metropolis before the pigstye voluptuousness of this semi-barbarism and ignorance. The very excesses of men of intellect and refinement, bring consequences with them that make, at least, a partial atonement to society, but what, except the groans of Africa, have we to set against the swill-tub prodigality, and brothel-house revelry, that constitute the unvaried circle of Creolean amusements?

"I tell thee, Edmunds, I am sick to my very heart, of this Creolean life; for I cannot live without society, and still less can I live in the society of these planters.

"This fine old venerable hermit here, his family, and his library, seem to promise something better, indeed, for the future; or I had half resolved, maugre[1] the impending maledictions of my father, just to make a short tour with thee to some of the most remarkable places in the island, and then to take French leave, as we call it, and turn my back upon St. Domingo, its plantations, its ignorance, and its rapacity, *for ever, and for ever, amen.*"

E. "If ever you propose such a thing to me, sir, I tell you before hand, that I shall certainly advise you against it, might and main; though at the same time I freely confess, that if I were in your circumstances, I verily believe it is exactly the thing that I should do myself.

"But perhaps, sir, the cure of your impatience may not be very distant. This foster-daughter, about whom you have heard and enquired so much, may prove a loadstone to fix the quivering compass of your heart. Nay, if I mistake not, sir (excuse my freedom), you are already half way at least, a second Geoffery Ruddel.[2] Are you sure, sir, you have penned no sonnets to this invisible Seraphina?"

H. "No, in good faith, Edmunds, there is no danger of that. Seraphina is one of the wonders of the island; and as such I am impatient to see her; but these female phenomena dazzle our imaginations too much to interest our

---

1 In spite of.
2 The twelfth-century poet and Crusader Jaufré Rudel of Blaye, who fell in love with the Countess of Tripoli on hearing reports of her great beauty and virtue, without ever having seen her.

hearts. Wonder has small affinity to love. The stupendous rocks we have visited this night we shall talk of, indeed, as long as we live; and who would not have seen them? But even Parkinson, with all his enthusiastic attachment to the wild and romantic, has built his cottage in this calm sequestered dell, with a soft lawn before it, and a few shrubs and fruit-trees around: and the cataract he prides himself in so much, is not to be seen from his windows.

"The softness of Marian, add but a little sentiment, and an ordinary degree of information (just enough to render her conversible), would be more interesting in a partner for life, than all the stateliness of philosophy, or the rapturous enthusiasm of the muse."

E. "Your logic upon this subject, sir, may be very sound, for aught I know to the contrary; for I am but a novice in these matters; but, as I see you are determined to stay here, and abide the experiment, I would not lay the odds against your changing your key before this time to-morrow."

H. "If I thought there were any danger of that sort, I assure you, Edmunds, I would lull myself to sleep to-night with the two last sentences of the Lord's prayer,[1] and make the best use of my heels as soon as I got up in the morning."

E. "You must repeat the whole of that prayer, sir, with the litany and ten commandments into the bargain, before you will be able to execute such a resolution."

H. "But who can this Seraphina be? Is she, I marvel, in reality, any relation to our venerable host?"

"I know not, sir," said Parkinson, smiling—for the latter part of the sentence fell upon his ear as he was re-entering—"I know not whether your question means to insinuate any particular kind of relationship: if so, the manners of the colonies may justify the suspicion; but to me, as an individual, it is injurious.

"*Free thinkers*, it is said, are generally *free livers*. It may be so in general. I am afraid the generality of mankind are such, let their opinions be what they will. But for my own part, I have been too happy in an early and virtuous attachment, to have given way to incontinence in my riper years.

"Seraphina is certainly not, in reality, my daughter; nor does any species of relationship exist between us, unless that may be called relationship which, originating in sympathy, has been so improved by esteem, on the one hand, and gratitude on the other, that the reciprocal feelings of paternity and filial affection have supplanted the desultory impressions of friendship, and the frigid sense of obligation.

"This is the only relationship that exists between us. A relationship as indissoluble, however, as that of nature. She is my daughter to the inheritance of the last shilling of my little property—I am her father to the last atom of that influence which experienced affection can properly desire to exercise over inexperienced innocence.

---

1 "And forgive us our trespasses, as we forgive them that trespass against us. and lead us not into temptation, but deliver us from evil."

"But I perceive you have a natural curiosity relative to the history of one who must certainly be considered as a sort of phenomenon—a literary Creole—a female philosopher.

"This curiosity, therefore (as far as it is in my power), I shall readily gratify; for Seraphina is superior to the desire of mystery. I know her too well to suppose she would be gratified by any other species of respect than that which rests upon the solid basis of personal merit."

CHAP. III.

The History of Seraphina.

The deserted Courtesan.—Eccentric benevolence.—Maternal struggles.—An infantine Portrait.—Interesting Associations.—The very Mother!!!—Dying Injunctions.—The Adoption.

"SERAPHINA is the reputed natural daughter of an eminent planter, formerly resident in Jamaica; but as she never seems to have been acknowledged by him, this is, perhaps, a disputable point.

"Her mother was a woman of very considerable attractions; by the influence of which (so long as her beauty, the most powerful of them all, continued to be unimpaired) she maintained herself in a considerable degree of affluence and splendour; but, like the generality of persons of her description, she was improvident: and the ravages of the small pox, with which she was attacked while in the very prime of life, having put a sudden and unexpected period to the dominion of her charms, her resources failed, while, her habits of extravagance still continuing, she was quickly reduced, together with two infant children, to the verge of the extremest misery.

"In this situation she did not fail to exhibit some symptoms of returning virtue: so far at least as related to the feelings of maternal affection. She made several efforts to obtain a subsistence for her children; threw away the airs and delicacy of a fine lady; applied herself to habits of industry, even in a state of society where it is disgraceful for a white person to be industrious; and, for the sake of her little babes, practised a degree of self-denial almost equal to her former prodigality. But all in vain—the brand of infamy was upon her; nor did even envy slight a face no longer fair. She was hated by the women because she had once been handsome, and neglected by the men because she was handsome no more.

"In this exigence, a proposal was made to her of a very trying, and a very extraordinary nature:

"A particular friend of mine, the Rev. Mr. Robertson, and pastor of the adjoining cure (for I held my cure at that time), happened to pay a visit to some friends in Spanish Town, where this unfortunate woman then resided; and it so happened, likewise, that her story, and her children, became the subjects of conversation at a table where he dined.

"Robertson had some excellent traits of character; and among the rest, one that can never be too much admired: namely, that he had always an abundant share of sympathy for those with whom nobody would sympathise but himself. The story of this magdalen, therefore, excited a particular interest in his mind. He visited her, and relieved her present necessities; but returned still more interested than ever, by the beauty, the helpless innocence, and the endearing sweetness of the little Seraphina.

"He had a daughter much about the same age, an only child, whom he determined to educate himself, and concerning the management of whom he had some strange crotchets; most of which were very eccentric, though many of them had a good deal of reason upon their side.

"In the education of this daughter he believed it would be a point of considerable importance that she should have a companion, and a rival, of correspondent years; and human sympathy conspired with parental policy, to point out the little maid in question as a proper object of his adoption. But the character of the mother was a grand impediment; for he knew the *vehement virtue* of his wife, and the insuperable objection she would have to suffering a *creature* of this kind ever to darken her doors. Once a prostitute, was always a prostitute, with her: for she had no notion that sins of this kind could be washed away with repentance.

"He, also, I believe, imagined (and perhaps with good reason) that the intercourse of a mother (and such a mother in particular) might interfere with his plans of education; and that it was necessary that he should have an undivided influence over the mind of his adopted pupil.

"He accordingly proposed to the mother to take upon himself to educate and provide for Seraphina in a comfortable and eligible way, upon condition that she should renounce all claim and interference with respect to her, and even quit the island (which he undertook to enable her to do), as the best security for the fulfilment of this part of her contract.

"It has cost me many a tear to hear my friend relate, as he often would, the struggle which this proposal produced. At length, however, maternal duty got the better of maternal tenderness; and the afflicted mother preferred a painful separation to the probable alternative of seeing the infant, to whom an eligible prospect seemed thus to be unfolded, unprotected, uneducated, and friendless, lingering in hopeless wretchedness, or perishing in the fangs of want.

"Seraphina was accordingly received into the family of my friend, and her mother and little brother were shipped away—for England, I believe—at least they were sent out of the island. It matters not whither; for they never arrived at their journey's end. They were swept from the deck by the breaking of the waves, or thrust over by the brutality of the seamen; or else she plunged in herself, in some fit of desperation—The tale I have heard leaves it doubtful which. However, certain it is she was drowned; and the child too, as I understand: at any rate, he has never been heard of since.

"Under the roof of this eccentric protector, I first became acquainted with this charming little innocent: and certainly, never had child the powers of fascination in a more eminent degree.

"She was then about four years old[1]—acute, lively, and susceptible. Her stature was tall and strait, her complexion healthful, her eyes large and expressive, their colour somewhat too dark for hazel; her eye-lashes long and thick, and her brows smooth and regular; her forehead had an ingenuous expansion, and her locks of brown, glossed with a tint of orient, played over her glowing cheeks.

"Then she had such kindness of manners!—such an ambition to please!—such a solicitude to oblige!—a sort of officious sensibility, which the cynical and the unfeeling might perhaps regard as troublesome; but which, to me, appeared to be the germ, and indubitable evidence of an amiable disposition.

"How much of this she derived from what we call nature—how much from accidents, we cannot trace—how much from some incongruous mixture of atoning virtues in the vicious disposition of her mother; and how much in the course of a few months might have been effected by the instructions and rational management of my friend (less thwarted with respect to her than his own child, by the opinionated perverseness of his wife); are problems I shall not attempt to solve. Suffice it to say, such was Seraphina; and as such she made an impression first upon my sympathy, and progressively upon my affections, which every visit more and more confirmed.

"Our affections sometimes depend upon very slight coincidents. Mind itself, what is it but association?—at least, it is by association that its affections are perpetually regulated. Without it, the most important things impress not; and with it, the most insignificant become important.

"The very name of Seraphina had a charm in it; and I am not philosophical enough to be ashamed to confess its power. No, no—that power had its foundations in the depths of human nature—in the best and strongest affections of the social heart—in those affections which reason herself must sanction, and moral rectitude approve.

"It is a sad digression I am about to make, Mr. Montfort; but you cannot enter into the feelings of the foster-father till those of the real parent shall be explained.

"I had been always very fond of children; but I never had but one.—Ah! such an one!—the image of my lov'd Amanda:—yet something more—in promise and in expectation at least, yet something more than even my Amanda's self!

"But she died, Mr. Montfort, just as she had completed her sixth year—that age so interesting, so engaging. Cut off—suddenly cut off in

---

1 The description of Seraphina parallels Thelwall's description of his daughter
   Maria, who had recently died, in 1799.

the very bloom of health and cheerfulness. Within a few short days bounding before me in sprightly vigour, all smiles, and grace, and loveliness, and stretched in expiring anguish upon this arm.

"Ah! Mr. Montfort—you who have never been a parent, cannot image to yourself the faintest resemblance of those pangs that accompany the death of so beloved a child—a child, whose acknowledged beauty, and acknowledged intellect, were the slightest links of my affection—whose amiable disposition endeared her to all hearts—who seemed formed to exist only for the purposes of benevolence, and whose contented temperance—whose voluntary self-denial, and promptitude of participation to all around her, even at those tender years, might have shamed the boasted morality of philosophers, and given philanthropy itself a model.

"Why should I recal the woeful remembrances of that season of horrors?—my sleepless solicitudes, while the event was yet impending—my self reproaches when it was past—the wild phrensy of my Amanda—my own vehement desperation—the pangs that never shall be quieted—the tears that never shall be dried?

"Her name, also, was Seraphina.

"I know not whether this coincidence suggested the idea; but, some how or other, I persuaded myself that this little fosterling bore a striking resemblance to my own ever-regretted babe.

"Oh, at that thought how all the father rushed upon my soul. I pressed the little stranger in my arms—I gazed upon her beauteous form—I repeated the name of Seraphina! while delight and agony struggled within me, and I wept such tears as might be expected to bedew the cheek of a parent who had witnessed, in reality, the resurrection of his child.

"I went home full of the impression—'I have found our Seraphina again, my love,' said I, somewhat wildly, 'I have pressed her to my bosom; lively, beautiful and affectionate! just such as she was snatched away from us so many sad years agone!'

"Amanda glowed, and wept, and shuddered; and feared, till I had explained myself, that something had turned my brain: and, indeed, it was almost turned, the imagination had shaken my frame so strongly.

"My enthusiasm so far awakened the curiosity of Amanda, that she was not easy till she had seen the object by whom it was excited. She, also, either by the force of prepossession or some actual resemblance, was struck with the same idea, and entered into all my feelings. Those feelings became gradually strengthened by habitude. Our intercourse with the family of Robertson became more frequent; the new Seraphina was constantly in our thoughts, and every time we beheld her the resemblance seemed to be more and more impressive. I gave her the little lessons I had written for our own little cherub, and which, till then, had been treasured as holy reliques. I taught her to repeat them with the same tone and gesture; in short, the Seraphina I had lost became a model to her whom I had found, till they were identified in my heart, and I felt as if I were again a father.

"The consequences of this attachment were not a little gratifying to my friend. The interest I took in Seraphina induced me to co-operate with him in his plan of education; and as each of us had, of course, some attainments in which the other was deficient, his daughter was benefited (or at least might have been so, if our care had not been counteracted by the foolish vanity of the mother), by a more extensive range of accomplishments and studies.

"In the mean time, Seraphina continued to thrive in beauty and stature; and the sweetness of her temper—the liveliness of her imagination—the acuteness of her discernment, and the rapidity of her attainment, commanded the love and admiration of all who knew her:—one only excepted. That one, however, was unfortunately Mrs. Robertson.

"This selfish and malignant being soon began to consider every thing that was done for Seraphina as a robbery of her own daughter. Nay, her husband was guilty of little short of blasphemy against Nature, according to her mode of philosophising, *in placing a nameless fosterling—a child of base origin! upon a footing of equality with his own flesh and blood*: in dressing her in the same attire, suffering the slaves and domestics to pay her the same attentions, and giving her the same indulgencies, accomplishments and education.

"I had, also, my objections to his mode of proceeding. But they rested upon very different grounds.

"'You are giving this charming innocent,' said I to my friend, a thousand times, 'the education, the accomplishments, the sentiments and feelings of a gentlewoman; and when you die, perhaps, you will leave her a hundred pounds to buy mourning.'

"To this I could never obtain any better answer than that 'it was easier to educate two than one; since there could be no emulation in solitude'; and that 'this emulation could never be properly supported, unless the competitors were educated as equals.'

"This, as far as related to his own daughter, might perhaps be good reasoning. But, then, Seraphina was to be sacrificed, that Mira might be accomplished: a sort of compromise, in which I could discover neither humanity nor justice. If I co-operated in his plan, therefore, it was because I had more extended views.

"While things continued in this situation, Seraphina entered her eleventh year: a period at which, in these forward climates, a young woman begins almost to be regarded as an object of desire; and at which the accomplishments, the manners, the conversation and sweet attractive graces of this fosterling, rendered her a formidable rival both to the fellow-pupil and the mamma.

"She had already borne away the prize in every fashionable accomplishment, and every intellectual attainment. 'Were the unfolding beauties of Mira, and the more matured, but not less emulous charms of Mrs.

Robertson herself, to be overlooked, while all eyes, and all hearts, were, at every assembly, paying their devotions to the form and features of this aspiring alien?' This was not to be borne.

"At this critical conjuncture, my friend happened to die. But he did not happen to fulfil my prognostication. He did not leave her a hundred pounds—no—nor a shilling.

"He died without a will: but, with his dying breath, enjoined his widow and daughter not to withdraw their friendship and protection from Seraphina, till she could be eligibly settled in the world.

"The promise, which the dying husband and father so importunately demanded, it was difficult for the hovering wife and kneeling daughter to with-hold, and the engagement entered into under such circumstances, superstitious terror induced them, however reluctantly, to fulfil.

"But *the tender mercies of the wicked are cruel:*[1] and where the will goes not with the act, it is possible to do more than violate one's promise while one is fulfilling it.

"The friendship of Mira, and the protection of Mrs. Robertson, soon degenerated into the most intolerable persecution: and the tyranny of the one and the imperious insolence of the other, now they were freed from the influence of that authority which had hitherto restrained them within the bounds of decency, broke out in such outrageous insults, and threw her to such a humiliating distance in those circles where she had hitherto been received as an equal, and treated with distinction, that the poor girl grew weary of her very existence.

"In the mean time, in pursuance of the intention of the deceased and their own inclinations, the family were preparing for England: the country for whose meridian, not that of the colonies, the education of Mira had been calculated, and Seraphina was rather ordered, than invited, to accompany them thither.

"Nothing, however, could have been more terrible to her imagination than the idea of visiting a strange country under such protection. And one evening, as I entered the room, in the presence of a large party, who were assembled upon a sort of farewell visit, she threw herself at my feet, and in the agony of her soul, and undisguised simplicity of her nature, entreated me to rescue her from her tormentors, to save her from the transportation with which she was threatened, and receive her under the protection of my roof till some situation could be procured, however humble, in which she might avoid the horrors of an unsupportable dependence.

"'My child! my child!' said I, lifting her up, and clasping her to my heart with an agony truly parental, 'be comforted. Your request imperfectly anticipates the purpose of my visit.

"'Thou knowest I have no child of my own. But my heart has room and capacity for all a parent's feelings. This void you—and you alone are

---

1 Proverbs 12:10.

capable of filling up. I have long considered you as my own—long adopted you in affection: and my Amanda, equally sensible of your merit with myself, has long confirmed the election. In her name I am now come to request of Mrs. Robertson to relinquish her future interest in your protection; and to invite you to share with us whatever our house and our fortunes can afford—not as a dependant, but as a daughter.'

"Poor Seraphina!!! how shall I describe her emotions. Alas! at the recollection I am overpowered by my own. Language forsakes me: and articulation fails.

"Pardon these tears, Mr. Montfort—a father's tears: for such I became from that day: a day the brightest in my existence, that only excepted which gave me Amanda, a blushing bride to my arms.

"Oh! you can never conceive the proud delight, the swelling satisfaction I have experienced in forming the mind of this lovely, this accomplished young woman—or rather in assisting its progress; for nature seemed already to have formed it to every thing that was good and excellent.

"I have told you already, that I have been almost from the first a joint instructor with my friend; and mine were from the first the instructions that were always attended to with the most affectionate assiduity: for Seraphina very soon began to feel that whatever Robertson did for her was done for the sake of his daughter, but that my solicitude was purely and simply for her own. Our satisfaction was therefore reciprocal when the task devolved entirely upon me. And never was task performed with more alacrity—nor ever was success more commensurate—I will not say with the expectations, but with the wishes of the tutor.

"You see, sir, with the name I have adopted the feelings of a parent; and you will forgive the loquacity of parental fondness.

"But the night wears fast away; and I shall weary you with an old man's prattle. Let me conduct you to your humble apartments.

"But first let me extort a promise from you, Mr. Montfort, that you will not depart till you have had an opportunity of apologizing, in person, to my wife and daughter for the disappointment which you have occasioned them."

With this request Henry very readily complied. And early in the morning Edmunds was dispatched to the plantation of La Soufriere; where he never arrived; while our hero, with a sort of mysterious impatience, waited for the expected interview with Seraphina, at that sequestered retreat to which she never more returned.

But for the causes of these disappointments the reader must be referred to the ensuing volume: being connected with matters of too much weight and importance to occupy the fag-end of a chapter.

END OF THE FIRST VOLUME.

VOLUME II

BOOK IV.
=========
CHAP. I.

Containing the military Exploits of our Hero during the Insurrection of the Negroes.

Chronological Notices.—Emancipation and Revolt.—Distracting Recollections.—The Insurgent.—Devastations and Horrors.—The Fugitives.—Apprehensions and Expedients.—Practical Distinctions.—Cruel Retaliations.—The Consternation at Cape Françoise.—The Departure from the Cape.—Nautical Logic.

IT seems as though fortune had predetermined to play at cross purposes with the hero and heroine of our history; and that accidents the most insignificant, and events the most important, were alike to conspire to procrastinate their predestined interview. We have already seen how a casual ramble to the brink of a romantic precipice chased from the remembrance of Henry an engagement into which he had been invited for the specific purpose of introducing him to the acquaintance of Seraphina; and, at the conclusion of the former volume, we gave some kind of mysterious intimation of the fruitlessness of those hopes which now detained him at the romantic retreat of Parkinson.

In order that the causes of this second disappointment may be the more accurately understood, it is necessary to apprise the reader that the eccentric ramble and interesting conversations, which formed the subjects of the preceding chapter, took place on the eventful evening of the 22d of August, 1795;[1] that very evening on which the insurrection of the Negroes first broke out in the settlement of St. Domingo; and that the village of Acul, the scene of their first enormities, was unhappily situated in an almost direct line between the quiet retreat of Parkinson and the hamlet of La Soufriere, where Amanda and Seraphina, were, at that time, visiting.

In a situation so sequestered, near as it was to the scene of action, it is not surprising that our hero and his host should remain perfectly unapprised of the event for many hours after the ravages and uproar had commenced; or that they should be calmly expatiating on the miseries of the unhappy slaves, at the very time when those slaves were satiating their vengeance in a severe retaliation, on the surrounding mansions and plantations.

---

1 1791, not 1795, which is probably a typo.

Rumour, that ill-tongued babbler, whether true or false, seeks not the lonely cottage of obscurity, till her garrulity has first been wearied in those more populous haunts where thousands of ears are stretched out to receive her accents, and those accents may be reverberated by a thousand tongues.

The first intimation, therefore, they had of this event, was from young Edmunds; who, returning somewhat earlier than was expected, came running up to them, and exclaiming, with eyes on fire and his whole frame in almost convulsive agitation, "'Tis done! 'tis done! the negroes have thrown off the yoke. They are breaking their chains on the heads of their oppressors."

"I am sorry for it," said Parkinson, with a sigh, "very sorry. The news you repeat with so much transport, fill my mind with the most terrible apprehensions."

Edmunds was petrified with astonishment. "And is it possible, sir," said he, "after what I have heard from your lips, that you can be averse to the emancipation of your sable brethren?"

P. "No, young man, no. I wish for their emancipation as eagerly as you can. I would die to emancipate them; but I cannot wish for their revolt."[1]

"And by what other means, sir," said Henry, "were they to be emancipated?"

P. "Not immediately, perhaps, by any. But never, never, most assuredly by these.

"The sympathy of mankind has long been flowing strongly in their favour; and the operation of this feeling, though slow, is ultimately certain. You shall see how quickly the excesses of their cruelty will give a contrary direction; while the improvident fury of their vengeance will inevitably destroy every means and provision for their success.

"Thus will their boasted freedom prove but the hideous phantom of a day; which, after it has been worshiped by the inhuman immolation of thousands of miserable victims, shall vanish from the sight of its deluded worshipers, and leave them nothing in return for their hazards and their atrocities but fetters and scourges, gibbets, and excruciating tortures."

E. "If you were a poor negro, sir, and had been stolen away from your parents, your friends, and your country; if you had been dragged in chains and fetters across the ocean, in a vile floating charnel-house, been sold to stripes and bondage by a vile man-stealer, been roused every morning from your slumber by the unpitying scourge, and driven like a brute beast to labour by some inhuman task-master; you, sir, I think, would have endeavoured to realize this phantom; you, sir, would have done, what I am sure I should, and what these poor negroes have."

P. "Perhaps I should, my honest lad, perhaps I should; but I should not have done wisely; because the probability is that I should have been too

---

1 Parkinson's extensive comments against revolution and violence reflect the ideas in William Godwin's *Enquiry Concerning Political Justice*, Bk. 4, ch. 1-3 (1798) (see Appendix B3b).

frantic with revenge and too blind with ignorance, to know how to serve the liberty I sought for.

"It is the hard condition of human wretchedness that the deeper we have sunk in misery, the less capable we are of emerging from it; or even of keeping ourselves afloat when the agitations of tumultuous waves may chance to have brought us upon the surface.

"How few are there who know how to redress the wrongs of mankind, but those who have little to redress!"

E. "And they, sir, are too selfish to be very active in the abolition of abuses of which themselves or their connections reap the profit."

P. "Their sympathy is indeed somewhat too tardy for our enthusiasm; but after all, Edmunds, it is the only resource of the oppressed. Slavery was once the portion of the mass of mankind in every quarter of the globe. From almost every nation in Europe it now has disappeared; yet in no single instance was slavery abolished by the insurrection of the slaves!"

E. "Alas, sir, what you say may be very true; but the history of Europe, I believe, is six thousand years old; and slavery still maintains its ground in Poland, in Turkey, and in Russia. When Sympathy shall have visited every corner of those countries, she will still have three quarters of the globe to traverse with the same snail-like expedition. In the mean time, sir, we reason, but the poor negro feels."

"Feels, Edmunds!" exclaimed Parkinson, as some shouts and groans came echoing along the rocks from a neighbouring plantation: "Do you hear those yells; those shrieks? Do you see those conflagrations?

"It is the white man that now feels. He feels the dreadful stroke of retribution.

"It is true he may thank himself. It is he who has taught those
>Bloody instructions, which, being taught, return
>To plague the inventor.[1]

"But let not this reflection root out our humanity. When the criminal is groaning on the rack, let us sympathise even with the criminal; at least, let us sympathise with those helpless babes who are now reaking on the sword of massacre, and those maids and matrons who are writhing in the abhorred embrace of brutal violation.

"Heaven and earth! Amanda! Seraphina!

"Where, where are they?"

So saying he ran, like one bewildered, to the eminence that overlooked the cataract, and cast his eyes around to behold the scene of horrors.

Henry accompanied him with equal agitation; while Edmunds followed with a slower pace; deeply impressed with the picture, which he felt to be no coinage of a wild imagination; and pondering in his bosom a thousand painful and wavering reflections.

Such observations from any other person, perhaps, might have had little effect. But he regarded Parkinson with a kind of veneration which disposed

---

1 *Macbeth* 1.7.9–10.

him to weigh, at least, every thing that came from his lips; and, in such a case, consideration is all that is necessary to make one feel correctly: at least where the heart is right: for though enthusiasm may sometimes transport beyond the bounds of reason, he who is not destitute of human sympathy will feel for sufferance even where he abhors the sufferer.

"It is from Acul! It is from La Soufriere!" exclaimed Parkinson, in an agony of horror. "Distraction! Amanda! Seraphina! Whither shall we run? What shall we do to save them?"

While he was thus rolling his bewildered eyes around in quest of he knew not what, he beheld the negro who had driven the carriage, entering the dell below, in apparent trepidation, and hurrying towards the cottage.

"Mozambo! Mozambo!"[1] shouted he; and flew down the precipice to meet him.

Mozambo's hand was armed with a reeking sword. A pair of pistols was tied round his waist with a handkerchief; and his arms were bathed in blood. There was a deathful horror in his countenance.

"My wife! my child! Mozambo," exclaimed Parkinson, with frantic impatience.

He saw the clotted gore upon the limbs and weapons of the negro. He recoiled a few steps. His heart died within him.

"Demon of hell! that blood?"

M. "'Tis white man blood. Me hab kill de tyrant. Him roast poor negro man no more."

P. "And Amanda! Seraphina! my wife, my sweet fosterling! thou hast murdered them also; and now, in mercy, art come to murder me.

"Be quick. 'Tis all I ask thee," continued he, presenting his throat.

"Kill massa!" said Mozambo, throwing away his sword, and falling at his feet.—"Kill good madam! Kill sweet missee! Oh! you kill Mozambo tink so. Me die, me save your life.

"Me hab save you Manda! Me hab save you Seraphina, now me come save massa."

P. "Saved?—Where?—How?—Where are they? Faithful Mozambo! where are they?"

M. "Dem hide in forest, by little river, where me hab boat for carry dem away dese tree day."[2]

P. "You knew, then, of this intended insurrection, before hand. And what had you to complain of, Mozambo, that you should join in these horrors?"

M. "Me complain, massa? Me not complain nothing. Me love massa. Me love madam. Me love missee. Me wish serve dem still. But me love

---

1 The name is from Wimpffen's narrative, in which a "Mazimbo" is a friendly slave who expresses "gratitude" to his white owner (186).

2 The Mozambo episode in which Parkinson's wife and Seraphina are saved is from Bryan Edwards, *Historical Survey* (3:80-81); see Appendix B2d.

poor negro man, whom cruel white man whip to die. Me love poor negro man, who hab no bed to lie but dirt; who groan, and sweat, and toil; eat fish dat stink like rot, and drink him tears. Dese me love, massa."

"And so do I, Mozambo," said Parkinson, the tears swelling into his eyes. "Would we could love them to some purpose."

M. "Me make dem free, or die."

P. "Generous Mozambo! it is pity that such men as thou art should not be free: and were all like thee, they might be so.

"But no: thy hands, too, are polluted, Mozambo: thou, too, hast murdered."

M. "Me murder him who murder. But me not roast him. Tyrant! Debbil! me not roast him neider. Me not scoff at him dying agony. Me not tell him laugh."

The circumstance required no further explanation. It was evident he alluded to a planter at no great distance, who having thrown his negro cook into the oven, for spoiling a favourite pastry, exclaimed, with barbarous exultation, while his lips were shrivelling in the heat, "See how the rascal laughs."[1]

Edmunds clenched his right hand, as if wielding, in imagination, the delegated sword of justice. He strode two or three yards backwards and forwards, swelled his chest, breathed with a more forcible aspiration, and erected his brow with a sort of stern enthusiasm.

Parkinson was stricken mute; and Henry rolled his eyes to heaven in an appeal of agonised devotion.

"But come, massa. Missee and madam tink long stay. Negromen tink Mozambo betray, if not make haste. Me save massa, me save massa friends," said he, pointing to Henry and Edmunds, "den me go back, and make my brederen free."

So saying, he conducted them out of the dell; and leading them into an unfrequented path, directed his course towards the forest.

"You see, sir," said Edmunds, exultingly, "these negroes are just, in the midst of their revenge. They do not torture indiscriminately! They execute the guilty; but they preserve the good!"

"Mozambo does so," replied Parkinson; "but all negroes are not Mozamboes."

E. "That, sir, is because all masters are not Parkinsons."

P. "There may be something in that, young man. But things are as they are, and the conclusion will result from the premises.

"Poor Mozambo! If he himself should fall a victim to the blind fury of those he is struggling to emancipate, who will may wonder at it. I shall not."

M. "Me do what me think duty, massa. Me bide the consequence."

---

1 Thelwall's 1793 Capel Court Society debate speech discussed the implications of a runaway slave being burned in a frying pan (see Scrivener, *Seditious Allegories*, 111-18).

P. "Generous Mozambo! I would it were possible that thou shouldst succeed. But blood and horror never led to freedom."

A confused uproar of shouts and groans interrupted their conversation. The shrieks of women and the screams of infants resounded upon every side; and the flames of surrounding conflagrations reddened the air.

"O God! O God!" ejaculated Henry. "Is this emancipation?"

Edmunds was mute and confounded.

"Haste, massa! haste!" said Mozambo, fearfully, "or negro men surround us before reach de forest."

The harbour of expected security was in sight: but the groans and shouts thickened upon them, and the clouds of dust raised by the trampling feet of fugitives and pursuers came rolling across their way.

"See! see!" said Mozambo, thrusting his master into the hollow of an huge tree, that was moldering by the way-side. "Negro men see white man, dem kill!"

Henry and Edmunds followed into the same retreat.

They were just in time.

Some families of white people came flying, within a few paces of the spot, before a tumultuary gang of negroes; who, armed with hoes, and cutlasses, and muskets, and fire-brands, struck down, with hideous shouts of exultation, all they could overtake.

Mozambo made a feint to join in the pursuit. But he returned to the hollow tree, as soon as the path was clear; and the fugitives resumed their route.

But what was their horror at the scene before them! The road was strewn with limbs and mangled carcases: with dead and dying: with women and with babes.

A wretched mother was seen weltering on the ground; and the infant she had, sheltered even in death, was still clinging to that accustomed breast which streamed, not with nutriment, but with blood.

"God of mercy!" said Henry, taking the babe in his arms, "what a sight is here!

"I trust Edmunds, that with all thy enthusiasm for negro emancipation, thou wouldst not be an actor in such deeds of horror."

"Indeed I would not, sir," answered Edmunds. "Indeed I would not. But if men of intellect, of information and humanity, sir, would have the disinterestedness to take upon themselves the direction and conduct of these movements"—

"They would be murdered too," answered Parkinson, interrupting him. "It matters not what may be the humanity of the leaders, while the followers are mere ignorant savages. Though you speak with the tongues of angels, the fury of vengeance is deaf and cannot hear. Barbarous ferocity will comprehend no logic but blood."

"Poor babe." continued he, taking it from the arms of Henry, "if it be our destiny to reach the boat in safety, Miranda shall cradle thee upon her bosom, and Seraphina be thy virgin mother."

They were now arrived at the very borders of the forest, and began to flatter themselves that the danger was at an end. But what was their consternation when, from that very forest, they heard the discharge of musquetry, and beheld flames of fire and curling volumes of smoke breaking from among the trees.

A small body of planters and militia had rallied upon that spot, and were attacking a body of negroes; who, with much more order and discipline than usual among them, were keeping watch upon the confines.

It was the troop of Mozambo.

The fire was instantly returned.

"Undone! undone!" exclaimed the poor fellow, in great perplexity. "White men beat negro, if Mozambo stay. White men kill Mozambo if dem take him.

"But negro men not shall kill massa."

So saying, he snatched the old man suddenly in his vigorous arms; and, sword in hand, hurried with him, into the midst of the conflict.

What were Henry and Edmunds to do in such a dilemma? Neutrality and retreat were alike impossible.

Henry yielded to the impulse of that sympathy which the recent scene had excited. He threw himself among the planters; and Edmunds, impelled by his attachment, followed where his master led; more, indeed, as a defender than a combatant.

A sharp conflict ensued; and the planters, overpowered by numbers, were slaughtered or dispersed through the forest.

Henry and Edmunds were among the fugitives. They escaped with difficulty from the fury of the victors; and with still greater difficulty avoided the additional misfortune of separation, as they fled among the inextricable labyrinths.

Their situation was now truly deplorable.

Strangers to the face of the country; driven, in they knew not what direction, by an infuriated foe, beyond all prospect of the boundaries of the forest, far from every human habitation, and from every means and prospect of sustaining nature, they were in danger of perishing by slow-consuming famine; or, even if they should chance to extricate themselves from this situation, and regain the open country, their complexions would be their inevitable warrant of execution, with the first party of the insurgents they might happen to encounter.

Reflections of this kind, it is true, are not very becoming in the hero of print and paper; who ought to be of those steady and confident beings, who care no more about being starved, or roasted to death, than they do about eating their dinners.

The feelings of Henry, however, were not always regulated by the figure they would make in a book; it having never occurred to him that he was to exist in one: and therefore, as his courage was rather of an active than of a passive kind, rather enthusiastic than philosophical, it did so happen, that these reflections filled and occupied his mind to a very considerable and very painful degree. In the midst of all his apprehensions, however, he was not forgetful of Parkinson; and all that he felt for his own situation was still more embittered by the uncertainty in which he was doomed to remain, relative to the fate of that venerable philanthropist, and of the accomplished Seraphina.

In this desperate situation, the only expedient that Henry could devise was to mark the position of the sun in the horizon, and, comparing it with the hour of the day, to endeavour to ascertain the eastern point of the compass; since it was from that direction they had entered the labyrinth, and in that direction lay the only part of the country they were acquainted with, namely, the vicinity of La Soufriere.

But where was their security when they had passed the confines of this wilderness?

How were they to avoid the fury of the insurgents, who in that very part of the country seemed to have concentrated their principal force?

"These are questions," said Henry, "we may discuss when we arrive upon the confines. Here we must inevitably perish."

"I have another expedient, sir," said Edmunds. "We cannot at any rate be more than a day's march from the sea. What I advise, then, is to turn our faces exactly in the opposite direction from that which you propose, and so proceed till we meet with some stream or other, which taking a northerly direction, may lead us to the shore. From thence it is not at all improbable that some opportunity or other may present itself of escaping either from the island entirely, or to some securer part of it."

Henry caught at the idea with eagerness. He did not, indeed, say as much, but he brooded in silence over the hope that chance might direct them to the very stream on which Seraphina was waiting to embark.

The thought gave fresh strength and vigour. Hope cheated itself into certitude; and the sprightliness of his mind returned.

Night, however, arrived before either brook or rivulet was descried: night and the solemn moon.

"With what different sensations," said Henry, "do we behold this luminary at this instant, from those with which we contemplated her last night. Yet the sky is as clear; her lustre is undiminished, and this dark irregular canopy, that breaks and intercepts her rays, chequering the turf below with rude mosaic, would, under favourable circumstances have been regarded as a pleasing diversity.

"But after all, they are the phenomena within, not those without, that constitute our enjoyments; and

"The pomp of groves and garniture of fields."[1]
like the vanities of courts, have little of the power to charm, when the imagination is disturbed with apprehensions, and the vindictive passions are afloat."

---

1 James Beattie, *The Minstrel* (1771), Bk. I, ix.

"I am glad, sir," replied Edmunds, "that your mind is composed enough to philosophise in this way. For my part, sir, I am thinking what we are to do for a compass now. I confess I am not master enough of the moon's motions to ascertain the cardinal points by her position in the heavens. I verily believe the best thing we can do is to get up into one of the thickest of these trees, and, in the securest attitude we can devise, commend ourselves to sleep till the sun rises."

Henry was not much in a humour to relish this advice. His imagination was full of Mozambo's bark, and of its freight; and he would willingly have pursued his way. He saw, however, no safe alternative, and therefore was about to comply; when their attention was diverted by a rustling among the thickets; and presently, still more so, by occasional flashes of scintillations of a sort of glow-worm light, which they soon perceived to be emitted from the burnished bayonets and musquetry of some military detachment.

Whether friends or foes were approaching, it was not possible to conjecture: but it behoved them to ascertain the fact, from some secure concealment without delay; for the trampling was now heard from a variety of quarters.

The silence and regularity of the march, soon convinced Henry that they were not insurgent negroes who were assembling. And as they were approaching nearer and nearer, he began to recognise the remains of that very corps in whose behalf they had been engaged in the middle of the day, and from whom they had been separated in the general rout. These were now rallying, by some preconcerted appointment, together with such recruits, both planters and regular military, as the magistracy had been able, upon such short notice, to call together.

To these Henry and Edmunds, accordingly, revealed themselves; and under their conduct and protection directed their course towards Acul.

Among those who joined them the next morning, in their rout, after they had repassed the confines of the forest, was a party of planters, from the neighbourhood of La Soufriere.

"How, young sir," said St. Valance, who conducted them, darting an enraged and suspicious look on Henry, "I did not expect to have met with you in such society. The season of your withdrawing so secretly from La Soufriere was critically chosen; and the sentiments you have so often supported, furnish a tolerable explanation of that ambiguous event. I supposed, of course, that you and your brother propagandist were gone to join your friends the blacks, and help on their glorious work of emancipation. Here, I trust, you cannot expect many proselytes."

"I know not, sir," replied Henry, warmly, "what you may have *supposed*. What you would *insinuate* is pretty clear. And, perhaps, it would not be inconvenient to you that the son of your partner should encounter the probable consequences of your insinuation. As for what you say about *my friends the blacks*, if friendship and commiseration are synonimous terms, know that I shall never be ashamed to confess myself the friend of the whole human race: of blacks, as well as whites; of the oppressor, as well as the oppressed. But you know nothing of my principles, if you suppose they would lead me into such scenes as these.

"It is true, I would not be the owner of a slave I had the power of emancipating, for all the wealth that has been scourged out of the backs of these poor negroes, since they were first introduced into the islands. But I abhor massacre and conflagration, under whatever pretence they may be perpetrated; and would preserve even the tyrant from the blood-thirsty vengeance of his revolted slave.

"I love liberty, Frenchmen, I confess, as dearly as you seem to love domination. But rape and murder are the tyranny I most abhor; and when the slave I compassionate becomes the tyrant I condemn, I am his champion and his advocate no more."

These sentiments of Henry would not have done much towards removing the insinuations of St. Valance, if the commander had not witnessed his gallantry during the late unfortunate engagement. But this was a commentary that rendered the text somewhat more intelligible; and, as he was a man of some moderation, for a military man and a creole, he very prudently interfered with his authority to put an end to the altercation.

"We have nothing to do, monsieur," said he, "with these disputes. The gentleman is an Englishman, has behaved with great intrepidity during the late conflict, and has escaped with difficulty the general massacre that has desolated this neighbourhood. If he is still willing to join his hand to ours, we shall honour him for his assistance. If not (by virtue of his country) he has a right to be protected in his neutrality."

The scale was now turned; but it settled no more than formerly, to the steady balance of justice. The whites retaliated, with interest, all the cruelties and massacres that had been perpetrated during the former day. Their course to Acul, and from thence to Cape François, was marked with carnage, with mutilations, and impalings. But the fate of the prisoners, such of them in particular as were suspected of having been leaders or agitators in the revolt, was horrid beyond description.

Several of these were tried in a very summary way, as soon as they arrived at the Cape. Some were ordered to be burnt alive; others to be whipt to death; and others again to be broken on the wheel. Punishments so horrible and barbarous, and attended with so many aggravations of cannibal ferocity, as presently revolted the pendulating mind of Henry, and made him heartily repent his co-operation with the inhuman planters. While, on the other hand, the immoveable fortitude with which several of those unfortunate victims endured their torments, excited an admiration that powerfully increased his sympathy.

As for Edmunds, he was almost frantic. He reproached his master; he reproached himself; and began to execrate an attachment that had led him to act against his principles. He even meditated to make atonement for his error by an immediate revolt to the insurgents.

While his mind was in this agitated state, an instance of unparalleled barbarity worked up his sympathy to a crisis.

It was the execution of Aboan, a Koromantyn negro,[1] one of the captive leaders of the insurgents; and who having been in his own country a man of some consequence, a chief, and a leader of armies, did not forget, upon this occasion, to support himself with a degree of magnanimity worthy of his former fame.

Taken in arms against his purchasers, and found guilty of endeavouring to regain his freedom, he was sentenced to be broken on the wheel, together with Otuba,[2] a principal associate in the revolt.

The place assigned for the execution was immediately under the window of the apartment in which Henry had taken up his abode. The victims approached the scaffold with an undaunted countenance; and all the inhabitants of Cape François thronged to the spectacle, breathing taunts, and insults, and execrations, and whetting the cruelty of the executioner by every excitement that barbarity could devise.

The torments of the sufferers were accordingly procrastinated, and aggravated, with every refinement of barbarity; till at last the executioner, weary himself, and disgusted with the scene of horrors, dispatched Otuba with a *coup de grâce*, as it is called; and, after a short pause, uplifting his mace again, was about to perform the same cruel kindness for Aboan.

But the cannibalism of the populace was yet unsatisfied. "Hold! Hold!" was re-echoed from a hundred tongues. The catastrophe was accordingly delayed; and the wretched Koromantyn, whose every joint was already dislocated, and every bone was broken, was abandoned to the sport and fury of the spectators; who, themselves becoming actors in the bloody scene, aggravated all his sufferings, and procrastinated his tortures; refusing him the wretched privilege of death.

But Aboan was yet unmoved. He did not supplicate; he did not groan. The sweat drops of agony, indeed, bedewed his mangled limbs; but his eye rolled defiance; and the only sounds that escaped his lips, were those of execration and contempt.

Thus hour followed hour, and torment succeeded to torment, till at last an English sailor, who served on board a vessel then in the harbour, happening to be on shore, and thronging, like others, to see the spectacle, burst through the crowd, and with characteristic indignation, and a hearty d—n at the cruelty of their French eyes, with a merciful twist of his handkerchief, released the wretched victim from intolerable sufferance.

"See, see what we have done!" said Edmunds, sobbing, as soon as the tragedy was completed: for neither words nor tears could find any

---

1 Aboan, a Koromantyn chief, alludes to *Oroonoko*, either Aphra Behn's narrative (1688) or Thomas Southerne's play (1695). Aboan is Oroonoko's male companion. On the planters' cruel executions of the rebels, see Edwards (3:83).

2 From Ottobah Cugoano, influential ex-slave and abolitionist who lived in London in the 1770s and 1780s; he was active in circles familiar to Thelwall.

vent before. "See what we have done, sir, and with whom it is we have joined!"

Henry was dumb with anguish.

"O that I were a negro," continued Edmunds, "that I might conquer or die with these brave fellows! It were better to die than live to see these horrors.

"I am weary of life, sir—I am blasted in my own eyes, to have combatted for these worse than monsters!

"There is but one atonement—only one."

The tears ceased to flow as he uttered this. His eyes rolled furiously. He knitted his brows; compressed his lips, with almost convulsive rigidness; and pressing his clenched fist upon his bosom, strode across the room in desperate meditation.

Henry understood his purpose; and, rousing from the lethargic dejection into which the horrid spectacle had thrown him,

"Nay, Edmunds," said he, seizing him by the arm; "thou shalt not go. By Heaven thou shalt not go! They will murder thee also, poor boy! Thee, also, they will murder, the black cannibals or the white.

"Let us fly, Edmunds—let us fly this hateful, this accursed land!—this land of reciprocal horrors!

"Not Seraphina, herself, were she all that busy imagination has been painting her, could longer detain me here."

Then, after a pause,

"We have done wrong, perhaps; yet wherewith have we to reproach ourselves?

"Hurried on by blind necessity; precluded from the possibility of neutrality; we chose between two terrible alternatives: and how could we have chosen otherwise?

"Could we, with that poor infant,[1] whom we had just seen baptised in its mother's blood, still screaming in our arms, could we have leagued ourselves with the murderers? Or could we have foreseen these horrors?"

"We might have foreseen them," replied Edmunds, with a voice almost inarticulate with anguish. "We might have foreseen them; because the same, and worse, have been perpetrated by our own country-men; if, indeed, it be not a sort of blasphemy against nature to suggest compatriotism or affinity between human beings and these creolean cannibals.

"O Jamaica! Jamaica! thou island of abominations and horrors! what conceivable cruelties are there with which those who insult our national virtue by calling themselves *English* planters have not polluted thee!

"But thirty years ago, sir—it is but thirty years—The story is notorious through the two hemispheres; and some of the actors in that bloody

---

1 An iconic image of the insurrection in atrocity narratives was a white baby impaled on a stake used as a banner by the rebels (Anon., *A Particular Account of the Commencement and Progress of the Insurrection of the Negroes in St. Domingo* 4; Edwards 3:74).

tragedy are still alive—But thirty years ago, sir;—you must have heard the tale—when Tacky, the Koromantyn chief, who had been taken prisoner in one of those detestable wars provoked for the purposes of this traffic, and sold to our vile man stealers!—when this gallant but unfortunate chief, indignant of his servile chains, and thirsting for revenge and liberty, roused the whip-galled negroes from their bonds, and led them to the disastrous conflict in which he was slain.[1] You cannot forget, sir, the burnings and the roastings that succeeded.—You cannot forget, sir, the two devoted wretches who were hung alive in chains, and left, for nine whole days, parching and frying beneath the vertical sun, till tormenting hunger, and more intolerable thirst, at length consumed their vitals.

"Tornadoes! hurricanes! and earthquakes! What inadequate ministers are we of vengeance! Ye roaring tempests and deluging inundations! how imperfectly do ye perform the biddings of eternal justice! Were ye indeed the instruments of moral retribution, what single spot of all these islands that the palm of man could spread over would continue to lift up its head from the Atlantic, and reproach the providence of Heaven!"

"Good God!" exclaimed Henry, terrified by his wild enthusiasm; "compose thyself Edmunds—for Heaven's sake compose thyself. Thy brain is turned by a too irritable humanity: thy feelings have overpowered thy reason. Let us fly, my poor lad, from scenes too terrible for our nerves to bear; let us shun the torrent of cruelty we cannot stem. Let us leave these bloody men to their reciprocal barbarities; convinced, from what we have seen, that the oppressions of these tyrants have rendered their slaves too vile for liberty, though yet not so vile as themselves."

From these heart-rending reflections, the attention of Henry and Edmunds was now aroused by the noise of fresh bustle and agitation without. They looked out of the window, and beheld the streets filled with consternation and terror. The inhabitants were running in all directions; the military collecting; and every thing evinced the apprehension of approaching danger.

In short, the negroes had rallied; the insurrection had broke out in fresh quarters; their numbers were hourly increasing; the whites, who had encamped themselves in such a manner as to form a chain of posts through the northern districts, had been overpowered, at two different places, and killed in great numbers; and the insurgents, flushed with success, were marching, in great force, towards the town.

Every preparation was, accordingly, making for defence. A retreat was anxiously secured to the ships in the harbour; on board of which the women, the children, and the infirm, were immediately conveyed, and whatever was portable of the most valuable effects of the inhabitants. All that remained were ordered immediately under arms, and even the mulat-

---

1 Tacky's Rebellion (1760) in Jamaica, an unsuccessful slave insurrection, seriously challenged the planters.

toes, more faithful to their pecuniary, than their natural interests, were entrusted on this occasion.

Henry and Edmunds, however, pleaded the privilege of foreigners and temporary visitants, and demanded exemption from the service. They did not stop here; but, in pursuance of their former resolution, applied immediately to the commandant, for permission to depart from the island.

"We have no power over you, sir, or over your attendant," replied the commandant, addressing himself to Henry; "and certainly shall consider it as our duty, as far as our distressful circumstances will permit, to facilitate your departure. We cannot, however, but be sorry, after the report that has been made of your conduct and intrepidity, on more occasions than one, to lose the honour of your assistance at this crisis."

"Sir," replied Henry, warmly; "when I drew my sword upon the behalf of those to whose laws I owed no allegiance, it was not to defend the interests of a father; it was to prevent cruelties and horrors, as I imagined, not, to promote them. This was my moral compact. This compact is now dissolved.

"As foreigners, sir, we interfere not with your internal regulations; as men, we will not participate in your crimes. We are natives of a country where the vilest criminal suffers only death; and we will not fight for those whose logic is racks and tortures."

This rebuke may be thought to have been a little imprudent, under impending circumstances. But to speak his mind with bluntness was at once the characteristic and privilege of an Englishman; and foreign authority bowed before the established right.

If it was not thought prudent to resent this answer, it was at least thought prudent to get rid, as soon as possible, of the man who had the temerity to make it; and, as it was found necessary for the general safety to send some dispatches to Port Paix and St. Nichola Mole, Henry was informed, that he and his attendant might be accommodated with an immediate passage to those harbours; in one of which he could not fail of meeting with some vessel or other about to depart for Europe.

Henry and Edmunds embraced the opportunity with pleasure; if pleasure be not too strong an epithet for that partial relief from the feelings of depression and horror of which their minds, in the present state, were capable.

They went, almost immediately, on board; and, before day-break the ensuing morning, took their final farewell of the atrocities of Cape François.

It was an additional relief to find among the crew of this vessel the English sailor whose sympathy had induced him to put an end to the sufferings of Aboan.

"Brave, good fellow!" said Edmunds, shaking him heartily by the hand, while they were talking of that tragical event, "I love and honour thee. Thou hast bowels of compassion, notwithstanding thy rough profession.

Thou canst feel for the sufferings of thy fellow being, whatever be their features or complexions."[1]

"Fellow beings!" replied the sailor; "avast! avast! master, none of that patter neither: though I am a rough sailor, and no scholar, I know larbord from starbord too well to enter that upon my log-book.

"As for fellow creatures, or fellow *beings*, as you call them, I hav'nt sailed so long in the fleet, without being able to know them by their rigging gun shot off. One may call a Scotchman to be sure, or an Irishman, a fellow creature; and so perhaps, for aught I know, one may a Welchman, or these here French fellows, or the like: but as for these black lubbers, why every body knows they are nothing but a sort of monkies: though they do jabber a little: and matter of that, I'll never believe but what the other monkies could talk too, if they would, as well as Christians; only they know that if people knew as how they could talk, they would be obliged to work also.

"But what of that? Man or no man, b—my eyes if I see why a monkey, or a dog, should be used in that way: and d— me if they shall, when I'm by, for all the mounseers in the world."

"Thou art a good fellow for that, however," said Henry; "but what makes you suppose that the blacks are not men as well as yourself?"

"Why as for that, your Honour," resumed the sailor, "when I was a boy, and used to go to church o'Sundays, I remember to have heard the parson there read from the pulpit, as how God created man in his own image: and I should be glad to know, sir, whether you or any man in his senses ever believed as how God Almighty was a blackamoor, and had great thick lips and a flat nose, like these here fellows?

"Besides, sir, did you ever know a negro that was able to climb aloft?"

This latter argument, in particular, was so conclusive, that neither Henry nor Edmunds ventured to make any reply. The latter, indeed, was somewhat impatient under the imputation thrown upon his sable brethren; but the former conceived it to be of little importance how erroneously the poor fellow might reason, so long as he acted right.

CHAP. II.

*The Adventures of a Coasting Voyage from Cape François
to the little Island of Margot.*

Coasting Scenes.—Sympathy and Sagacity—An afflicting Spectacle.—
The Rescue.—The Island of Margot.—Nautical Remonstrances.—Indications of a susceptible Heart.—The Forlorn-hope.—An interesting Conjecture.—The new Leander.—The mysterious Disappointment.—

---

1 The British sailor resembles the character of Williams, a similarly plain-speaking figure in Thelwall's play *Incle and Yarico* (1787).

The Inscription.—Romantic Visions.—The Boat.—The imprudent Messenger.—The Sailor's Panacea.—Retrospect and Explanations.—The Delusion.—The fortunate Coincidence.

THE Captain of the vessel, among other things, had it in commission to keep as near to the shore as possible, that he might observe what was passing, and be in the way of collecting occasional information.

Conformity with these instructions, occasioned our voyagers to be spectators of many a scene of horror. Devastation and ruin strode along the coast; and, as far as the eye could reach, it was every-where presented with desolated villages and plantations.

But when they had passed by the narrow mouth of the bay of Acul, objects began to present themselves still more afflicting to the sympathising heart. Crowds of unhappy wretches, who had escaped the general massacre, and hid themselves among rocks and caverns from their pursuers, came flocking to the beach, stretched forth their hands, in supplication to the passing bark, as if solicitous to be received on board.

Henry supposing that this circumstance had not been attended to by the captain; immediately applied to him, and offered his assistance in the talk of mercy.

"Softly a little, Monsieur Anglois," said he, "that fetch won't do: for who knows," continued he with a significant look, "but that some of these d—d friends of the blacks, who have found their way among us, may have some lurking trick under the mask, for cutting our throats and giving up the ship's stores to the insurgents."

"Despicable poltroon!"[1] exclaimed Henry, with great indignation— "unsympathising barbarian! are these the vague and shallow pretences under which you shelter your inhumanity, when your fellow-creatures— your country-men, are imploring your assistance? Is this the gallantry of a French officer?"—

"Mighty fine, young gentleman," exclaimed the captain interrupting him; "mighty fine! all this sounds very pretty I confess. But d— me if (when treason is in the wind) I'll trust your prating fellows the length of my nose."

But notwithstanding the perverseness of the commander, the importunities of Henry were not entirely disregarded. He indeed being a confused and muddle-headed fellow, and having more than half intoxicated himself with copious libations of *kill devil*,[2] thought to shew his sagacity, after certain hints he had received from his employers, by suspecting he knew not why, and guarding against he knew not what. It was enough that he was always suspicious. It mattered not whether the circumstances of the case were such as could furnish any possible grounds of suspicion.

---

1 Coward.
2 Rum.

But others of the crew were not so wise. To them it was evident that the proposal of Henry could originate in nothing but humanity. Shame co-operated with sympathy. They were abashed at the idea that a stranger should have more commiseration than themselves for their unfortunate countrymen; and began to importune the captain to lend, at least, so much assistance to the distressed inhabitants, as might enable those who had escaped to the sea-shore, to take refuge on board the vessel, and not to leave them to perish in those rocks and caverns, where famine must devour whom the sword and the conflagration had spared.

During the altercation, the shrieks and shouts and conflagrations had been renewed at no great distance from the shore. But now a spectacle was presented at which all that was not petrified in the heart of man could not fail to melt within him.

Two females, defended by a single negro, whom some stronger sympathy seemed to have prevented from joining his countrymen, were chaced among the rocks by a party of the insurgents. They were overtaken. The faithful negro was immediately struck down, torn into an hundred pieces, and his quivering limbs tossed up in the air, with shouts of inhuman exultation.

For the women, one of them in particular, a more dreadful fate seemed to be reserved. They were immediately rifled and stript, with the most exulting disregard of those feelings of modesty, which now seemed to prevail over every other terror.

But rapacity was soon succeeded by another appetite. The younger of these unhappy victims, who might have excited, in less savage bosoms, all the tender sympathies of the purest and most ardent affection, fired the licentious passions of these barbarians; and each, with equal vehemence, claimed the consummation of his ferocious desires.

Even the most atrocious acts, however, require some subordination for their accomplishment. In the present instance there was none. All were alike inflexible—alike importunate; and uproar and contention, accordingly, ensued: during which time the poor maiden, half dead with terror, was sometimes seized by one, and sometimes by another; and sometimes dragged in different directions, by the brutal competitors, till she seemed in danger of sharing the same fate that had fallen upon her sable protector. At length an athletic negro, more powerful than the rest, had snatched her up in his arms, and was bearing her away in imagined triumph, when his weaker, but unencumbered rival, recovering one of the hoes, which had been thrown aside during the conflict (for many of the insurgents had no other weapon), levelled it with such fury at his head, that it cleft him to the very chin; and the ravisher and the intended victim fell together at the feet of the conqueror; who, in his turn, was preparing also to seize upon his fatal prize; and, at equal hazard, to attempt the gratification of his inhuman appetite.

Disgusted as he was with the conduct and character of the whole creolean race, and heartily as he had repented his co-operation with them,

Henry was not of a temperament to endure such a scene as this. On the contrary, frantic with sympathy, and hopeless of any co-operation from the captain, he drew his sword; and shouting to all who had not the souls of cannibals to follow him, he plunged into the sea; and being an excellent swimmer, made directly towards the shore.

Poor Edmunds, whose sympathy was also awakened, and whose attachment for his master revived with double force when he saw him in this perilous situation, was driven almost to desperation.

What should he do? He could swim no more than a stone. "Must he stand upon that accursed deck, and see his generous master perish before his eyes?"

Fortunately the honest sailor, of whom we have already made honourable mention, and whose sympathy was equally excited, had a more rough and active way of displaying it.

"D— your eyes, you land lubber," said he, "don't stand blubbering there; but bear a hand, and help me to heave the boat out."

The thing was no sooner said than done. The boat was heaved out; and Edmunds, the English tar, and one Frenchman, leaped into it, while the captain kept roaring out, "Mutiny! mutiny!" but not a soul would interfere to prevent them from accomplishing their purpose.

Henry, and the boat's crew arrived on shore at the same instant. It was a critical instant; that in which the victorious negro already, in imagination, believed himself possessed of his wretched, his almost expiring prize.

Of course, Henry and his associates did not pause for a single moment. The former in particular, breathing an invincible spirit of vengeance, rushed to the scene of action, while the others, shouting and denouncing death, as though they had grasped the thunderbolts of heaven, followed him with equal ardour.

In an instant the sword of Henry laid the sable ravisher breathless by the side of his vanquished rival; while the other assailants scattered the astonished and disorderly negroes; who, imagining that the whole ship's crew, and all the thunder of their cannon, were let loose upon them, fled with the utmost precipitation, leaving behind them, not only the apparel they had just made prize of, but all the plunder they had collected in the burnings and devastations of the day.

Of these, the two sailors, with true professional avidity, began immediately to make prize; loading themselves with whatever was rich and gaudy, till their arms could grasp, and their shoulders sustain no more.

Henry, in the mean time, was more benevolently employed. For a few seconds, indeed, he could not avoid gazing, with admiration and tenderest sympathy, on the naked beauties of the maiden whom his heroism had rescued from worse than death; but who still, overpowered with horror and apprehension, lay motionless upon the earth, utterly insensible to her own situation, and to the events that had just taken place.

All the delicate feelings, however, which belong exclusively to the refined and cultivated understanding, rushed immediately upon his heart.

He averted the unlicensed eye; and snatching a loose garment, wrapped it, in the best manner he could, around her, and bore her in his arms to the boat.

Edmunds followed, with such wearing apparel as, lying nearest the spot, appeared most likely to have belonged to her: and the two sailors having also joined them with *their share of the honour*, Henry proposed that they should immediately take to their oars, and endeavour to regain the vessel, which already, with an unslackened sail, had passed the little island of Margot.

"What, to be hanged for mutiny and desertion!" replied the tar, "that the hulking lubbers on board may share our prize-money? Avast heaving, my boys: the wind will never answer in that quarter neither."

Henry no sooner understood the circumstances under which the boat had been seized, and the two sailors had followed him in the adventure, than, considering the character of the captain, the reasonableness of the apprehension appeared in all its force.

But what was to be done? What less than inevitable destruction awaited them on the shore?

There was but one alternative. It was to cross over immediately to the little island of Margot, that lies at the distance of only two or three miles from the shore, over against the port of that name. Thence it was supposed they might probably, in the course of the day, or the next, at farthest, discover some other vessel, by which they might be taken on board, with less hazard to the two brave men who had been so instrumental to the success of the expedition.

The unhappy maiden was still but imperfectly recovered from her swoon, when they arrived at this inhospitable retreat. Henry placed her with her face towards the refreshing breeze, that was just springing up from the sea, and at the entrance of a little natural harbour, formed by the luxuriant vegetation of the climate. He chaffed her temples with his handkerchief, and moistened her lips with some spirits, several flasks of which the sailors, with sagacious nostril, had discovered among the spoil. These attentions soon restored her so far to her faculties, that she began to breathe with greater freedom, and exercise, though with considerable tremor, the powers of articulation.

"Where am I?" exclaimed she, staring around with a sort of vacant horror: "where am I? Into what hands has my unhappy destiny at last consigned me?"

"You are in safety, madam," replied Henry, with respectful modesty; "in the care of one who, though a man and not insensible to the power of beauty, knows how to respect the innocence he has preserved."

"And those cruel negroes?—Where, where are they?" continued she, with convulsive agitation.

H. "They have paid the price of their enormities, madam, without accomplishing their wicked purpose. The most audacious of them fell by this arm, and atoned, with his life, for the violence he offered you."

The lovely Creole felt the full force of these obligations. She was about to overwhelm him with a profusion of thanks, for her heart stood ready at her lips, when her eye (averted by modesty from the ardent, the fascinated gaze of Henry) fell upon the gown that was wrapped around her.

"Heaven and earth!" exclaimed she, "this garment! how came I in this garment?"

Henry preserved a modest silence: withdrawing his eyes, that his looks might create no unnecessary embarrassment, Edmunds observed the like delicacy.

As for the sailors, they might perhaps have considered it as no bad joke, to let the young lady know who had been her tiring woman;[1] but they were quarrelling at a distance from the harbour, over the division of the booty.

"And where—where is the owner?" continued she, in a tone of frantic desperation. "My poor devoted Morton! where is she?"

To those who are not acquainted with the power of one certain impression, at Henry's time of life in particular, to efface all other reflections, and all other recollections, it may perhaps appear surprising that certain circumstances which this question immediately brought to recollection, had never occurred before. Certain, however, it is, that his sympathy for the more alarming situation of the younger sufferer having, in the first instance, predominated in his mind and directed his efforts, he no sooner beheld the charming symmetry of the form he had rescued, and felt the pressure of her arms, as she clung (unconscious what she was doing) to the neck of her deliverer, than every other circumstance vanished entirely from his mind. The companion of her sufferings, and, with her, every idea, of the present or of the future, but what related solely to her safety, and to her accommodation, were entirely forgotten; nor did even the apparel that he had snatched from Edmunds, and laid with assiduous delicacy the side of his lovely protegé, bring to his recollection the circumstance that there was yet another person, about whose destiny both gallantry and humanity would have dictated some anxiety.

He saw the garments that he imagined had once enfolded the charms of this incomparable beauty, and he seized the whole heap, without ever recollecting that there were more than belonged to her: as indeed he would have done, if the whole wardrobe of all the ladies of St. Domingo had been spread before him.

This impassioned enquiry was, therefore, like a thunder-clap in his ears. He awaked as from a dream:

"*Where is the owner?* Good God!" exclaimed he, "ah, where indeed? What has become of her, Edmunds? Heaven and earth! what has become of her?"

Alas! Edmunds had been as forgetful upon this subject as himself. His solicitude had been as undivided, though his heart was not so deeply impressed.

---

1 Lady's maid.

"She is dead, then! She is murdered! Violated and torn to pieces by those horrid cannibals!" exclaimed the afflicted maiden. "My Morton! my poor, faithful Morton! What the torrent had spared, these monsters, more inhuman, have devoured.

"All! all have perished!—All that I have ever loved!—all that have dared to love me!"

"Be comforted, lovely mourner!" said Henry, with great solicitude; "compose your troubled spirits, and let us hope."

"Hope!—comfort!" exclaimed she, interrupting him, with a fearful wildness of tone and gesture—"What are they? There is no hope, no comfort, left for me.—Oh! on what misplaced link in the infinite chain of necessities hang my disastrous fortunes?—All to perish—all—parents, friends, protectors—all!"

"O! say not so, fair excellence!" replied Henry, with impassioned tenderness—"You have yet one friend, if he is not unworthy that distinction—one protector, who is ready to die a thousand deaths—"

"Oh! you are all kindness—all heroism and generosity!" replied she, clasping his hand, with an agitation of mingled passions, and looking at him with great interest. "My friend, indeed!—My preserver!—If such things there were, my guardian angel!

"But fly me—shun me—the spell of evil destiny is upon me, and upon all that would dissolve the charm.

"Leave me—oh! leave me, ere your better fortunes become identified with mine—ere my baneful gratitude shall have learnt to love thy virtues—and thou perish like all that I have loved:—like those more than parents who were whelmed in the fatal torrent—like the gallant negro (that mind magnificent in slavery!) whose limbs are yet quivering on the shore—like my poor Morton—poor, faithful Morton!—She saved my life, at the peril of her own; and I—agony to think upon!—I have fled for safety in the arms of a stranger, and left her to the most horrible of deaths!"

"Saved your life!" repeated Henry, collecting all his firmness, as if meditating some desperate enterprise. "And did the friend I have left unprotected upon yon shore of horrors, hazard her life for the preservation of yours?"

"O yes! she did!" replied the distracted maiden. "During the horrors of the last fatal night, the rapids that swallowed up my beloved parents, had overwhelmed me, also, but for her."

"Then shall she, also, be preserved!" exclaimed Henry, with great enthusiasm. "Be comforted, lady! be comforted!

"Thoughtless recreant that I am! I find I have performed but half my duty. But I will fulfil it immediately. Either you shall hear at least the fate of your friend, or Henry Montfort is a breathless corpse."

He did not wait for a reply, but hurrying away, together with young Edmunds (who was inseparable from his side, in the hour of agitation or danger), to the brave companions of the former adventure,

"To your arms! to your arms, my boys!" exclaimed he; "we must back again to the opposite shore immediately."

"The devil we must!" said honest Ben, hiccuping. "Why, in what point of compass does the wind lay now, noble captain? Have we left any of the rum behind us?"

"We have left one of the women behind us," answered Henry, with great impatience.

"Well, and what o' that?" replied Ben, hiccuping again and staggering; "that's a vessel won't founder easily in these storms, noble captain; though she has lost her rigging. If one may judge of things by their appearances at a distance, she is not in much danger of being ravished."

H. "But she may be murdered, barbarian!"

B. "No hard words, noble captain—no hard words. That's a squall I won't spread my canvas to, d— me. But as for the woman, I'll warrant the squadron we've been alongside of will never pour broadsides into her. I saw her myself scudding full before the wind, with not a sail in chace, while we were launching our pinnace.[1] I'll be bound she's either in tow by this time, or has dropt her anchor in some safe harbour or another."

H. "Then must we go back, and seek her out."

B. "Seek her out? Splice my timbers! I'd as soon calculate the ship's way without compass or log-line!"

Henry, chaffed with impatience and indignation: "We will go without thee, then," said he.

B. "Nay, nay! noble captain; if you are determined upon a voyage of discoveries, let's look to the rigging" (taking up a flask), "and be with you. It shall never be said that Ben lay hulking at his moorings, while the flag ship was beating against wind and tide, and hung out the signal for assistance."

The disconsolate maiden had scarcely arrayed herself (in the inmost recesses of the bowers); scarcely had the waves, that washed the tranquil beach of Margot, closed over the track of the keel, when she began to repent that she had suffered her deliverer to seek again the shore of dangers and of horrors, upon what further reflection represented as so hopeless an adventure.

She would have called him back, but her voice was too feeble to overtake the flying bark: the sea was too loud to give audience to such plaintive melody.

"Montfort! Henry Montfort!" said she, sighing, as she stood a motionless statue, and followed her faithful adventurers with her eye.

Wherefore it was that she repeated this name a thousand times, and every time with deeper aspiration; why the trickling tear sometimes filled the intermediate pause; why, before the bark had even reached the opposite strand, she so prematurely bewailed the untimely fate of her champion, and repined against that cruel destiny that doomed her to be the

---

1 Smaller boat on a larger ship.

destroyer of ALL who interested themselves in her preservation; and finally, why it was, that, while she pronounced this word ALL with so much emphasis, it was the image of Henry alone that presented itself, in vivid colours, to her mind: these are questions we must leave to be determined by any young female of sixteen or seventeen, whose ingenuous disposition has never been chilled and sophisticated by the parades of vanity and ambition, and the sordid maxims of an avaricious world.

Certain it is that gratitude (whether a virtue or a vice)[1] is one of those feelings which uncorrupted natures have the greatest propensity to indulge:—certain, also, it is, that this sentiment would rarely be cherished with less complacency in the bosom of a young female, at the age we have just described, in consequence of its having been inspired by the conduct of a young man of accomplished manners, with a pair of expressive and penetrating eyes, an expansive brow, a clear and glowing complexion, and a commanding grace and elegance of form.

But whatever was the nature and origin of these feelings, they were presently to be aggravated and enflamed to the wildest excess of anguish.

The boat had not long discharged its freight upon the shore, before the neighbourhood of the place where it had landed was evidently a scene of tumult and contention. The flash of fire-arms was distinctly seen by our lovely solitary; and, at length, the report of distant musquetry rolled slowly and sullenly upon her ear.

"He is dead! he is dead!" said she, with frantic agitation: "I have sent the gallant Montfort, also, to an early grave! It is the destiny of all those who interest themselves in my misfortunes to perish for their generosity—to be virtuous, only that they may be unfortunate—and loved, that they may be lamented!"

Heart-broken by these reflections, she threw herself disconsolately on the stony beach, and called upon the waves to cover her.

Henry and his companions, however, in the mean time, were not engaged in the conflict she had imperfectly witnessed. They had hastened from the beach immediately upon their landing, and pursuing the track that was pointed out to them by honest Ben, advanced as far as *Port Margot*, to see if the fugitive had taken refuge there. But the habitations of this port were desolate. Silence and solitude brooded over the embers of obliterated inhabitations, and even vegetation had perished in the general conflagration of revenge.

Even the enthusiasm of Henry was now at a stand. The universal desolation of the country baffled all his hopes, and disconcerted the crude projects which he had so hastily devised.

"What track to trace her by?—What means of enquiry?—Which way to turn?" said he, musing, in an attitude of embarrassment and despondency.

---

1 William Godwin's *Enquiry Concerning Political Justice* (1798), Bk. 2, ch. 2, controversially offered a critique of gratitude as symptomatic of aristocratic oppression.

"Why as for turning, noble captain," said Ben, "if I might advise, our only course is to steer back to the place we came from, and secure our boat, before the enemy takes her in tow."

H. "What!—and return to the disconsolate maiden, after all my boasts and promises, without her poor faithful Morton?"

"Certainly not, sir," said Edmunds, "if you can point out any means by which our search can be further prosecuted, with even the most distant prospect of success.

"But where are we to seek? By what suggestion may we hope to be directed?

"As for shelter of human habitation—here she can never have found it. All around is a smoking desert.

H. "She may have hid herself in the caverns of rocks—in the tangled labyrinths of these woods and forests."

E. "Granted. But in this infinitude of intricacies and possibilities, what instinct shall guide us to the particular cavern, she may have chosen? By what clue shall we be assisted to tread the particular maze she may have trod?"

H. "We will disperse ourselves, in different directions; and call upon her name, at every step. Should any of our voices happen to reach her, it will be an assurance of safety, and draw her from her retreat."

Ben. "Yes, noble captain, and it will be a notice to the enemy where they may find us too much scattered to form a line of battle against them. So that they may bear down upon us at vantage, and rack our single hulks, fore and aft, till we all founder.

"But d— me, you're a heart of oak, and I like you. Never shall Ben hang a-stern when there's danger afloat: So give the signal, my boy, and let's slip our cables at once. Give me the commander that fights all that comes in his way, without counting either guns or metal; and when he can hold out no longer, grapples at once with the enemy, and blows up both ships together."

E. "That may be very well, Ben, when one has no convoy under one's care. But if we should all of us be blown up, in this random cruize, what is to become of the prize?"

B. "Prize?—O! as for that, never mind the casks, my boy—we shall want neither rum nor brandy when it is once come to that."

Henry understood the hint more correctly—

"Ah! what indeed! Poor desolate and unprotected maiden! what indeed! Alone and comfortless on a desert island—where human consolation never perhaps may reach her.

"Let us return, Edmunds—Let us return immediately. Let us shout the name of Morton in our way, that if she is hid among these rocks she may answer to the invitation; but let us hasten again to the island of Margot."

E. "And who knows, sir, who it is that we may happen to find there!"

H. "Who it is! Edmunds!—Who?—What do you mean? Your question seems significant."

E. "I mean, sir, that there seem very strong grounds for the suspicion, that this fair Creole you have so gallantly rescued, can be no other than the accomplished Seraphina."

H. "Seraphina! Seraphina!!!

"Let me consider.—Seraphina!

"But for certain melancholy associations, Edmunds, I could almost wish to persuade myself—

"Seraphina!!!

"Oh, Edmunds!—if it should be so!

"But what are your grounds, Edmunds, for this conjecture?"

E. "The place where we first saw her—so near to the little river that empties itself at port Margot:—the direction in which they were flying—apparently from the neighbourhood of that river:—the rapids that swallowed up her *more than parents*; all alike recall to my remembrance the story of Mozambo's little bark."[1]

"Good God!" said Henry, shuddering, "and that poor negro, then, whom we saw so inhumanly torn to pieces—"

E. "Was, I fear, Mozambo. At least some faint traces of resemblance that struck me from the distance whence we saw him have occasioned the prophecy of the venerable Parkinson to be ringing, ever since, in my ears.

"The wanton fury of his executioners prevented me from satisfying these doubts; and indeed our attention was absorbed by Seraphina herself: if Seraphina indeed it be whom your valour has so fortunately preserved from violation."

H. "Good God! if it should prove so!—Old, venerable Parkinson!—intrepid, faithful, generous Mozambo!!!

"What a commentary is here upon the text of our enlightened and philanthropic host!

"But the name, Edmunds!—It is not Amanda—it is not Mrs. Parkinson we came in quest of; but Morton. What connection could Seraphina have with the name of Morton?"

E. "Why, that is a difficulty, I confess, sir; but not absolutely insurmountable. Amanda and Seraphina were not the only females in the family—and her parents—her *more than parents*, you will recollect, were both of them overwhelmed. But there was a nurse, sir, an old white servant, whose attachment was particularly marked in the narrative of the venerable Parkinson. Why may not this faithful Morton—"

H. "It must be so, Edmunds—by Heaven, it must be so! The lovely Creole I have preserved from massacre and brutal violation, is no other than the incomparable Seraphina; and she whose matchless beauty has

---

1   The story of the attempted escape of Morton and Seraphina, aided by Mozambo, is taken from *A Particular Account of the Commencement and Progress of the Insurrection of the Negroes in St. Domingo* (7-8), or Bryan Edwards, who repeats the same story (3:80-81).

awakened these emotions in my heart, is the same whose transcendent merits had already engrossed my admiration!"

These reflections of course made him hurry, with increased impatience, towards that part of the shore where he expected they should find their boat. But, alas! the beach was scattered with recent slaughter, and the boat was no-where to be found.

Terror and consternation seized upon the minds of the whole party. As for Henry, he was absolutely frantic; and took accordingly a desperate resolution, which nothing but phrensy could have inspired.

We have already observed, that he was an excellent swimmer; and the reader has seen with what adventurous intrepidity he plunged into the sea, in the preceding part of this eventful day.

In the present exigency—worn as he was with incessant fatigue and the want of proper sustenance, he determined to appeal again to the same expedient.

In vain did his companions remonstrate that not a soul of them could swim but himself; that his strength was already impaired; that the damps of night had succeeded to the fervours of day; that the dimness and indistinctness of the light might occasion him to miss the island, and get into the main ocean; where, according to the nautical phraseology of Ben, "be the vessel ever so tight, beating about without compass or steerage, he was sure to founder at last"; and that, even though he should arrive in safety across a strait of two or three miles, destitute of the means of making a fire, or procuring any of the necessaries his situation might demand, the probability was, that he would contract some fatal disease that would put a premature period to his existence.

Equally vain were the entreaties and even the tears of Edmunds.

The thoughts of Seraphina, and of her cheerless and unprotected situation, and the thousand chimerical fears which haunt the imagination of a lover, outweighed all other considerations; and leaving his companions to make their way, in the best manner they were able, to Port Paix (the nearest place where any assistance could be rationally expected), he fortified himself with a moderate cordial, from a flask which Ben had been provident enough to bring with him; and then stripping off every thing but his drawers and calico jacket, he plunged, without more deliberation, into the sea.

Fortune and vigorous constitution favoured his presumption. He arrived in safety upon the little island, and calling on the name of Seraphina, ran immediately to the bower.

But the voice of the lover fell not on the ear of his beloved; the form that had been a lamp to his imagination, and a beacon to his heart, met not his eager glances on his arrival. Seraphina was no-where to be found.

What language can do justice to his distraction!

He ran from bourne to bourne. He explored again and again every nook and crevice. He called; he shouted, till the rocks of the opposite coast mocked him with their echoes; and still, indefatigable in exhaustion, and hoping amidst despair, he repeated the same round with the same diligent anxiety, and wore away the night in unavailing search.

At length, faint and over-wearied, he sat himself down disconsolately in the arbour, where he had expected to have found Seraphina, and listening to the deep roar of surrounding waters, he brooded a thousand visionary disasters, till slumber closed his eyes.

CHAP. III.

The Conclusion of the Adventures in the Island of Margot.

The Inscription.—Romantic Visions.—The Pocket-book.—The Boat.— The imprudent Messenger.—The Sailor's Panacea.—The Delusion.— The fortunate Coincidence.—Tender Solicitudes.

THE fatigue of his body could not so far overcome the uneasiness of our hero's mind, as to secure him a continued or refreshing sleep.

Restless and perturbed, he was perpetually starting, in feverish apprehension, from some dream of horror, in which Seraphina was constantly represented as falling from precipices or ingulphed in whirlpools, from which, with feet rooted to the ground, or withheld by some mysterious impediment, he struggled in vain to attempt her preservation.

At length, weary of this state of dozing, delirium—distracted rather than refreshed, in very wretchedness of soul, he lifted his head from his mossy pillow, and cast his languid eyes towards that glorious luminary which was now beginning to climb up the arch of heaven, and scatter light and nutriment and joy, "to all," said Henry, "but to me!"

He was unjust. It had something to communicate to him also, even in this arborous chamber where he lay.

Almost the first object that presented itself, as he cast his eyes around that scene where formerly he had beheld his Seraphina, was a monumental wreath of flowers, suspended from one of the boughs: such as he had sometimes observed in the village churches in particular parts of England. To this was also attached a paper, with some verses, apparently written by a female hand.

"It must be her's!" exclaimed he, seizing it with great eagerness. "This may perhaps explain the mystery."

Whether it did so, or what else it explained, the reader shall judge for himself; for it was as follows:

INSCRIPTION.

Stranger, whate'er, to this sequester'd bower
Whom chance, or dire necessity, may lead,
O hold it sacred ever. 'Tis a spot
Holy to saddest sympathy—to love

Nipt in the tenderest bud of infant hope,
Ere yet its joys could blossom.
                        Here the breath
Of Henry, sweeter than the pregnant dews
Of aromatics, when the western breeze
Awakes the morn, call'd back the fleeted life
(Life worth the care when it was Henry's gift)
To Seraphina's breast. Here too his eye,
Persuasive in mute eloquence, reveal'd
The welcome tale of passion; and the tongue,
Persuading what it speaks not, sweetly stole
Into the soul's recesses, and infus'd
Its thrilling softness in a virgin heart,
Till then of love unconscious.
                        Bow'r most blest
Were these thy sole memorials—could we here
Close thy brief legend, guiltless of the tears
That flow'd for Henry lost. But here, alas!
Breath'd the unwilling maid the frantic wish
(Frantic with hopeless sympathy), that steel'd
His arm to new adventure: and even here
She, most disastrous! for his lov'd return
Sigh'd, vainly anxious.
                        He no more returns—
No more beneath the fragrance of this bower
Breathes the soft sigh, of magic power, to wake
The sentient chords of nature, and inspire
Life and the living warmth of virgin love
Even in the death-chill'd bosom. He, alas!
For her, untimely, on yon savage shore,
Fell by barbarian hands.—His beauteous form,
In all the bloom of manliness that left
This scene, ill-omen'd, and this aching side
(That with prophetic terrors heav'd too late—
Too late recall'd him anxious), breathless lies,
Gash'd o'er with wounds; with not one pious hand
To heap his ashes in the funeral urn,
Or mark the spot that holds him? Even she—
The cause of all his perils, torn away
By too officious friendship, lacks the power
To do the last sad office; with her tears
Bathe his wide-yawning wounds, and print the kiss
Of agonized affection on those lips,
Clay cold, alas! and lifeless, or those eyes
Which never more from the informing soul
Shall beam ethereal virtue—now extinct.

Stranger (if ever stranger sojourn here),
Drop thou the pearly tribute (Henry so
Had wept o'er thee, so fallen!)—drop the tear
In sympathizing sorrow o'er this wreath—
This frail memorial! and, with pious hand,
Renew the rustic offering; and devote
To Henry's shade, and Seraphina's love:
While she (chance-wafted wanderer!) afar
Bears the dear image, and her joyless youth
Devotes to virgin widowhood and woe.

With what tumult of mingled sensations Henry perused this mysterious paper, may more easily be conceived than described.

Seraphina, it seemed, was still alive!

But to what distant region might she, perhaps, be flown? How was she conveyed? And who could be those friends who having abused her ear,

"By a forg'd process of his death,"[1]

had torn her, reluctant, from the sequestered island?

She had perceived, also, and she returned his passion!

But what availed to him the knowledge of these flattering circumstances?

Should he ever again behold that form, upon which his imagination feasted with insatiable delight? Should he ever enjoy the sweets of communion with that refined, that elevated, that expanded, and cultivated mind?

No: he was unworthy of such happiness. His adverse destiny precluded all such hopes. He was doomed, perhaps, forlorn, and desolate, to perish in that unfrequented island, far from the consoling sympathy of an affectionate mother!—far from his Seraphina!

These, and a thousand tormenting reflections, came hurrying across his brain. But others, of a very different description, occasionally intruded themselves; and he alternately glowed and shuddered.

Seraphina lived!!! Seraphina loved!!! This was something, in the favourable scale of fate, to balance against his apprehensions and misfortunes; something to sustain and calm his agitated spirit, and enable him to endure existence, till Edmunds (if Fortune were disposed to give earnest of her future favours) might arrive, with some vessel or other, and enable him to pursue the lovely mourner:

"And pursue her he would, to the utmost extremity of the poles; though it were but in a common wherry-boat!!!"[2]

Full of these romantic ideas—the hyperboles of youthful passion—he perused again and again, with still increasing delight, the expressions of ingenuous sorrow by which they had been excited. He printed a thousand

---

1 *Hamlet* 1.5.768.
2 River or canal boat, transporting people or goods.

kisses upon every tender syllable, and luxuriated in all the hopes and coinages of an enthusiastic temperament, till imagination realised every wish, and the cheated senses yielded to her dominion:—till rocks and seas appeared already past, tempests encountered, and every danger and difficulty overcome; and Seraphina, with all world of charms, personal and intellectual, and all her heaven of softness, was yielded to his impatient wishes.

Happy infatuation! Realities were forgotten.—His senses were closed to all the horrors of his actual situation, and his fancy luxuriated in nothing but

"Day dreams whose tints with sportive pleasure glow!"[1]

The scenery of romance and the descriptions of poetry seemed realised by the magic of his empassioned enthusiasm. The little island of Margot was another paradise; the world of felicity was begun again: and Seraphina, another Eve, was surrendered in bridal purity to the arms of her second Adam; while

"All heaven
And happy constellations on that hour
Shed their selectest influence."[2]

He cast his eyes upon the surrounding scenery, and fancy still pursued the illusive vision. It was a scene of enchantment!—an Arcadia! a Paradise indeed! fit region for the blessed! an empire—a continent for those who were all the world to each other.

"What couch!" exclaimed he, "what canopy could love require but this delightful bower, formed as it is, in the careless elegance of nature, with twining tendrils of withs,[3] and pendulous shrubs, and scented briars that bow beneath the burthen of their own variegated floriage? What palace can he covet but this clump of stately trees, whose leafy roof, propt on the smooth and towering trunks, the vanity of profusion may imitate, but art can never equal? What domain could he enjoy beyond the boundaries of this little isle, with its miniature diversities of hill and dale, champaign and shade—with the boundless ocean in prospect, on one side; and, on the other, this narrow strait?—and finally, what society could he wish—what society would he suffer, beyond that gentle intercourse, of souls—that reciprocation of thoughts, of desires, of sympathies—those intercourses of unbounded confidence that constitute the intellectual fruition of united hearts.

"World! and thy giddy vanities! thy toils, thy tumults and savage wrongs, farewell! we renounce thee for ever. Solitude and seclusion shall henceforth be our society—if that can be called solitude where all that is estimable is concentrated.

---

1 Samuel T. Coleridge, "Kisses" (1796), l. 9.

2 John Milton, *Paradise Lost*, 8:511-13.

3 Any pliant twig or bough, as of willow or osier, and more specifically the creeping plant *Heliotropium fruticosum*, of Jamaica, used for making baskets.

"Flow on, thou vast separating ocean! Embrace us still around with thy green splendours. Still heave and swell in all thy variegated sublimities! Let the wild conch of the triton still resound—roar in rude tempests to the maddening world; but plain and brawl, as now, in gentlest murmurs on our beach; for this is the stormless residence of love! The region of sequestered virtue! The little universe of Henry and Seraphina!"

While he was thus raving and soliloquising, in a state of mind little short of insanity, his eye glanced for awhile (by chance or by natural sympathy) on the chaplet, which he now regarded, not as a funereal but a hymeneal trophy; when, half hid by the little sprays that trailed along the ground, he thought that he discovered the shining clasp and morocco covering of a pocket-book.

He stooped. He was not mistaken.

"Whose should it be?

"It must be Seraphina's!"

He opened it—he beheld—he kissed the name with fond idolatry. He hugged it in a transport to his bosom.

He explored its contents.

What lover in such circumstances could have done otherwise? Say, ye fastidious slaves of ceremony—who know nothing of morality but its decorums—of manners, and what ye call politeness, nothing but the forms—could even you have neglected, at such a time, the opportunity of diving a little deeper into the secrets of a heart, a part of whose invaluable treasures you had already so undesignedly discovered?

But the pocket-book of Seraphina had no secrets to divulge. It was a page of purity: the tablet indeed

"of a virgin heart
"As yet of love unconscious."[1]

In one place some flower, or some curious plant, lay folded between the leaves; in another the pencil had sketched some prominent beauty of the landscape—some rock of romantic form—some water-fall—some clump, gay in the luxuriance of youthful vegetation—or the fading foliage of some time-shattered tree. A third was conscious of some effusion of the muse; but it was a strain, for purity at least, which vestals might have chaunted at the altar, while angels bent down their ears to listen—a strain of rapture waked by the beauties of surrounding nature, and animated by the generous sympathies of a feeling heart.

These were decisive traits: and though Henry was no pupil of Lavater's, he had as firm a faith in the physiognomy of a pocket-book, as ever that penetrating visionary had in the form of an eyebrow or a contour.[2]

---

1 Probably Thelwall's own poetry.
2 Johann Kaspar Lavater (1741-1801) wrote *Essays on Physiognomy* (1789), translated from the German by Thomas Holcroft (1745-1809), friend of William Godwin and fellow treason trial defendant in 1794. When Thelwall edited and wrote for the *Biographical and Imperial Magazine* (1789-92), Lavater received considerable attention.

Beneath the inner clasp of this pocket book he found also, another treasure. The travelling inkstand, and the silver pen with which Serphina had written the inscription which had given birth to all his visionary raptures.

This was inestimable. He also, was inspired; and Seraphina was his muse. Seizing therefore the pen, with a sort of divine enthusiasm, and, recurring to the romantic project he had so lately been brooding over, he wrote the following rhapsody on the back of the very paper that contained the little poem of Seraphina:

ADDRESS

To the Bower of Margot.

Bow'r of delight! beneath whose fragrant shade,
Gay with profuse luxuriancy, the Fair
First wak'd—first felt—first own'd (tho' but to thee,
In sweet sequester'd privacy) the pang
Of love reciprocal, and mourn'd, as lost,
Joys yet untasted—joys that provident Fate
Treasures, with brooding avarice, till Time
Mature their full increase; that so the hours,
Love-crown'd, that, in Fruition's saffron robe,
With bridal gaiety, come smiling on,
With ample restitution, may atone
The wrongs of adverse Destiny; and Love
Repeal Misfortune's malice!—
     Blissful bower!
Yes thou, who knew'st Love's sorrows, thou shalst know
Its boundless raptures: and this gorgeous pomp
Of aromatic fragrance, that to earth
Bends from its arching canopy, with sweets
Curt'ning the mossy couch (fit veil to shroud
Connubial mysteries!)—These pendant sprays,
That shook responsive to the deep-drawn sigh
Of virgin widowhood, again shall wave,
With more congenial tremors, in the gale
Of bridal aspiration!—the rich gale
That with surpassing sweetness shall outshame
Thy spicy odours—the rich gale that flows
Even from the living censor of the heart,
And with imperishable sweet embalms
My Seraphina's love.
    "Wave then, ye sprays,
In prouder fragrance! twine in closer folds
Your wanton tendrils, ye, whose feminine sweets

Cling for supportance to the neighbouring boughs
That bend to your embraces! Shrubs and flowers
Throw all your blossoms forth, and deck the couch
In more profuse embroidery, that so
My fair may view ye with complacent eyes,
And, not unworthy, this the temple prove
Of Henry's bliss and Seraphina's love."

Henry had but just finished this poem, when all visions seemed in a manner to be realised by the arrival of the boat, the loss of which had been the source of so many perplexities, and so many difficulties and dangers.

The paladins[1] of our knight adventurer, had pursued their journey without interruption; for the revolted negroes were driving from all parts, with so universal a concurrence, towards Cape François, that the neighbourhood of Port Paix was, at present, unmolested.

In that port they found their lost boat; and in that port they found, also, what made them hurry back to the Isle of Margot, as fast as their arms could pull them.

Their fears for the safety of Henry were at an end as soon as the boat had brought them in sight of the little bower: for at the entrance of that bower they discovered him also. As soon therefore as the keel brushed against the beach, Edmunds leaped upon shore, and ran, open-mouthed, with his intelligence; while Henry, with a staggering pace and agitated frame, made a feeble effort to meet him.

"They are found! they are found!" exclaimed the young enthusiast, with almost breathless impatience. "Morton is found! and Seraphina is found! They are waiting for our return, on board a vessel bound for England; and I have secured you a passage to accompany them."

Poor, honest, enthusiastic Edmunds! How quickly was all this exulting transport converted into astonishment and horror!

The flushed cheek of Henry changed, while he was yet speaking, to the deadly paleness. His eyes closed; his lips became convulsed; a sudden tremor seized upon all his limbs, and he fell motionless upon the earth.

Worn by incessant and intolerable fatigue, which for almost two days he had endured, without any other sustenance than a single mouthful of spirits; exposed to the night dews, upon the bare ground, with no other covering than his drenched jacket; deprived of the refreshment of sleep by the excessive agitation of his mind; and tost and torn by contending passions, the reader has already seen how the warmth of his imagination and the sensibility of his temperament had been worked upon by the momentoes which the affection and the agitation of Seraphina had occasioned her to leave behind her. Nor will he be surprised that the delirious enthusiasm which succeeded, should so far over-power the vigour of his constitution, that it should be incapable of sustaining the increased excitement

---

1   Knights. Sarcastic allusion to the twelve peers of Charlemagne's court.

and assurance of delight produced by this torrent of abrupt and interesting intelligence.

Edmunds, in a voice of frantic terror, immediately called for assistance to his companions, who while he was posting with the joyful intelligence to his master, had hastened, with no less expedition, to the spot where they had left their booty on the preceding day.

It was not the intention of our tars that it should be lost; and, their eyes informing them, as soon as they landed, that it was still in the place where they had left it, they had crowded all their sail and steered their course accordingly.

The cries of Edmunds, however, occasioned them immediately to tack about and bear down upon the spot whence they had received the signal: in plain English, they hastened immediately to his assistance; and Ben, without any deliberation, applied his usual remedy (the brandy cag)[1] to the mouth of Henry.—This being, indeed, the sailor's universal specific, in all accidents, and for all disorders.

In the present instance, the medicine operated in a favourable way. Exhausted nature revived under the powerful stimulus; and, in a little time, Henry was sufficiently recovered to be helped into the boat, that was to convey him to the port, where all his hopes and anxieties were concentrated.

Still, however, he was in a very debilitated and alarming state: almost incapable of swallowing the nutriment that was offered him, and talking occasionally with a degree of wildness that absolutely terrified young Edmunds.

Under these circumstances, Ben presented his specific again and again; and was not a little indignant at the stupidity with which Edmunds approved the obstinacy of Henry in rejecting the prescription: for Ben had as hearty a conviction as any Jack Tar, in the British, or any other navy, that "if brandy would not save a man, nothing else could."

Edmunds, however, with what reason let the reader himself determine, had much greater confidence in the operation of the welcome our hero was sure of meeting, at his arrival on board the vessel, from the lovely Seraphina.

About the recent adventures of this our acknowledged, heroine, we suppose the reader has, by this time, begun to feel no inconsiderable degree of curiosity. This we shall accordingly proceed to gratify; entering, at the same time, so far as necessary connection obliges us, into some particulars relative to certain of the subordinate, though not unimportant characters of this our tragi-comic drama.

We begin therefore with

"THE FAITHFUL MORTON,"

who was, in reality, no other than the mysterious nurse Edmunds had conjectured her to be.

---

1 Small cask or keg.

In the midst of that scene of horror formerly described, she had no sooner found herself disengaged from the gripe of the ruffian negroes, and their attention exclusively engrossed by Seraphina, than, yielding to "those natural fears that flesh is heir to,"[1] she seized the opportunity (as Ben has already explained) of consulting her own safety by a precipitate flight.

She fled not, however, so far, but that, from the rocks among which she concealed herself, she was able to discern (though not what was actually passing on the shore) yet the boat of the victorious adventurers conveying Seraphina to the little Isle of Margot. But some of the vanquished negroes, flying, at the same time, almost by the very entrance of her retreat, she was prevented from making any immediate use of her discovery.

After some time, however, all continuing quiet, she quitted her retreat, and having clothed herself in the apparel of an unfortunate planter, who had been murdered by his own slaves at the door of his casa, she ventured to approach the beach, in quest of some more contiguous place of concealment, from which she might have a better opportunity of taking advantage of the appearance of any boat or vessel; if any such should pass within hailing, to facilitate her escape, and that also of the sojourners at Margot.

A retreat of this description she at last discovered; and, on entering it, found it already occupied by a party of fugitives, one of whom she immediately recognised to be an English Creole of the name of Maroon.[2]

This young man, whom the inevitable decrees of destiny have foredoomed to make some figure in the future pages of our history, was at that time, in his capacity of a coaster, or contraband trader,[3] upon a *visit* to St. Domingo, and happened to be one of the party at Rabeau's on that fatal evening which Henry was also to have spent at the same place.

Morton, also, by the contrivance of Mozambo, had been brought thither, that she might be ready as he pretended, to wait upon her mistress; but, in reality, that she also might be preserved in his little bark.

There she accordingly had seen Maroon; and had observed, with particular satisfaction, the marked attentions he had paid to Seraphina.

Society in dangers and difficulties is always acceptable. But this rencounter appeared to be particularly fortunate, since there could be no doubt that the interest he felt in behalf of Seraphina, would stimulate him

---

1 *Hamlet* 3.1.62-63.
2 The character's name is usually "Moroon" but the "Maroon" spelling indicates the importance of the maroons, slaves who escaped to form their own societies. Another West Indian meaning of maroon was wild hog (Wimpffen 246).
3 Coasting usually refers to smuggling, but Moroon is also involved in "the trade of kidnapping" (see p. 365), alluding to the practice of press-ganging, or forcibly enlisting others into military service.

to embrace with ardour, every means that accident might offer, or circumstances enable them to devise for her relief.

While they were keeping due watch, from this hiding place, they beheld, with considerable satisfaction, the boat returning from the island of Margot. But the shouts and cries which, at the same time, gathering towards them, from several directions, deterred them from quitting their retreat.

They saw, however, the three men who landed from the boat hastening up an avenue between the rocks, heedless of the surrounding uproar; and, not many minutes after, beheld the same number, and as they imagined, the same persons, driven down, from the same direction, by a party of negroes armed with pistols and firelocks.

A conflict ensued. The fatal discharge took place, which Seraphina had, also, heard; and the whites were slain.

When all was quiet again, Morton, and Maroon, and his companions ventured forth from their den; and seeing the combatants lying mangled and breathless on the ground, they hurried into the boat, and rowed immediately across to the sequestered island. Here they found Seraphina, stretched upon the beach, in the disconsolate manner already described. Their tale confirmed her suspicions; and her sensibility vented itself in all the frantic expressions of self-condemnation and despair.

At length they prevailed upon her (more indeed by force than by persuasion) to quit the disastrous island, and accompany them to Port Paix.

But before she would suffer herself to be torn-away from the bower, which she now considered as the mausoleum of her brave deliverer, she called upon the muse to soothe her agonised heart with dirgeful melody; and penned the tender memorial, with the fate of which the reader is already acquainted.

At Port Paix, they had the good fortune to meet with a vessel which was preparing to sail for England; and which (to let the reader into an important secret) had been fitted out by certain opulent planters of the island, for the purpose of conveying proposals of putting the colony under the protection of the English government.

On board this same vessel, not long afterwards, Edmunds also arrived, and was discovered by Seraphina, while he was actually bargaining for a passage for her as well as his master and himself.

Their mutual surprise—their mutual enquiries, and the throng of consequent sensations, particularly in the mind of our heroine, the reader will in some degree conceive. But the maiden must have loved, and loved like Seraphina—and must have been fashioned, moreover, with those strong and powerful sympathies, that peculiar susceptibility and ardency of mind, which so peculiarly distinguished this enchanting daughter of the fervid clime, who can do justice, in her imagination, to those alternate hopes and terrors, those generous solicitudes and melancholy apprehensions that shook the sensitive frame of our heroine, as she revolved the circumstances that had been described by Edmunds, and the perils that her Henry had to encounter.

Neither did a maiden blush fail to diffuse itself over her cheek, when (in the absence of more painful apprehensions) she called to mind that paper, and those undisguised confessions of a susceptible heart, which by this time, perhaps, had fallen into the hands of him from whom the decorums of the world would have enjoined their most solicitous concealment.

At length the boat that had been dispatched to Margot was seen returning to the harbour.

"If Henry were on board, how should she meet his eye under the embarrassment of these remembrances?—

"If he were not there, what eye could she ever endure to meet again?"

She flew, with anxious curiosity, to the deck; and, far as her eyes could strain, began to count the passengers.

"There were four!—there were four!!!"

The exclamation was no sooner uttered, than, clasping her hands in terror, "Alas, there were only three!"

And then it was *four*—and then it was three again: for it was not Seraphina that counted: but it was Hope: and it was Fear: and the simplest calculations of arithmetic are varying and uncertain when these are the arithmeticians.

But now, both hope and fear were lost in certitude. The boat came under the steerage of the vessel; and four were the passengers that mounted up the side, upon the deck:—Edmunds, and the two sailors,—and Henry.

But what a Henry!—

Where was that manly beauty—that commanding grace—that easy, cheerful dignity—that gallantry of deportment—that ardent voice, and glowing animation of feature and complection that distinguished the champion, the preserver of Seraphina?

Alas! they were flown!

Languor and debility supplied their place. A deadly paleness was spread over his cheek, into which even the presence of Seraphina could scarcely recall a transient glow of animation: and his eyes alone (those dark, rolling, majestic orbs, which had penetrated the soft soul of the virgin) preserved their expressive tenderness, and a portion of their fire.

Seraphina burst into an agony of tears.

Speak to him she could not. But she presented her arm (whiter than the lillies of Sharon[1]) for him to lean upon; and, sad and silent, assisted the faithful Edmunds to conduct him to the cabin.

She seated him in the chair. She propped him with a pillow.—Let heartless prudes enquire what couch she snatched it from. She assisted the refreshing breeze with the motion of her fan, she chaffed his temples with her gentlest hand, and performed every office with such prompt solicitude, that there was no room for any care but her's.

---

1 Song of Songs 2:1; also a white flower.

"I am come, my Seraphina!" said he, at length, with a feeble voice, "I am come to die in those arms (if that be not too great a felicity for me to hope) in which alone I could have wished to live."

Seraphina laid her hand upon his heart. She hovered over him with a look of undisguised affection; and her soul came streaming from her eyes.

"O! do not weep!" continued he—"do not weep for me, my Seraphina. I am not worthy of those tears."

She fell in an agony upon his neck: in such an agony as bosoms like Seraphina's alone can feel—as bosoms like Seraphina's can alone conceive.

Edmunds caught the infection. His sympathising heart throbbed with a degree of anguish he had never before experienced. He joined his tears with those of Seraphina.

"And mourn'd the living Hector as the dead!"[1]

---

1 Pope's *Iliad* 6:647.

BOOK V.
=========
CHAP. I.

The Hero and Heroine proceed on their Voyage towards England.

The true Panacea.—Prudence and Sympathy.—Affecting Remembrances,—Amanda.—A Tale of Woes—The Stratagem;—The Bark;—The Babe with bloody Hands;—Rocks and Rapids;—Heroism of Attachment.—Estimates of Life.—Vows and Protestations.—The Song.

IF there is no balm in Gilead[1]—is there none in the tears of love?

They know little of the nature of man, physical or moral, who are sceptics upon this question;—little of the affinities, reciprocations, and dependencies that exist between the corporeal mass, and what is called the intellectual essence!—little of the power of fancy, of sentiment, of passion over the circulation of the fluids, and the tone or relaxation of the fibres.

Yes—there is a medicinal power in the tears of beauty! There is a medicinal power in the soft pressure of a hand beloved! In the heavings of the sympathising bosom, or the pitying glance of an eye, there is frequently more real efficacy than in all the prescriptions of the college, and all the ingredients of "the materia medica."[2]

Those who have never felt the truth of this, have feelings little to be envied—have little to recommend them in the tenderest relationships of life. One might see their judgments, perhaps, in Change Alley, or the Courts of Westminster,[3] but it would be difficult to associate with them in the circles of domestic endearment, or upon the footing of an ingenuous and confidential friendship.

Henry was not one of these characters. There was in his composition—but the reader knows what there was before this; or it is time that I should fling away my pen. Suffice it to say, that if (in his own words) he "came to die in the arms of his Seraphina," he found that in her presence there was life. His perturbation was soothed by her tender solicitudes, and the feelings by which he was oppressed found vent in a shower of tears:—of tears that could only have flowed in concert with those of beauty—in sympathy with those of Seraphina.

---

1   Jeremiah 8:22: "Is there no balm in Gilead?" i.e., "Is there no remedy, no consolation?"

2   Medieval Latin for "medical matter"; the phrase refers to the branch of medicine that deals with remedial substances. Dioscorides's *Materia Medica* (1st century CE) gives the properties of some 600 medicinal plants and animal products.

3   Change Alley: London street that was the site of gambling in South Sea and other stocks; Courts of Westminster: Westminster Hall was a court of justice until the nineteenth century.

Not that his constitution immediately recovered from the shock. Æneas limped awhile, although the restorative ambrosia of his goddess-mother had been infused into the wound;[1] and the health of Henry, continued for some time in a state of langour, though Seraphina pitied, wept, and loved.

Perhaps, however, his recovery was more rapid than he himself desired: for Seraphina was his nurse.

Yes, she it was who, during the whole of the else-tedious voyage, hovered over his pillow in the hour of restlessness or of langour—who watched his slumbers, sweetened his repast, and ministered the healing draught, with looks and words more healing.

Not that the faithful Edmunds was tardy or inattentive: but what could the faithful Edmunds do better, than leave undone whatever could be done by Seraphina?

Perhaps, the fastidious reader may be inclined to say, that these marked attentions of our heroine were not very prudent. And the pupils of Dr. Gregory,[2] (who consider it to be as indelicate for an English Lady to have any *heart*, as that Don Fererlo Whiskerandus of an ambassador, in that well known anecdote of hosiery, did for a queen of Spain, to have any *legs*[3]) may simper out an "o'fie!" or an "o'la!" and wonder how the *strange creature* could expose herself so.

"Let a man know that one loves him?—No, NOT EVEN THOUGH HE WERE YOUR HUSBAND!"—"*It is* INDELICATE!"

These are cogent reasonings, undoubtedly; and upon *self-evident principles*! and prove, no doubt, that the blushing bride who has yielded the possession of her person to the enamoured bridegroom, upon any other considerations than those of *interest* or *convenience*, is a sort of concubine; and that if she has been so unfortunate as to conceive some degree of affection for the man to whom she has vowed eternal fidelity, it is a sort of criminal misfortune, for which nothing but a life of hypocrisy can atone.

But to what purpose should Seraphina now appeal to such hypocrisy?—To what purpose affect the coyness of reserve. Concealment was, in her case, impossible. In the hour of agonised emotion (under cir-

---

1 In Book XII of the *Aeneid*, Aeneas is wounded in battle by an arrow that his physician cannot remove, and his mother Venus heals the wound with a magical concoction.

2 See his Legacy to his Daughters. [Thelwall's note] John Gregory (1724-73), Scottish physician and author of *A Father's Legacy to his Daughters* (1774), an influential conduct book for young women.

3 Don Ferolo Whiskerandos is a character in Richard Brinsley Sheridan's burlesque satire on stage conventions *The Critic*, first performed in 1779. The anecdote to which Thelwall alludes may be the one recorded by David Hume in his "Essay XIX: Of Polygamy and Divorces," where he remarks that jealousy is sometimes carried so far in Spain that it is considered indecent to suppose that a woman of rank can have feet or legs.

cumstances in which it was no longer *indelicate to feel*), she had whispered her attachment, in the deepest sequestrations of solitude; and groves and bowers had revealed the tender secret.

It may be said, indeed, that this very circumstance rendered prudence and precaution so much the more necessary, and that *decorum* would have balanced the confidence of the lover by the rigid circumspection of the mistress.

But assuredly it ought to be remembered that Henry was somewhat more than the lover of Seraphina—that he was also her benefactor—that obligation had preceded passion—that he had been the champion of her honour, and the preserver of her life, before he was the vassal of her charms. And surely, there is nothing so very criminal in love as to cancel all the prior claims of obligation, and preclude the returns of gratitude.

In the bosom of Seraphina, at least, it had, certainly, no such operation. Might she not consider, therefore, that in so ill an hospital as a ship at sea, where proper attendance is difficult to be had, some solicitude, on her part, was due towards the preservation of one, who had encountered every difficulty, and rushed through every danger to protect and rescue her? And might she not, also, consider (without any very unpardonable heresy) that there are some situations and some circumstances in which the decorums of life are to be regarded as inferior to its duties?

But was not "the faithful Morton" arrived at a time of life more calculated for the performance of duties of this description? Granted. But would her solicitudes have been equally tender, or equally efficacious? Or, might not "the faithful Morton," have become too much the confidant of a rival, to be a willing, or an acceptable attendant upon the couch of Henry?

Not to pro and con, however, with the reader, any longer upon this subject,—a subject, on which in the course of the present book, the heroine herself will have an opportunity of delivering her own sentiments—let us concede, at once, that neither the character nor the habit of our heroine were very favourable to nice calculations of this description. They

—"Were not of her soul, nor understood!"[1]

The child of Feeling and Intellect, rather than Custom and Discretion, prudence was, of all the virtues, that in which she was least proficient: for it was one in which, protected by seclusion, and guarded by the fostering providence of Parkinson, she had hitherto been little exercised: nor was she of a character, altogether, the most likely to be very docile to such discipline.

Her temperament was ardent as her nature was unsuspicious; her heart was sympathising and unsophisticated, (ill fashioned for the little frauds and coquetries of feminine policy!)—and in her mind was more of genius than of subtlety, and a capaciousness perfectly incompatible with the

---

1 Pope, *The Iliad of Homer* (1715-20), Book XXIV, l. 56.

sordid wisdom that considers only self! Add to which, that the singular circumstances of her education had conspired to give a tone of independence to her mind, which those who are very fond of what they call amiable weaknesses might consider, perhaps, as somewhat more than feminine; while the seclusion of the recent years of her life, and the precepts and example of her beloved foster-father, had alike disposed her to consult, in her motives of action, rather the deliberate whispers of internal approbation, than the noisy echoings of a babbling world.[1]

But of this, and of its consequences, enough hereafter.

Suffice it, for the present, to observe that in this instance, in particular, she listened to no other suggestions than those of sympathy and affection. The life of Henry was the first object of her solicitude; and in that solicitude, all other considerations were swallowed up. Not that Morton (as will be seen hereafter) was forgetful of more prudent councils. But whatever influence Morton might otherwise have possessed over the mind of our fair Creole, her admonitions, on the present occasion, effectually lost their weight, on account of the evident solicitude of the monitress to promote the views of Moroon, in preference to those of Henry. So that the only effect produced by her hints and ill-timed suggestions was, that she herself was in a manner precluded from those tender interviews the imprudence or the indecorum of which her presence might in some degree have obviated.

In the mean time, the reader may be well assured that the tenderness of these interviews did not consist in the mere mute pathos of the ordinary sick-bed: that the intercourses of our hero and heroine were not confined to the silent solicitudes of the nurse, and the fretful acquiescence of the patient; and that Edmunds—affectionate and faithful Edmunds, was not satisfied with merely pouring out a medicine, or rinsing a tea-cup, like the retainer of an hospital or infirmary.

They had, on the contrary, much to enquire, much to communicate, and many sympathies to indulge. Some of their conversations, accordingly, were much too interesting, and too much connected with the main business of our history, to be passed over by us in silence.

Among the earliest of these, some would of course relate to the heroism and unhappy fate of the generous Mozambo; to the orphan babe, whom the reader we trust has not forgotten; and to the circumstances of the melancholy catastrophe of Parkinson and his Amanda.

"Alas! my Seraphina!" said Henry, pressing her hand, as she reclined by his bed-side, in the little cabin, while Edmunds sat pondering at his feet—"what confidence can we have in the recompense of virtue in this life, when we think upon what we have seen, and what we have lost?

---

1 Cf. Thelwall, "Lines, Written at Bridgewater," where Thelwall refers to "honours emptier than the hollow voice / That rings in Echo's cave; and which, like that, / Exists but in the babbling of a world / Creating its own wonder" (*Retirement* 131).

"But tell me, dearest girl, if the recital will not tear too much thy sympathising bosom—tell me all the sad story of your misfortunes—all the circumstances of your escape, and of the fate of your benevolent patrons.

"With the substance of the tale, indeed, we are already imperfectly acquainted; but every minutest incident that is connected with the history of Seraphina, and with the catastrophe of so divine a character as Parkinson, must of necessity be interesting."

"Aye—and of such a one as Mozambo too, sir," continued Edmunds.—"Virtuous Mozambo! who is, alone, a sufficient instance that the noblest qualities of the soul can be nourished in the sable breast of a negro, as well as of the lordly white!"

"Oh! they were indeed," said Seraphina weeping, "according to their respective capacities, each in his way, most virtuous. Nor would the good Amanda—if you had known her, Henry, have excited a less generous admiration.

"She had lost, indeed, that for which alone your sex are apt to be interested in ours. Time had disrobed her person of those charms that once fired the hearts of contending rivals; but the beauties of the soul still beamed conspicuous in her countenance; while her conversation, cheerfully sage, and benevolently free, gave charms to instruction, and made even the relaxations of hilarity contribute to the amelioration of the heart.

"She was worthy—Could panegyric say more in her behalf?—She was worthy to be the partner of that good man in whose bosom, for more than thirty years, she had been cherished with unabating affection; and in whose embrace (oh merciless waves!) she perished."

Then after a pause—

"You know, it seems, from the conversation you had with my lamented foster-father, the circumstance of our visit at La Soufriere on the fatal night when this terrible insurrection broke out.

"The evening was most ominously dull. It lacked the guest that should have made it otherwise. But, oh! how was it concluded!

"Mozambo had disappeared, as soon almost as we entered the casa. He was busy, as it afterwards appeared, in collecting and marshalling the gangs over which he was to have the command.

"At length—it was drawing towards midnight, though the company was not broken up—Mozambo again appeared.

"There was a sort of wildness and embarrassment in his countenance, so unusual, as to dispose us readily to credit any dismal tale he might have to tell: and his dismal tale was ready.

"'O madam! missee!' said he, 'you must home mediately. Poor massa ill.'

"'Ill!'" exclaimed we. We did not pause to enquire from whom he had received his intelligence; but, the mules being already harnessed, hastened into the coach—Amanda, and myself, and Morton.

"Mozambo drove us away as fast as the mules could be made to go. But what was our surprise—what were our apprehensions, when, instead of striking into the road that would have conducted us to the retreat, we perceived him just turn his face towards it, as in some agitation, and then whip on the mules towards the wildest part of the neighbouring country.

"'Where are you going, Mozambo?' exclaimed Miranda;[1] 'what have you missed your way?'

"'O madam! missee!' replied Mozambo, 'me not drive you home. Massa no ill. Me save you from black men make insurrection to kill the whites.'

"'And my husband!' 'And my father!' exclaimed Miranda and myself at the same instant.

"'Me save massa too,' replied Mozambo; and lashed away the mules, urging the slow-paced animals to a degree of exertion of which they had never before seemed capable.

"At length we had got so far into the forest that the mules could proceed no farther; and Mozambo, alighting and letting us out of the coach, immediately fell at our feet, and began to implore our pardon, with the most fervent expressions of gratitude and affection.

"He would save our lives, he said, and he would save his master; or he would perish with us; but he could not see the sufferings of his fellow-negroes!—indeed he could not.

"Poor fellow! we could not blame him. I do not blame him now. My sufferings have not altered my sentiments; nor the wrongs I have endured obliterated my sympathy. The atrocities of revolted slaves, can never reconcile me to the tyranny that made them so atrocious!

"In short, we forgave him very freely. I believe, I even wished him success. I am sure I did so in my heart: for I dreamt not of the cruelties that would render success impossible.

"But I expatiate. Suffice it to say, that Mozambo conducted us to our place of concealment, on the banks of the rapid river, that, running through the wild and savage woodlands, empties itself into the sea at Port Margot. Here a boat, that Mozambo had prepared, was ready for our reception; and here we tarried, while he hastened to the retreat for that venerable man whom I called my father; and who, in all essentials of care and solicitous affection, was more than a father to me.

"I need not mention to you the conflict that took place upon the borders of the forest. Mozambo, still faithful, brave, and generous, performed the part of a hero to his countrymen, and of a guardian and preserver to his former master.

"But, alas! he preserved in vain! In vain did he conduct him unhurt through the conflict of contending armies. In vain did he restore him once more to our anxious wishes. In vain did he conduct him to the bark; and, with a thousand blessings and protestations of zeal and attachment, bid him be safe and happy. A short respite was all that the zeal of Mozambo

---

1 A mistake for "Amanda"; the reoccurrence of the error a few lines down suggests that Thelwall may have originally named the character Miranda.

could procure from destiny; and he escaped the fury of cannibals only to be swallowed by the merciless flood."

"And the poor babe?" said Edmunds.

"Aye, the sweet babe! But you shall hear.

"The report of musketry had reached us in our hiding-place, while we were waiting, with anxious expectation, for the return of Mozambo with my father. Judge what was our agitation!—what our terrors! At length, however, they appeared—safe—unhurt—and in the arms of the latter the sweet innocent you enquire about.

"Ah your solicitude was vain, my Henry. He too was doomed to perish.

"Amanda and myself both stretched out our arms to receive him. Parkinson consigned it to Amanda; and she lulled it in her bosom, while he related, in few words, the circumstances under which it had been found, and by whom. I need not tell you, we were interested. Perhaps we were interested the more on account of him who had preserved it: for such associations have great power over the affections; and we had heard enough both in praise and condemnation of Henry Montfort to give him an exalted place in our esteem.

"In the mean time, Mozambo placed us in the bark; bade us, as he thought, a last farewel; and, wiping the tears from his eyes, turned round to rejoin his confederates.

"One of those confederates he had left with us: an experienced boatman, as he said, and well acquainted with the river: for himself, his troop expected him; and they could not act without him.

"For a while, we glided smoothly, though rapidly along; but at last, whether by mismanagement or some unexpected swell of the river, the boat was driven from its midway course; and, being whirled and entangled among the rapids, dashed against a rock, and was engulphed in the eddying pool.

"But this catastrophe was not instantaneous.

"Destruction yawned upon us some time before it devoured; the eddies driving and heaving us from side to side, powerless of all precaution, and conscious of inevitable fate. Our pilot, indeed, as soon as he perceived it impossible to control the eddies, sprung from the boat, before it was too far entangled; and being, like the generality of negroes, a very powerful swimmer, he regained the shores; while Parkinson, in an agony of affection, clasped his shrieking Amanda in his arms, and turning a last pitying glance upon me, awaited his fate in silence. And they perished!—Both perished—They and the sweet babe: swept away into the ocean of eternal oblivion: never to be seen again!

"I too had perished," continued Seraphina, after a tearful pause, "but for this Morton: this mysterious Morton: whose attachment, in some instances, appears almost like devotion; although there is not one point of sympathy, in our characters or sentiments, to account for this phenomenon.

"The rock against which we had bulged is a long, irregular, and narrow slip, that seems, at some former period, to have been separated from the lower bank by the weight and fury of the torrent, and the less tenacious earth beyond. Its ridge is adorned with a mild luxuriancy of withs[1] and underwoods;[2] and, in several places, by some majestic trees, probably anterior in their growth to its insular separation; and which still, venerable in decay, seem to frown triumphant over the revolutions of elements that have raged for generations around them.

"Under other circumstances, it would have been a scene of impressive and awful delight: as it was, its singularities were connected with events of too much importance ever to be forgotten.

"Upon this romantic ridge, Morton happened to be thrown; and being, as you perceive, a woman of uncommon strength of frame and constitution, she struggled up the crags to the top, beyond the reach of the waters. In the mean time a strong eddy had whirled me several times around, engulphed me down, and throwing me again upon the surface, the stream was bearing me away by the edge of this ridgy island."

"And I not there!" said Henry, shuddering—"I not there!"

"No, Henry—but Morton was," continued Seraphina: "and, though in many respects, one of the most timid and irresolute of her sex, affection rendered her heroical: and seizing a pendant with in one hand, she plunged into the water, caught me in her other arm; and with no better hold or safeguard, dragged me, almost senseless, up the rock.

"Oh! Henry! Henry! what an hour of horrors was that! and what an evening! what a night succeeded!

"How my poor heart throbbed within me!—with how wild and terrible an anguish! when, rebuking the officious heroism of Morton, I compared what I had escaped from with what I was. Pent up in desperate and insulated security!—walled and imprisoned by that hideous torrent which had overwhelmed all that, as yet, was dear to my afflicted soul, 'Why didst thou, Morton,' said I, 'why didst thou compel me to be sensible to these miseries?—to live to anguish, and to terror, when every joy is dead, and hope and consolation are no more.'"[3]

She paused a while. Her tears would not permit her to proceed.

"Be comforted, my Seraphina!—be comforted!" Henry would have said: but his own sobs choked up his utterance, and "be comforted," died upon his tongue.

He could but press her hand; and look with eloquent compassion in her eyes; mute and inconsolable himself: while Edmunds was inconsolable as either.

"At length—oh Henry!" continued she, with a mixture of agony and tenderness, "when I recollect these things—when I recollect what since

1   See p. 188, note 3.
2   Small trees or shrubs growing beneath higher trees.
3   This scene evokes Thelwall's feelings on arriving at his Llyswen farm, whose site (at a double-hairpin bend in the Wye river, with rapids above and below it) matches the earlier description of the eddy that claimed Amanda and Parkinson and the ridge above it to which Morton escapes.

has passed—when I consider what thou hast suffered, my Henry, and for whom, I scarcely know, even yet, whether the gratitude I feel to this woman is not irrational—whether this gift of life be in reality worth my thanks.

"Amanda! thou more than mother! generous, venerable, benevolent Parkinson! thou three times more than father! can I ever cease to remember ye—to venerate—to deplore? Ye had no natural punctures—no secondary self-love—no goading vanity—no dread of the world's reproaches, or of reproaching conscience, to urge your solicitude, and dictate your more than parental tenderness and cares. All was pure spontaneous benevolence—elective voluntary kindness. And yet, what parents ever loved so?—what daughter ever was so blest?

"And ye are gone!—gone to the watery grave. And these hands that, in some distant day, ought to have smoothed the pillow beneath your heads, and closed your eyes with filial solicitude—these hands were engaged in selfish struggle with the eddying waves; while ye, unaided and unregarded, were swept from my side and perished.

"Why participated not I of your peaceful oblivion?

"Were it not better Henry, to drink of that cup, to have drank of which is to taste of bitterness no more, than to weep over the graves of those we love, and linger in this feverish world?—where all that we most delight in, and every felicity we enjoy is held upon the tenure of constant apprehension, while misery frequently overwhelms us with so inevitable a certitude as mocks the illusions of hope.

"Amanda!—Parkinson!—What power in nature can restore *them* to this afflicted heart!

"How many are the accidents (even could mortality be thrown out of the calculation) that may tear the sole remaining consolation from these arms?"

"Hast thou one consolation yet?" said Henry, pressing her hand to his heart—"one solitary consolation? and did the bower of Margot whisper to me what that was?"

Seraphina was silent. Her eyes were silent too: the bashful lids had muffled them. But a blush confessed her meaning.

"And can Seraphina," continued he, "doubt of the truth or constancy of Henry?

"What accidents!—What power of Destiny!

"*From those arms?*—May Henry hope to dwell in that elysium? and can there be an event, but that which your attentions have averted, can tear me from such beatitude?

"Ah no, by heaven!" continued he, raising himself in his bed, and clasping her hand between both his own, as he lifted up his eyes—"By that great power I worship there, nothing but death—no accident, no influence, no authority on earth, shall tear me from Seraphina!

"Bear witness for me, Edmunds—or against me—be thou my *accusing spirit*—brand me with infamy—blot me as a contaminating pestilence, if ever I forego my Seraphina, or become a traitor to such unexampled excellence!"

"O compose thyself," said Seraphina, terrified by his earnestness— "Still that poor heart! I will believe thee, Henry; as far as depends on thee, I will believe.

"This bosom is not suspicious, Henry. It used not to be fearful.

"Thou seest with how undisguised—perhaps, how censurable a simplicity (Morton at least will tell me so), I confide in thy integrity and virtue.

"But I cannot practice looks in the smooth mirror of decorum, and dress up my heart with falsehoods. The pupil of Parkinson and Amanda, would make but an indifferent hypocrite, even if accident had not precluded hypocrisy. Neither can I feel by halves, and mingle the tenderness of love with the bitterness of suspicion.

"But my heart is agonised and depressed by a thousand painful recollections; and the remembrance of what I have suffered, makes me fear that I have every thing to suffer.

"But compose thyself my dear Henry! calm thy perturbed spirit. My agitation has overpowered thee: and the catastrophe of this tragic tale would now be more than thou couldst bear: more than I could relate with calmness and collection.

"I will lull you to slumber—I will lull the perturbation of my own mind with some gentle strain—some touch of soothing melody; and, then, in the morning, I will conclude the mournful story; and our mutual tears shall perform the funeral obsequies of departed worth."

H. "Hast thou a voice then, Seraphina, for any minstrelsy that chimes not with the heart?"

S. "No, Henry, I am no actor in that organ more than in others. I cannot sing but as I speak, from a sort of spontaneous emotion. Music has no charms for me that has no passion in it; and both the tune and the sentiment must harmonize with the state of my feelings, or I cannot execute the simplest melody.[1] But such a strain you shall have.

"Did you find no little prophetic theme in the pocket book, that might suit the occasion, and soothe the present wildness of our anguish with a sort of medicinal melancholy?"

Henry recollected it well. "O rocks and pendant woods!" said he, repeating.

"It is that I mean," said Seraphina; and, with a voice most tremulously plaintive, she sung as follows:—

"O rocks and pendant woods! that throw
O'er Limbé's stream a deep'ning shade,
And tinge the eddying foam below
With melancholy hue!

---

1 Seraphina's remarks reflect Thelwall's own musical taste and theory.

Well may your awful gloom the soul pervade,
And claim the pious tribute due
To human woe!

"O stream that 'mong the rocks below,
With loud lament and deep'ning moan,
Art wont in endless course to flow!
Those moans my tears renew,
Well dost thou wail of peace—of pleasures flown,
Or pangs that hopeless myriads rue
Of human woe!

"But should I e'er these haunts forego—
These dark-brow'd rocks, this eddying tide,
For scenes where wayward passions flow,
Rapacious, fierce, and rude!
How to the throbbing heart, from every side,
Would then the deeper moan intrude
Of human woe!"

The strain was indeed medicinal; and, if it brought not sleep, it produced at least a melancholy tranquillity; no ill preparative for the reception of that balmy power; whose presence it was now thought proper to compel by a charm of more potency. This no sooner began to operate than Seraphina retired, as she had promised, to her own cabin—not to enjoy herself, indeed the same tranquil blessing, but to hear what the reader will meet with in the course of the following chapter.

CHAP. II.

In which the Adventures and the Voyage are continued
till the Arrival of the Ship at the Madeiras.

Designs of the faithful Morton.—Moroon.—The Adulteress.—The Ways of Wealth.—Dazzling Prospects.—Female Politics.—Speculations of Love.—Prudent Admonitions.—Moral Indignation.—Midnight Meditations.—Morning Devotions.—A Night of Horrors.—Mozambo.—Mute Acknowledgments.—A critical Similitude.—The Troubadour and the Widow of Tripoli.—The Madeiras.—Deportment of Morton.—Moroon.

IN the early part of the first chapter of the present book, we took some notice of the solicitude of "the faithful Morton" to advance the designs of Moroon upon the heart, or rather the person, of Seraphina, in preference to those of Henry. As we have already given one instance of the heroic attachment of this matron, which certainly entitles her to no small degree of favour, we feel it a sort of duty to rescue her, without further delay, from any injurious suspicions that might arise in the mind of the reader, by declaring, that in this preference she was influenced by motives which (as far as related to herself) were purely disinterested: as completely so, at least, as those of many pious mothers who sacrifice the happiness of their daughters for the sake of a splendid establishment.

The welfare of Seraphina was her only object: and few are the parents who would have proceeded upon better calculations than those of this zealous attendant.

Moroon, though a younger man than Henry, had no capricious father to oppose his union, or to disinherit him upon disobedience. The property he possessed was such as to dread no comparison with the utmost expectations of his rival. It had, also, the advantage of being in a state of very rapid increase; and of dreading no diminution from the insurrections and ravages that shook the devoted settlement of St. Domingo. It stood upon a firmer and broader basis: for he was largely engaged in the two most profitable branches of West-India traffic; a traffic that embraces the whole of the islands; having vessels "on the coast," and vessels in the contraband:[1] and he was said to have an establishment at Bridge-town in Barbados, which surpassed the usual measure of luxurious ostentation, even among the most proud and prosperous of the creolean race.

With all these advantages, he was solicitous (with Morton at least, for he had not mustered courage enough to talk to Seraphina upon the subject) for an immediate marriage.

And what was there to set in opposition to the proposal? Nothing—or what a *prudent* guardian (and Morton was as prudent in this respect as any guardian of them all) would consider as less than nothing—his temper; and his moral character.

With these it is proper the reader should be, in some degree, acquainted. They shall form the subject, therefore, of some of the ensuing pages.

He was one of those many deserted and friendless beings who, amidst the neglects and indifference of those of their own class and complexion, have been fostered by the more generous sympathy of the Mulattoes: a set of people in whose composition vices the most atrocious, and virtues the most rare and disinterested, are frequently so confused and blended, that it is sometimes equally difficult to condemn with sufficient abhorrence, or applaud them with sufficient ardour.

By a woman of this cast he had been taken into protection while he was quite a child, and had been introduced to her husband, a mulatto of very considerable property, and very extensive connections, both in the African trade, and that illicit commerce, which we already hinted is carried on by all the colonies and dependencies of the respective European states.

With these people he had lived till he was about sixteen years of age; and by their liberality had received whatever education the islands could

---

1 See p. 76, note 3.

afford. He had been, also, confidentially entrusted by the husband, and initiated in all the lucrative mysteries of his two-fold commerce.

About this time, however, the wife, who felt herself more neglected by her husband than she had a disposition quietly to endure, began to cast her eyes for redress upon the attractive form and amorous complexion of her foster-son; who, as far at least as features and proportions will go, might certainly be regarded as a very handsome young man.

Moroon was not insensible to her advances. Gratitude was not so strong a sentiment in his mind as to preclude the admission of a more ardent feeling: nor was he so dull as not to perceive, that to neglect the proffered kindnesses of the wife, was to provoke her to seek some means of ruining him with the husband; while by being subservient to her gratifications, he could scarcely fail of promoting his own future interests.

In short, a criminal commerce took place; and that criminal commerce was detected by the injured husband.

The mulatto gave full vent to all the unbridled passions of his cast; and the death of both the criminals would have atoned for the crime, if they had not disappointed his vengeance by a timely retreat to the woods.

What consultations might there pass between them, it is impossible to say: but some detached and solitary facts are notorious: and these we shall relate: leaving the reader, as the world was left, to suggest the connecting links of the series, and form conclusions for himself.

It is known that some few years before when the fondness of the husband was yet undiverted by any other attachment, he had made a will, in which he bequeathed the whole of his property, without restriction or condition, to the disposal of his wife.

It is known that this wife ventured to return home the very night after the discovery of her incontinence, from the dreaded consequences of which she had fled.

It is known that the husband was that very night prevented, by sudden death, from executing his design of altering the will in question: and

It is known that the adulteress was found in the morning, weeping and wailing, by his bed-side, with the will that yielded every thing to her disposal, in her possession.

It is known, also, that young Moroon returned to console the unhappy widow, even before the corpse was taken out of the house; that they continued afterwards to live together in the most open and undisguised intercourses of criminality; and that the young gallant attained, in a little time, so complete an ascendency over the mind of his mistress, that partly by legal transfers, and partly by encroachments, the whole property came to be vested in his possession.

In a civilised country (properly so called), such circumstances would not have escaped the jealousy of legal enquiry. But in such a state of domination as prevails in the West-Indies, what has the watchful spirits of the law to do with these private passions and private transactions? So long as the negroes are kept in orderly obedience, and the subordination of classes and complexions is duly preserved, Juridical Polity is satisfied; and her Argus-eyes[1] may wink over the offences that relate only to the lives and morals of the people.

Besides, the deceased was only a mulatto; and the eventual successor to his property was evidently uncontaminated by any "relationships upon the coast." The reciprocations of patronage and dependence that heretofore subsisted between them, was an unnatural derangement of the established order of things. What had the *white* Creole to do with enquiry, under such circumstances? Should he, with impertinent curiosity, endeavour to develop the nature of the *accident* by which things had been restored to the standard of decorum and propriety. Nay more, what evidence could have been brought into a court of justice upon this subject? None but the testimony of negroes and people of colour; and who does not know that in a case where the life and property of a *white* might chance to be implicated, the unseconded evidence of these can never be admitted at the West-Indian bar?

The property which had been thus transferred by the amorous liberality of our mulatto widow, the gallant neglected no opportunity of improving. Young as he was, he was a perfect adept in commercial mysteries; and he had an avidity at accumulating, only to be equalled by the voluptuous ostentation with which he gratified his own vanity and appetites, and the solitary sordidness with which, to the utmost of his power, he precluded all participation in his enjoyments.

With such propensities and such opportunities, those who know the world, and the West-Indian world in particular, need not to be informed with what rapidity immense opulence was to be there acquired.

Of the woman, however, whose crimes had been the ladder of his fortunes, he was most completely weary. Probably his conscience might now find time to reproach him with the horror of the connection: for his mistress had nothing more to give!

But, as he knew very well that the revenge and jealousy of a mulatto-woman are not to be trifled with, he determined to quit, at once, the connection and the country; believing, that while his present lucrative branches of traffic might be carried on by agents on the spot, he might employ a part of his capital to no less advantage in the metropolis of England; where his appetites (if he had been rightly informed) might at the same time be gratified with a more extensive range of luxurious indulgences.

Previous, however, to his returning home (for so the Creoles, by a curious piece of Hibernianism,[2] describe their settling in a country and a hemisphere they have never seen before), he determined to visit the different islands where his commercial connections lay, to settle arrears, and adjust his future arrangements.

---

1 Argus was a mythological giant with a hundred eyes.
2 Irish idiom or expression.

Upon such errand it was that he was visiting at Rabeau's, when he chanced to meet with Seraphina.

He saw: even he admired: he loved,—nay, inconsistent as it may appear with some other parts of his character, he loved with fervour, almost with phrensy.—He loved like one who (dulled as they might be by education, by habitude, and association) had nevertheless some latent energies in his composition—or at least had the energies of passion. It was not a very sentimental passion indeed: but it was passion fixed and individualised. In other words, he conceived so vehement a desire for the possession of her person, that, among other desperate things he would have done to obtain it, he meditated the design of marriage.

Morton, as has been seen (who had a penetrating eye for discoveries of this description), perceived the first dawn of this attachment, during the visit at Rabeau's; and had hailed it as the promise of a day of future splendour to Seraphina.

The force of this attachment she soon had reason to be satisfied, she had not overcalculated: for during their retreat in the cavern, whenever his terrors so far subsided as to leave him breath enough for such conversations, the charms of Seraphina were his constant theme, and no sooner was the boat pushed off towards the isle of Margot, than the confidence of security letting lose his tongue, he began to be very explicit with the duenna upon the subject; and very importunate with her to make love to the young lady for him: for it was a thing that, to a female of such character and description, he knew not how to make for himself.

To this commission Morton was by no means averse. Her attachment to the family of Parkinson had been purely on the score of Seraphina; and her solicitude to promote her prosperity in the world, was not diminished since she had seen these benevolent guardians swallowed by the whelming waves.

But Morton was on the wrong side, as it is called, of forty; and her ideas of prosperity were not precisely the same with those that may be entertained by some of our younger readers. She conceived, accordingly, that a matrimonial connection with such a property as Moroon's, would be a very eligible thing; but the bringing it about was no such easy matter; for she foresaw that, in the first blush of the business, at least, a man of Moroon's character was not likely to be a very acceptable suitor to a woman of Seraphina's romantic turn of mind:—for romantic is the epithet that *prudence* never fails to apply to all that is disinterested and noble in human nature.

She determined, therefore, even before she had seen her fair ward, and, of course, before she had the least suspicion of any prior attachment, not to drop the most distant hint of the purposed addresses of this gallant, in the first instance; but to contrive, some how or other, to get them fairly embarked together, on board some European vessel, and then, by degrees, unmask her battery, when she could not possibly be baffled by a retreat.

The discovery of Seraphina's affection for Henry, and the distracted state of her mind, on the supposition of his having been slain by the insurgents, of course, did not incline our duenna to change her plan of operations; neither did they produce the least abatement of the fervour of Moroon's attachment: which, we may be sure, was not over-clogged with sentimentality and abstract refinements. It was her person, not her heart, that he desired; and so that he could but obtain the former, it mattered not whether the other were in the grave, or at the antipodes; provided that he who possessed it had no opportunity of producing the pledge, and claiming the other part of the bargain.

The first care of Moroon[1] was, therefore, to persuade, and almost to compel Seraphina to quit the isle of Margot; and afterwards to influence her to take her passage to England, in company with their friendly protector, on board the vessel which they fortunately met with in Port Paix.

"What shall we do, my dearest Seraphina!" said she, "in this land of horrors? Where now shall we seek for security? Who shall console?—who shall protect us here?

"But though you have lost your dearest friends, let us not lose the opportunity of securing that which may enable you to befriend yourself.

"I know the generous intention of your departed patron. I was a witness to the will he lately made in your favour. Let us repair to England, then, and seek out his agent. In all probability the counterpart may have been transmitted to him. If not, the claims of kinsmen may be suspended, by my testimony, till the returning quiet of this place gives an opportunity of having it properly searched for; and the property, at least, which was destined for your future comfort, may be preserved."

To this argument, which Morton regarded as of unquestionable potency, the ear of Seraphina was deaf.

Fortune and future subsistence were things she could not brood upon. Life had to her no prospects; and therefore no futurity.

But, "if she might not be permitted to weep away the wretched remnant of her existence in that bower, where her eyes had first encountered those of Henry—if she might not be permitted to seek his mangled body on the fatal shore where she had sent him, to perish by a miserable death, climes and regions were to her indifferent; and she had little repugnance at being torn from a polluted country, already guilty of the untimely death of Parkinson and Amanda; of the faithful Mozambo; and of her gallant Henry."

The arrival of Edmunds, and afterwards of Henry, while things were in this state, was of course not quite as acceptable to Morton as to Seraphina. Our duenna, however, had her notions of things derived from her own experience, and she did not, therefore, abandon her designs.

It was necessary, however, that her inexperienced mistress, or ward— for the connection was now of so ambiguous a nature, that it is difficult to

---

1 A mistake for "Morton."

say in what relationship she considered her—It was necessary however, so to play the cards that this inexperienced creature should not be provoked, rashly and inconsiderately, to throw herself under the protection of her lover, and embark on board some other vessel; and Morton, therefore, evinced not the slightest disapprobation of her conduct, till they were out of the harbour. Then, indeed, she imagined herself secure of having time and opportunity enough to bring the child to reason. For as for that love which defies all reason—she herself (though not extravagantly overdone with rationality) had never known it. She believed it to be the exclusive attribute of the other sex; and as for the tears, and faintings, and hysterics of young ladies upon this subject, she believed them to be of precisely the same description with those into which they will occasionally fall about a gauze flounce or an assembly ticket, and to be just as easily cured, by persuading them to be still more desperately in love with some other gaudier, and more attainable bauble.

That her reasoning might have been applicable enough to more young ladies of sixteen or seventeen than one in the world, may probably be readily believed. But whether Seraphina was one of the number, the reader may judge for himself.

Be this as it may, the die was no sooner cast, or, in other words, the anchor was no sooner weighed, than our duenna began to unmask her batteries, or at least to throw a few hand grenades,[1] or so, against imprudent attachments and indecorous behaviour, and the like.

We have already noticed the effect of these first interferences. Morton, however, was not discouraged. She thought it absolutely impossible that any young woman in her senses, situated as Seraphina now was, could think of rejecting such an immediate establishment as Moroon had it in his power to offer, when all the advantages of that establishment were set in a proper point of view before her. She determined accordingly to try the effect of her eloquence upon the subject without delay; and accordingly, as soon as Seraphina returned to her own cabin, from the tender scene we have so recently described, she began to address her as follows.

"I trust, my dearest Seraphina, that it is not at this time necessary that I should make protestations of my zeal and attachment to you, or my anxiety to promote your interest. It is now about five years since, on your account, and yours only, I entered into the family of Mr. Parkinson, and, devoted as I was to your service, removed with them to this strange island, and their solitary hermitage."—

"Surely, my dear Morton," said Seraphina, interrupting her, with a look and tone of affection, "it is not necessary to recall these, the smallest of the obligations I owe you, to my remembrance. You do not suspect me, I hope, of being deficient in gratitude or tenderness towards you? In an essential point, where my own heart must judge for me, I have not,

---

1 The expression is not in fact anachronistic: the *OED* notes that since the seventeenth century it designates an explosive missile thrown by hand.

indeed, implicitly followed your advice. Implicit following, you know, is one of the maxims which my departed foster-father never taught.

'Not such the precepts from his lips I drew.'[1]

But do not therefore suppose, that I have forgotten the affectionate attendant—the companion, the benefactor, the preserver."

"Ah, my dear Seraphina," resumed Morton, with emotion—"by the dearest of those names, and by one still dearer, if I dared to name it, I would conjure you to consider, what interest but yours I can possibly have, in any advice I may be disposed to give you."

S. "None, Morton—none. But you may mistake my interest. You may seek to promote the happiness of youth by recommending that which youth can neither desire nor relish. You may wish me to anticipate the ambition of maturity, or the rapacity of age, which, as yet, at least, are crude and indigestible to my nature, and neglect the more generous feelings of uncorrupted youth, which hereafter I may have no appetite to enjoy: and you may call it wisdom to tear the unripe fruitage of winter from the bough, while the perishable treasures of the summer are yet untasted."

M. "Ah, Seraphina! be not so overgreedy of these summer sweets, as to forget that winter will come, and will require her less perishable stores."

S. "The stores of virtue, Morton. I trust they shall be treasured here."

M. "Will the world say you are treasuring them now, Seraphina? Will the world call it virtue—call it discretion—call it decorum, to be sitting day and night by the bedside of a young man—a stranger, whom you had known only a few hours before you gave way to these familiar attentions."

S. "A few hours, Morton!!!—Heaven and earth!—but what hours!—Under what auspices did that acquaintance begin, of which you speak so irreverently?

"A few hours!!!—And are there then no circumstances of attachment that preclude the vulgar measurements of time?—no proofs of merit—no claims of gratitude of such spontaneous growth, as, in all moral calculation, to make minutes more than years?"

M. "Ah, Seraphina!—The world will make no allowance for these circumstances."

S. "Will it not? It is a vile world then, Morton! and thanks to the benevolent instructions of the lamented Parkinson—thanks to the privacy and sequestration in which I have spent those docile years, which are most decisive as to our moral feelings—thanks to those generous sentiments I have inhaled in silent converse with the time-honoured dead, with the intellect and virtue of a better age, I am not one of the world's family; nor will be so. From the fountain of my own heart—from the store-house of memory, I can draw those simple but salubrious resources, that render me independent of the luxuries, the gauds, and the flatteries, and, therefore,

---

1 William Shenstone, "Elegy XXVI. Describing the sorrow of an ingenuous mind, on the melancholy event of a licentious amour," l. 88.

of the opinions of that world. The heart of my Henry and the bower of Margot are universe enough for me; and, in the mere scorn and hatred of such a world as thou hast depicted, Morton, I would attempt to realise the vision suggested by the fond delirium of my generous preserver, rather than bow the stubborn virtue of my spirit to sentiments so depraved and corrupted."

M. "Ah, Seraphina! these romantic notions will ruin you.

"If you could live upon the wild berries that grow in that fatal bower, they might do very well. But you are going to a country, in which scraps of old-fashioned learning, and quotations from the poets and philosophers of antiquity, will be of little value, unless they are written on the back of bankers' drafts.

"You are young, and you are handsome; but, at best, you are not rich—perhaps you are entirely destitute. You have your fortune to make in the world; and that cannot be made but by courting the world's opinions.

"But what must be the result of your present conduct? Your character will be blown upon by the passengers—your reputation will be blighted before you have well set foot on the shore of England—and your prospect of an advantageous establishment will be destroyed for ever."

S. "And what is fortune, Morton?—what are establishments—what is character, and even life itself, unless they are enjoyed with my Henry?"

M. "Strange infatuation child!—this might be in character, indeed, if Henry were talking of you.

"But what is this Henry?—A proper man I confess—if one may judge of him in his present state of health? A man, also, of pleasing manners and conversation—and, I make no doubt, infatuated enough with your beauty to do any foolish thing you might desire. It is the privilege and prerogative of man, nay he sometimes calls it his glory, to play the fool at our bidding. Nature has given him personal force, and the laws of society have given him property and power; but Heaven, to counter-balance these advantages, gave us beauty, and education gives us art, to compel him to lay his boasted superiority at our feet, and throw every thing away again for our amusement.

"Happy is that woman," continued she, pulling out a little pocket-glass, and examining the wrecks of her own face, with a sigh—"Happy is that woman who makes the most of the power of her charms, while they last—for they are frail and perishable.

"I once had beauty, Seraphina!—not like yours, indeed; no, not like yours, my child!—I see renewed——I—I confess with——I—I—that is, as I was saying, Miss Seraphina, What is this Henry?—a gentleman—a man of fortune, I confess: but of fortune encumbered by the caprice of a father, who, if Henry should be romantic enough to marry you, would disinherit him to a shilling, perhaps, and leave you to—love and beggary.

"Come, come, Seraphina, you have a wiser choice to make; and one that might be, to the full, as pleasing, even to the eye of youthful fancy. Montfort, we will admit, is a very handsome young man; but, is not Mr. Moroon to the full as handsome?"

S. "Yes! in the moral beauty of expression, particularly, Mrs. Morton!!!"

M. "Expression! romantic nonsense! Are not his limbs as well put together? his features as well formed? his complexion as clear? But the provincial bashfulness of eighteen is not so profuse of amorous compliment, I suppose, as the more cultivated assurance of two-and-twenty, with all alliances and aids to boot, derived from an education in the public seminaries of England. That's the matter.—But then, to counter-balance this, has not Moroon a fortune in immediate and actual possession—unbounded—unincumbered?"

S. "Is his conscience no incumbrance, think'st thou, Morton? Is there no mortgage there? Is the infatuated adulteress whom, if report belies him not, he stimulated to murder her injured husband, and then plundered her of the rewards of that deed of horror—Is she no incumbrance, Morton?"

M. "Calumny! calumny! my Seraphina—Or suppose it were all true as the Gospel itself—In the name of wonder, what has a woman to do with the manner in which her husband procured his property? It is enough for her that he has it.

"I never heard of any law, as yet, that tendered the wife accountable for the actions of the husband.

"Will you—or will Mr. Moroon himself, be respected by one person of consequence the less upon such accounts? Will you have a carriage or a flambeau[1] the less around your door, when you give your routs and public entertainments? Will you have a bow the less from the side-boxes?[2] Will stars and garters[3] consider themselves as contaminated? Will the gentry and nobility of England be more backward in associating with you? Will the foolish populace gaze with less empty admiration on the splendour of your carriage, or the sumptuous decorations of your attendants?"

Seraphina was silent. Why she was so, let the reader conjecture for himself. Morton, of course, concluded that she was dazzled by the picture, and began to feel conviction.

"Come, come," continued she, accordingly—"think again, my dear child! upon this subject—and think more reasonably—Think of the liveries, the equipages, the palaces, the splendour, the consequence, the enjoyments, the opulence, the dignity, the respectability that would be the enviable and envied lot of the wife of Mr. Moroon.

"And it is for the purpose, my dear Seraphina, of laying all these advantages at your feet, that he has broken through every connection—has relinquished, for ever, his native country, and embarked with us in our voyage for England; and, that you may have no doubt of his sincerity, he has importuned me, day and night, to propose to you an immediate mar-

---

1 A lighted torch.
2 A box at the side of a theatre.
3 Decorations of the English knighthood.

riage. You have nothing to do but to name the earliest day you please, after our arrival in England, and the terms of the settlement you require; and he pledges himself, by my lips, to make you mistress of his hand, his heart, his fortune—every thing that your utmost ambition could suggest, or that any heart of the fondest mother could possibly desire for you."

"A mother! a mother!" said Seraphina, emphatically, and looking upon Morton with a severity she had never assumed to any human being before—"You play the mother rarely. But if I had a mother, let me hope, for the honour of human nature, that she would wish me something better than all this—She would wish me a husband who himself was virtuous, and who had the power to make me happy.

"And if she could not discriminate between pageantry and honour—between opulence and respectability—between the sacred intercourses of conjugal affection, and the hireling baseness of a legalised prostitution,[1] I should discriminate between obedience and duty; and shun her society, lest I should become contaminated with her vices."

If Morton had known human nature, she would have spared her tongue the trouble of this oration; and her cheek the confusion of this rebuke. But Morton only knew herself: which is all, by the way (or something more than all), that appears to be known by many of those great philosophers who write dissertations, by the wholesale, on the government of the passions, and the theory of the human mind.

But the reply of Seraphina, and the settled indignation with which she turned away from her, and, without uttering another word, retired immediately to her couch, taught our duenna at least one lesson.

She perceived, that she must either relinquish the cause of Moroon, or her interest in the affections of Seraphina. She perceived, indeed, that she had already shaken the very foundations of that interest; and, in the bitterness of repentance, would, if possible, have trodden back the steps she had taken. But if this was impracticable, she resolved, at least to make all the atonement in her power;—to cut off all intercourse with Moroon, during the remainder of the voyage; to acquiesce, with a good grace, in an attachment that appeared indissoluble; and leave Seraphina, for the present at least, to the government of that discretion, by which alone, it was evident, she had determined to be regulated.

In the mean time, the dialogue did not act as a very powerful narcotic on the sensitive nerves of Seraphina. On the contrary, it strewed her pillow with thorns, and made her bed a couch of restlessness and painful agitation.

"What a woman was this! and what depraved and abominable counsels had she given!

"And yet for her it was, that Henry was a second time exposed to the dangers and horrors of that fatal shore! Through her it was that those dif-

---

1 Seraphina echoes Wollstonecraft's description of marriage as "legal prostitution" (*Rights of Woman* 286).

ficulties and hardships were encountered that produced the present alarming derangement of his health.

"Unjust and profligate!

"And yet to me, at least, the deportment of this woman has been zealous and affectionate. O! rocks and rapids of the fatal stream of Margot!—how affectionate!

"Yet mere humanity—the spontaneous feelings of a powerfully excited sympathy (of which the most vicious characters are not always deficient) might have dictated that exertion. But can mere, transient, momentary sympathy account for those lesser, but reiterated and unwearied, and therefore more demonstrative, proofs of attachment, of which a review of the five last years presented an almost uninterrupted series?

"But what can there be in the composition of Seraphina to excite the partiality of a woman of such principles, and such feelings?

"Is not the attachment of such a character a misfortune—almost a degradation?"

These and a thousand like reflections agitated her mind with respect to Morton. On the score of Henry, her feelings were still more poignant.

All that Morton had advanced for the purpose of weaning her from her attachment, had increased her sympathy, and consequently had given additional ardour to her affection.

"But was her love to be more ruinous than her hate? Was Henry to be disinherited for her? Was her gallant preserver to be ruined and destroyed by her scorpion gratitude?"[1]

The thought was intolerable; and, in the benevolent enthusiasm of her soul, she meditated a thousand disinterested projects, and formed as many fine-spun plausible resolutions; and then, mistaking the imagination for the act, she soothed her perturbed bosom with congratulations on the disinterestedness of her conduct, and the heroical sacrifices she had resolved to make.

"She would watch his sick couch with the solicitude of a *sister*—She would heal him with her sympathy—She would restore him to health—to a fond mother—to fortune and to friends; and then fly, with her disastrous love, far from him and from all human society, engrave his name upon some tree, and trace his portrait on the leaves of that little pocket-book which had been pressed to his bosom in the Isle of Margot, and soothe her melancholy with the recollection of his heroic virtues."

Morning at length arrived; and the lovely Creole quitted her sleepless couch, and repaired to the cabin of Henry.

The cordial had done its duty. He was still asleep: and Edmunds, wrapt in a sort of military cloak, slumbered on a trunk beside him.

---

1 The phrase alludes to the popular belief that if a scorpion were surrounded by fire it would sting itself to death with its own tail. In his poem "Lines, Written at Bridgewater," Thelwall describes "a World most scorpion-like, / That stings what warms it" (*Retirement* 127).

Seraphina drew near. The cheek of Henry was less pale. A healthful dew was perceptible upon his brow; and his lips had regained their colour.

O, where was now the *sister-like* solicitude?—the feeble sympathy—the chilling warmth of relative affection?—Alas! these platonic visions, suited not with the temperament of Seraphina. She felt the lover in her heart. She felt the genuine touch of nature; pure and unsophisticated—warm as her climate, and artless as her years: yet chaste as sainted purity ought to wish—for it could have *but one* object—and nature meant it ONE!

She hovered over him, for a while, with all her soul in her eyes; watched the motion of his breath—(it was soft and regular);

"Fell to such perusal of his face
As she would draw him";[1]

and printed—Will prudery forgive her? No eye beheld it—Henry never knew it—She printed one soft kiss upon his lip; and, throwing herself upon a chair by his side, in an agony of recollection:

"And must thou never be mine, Henry?" exclaimed she.

Her poor heart had burst, had not her tears relieved it.

Henry began to stir. "Edmunds!" said he, stretching out his hand. It was met by that of Seraphina.

She dried her tears.

"Art thou still there, my angel? Thou hast deceived me, Seraphina. Thy eyes tell me thou hast not slept."

"I have not slept, Henry," said Seraphina. "But I have not deceived thee. I laid my head upon my pillow: but sleep was not there. Morton
—'Has murder'd sleep!'[2]

"But you are better, Henry—are you not?"

H. "How can I be otherwise? I shall be well too soon: for then I shall lose your attentions, Seraphina. My consolation, however, is that, if I do, I shall grow ill again.

"But let us awake young Edmunds. I want refreshment. He shall boil my kettle, and you shall make my tea. And I believe, Seraphina, notwithstanding the narrowness of my apartment, the greatest monarchs in the universe have seldom had so much intellect, or so much virtue, employed in such offices about them."

Neither Henry nor Edmunds were forgetful of the promise of our lovely Creole; nor backward in their enquiries into so much as yet remained untold of her perilous adventures, and the fidelity of the generous Mozambo.

"Alas!" said Seraphina, "my mind has been so torn and harassed by conflicted passions, and every part of that dismal tragedy is so fresh in my remembrance, that I can scarcely recollect the circumstances with which I formerly concluded."

---

1 *Hamlet* 2.1.88-89.
2 *Macbeth* 2.2.51.

"You left off, madam," said Edmunds, "at a part which, had it come from any tongue but your own, would have left the hearer in the most anxious state of alarm and suspense. You had just escaped, by the assistance of Morton, to the narrow rock that divides the fatal torrent."

"I had so," said Seraphina—"and there I must begin again.

"All that was left of this disastrous day, and all the night of horrors that succeeded, did we remain on this insulated ridge; dripping and comfortless—shuddering in the dank gale, and shuddering more with horror of our situation.

"No tread of human foot—no sound of human voice, could here relieve our solitude. Instead of these, the circling torrent roared hoarsely in our ears, dashing its white spray in showers around us, and adding a misty obscurity to the fearful melancholy of the scene.

"For me: imagination was diseased. I listened to the deep and solemn roar, till every wave that broke against the rock seemed to waft the death groans of my beloved patrons: and Fancy, that believes against conviction, and realises impossibilities, beheld their departed spirits in every gleam of moonshine reflected by the surrounding vapours.

"Morton was more calm. She expected with confidence the return of the negro who had escaped: and she was not disappointed. The morning came; and with the morning Mozambo, and our disastrous pilot; for the latter had marked our escape to the ridge, and brought our guardian angel to our relief.

"Fastening a with around his waste, and giving the end of it to be held by his companion, Mozambo plunged into the water, and, partly by swimming, and partly by the hawling[1] of the with, brought first one, and then the other of us to the shore.

"But Mozambo was not yet contented with the dangers and difficulties he had encountered; and, instead of waiting for our thanks, with a look of mingled anguish and distraction, twice more did he plunge into the torrent, twice more swim to the insulated ridge, and twice return to us with empty arms.

"'What art thou doing, poor fellow?' said I, as he was plunging the last time—'there are no more to save!'

"'Me honour dem dead,' answered Mozambo, 'me not save dem 'live!'

"It was an act of devotion—a tribute of heroic gratitude to the memory of the departed: and happy are they, who by such unavailing, but innocent observances, can relieve the anguish of their overburthened minds; and substitute the melancholy satisfaction they apparently bestow to the pangs, not less unavailing, of never-ceasing regret!

"The poor fellow now dismissed his companion, and conducted us to another hiding place, somewhat lower down the river; where he entreated us to remain till he could procure another boat, at a place where the stream, becoming both deeper and wider, was of course more tranquil.

---

1 Or hauling.

"Here through two hideous days, and two successive nights (consumed in feverish fluctuation, between apprehension and regrets), he repeatedly visited us; always by stealth; and sometimes in great apparent trepidation; bringing us whatever was necessary for our subsistence; and cheering and consoling us, the best he could.

"And some consolation he did impart. There is a pharmacy in genuine benevolence that is potent in wounds of the heart: and they must lack something of a well-regulated feeling, whose worst sorrows are not, partially at least, alleviated by the contemplation of a disinterested act of virtue.

"At length Mozambo informed us that he had procured a boat; which was stationed not far below us; and in which he proposed to be himself our conductor to Port Margot.

"Under his guidance we accordingly began to trace the margin of the river, to the spot proposed. But our disasters were not yet at an end. The boat was gone; the whole country towards Port Margot appeared to be in conflagration; and escape in that direction was absolutely impossible. Even retreat to our former hiding place was now precluded. Straggling parties of the insurgents were seen in every direction, acting without plan or concert, and driven without leaders, from plantation to plantation, merely by the blind impulses of revengeful fury.

"All was excess and cruelty; and insurrection seemed to become formidable to others in proportion as it became impotent to its own purposed end.

"Poor Mozambo, beheld this scene with an accumulation of afflictions.

"'Oh, misse! misse! how me save you now?' exclaimed he,—'how me do negro men good?—

"'They will not obey their leaders,' said this penetrating savage; 'they will kill the white men first, and then they will kill themselves. But come, misse; come, we will try to escape to the rocks by the seaside. There you may hide in the chinks till Mozambo can get another bark to carry you away.'

"It was in attempting to execute this advice, that we fell in with one of those desultory gangs, of banditti, rather than insurgents, whose horrible ravages were deforming the whole country.

"From these infatuated wretches what had we to expect?—We were whites! Our complexion was a sufficient crime: and what was still worse for us—we were women.

"In vain did Mozambo call out to them that he was himself a captain of insurgents; and that we were *good people, love negromen, and save their live*. He was a traitor and a deserter, that was taking part with their tyrants!—He himself should die.

"You know the horrible catastrophe.

"Poor, faithful, generous, Mozambo! thou hadst the best parts of what we call hero in thy composition. The soul of the negro wanted but a little assistance from knowledge and cultivation, and a most favourable sphere of action, to have ranked among the worthies who challenge the admiration of mankind.

"But what was thy fate? And what might have been mine?"

She turned her tearful eyes upon Henry as she uttered this, with inexpressible tenderness.

It was not gratitude. It was not love. It was something more divine than either—or, to speak more accurately, it was something so divine as nothing but the intimate union of those passions could inspire.

What thanks—what recompense could have been equal to such a look?

Though Henry had bled at every pore, and every joint had been dislocated on the rack, he would have considered himself as overpaid. Yet he did not say so.

There are situations undoubtedly, in which, "from the abundance of the heart; the tongue speaketh";[1] but there are others, also, in which the tongue is mute because the heart aboundeth overmuch.

Such was, at present, the case with Henry. He answered not: but pressed the hand of the weeping maiden to his bosom;

"And sigh'd and look'd unutterable things!"[2]

It was said of Mallet's "Life of Lord Bacon," that the "biographer seemed to have forgotten that Bacon was a philosopher, and that if he should write the Life of the Duke of Marlboro', he would probably forget that Marlboro' was a general."[3] With the same sarcastic spirit of criticism, perhaps, it may be observed that we are writing a book of voyages, and seem to forget that our hero and heroine are at sea.

True it is, indeed, that neither our logbook nor our journal of the weather are very regularly kept: but then it is to be remembered that our business on board is simply with a youth of little more than one and twenty, and a damsel of somewhat less than seventeen, both equally smitten by the blind archer; and whose thoughts had neither steerage nor compass, but what was to be looked for in each other's eyes.

And what are squalls or calms—what are favourable or contrary winds—what is the length or the shortness of a voyage to a pair of lovers embarked in the same vessel, and for whom the shore has nothing to offer but those reciprocations of confidence and affection which, in defiance of winds and waves, they can enjoy, without interruption, at sea?

Suffice it to say, that the progress of the vessel was as slow as that of the affections was rapid; and that the improvement of the health of Henry kept a sort of middle pace between the two.

---

1 Cf. Matthew 12:34 and Luke 6:45.

2 James Thomson, *Summer* (1727), l. 1188.

3 David Mallet, *The Life of Francis Bacon, Lord Chancellor of England* (1740). The quip by William Warburton (1698-1779), bishop of Gloucester and religious controversialist, is recorded in Samuel Johnson's *The Lives of the English Poets* (1779-81). John Churchill, first Duke of Marlborough (1650-1722), was an army officer and politician.

In the mean time his little cabin was conscious of many a conversation that called forth all the finer emotions of the soul.

Love, exalted by generous sentiment, mingled with the refinements of taste, and the enjoyments of intellect; and friendship, humble friendship! sometimes contributed its mite to the full treasury of happiness, and diversified the felicity it would not interrupt. In other words, Edmunds, who of course, and of necessity, indeed, was frequently of the party, was constantly endearing himself to our hero and our heroine, both by the simplicity and the enthusiasm of his character; and still more by the proof of his attachment to them both.

"Well, sir," said he, after they had been walking together for some time upon deck, one clear and tranquil evening, "I think I may now venture to congratulate myself upon the assurance that the tragedy of Jeffery Rudell[1] will not be acted over again to the catastrophe on this occasion; though to say the truth, sir, I was very much afraid of it at one time."

"This Jeffery, it seems," said Henry, smiling, "is a very favourite hero of yours: though his story, Edmunds, is not, I believe, very popular, at this time. Love, my Seraphina! in a few romantic bosoms alone excepted— pure disinterested love, like the knight-errantry it prompted, is superseded by the calculating commercial spirit of the age.

"Prithee, good lad, where didst thou become acquainted with this amorous troubadour?"

E. "Why truly, sir, my researches have not been very profound. In our good country, you know, knowledge is only to be obtained by those who can afford to purchase it. I had my information, where many a poor lad gets a mouthful of knowledge, now and then, to whet rather than satisfy his appetite—that is to say, in a twelve-penny magazine.[2]

H. "Prithee, let us hear the story, Edmunds; perhaps it may be new to Seraphina; and as it is I believe, an undoubted truth, it is not incurious. As a fiction, it would be too wild and extravagant to interest the hearer."

E. "Not if the hearer had our experience, sir.

"But will you have the story, madam, in verse or in prose? for I met with it in both shapes, in the miscellany in question. For my own part, I confess, the former clings most to my remembrance; and perhaps it har- monises best with the story: for the fact itself may be regarded as one of the poetical flights of Nature: such as she occasionally indulges herself in, both in her physical and moral operations; whatever your mathematicians and necessarians[3] may say to the contrary."

---

1 See p. 150, note 2.

2 A magazine costing only twelvepenny or twelvepence, that is, of small value. The remark reflects Thelwall's lifelong interest in the magazine as a medium of self-improvement.

3 Aka a necessitarian; one who believes in the doctrine of necessity, the philosophi- cal doctrine that human action is constrained or determined by inexorable laws of cause and effect. Godwin famously advocated the doctrine of necessity in his *Enquiry Concerning Political Justice.*

"You have only changed the sex of Deity, I perceive, Edmunds," said Henry, smiling, "not dismissed the essence."

"True," said Seraphina, "and his philosophy is as unsound as his theology. These eccentricities, or *poetical flights of Nature*, as he calls them, are, in reality, only the comets of the moral system, and like those of the planetary, are the results of necessities as invariable as the more vulgar phenomena, only that our observation has not been sufficiently extensive, to embrace the more capacious orbit of their revolutions."

E. "This, by the way, madam, is only a presumption, as I conceive; for how are we to know—"

S. "We will dispute this point another time, Edmunds. But in my present turn of mind, I have more inclination for the poem than the argument; and would rather converse with Jeffery Rudell than Sir Isaac Newton.[1]

"You have excited my curiosity. Be kind enough to gratify it."

E. "With all my heart, madam. The poem (if my memory serves me rightly) is as follows; and you will please to recollect that the sonnet, which is introduced, is, in reality, a sort of translation of one of the little poems written by the Troubadour himself during his romantic voyage to Tripoli."[2]

JEFFERY RUDDEL.

"The Bard whose fam'd Provençal lyre
    Could challenge Petrarch's[3] softest praise,
Now feels, alas! a wilder fire
    Than erst awak'd his sportive lays.

"Lo! Fancy's favourite—Fancy's child,
    O'erpower'd by Fancy's fond regard!
O! had her visions less beguil'd,
    Nor cherish'd thus to wound the Bard!

"Or, O! that, else, enraptur'd Fame
    Had never in the enthusiast's ear
Proclaim'd Tripolia's lovely dame;
    The tender cause of pangs severe!

---

1 The works of Sir Isaac Newton (1642-1727), natural philosopher and mathematician, marked the culmination of the scientific revolution.

2 The source of this English translation of Rudel's verse is untraced; it may be Thelwall's own composition.

3 Petrarch (Francesco Petrarca) (1304-74), the most popular Italian poet of the English Renaissance, best known for a long series of lyrics in praise of his beloved Laura.

"For oft, as echo swells the theme,
    O'er-sentient fancy feels the fair
Reveal'd in many a waking dream—
    The matchless form!—the graceful air!

"With more than fam'd Pygmalion's[1] art,
    His thoughts the bright perfection drew;
With more than fond Pygmalion's smart,
    He fights the imag'd fair to view.

"He bids the canvas court the gale,
    Propitious to his ardent flame;
He bids the oar assist the sail,
    And waft him to the lovely dame.

"But spreading sail, nor feather'd oar,
    Are wing'd alas! with lovers' hopes;
And, eager for the happy shore,
    His feverish soul impatient droops.

"Now languid flows the poet's strain,
    Desire inflicts his restless stings:
Till, sinking with the hopeless pain,
    Thus, to his harp, the lover sings:

'Fain would my pensive soul be free;
    'Yet Death thy wish'd oblivion stay
'Till these fond eyes my love shall see—
    'My love, alas! *so far away!*

'But, ah! how many a doubt alarms!
    'Will she not scorn, ye Muses, say,
'The bard who roves to hail her charms
    'From native home *so far away?*

'O thou, creation's genial Lord,
    'Who mad'st whate'er these eyes survey,
'And her, thy master-piece ador'd,
    'The dame I love *so far away—*

---

1   According to Ovid's *Metamorphoses* (1st century CE), this legendary sculptor and
    king of Cyprus fell in love with his own ivory statue of an ideal woman. In answer
    to Pygmalion's prayer Venus transformed the statue into a woman, whom he
    married.

'O give me yet to baffle death
  'Till at her hallow'd feet I lay,
'And yield in murmur'd sighs, my breath
  'To her I love *so far away*.

'Tho' pale disease awhile refrains
  'Upon my drooping frame to prey,
'Yet still I feel a thousand pains
  'For her who dwells *so far away*.

'No other form can joy impart.
  'To her I'll tune my parting lay.
'Cold is to all but her my heart,
  'Or be they near or *far away*.'

"Thus Rudell sung, and o'er and o'er
  Repeated oft the plaintive strain.
His prayer was heard. Tripolia's shore
  'Twas giv'n the drooping bard to gain.

"The fair one meets him on the strand.
  Her looks the pitying heart bewray.[1]
Eager he clasp'd the proffer'd hand:
  Then sigh'd his soul—*far—far away!*"

The subject came too near to the hearts of our lovers to leave their judgments at liberty for any very severe criticism. Numbers were not requisite, in this instance, nor the embellishments of fancy, to awaken their sympathy. They sympathised relatively, as it were—as the mother sympathises over the sufferings of her child; merely because it does suffer; not like the stranger, who must be tricked into pity by the exaggerations of eloquence and the plaintive harmony of well-arranged syllables.[2]

Thus rolled the hours, the days, the weeks, the moons, till the vessel, with snail-like expedition, arrived at the Madeiras;[3] where it touched for the benefit of water and fresh provisions: having been driven out of its due course by the stress of unfavourable weather.

Morton in the mean time threw no further impediments in the way of this tender intercourse; but on the contrary, as if desirous of making the

---

1 Expose or reveal.
2 The passage echoes Adam Smith's definition of sympathy in *The Theory of Moral Sentiments* (1759) as the sharing of another person's feelings when imagining oneself in the other's situation. Smith illustrates the definition with reference to "the pangs of a mother, when she hears the moanings of her infant that during the agony of disease cannot express what it feels" (12).
3 Portuguese archipelago in the North Atlantic.

only atonement that could restore her to the confidence and affections of Seraphina, she seemed anxious to give the lovers every opportunity in her power, of enjoying the sweets of reciprocal confidence, uninterrupted by the eye—unparticipated by the ears even of officious friendship itself.

This alteration in the conduct of the duenna, did not escape the observation of the creolean rival: nor did it fail to stir in his bosom all the gloomy and resentful passions of his nature. He had been at the outset of the adventure very confident of success. It is true, that making love (to a woman of character and virtue) was a business he did not understand. But he had supposed that this, like any other bargain, might be conducted by a confidential agent, and that a woman, of course, like any other commodity, might always be bought out of hand, if you were not ready to bid high enough, notwithstanding a previous contract might have been half concluded.

What could prevent him then? His agent was an adept in this species of contraband; and he had immeasurably outbid, with the tempting advantage of prompt payment, all that his competitor could promise, with the hazardous necessity of a long and uncertain credit.

He no sooner, therefore, perceived the coldness of Morton, than he suspected that he must have been outbribed by his rival, and consequently betrayed; and he proceeded, accordingly, to load the duenna with the most costly presents; and to offer her, her own terms in remuneration of her trouble, if she would bring the business to the desired conclusion. His presents she very readily accepted; thinking, perhaps, that she had sufficiently earned them by what she had already done: but she as explicitly declined all further interference in the affair—informing him that it was evidently the fixed determination of her fair ward to give no ear to his proposals; and that she should lose all her confidence, and all her affection, if she ventured even to hint at so disagreeable a subject any more.

From that time, Moroon meditated nothing but revenge. But, malignant and watchful as his feelings were, he could neither find nor create any proper occasion effectually to discharge his malice; nor even, during the whole of his voyage, to disturb the confidence of the lovers, or retaliate upon Henry the jealous torments of his own breast.

Like another devil in Paradise, his mind was torn and lacerated by the sight of happiness he himself could never hope to enjoy; but as he found himself incapable of casting them out from their felicity, he very wisely determined to cast out himself; and, accordingly, took the present opportunity of landing with all his baggage at the Madeiras, and deferring the prosecution of his voyage to England.

This, indeed, might have been the more readily expected, on account of certain traits of his character, not reckoned indeed among the *high* heroical, but from which, perhaps, many much more celebrated heroes have not been entirely exempt.

In short, nature had not forgotten to mingle in his composition a due proportion of those precautionary feelings, to which she has prudentially entrusted her preservation. Never were instinctive apprehensions more diligent, or keener sighted; nor ever centinel on the watch-tower of a beleaguered city more ready to give warning of the most distant danger. If they were censurable in any thing, it was only in a too scrupulous discharge of their duty: or, more strictly speaking, in occasionally sounding the alarm bell, as in the present instance, when the enemy was not in motion.

To descent from allegory to unsophisticated prose, Moroon had conceived a very terrible idea of the courage and impetuosity of Henry; and, as he himself would have made no sort of scruple of taking any sort of revenge upon our hero, from which he was not prevented by his own timidity, he was seriously apprehensive lest his rival (who had, apparently, no restraints of that description) should, upon their arrival in England, take the liberty of calling him to account, in what is called a *gentleman-like manner*, for his presumptuous pretensions to Seraphina. He thought, therefore, that a better opportunity than the present could not be expected, for preventing the possibility of an *explanation*, for which he was so ill prepared.

CHAP. III.

Adventures in the Bay of Fonchiale.[1]

An extraordinary Project for preserving a young Lady from Ruin.—
The Matron worldly wise.—The double Seduction.—The platonic
Attachment.—Old Heads on young Shoulders.—A Dissertation on
grey Beards.—Filial Remembrances.—The snare.—The Portrait.—
Reciprocations of Tenderness.

IT had been well for Seraphina, if the zeal and affection of Morton had been as uninventive as the jealous malignity of Moroon. But her faculties were more accommodating, and she had to work with more malleable materials. She began, about this time, to have certain views, of which it is necessary to enter into some explanation. True to her original object, that of promoting the interests of her ward (that is, interest, simply and properly understood, according to the dictionary of Lombard-street[2]); and perceiving the absolute hopelessness of accomplishing her purpose according to her first design, she began to vary her means in order to secure her end; and to consider in what way the present attachment might be rendered most advantageous—or, rather, least disadvantageous: for she had no doubt (but for the infatuation of Seraphina to the person of Henry) that her charms, her accomplishments, and her understanding might claim any match, or any rank whatever in society to which she

---

1 Aka the Bay of Funchal, in the Island of Madeira.
2 A London street that was a centre of banking and mercantile transactions.

might think proper to aspire. "But the thing was irremediable. The ardour of a tropical climate, and the romantic nonsense which seclusion and Parkinson's ridiculous system of education had conspired to foster in her mind, had turned the girl's brain, and rendered her perfectly indocile to all prudent advice or government. All therefore that could possibly be done was, to prevent her from being absolutely ruined by her unfortunate passion."

And how was this to be effected, thinkest thou, gentle reader?—Truly the project was extraordinary—the idea was indubitably original; and deserves enrolment among the ingenious, and patented inventions of the day. In few words, the wily politician Morton, out of pure, sheer, outrageous zeal for the interest and welfare of our heroine, entered into "*a conspiracy with herself*" so to bring matters to bear, that this innocent and amiable young woman should become, not the wife, but the mistress of her impetuous, but undesigning lover.

Yet, strange as this method of averting the ruin of a young lady of seventeen may, by some at least, be thought, upon Morton's system, the design was perfectly consistent.

She considered, as has been already seen, the intercourse between the sexes merely as a piece of chicanery; in which the female was to gratify her ambition and promote her worldly prosperity, by playing upon the infatuation of the other sex. Had Henry, therefore, been in present possession of his fortune, or independent in his expectations on the caprice of others, no Argus[1] could have been more watchful of the chastity of her fair ward, or more sedulous to preclude the lover from all opportunities of obtaining the gratification of his passion, till *the price of matrimony* had been solemnly and legally paid. But the character of old Montfort was well known. He had been for some little time a resident at La Soufriere (as may be concluded from what was said upon the subject of his second voyage, towards the conclusion of the first book of our history), previous to his return to Jamaica: and all his dispositions and peculiarities, as well as those of his son, had been subjects of general canvass, in that part of Saint Domingo, as soon as the latter arrived at the plantation. Morton, it will be readily believed, was one of those who always took care, every time she escaped from the retreat, to make herself mistress of all the news, and scraps of secret history (true or false), that were afloat in the settlement. She, accordingly, was in possession of all that was generally known about that capricious and crabbed old gentleman: and she rightly concluded from the premises, that should Henry marry Seraphina, without this old gentleman's consent (and it was clear to her conception that with it he never would marry her), he would, at a dead certainty, be totally and absolutely disinherited.

Now as for that thing called virtue in the world, in any of its shapes or denominations, Morton was one of those profound philosophers who

---

1 See p. 210, note 1.

considered it altogether as a mere bubble[1]—the phantom of fools, and the stalking-horse of those who have wisdom enough to aim at better things. She would not, it is true, have committed a robbery—for she abhorred a rope; or a murder—for she was afraid of ghosts, and of the devil (and indeed, to say the truth, she was by no means deficient in human sympathy); but as for becoming a sort of accessory after the fact, the reader has heard already, from her own lips, how little any thing of that sort would have troubled her conscience.

With respect to female chastity, in particular, this was a bubble of bubbles—a commodity in which she would have trafficked, at any time, wholesale or retail, with as little remorse as though she had been a West-Indian by birth, and all womankind had been negroes. And she did verily believe that no rational woman (whatever rout might be made about it) did ever set one-shilling value upon it, further than as it might be subservient to her more essential interests.

Mistress and wife she considered as terms of perfect indifference, any further than as certain valuable privileges appeared to be attached to the condition of the latter; but which she regarded as more than counterbalanced by any material difference in the condition and property of the persons with whom the respective connections were to be formed. Thus, to be the wife of my lord, was certainly more eligible than to be his mistress; but the mistress with a splendid equipage was still more superior to the wife in a hackney-coach: or, to come home to our case at once, it was better to be the mistress of Henry Montfort, while his fortunes and expectations were unimpaired, than to aspire to the idle distinction of being his wife, at the expence of his being disinherited, and stripped of all that could make the connection (in any shape) *rationally eligible.*

But Morton had recently seen sufficient reason to conclude that her mode of reasoning was not of the most convincing nature to Seraphina; and she feared that her arguments, on this head, might appear as inconclusive to *so romantic a girl* as those she had advanced in favour of Moroon; and consequently, instead of bending her to her purpose, might, in reality, put her so much the more upon her guard. She prudently determined, therefore, to put her trust in stratagem, rather than in logic; and neglected no opportunity of fanning the flame that glowed in the ardent bosoms of these lovers; or leaving them to indulge their tenderness in all the privacy that amorous stealth could wish for.

Nor did she even rest here. She marked the impetuosity of Henry's passions; and determined to play upon them to her purpose. To him, therefore, when she happened to meet with him alone, she would occasionally unbridle her tongue in all the wantonness of description, lavishing her praise on the form and personal attractions of her fair bed-fellow—the softness of her bosom, the fine proportion of her limbs, the symmetry and harmony of their combination, and the spotless purity of that pale half-

---

1 Something unsubstantial, worthless, or delusive.

blushing tint which was diffused over and gave animation to the whole,— these and every like topic would she occasionally introduce that could rouse the youthful passions and stimulate desire to madness.

Could the passions of Henry have permitted him to see through this artifice, his generous virtue would have taken the alarm, and his abhorrence of the baseness and treachery of the duenna would have rendered him the circumspect guardian, rather than the betrayer, of the innocence of the ward. But Morton (for reasons that it would not be difficult to suggest) happened to understand our sex better than her own; and she contrived, accordingly, so to play her cards that the suspicion of any design in these conversations never once entered the head of our lover.

In the mean time she had a very different game to play with Seraphina. The person of Henry, indeed, was every now and then to be introduced into conversation, as a subject of rapturous panegyric: but this was to be touched with a much more delicate hand. The main battery of her artifice, in this quarter, was directed against the generous sympathy that formed so conspicuous a trait in the character of our heroine.

"Well," would she say sometimes, as they sat at work together, "this Henry is certainly a noble fellow, my Seraphina: and his attachment to you surpasses all I ever met with, either in actual life, or in romance, I cannot wonder at the passion you feel for him; nor blame you, hardly, for your determination to reject, for his sake, more advantageous offers.

"But is it not a pity, my dear Seraphina, that so charming a young man should be ruined by so unfortunate an attachment? Tell me truly now, does not your conscience sometimes reproach you, when you think of the probable consequences of this union? and that this elegant youth, who has been nursed in the very lap of splendour and luxurious indulgence—for this one act should be disinherited, by the fantastical curmudgeon his father, and reduced perhaps to absolute want and wretchedness?"

It is not impossible but that these suggestions were intended as appeals to the prudence, as well as the sympathy, of our heroine. Certain, however, it is, that it was in the latter point of view only that they were either felt or understood, and as such they never failed to make a powerful impression on her mind, and throw her into a state of the deepest melancholy and dejection.

Under this dejection she never failed to recur to her former resolution of making a disinterested sacrifice of her happiness to what she considered as her duty, by flying for ever from the presence of Henry, as soon as they arrived in England, and burying herself in some obscurity, where she might

"Mourn in virgin widowhood her fate."[1]

And this resolution never failed to last, till the presence of Henry scattered it to the winds. Morton had sufficient reason to congratulate herself on

---

1 Possibly from Sir William D'Avenant's *The Siege* (1673), 5.245-55.

the progress of her machinations. The desires of Henry became evidently more and more impetuous, and the sympathy of Seraphina more poignant; and the wily politician began to persuade herself that there was but one impediment to the full accomplishment of her design.

This impediment was no other than the watchful solicitude of young Edmunds. This generous enthusiast had conceived, as may already have been apparent, a very considerable degree of attachment for our charming Creole. He looked upon her indeed as a sort of divinity—a being more exquisitely perfect than belongs to the condition of humanity; and he contemplated her many excellent qualities, and even her person, with a degree of satisfaction which, if Henry had known it, might almost have made him jealous.

In short, the sentiment he felt for her only was not love, because it had a spice or two of awful admiration more than consists with the familiarity of that passion; or, to discriminate more accurately, he loved with devotion, as Henry did with desire.

He loved, also, the cause of virtue; and some of the pathetic scenes that had passed between Henry and Seraphina in his presence (particularly when the recollection of the circumstance of their first interview—the adventures in the bower of Margot, or the catastrophe of the venerated Parkinson, tore them with conflicting passions, or dissolved them in tender woe), had excited his apprehensions.

Upon such occasions he had seen the guardless lovers, not unfrequently, heart throbbing to heart in equal sympathy, and locked in mournful embraces.—Yes, they were mournful: the embraces of agonised affection—of tenderest sorrow. But he saw the fire that scorched beneath their tears; he knew the ungovernable passions of the one—he saw the unbounded confidence—the unsophisticated simplicity of the other; and he trembled for the virtue of Henry and the innocence of Seraphina.

These are grey-bearded reflections for a youth of eighteen!!!

Grey bearded?—I fear they are reflections that grey-beards rarely indulge—unless, indeed, the innocence endangered is found within the pale of their own relative attachments—a daughter! or at most a niece! Such instances excepted, it is not to the experienced sordid ones that we should send endangered virtue for protection. No: it is from the ingenuous ranks of youth—of youth as yet untainted by the world, yet warm with generous sympathy, and flushed with the gracious modesty of nature, that purity, if any-where, must expect her champions; not from the veterans, who have been trained and exercised in the frontless vices, which who mixes with mankind must assuredly encounter, and from which, who mixes much is in much danger, at least, of contamination.

The tender familiarities that began in sorrow—and it is in sorrow that these dangerous familiarities are aptest to begin—It is in the tears of sympathy that seduction seems fondest to embathe herself.—These tender familiarities, rendered habitual in the hours of melancholy, were of course not entirely forgone as grief subsided. Innocent of designed impropriety, the infatuated lovers guarded not their hearts against the danger of unpremeditated surprise; nor ever seemed to reflect that there is within the youthful bosom a power, which, if it be once suffered to make presumptuous head, it is not in the government of youthful virtue to control.

But, alas! the conspirator within was now provoked and assisted by the intrigues and confederacy of a powerful enemy from without.

The reader, will of course, perceive that we allude to *the faithful Morton!*

As lookers on, it is said, frequently see most of the game—for they have no cards of their own to mind, and no passions to blind them—it will not appear extraordinary that this youth should penetrate further than the lovers themselves into the designs and machinations of this woman. He soon indeed began to look upon her as not much better than one of those convenient lady abbesses who initiate young novices into the nunneries of King's-place, or the cloisters of Covent-garden;[1] and, as it was not possible that he should look so far into her bosom as to perceive the whole of her motives, he even concluded her (as we generally do conclude the vicious part of mankind) to be many degrees worse than she actually was; and imagined that she wished to betray the virtue of her ward, for the despicable purpose of making, at some future time, a merit of her treachery, and pleading it as a recommendation to personal rewards and advantages.

These suspicions, as he had no confirmations, he did not, however, venture to express. But he watched, with more particular circumspection, the conduct of the lovers—knowing that Adam and Eve were likely enough to fall without the addition of a serpent to tempt them.

He determined, also, to take the earliest convenient opportunity of remonstrating with his patron upon the danger of his situation, and making some powerful appeals to his generosity and his virtue.

Such was the posture of affairs—such the designs and feelings of the parties, when the vessel arrived in the bay of Fonchiale; the sole harbour of the ridgy, but luxuriant and beautiful Island of Madeira.

While the ship lay here at anchor, it, of course, soon became almost empty of its living cargo; who, scattered over the beach, or up the country, luxuriated in the pleasure of treading, once more, upon firm land; or were busily employed in procuring the rich wines or more salubrious water of the island: for Bacchus and the nymphs[2] both revel here; and in equal triumph.

Henry, the while, pensive and perturbed, indulged his feelings in a solitary walk upon the deck. He cast a transient and a vacant look over the delicious beauties of the scene.

The chaffing[3] surge, the moon-like bay, the castle on the rocky promontory, the town upon the beach, its public buildings, and its sacred

---

1   Edmunds, in other words, regards Morton as a procuress. Thelwall alludes here to a two-volume book about London brothels entitled *Nocturnal Revels, or the History of King's-Place and Other Modern Nunneries* (1779).
2   The god of wine (an allusion to Madeira's wine culture).
3   Probably a mistake for "chafing," meaning fretful or raging when used of the sea.

spire, and the rich varieties of farm and vineyard, cottages of the wine-presser, and mansions of the planter, that decorate the whole southern declivity of this insular mountain, from east to west, from the base to the very summit—these had no charms for Henry. Even Seraphina was for a while forgotten: for his heart was straining homewards; and Britain was a load-star[1] of his eyes. Yet not the clod—not the dull circumstance of native earth—no nor

> "The valleys, fair as Eden's bowers,
> "That glitter green with sunny showers,
> "Or grassy uplands gentle swells,
> "Echoing to the bleat of flocks—
> "Those grassy hills, those glittering dells,
> "Proudly ramparted with rocks!"

COLERIDGE[2]

Not these were the objects of his solicitude. It was filial emotion that, stirring in his breast, made him impatient even of the short and necessary delay that now kept the furled sail idle upon its mast, when the wind, veering to a favourable point of the compass, invited them abroad.

Henry, indeed, had never been forgetful of his mother beyond the measure that the circumstances he was placed under might reasonably excuse. But now she rushed upon his soul, with all that ardour of affection to which her maternal virtues so eminently entitled her: and the thought of what she might suffer, should the news of the terrible insurrection in St. Domingo (as in all human probability it must) reach her anxious ears before any intelligence of his safety could arrive, filled him with the most heart-rending apprehensions.

From these painful reflections Henry was suddenly aroused by the voice of Morton.

"What you in tears, too," said she. "Mr. Montfort! For Heaven's sake, what is the matter with you both? I verily believe that you will kill my poor girl."

"Good God!" exclaimed Henry, starting from his reverie.—"Kill my Seraphina! For Heaven's sake, Mrs. Morton, what do you mean? Is any thing the matter with Seraphina? What?—Where is she?"

M. "Nay, I know not what is the matter. You will neither of you make me your confidant. But the poor girl grows so melancholy of late, and so takes on her, and weeps, and sighs, that I verily believe she will break her heart before we get to England."

H. "Heaven and earth! But where is she, Morton?"

M. "She is weeping by herself in the cabin."

Henry flew like lightning.

Weeping indeed. The beauteous virgin was overwhelmed in tears—abandoned to an excess of woe that looked almost like derangement.

---

1 A guiding star, especially the pole star.
2 "Ode to the Departing Year" (1796), ll. 123-28.

Morton had been lecturing, with more than wonted energy, on the impendent[1] ruin of Henry; and she had worked herself, accordingly, into a more than ordinary degree of resolution to sacrifice her attachment and herself to the welfare (her heart would not suffer her to call it *happiness*) of the man she loved. But though a sentiment of imagined rectitude dictated the resolution, the indocile heart revolted; and torn and agonized with the excess of contending feelings, she yielded up her tender bosom a prey to anguish and despair.

H. "For Heaven's sake, my dear Seraphina! what is the matter?"

S. "Ah do not ask me, Henry—I must not tell you yet."

H. "Not yet?—And has Seraphina then a secret she would conceal, even for a single hour, from the knowledge of her Henry? Unkind and cruel Seraphina! How have I forfeited that generous confidence you could once repose in me?—How have I offended?"

S. "Oh! you have not offended. You are all goodness, all kindness, all generosity and truth.—But Seraphina, alas! is wretched!"

H. "Oh Heaven! Seraphina wretched, and I not know the cause! Is there some grief that Henry cannot cure? At least, let me know it, Seraphina! Let me share it with you; that participation may render it more tolerable; or, at worst, that we may die under it together."

S. "Die!—No, no—my Henry, *thou* shalt not die. Live thou to fortune and to happiness; unblighted by the disastrous love of Seraphina. I will die alone, my Henry. I ought to have died before I brought the weight of my unhappy destiny upon your head: then ought I to have died when my beloved foster-parents (oh! ever to be lamented—honoured pair!) were whelmed in the merciless flood. Some hours of illusive blessedness, it is true, I have since enjoyed—O Henry! *how blessed* some of them have been!—But what a price hast thou paid for them?—But thou shalt pay no more, my Henry! I will not bring destruction to thy arms! A friendless orphan! I will not render Henry, also, friendless! No: I will die guiltless of that, at least."

H. "Can Seraphina die, and Henry live? Alas! what meanest thou, my Seraphina? What desperate project do you harbour in your bosom, that drives you thus to distraction?"

S. "No; nothing desperate, Henry. I am not desperate. I talk of death, indeed—for it is death to live without you. But I will not die. I will live to pray——

"Ah! no—I have no power to pray to.—I lack the wretch's privilege of believing that Nature will change her order for my tears!"

H. "O Seraphina! tell me, I conjure you—by all the love we have vowed together—by all our promised bliss—unconsummated hopes, I conjure you, tell me what is the meaning of this distracting wildness. Kill me not, Seraphina! kill me not with these bewildering suggestions—these heart-rending apprehensions."

---

1 Or impending.

S. "Kill thee—O! no Henry. To prolong that dear life one hour, I would brave all the deaths that you have braved for me. No: I will watch thee, I will soothe thee still; yet, yet a little while I may do so. I will lull thy aching head upon this bosom, if, when it aches, it can find quiet there; and sing thee, when you art over-watchful, to thy slumber—This will I do till you arrive at that native country and that home where you have a kind, a generous, a noble mother. And then——"

H. "What then? my Seraphina! Then you will have satisfied your conscience: you will have paid, with interest, the debt of gratitude; and may fly, without self-reproach, to the arms of some wealthy Moroon, to shelter you from the more insatiable claims of love—Then you will leave to that beloved mother, to whose virtues you do so much justice, the sad office of closing these eyes by which the light of life can no longer be endured, when deprived of their Seraphina!"

S. "O Henry! unjust and cruel Henry! you do not think so meanly of me. You do not so suspect your Seraphina. I need not vow—If there were any thing more sacred to me than my love and my integrity, I need not call on that to witness for me. You know there is no room in this sad heart for any image but that of Henry. No, Henry, no! In the obscurest depths of solitude (a mourning vestal for your sake), I will treasure *this* dear, loved image; I will clasp *this* faint resemblance to my bosom; kiss these unconscious lips: and, night and morning, will still the throbbing anguish of my soul with the soothing recollection that I preferred the welfare of my generous deliverer, to every selfish consideration and prospect of my own felicity."

Henry turned his eyes, for the first time, from hers. It was the little pocket book she was clasping to her heart. Her pencil had traced his miniature resemblance upon one of its innocent pages, to which her feelings had dictated the following

INSCRIPTION.

"Ah form belov'd!—by me belov'd in vain;
Tho' not with sighs unanswer'd: my hard fate
Dooms me, ill-omen'd! with pernicious dower
(Most like the baleful ivy, whose embrace
Blasts the fair tree it hangs on), to confer
Hate where I love, and, with disastrous touch,
Chill where I ought to cherish; or, afar,
In maiden widowhood, to shun those arms
Where bliss alone is folded. Be it so——
I not with scorpion gratitude shall taint
The bosom that has warm'd me. World, farewel!
And thou the world's best treasure! I can pine
Joyless myself; but not to him I love
Bring joyless poverty, or blight the hopes
Fair blossoming on this most flourishing stem

By my contagious foldings. Rather thus
Trailing on earth, supportless, will I drink
The dank cold dews of solitude, and droop
(Since droop I must) yet guiltless of thy bane."

Henry seized the book, with gentle violence. He saw—he read. He clasped the blushing mourner to his bosom.

"O Seraphina! victim of thy own excessive virtue! unjust from too keen sense of justice! and cruel from intended kindness; are these the melancholy visions with which you torment your too-sensible spirit? Is it thus you would promote the welfare of your Henry?

"Has Henry then no heart? Would Seraphina sacrifice her happiness to his prosperity? and could Henry consent to be prosperous by such a sacrifice?"

Then, after a pause—"O Seraphina! Seraphina!" continued he, "how has thy zeal for virtue blinded thee to that good, without which virtue is not? How has thy excessive generosity prompted thee to that which would have been most ungenerous! For Henry's sake you would have killed your Henry."

S. "Killed my Henry!"

H. "Yes, killed him, Seraphina! For by that great Power whom I believe to have made and to sustain me—By him I swear I will not live without you—cannot, Seraphina! It were not life—It were misery not to be endured—

'Trailing on earth supportless!'[1]
"God of heaven! Rather that earth shall drink the ruddy drops that warm this heart—Rather these eyes———"

"O peace! my Henry, peace!" exclaimed she, weeping, and throwing her arms around his neck, "I will not leave you—indeed I will not. Have I torn you thus? rent the dear bosom that I would have soothed? and driven you to delirium? I will not leave you. If you are so infatuated with ruin, take—take it to your heart; enfold it there. It is there it loves to hang.

'Misfortune is enamoured of thy parts!'"[2]

"O call it not misfortune, Seraphina!" replied Henry, kissing away her tears. "Call it not ruin. It is heaven to hold thee thus. To fold thee, thus unreluctant in my arms, to print this unrejected kiss upon those lips—to feel the gentle pressure of thy sweet bosom, thus heaving against my heart.—What can the displeasure of a father deprive me of, for which this—even this, is not an ample recompense?"

S. "Oh! Henry!"

H. "Oh! Seraphina! Sigh not again in sadness, my love!—no, not in sadness. We will not part. No; never while we have life. You are—you shall be mine. There is no power shall part us."

---

1 Henry quotes Seraphina's pocket-book inscription back to her.
2 *Romeo and Juliet* 3.3.2.

He printed a thousand glowing kisses upon her lips. He strained her, with fonder ecstasy, to his bosom. He gazed upon her blushing charms; and kissed, and pressed again; and sighed with ineffable fervour.

The heart of Seraphina was full. It was full of tenderness—of confidence—of unbounded love.

Sigh answered sigh, and endearment succeeded to endearment.

Edmund was not there: and Morton would not interrupt so interesting an eclaircissement.

The hours rolled insensibly away; and the thoughts of separation fled, like the sad dream of yesternight; never to be realised; never to be renewed again.

END OF BOOK THE FIFTH

BOOK VI.

CHAP. I.

Containing, among other Matters, the Arrival of the Lovers in England;
the Renewal of the dissipated Career of Henry;
and the fruitless Researches of Edmunds after Parkinson's Will.

The faithful Morton.—Parting Remembrances.—Honest Ben.—Old
Acquaintance renewed—Amelia.—Symptoms of Decay.—Nerissa.—
Mellowing Tints of Time.—The reverend Emanuel Woodhouse.—
Female Eccentricities.—The Apartment.—The fruitless Enquiry.—
Consolatory Prospects.—Painful Apprehensions.—The Knock physiog-
nomical.—Effusions of Simplicity and Enthusiasm.

THE ensuing day, the wind now continuing to be favourable, and the necessary supplies, together with the crew and the remaining passengers,
being all aboard, the vessel weighed anchor once more; and, without
further delays or interruptions, arrived in the British port. Nor did any
other circumstance worthy to be recorded occur during this part of the
voyage, except a partial degree of coolness, on the part of our hero, in his
deportment towards young Edmunds, and the growing influence of
Morton, who appeared to be making considerable advances in the confidence of both the lovers.

To her it was that Henry entrusted the important business of obtaining
proper apartments for the reception of his Seraphina; to her care he com-
mended her, with the most anxious exhortations to zeal and fidelity, and
the most solemn engagements on his part of liberal protection and unalterable friendship.

Neither was he forgetful of the humble companions of his heroic enterprise. Honest Ben and his French comrade were amply rewarded for their
valour; and the former, in particular, did not bid him farewel without a
nautical prayer or two, in the rough style of affectionate sincerity, and a
hearty wish that his honour were in his majesty's service, that he might
stand to his gun under his honour's command, so long as his limbs lasted.
"But no doubt," added he, "your honour will now make interest to be promoted to the command of the Seraphina, as soon as you can; and, having
seen so much sharp service, will wish to cast anchor, as one may say, and
be port-admiral for the rest of your life."

Henry smiled at his technical cordiality and characteristic bluntness;
and, having fulfilled these lesser duties, with a bosom throbbing with all
the ardour of filial emotion, he hastened to the beloved home of his
infancy.

The feelings of the reader will anticipate his reception—will anticipate
the joy, the transports of a doating mother, and the corresponding emotions of an affectionate son.

But, alas! the joy of their meeting was transient and deceptive. The constitution of Amelia had never, in reality, possessed that vigour which her exterior appearance had indicated. An incurable cancer had been preying (for some years) upon her vitals; the knowledge of which, from a feeling of maternal tenderness, she had carefully concealed from Henry; but which had been fed, during his absence, by the anxiety of her mind, and aggravated by the wildness of her agitation, during the terrible interval that had passed between the first rumours of the insurrection in Domingo, and the news of his safe arrival.[1]

No apprehensions of this kind, however, dashed in the first instance the happiness of Henry; for the glow that health imparted not, was supplied by maternal delight, and from the presence of him for whom her soul had so long thirsted, debility appeared to vanish. Nor were these flattering appearances the mere transient effects of a solitary impression. The safe return of that only individual in whom her heart had consolation or delight, was indeed a cordial of such efficacy, that if any thing could have redeemed her constitution from the encroaching poison of so inveterate a disease, it was undoubtedly this circumstance.

It is even probable that her eager desire to live, now that life had once again an object worth living for, might induce her to believe that her strength was so far renewed as to justify the expectation of a protracted date. Certain it is, that the presence of Henry never failed to impart a partial glow and clearness to her complexion, and an animation to her eyes, well calculated to produce, even in her own mind (had she contemplated her features in those flattering moments), impressions not unfriendly to these suggestions. And although sometimes the lurking enemy within, would so far operate, even upon these exterior appearances, as to agitate the filial bosom with painful sympathy, it was long before Henry conceived any very alarming apprehensions for the life, or even the health, of this affectionate parent.

The reader will naturally conclude that this delusion was somewhat the more easily adopted from the circumstance of the divided state of our hero's affections.

Even those of our readers who carry their notions of filial duty to the highest extent (such of them at least as are not yet approaching to their grand climacteric[2]) may, perhaps, be disposed, under the particular circumstances of the case, to excuse a young man of two-and-twenty, if, even in the midst of parental endearments, the feelings of the lover would sometimes preponderate; and the ardour of youthful passion urge him

---

1   Amelia's anxiety evokes that of Thelwall's mother during his imprisonment under
    a charge of high treason in 1794. Thelwall attributed her death the following
    spring to this period of uncertainty and separation (see, e.g., *Politics of English
    Jacobinism* 102).

2   "[A] year of life, often reckoned as the 63rd, supposed to be especially critical,"
    when a person is particularly liable to a change in health or fortune (*OED*).

somewhat frequently to fly from the monitory solicitudes of Amelia, to that more delightful intercourse of souls which could alone be participated with his Seraphina.

The progress of apprehension in the mind of Henry was not, however, resigned to the mere operation of his own observations. He had frequent hints upon the subject from an old acquaintance whom the reader (after so serious an introduction) may probably be surprised never to have heard of again for so long a time. We allude of course to the humble friend, and *intended* confidant of Amelia—the fair Nerissa—a lady, we confess, whose character and conversation is not so entirely to our taste as to induce us to be perpetually courting her society, but whom, nevertheless, we are not in the least danger of forgetting. But the fact is, that for some time, independent of the period of our absence with our hero in the West Indies, we were little in the way of falling in company with this damsel: however desirous we might have been of that honour.

Her intimacy with Amelia was suspended by the return of Montfort: for Nerissa, as the reader will remember, was then young enough to be, even on that account alone, a sort of temptation in the way of a veteran debauchee of five-and-forty. She was, in addition to this, somewhat pretty: and, in her manner, at least, had a sort of yielding softness, not the best calculated, perhaps, to discountenance the presumptuous hopes of libertinism.

The looks and deportment of Montfort soon made it, at least, probable, that he should presume upon these calculations. And though Amelia was not jealous for herself—(she had soared to better feelings) she was most solicitously so for the innocence of a young female, whose unprotected situation, while it laid her but too open to such attacks, should have rendered her sacred from every unhallowed thought.

The departure of Montfort a second time to Jamaica, produced a renewal of that personal intercourse, the interruption of which had occasioned no abatement of the generosity of a benevolent patron.

Nerissa became, once more, a frequent inmate in Grosvenor-square. She regained not, however, in so ample an extent, the confidence of her penetrating friend. Nine years of that sort of experience to which a solicitous dependant must of necessity have been exposed, had produced some alteration of character; and time is an artist that does not always improve the pictures that are submitted to the retouches of his pencil. His lines are apt to be somewhat harsh; and his colouring a little opaque; and though he sometimes endeavours to conceal his blemishes by the glare of embellishment, and the varnishes of art; the blotches are but so much the more conspicuous to the eye of the genuine connoisseur, who searches in vain for the harmony and simplicity of the original design.

These circumstances were not of sufficient importance to interrupt the thread of our narrative at the time when they occurred: being no way connected with the history of Henry, either at Eton or the University. But now, as, upon our return from a long voyage, we find it necessary to introduce the reader again to some of his *old friends*, we think it not amiss to apprise him how far he must expect to meet them *with new faces*.

Nerissa being now very much about the person of Amelia, and consequently not entirely unacquainted with the state of her health, thought it not amiss to give him some hints (though not very direct) upon this subject. They did not, however, make the impression they deserved, because being accompanied with some officious suggestions of the propriety of his spending much more of his time at home; and Nerissa having, on many occasions, appeared exceedingly solicitous of intruding herself upon his society, he looked upon the whole, in some degree, as a piece of artifice; his youthful vanity entertaining certain suspicions, which, whether well or ill founded, did not in the least dispose him to listen to these moral admonitions, or be more assiduous in his attentions at Grosvenor-square; or less so in the noiseless retreat at Somers-town.[1]

Happy would it have been for our hero, if, upon his return to England, his time and his affections had been only thus divided: Seraphina and Amelia—the mistress and the mother, had conducted through different roads to the same ends of virtue and utility; "and purpled o'er his name with deathless glory."[2] But unfortunately the voyage that restored him to his native land, restored him, also, to many of his dissipated companions, to the habits and prodigal propensities of his youth. The dissipations of St. Domingo had not sufficient intellect or refinement for his seduction. Abhorrence of the whole state and organization of society there, and his contempt for the talents and attainments of those with whom alone he must have associated in the career of prodigality—the novelty of surrounding objects, and the restless dissatisfaction of his mind under the arrangements of La Soufriere, had altogether conspired to give a new turn and bias to his character. Solitude and romantic scenery had awakened the reflective powers and energies of his mind; which, cherished by the enthusiastic morality of young Edmunds (the only being he had met with for a considerable time who had rationality enough to give interest to conversation), had expanded and matured into a sort of philosophical and heroic virtue, which we trust, together with the ingenious ardour of his passions, cannot have failed to recommend him to the affections and admiration of the reader. But the unsteadiness and inconsistencies of his early character, we suppose are not forgotten: and when these are recollected, it will not appear surprising that the recurrence of former associations should produce a re-action of former foibles: that the peccant

---

1 Or Somers Town: area of London (in the present borough of Camden) where Wollstonecraft lived with Godwin from their marriage until her death in 1797.
2 Aaron Hill, *The Fatal Extravagance* (1721), Act 3. (Thelwall may in fact be quoting from Act I of F.G. Waldron's *The Prodigal* (1794), an adaptation of *The Fatal Extravagance*.)

humours,[1] upon the repetition of their accustomed stimuli, should taint once more the frame and system of a mind, whose apparent convalescence had been the effect of temporary regimen, rather than a radical cure.

But the progress of the disease unfortunately was not resigned to the simple influence of these natural causes. As though the original virus were not sufficient to ensure a relapse, provocatives were artfully administered, to enflame its malignancy, and overpower whatever vigour might have remained for its counteraction in the sounder parts of the constitution. The reader will not feel himself very much surprised when he is informed that we allude to the artful and seductive machinations of the Rev. Emanuel Woodhouse.

This sordid and saturnine[2] conspirator was no sooner informed of the return of Henry, than, considering his functions of superintendence also as renewed, he began to regard it as an indispensable duty (to himself at least) to take the best care he could that his office should not appear in the eyes of his employer, either unnecessary or unimportant.

His first care, accordingly, was to apprise, in a circuitous manner, all the most prodigal of the former companions of Henry, of the circumstance of his return; those, in particular, who blending the fascinations of genius with the propensities of voluptuous dissipation, were considered as the most powerful instruments for the accomplishment of his designs.

Nor were any means of seduction, any provocatives of appetite neglected, when they could be thrown in the way of this heedless young man, without suspicion of the design, or of the author.

The pride of Henry co-operated but too powerfully with the intrigues of Woodhouse. Could Edmunds have been heard, the moral Edmunds would have advised a more prudent course. But he alas! was no longer of the privy-council.

The decline of his influence has been already marked: and though, in the first instance, the alteration in the deportment of his patron consisted only in a sort of cautious shyness (the causes of which the mind of the reader may, perhaps, with little difficulty suggest), yet the progress of alienation is apt to be as rapid as that of affection; and, European habits of feeling recurring with the return of European opportunities of intercourse, Henry soon began to revolt from the idea of that amphibious[3] sort of association which confounds together the servant and the friend. In short, he began to recollect that he was himself a man of family and

---

1 In ancient and mediaeval physiology, the humours were the four chief fluids of the body—blood, phlegm, yellow bile (choler), and black bile (melancholy)—thought by their proportions to determine a person's physical and mental qualities and temperament. Peccant humours are unhealthy or diseased.
2 Cold and gloomy, like a person born under the planet Saturn.
3 Connected with or combining two classes or qualities.

fortune, and that our moralist was nothing but his servant: a recollection for which the more fashionable part of our readers will not be very angry with him; but which may be found, in the sequel, to have been the source of many an intemperate folly, and many a bitter emotion of self-condemnation and remorse.

It will be readily imagined that the career of dissipation, in which Henry was thus engaged, was beheld with equal affliction by Amelia and Seraphina. The latter, indeed, exerted all the influence of her charms to allure him to the paths of virtue; and endeavoured, at once by the innocent cheerfulness of her deportment, and the calm retirement of her own life, to convince him that there are pleasures within the pale of temperance and reason, which are not to be equalled in the noisy circles of riot and profusion.

Unfortunately these exertions were not as successful as they were meritorious. They influenced not the conduct of him in whose behalf they were made, but they influenced (as the efforts of virtue are too apt to do), in very unfavourable way, the happiness of her who made them.

Henry was now in a whirl from which he had neither the power nor the inclination to extricate himself; and such was the infatuation of youthful folly, that his heart was full of dissatisfaction because his lovely monitress would not plunge with him into the same giddy vortex.

Nor was our hero the only person with whose taste this philosophical seclusion did not entirely suit. Morton considered it as a folly that amounted almost to crime to neglect, in this manner, the proper enjoyments of youth; and, with such charms as those of Seraphina, to forego the adulation she might have commanded in the circles of dissipation; and, with all the splendour and enjoyments of a gay metropolis within her reach, to devote herself to the same dull retinue of books and pencils, and papers, and pens and ink, that had relieved her loneliness in the retreat at St. Domingo.

In the first instance, indeed, our good duenna had arranged these matters in a more rational way. Presuming on the infatuation, as she called it, of the lover, and her own penetration into the foibles of his character, she had procured a splendid suit of apartments, in the most fashionable part of the town, and was proceeding to form a correspondent establishment—intending indeed, that the residence of Seraphina should be the centre of *all* the pleasures of our hero.

But this eligible arrangement (consistent as it would have been with the wishes of Henry) was immediately counteracted by the perverseness of the very person for whose enjoyment and advantage it had been concerted.

Seraphina no sooner beheld the apartments that had been engaged for her, than a thousand revolting impressions rushed upon her mind.

"Is this," said she, "a proper habitation for an alien and an orphan, whose sole business, in this gaudy city, is to endeavour to secure a little property of two or three hundred a year?"

"It is a proper habitation," replied our sage duenna, somewhat archly, "for the friend and fair companion of the opulent Henry Montfort."

"Mistake me not," rejoined Seraphina, with some degree of severity—"mistake me not, Morton—nor judge of my heart by the corrupted standards which you seem alone to have consulted. I am, indeed, the friend of Henry Montfort—this breast alone can ever know with how dear a friendship I have loved, and shall continue, till death, to love him. He is, indeed, my friend—my only friend; and, unless the merciless torrent could restore what is devoured, my heart is so full of him, I cannot wish for any other. I acknowledge, with pride, the mutual affection that glows within our bosoms; and I glory in his generous protection. But this friendship, this affection—call it by what ardent name you please—shall never be a snare to his unwary passions—a mildew on the promised harvest of his nobler virtues. I know enough from himself—I know enough from the gossip tales you gleaned in the neighbourhood of La Soufriere, of the failings and irregularities of his character; and I perceive with indignation the uses you would have me make of them. But I will not be his Lais, or his Phryne.[1] I will not seduce him again into habits of dissipation and extravagance; nor, aiming at the meretricious splendour of the courtezan, be suspected of having sold to vanity, what never could have been yielded but to love.

"No, no, Morton, procure me some apartment, consistent with the expectations which the generosity of my departed foster-father has given me a right to cherish; where the confidence of affection may be indulged without derogating from the independency of the soul; and Henry may perceive that he is beloved for himself alone."

Outré[2] as these sentiments appeared to our duenna, it was in vain that she resisted them. Another apartment was procured; and afterwards a small house, or rather a neat cottage, in Somerstown; and Seraphina (after a transient survey of the novelties that surrounded her) contemplated from a distance those scenes of splendour and dissipation, for which the state of her feelings and the circumstances of her education had given her so faint a relish.

In the mean time, the faithful Edmunds was employed in a diligent but unavailing research after the agent in whose possession the will of old Parkinson was expected to be found.

With the credentials for this research, indeed, he was very imperfectly supplied. Almost all that was known of this agent, either by Morton or Seraphina, was his name and his profession; and in a profession so numerous (that of the law), this in fact was knowing nothing at all; and as Parkinson had never possessed much of the pride of pedigree, and had been separated from his family very early, and under circumstances but

---

1   On Lais, see p. 77, note 2. Phryne was an Athenian courtesan of the 4th century BCE.
2   Extravagant or unconventional.

little favourable to endearing remembrance, little assistance could be had towards removing the difficulty from the recollection of any conversations about them.

At length, an attorney of the name was heard of, who was believed to have had some connections and transactions in the West Indies; and who had been considered as a man of great punctuality and very fair character; till, having lately involved himself in some gambling speculations, he had become implicated, by suspicion at least, in a forgery of very extensive amount; in consequence of which (as was believed) he had suddenly disappeared, together with his clerk, who was therefore supposed to be implicated in the same conspiracy, and was concluded to have escaped out of the nation.

No tidings, however, could be learned of what had become of his papers. By some it was believed that he had hastily consumed every document, of whatever description, he was in possession of, in one promiscuous conflagration, lest any thing that related to the forgery should inadvertently escape; others, on the contrary, affirmed, with as much confidence as if they had been in the secret, that he had conveyed away all the title-deeds and other papers of his clients, that he might make some future use of them to his own advantage. However this may be, certain it is, that after the most diligent enquiry, Edmunds found it utterly impossible to procure any sort of information that could positively ascertain the fact, whether this were the agent in question. Much less could he obtain any clue that might lead to the ascertainment of security of the property which Parkinson had bequeathed.

Thus, for the present at least, the chace was effectually at an end; all track and scent of the game being absolutely lost; and the trusty Edmunds, after having consumed between five and six months in traversing town and country (in visiting sea-ports where the fugitive was said to have embarked, and distant counties where he was reported to have relatives and connections), returned upon his steps, rather wearied by ill success than by exertion, to detail the chilling narrative of his disappointments.

At first, indeed, he was not very much dejected. While he perceived any hopes of attaining his object, he had pursued it with the ardour and enthusiasm natural to his character. But when hope was no more, he began, like a good philosopher, to seek for consolation; and to question the importance of that which it was impracticable to attain.

"Well; and, after all, what does it signify," said he, to himself; "it is but two or three hundred a year; and Henry Montfort will have enough for both; if he will but have patience to wait till the old man dies: and as, by all accounts, he is a debauched old rogue, with a crazy sort of a constitution, who knows what the climates and diseases of the West Indies may do for us? Or suppose he should even take it into his head to make a long life of it; there is something in the power of the mother; and she is too noble-minded to discard her son, for following, in such a case, the dictates of nature and of virtue."

These prospects, while they lasted, set the mind of our enthusiast perfectly at ease. But the consolation was rather flattering than permanent.

Some painful doubts intruded themselves on the score of Henry himself.

"Was he unaltered and unalterable in the disinterested purity of his attachment? Had the dissipations into which he had plunged, since his return to England, left his moral principles uncontaminated? or might not he, who in the solitary retreat of Margot, or in the hours of melancholy and languor, had loved like the friend and champion of virtue, have learned, in the gaiety of health, and amidst the licentious prodigalities of a corrupted city, to desire like a sensualist; and, like the sordid votary of appetite, to seduce, to abandon, and destroy?"

The morals of those with whom he associated, as far as Edmunds had found opportunities to observe them, during the intervals of more important enquiry, seemed but too well calculated to countenance these suspicions: and indeed his whole conduct towards his lovely protegé[1] (now that Edmunds was at leisure to consider it) appeared in a very ambiguous point of view: nor was the recent alteration of his deportment towards our enthusiast himself calculated to remove the impression.

"It is true," said Edmunds, meditating, "that new situations beget new habits and new feelings. Henry Montfort is a man of fortune and accomplishments. He is now surrounded by young men of his own rank and condition in society; of similar talents and correspondent education; and the humble Edmunds must not expect the same condescensions and familiarities in the metropolis of Britain, as amidst the intellectual desert of La Soufriere.

"But if this were the only motive of the alteration, are there not hours and situations in which the pride of rank might unbend a little, without derogating from its dignity? Does he not so unbend with servants whom, in other respects, he places at a much greater distance? for, to do him justice, his deportment, in many particulars, is rather that of a patron than a master; and, this reserve excepted, I have felt in his service none of the degradations of servitude.

"But Seraphina—why is it that whenever she is mentioned, or aught that concerns her interests—why is it then, in particular, that his looks, his tone of voice, his authoritative brevity, and his whole chilling deportment, should perpetually remind me that he is a master, and I am but a servant?

"Is it upon that subject alone that I am least worthy of being a confident?[2]—or, rather, that he is least worthy to confide? Why have even his instructions, with respect to this enquiry, been communicated at second hand?—by the lips of this suspicious Morton?—Is she a being in whom it is less degrading to confide, than in the humble Edmunds? He does not think so."

---

1 A person who receives the protection, patronage, or guidance of another.
2 A friend in whom one confides.

Full of these painful reflections, Edmunds arrived at the humble habitation of our heroine.

He knocked.

His hand was heavy as his heart; and the sullen door seemed conscious of unwelcome salutation.

Could that fine personification of Horace be realised, and death were actually to beat at our doors, after the fashion of an old Roman visitant, scarcely could the stroke of his fleshless heel against the pannel, be more thrillingly ominous.[1]

The servant opened the door with trepidation; as though she had expected to see a ghost: and Edmunds stalked by her, as though he had been actually one.

Seraphina was alone.—Alone, and sad, and pensive. The thump of the knocker had startled her from a painful reverie; and she looked around for some messenger of evil tidings.

Edmunds was introduced; and with a dismal countenance related his disheartening tale.

"And what resource have we now, Edmunds?" said she, when he had finished—"What further can be hoped or done?"

"Nothing, madam," answered the poor fellow, "that I can devise, till we can receive intelligence from St. Domingo: our intercourse with which, if report says true, is not likely to be very difficult. We might write to the planter Rabeau, and to St. Valance, either of whom, if they be alive, would surely interest themselves so far as to have some search made after the papers of your venerable foster-father; which, considering the remote and sequestered situation of the retreat, may possibly have escaped the burnings and devastations of the insurrection. Nay, indeed, madam, it is not unlikely that Monsieur Rabeau (considering the connection that subsisted between him and Mr. Parkinson) should himself be in possession of the documents we are enquiring after.

"Or, supposing the worst, madam," continued the honest fellow, assuming a tone of cheerfulness—"Supposing that you should never hear of the will, or the property either, so long as you live; I had been thinking that it does not much signify, after all.

"What is the difference of two or three hundred a-year, madam, to Mr. Henry? who, in all probability, when the old gentleman is once out of the way, will have twice as many thousands: and, at any rate, you must have waited, I suppose, madam, for that event; as you would hardly have thought of hazarding the consequences of his displeasure.

"In the mean time, madam, considering the union of sentiment that subsists between you—considering the circumstances of your attachment, and the mutual sufferings you have endured for each other, why should you feel yourself hurt, madam, in sharing, even at present, a portion of the

---

1 Horace, *Odes* I.iv.13-14.

better fortune of one who waits only for the opportunity of being at liberty so to do, to make you an equal partner in the whole?"

"Does he so wait?—Are these his meditations *now*?" exclaimed Seraphina, unconsciously: for her heart was overpowered by its emotions; and its whispers became audible.

She walked about the room: absent and disordered. Her hurried step and agonizing eye were full of Henry. Edmunds was not seen. His voice, for a while, fell unheeded on her ear; and the present was obscured by the absent.

"Or—or—or," continued Edmunds, hesitating—"Or, madam—could it be supposed, madam! for a single moment, madam!—as sure it cannot, madam!—that Mr. Montfort, madam!—should, should, madam!—should prove ungrateful, madam!—Were it possible that those profligate and dissipated young men (pardon me for the suggestion madam)—were it possible they should draw him so far aside from those noble principles he once fostered with generous ardour in his heart, as to make him forgetful of all the solemn oaths he has so often repeated; and of those still more sacred obligations which require not the force of oaths to make them binding upon the consciences of good men; yet, madam, I would continue to be your servant: and what poor service I can render, you shall never want.

"I would receive your orders and execute your commands, and I would labour night and day, with my head and with my hands—(I have turned the means over in my mind again and again, madam, since this last disappointment), for your support and comfort.

"I would write for the booksellers, madam (for I have been thinking that I could compile a history, or a book of travels, or teach a German ghost or an incubus to talk English, as well as some of those who get a very good livelihood by it); or I would write your history, madam, under some fictitious name, and call it a novel; and I am sure every body would read it; for every body would weep over it.[1]

"Or, when I had exhausted myself in this way, I would write for the merchants, or write for the lawyers—and, for aught I know, this might be the more profitable employment. And all that I earned should be yours, madam: for you are worthy of more than I can do for you; and the only reward that I would ever wish, should be the satisfaction of seeing that you were happy, and the consciousness of having discharged, with fidelity, the functions of an humble friendship, to the most amiable and most excellent young lady that ever was persecuted by the malevolence of fortune."

---

1 Edmunds's catalogue of literary genres includes gothic novels, also called "German tales," which were extremely popular during the second half of the 1790s. The passage alludes to the genesis of *The Daughter*, which Thelwall began writing around the time he finished his Arthurian romance *The Fairy of the Lake* (featuring a rather eloquent Incubus). Like Edmunds's proposed sentimental novel, *The Daughter* was published under a pseudonym ("John Beaufort, L.L.D.").

Seraphina listened to this harangue—or rather to the latter part of it—with sensations that cannot readily be conceived. Painful as it was, she could not interrupt it; for it was the effusion of honest sympathy. It had the stamp of sincerity upon it. It was in unison with that mingled simplicity and enthusiasm which constituted, in every stage of action, the prominent feature of the character of young Edmunds. She paced about the room, therefore, in considerable perturbation, struggling with her emotions till he had concluded: and then fixed her eye upon him, for a few seconds, with a mixed expression of benignity and anguish—

The man she loved with such unbounded confidence, out-stripped in virtue and magnanimity by his servant—

How heart-rending!—how degrading!

"Generous Edmunds!" said she—"Poor, faithful, enthusiastic visionary!" Then, turning suddenly away, "O Henry, Henry!" she exclaimed; and bursting into a shower of tears, she threw herself with her face upon the sopha.

There was an emphasis in this short ejaculation that spoke most forcibly to the suspicions of poor Edmunds. His inquisitive eye glanced over the form of the lovely mourner; and he fancied that those suspicions were confirmed.

He wept in silence; and his heart bled within him.

Morton, who had been absent from home during the whole of this interesting scene returned at this instant.

"Good God," exclaimed she, "what is the matter? my dearest Seraphina! what is the matter? What has this messenger of ill things been saying to you?"

Edmunds glanced his eye upon Seraphina; and then, turning with a reproachful sternness upon the duenna, hurried out of the room, to give vent to the feelings with which he struggled.

CHAP. II.

Containing a Dialogue between Seraphina and Morton; and another between Henry and young Edmunds.

Discretion and Independence.—Retrospects.—The intrepid Remembrancer.—Returning Virtue.—Classes and Distinctions.

MORTON seated herself by the side of Seraphina; and hovered over her for some time, in silent endearment: a silence that proceeded partly from sympathy—for the reader, of course, will give her credit for not being entirely indifferent to the feelings of Seraphina; but partly, also, from that policy of which, likewise, she is in no great danger of being regarded as entirely destitute.

In short, Morton had a part to act—as the reader will hereafter perceive. She waited, therefore, to receive her cue, that she might know in what manner to begin.

But the grief of Seraphina was not of that description which vents itself in communication or complaint: or Morton, at least, stood not, at present, in that high station of confidence, to induce her to unbosom her emotions. The latter, therefore, however contrary to the manner in which she had wished the drama to be cast, was obliged to play the interlocutor herself.

"I perceive, my dear Seraphina," said she—"I perceive too plainly, that all our hopes, concerning the property, are at an end. But this is not all, my dearest lady—I am sure this is not all. Some other cause there must be for the excess of the present emotion. The officious impertinence of this Edmunds"—

"Peace, babbler!" exclaimed Seraphina, interrupting her, "nor profane the virtue of that generous enthusiast. If your conduct had been half as widely removed from officiousness, or you had been actuated by one tythe of his fidelity, Henry would still have loved; and I had not been wretched."

M. "Oh! madam!—Seraphina! wrong me not—do not torment yourself with these injurious suspicions. If I have been too officious, it is the excess of my affection that has made me so. But I have never been unfaithful; nor has Mr. Montfort ceased to love."

S. "Yes he has, Morton. I feel he has. At least he has ceased to love as I can alone endure to be beloved.

"I have lost my value in his eyes; through you I lost it; if not by your treachery, at least by your indiscretion.

"What is his affection now, but a feverish fluctuation between appetite and indifference, which my principles revolt at, and my pride disdains? Not such the love that I have borne for Henry. Not such the love that Henry once bore for me.

"But let him cease to love: I can forgive the fickleness of appetite: if he will but restore to me his esteem.

"Be but my friend. I ask no dearer name—
"Be that the meed of some more artful fair:
"Nor would it heal my grief, or chace my shame,
"That pity gave what love forbade to share!"[1]

M. "Aye, there it is, madam. You have been reading those vile poets till your brain is turned. I wish to God the attorney general would prosecute them all in a lump.[2] For it is they (after all) that put the foolish romantic notions into people's heads, that do so much mischief in the end, and create so much confusion. I never knew any body that was addicted to the study of those foolish books, that did not become totally unfitted for the state of society in which we live.

"In the name of wonder; what can you possibly desire that you may not command?"

---

1 William Shenstone, "Elegy XXVI. Describing the sorrow of an ingenuous mind, on the melancholy event of a licentious amour," ll. 81-84.

2 An allusion to the many prosecutions for seditious libel in the early 1790s, notably that of Paine for *Rights of Man* (1791-92).

S. "The esteem of Henry; which I am sure I merit. The esteem of myself; which no conviction can give me, while I am deprived of his."

M. "And does he not esteem? does he not love? What better proofs could any reasonable woman require? What bounds have there been to his liberality, but what have been opposed to it by your fastidious prejudices? With how much delicacy has he eluded—with what indignant generosity has he overleaped those bounds?—What indulgences has he not forced upon you?—What presents has he not lavished?"

"I will receive no more of them," said Seraphina, rising from the couch, and assuming an air of dignity and composure—"I will not be finessed into degradation. I will return them all.

"Poor Edmunds, thou hast taught me an useful lesson. Would'st thou toil and drudge for me? and can I not labour for myself? Can the attainments of solitude be turned to no account in this world of population? Were the accomplishments I owe to the fostering care of the generous Parkinson, designed only as superficial ornaments?

"The mind that is resolved to be independent, will always find within itself the resources of independency."

M. "O for shame! for shame, Seraphina! and can you cherish, even for a moment, a thought of such ingratitude?—

"Independency! who have you but yourself to thank that you are not independent? Has not Mr. Montfort been repeatedly anxious—Is he not solicitous now to make every settlement in his power, to provide for this independence, till the death of his father shall leave him at liberty to follow the dictates of his heart?"

S. "Name it no more, Morton—I charge you, name it no more. Shall I be bought like a slave—shall I be hired like a courtezan? Has Seraphina made a market of herself, that she should higgle[1] with lawyers, and set her hand to a deed of bargain and sale, amidst the sneers of barristers, and the significant glances of attorneys' clerks?"

M. "And prithee, my dear child! might not these romantic objections be urged with equal force, against almost every marriage settlement that ever was executed? What are they but deeds of bargain and sale?—the commodity in general having been regularly, and wisely, knocked down to the highest bidder?"

"There may be many wives, for aught I know," replied Seraphina, with dignified contempt, "who, in reality are nothing but purchased concubines: but whatever name the censorious world may give to Seraphina, she shall never be degraded to their rank.

"But is this, Morton, of all seasons—is this a time to talk of settlements—when the heart of Henry is itself unsettled? When he is become cold, and distant, and almost a stranger?—Shall I accept his bounty, when I have lost his love?"

---

1 Or haggle.

M. "You have not lost it, Seraphina!—you have not lost it. Though I confess your inflexibility, on a point not less connected with your own consequence than his happiness, diminishes your influence, and may endanger his attachment. Why will you thus obstinately seclude yourself, and be wedded to this lowly privacy? Is this an apartment fit to receive the visits of the splendid Henry Montfort?"

S. "I disdained not to visit him in the narrow cabin; and to watch by the side of his hammock, when a trunk was my only couch."

M. "Aye, and believe me, child—Doubt not the power and fascination of your beauty; in the vilest dungeon of pestilence, if you were there confined, he would fly to visit you. But here, it is perverseness; not necessity. Why should you disdain the splendour with which he is fascinated? why shut yourself up in obscurity from his friends, and fastidiously avoid all communion and participation in his pleasure?"

S. "Because the habits of my life have given me a relish for pleasures of a more exalted nature—Because I will not be instrumental to the ruin in which he is involving himself—Because I will not be enrolled in the list of courtezans, or tainted with the depravity of their manners.

"What is become of the generosity of Henry, when he could urge such a proposition? Were it ever his intention to make me his wife, would he wish me to be acknowledged as his mistress?

"No, no: he has ceased to consider me in that point of view. He, too, is the slave of forms and ceremonies—He, too, believes that the bond of conjugal chastity exists not in the purity of the heart, but in the gingle of mystic phrases—and that the intrinsic excellence of virtue resides not in the essence, but in the name.[1]

"Well, be it so—Love, gratitude, and unsuspecting confidence (three cardinal vices in this well-reasoning world), have degraded me from my rank in society: shall I be deprived, then, of the privilege of living beyond the pale of association? Is Henry not contented with the private consciousness of his victory? Must I be dragged in triumph at the chariot-wheels of the conqueror? and be exposed to splendid derision?

"But no more of this, Morton. Your morality (thanks to the generous instruction of a better tutor) is not my morality: your prudence is not mine. I am resolved; and will waste my breath no more in these degrading altercations. The next word I hear from you upon this subject, shall be the last that, upon any subject, I will ever hear.

"I know it has originated all in you. The unprompted heart of Henry never could have conceived a thought of so much baseness.

"But you are dissatisfied with this life of privacy? You love not books and solitude and meditation and lonely walks. The glare of publicity—the splendour of dissipation alone has charms for you.

"Go then, Morton; go. Why should my tales and peculiarities be a bar to your happiness? I have no right—no wish to fetter you. Go: you are free

---

1 Cf. Appendix B2b.

as air. Your talents would be useful to a mistress of congenial dispositions; and among the Aspasias[1] of some of those dissolute companions of my deluded Henry, to whom you would have me give entertainment—(perhaps in the service of some newer mistress of Henry himself—some more practised fair one, who may not happen to be troubled with any of my eccentricities and romantic foibles) you cannot fail to meet with a situation more congenial to your views, and more consistent with your interests.

"For me, in the new arrangements that my altered circumstances may require, I shall not want your services. I must learn to contract my simple wants into a yet narrower compass, and wait upon myself."

"Oh! do not kill me, my child! oh! do not kill me!" exclaimed poor Morton, clasping her in her arms, and venting her agony in a shower of tears—"Oh! do not kill me with such language—with such thoughts! I have not followed you for six successive years, from clime to clime—I have not snatched you from whelming torrents, and clung in faithful servitude to your changeful fortunes, to leave you at such a time, and in such a state of mind; or to think of any interests, or of any happiness, that is not connected with yours.

"No: Seraphina! no: life of my life! and comfort of my eyes! I will not—cannot leave you: no, never while I live!"

"Mysterious woman!" said Seraphina, looking steadily upon her, with an equal expression of sympathy and wonder—"how can I believe you?—or how suspect?—Why do you cling to my arm as if it were a part of you, and look into my eyes as if your soul were there?

"What can be the meaning of all this? your tones and gestures thrill me with a sort of horror!"

M. "Oh! do not ask me. Ask nothing: for my brain is giddy. Only let me be your servant still—your fond, faithful, servant. Only believe that I have been sincere in my prayers and wishes for your prosperity; and if you cannot be happy in the way that I would have made you so, consult your own discretion, and endeavour to be happy in your own. But do not bid me leave you. However your fortune, or your own wayward temper may dispose of you, let me feast upon you with these eyes, and follow you through all the mazes of your destiny, and I will bow contented. You are mistress of your own motives; and I will oppose you with my officious solicitudes no more."

While this dialogue was passing in the apartment of Seraphina, another not less important was maintained, with equal earnestness, in another place.

Edmunds, whose sympathy, as may have been remarked, was not of the mere passive kind, no sooner quitted the room, upon the entrance of the obnoxious Morton, than he hastened, in the temper of mind, and under the impression produced by the deportment and ejaculation of Seraphina, immediately to Grosvenor-square.

---

1 See p. 77, note 2.

It was past mid-day, indeed, but Henry was not out of bed. The night had been spent in prodigal intemperance, and his aching head was paying the accustomed penalty upon his pillow.

Edmunds proceeded, however, without delay to his chamber; Henry started from his imperfect slumber; and appeared to be somewhat confused when he perceived who was approaching.

"Well, Edmunds," said he, recovering from his embarrassment, "and what news do you bring?"

E. "Bad enough, sir; but not so bad, I am afraid, as the news that I come to hear. Our hopes are at an end. Seraphina, in point of fortune, at least, is destitute; perhaps she is destitute, also, of a friend."

H. "How, Edmunds? of a friend!"

E. "Aye, sir, if the name be properly understood: for there be those who arrogate it to themselves who are, in reality, the worst of enemies."

Henry was abashed.

"True Edmunds. But I hope—But Seraphina—Prithee, lad, tell me your story as briefly as you can: for I would fain sleep a while."

E. "No sir: you cannot sleep. You do not hope it, sir. But you would get rid of me, lest something I should say that might awaken thoughts—"

H. "Edmunds!"

E. "Well! well! sir;—the tale shall be as brief as you desire. I have hunted this fugitive attorney, from inn to inn, from sea-port to sea-port, and from county to county; but have not been able to gain the least shadow of intelligence of him or his papers, of the property or family of Parkinson: and now I have not the slightest clue to conduct me any further in the labyrinth.—

"This, sir, is all my story. But—but now—sir—will you—may I—I—"

Henry perceived by his hesitation what he was endeavouring to introduce; and shrinking from the apprehension of remonstrance or enquiry, "No, Edmunds," said he, "I will not, nor may you at present: for my head aches so vilely that I cannot talk."

"Your *head* aches, sir!" repeated Edmunds, pacing about the room—"Alas! sir—Seraphina's head aches, and her *heart* aches too! It is there that all *her* aches begin."

"Seraphina's heart!" resumed Henry, struggling with his emotions—"Seraphina's heart—Edmunds! And did she take the disappointment so hardly?"

E. "Would she had nothing harder, sir, to take!—that in the cup of her misfortunes there were nothing more bitter than the dregs of poverty!

"O! sir! sir!—Mr. Henry! have you been as assiduous, of late, to this all-deserving—*all-confiding* excellence as you used to be?—And is there not, sir, a cause—should—*should* have made a generous man still more so?"

These were the questions that the heart of Henry was not prepared to meet. Fortunately, however, he was at liberty to call in the dignity of a master to his relief; and to silence enquiry by the clamour of violated authority. Smothering his confusion, therefore, in a shew of anger,

"And pray, sir," he demanded, in a tone of hollow stateliness, "by what authority do you put these interrogatories? Have you forgot yourself? and what you are? and who I am?"

E. "No, sir, I have not forgotten (where no superior duty interferes, I will remember it with all lowliness) that my unfortunate circumstances have reduced me to a state of servitude, my admiration of your most excellent qualities, induced me to intrude my services upon you. And I trust, sir, you have had no reason to repent the condescension with which you yielded to my importunities: for though I can boast of no attributes, particularly appropriate to the class of society I have fallen into, but those of zeal and fidelity, I trust that in these, at least, I have not been found deficient."

H. "Are you under accusation, Edmunds, that you enter so elaborately on your defence?"

E. "Why yes, sir; as for that, I am under accusation: the worst of accusations; for I am charged with no particular offence; and, therefore, can clear myself by no process of vindication;—a circumstance, sir, that may always suggest a suspicion, at least, that the accuser is more criminal than the accused.[1]

"Yes, I am under accusation. Your eye accuses me, sir; for it shuns me, when I would approach you with my accustomed services. Your ear accuses me; for it is closed against the professions of my honest zeal: and your whole deportment accuses me, so different from that confidence with which you formerly condescended to honour me.

"But this, sir, is not the subject I would talk about."

H. "If your services have not been properly rewarded, Edmunds, let me know the price you set upon them. I would not be parsimonious in these matters."

E. "Oh! sir—wound not my heart with these insinuations; nor artfully draw me aside to the consideration of mere personal feelings, till I have discharged my conscience of the more sacred duty I owe to Seraphina, and to you.

"It is true, I am your servant, sir—I have eaten your bread; I have received—not your wages, indeed (your liberality has precluded the appellation of that degrading term), but your bounty. As such, I am subject to your orders, and must perform all your honourable biddings. But as you, yourself, once told me, sir, in an hour of generous condescension, mine is no serving mind. Fortune, and not Nature, has made me what I am: nor is the spirit of subjection enough within me to make me suppose that these are the only relationships that subsist between us. I cannot forget that we both of us are men; and as such, have solemn obligations to perform, at once prior and paramount to these artificial distinctions.

"*O! rocks, and pendant woods, and eddying foam* of Limbé!—

---

1   The passage may allude to the Treason Trials of 1794 and the delay of almost five
    months before the prisoners learned the nature of the charges against them.

"O sequestered retreat of the venerable Parkinson!—

"O! bay of Acul, and never to be forgotten isle of Margot!—

"Are there no associations, sir, connected with those scenes, that may give some little licence to the tongue of the lowly Edmunds?

"Can you forget, sir—ah! can you forget that hour, when on the fatal coast between Acul and Margot, in the midst of a tremendous scene of dangers and of horrors, we combated, side by side, to rescue an endangered innocent, who, in every particular of form, and intellect, and virtue, so far surpasses all that mine eyes have ever beheld of human excellence, that many and many a time I have said to myself—*if there be such a thing as divinity, it must be feminine; and this is she?*"

Henry was moved. His heart echoed the panegyric. He almost envied the tongue that gave it utterance.—

"Well! well, Edmunds!"

E. "Well, sir! The conflict was common. The laurel and the prize were yours. You know, sir, with how sincere an ardour I laboured to preserve them to you. My humble fortune would have prevented me from looking so high, even if your more happy accomplishments had not already fascinated the innocence your valour had preserved.

"My feelings, sir, knew the subordination of my circumstances; and my trembling devotion was satisfied with worshipping in the vestibule, while the sacred communion of the sanctuary was all your own. But if the priest himself should turn incendiary, or plunder the shrine he has been entrusted to defend, shall not the lowest devotee be permitted to call out *sacrilege!* and deprecate the impious treachery?"

"Ha! ha!" said Henry, somewhat convulsively—for conscience began to be rather turbulent; and his pride was obliged to ask alliance of his wit, to keep the internal enemy in order—"ha! ha! I congratulate you upon your conversion, Edmunds—you have been studying the prophets I perceive; and have learned to speak in parables.—*And Nathan said unto David, Thou art the man!*[1] Ha! ha! well said, old Nathan!—Verily! verily! I admire the prophetic length of thy beard!"

E. "Ah! sir, I would the tale were realised to the conclusion, for David's heart was not entirely obdurate to the puncture of human sympathy; and he, we are told, repented. But the moralist of Limbé—the champion of Margot, rendered callous by profligate association, silences his conscience with a ribald's[2] laugh, and triumphs in the reproach of guilt.

"But your gestures, sir, are ill companions to your pleasantry; and your mirth, I perceive, is changing into rage.

---

1 2 Samuel 12:7: Nathan prompts David to self-condemnation (for his affair with Bathsheba and murder of her husband Uriah) by telling him of a rich man who killed the only lamb of a poor man rather than slaughter one from his own numerous herd. David angrily declares that the rich man deserves to die for his lack of pity, upon which Nathan informs him, "Thou [art] the man."

2 A person who speaks, jokes, or behaves in a rude or lewd way.

"O sir!—my master!—my once noble master! what a spectacle is this! to see a mind like yours thus tossed in feverish agitation from pride to wrath, from wrath to ribaldry, convulsed and writhing in disgraceful tortures, rather than patiently endure the salutary application that would restore it to the sanity of virtue.

"What is it that I would say, that would be dishonourable for you to hear? and who is the speaker, that you should think it a degradation to listen? A nameless youth, indeed, destitute alike, of fortune and connections; but one who has been, heretofore, ennobled to your confidence; and encouraged by your better example in the career of humanity and honour. He it is who conjures you not to derogate from the remembrance of your former virtues!—who warns you to beware how you destroy and abandon that confiding innocence which you are bound, by every sacred obligation, to protect!—how you degrade the most excellent, the most exalted, the most amiable of human beings, to a situation the most despised and lamentable—a situation that precludes all condition and estimation in society; and annihilates, of course, all the powers of utility, however extensive—all the functions and influences of the most exalted virtues!

"Ah, sir!—the injurious world, it is true, gives licence and privilege to our sex,

"And man the lawless libertine may rove
Free and unquestion'd through the wilds of Love";[1]
may practise every species of aggravated treachery; and, reducing seduction to a science, may triumph in the spoil of innocence, and the tears of confidence betrayed; while the injured female, whose only crimes are an affection that could not suspect, and a simplicity that could not disguise, is left to the heavy penalty of contrition and despair, of infamy and irretrievable ruin. But will the silent whispers of the heart echo this popular clamour? Will they condemn the victim, and absolve the criminal? Or could you, sir, lay your head upon your pillow, and reflect without madness on having betrayed the boundless confidence of an innocent maiden, who in every thing, but the excess of her passion for you, had a virtue exalted beyond the frailty of humanity, and a mind that was superior to all blemish?

"Ah! such a one, sir—such a one—could you, sir, of all mankind, deceive, dishonour, and destroy!"

Henry was almost overpowered. He endeavoured to raise a laugh: but this resource had been exhausted by the last requisition. He applied to sophistry: but sophistry was unable to bring her forces into the field without a considerable subsidy from the animal spirits; whose funds were, at this time, in a very deplorable state. Even pride itself, though it still kept guard in the citadel, was too weak with its wounds to venture into the field of action.

---

1   Nicholas Rowe, *The Tragedy of Jane Shore* (1714) 1.2.191-92.

In short, Henry continued, for a considerable time, in a very painful state of mind; silent and fluctuating; unable to determine either what to say or do; reluctant to yield, and yet incapable to defend.

At length, forcing a sort of sneer upon his lip, in a tone of voice midway between jest and seriousness, "This is strange cant," said he, "me thinks, Edmunds, for a lad, of your principles!"

E. "Cant!!!—Principles!!!

"And what, I pray you, sir, are the principles of those who have taught you to consider this cant?

"Principles, sir!—My principles!!!

"Alas! how little are they acquainted with the motives of human action who would gauge our morality by the rule of a few speculative opinions!—whose narrow-minded bigotry would damn by sects, and absolve by creeds and ceremonies! How multiplied are the springs that set in motion that complicated machine the human heart, of which belief is, at any rate, but one!

"If I mistake not, sir, the laws and operations of that mysterious organ, feeling and reflection are the elements of all practical morality: and he who is destitute of these, is sure to be a scoundrel, whatever be the articles of his belief.

"These elements, sir—pardon me if I am too warm: the cause is my sufficient apology—These elements cannot long subsist, but in intimate union. They must be fostered by sentiment and cherished by the association of congenial minds; for the noblest feelings will soon be overwhelmed in the career of thoughtless dissipation; and the companion of Falkland and Mordant[1] was but a suspicious guardian of the innocent Seraphina."

"Falkland and Mordant, sirrah!" repeated Henry, starting up in great choler[2]—"trespass not too far upon my patience, Edmunds; nor abuse the indulgence I have extended towards you. Falkland and Mordant!—who, I pray you, sir, has given you authority to question the propriety of my connections, or canvass the characters of my friends?"

E. "Those accidents, sir, that rendered me joint protector of the life of Seraphina—that zeal which prompted me (for I thought it for your mutual happiness) to restore you, when separated, to each other—that confidence, with which I have been honoured by you both, and those solemn protestations you have called upon me to witness—all—all have authorised me to guard, with a lowly, but yet jealous fidelity, the honour and happiness of my most accomplished mistress; and to warn you against those connections, the contamination of whose unprincipled licentiousness may be dangerous to your virtue, and ruinous, in its consequences, to her.

---

1 Mordant is also the name of a character in Thelwall's essay "The Sceptic," serialized in the *Biographical and Imperial Magazine* in 1789-90. The name Falkland is shared by the aristocrat who persecutes his servant in Godwin's novel *Things As They Are; or, the Adventures of Caleb Williams* (1794).

2 Anger, heated temper.

"Bear witness for me, Edmunds—or against me! Be thou my accusing spirit! Brand me with infamy—proclaim me as a contaminating pestilence if ever I desert my Seraphina, or betray the generous confidence she reposes in me!"

H. "And have I, Edmunds—have I deserted?"

E. "I know not, sir, how far this may be answered in the negative: but I find you do not dare to enter upon the enquiry, whether you have not *betrayed?*

"But the boldness of my speech, it seems, offends you, sir: and my language, though not free enough for your conscience, is too presumptuous for your pride. It is not sufficiently respectful for the humble Edmunds. It suits not the accidental predicament in which (in the view of society) I stand.

"Perhaps it does not, sir—perhaps, in the dignity of the cause, I have forgotten the insignificance of the advocate; and I ought to apologise for the indecorum.

"Perhaps my appeal might have been more forcible, if my language had been more submissive: and if the advocate of Seraphina could have degraded her by supplications, Henry Montfort might have condescended to feel. But I am no practised pleader, sir. I am just the same unsophisticated enthusiast that I was when, following a master who was all virtue, generosity, and honour, I plunged into the thickest ranks of danger, and combatted in the cause of innocence. I speak now, sir, as I acted then, from the impulse of an honest passion. And if my language has been somewhat intemperate, yet misery has its privilege as well as rank: and miserable is the lot of Edmunds!"

The tears rushed into his eyes. He turned away to conceal his emotions; while Henry, who, in the conflict of pride and feeling, had maintained the dialogue with considerable difficulty, began to give way to his.

"Miserable!" said he faltering—"Art thou miserable? Poor boy! And what hath made thee so?"

"The misery of Seraphina!" sobbed poor Edmunds, scarcely articulate, from the excess of feeling—"The misery of Seraphina!"

"Of Seraphina!" repeated Henry, with increased emotion; "and has she complained to you, Edmunds?"

E. "Complained!!! Seraphina complained!!!

"No—no, sir. She is still unaltered, if you are not. She is too generous to complain—too noble to complain. But she has called upon the name of Henry with such a look, and such a tone of voice, as made me wish that I should find him dead: for never could the name of *that* Henry whom I once reverenced and Seraphina loved, have been so accompanied, while *he* was yet alive."

Henry was completely subdued—Whatever of pride or libertinism had hitherto maintained their ground against the attacks of sympathy and conscience, fled at this powerful charge. Nature stormed at his heart; and Virtue was again triumphant.

He threw himself backwards in his bed, clasped his hands over his eyes, and uttered a deep groan.

"Ah! sir"—continued Edmunds, who saw that Contrition was awaking, and was not willing that she should go to sleep again—"Ah! sir, if you had seen this angel, with what patient resignation she listened to the tedious tale of my disappointments—if you had heard the deep sigh, and marked the pensive look, that seemed to say, *Well then I am destitute!*—I will not say your heart would have bled—mine did that, who never breathed vows of love to her!—but you would have clasped her in your arms, and called her Mrs. Montfort, and never have closed your eyes again till you had made her so."

Henry took his hand from his eyes; and fixed them, full of tears, upon Edmunds—

"And did she look so dejectedly, Edmunds?"

E. "Aye, sir—as who should say—*I have no friend to help me!* And when I talked of you, and your generosity, and your affection, she rose from her seat, and went to the window, and then came away again, as not liking to be seen; and walked to and fro, so wildly; and though I could perceive that she struggled against her tears, her eyes so swam, and rolled about the room, from place to place, and her bosom heaved so wildly, I could not bear it. I was sure all was not right."

The agitation of Henry increased as he proceeded.

"No, sir," continued Edmunds, "I could not bear it. So I offered to work for her myself—to write for her, and labour for her, and be her servant; and do the best I could for her support and comfort."

"Didst thou? poor Edmunds!" said Henry smiling in the midst of his anguish, at this simplicity. "And what did she say to that?"

E. "Oh! sir—she turned her eyes upon me with such a look—so divine, and yet so distressing—Painters should have copied it, if they would give us an idea of weeping angels!—and then, turning suddenly away, *Oh! Henry! Henry!* exclaimed she (but it is impossible to describe the tone in which it was uttered): and, incapable of restraining her tears any longer, she threw herself upon the sopha, and abandoned herself to an excess of woe.

"Oh! sir—I cannot tell you what I felt—or what I suspected. But my eyes travelled involuntarily over her form, as it lay stretched before me.—

"Alas! sir—I see, by your confusion, that you understand me. Oh! I would rather, a thousand times, have felt a dagger at my heart, than have felt the sensation of that moment!

"Morton came into the room at the very instant. I did not stop to curse her. I could not curse in the presence of Seraphina: though I know it has been her plotting."

"O, Edmunds" exclaimed Henry, striking his hand against his heart, "you have planted an hundred daggers here!"

E. "No—no, sir; I do not remind you of your wounds. It was your own hand that inflicted them.

"And could Henry Montfort, sir—the gallant Henry Montfort—the hero and the philanthropist—the moralist of Limbé—the attentive pupil of the venerable Parkinson—the enthusiast of Margot—could he become the betrayer of that innocence he enlisted himself to preserve? Could he protect from violence only that he might destroy by fraud? and abuse the influence of an unbounded confidence, to the ruin of the most excellent piece of nature's workmanship that virtue ever dignified, or intellect informed?"

"Oh, she is all," exclaimed Henry, in a transport of enthusiasm—"all that you have said of her, or that language can describe!"

E. "Or if the impatient fervour of desire, and the arts of that old mother convenience[1] there—that Morton, had drawn him aside from the paths of virtue, could he have deserted because he had seduced—and have abandoned a prize so rare and so inestimable because it was completely in his power?"

"Nay!—nay, Edmunds" said Henry, eagerly, "accuse me not of a barbarity of which I could never have been capable. I never thought of desertion. No: I could not have relinquished my Seraphina. I would not have forgone that heaven of softness and of every excellence—no—not for the universe! Though, I confess, some devil's thoughts have, of late, been busy with my brain, which you, like my guardian angel, are come to chace for ever. Ask me not what they were, Edmunds: but help me to dress myself. (A curse upon these headaches, and those infernal revels of libertinism and intemperance, of which they are the slightest evils!) If I have wounded the bosom of Seraphina, even your enthusiasm shall be satisfied with the atonement."

The heart of Edmunds danced at this assurance.

"Would to Heaven, Edmunds," continued Henry, "that either you had been born my equal, or that my mind could fairly overleap the prejudices that make the gap between us: for I was never half so much of a moral and intellectual agent as when you were my only confident and companion.

"A plague of these distinctions and separations! And yet there is something in birth, after all, Edmunds; or at least in the education that accompanies it. But why should not your capacity and virtue be as good a parent of gentility as the plantations of the slave-dealer, or the banker's hoards?"

E. "I am not casuist enough, sir, to settle these points: but if Seraphina has not sufficient influence, what could be hoped from me?"

H. "Alas! Edmunds—this virtue is a slippery sort of companion. Like a debtor in the hands of the catchpole,[2] it wants guarding upon both sides; and a friend and confidant with virtuous dispositions, of our own sex, is as essential as of the other. We must be chastened (at least I must), as well as allured, to rectitude; and the female who loves like Seraphina,

---

1 "Convenience" here refers to Morton's opportunism, particularly in encouraging Seraphina's and Henry's sexual relationship. See p. 233, note 1.

2 A sheriff's officer or bailiff.

is too partial, and too tender a monitor to keep the intemperance of youthful dissipation in awe. I am thinking, Edmunds, if the restraints of inequality of situation were removed, you would not be likely to be very vehemently reproached for this failing.

"But get you away into the library, and calm the turbulence of your spirit with a little philosophical society: and, by the way, as you have yet no establishment in the household, I care not if, from henceforward, you consider it as your province to keep the poets and philosophers in order. My mother, I dare say, will have no objection to confirm the appointment.

"In the mean time, Edmunds, when we meet again, infidel as you are, you shall congratulate me on my regeneration."

CHAP. III.

The Reconciliation of the Lovers, and the Death of Amelia.

The extraordinary Contest.—Amelia.—The Prospect blighted.

THE reader will readily conclude that the reparation alluded to by Henry, in the preceding chapter, could be no other than an immediate marriage. It was, indeed, with the determination of concluding his apology for his recent conduct with this proposition, that he hastened to the cottage of Somers-town; and, as the suit was urged with all the zeal and ardour of sincerity, it will be, of course, expected that the business was presently agreed upon; and that nothing remains but to procure the licence, the Bride's-maids, and the wedding suits, and bring our history to its immediate and happy conclusion.

But this was far from being the case. Impediments arose where, by the generality of readers, they would be least expected—in the bosom of the intended bride. Not that Henry had any difficulty in making his peace. Seraphina loved with too much tenderness to be reluctant to forgive—or, more properly speaking, to forget: for her gentle bosom was incapable of harbouring resentment, even while the wrong continued; and in the traffic of submissions (yielded or received) it was not in her nature to delight.

Her objections originated in a much more generous principle. The raven notes of Morton, "disherison[1] and inevitable ruin!" had not been croaked in her ear to no purpose. Perhaps it had operated in some degree (as, doubtless, it was meant to operate), in influencing her sympathising nature to those too tender condescensions that followed the pathetic scene in the harbour of Fonchiale. At any rate, it had certainly no small degree of influence in reconciling her mind to the consequences of that interview; and, in every mortifying occurrence that resulted from her situation, she consoled herself with the idea of having made a generous sacrifice to the interests and welfare of the man she loved.

---

1 Or disinheritance.

These considerations were far from being weakened in their influence at the present time. On the contrary, they pressed upon her mind with additional force. She saw that Henry was perfectly disqualified to struggle with the circumstances under which the displeasure of his father might eventually place him. Her own prospects, with respect to the property bequeathed by Parkinson, appeared to be entirely blighted: and, in addition to these, she considered the circumstance to which we have more than once alluded, as precluding, in a considerable degree, the respectability which it is the object of the nuptial ceremony to secure; while, at the same time, it would inflame the irritation of those who, under any circumstance, were likely to have been averse to the connection.

"No, no, my dear Henry!" said she, "it is now too late and too early to think of such an union. If, indeed, the indiscretion of that fatal evening could be recalled, and I could come a maiden bride to your arms, pure and untainted in the world's esteem—if that little property (small as it is), which I expected to call my own, were in my possession, and Henry felt himself impatient of a suspense, in which the tenderness of the lover and the duteous wishes of the son were waging perpetual warfare—then would I say at once, with the frankness and sincerity of my nature, 'Take me, my Henry! lead me to your altars; initiate me in your mystic ceremonies; and let me assume the rank that belongs to me in the scale of society; unstigmatized by envy, nor derided by folly. Take too my little property—tear yourself from the companions that are unworthy of your conversation—from the dissipations that enfeeble your intellects and disgrace your virtues; and, with this, let us maintain ourselves in philosophical independency; with a narrow circle of homely friends, and a few books for the amusement of our leisure hours; and imitate the frugality of a better age.'

"But as the matter now stands, marriage can give us nothing that we may not command without it. Henry would be ruined; but Seraphina would not be advanced.

"Trust me, my love! it is not worth the sacrifice. My habits are fixed. The name of wife could not draw me from this seclusion; and, while the seclusion lasts, that of mistress can never reach me. If Henry will be true, I can be happy in this little cottage. If he will not, what parchment bond can make him so?—what register or certificate can console me for his affections lost?

"No, no, Henry!—taught from my infancy, to look for my resources within myself, I stand not in the predicament of others of my sex, who if they are excluded from the society of those who have the world's respect about them, fall, of necessity among the abandoned and the vile. My love of retirement insulates me (as it were), upon an eminence, where the vapours of contagion cannot reach me; and, in a region of contamination, I can still be pure.

"The penalty of my situation is but being, for the sake of Henry, the solitary recluse I used to be while Henry was yet unknown."

This reasoning was far from satisfactory to the mind of Henry. The moral lessons of Edmunds had made a deep and permanent impression; and a sense of the unworthiness of his recent conduct, was a lesson still more impressive. Besides he had elated his imagination with the prospect of an action that had an air of disinterestedness and magnanimity: and when an idea of that description had once got possession of his mind, it was a part of his character, that it was not readily to be driven out again.

The objections of Seraphina appeared at once so delicate and so magnanimous, that they inflamed his ardour for the accomplishment of his purpose; and he determined not to be outdone in generosity.

At length an expedient was suggested for the settlement of this amicable difference; perhaps the most prudent that could be devised; and which Henry was highly censurable for not having appealed to immediately on their arrival in England. This was no other than to lay the whole circumstance of their connection before Amelia; and, premising only their mutual determination never to be separated, to abide by her advice, as to the line of conduct they should pursue.

The prospect (however obscure) of being received as a daughter by such a woman as Amelia, was too delightful, and the proceeding altogether too frank and honourable, for Seraphina to make a single objection; and Henry was so confident that the sympathy and generous principles of his mother would fall in with the current of his present wishes, that he pledged himself to abide by the consequences of her decision.

The appeal was to be made immediately on her expected return from a visit she was then making to a particular friend at a few miles distance from the town.

One circumstance, indeed, there would be in the introduction of the affair, that Henry felt particularly awkward. In the narrative of his adventures, of course, he could not avoid some mention of the conflict in the bay of Acul. But he had omitted several of the most interesting incidents in the Isle of Margot; and had given it to be understood that the lady he had protected was left at Port Paix. He would now have his insincerity to acknowledge: a circumstance to which his pride was exceedingly reluctant. But his affections were now flowing in a nobler channel; and their current was too strong to be stopped by such impediments. He determined to throw himself, with a full confession of all his aberrations and motives, on the indulgence of an affectionate mother, and to claim her concurrence in the reparation he proposed to make to the violated confidence of Seraphina.

It may readily be conceived, with what facility our lovers (upon the strength of this project) deluded themselves into the most pleasing expectations, and soothed their imaginations with the most flattering visions:— with what ardour Henry expatiated on the virtues of an enlightened and indulgent parent (a subject upon which he had been heretofore by no means silent); and with what eagerness Seraphina anticipated the delight of calling a new Amanda by the name of mother.

But these delightful prospects were unexpectedly dissipated by the sudden appearance of Edmunds; who, with equal hurry and agitation of delivery, summoned our hero to his acknowledged home, to take his last farewell of an expiring parent.

The disorder with which Amelia had so long and so vainly struggled, had been for some time rapidly approaching towards its fatal crisis. She had persuaded Henry (perhaps she had persuaded herself), that the loss of appetite and the continual hectic fever, that had for some time exhausted her strength, were the temporary effects only of some cold, or casual derangement of health; and it was in conformity with this statement, that she had yielded to the pressing invitation, which (through the medium of a change of air) seemed to promise the removal of these symptoms.

But the case was too deeply seated to be influenced by palliatives; and these symptoms were succeeded by others of a still more alarming and decisive nature. The sudden rupture of an artery gave warning of the general decay of the system; and the faintings and convulsions that succeeded, yielded only a short interval of imperfect convalescence; during which she insisted upon being immediately conducted home; that she might breathe her last accents in the ear of her beloved Henry, and die in his presence for whom alone she had a wish to live.

Scarcely was she conveyed into the house, when all the alarming symptoms again recurred, with additional violence; and all who surrounded her, began to look for her hourly dissolution.

Under these circumstances, Henry, of course, was anxiously enquired after: but not an individual in the house could give the least information whither he had gone, or where he was likely to be heard of. Edmunds, the only person that was in the secret, had taken himself out but a few minutes before; and it was not till after being searched in an hundred different places that this faithful enthusiast was at last discovered, in a coffeehouse,[1] pouring with eager eye over the debates of the National Convention,[2] and balancing, in imagination, the fate of Europe.

Allies and republicans, Maratists and Girondists,[3] however, vanished from his recollection, the instant he was informed of the alarming state of affairs, in the contracted, but more endeared circle to which he was attached.

---

1   In the seventeenth and eighteenth centuries coffee houses, where coffee and other refreshments were supplied, were frequented for political and literary conversation and the circulation of news.

2   Assembly elected in France in 1792 to draw up the country's republican constitution; it governed until 1795.

3   Maratists were supporters of the French populist journalist and republican Jean-Paul Marat, assassinated in 1793; Girondists were members of the moderate republican party in the French assembly from 1791 to 1793 (its leaders were the deputies from the department of the Gironde).

He flew immediately to the place where he imagined that Henry was to be found. He did find him, as has been already described, expatiating on prospects of approaching felicity, and, with a look and a word, transformed all his joys to anguish.

He sprung, without farewel, from the side of the afflicted Seraphina. He hastened into the hackney-coach that had brought the unwelcome messenger. He was driven, as fast as the horses could be lashed along, to the now melancholy mansion in Grosvenor-square.

He arrived—too late to receive the last injunctions of an expiring mother.

She was already dead.

Nerissa met him in the hall; and, with an air of mixed embarrassment and concern related the dismal tidings. She had received the parting breath—She had closed the eyes of the best of mothers and the best of friends. She had been entrusted to convey the last blessing, and the last admonition of agonised affection, to the afflicted Henry.

Henry was stupefied, at first, with his anguish. He stood motionless for a while—the tears did not flow—the heart scarcely heaved—the breath passed not perceptibly through his nostrils.

At length, with a burst of voluble affliction he rushed into the fatal chamber; and, throwing himself down upon the breathless corpse, washed it with his tears; and vented the phrensy of his soul.

It was with difficulty that he could be torn away from the scene of horror by the solicitudes of Nerissa and the domestics; and but by the slow progress of time alone, could his wounded mind be restored to its accustomed peace.

Seraphina was informed by Edmunds the next morning, of the fatal catastrophe. She mourned over her blighted hopes. She mourned still more bitterly over the irremediable loss that Henry sustained—She mourned over the loss society had experienced in so excellent a friend to virtue and misfortune; and, in the bitterness of her heart, recurred to the impressions upon which the reader has heard her dwelling, upon former occasions.

She questioned the value of life; and lamented, once more, that she had not been destined to share the peaceful oblivion of Parkinson and Amanda!—that she might not be permitted to participate in that of the revered, though unknown Amelia.

END OF THE SECOND VOLUME

T. Davison,
    White-Friars.

VOLUME III

BOOK VII.
=========
CHAP. I.

Containing the Space of somewhat less than a Year, from the Death of Amelia, to the Arrival of Intelligence of the Death of Montfort in the West-Indies.

Self Condemnations.—Irrational Resources.—Disappointed Hopes.—
Technical Precautions.—Disinterested Perseverance.—The Parasite.—
Wheels within Wheels.—News from Jamaica.—The Express.

OF all the afflicting forms in which grief is apt to array herself on the death of those we love, most undoubtedly the least supportable is that of self-reproach. Yet who is he that, having lost a beloved parent, an affectionate partner, or a darling child, looks back upon the sad catastrophe without sometimes saying—"This—this might I have done which I omitted"—or, "That I did which ought never to have been done?"

Henry had his share in this portion of bitterness.

The incurable nature of the disease of which Amelia had died, left him not, indeed, at liberty to suppose that any attentions of his could have preserved her life.

"Yet they might have protracted it!" said he to himself, in the anguish of his heart—"or, at least, I might have rendered her closing days more comfortable. Ah! why was I blind to those alarming symptoms?—why proudly inattentive to the voice of friendly reproach?—why did I suffer the suggestions of youthful vanity to render me deaf to the well-founded apprehensions and admonitions of Nerissa.

"And is this—even this, the heaviest part of that misconduct of which I have reason to accuse myself?—might not those frequent uneasinesses and agitation of mind with which my irregular conduct afflicted the best of mothers, have tended, in a considerable degree, to the fostering— perhaps to the formation of that cruel disease, which has brought to so premature a termination her invaluable life?"

It had been happy if these reflections (whether well or ill founded) had produced any permanent amelioration of character: If those habits of dissipation which he now bewailed, as the frequent sources of maternal affliction, had been superseded by more rational pleasures, and dispositions of a more regulated nature.

But whatever stress divines may think fit to lay upon the virtue of repentance, a little knowledge of mankind will soon convince us that it is much more efficacious for the endowment of monasteries and hospitals, than for the practical correction of the heart. Reflection, indeed, may influence us in the closet: but habit is imperious when we mingle again with the accustomed circles of business or of pleasure; and, in the moral, as the physical world, action is more frequently decided by the stimuli of custom than the boasted volitions of reason.

This was particularly conspicuous in the conduct of Henry, upon this occasion. It had been long an inveterate practice with him to bury all uneasy reflections (from whatever circumstance they might arise) in dissipated and intemperate gratifications. It was, accordingly, not difficult for his accustomed associates (when the first torrent of his affliction began to subside) to draw him to his accustomed remedies.

He was so drawn. Reflection was uneasy. He fled from it. He drowned it in the circulating bowl. That which at first did but overwhelm his melancholy feelings, renewed in time the full but irregular tide of his animal spirits. He launched into every pleasure; he engaged in every extravagant pursuit; and having thus abandoned himself again to prodigal excesses, he seemed to indulge in them beyond all former bounds.

Another circumstance, that happened within a few months after the death of Amelia, assisted in impelling his mind to these irregular resources.

Seraphina, whose situation is now no longer a secret to the reader, was seized, at the accustomed time, with the pangs of child-birth. She endured a mother's throes; but she felt not a mother's transport. One faint scream, indeed, ascertained the vitality of the infant, and flattered paternal anxiety with delusive hopes; but, in a few minutes, it was seized with convulsions and expired.[1]

This was scarcely a more grievous disappointment to Seraphina herself than to Henry.

He had a heart not unsusceptible of paternal emotions. He had anticipated many delightful sensations from that new and endearing relationship. He had wished particularly for a daughter, (for a little Seraphina!) and a daughter it was. But the messenger who brought the welcome tidings, had scarcely time to return to the chamber of her mistress, when she was dismissed again, to chill his rising transports with the intelligence, that the object of those transports was no more.

Henry had now a new affliction to soothe with his accustomed antidote: and, what was worse, the links were weakened that held him to more virtuous pleasures.

Hitherto he had been very assiduous in his attentions to Seraphina. His dissipations were rather accidental than steadily pursued—the consequences of the allurements and invitations of others, more than of his own spontaneous inclination. His visits to the retreat were long and frequent; and he soothed his anguish for a beloved mother with the solicitudes of conjugal tenderness, and the prospects of paternal endearment.

---

1 A reversal of the fate of Wollstonecraft, who died on 10 September 1797 of complications resulting from the birth eleven days earlier of her daughter, the future Mary Wollstonecraft Shelley.

During this interval of moral convalescence, he had been again solicitous to obtain the consent of Seraphina, to an immediate marriage.

By the death of Amelia he had become possessed of some property, independent of paternal caprice. All that by marriage settlement was left at her disposal (with the exception only of a few small legacies, to Nerissa, and two or three old-standing servants) she had bequeathed to him: and had secured her bequest, and identified the object of it, with a mingled precision of a legal and endearing description that was not a little remarkable.

The will was written by her own hand: and it appeared as though the law books which, during the last three or four years of her life, she had accumulated and consulted with so much diligence, had been procured for the express purpose of enabling her to perform this last office of maternal kindness with a punctual formality, that might leave open no door for evasion or litigious dispute. Even technical men, when they heard the instrument read, marvelled at her elaborate preciseness, and said that she had been careful overmuch.

Henry was thus described—

"And all the rest and residue of my property, which by the terms of the marriage settlement," &c. &c. "I am entitled and empowered to dispose of by my last will and testament, I do hereby give and bequeath to my dearly beloved son, Henry Montfort—he who at the time of the date of these presents resides with me in the dwelling house where this my last will and testament is made and executed, performing all the duties of an affectionate son; and who, from the day of his birth, has been my sole joy and consolation, in all my trials and afflictions; and from that time to the present hour (saving and excepting those intervals which were devoted to the acquirements of science and accomplishment in the Colleges of Eton, and Christ Church, Oxford; and saving and excepting, also, the anxious season of his voyage to St. Domingo, and temporary residence there) has been my constant inmate and companion; sweetening the otherwise bitter cup of life; which for his sake, and his alone, I feel myself reluctant to forego."[1]

"If she had left twenty sons behind her, and they had all been christened by the same name," exclaimed the gentlemen of the long robe, "she could not have distinguished her favourite legatee more precisely."

The property, indeed, with the immediate possession of which he was vested by this will, was very inconsiderable, in comparison with what he might expect at the death of his father; and Henry's general habits of life seemed very well accommodated to the size of its utmost expectations.

---

1 The language of Amelia's will reflects Thelwall's early legal training.

Upon this basis, however, when the first transports of his grief had subsided, he began to importune Seraphina for her consent to their legal union.

"Let us delay no longer, my love," said he, "the fulfilment of those preliminaries which may enable the virtues of Seraphina to shine forth in their proper lustre, and place her in the rank to which she is entitled in society. Melancholy, indeed, and ever to be deplored is the event that has enabled me to say so—but we have now an independence, even though my father should be inexorable in resenting this act of justice and of virtue."

"An independence, indeed," answered Seraphina, "more than my ambition ever aimed at, or *my* habits would require. But is it such as *you* can be independent upon?

"Alas! I fear it is not?

"Try—try the experiment first, Henry. Contract your desires. Reform your habits of expense and dissipation. See if you can reconcile yourself to that simplicity of life and manners—that sequestered and philosophical retirement which a contracted income might require.

"O! that you could do so, my Henry! O! that you could!

"Why have you not the fortitude—the wisdom to make the effort? Why has not Seraphina the power to lure you to those paths of peace?"

H. "Doubt not your power, my enchanting Seraphina! Be thou my constant monitor and companion, I will be every thing you can wish."

S. "I needs must doubt, Henry, what I have so often seen to fail. Yet cannot I but wonder that, with powers and faculties like yours, you should want inducement to change your line of conduct.

"Are there no pleasures thinkest thou, Henry, without the pale of dissipation and expense? Among those complicated powers and faculties that constitute the intellectual agent, man, are there none that are capable of ministering to his delight, but the grosser ones of sense?

"I would not be a preacher, Henry. I would not exchange the gaiety of my youth, or the softness of my sex, to appear an antiquated pedant in the eyes of the man I love. Yet once in my life, let me yield to the powerful stimulus that seems to prompt my tongue.—Let the mistress be awhile forgotten, while I perform the solemn duty of a friend; and, in the voice of moral exhortation, call upon you, my dearest Henry! to tear yourself from those profligate pursuits and dissipated companions with which you are so unworthily engaged.

"O! try with me, the sweets of a more rational intercourse! Let us commune with the time-honoured dead—let us imitate the frugal virtues that, in the illustrious examples of antiquity, never fail to excite the admiration of the dissipated and the prodigal. Look more to intellect, my Henry, and less to sense—walk with the philosophers and the muses, instead of revelling with bacchanalians.

"Let not the Orphic tongue be rendered mute by those licentious passions that tore the Thracien bard at Rhodope.[1]

"Assume that higher port of character for which the organizing power of nature, and the instructions of your most excellent mother, have conspired to fashion you. Qualify yourself for those public utilities to which (in this season of alarms and innovations, when the frame of social nature totters, and the foundations of existing institutions seem to be shaking under them) every man of intellect and virtue should consider himself as liable to be called; and, if your active mind still pants for variety, and the levity of youth must have its relaxations from serious pursuits, let the pleasures of fancy diversify those of science; and let not the delirious visions of the bower of Margot be the only effusions of your pen that may gratify the taste, and rouse the tender feelings of posterity.

"Ah, Henry! if, in consenting to become your wife, I could assure myself, that I should bestow upon you, as my dowry, the steadfast, the unrepining resolution to adopt and persevere in this advice, with how much joy—with how proud a consciousness of disinterested rectitude would I embrace your present proposal! For with such resolutions, and such tastes, thou would'st be more happy—ah! three times thrice more happy, with this comparatively humble independence, than all the wealth of your father can ever make you, while you continue your present career of dissipation and prodigality."

Henry listened to his lovely monitress with a charmed attention. He gazed upon her with a sort of awful delight. The animation of her delivery—the elevation of sentiment that glowed within her bosom and beamed through her eyes, gave the heightening touches of expression and moral loveliness to the beautiful symmetry of her features.—He called to mind the strong language of Edmunds, upon a recent occasion. His heart—his voice adopted it—

"*If there is such a thing as divinity,*" exclaimed he, "*it must be feminine; and this is she!*"

Seraphina blushed at the extravagance of the compliment. She blushed too at the novel character she had assumed, and at the recollection of the fervour with which she had spoken.

"O! Seraphina!" continued he, snatching her to his bosom, while his eyes overflowed with emotion, "by what new methods would'st thou persuade me to look for no heaven beyond what is sometimes to be found on the sphere upon which we move?—why convince me, by so divine, so dangerous an example, that there is a morality of the heart beyond all that creeds and systems could ever teach?

---

1   The bard Orpheus, famous for his failed voyage to the underworld to rescue his wife Eurydice, is typically associated in Greek mythology with Thrace, the region of northern Greece where he was born and died. Some versions of the Orpheus myth attribute his death to the Maenads, ecstatic female followers of the god Dionysus.

"If such are its effects, proselytise me to this new faith. Let me worship the moral divinity that dwells within, and leave to gownsmen the mystic jargon of their schools."

S. "Worship what you will, Henry, so you do but cease to deify the gross pleasures of sense."

H. "But, no—it is all illusion. Heaven moves within thee. Thou art thyself the organ of that power of whom thou are unconscious. Divinity speaks through thy lips; and so speaking, becomes still more divine!

"And can I listen to thee, and not be all that thou wouldst have me?

"Ah! no. Your accents have sunk into my heart. Like chemic fire[1] they have transmuted it, and turned its base alloy to the pure ore of virtue.

"I will be no more—I *am* no more the thing you have reprehended— the sordid slave of dissipation and luxurious appetite! I will believe that I have within me the powers that you ascribe. I will believe, that *if I have them*, they may be called forth. And thou, my lovely monitress—my friend!—my mistress! my wife! by the last, and best, of those dear names, shalt guarantee my reformation—at once my companion and my example in this new and more rational career!"

"O! Henry! Henry!" exclaimed she, returning his embrace with glowing tenderness, "how blest were Seraphina should this resolution last! How dear, how doubly dear wouldst thou become to this fond heart!— Ah! dearer by far, ten thousand times more dear (if such multiplication of tenderness, indeed, were possible) than even at that hour, when, over-powered by its emotions, and betrayed by conspiring circumstances, I sur-rendered to your importunities, and as the fervour of your protestations led me to believe, to the peace and tranquillity of your mind, my virgin honour, my innocence, my all of future hope and destiny!——The world will add—of virtue also."

A tear or two stole from either eye, as she uttered this. Her heart swelled with its emotions. She felt that the censure of the world is some-thing—even when the judgment revolts from the principles upon which that censure is founded.

Henry kissed away the drops that bedewed her cheek.

"Repent not of that hour," exclaimed he, "my Seraphina!—nor of the many many hours of heart-racking suspense and apprehension that it has spared me. If ever there was a season when you might have repented; that season is now gone by. This day, my love! this day shall see you the wife of Henry Montfort—The world shall acknowledge you as such—Shall commend my choice, and envy my propitious fortune."

"No, Henry, no," replied she, resuming an elevated firmness of tone and gesture—"No. It was not by *professions* that you won this heart; nor by professions shall you gain this hand.

---

1   An allusion to the pseudoscience of alchemy, which sought to transmute base metals into gold by means of an alkahest, a hypothetical universal solvent also known as the "Fire of Hell."

"I know your sincerity, Henry—but I know your weakness. If in the hour of passion I betrayed myself, I will not, in the hour of passion, betray you, also.

"You are moved, my Henry, strongly moved—as your generous nature is apt to be, when that which is good and amiable is set before you: but the cool considerations of judgment must sanction these feelings, before I suffer you to act upon them; and experience must have proved, both to yourself and me, that you are capable of adopting the system which under the influence of those feelings you so enthusiastically approve, before you pass the Rubicon[1] of all your hopes, and shut yourself out from these prospects so indispensable to your present habits.

"Nay, protest not, Henry—endeavour not to enforce upon my heart a credulity to which it is already but too much disposed.

"I am interested enough in the belief of your reformation. I have reason enough to wish what you so generously desire: for I confess my situation is somewhat irksome. My solitude when you are absent (and you have been too often so——It is the first time I have reproached you, Henry—and it shall be the last)—My solitude is rather too absolute; and this Morton—whom I cannot comprehend—whom I cannot approve—(I pray you make not *her* your confident,)—and whom yet I cannot shake off, affords not much relief to its occasional dreariness.

"There is a pang of loneliness, Henry. This heart has often felt it: and since the loss of your excellent mother (the aspiring hope of whose society and friendship was no sooner lighted up than it was so fatally extinguished) I have felt, I think, more than ever, the growing desire of social intercourse—the happiness that is to be enjoyed in a small circle of enlightened and congenial minds. But even this, and all that could result from my acquiescence with your present wishes, might be bought too dearly. It would be bought too dearly, if Henry should repent—if his accustomed habits should return upon him, and conspiring with the resentment of an inexorable father, should involve him in misery and ruin.

"Never, never shall you accuse your Seraphina with being the cause of such calamities as then might overwhelm you.—Never, never shall you say—never, never will I expose myself to the anguish of suspecting the glance of your eye, in some distempered moment, of so suggesting—*This, this do I owe to thee, O Seraphina!—To thee and our disastrous union!*

"She is gone, Henry! to whose decision we agreed to refer this controversy. She is gone without pronouncing judgment: and with her is gone the main stay and prop of all my hopes of fixing you in wiser habits.

"Our united efforts might have done much. Mine, solitary and unseconded, nothing.

---

1 A point of no return (from the name of the river whose crossing by Julius Caesar marked the beginning of the war with Pompey).

"She could have made use of many arguments (they would have been generous in *her*!) which I cannot. This once, Henry, I have appealed to exhortation: for the occasion led me to it without premeditation or design. But I cannot repeat such admonitions, or lay in wait for the proper seasons of enforcing them. I love too tenderly to play the monitor. Besides I have an interest of my own at stake, and that must chain my tongue: for I cannot endure to be suspected, or even to suspect myself of lying under the suspicion, of a selfish motive."

It was in vain that Henry endeavoured to remove these objections. They were not to be removed by words. Time only and experience could remove them: the experience that he had changed his habits.

Of this, indeed, at first, there were considerable indications. The dialogue, as has been stated, took place some time before the disappointment of those paternal hopes that had begun to glow in the bosoms of our hero and heroine; nor was the conversation concluded without many allusions to the prospects and expectations they had reciprocally formed with reference to the interesting event they looked forward to.

This was a theme upon which Henry loved to dwell; and the emotions it frequently excited were an excellent comment upon the text of Seraphina that *there were pleasures* (aye and those of a very exalted nature) *without the pale of dissipation and expense.*

But these pleasures and these prospects were of short duration. Upon the disappointment of his paternal hopes, he sunk into that state of dejection and melancholy to which, upon every visitation of misfortune, he was too much inclined: and to rouse himself again from this despondence, he applied to his usual resources, the society of his former boon companions, and the revels of thoughtless profusion.

The admonitions of Seraphina were soon forgotten. The philosopher—the poet—was no more. And, as in the physical frame, where any constitutional infirmity exists so intimately blended with the vital fibre, as to admit of palliatives only, instead of cures, every successive relapse is apt to be attended with a more obstinate and more alarming crisis, so in this intellectual relapse, the moral infirmity of Henry appeared to have become more alarming, and this reformation more hopeless for ever.

It has been hinted, already, more than once, that this infirmity of Henry was not left to its own simple constitutional progress: that from time to time fresh fuel was artfully heaped upon the languishing fire of his disease, and the feverish thirst of dissipation provoked by inflammatory stimulants prepared by the designing hand of unsuspected enmity.

The real though secret ministrator[1] of these provocations was still, as heretofore, the reverend Emanuel Woodhouse; who, that he might the better perform the two-fold duty of diligently reporting all the irregularities of Henry, and as diligently providing that he should always have something to report, had quitted the learned shades of Oxford, and fixed

---

1   One who ministers or administers something.

his residence in the metropolis; in one of the Inns of Court:[1]—a convenient distance, from which this great mathematician and astronomer could
so manage his machinery, and direct his *telescope of Espionage,* as to be able
at once to influence and distinctly observe whatever was going on in the
neighbourhoods of Grosvenor-square and Somerstown, without appearing to turn any particular attention towards those latitudes.

Among the most distinguished of those profligate associates who had
been lately intruded upon Henry by the circuitous machinations of this
goodly divine, was a young man of the name of Lewson,[2] whose taste for
dissipations which his circumstances could ill support, rendered him a
very fit instrument to play upon the foibles and urge on the ruinous follies
of any prodigal youth of fortune or expectations that might happen to fall
into his hands.

He was, moreover, particularly qualified for the task he was now to
perform. To a prepossessing person, the vivacity of youth, and a more than
ordinary share of the polish of fashionable manners, he added the advantages
of travel, some of the attainments of elegant literature, and a versatility and
promptitude of mind that might almost pass for genius. On the other hand,
he was destitute alike of all moral principle, and all delicacy of feeling—keen
in the pursuit of every voluptuous enjoyment, careless at whose expense his
pleasures were supported, and ready enough to overleap all bounds of obligation or decorum that stood in the way of his gratifications.

So much of these dispositions as related to extravagance and dissipation, seemed to be a sort of hereditary infirmity; and the contagious association seemed to be somewhat hereditary also.

His father had been, heretofore, one of the companions of old Montfort. With unequal resources he had plunged into equal prodigalities; and,
as the habit was too inveterate to be checked by the first approaches of
embarrassment, he had proceeded in his career, supplying his present
necessities by such expedients as presented themselves, till, a little before
the time of which we are now speaking, his credit became completely
exhausted, and his circumstances involved in difficulties that were
absolutely inextricable.

Thus situated, incapable of pursuing his wonted pleasures, and *persecuted* (for he so called it) *by the importunities of his creditors,* he took a resolution, which, to his family at least, appeared to be honourable and generous, whatever might be the opinion of those tradesmen and other
creditors who were thus disappointed even of the hopes of a dividend
upon their demands. He made over, by deed of gift,[3] so much of his prop-

---

1   The four sets of buildings in London belonging to the four legal societies that had
    the exclusive right of admitting people to practice at the bar.
2   Lewson (like Mordant) is also the name of a character in Thelwall's essay "The
    Sceptic," serialized in the *Biographical and Imperial Magazine* in 1789-90.
3   Legal document by which one person transfers property to another without
    recompense.

erty as was yet in his power to his only children (a son and daughter) and suddenly disappeared: whether by flight or suicide was not otherwise ascertained, than by the general conjectures of the circles in which it was canvassed.

Be this, however, as it may, he left behind for his two children (together with their small fortune) an instructive example by which they might have regulated their future conduct.

This example was not lost upon them: though the moralist perhaps may be of opinion, that they did not make precisely the best use of it that might have been desired.

But their characters, in some respects, were already fixed. Habit and association had determined their pursuits. They had not, however, determined them to an implicit adoption of every part of the paternal disposition.

In this disposition they had observed certain foibles that did not very well accord with existing circumstances; and to which, indeed, they persuaded themselves, exclusively, to attribute all his *misfortunes.*—These were frankness of mind, a promptitude to sympathise and bestow; a readiness to confer; a proud reluctance to the receiving of obligations; and some two or three more weaknesses of the same family and complexion. Dismal qualifications for a gentleman with a contracted income!

Lewson was about two-and-twenty, and had just returned from his foreign tour,[1] when, under these circumstances, and with these reflections, he found himself master of his own and his sister's destinies. His tastes and pursuits had been hitherto such as might have been expected from his education; and, as his father had thought it no part of his duty to confer with his children on the situation of his affairs, his expectations had been such as to lay him under no uneasy restraints.

What, therefore, was to be done, now that he was awakened from his dream of opulence and pleasure, and looked round on the actual situation of his affairs? "Turn hermit?—bookworm?—moralist? and cry out against the pleasures and enjoyments which it is no longer in my power to indulge!"

This was not the *species* of hypocrisy to which his nature could most readily accommodate itself. It was of too grave a character: elaborate in practice, and barren of remuneration. There were other lines of conduct that ran more parallel with his habits and desires.

He did not want penetration. He had observed how much the sympathy of mankind flows in the narrow channels of ranks and classes; and that many of those favoured sons of opulence and dissipation, whose palms are clenched against the vulgar appeals of indigence and misery, will yet unfold the full amplitude of their generosity to support the prodigal pleas-

---

1   Or Grand Tour: an educational tour of the principal cities and places of interest in Europe undertaken in the eighteenth century by young men of good birth or fortune.

ures of a companion of their own rank and circle. To the foibles of these, therefore, he determined to apply; and he did apply, with such success, that, without breaking further into the capital of his contracted fortune, he continued to indulge, with even increased avidity, in all the dissipated excesses of his days of imagined opulence.

Such was the principal agent pitched upon by the Rev. Emanuel Woodhouse to complete the ruin of Henry, which for some time past, and for very substantial reasons, he had very deliberately and elaborately planned.

This holy man, who perfectly understood the character of the parties, concluded that nothing more was necessary than to bring them together, and the business would assuredly be done.

Now Woodhouse was, in his way, a man of some celebrity and importance—extensive in his erudition, and of a penetrating sagacity; and, though cynical and saturnine in his general disposition, he possessed, when he chose to call them forth, some powers of conversation, and a fund of various information and remark. He had, of consequence (like the generality of those who have any reputation for talents of learning), his little system of satellites that revolved around him; dependent, as it were, upon his motions and attractions for their position in the visible hemisphere. In other words, he had his toad eaters—his Baretties, and his Boswells,[1] who echoed his sarcasms and retailed his opinions in whatever society they happened next to fall.

Upon one of these, who never ventured to shew himself in any afternoon party, till he had furnished his empty cranium by a morning visit to the chambers of our sagacious divine, he accordingly fixed as the first spring for setting his complicated machine in motion.

The retailer of second-hand witticisms (who was never unprovided with a pocket memorandum-book to note down, at the end of every visit, whatever had been dropped in scattered hints, or poured out in the full tide of inspiration from the oracular tripos[2]), being engaged to dine with a large party at the house of a gentleman (to whom Lewson was at that time a sort of constant hanger-on), had appealed to his accustomed means of qualifying himself to shine with becoming lustre on the occasion.

Our reverend Machiavel,[3] who perfectly understood the object of these visits, and had made frequent use, in divers circles, of the reflective

---

1 Giuseppe Marc'Antonio Baretti (1719-89): Italian writer who sought to promote Italian language and culture in England, where his many influential friends included Samuel Johnson. James Boswell (1740-95): friend and biographer of Johnson. Thus the reference is to a constant companion or attendant, especially one who witnesses and records what a person does. A toad-eater is a flatterer or sycophant, a toady.

2 Or tripod: a three-legged vessel at the shrine of Apollo at Delphi, on which the priestess seated herself to deliver oracles.

3 "A person who acts on principles recommended, or supposed to have been recommended, by Machiavelli in his treatise on statecraft; an intriguer or schemer" (OED).

loquacity of his visitor, soon put himself in possession of the two leading facts, where he was engaged, and who were to be of the party; and then, taking his scent accordingly, he began to beat about the bushes (animadverting, in his cynical way, first upon one character, then upon another of their mutual acquaintance, without apparent connection or design), till, at last, he started the purposed game, and mentioning the name of young Montfort, began to dwell with some pleasantry upon that particular foible which rendered him the easy dupe of every bankrupt prodigal, who was disposed to enjoy the fashionable pleasures of the day without means to support the expense.

The event justified the expectations of our polite calculator. Our camelion was accomplished with the character of the day. Sarcastic humour was to be his sort, and Henry Montfort the butt of his raillery. Nor did he fail to repeat (almost verbatim) the lesson he had been taught; and with an ease and effrontery that passed for originality with those who did not know him, and affected the risible muscles of the whole party.

Lewson was particularly attentive. He had *squeezed one orange pretty close*; and was beginning to apprehend that he might soon become a little husky, if he had not convenient opportunity of fastening upon another. In other words, he had been so long a sort of expensive appendage to the dissipated pleasures of his present patron, that he began (not without foundation) to suspect him of meditating a moral reformation, for the express purpose of getting rid of so costly an incumbrance.

The description of the prominent foibles of Henry, was therefore very inviting. It was the very longitude he wanted to discover. His resolution was accordingly taken. A new friendship was to be cultivated without delay; and Mordant, who was of the present party, listened very readily to the first suggestion of his desire to be introduced: the fact being, that, although he was very much pleased with the company of Lewson, he was somewhat apprehensive that he might have fastened upon him; and he was, therefore, very well pleased with the opportunity (according to his own quaint mode of expressing himself) of hanging the hat upon another man's peg, since, though somewhat too heavy for his brows, it was too good to be thrown away.

Such were the companions with whom Henry was indulging in the full career of dissipation, when intelligence arrived, both through the medium of public prints and private communication, of the death of old Montfort, by the yellow fever, then raging in the island of Jamaica.

Filial emotion checked for a while the extravagance of youthful folly: for, though the conduct of Montfort, as a father, had never seized upon the affections of Henry with that impressive force with which they had been attached to by the maternal tenderness of Amelia, he felt the obligations, and gave way to the sorrows of a son; and inebriate levity was lost in pensive gloominess and regret.

He had just returned from the mid*night*—or rather mid-*day* masquerade (for it was verging towards that time before he separated from *all* the party with which he had been there carousing) when the news was first communicated by the officious friendship of Woodhouse.

He read—he did not weep—but he felt a sudden damp upon his heart. He sat himself down upon a chair, and resting his head upon his hand, gave way to the benumbing sensation. His corporal frame seemed to sympathise with the state of his mind. Languor and debility succeeded to the feverish impetuosity of an over-stimulated pulse. In short, he sickened, and took to his bed.

Finding himself no better in the evening, he began to be somewhat alarmed. The thoughts of Seraphina too came rushing on his soul—and calling for pen and ink, ordered the coach, and desiring Edmunds to hold himself in readiness to do a welcome errand, as soon as it arrived, he set up in bed, and wrote the following letter.

"Dearest Seraphina,

"I write this from my sick bed, to which I have taken within these few hours; but from which, if I may judge by my sensations, I shall not soon rise.

"My father is no more.

"I received the intelligence on my return from a scene of riotous folly, in which I had been dissipating, with too much profusion, both my animal spirits and my health. Perhaps, if I had not taken so much pains to conceal it from myself, I should have discovered some time ago, that the latter was not in a state to bear the freedoms I have been taking with it.

"The shock I received from the abrupt communication of this unexpected event, has brought the latent disease into action. I droop—I feel it fastening upon my vitals; and beneath this roof of vacant ostentation, there is no one to watch by my bed-side with that medicinal solicitude that once made the hammock of sickness in the narrow cabin, a couch of enviable repose.

"O! come to me, my love! my angel of consolation! come with healing on thy wings: for it is thou alone canst heal me.

"If this sudden sickness had not prevented, I would myself have hastened to conduct you—not as Seraphina Parkinson, but Mrs. Montfort: but fate defers a while this proof of my fidelity—this completion of my happiness.

"Come then, my love! once more let the heart of Seraphina dispense with forms that obstruct the happiness of her Henry. Come, and, with thy looks of love and of forgiveness, charm away this envious disease, which is now the only obstruction to our indissoluble union: or, if that may not be, come, at least, and soothe the last hours, and receive the latest breath of

Thine to the final ebb of life,

HENRY MONTFORT."

It is scarcely necessary to inform the reader with what emotions Seraphina perused this letter—

"And is he really so ill, Edmunds?" exclaimed she, with a look of wild anxiety.

E. "Very ill, indeed, madam, considering how suddenly he was taken. But I hope not dangerous. We have brought him round again, madam, when he was much worse."

S. "Bring me my cloak, Morton—Haste! haste! Let me fly to him this instant."

Morton's heart was all on pit-a-pat from the instant she beheld the carriage, with the liveries and armorial bearings of Montfort at the door: for she immediately concluded that this publicity must augur some happy change. She obeyed the order, therefore, that indicated the resolution of Seraphina with the utmost alacrity; not doubting (whatever might be the occasion of the summons) that when her mistress was once fairly set down in Grosvenor-square, means would easily enough be found to prevent her returning to her odious solitude. But as soon as she came to understand the whole of the business—that old Montfort was dead, and Henry, full of qualms, upon the bed of sickness, her tone was instantly changed.

It immediately occurred to her that this was an opportunity not to be lost. That Seraphina had nothing to do but to affect a little coyness, and Henry might be brought to whatever terms they pleased: the indispensable preliminaries of which now appeared to be, that the invitation to treat should be accompanied by a clergyman and a special licence. She therefore began immediately to raise objections and delays—to start doubts, and suggest suspicions, and put her countenance in form for grave and matron-like advice. But Seraphina, with an indignant look, giving her hand to Edmunds, hurried to the carriage, without so much as bidding her to follow; and Edmunds was not without hope that she would actually have been left behind. Indeed she was likely to have been so: for the footman was shutting the door, and Seraphina showed no inclination to stop him, if the good duenna had not mended her pace, and lifted up her voice in earnest importunity for admission.

CHAP. II.

Containing only a short space of time; in which, however, the Hero will make considerable progress in regaining the good opinion of the reader.

The Closet.—Grateful Remembrances.—Old Scenes revived on a new Theatre.—Delays and Difficulties.—Consultations and Counsellors.— Amiable Solicitudes, and generous Resolutions.—Propitious Appearances.—

THE indisposition of Henry was so much the more obstinate, as the morbid humours had been long collecting before the symptoms made their appearance in the constitution.

The attentions of Seraphina, however, had lost no part of their medical influence. In a little while he began gradually to recover; and though the perfect restoration of his health was a work of time, it was not long before he appeared to be out of danger, and was able to take some exercise in the open air.

Seraphina took this opportunity of gratifying a curiosity, which, ever since she entered the house she had continued to cherish, by a visit to the closet or private study of Amelia: an apartment which, from several scenes that the reader will remember to have passed in it, could not fail to have been a subject of frequent conversation between our hero and heroine.

In the place itself there was little that was remarkable. It was merely a small, but convenient apartment, connected with the library by a long avenue or gallery; and approachable on the other side only through that suite of rooms which Amelia herself had formerly used to occupy. In this the select library of Amelia—a small, but valuable collection, was arranged.

This was a sort of consecrated temple. Every thing in it was sacred from innovation or removal. The books, the papers, the writing-desk—the very chair in which she used to sit—all seemed as though they had been suffered to remain in the very posture in which she had left them, and they had so been suffered.[1] Their disposition had been preserved with a sort of superstitious veneration; and the same servant, who used exclusively to wait upon her during the studious hours she spent in that recess, still defended it with pious reverence from the pollution of the cobweb and the moth; and ever as she brushed the untenanted walls, and wiped away the dust from the chair, a memorial tear stole down her cheek, and she breathed the murmured sigh of regret.

With what sensations did Seraphina behold this scene! With what sensations did she hear the simple tale of garrulous affection, from which she collected these particulars.

The impression at first was deeply aweful. Her eyes travelled slowly round from object to object—and every thing appeared to be invested

---

1 I am informed by an intelligent friend, to whom I happened to have an opportunity of reading this while I was correcting it for the press, that there is a scene very similar to this, in many particulars, in Mrs. Radcliffe's Mysteries of Udolpho. It is necessary, therefore, for me to declare, that I have been unfortunate enough never to have seen any of the novels of that celebrated lady, and to have been even ignorant of the very nature of those performances, till the recent conversation of the abovementioned friend gave me a sort of second hand acquaintance with them, and whetted a curiosity which, in my remote obscurity and double exile from books and from the world, I have no opportunity of gratifying. The coincidence, therefore, striking as I understand it to be, is simply and purely accidental: to make use of an Hibernianism, I have been unfortunate enough to imitate what I never had the good fortune to see. [Thelwall's note] The "intelligent friend" may have been the London publisher of The Daughter, Richard Phillips.

A similar scene occurs in The Mysteries of Udolpho, Vol. IV, Ch. 4, when the orphaned heroine Emily visits the death chamber of the late Marchioness de Villeroi. The editors are grateful to Margaret Anne Doody for her help in identifying the scene. On Thelwall's "double exile from books and from the world" between 1797 and 1800, see the Introduction, pp. 9-12.

with a sort of venerable solemnity. All was full of Amelia. It seemed as though her spirit still hovered and presided there: and her form (such as imagination fashioned it) rose before the intellectual eye of Seraphina.

These awful impressions were presently succeeded by others of a more tender nature. In the objects that presented themselves she began to look around for images not of the form, but of the mind of its departed tenant. In these she could not be mistaken. That mind was impressed upon every thing. Every thing conspired to confirm and strengthen the impression which the frequent conversations of Henry had made of her liberality, her understanding, and her many virtues.

"O, such a mother!" exclaimed she, as these reflections and remembrances rose upon her mind—"O! such a mother! and I not know her!"

The soul came streaming from her eyes. She burst into an agony of exclamation. She threw herself down in the chair.

This, in any other person, would have been a sort of sacrilege. But Seraphina had wept herself into the heart of the kind-bosomed menial, and her whole deportment had interested her so much, that she seemed to think her not unworthy to fill the place that had been heretofore so distinguishedly occupied. Add to which, that as the good waiting-woman had got a sort of notion (which indeed Edmunds had taken some pains to propagate, as a kind of secret, among all the servants) that Seraphina had for some time been privately married to her master, which was to be publicly announced as soon as the customary season of mourning would permit, she was, perhaps, not displeased with any indications that seemed to suggest a similarity of character between her late and her present mistress.

"Ah! madam," said she, sobbing—"there our poor dear mistress as was, used to set for many a long hour—and there sometimes she used to write; and in that desk she used to lock up what she had written so carefully. And there she had used to keep something—I don't know what it was—but it was a parcel of writings, that she used to read so often, and so weep over—I am sure it must have been something about Mr. Henry: for she never wept about any thing but him—except, indeed, when she met with any thing very melancholy in a poetry book, or heard of any poor body's misfortunes.

"But then that was all very different from this. For, as for the story-books, when she had made herself melancholy enough with them, she would shut them up and give them to me, to put them in their places again. And then she would begin to smile, and look so comfortable, and walk two or three times up and down the long passage here; and then return to some of those great large books that she used to be so thoughtful over.—*Ah!* thought I to myself, many's the time, *Ah! that I had been a schollard!*[1] *that I might have read melancholy stories to make me cry so, and be so happy.* And then, too, my poor dear mistress used to tell me that they

---

1 An illiterate or dialect word for "scholar."

did the heart good, and made us kind and compassionate. And I am sure there must have been something in it—She was so good, and so kind, and so compassionate herself: for when she heard of poor people's misfortunes, as I was saying just now, madam, and used to cry about them, she would put her hand into her pocket, and give me something to take to them; and then her tears would stop, and her countenance would so brighten.

"But she never smiled and looked comfortable, and her countenance never brightened after reading them there papers that I was talking about, in that little desk. I could never bear to mention it to my young master yet: for he always weeps and looks so melancholy when any thing puts him in mind of my poor dear lady. But to be sure it must be about him—or else about that madame Louisa that my mistress used to talk about to Nerissa.

"Ah! that was a sad story, madam—but then, to be sure, we servants have nothing to do with such things—and my old master is dead and gone for *sartin*[1]—and every back must bear its own burthen—but I am afraid it was a black piece of business for all that.

"And so, as I was saying, madam, my dear good mistress used to sit in that chair just where it stands, madam. And, since she left us, madam, to go to a better place—for if she is not in heaven, I am sure we can none of us have any chance of going there—nobody has ever set in it before. I thought I could never have born to have seen any body set in it. But I do think you are so like her, madam! And I hope you will set there often, madam," (continued she, curtsying) "and—and—and that my master will be very happy, madam," (curtsying again) "and that I shall look to this room, madam, and dust it, and keep it in order all the days of my life—for I know all the ways of it, madam—and it would be like losing my poor dear mistress a second time to leave it, madam!"

Seraphina, to whom this long tale about nothing[2] (as some heartless being perhaps might call it) had not been without interest, either from the matter, or the manner in which it was told; but who, on the contrary, had listened to it throughout with fixed attention, and a variety of powerful emotions, was touched by these broken sentences, almost as much for the teller as by the tale. She fixed her eyes with benignant sympathy upon the face of the embarrassed maiden. She smiled encouragement.

It was an April smile—as much of shower as of sunshine. But it cherished the spring of hope in the fearful heart of Nanny; who curtsied, and thus resumed—

"No, madam, nobody has ever set there before, as I said. Nobody has ever been in the room, only my master, sometimes, and myself—except Miss Nerissa, who was very busy here for a little while, as soon as my poor mistress was dead. But I could never understand what she was about—for, when I came in afterwards, I could not see that any thing had been moved.

---

1 An illiterate pronunciation of "certain."

2 *Macbeth* 5.5.26-28.

"I suppose it was something that my poor mistress told her to do when she was dying: for we were all of us ordered out of the room; so that nobody could hear her last words besides. For she was very fond of Miss Nerissa; and very good to her; though, I believe, towards the last, she was no better than she ought to be: and the servants all say she wanted to draw in my young master, for all she was so much older:—but I hope my master has done better, madam," concluded she, curtsying very low.

Though some of the hints and insinuations in this harangue could not but be a little embarrassing to Seraphina, yet, upon the whole, those very parts were not displeasing. It was pretty evident upon what footing she had been placed in the estimation of the servants; and she believed it not difficult to conclude who had been at the pains of setting her in that favourable point of view. But that which principally filled her mind was the vivid impression of the philosophical and benevolent character of Amelia, which the little anecdotes and characteristic declamation of Nanny had produced.

It was a painting, indeed, somewhat in the rough, and by a pencil not very well skilled in the more delicate touches of the art; but the draught was evidently from nature, and the outline had all the characteristic marks of a genuine resemblance.

From that time our heroine took every opportunity of visiting the little study: and while she turned over the pages of Amelia's favourite authors (which from a variety of indications it was not difficult to discover) and noted the leaves she had doubled, and the passages she had scored, she seemed to enter more intimately into her tastes and feelings; to become acquainted, as it were, not only with her thoughts, but with her heart and habits; and, in short, to enter into a sort of familiarity after death, with one who in life had been esteemed and reverenced, although she had been never known.[1]

In the mean while, these were not the only intellectual pleasures enjoyed by Seraphina, in this new abode; nor this the only apartment in which the flow of sentiment was indulged. The reign of virtue and reason over the heart of Henry seemed to be again restored. All the affections, and all the habits that had rendered him heretofore so amiable seemed to revive, and the powers of his mind to expand.

With such a companion as Seraphina, it was impossible not to aspire to be an intellectual being; and the unsettled state of his health formed a further barrier of separation from the prodigal companions who might have seduced him to other pursuits.

Edmunds (besides what he felt on the score of sympathy and affection for the interests and happiness of the parties) was not without his share of

---

1 As in Wollstonecraft's *The Wrongs of Woman: or, Maria* (1798), in which the heroine falls in love with Henry Darnford by reading his marginal notes in various books. Thelwall's later elocutionary theory likewise emphasizes the importance, in recitation, of entering into the feelings of an author.

the advantages of this change. He regained his former footing and esti-mation. The library became a common sitting-room, both for the valetu-dinarian and his nurse. The familiarity with which the latter always con-versed with the librarian, chastised the magisterial pride of Henry; and this moral triumvirate[1] renewed, in this stately temple of the Muses, the delightful and instructive recreations for which, at a former period, neither the little cabin had been too narrow, nor the reeling deck too per-ilous or incommodious.

These conversations were much too interesting for any of the parties to be very eager to interrupt the opportunities of enjoying them. Henry was particularly anxious to create every delay, and oppose every impediment to the return of Seraphina to her retreat. He imagined, or he pretended, that he felt the symptoms of relapse whenever it was talked about; and the tenderness of Seraphina was prevailed upon by complaints of loneliness, and apprehensions of febrile dejection.

Edmunds himself, though he saw very clearly the awkwardness of Seraphina's situation, joined his endeavour to prevent her departure. He knew the weakness of Henry. He feared that, if left to himself, the harpies of dissipation would soon be hovering again around; and he knew how easily all his virtuous resolutions would again become their prey.

He ventured to suggest these apprehensions to Seraphina. She felt their force. But she felt also the embarrassing dilemma in which she stood.

"Her continuance under the roof of Montfort, from the time of his recovery to that appointed for their marriage was certainly neither very decorous nor discreet: but were the morals and welfare of Henry to be outweighed by consideration of decorum? Besides, was not the indeco-rum already committed? Would the tattle of the neighbourhood be silenced, or the suspicions of the world be removed, by her retiring again to her former privacy? Was it not inevitable that she should already have been traced from Somerstown to Grosvenor-square? and would she not be traced from Grosvenor square to Somerstown again, and identified, whenever she should re-appear as the acknowledged wife of Henry? Besides, was it her intention to act a hypocritical farce to conceal what, in her heart, she did not consider as a crime? Was she going elaborately to impose herself upon others for what she was not, or to conceal what she really was? For herself, it was sufficient that in act and thought she had been faithful and immaculate to her Henry. Was it not enough for society, that she was about to conform to its institutions, and bow to its estab-lished ceremonies?"——

These considerations, though they did not actually decide her to comply with the entreaties of Henry, the persuasions of Edmunds, and the instigations of Morton, to return no more to her solitude, were productive

---

1 Writing to his wife in July 1797 from Nether Stowey, Thelwall referred to himself, Wordsworth, and Coleridge as a "literary & political triumvirate" (rpt. in Davies, *Presences* 296).

at least of an irresolution and delay which had ultimately the same effect.

It is not ascribing too much to the influence of those impressions of mere sentiment that are seldom admitted into our reasonings, to say that the attachment she had conceived for the little study and the chair of Amelia, had something to do in that indefinite procrastination with which she continued to adjourn the consideration of her return.

Morton neglected no means of encouraging this procrastination. Unwilling as she had been, under existing circumstances, that Seraphina should, in the first instance, come to the house of Henry at all, without previously propounding such terms as she then imagined might have been dictated with ease; now that she was there, she wished her to remain to make sure of what she could, and to avoid, at any rate, the renewal of that life of moping solitude, of which, for her part at least, she had long been so completely tired.

Still, however, she endeavoured to persuade her to make all things sure before the perfect recovery of Henry's health; and by a *private* marriage (by which the scruples and decorums of the world, with respect to the seasons of what is called mourning, would be evaded) to put herself out of the hazard of future caprices, or cross accidents.

But, independent of that kind of repulsion with which she had, by this time, come in some degree to revolt from every advice (as necessarily selfish and disingenuous) that proceeded from the lips of Morton, the project itself was perfectly inconsistent with her views and principles.

Situated as they were, a private marriage was no marriage at all, in her estimation. It was not the bond of security that she desired. Like another Eloisa,[1] she despised all security but the bond of the heart. The publicity—the general recognition—the open assumption of that rank and respectability in society which might give her virtues room to expand, and restore her to the free exercise of the utilities in which her soul delighted— these were her objects—her motives to the purposed marriage: these were her inducements to comply with formalities which, abstractedly considered, she looked upon as neither rational nor moral.

It was not by a *stolen marriage* that those were to be obtained; but by a marriage in the open eye of day: and on nothing short of these would she condescend to bestow a thought.

The mind of Edmunds, however, was at the same time occupied with the same apprehensions that possessed the imagination of the duenna. From his knowledge of the frailty, he dreaded the fickleness of Henry; and though he never once dreamed even of the possibility of an alienation of his affections, he feared least the return of prodigal propensities, and the seduction of prodigal society, might persuade him to rest satisfied with the possession, already apparently secured, of the person of our heroine; to

---

1 Rousseau's epistolary novel *Julie, ou la Nouvelle Héloïse* (1761; translated as *Julie, or the New Heloise*), sometimes referred to as his *Eloisa*, was one of the period's most popular works of sentimental fiction.

the neglect of that more ample enjoyment of the social and intellectual intercourse which an union publicly sanctioned and avowed, could alone secure.

Of this he was the more apprehensive, as the circumstance of her residence at Grosvenor-square could not fail to give a degree of publicity to the connection, that might let loose the tongues of prodigals, who (if not for some sinister interests of their own, at least from the mere love of prodigality) might attempt to laugh and ridicule the too irresolute Henry out of the idea of pursuing a path of duty and of honour, so remote from the beaten track of fashionable morality: and he was perfectly aware that the longer the marriage was delayed, the more powerful the arguments that might be urged against it.

It was from these considerations that he presumed (though with that modesty which, when this moral indignation did not happen to be excited, he was not unsolicitous to preserve) to expostulate with our hero upon the embarrassing situation in which Seraphina was placed.

He took his opportunity, as he was attending him to his chamber (after a very interesting conversation had been prolonged somewhat beyond the hour of prudence;) and appealing to that mingled admiration and tenderness that filled the soul and overflowed the eyes of Henry, gave vent to the enthusiasm of his own feelings, and the suggestions that agitated his mind.

Henry heard him, with pleased attention, to the end.

"You anticipate my purpose, Edmunds!" said he—"and I am glad to find it thus anticipated. Believe me, Edmunds, nothing on earth is so delightful to my feelings as to observe the interest that all around her evidently feel in behalf of my Seraphina.

"Ambiguous as the situation is in which she stands, how is that respect, which my authority might command for her, superceded, in every person in the house, by that devotion of the heart, that mingled love and veneration, that flows from her own amiable dispositions and deportment!

"I will no longer be the slave of customs and decorums. She has never been so when my happiness or welfare was at stake. I will no longer forego the triumph of such a conquest—the distinction of being known as the possessor of such a heart—the happiness of participating to others those pleasures of intellect which the conversation of Seraphina can so eminently display.

"What are the forms and ceremonies of the world?—These trappings of superstition!—these exterior mockeries!—that for them the living interests of the heart, and the duties of morality should be suspended?

"I can lament the loss of a father—I do lament it. All the feelings of nature are not absorbed in one. But what advantage can his manes receive from *the inky coat*, and all *the trappings and the suits of woe*,[1] that for the

---

1 *Hamlet* 1.2.76-86.

sake of an accustomed perseverance in the assumption of these forms, Seraphina should be exposed to all the irksome sensations with which her present situation must inevitably be attended.

"I will delay this celebration no longer, Edmunds, than till my health is sufficiently established to perform it with that publicity that belongs to an act that fools may scoff at, but that honour and virtue must applaud."

While those who had always professed a personal attachment and interest in the welfare of Seraphina, were thus unanimous in expediting a marriage that alone seemed necessary to the confirmation of her happiness, one even, who had never seen her face, and who, neither from his *professional* nor *moral* character could be suspected of any particular partiality for her principles or her conduct, was, also, conspiring to urge forward, with as much speed as might be, *a consummation so devoutly to be wished.*[1]

This (extraordinary as it may appear) was no other than the Reverend Emanuel Woodhouse; who, among other sage expedients, had even endeavoured, through the medium of anonymous letters,[2] to influence Lewson, by specious arguments and prospects of personal advantage, to be instrumental in bringing about that desirable event. So that all planets appearing to be propitious, it might seem that, now at least, it was time to prepare the bridal robes; and bring our history without further trouble to an immediate and happy conclusion.

But not so smooth, even yet, is the destiny of our heroine. Hope smiles from the helm, indeed, as she looks down upon the flattering calm that is every where spread around; and the halcyon peace[3] seems to be building her nest upon the wave. But all is deceitful. "The exulting demon of the storm"[4] broods in secret among the deeps; and tempest and shipwreck are prepared.

---

1 *Hamlet* 3.1.64-65.

2 In pre-revolutionary France *lettres de cachet* (or letters of cachet) were warrants for the imprisonment of a person without trial at the pleasure of the monarch.

3 The halcyon is a mythical bird fabled to breed around the winter solstice in a nest floating on the sea, which it charms to calmness.

4 Although this exact phrase does not appear elsewhere in Thelwall's oeuvre, it is probably a self-quotation from drafts of his unfinished epic *The Hope of Albion*, which he was composing at the same time as *The Daughter*, and which features a shipwreck scene in which a fiend-like "chastening angel" exults in the storm about to break over the hero.

CHAP. III.

Plans of Lewson and his Confederates to recall Henry
to the career of Dissipation.

Machinations and Dilemmas.—Dr. Pengarron.—The Physician
advised.—The Prescription given.—The Prescription followed.—
Operation of the Prescription.—Symptoms of Infidelity.—Self Condemnation.—Shrewd Conjectures.—The Discovery.—Traits of Gallantry.—
Abrupt Communications.

THE cold return Henry's dissipated companions met with, for all their
inquiries and solicitudes about his health, was the symptom which to
them appeared most alarming. Among these there were several who, one
way or other, had too deep an interest in his follies to suffer him to be
reclaimed from them without an effort. This as has been seen already, was
particularly the case with Lewson; and so far was he from listening to the
suggestions in the anonymous letters of Woodhouse, that when, in consequence of those letters, he had set his engines to work, and made himself,
in some degree, acquainted with the character of our heroine, he began to
consider the match he was instigated to promote, as the inevitable fore-
runner and confirmation of the change so much dreaded; and consequently, in every point of view, as the greatest calamity that could befall
him: and he determined at all events to interrupt, and if possible to
prevent it.

But how was this to be done? The society of Seraphina was the pledge
of moral perseverance; and to persevere in morality was to marry
Seraphina! How to separate these adamantine links?

This was a problem of great difficulty; and the more so as it seemed, in
this *practical* as in certain *theological* syllogisms, that the conclusion must
be arrived at before the major proposition could be established. In other
words, the influence of Seraphina must be undermined before the
machines could be set to work that were to undermine it.

At length, however, the active imagination of Lewson hit upon the
project, as bold as it was profligate. This was no other than to make the
physician who attended upon Henry, an instrument in the promotion of
a plot which he saw no other practicable means of accomplishing.

He knew that this gentleman, Dr. Pengarron,[1] (a very worthy ornament of a very useful body,) independently of the confidence that was
placed in him in a professional point of view, had lived in the habits of
friendship with the family of Montfort, particularly with Amelia, to the
last hours of her life; and that professing, in all companies, a very

---

1   Thelwall seems to be suggesting that the doctor is Welsh. "Pen," the Welsh for
    "head," is common in Welsh and Cornish place names; Garron Pill is an estuary
    in Pembrokeshire.

sincere respect for her memory, he regarded Henry in a very different point of view from a mere ordinary patient; and had some anxiety about every thing that concerned his welfare. He knew him, also, to be one of those magisterial old gentlemen, though his heart was full of benevolence, who are still so much attached to the maxims of the old school, as to think that youth has nothing to do with the choice of its own line of conduct and means of happiness—and that it is the duty of years and experience (by authority when that is practicable, and, where it is not, by chicane and finesse, in which indeed our doctor somewhat delighted) to preside over the inclinations and dictate the conduct of the young.

To him therefore he thought it not difficult to make out such a story, well countenanced by probabilities and appearances, as should influence the old gentleman, from his own views of friendship and moral propriety, to lay, in his professional capacity, the foundations of the superstructure of fraud which Lewson had determined to raise; the more especially as he had learned, upon inquiry, that this son of Esculapius[1] had already advised (though not with the positiveness that might be necessary to ensure obedience) the very measure he now wished him to enforce.

He determined, accordingly, to wait upon Dr. Pengarron in person; and having introduced himself and made known his name, he proceeded as follows:—

"My calling upon you, sir, thus abruptly, may, I am afraid, appear somewhat intrusive—but the cause must plead my excuse."

"Umph—Umph! the cause, sir," answered Pengarron, with a mixture of pedantry and raillery—looking him in the face at the same time, and feeling his pulse; "it is very rarely, sir, that a patient is acquainted with the cause of his own disorder—that is to say with the real nature of the disease; or, as some definitions have it, with the disease itself. But if you will be kind enough to make me acquainted with the history of the symptoms, together with your general habits of body and way of living, as to diet, regimen, secretions and excretions, I make no doubt that I shall be able to understand the cause for you—that is to say, the *causes*, remote, proximate, and predisposing;[2] and from thence to make out my prognosis and diagnosis, and prescribe accordingly."

L. "You mistake me, sir, this is not my business. I have no symptoms to confer about. Thank heaven, I am very well."

P. "Umph!—So much the better, sir; then you do not want any assistance; and I may drink a glass of wine the more in peace and comfort."

---

1 Esculapius (or Aesculapius), son of Apollo, was the Roman god of medicine.
2 In *An Essay towards a Definition of Animal Vitality* (1793) Thelwall identifies the "pre-disposing," "remote," and "proximate" causes of life, namely, matter susceptible to a vital stimulus, the stimulus itself, and the resulting "meliorated or altered state of the organized frame" (*Selected Political Writings* 1: 17).

L. "Yes, sir, I do want your assistance:—and in an affair that materially concerns the future welfare and happiness of one for whom you are well known to entertain a very sincere friendship."

P. "Hum!—I understand who you mean, I suppose, sir; but you and I shall not tug in the same harness there I fancy. I am somewhat in years to be sure master Lewson: but I do not yet, thanks to my stars, belong to the rotten-row squad. We shall not tug together there, sir."

L. "I presume to think we shall, sir. You are I believe at once the physician and the friend of Mr. Montfort."

P. "Umph! Aye! I supposed it was in that quarter. Why yes, sir—yes, I do take some pains, I believe, sometimes, to restore him to the health which some persons, Mr. Lewson, take as much pains to destroy. A murrain[1] to such prodigals and blood-suckers—A murrain!—But what of that sir?"

L. "Why, with your pardon, sir—I suspect, that notwithstanding your professional skill and known discernment, you are not acquainted with the whole of his disorder."

P. "Hum! but you, I suppose are. You are his house physician I presume; and have watched him in his paroxysms. If report says true, Mr. Lewson, you have neglected no opportunity to feel his pulse."

L. "Whatever report may say, sir, I trust I shall prove myself, by this visit, to be a sincere friend both to the morals and interests of Henry Montfort."

P. "Umph!—morals and interests!—Umph! Umph!—morals, Mr. Lewson—Umph!—morals and interests!"

L. "Yes, sir—his morals and interests. Could I be more essentially his friend, in these important points of view, than by endeavouring to rescue him from the arts and fascinations of a strumpet—a stale,[2] who, after having lived with him for upwards of two years, as a hired prostitute, and assisting to anticipate a considerable portion of his fortune, is now endeavouring to grasp the whole; and hovering over his sick bed with pretended solicitudes, and other meretricious artifices, is inveigling him into a marriage ruinous to himself and dishonourable to his family?—a being, sir, who, presuming, it should seem (as the world is too apt to do), upon certain foibles and irregularities in my character, attributes views, and vices, and meannesses to me, at which my soul revolts; and thus, sir, by the hands of her anonymous agents, endeavours to seduce and bribe me into the baseness of becoming an instrument to her detestable designs?

"But no, sir, no, (continued he, assuming the swelling port of moral dignity) I am not the being I have been represented. Let this action bear testimony for me, I am not to be tempted, by views of personal emolu-

---

1 A plague or pestilence; when used in imprecations a murrain can refer to a misfortune more generally.

2 A term of contempt for an unchaste woman.

ment or advantage, to betray the moral and temporal interests of my friend."

So saying, he produced the anonymous letters already mentioned; and giving the Doctor just time to peruse them, he thus proceeded:

"Is it not friendship—is it not duty, to endeavour to frustrate such arts as these—to snatch from infamy and ruin a heedless young man, who, deprived of the advantages of that restraint and government of which youth so perpetually stands in need from the superintendence of years and experience, is left the unprotected prey of such harpies?—and, what is equally mischievous, of his own intemperate and untutored passions?"

P. "Well, young man! You talk it away very finely, I confess. But pray what does all this drive at? How does it concern me?"

L. "To your reputation, sir—to the speedy restoration of your patient's health—to that interest you have in his welfare, and the esteem in which you hold the memory of his excellent mother, it may be matter of much concernment.

"In short, sir, there is good reason to believe that it is entirely owing to the influence and the interference of this Siren[1] that my friend has not hitherto attended to the advice I understand you to have given him, of repairing to some watering-place for the restoration of his health."

P. "Umph! Umph! How sir? Umph?—His harlots meddle with my prescriptions? A murrain upon them!—His harlots?—"

L. "Yes, sir—even so. Having by a long train of artifices inveigled him into the infatuated design of marrying her—"

P. "How—How? Marrying her? The son of Amelia Montfort marry his harlot?—Umph!"

L. "Yes, sir, of marrying her; and fearful of the influence that absence, reflection, and the advice and interference of his friends might have in frustrating her designs—and at the same time considering that following her prey about from place to place, to prevent him from eluding her snare, might not be very consistent with her hopes and expectations of being received hereafter as his wife, in the circles to which she aspires, she has hitherto, it seems, persuaded him to turn a deaf ear to your excellent advice in this respect."

P. "What, and this cockatrice[2] lives in the house with him?"

L. "Aye, sir, privately. She is never to be seen. She and her old harridan[3] of an aunt (or whatever be the convenient name she may pass under). They seized their opportunity, it seems, and came to pounce upon him as soon as they heard that he was ill. Auntee, however, is not quite so

---

1 In classical mythology, a fabulous monster, part woman and part bird, who lured sailors to their destruction by singing.

2 Another term of reproach for a woman, meaning prostitute or whore (from the name of the mythical serpent reputedly hatched from a cock's egg and able to kill with a mere glance).

3 A haggard old woman, particularly an unchaste one.

private: and a curious old bawd[1] she is, I assure you. One may judge of the cattle by the driver."

P. "And these commodities—a murrain upon them! presume to counter-order my prescriptions! I am not to know what is best for my patient? My patient is to neglect my advice, and follow that of a harlot, who would send him out of the world that she may enjoy his fortune!"

L. "Just so, sir. And then the blame of his death is to fall upon you, sir."

P. "But it shall not, sir. But it shall not, sir. I will visit him no more. Let him get whom he will to be under physician to his harlot. Doctor Pengarron will not. I will go near him no more."

L. "And so, sir, you give up your infatuated friend to the government of these abandoned women?

"Surely, sir, you have too much regard for the memory of Mrs. Montfort—you have too much regard for her deluded son—you have too much regard for those sacred maxims of morality that dictate to years and experience the indispensable duty of counteracting the head-strong passions of youth?

"At least, sir, (if I may presume to offer my opinion) it might be very important for you to visit him once more; and (if you find it still not inconsistent with the state of the case) you might then make a generous effort so requisite on the side of years and experience to counteract the headstrong passions of youth. You might enforce your former advice, sir, in a more decisive style; and then, to be sure, sir—if you were not attended to, you might feel yourself at liberty to leave him to his fate. You and I, sir, at least, shall have the conscious satisfaction of having done our duty, whatever may be the result."

P. "Hum! You are right, young man!—you are right. He shall go to Brighton[2]—he shall go—or his harlot may be his physician for the future, for doctor Pengarron will not."

L. "Sir, you speak like a conscientious physician, and a benevolent friend. This, sir, is acting like the guardian of youth.

"I need hardly request you, sir, not to drop the least hint about this interview. Let me not suffer in my friendship, by endeavouring to preserve my friend."

P. "Umph!—Why, no; that would not be right, young man!—that would not be right. Besides, it would weaken the influence of my advice."

Lewson, of course, was highly delighted with the facility with which Dr. Pengarron fell into the snare he had spread. Every thing now appeared to be in his own hands again. Mordant, and Falkland, and the rest of the *mere prodigals* of the party, were already at Brighthelmstone.[3] Into the

---

1 A procuress or female brothel-keeper.
2 Brighton, on the south coast of England, was a fashionable resort, especially from the middle of the eighteenth century when bathing and drinking seawater came into vogue as medicinal treatments.
3 An older name for Brighton.

hands of these Henry would be sure to fall; and they would be sure to begin the great work, which himself, and others, who had more powerful motives for their industry, would not fail to complete. The reign of dissipation would be renewed; and then—but what then the reader will hereafter be informed.

His project could not have been set in motion more opportunely: for, the very evening after the interview with Dr. Pengarron was that in which the interesting conversations, noticed in the latter part of the preceding chapter, took place: and Henry, exhausted by prolonging the conversation to so late an hour, and by the agitation and fervour with which the harangue of Edmunds had stimulated him to express himself, spent a night of more sleepless and febrile agitation than he had experienced for some time before: so that, when the Doctor arrived, he found him considerably relapsed. This Pengarron failed not to attribute to the neglect of his former advice of sea-bathing and change of air. He concluded with prescribing what for the present appeared to be necessary; and informing Henry, in a very decisive style, that if he did not, as soon as he had got a little better again, remove to Brighton, and avoid the exhausting stimulus of female society, for his part, he must cease to stake his reputation as a medical man by attending upon him any more.

"Yes, sir, I say their very conversation—their very presence must be avoided in the present state of your health—for, from the general irritability of your constitution, and the morbid sensibility of your fibre, at this particular time, the very sight of a desirable object is exhausting—is injurious—and must be avoided. You must have nothing but men servants about you, and old women of sixty, that your blood may be kept temperate, and your mind composed."

Why the Doctor was so emphatic in this part of his prescription, the reader will be perfectly aware, though Henry knew not how to comprehend.

Neither did he understand much better the rationale of the practice. Empirically, at least, the evidence was against it. He was conscious, from repeated experiment, that the society and solicitudes of one particular female at least were conducive, not an impediment, to the recovery of his health: and accordingly, though he readily submitted to the alleged necessity of the journey and sea-bathing, he importuned Seraphina that the ceremony might be immediately performed; to the end that she might accompany him whithersoever he might be ordered.

Edmunds joined in this proposition most heartily; and Morton, of course, was no less eager. But Seraphina would by no means consent.

Desirous as she would have been to have accompanied Henry, and ready (as heretofore), if her solicitudes had appeared to be necessary to his health, to overlook, for such considerations, the pruderies of decorum, she could not persuade herself, at present, that there was any occasion for sacrifices either of discretion or principle. She saw that

Henry, notwithstanding this temporary relapse, was in a fair way of recovery; and though from motives of delicacy she never suggested any thing of the kind, she regarded the prescribed journey, altogether, as little more than compliance with the quackery of fashion, which might very well have been dispensed with: and, as for what related to Henry's proposal, "It should never be supposed that she had taken advantage of his weakness, in the season of sickness and dejection. Their marriage, whenever it took place, should at least be evidently, to all the world, the act of his deliberate judgment; when the faculties of his mind were unclouded by illness or calamity, and he could not even be suspected of being influenced by any other motives than affection sanctioned by reason, and the settled sense of moral propriety."

Edmunds bit his lips at this discourse. To him it looked like arguing only one side of the question. He considered into whose hands it was at least possible that Henry should fall during this separation; and he knew the artifices that would be made use of to dissipate all his goodly resolutions, and bring him back to his former habits.

But these were not topics into which he could presume, uninvited, to enter; and he suppressed the apprehensions he could not discard. His heart was heavy, but his tongue was silent.

Seraphina, however, easily yielded to the entreaties, in which all parties conspired, not to return to the cottage at Somerstown, but to retain the station to which, according to the present arrangement, she was so shortly to be legally, as she was already morally entitled; and to which, as has been already observed, the whole household had been instructed, tacitly at least, to recognize her claim.

Every thing being thus adjusted, Henry departed for Brighthelmstone, promising speedily to return in the full gaiety of health (to which he had no doubt that he should quickly be restored), and lead his lovely Seraphina to the altar at which he had already devoted his sincerest affections.

The apprehensions of Edmunds were too fatally realised. The health of Henry was indeed very shortly reinstated; but his mind's health became again the prey of contagious diseases.

In such a place as Brighthelmstone, the seductions of dissipation can never be wanted; and it has been already observed, that several of those dissipated young men, who had been the accustomed associates of Henry, in all his irregularities, were already at that place.

With these he was presently surrounded; and, as his strength and vivacity returned, with these he gradually declined into all his former habits: at first, reluctantly, indeed, and from the mere want of the resolution of repelling entreaty and resisting ridicule: but inclination returned, and strengthened with the practice. The pleasures of sense, not so much because they were sensual as because they were present, prevailed over, the purposes of virtue. The clouded optics of Henry could not pierce through the mists of passion that surrounded him, to dwell upon the intellectual prospect that was remote; and virtue and Seraphina lost their influence upon his mind, not from the want of attractions, but of vicinity. In short, before the time prescribed by Dr. Pengarron for his residence at this place had expired, prodigality had completed its triumph.

Lewson had watched his time. From an associate of congenial mind he had particular information of all that was passing; and when he perceived that every thing was so far prepared, that his presence, instead of exciting suspicions, would be regarded as a desirable event, he, also, had an indisposition that required change of air and sea-bathing, and accordingly set off for Brighthelmstone without delay: with what further projects, and how accompanied, will be unfolded in proper time.

The arts, the vivacity, the talents for wit and ridicule of this prime minister of seduction completed what the Falklands and Mordants had begun. Henry rushed again with unbridled neck upon the course of dissipation and intemperance; and renewed, even with increased avidity, all the follies of his former career.

To this career there were now no longer any impediments. Every barrier was removed. His ample means seemed to offer an inexhaustible resource of pleasures—and there was no one to censure—no one to control.

Seraphina, indeed, sometimes intruded upon his remembrance. In the hour of languor and exhaustion—in the silence of the night, her sweet confiding innocence, and the moral dignity of her soul, seemed to reproach his frailty: but he appeased the angry vision with the promise that this career would soon be over; that the appointed season approached, that was to restore him to reflection and intellect, and, by renewing his delightful intercourse with the inestimable object of his attachment, was to preclude the necessity of other pleasures.

But these visitations and these reflections became gradually less and less frequent; till at last, they were entirely discontinued. Other visions obtruded; the appointed season of return passed by unheeded: new temptations and new pleasures prolonged the fatal residence at Brighthelmstone; and Henry continued to wanton through all the regions of excess, and yield himself up, without further effort, to every temptation of unlawful pleasure.

The scene of these excesses, indeed, was soon shifted: but the character of the performance continued to be the same. Care was taken before the party returned for London (for it was as a party they returned), that Henry should be engaged eight or ten deep, as it is called, that he might have no time to reflect, and disentangle himself from his renewed connection, on his first arrival. And though the interview with Seraphina, and the scrutinizing glances of the moral Edmunds, covered him with some confusion and embarrassment; yet, as some one of the party never failed to call upon him at the appointed hour, to refresh his reluctant remembrance, those engagements were too punctually fulfilled: not without promises to himself, however, to Seraphina, and even to Edmunds, that, when once he had got to the end of them, he would enter into no more. Nay, he even declared as much to his companions themselves.

But this end never came. For the first two or three days, indeed, this whim, as it was called, was humoured by the confederacy, and no further invitations were pressed upon him. But the heart was no sooner off its guard, than this precautious indulgence was discontinued; invitation grew out of invitation, and party our of party, in its accustomed course; and every object that could awaken self-reproof came to be considered as irksome—to be neglected—to be studiously avoided.

How shall I describe the scenes in which the infatuated Henry was now incessantly engaged? how trace him through all the versatilities of dissipation?—now blaspheming at the gaming-table, the prey of sharpers! now strewing the fascinations of taste over the paths of prodigality, and alluring the circles of elegance with his masquerades, his ridottoes, his fêtes[1]—anon dissolved in voluptuousness, in the recesses of fashionable obscenity, or mingling in the orgies of bacchanalian revelry—perverting his conversational talents to the most licentious topics—overwhelming reflection with the most costly and stimulating libations—and even debasing himself by all the follies into which youth is so frequently betrayed by inebriation and profligate society!

But these are descriptions upon which I have neither leisure nor inclination to expatiate. As they fall in my way I may perhaps, occasionally give them a casual glance. But my soul delights not in them; and perhaps the interests of morality would not be promoted by the delineation. Suffice it, therefore, to say, that every folly unbridled appetite could rush into, and fashionable example sanction, was indulged without restraint, and that the thoughtless Henry appeared to be hurrying with rapidity down the precipice of irreclaimable immorality.

The situation of Seraphina now became more embarrassing, as well as more painful, than ever.

She knew not, indeed, the full extent of Henry's prodigality. Her seclusion prevented her from being the witness of his extravagant follies; and that generous indignation, with which she repelled the officious loquacity that loves to wanton in tales and descriptions disadvantageous to the repute of others, shut out the reports with which even that seclusion would otherwise have been disturbed. But the indications were too strong to leave her totally unacquainted with the growing evil: and there were some to which even the silence of the little study (the scene of all her solitary pleasures—or solitary reflections) seemed itself to bear too pertinent a testimony; and which appeared, indeed, not very equivocally, to indicate a growing depravity of the heart.

As some months were now past since the intelligence of the death of Montfort—and as the health of Henry was evidently and completely

---

1 A "ridotto" (Italian) is an entertainment involving music, dancing, and sometimes gambling; a "fête" (French) is a large-scale entertainment or festival.

reestablished—it became natural to expect that he would be importunate for the fulfilment of those engagements, the accomplishment of which had only been delayed for these events.

But, alas! how inconsistent is the heart of man! Now that objections and difficulties were all removed, the ardour of our hero—Hero! shall we call him?—No: Renegade and Apostate be his title from hence forward—His ardour began to cool. The Moralist seemed to have fled with the Valetudinarian—the devotion of the Lover to have subsided with the grief of the Son.

Since his return from Brighthelmstone, the subject of marriage was never mentioned but once, and that only in a slight and general way: and, what was still more distressing, his attentions began to slacken. His deportment grew comparatively distant and cool: and Seraphina found herself daily more and more estranged from his society; while her wounded mind was left, in long intervals of solitude, to brood over the apparently not very distant prospect of total and final separation.

This separation, indeed, she began to consider as absolutely necessary for the vindication, even in her own eyes, of her insulted honour. Resident under his roof without the public sanction and acknowledgment of that character which alone could render their cohabitation respectable, she perceived that she must of necessity be declining, with no very gradual pace, into that rank and estimation with all around her which her soul, not less from a thousand moral considerations than from a sentiment of generous pride, abhorred.

Her mind was not slow in discovering the only sad alternative; nor (ardent and unbounded as was her affection for the ungrateful Henry) was her resolution intractable to the dictates of her conviction.

Now it was that she began seriously to repent of not having returned to Somerstown, as soon as Henry was evidently out of danger. Now it was that she began to accuse herself of weakness and irresolution, in yielding to the temptations of those innumerable inducements that surrounded her—to the seduction of those newly unfolded pleasures, and those growing habits of attachment to every thing that presented itself, in this her promised mansion—and postponing, in the enjoyment of these little pleasures (so trifling in detail, so potent in combination), the serious deliberations of wisdom and propriety, till those deliberations began to appear to be too late, and as such were ultimately discarded.[1]

When such a train of reflection is once begun, it very rarely happens that it is soon exhausted. Self-reproach (the comparison more frequently of melancholy than of reason) is a monitor much more easily provoked than silenced. The mind, ingenious in its own torment, when once stretched upon the rack of recapitulation, finds it easy to prolong the pang. Memory travels backward from event to preceding event, and from

---

1 In *Political Justice* Godwin discusses cohabitation as a potential impediment to individual rational judgment. See Appendix B3b.

error to error, till all appears to have been erroneous, and repentance seems to discover the materials of condemnation in all.

So fared it with Seraphina, whose maturer experience, in this season of affliction, sitting in judgment upon the inexperience of past enthusiasm, arraigned those generous emotions and those results of indiscretion which heretofore she had regarded as the proofs and triumphs of an uncorrupted soul.

Alas! educated, as it were, in abstraction, she had considered every question of morality only in an abstract point of view. With a system of action deeply engraved upon her heart, that consulted only the happiness of others, she had not considered how essential to the permanency of our exertions for that happiness, it is to provide for the security of our own; and, with feelings alive to every generous sympathy and emotion, she had never considered that generosity may become bankrupt from too inconsiderate a profusion; and that, when the heart has not wherewithal to support its own tranquillity, its benevolence to others must expire in a wish and a sigh.[1]

She mourned therefore alike over her lost utilities and her hopes; and reproached herself, in the bitterness of heart, for having despised too much the prejudices and false opinions of the world, without considering how much opinions (while established), however false in themselves, must necessarily operate upon the moral and intellectual capabilities of the individuals to whose conduct they may attach.

Morton, in the mean time, was not without her perturbations. She also began to drink of the bitter draught of repentance. She saw the consequences of her crooked politics. Her machinations appeared to have frustrated the very object to which they were directed. She could not but reflect that if she had been the guardian, instead of the betrayer, of the innocent Seraphina—or had even left the youthful passions of the lovers (once, even in the bosom of Henry himself, as full of purity as of ardour) to their own unprovoked and unperverted course, using her influence (if necessary at all) only to delay their marriage, that the marriage would now inevitably have taken place—that she should have seen her lovely ward eligibly and happily established in that affluence and splendour, to place her in which had been the sole motive of all her arts and anxieties; and in the legitimate possession of all that fortune, connection, and condition in society can command.

Still, however, she "laid the flattering unction to her soul,"[2] *that she had done all for the best*; and that the miscarriage of her designs was to be attributed not to their impolicy,[3] but to those unforeseen events that so often frustrate *the best intentions*; and to the perverseness and intractableness of

---

1 Seraphina's realization can be read as a critique of Godwinian philosophy. See the Introduction p. 32.
2 *Hamlet* 3.4.145.
3 Their quality of being impolitic or their inexpediency.

her pupil, who would not be induced, by any arguments, to turn the varying circumstances, as they arose, to the advantages that they seemed to point out to her.

This intractableness she thought had now a severe lesson; and she doubted not but that Seraphina would be at last disposed to listen to more prudent councils; and, if so, she still made herself confident that, so far as related to his conduct towards her (which was all our good duenna cared about), Henry might be reclaimed; and all might yet be well.

Her calculations in this respect were not altogether unauthorised—nor her premises mere presumptions. Keen and penetrating in researches of this description, she perceived from a variety of symptoms that the affections of Henry were rather diverted, than permanently alienated:—that, plunged in a career of dissipation, in which Seraphina had so obstinately refused to mingle, and intoxicated with that perpetual whirl of splendour and diversions in which he had now so unlimited an opportunity of indulging, the pensive recluse was easily banished, for a while at least, from his remembrance, while the more obtrusive charms of some female of congenial habits, glittering before his eyes in all the meretricious glare and vivacity to which he was so much attached, excited his incontinent passions and dazzled his imagination.

It was not long before these suggestions were fully substantiated. It was as she suspected. Seraphina had a rival in the circles of fashionable dissipation—a rival, formidable from personal attractions—but still more so from her proficiency in all the fascinating arts and accomplishments of the most refined coquetry; a rival, who, having the art to suppress her own passions while she was displaying every blandishment that could excite and agitate those of her admirer, had succeeded in dividing and, at times, almost engrossing the affections of the wavering Henry; in whose unstable mind (perverted as it was at this particular season) the charm of yet untasted novelty had of course its particular attractions.

Some degree of this fickleness and infidelity was, indeed, to be expected from the course of life in which Henry was engaged. From what is already known of his character, it will be concluded that the whole of his time would not be devoted to the orgies of Bacchus, or the revels of the *venal* Cytherea.[1]

We have already described him as surrounded with the fascinations of taste, and alluring the circles of elegance. Into these circles he would of course endeavour to draw as much of female loveliness and elegance as was in his power: and that power was by no means very limited. The manly beauty of his person, the polish of his manners, the charm of his conversation, and the flow of his natural spirits, never failed to attract those attentions so seductive to the youthful heart.

He was, indeed, the general admiration of the accomplished and the fair—all fans fluttered round him—all charms were spread to allure his

---

1 See p. 133, notes 2-3.

attention—all ears were open to the sprightly effusions of his wit, his gallantry, his sportive vein of anecdote, of raillery, of description.

Henry was not insensible to these attentions. He was not over-scrupulous in improving the favourable impression his person or accomplishments might make. His intercourse with the sex was an almost perpetual courtship. His youthful vanity made him ambitious of a sort of tender interest in every lovely bosom that heaved and fluttered before him; and his youthful desires, occasionally at least, panted for the possession of every beauteous form that fascinated his eyes, or warmed his imagination.

In the midst of his amorous dissipation he had never entered, it is true, into any deliberate plan of seduction. Perhaps his heart was too much distracted by the multiplicity of its impressions to engage so elaborately in the pursuit of any individual passion. But in such fashionable circles as those in which he moved, it followed, of course, that intrigues and assignations should sometimes fall in his way, with such facility, that seduction might seem to have been precluded by what, if we were disposed to cover the deformity of vice with the softening shade of alluring verbiage, might be called the spontaneous reciprocation of tender wishes.

So long as the looser affections continued thus to be distracted by a variety of equal claims, the more refined emotions were not precluded; and there were times and seasons (and those at first recurred with considerable frequency) when virtue and Seraphina had more lustre in his eyes than all the blaze of meretricious charms. But in this routine of levity and fascination, as sensuality became more habitual, and sentiment declined, objects inevitably intruded themselves upon his observation that concentrated, more or less, the scattered rays of unlawful desire, and accordingly produced, for a time, a more serious alienation of that loyal affection which was due to the heroine of our story.

In short, as the quaint and jocular Mordant sometimes expressed himself, "Henry was a very *tinder-hearted* fellow, and the devil was in it if, in time, he did not meet with a *match.*" With such a match, in fact, Henry had met, or rather such a one had been provided for him; and the flame that had been kindled had so parched up all moral principle, as to threaten the final conflagration of a precipitous marriage.

This was indeed somewhat a more serious part of the story than Morton had been prepared to hear. She had felt herself perfectly assured that Seraphina's hold upon the heart of Henry was permanent and immoveable; that levity and incontinence might lead him at times astray, and her perverse attachment to moping at home over books and pictures, might drive him, for mere relaxation, and the love of show and gaiety, into the arms of some temporary rival; but that there could be no sort of danger of his rushing upon an act, which, from what he knew of Seraphina, he must be very well assured would divorce him from her society for ever.

Hitherto, therefore, she had consoled herself with the idea, that Seraphina, at the worst, had only to open her eyes to the necessity of falling into his taste for gaiety and splendour, and of playing off a few female arts (in which she might be easily instructed), and she would be, at all times, able so far

"To lure this tarsel gentle back again,"[1]

as to obtain a handsome establishment at least as his permanent mistress, if not in the more eligible character of his wife: and, as for those finer feelings, and that magnanimity of character, which might occasion our heroine to prefer all the horrors and anguish (perhaps the *disorganising pang*) of an absolute separation to the dignity of such a compromise, all that she had witnessed, in so many circumstances and situations, were not sufficient to suggest to her the possibility of the existence of such romantic feelings.

She had begun, however, to consider the malady as assuming an appearance somewhat alarming; and thought it high time to make herself perfectly acquainted with all the symptoms, that she might proceed to prescribe accordingly.

For this purpose it was necessary to apply to that "surly enthusiast," for so she called him;—the now despondent, melancholy Edmunds; whom, though totally estranged from the confidence and conversation of Henry, she knew to be not the less diligent and watchful to make himself acquainted with every thing that passed that might concern the interests and happiness of Seraphina.

It was with this view, indeed, and from the hope that in the flux of unforeseen events he might yet be able to seize upon some opportunity of serving his beloved mistress, that this worthy and excellent young man continued to submit to the irksomeness of a situation which the altered conduct of Henry had rendered otherwise insupportable.

Between our sage duenna and this honest enthusiast, it is very well known that there was no very great degree of cordiality: and though they now resided under the same roof, their interviews were not very frequent; nor their conversations very familiar or interesting. In short, they avoided each other when they could; and when they met they seldom spoke.—Scientifically speaking, they were kept asunder by the *repulsive attraction of antipathy*—Edmunds might be said to hate, and Morton to fear.

Not being able, however, to penetrate into the interior of this labyrinth by any other clue, the duenna put so much restraint and violence upon her feelings as to resolve to throw herself in his way; and, for the sake of the information she desired, to encounter the formidable terrors of his eye.

But it was not the terror of his eye alone that she had now to encounter. Her inquiries let loose, also, the still more formidable terrors of his tongue.

She could not have accosted him in a better humour. Suspicions of the most serious nature had been for some time afloat in his mind: and he had

---

1 *Romeo and Juliet* 2.2.159. "Tarsel" is a variant on "tassel," a male hawk.

made repeated efforts to intrude himself into every circle, and worm himself into the confidence of every person, that could minister information on the subject of his apprehensions. He had even made pot acquaintance with the varlets of the suspected parties, and from one of those had just parted, full fraught with intelligence that left him no longer under any doubt of the conspiracy that had been formed for the infatuated Henry, or the facility with which his corrupted and alienated affections had fallen into the snare.

Alarmed at the intelligence he had received, and stung with generous indignation, almost to madness, he had hastened home breathing execrations against all jilts, and libertines, and old convenient duennas, in a breath; meditating he knew not what, and threatening he knew not whom.

In this disposition, his communications of course were more blunt than explicit. Honouring the affrighted querist[1] with no better appellations than bawd and procuress, he asked her in plain terms, how much she had received for betraying the innocence of Seraphina to his libertine master? protesting, at the same time (with a sort of delirious extravagance of tone and gesture), that he would rob on the highway, or sell himself to a slave-merchant, but that she should have double the sum, if she would do the same good office for Melinda.

With what kind of sensations Morton listened to this salutation, the reader may readily conjecture. Her curiosity, however, got the better of her resentment; and calming the fury of her countenance, "Melinda," repeated she—"What of her?—Who, what Melinda?"

"*What Melinda?*—The devil's Melinda!" replied he—"for there need be twenty devils to deal with such a sorceress—Such a Melinda as wants only just such an old mother Convenience as thou art, for her waiting-woman, to make her all that the paragon of jilts could wish to be.

"But hie thee into her service, good bawd! Pretend affection for her, also, good cockatrice! and worm thee into her confidence. And then—do thy office dexterously—Make the coast clear, and bolt the door, that thou mayst put them to bed together decently. Dost thou hear?—Put them to bed in time; that the charm may be dissolved before the knot is tied; or Melinda is Mrs. Montfort;—and Seraphina—oh I could tear——"

Tears drowned his indignation. He turned abruptly away; ran up stairs, and left the astonished and petrified duenna to collect what she could from his incoherent ejaculations.

Too much, indeed, was perfectly intelligible.—

"Married!—Melinda Mrs. Montfort!" exclaimed she almost breathless—and then, after a pause of some minutes—"Henry Montfort marry?—Marry Melinda?"

But it was necessary, to counteract this, to know something more: and first and foremost to know who and what this Melinda was. Little therefore as she had reason to be gratified with the epithets and appellations

---

1 One who asks or inquires.

with which she had been honoured, she determined to follow Edmunds to his own chamber, whither he had retired, and prevail upon him, by whatever submissions, to explain all he knew of this affair, and all that he supposed.

Edmunds was subdued by the meekness with which she bore his reproaches. He was touched with some degree of sympathy for the anxiety she expressed; and recollecting that, at any rate, she would certainly be well disposed to do all in her power to frustrate this meditated match, he very freely communicated to her all that he knew of what will be found in the ensuing chapter.

BOOK VIII.

=========

CHAP. I.

The Amour between Henry and Melinda; comprising, in point of time, only the distance of a few weeks beyond the preceding Chapter.

Sketches of Elegance and Fashion.—Plots and Counter-Plots.—The Ridotto.—Elevated Morals.—Progress of Infatuation.—Triumphs of Coquetry.—The Coup de Main.—A Bacchanalian Prelude.

IT will be no great matter of surprise, we suppose, to many of our readers, to be informed that the Melinda with whom they are about to become acquainted, was no other than the sister of Lewson.

This young lady, who had the reputation of being a first-rate beauty, had, besides her personal attractions, some very conspicuous advantages, which the generality of young men of *rank and spirit* would undoubtedly consider as giving her a decided preference over so strange and rusticated a being as our unfortunate heroine.

She could not write poetry, indeed, nor had she much taste for any other species of it, than that which might be set to music by some Italian, or Italianised composer:[1]—but, she had inspired some of the very best that, for three or four years preceding, had covered with laurel the death-less names of Honourables and Right Honourables—the Sapphic Baronets[2] and rhyming Peers of the day. Neither could she rival the pencil of Seraphina in the painting of portraits, or the delineation of the pictur-esque scenery of nature; although not entirely unacquainted with the science of colouring, nor unadmired for the skill with which she would occasionally add a few heightening touches to a fine specimen of art. Still less did she aspire to the reputation of some other impertinent sciences, that had been cultivated with so much success by *the Recluse of Limbé*. But then she had her accomplishments of *a higher order!*

She had been trained, from her infancy, in all the exercises that give the finishing turn of elegance to the limbs and motions of the body; had been familiarized, from her cradle, to the circles of rank and elegance that alone can give the stamp of currency to address and manners; and had been early initiated into every science and mystery of fashionable life, by a very fashionable mother.

She was acquainted, of course, with all the etiquette of the card-table, and the drawing-room; knew how to assume the easy familiarity, and display all the graces and the accomplishments of her order—could out-

---

1   Italian opera was popular among the upper classes in London at this time, making it a target of patriotic and radical critiques.
2   A "Sapphic" is a type of classical lyric poetry named after Sappho of Lesbos, who composed such poetry.

shine all her rivals in the ever varying decorations of fashion, and had, more than once, enjoyed the distinguished honour of setting the mode in bonnets, plumes, and turbans; points, festoons, plaits, flowers, and furbelows; and all the innumerable decorations of female paraphernalia.[1]

She could moreover dance, and sing, and play upon the harp, with a degree of taste and execution not frequently to be met with among mere lady performers. In short, she was the very paragon of taste, the arbitress of elegant amusement—the blazing star of fashion!—the delight, the life, the pride, of the ball, the masquerade, and the ridotto. And so completely had she been admitted to have outshone all her rivals, that nothing was the ton[2] that Melinda did not approve; and drums, routs, and public assemblies lost a part of their splendour when Melinda was not present.

Since the disappearance of her father, indeed, she had, for some time, been rather under a cloud. She had been obliged, by the prevailing malice of her evil star, to relinquish, to more fortunate, though less skilful rivals, the expensive honour of leading fashions at birth-day balls and operas; and, deserted by the swarm of lovers that used to flutter around her, in the sunshine of her better fortunes, she began to sink into despondency, under the mortifying imagination, that all her charms and attractions, and all that fund of *elegant science* and invaluable accomplishment, which it had been the important business of her life to cultivate, were doomed to be buried in the shades of obscurity, and lost in the dull circles of private domestication.

But the connection of her brother with Henry Montfort seemed to open the way to better prospects.

It was indeed by no means the intention of Emanuel Woodhouse, when he projected the familiarity of Lewson and Henry, that the sister should play an underpart to the comedy he was plotting: on the contrary, as has already been observed, and the reasons of which will be divulged hereafter, it was an important part of his design to hurry on the match, which he understood to have been in frequent agitation, with the lovely heroine of our story: and, for that purpose, he had set all his engines to work to keep, in this respect, the moral enthusiasm of Henry awake, and the main current of his passions from being diverted from their proper channel: and we have already seen through what dark alleys of crooked policy he had ventured to proceed in order to influence Lewson to be instrumental in bringing about that desirable event.

But Lewson soon began to give entertainment to a better project. The facility with which he rendered both the purse and credit of Henry sub-

---

1 "Points" are pieces of lace or needlework; "festoons" are ornamental chains or garlands of flowers or leaves, usually suspended in a curve between two points; "plaits" are decorative braided strands of cloth; a "furbelow" is the pleated border of a petticoat or gown. "Paraphernalia" refers to articles of dress or adornment, especially those associated with a particular activity.
2 Fashion or vogue.

servient to every demand of his own necessities and dissipations, soon suggested the idea, that such a *friend* might be still more valuable and important in the management of his sister; and considering the dispositions of Henry and the attractions and qualifications of Melinda, he had no doubt, if she were once brought, in all that splendour of taste and gaiety and decoration, in which she so much excelled, within the sphere of his observation, that she would infallibly fascinate his attention, and soon obliterate from his heart the feeble impression of those rival charms, which the letters of Woodhouse had led him to conclude, must in some degree have palled upon the satiated sense, by the unrestrained possession of upwards of two years.

This project was no sooner suggested to Melinda, than the glow and animation of her some time fading features began to revive. Conscious of her power, charmed with the generous character of her intended lover, and secure of victory over such a heart, she began immediately to enjoy in imagination the splendours of her approaching triumph. Her fertile genius expatiated on new and untried forms of bonnets, and bandeaus, of turbans, plumes and kerchiefs. The ideal manteau[1] flowed in fresh forms of attractive elegance, the ringlets twined and braided in a thousand fascinating directions—the ivory neck was alternately exposed and concealed—the bosom heaved—the fan fluttered—the eyes sparkled or languished, as occasion best required—the smile, the blush, the dimple, were all at command. Even the sigh, and the reclining neck, and the graceful tear of sensibility, prepared to fall over a fading flower or a crushed butterfly, were all rehearsed, and got in readiness to answer their respective occasions. And, lo! the new æra of splendour was about to begin.—The gala invited—the concert staid[2]—the ball was at a stand—beaux admired! belles envied! and the opera-house was all in a gaze!—

"Visions of glory, spare my aching sight!!!"[3]

In short, milliners, mantua-makers,[4] jewellers, feather-merchants, and fashion-mongers of all descriptions presently surrounded her, as heretofore. Ways and means were resorted to, out of the beaten track, to supply the extraordinary exigence, and all the panoply of Cytherean[5] warfare was presently supplied.

Thus accomplished, and thus accoutred, she accompanied her brother, as soon as the project appeared sufficiently ripe for execution, in his excursion to Brighthelmstone.

---

1   Loose gown worn by women in the eighteenth century.
2   "Staid" appears to be used as a verb here, suggesting that the concert momentarily stopped.
3   Thomas Gray, *The Bard* (1757), line 107 (with exclamation marks added by Thelwall).
4   A milliner designs, makes, or sells women's hats; "mantua" is a variant of "manteau," defined above.
5   See p. 133, note 2.

The forces thus arrived at the destined place of rendezvous, the ground was presently reconnoitred; and every thing appearing favourable to the designs of the confederates, an approaching ridotto was fixed upon for the opening of the campaign. The enemy was to be unexpectedly attacked. The fortress was to be stormed by surprise: and the heart of the Amazon[1] throbbed for the hour of assault.

The hour at length arrived. The assault was given. All the whole artillery of sighs, and smiles and blandishments—all the enginery of feminine lures—the stratagems of feints and mines and masked batteries—and the whole tactics of seduction were played off with infinite address. Victory appeared to pay over the banners of the assailants: and a powerful impression was evidently made.

In plain English, Henry was fascinated by the charms, the splendour, the vivacity and evident accomplishments of the fair stranger; and his admiration was not diminished when he discovered her to be the sister of *his friend*.

"Your sister, Lewson!" exclaimed he, "under what cloud have you contrived to keep this day star of beauty and elegance so long enveloped?"

"Our present circumstances," replied Lewson with an affectation of candour, "do not permit her frequently to appear in public, in a manner suitable to her taste and education. Besides, she is not for all eyes; and though, having brought her to this place, for her more perfect recovery from a recent indisposition, I could not deny her, for this once, the gratification of paying her respects to my best of friends, yet I know the line of conduct our declining fortunes dictate, and what duty requires of me as a guardian of my sister's honour."

Henry understood this hint, as Lewson intended he should understand it, as a sort of covert insinuation that he was not to expect to meet with Melinda again in such circles. What followed, also, was just in the succession that was expected: for, from that time forward, Henry hardly ever engaged in any scene of pleasure, in which it is customary for females of character to mingle, without laying his commands on Lewson to use his best endeavours to prevail upon his sister to be of the party.

Melinda was not deficient in improving the opportunities thus presented. She called forth all the resources of her mind. She indulged her fancy and her caprice, in all that playful versatility which is so apt to captivate the young, the dissipated and gay; and, penetrating into the character of her new admirer, she accommodated herself so completely to his tastes, and directed her attention so dexterously to his prevailing foibles, that it was not long before he himself occasionally mistook the fever of imagination with which she had inflamed him, for an ardent and deep-rooted passion; and there were hours of infatuation and delirium in which he meditated designs that could not but have eventually proved as inconsistent with his own happiness, as injurious to the disinterested affection and prior claims of Seraphina.

---

1 The Amazons were a mythical race of female warriors.

Melinda was, indeed, in every respect, the sort of being best qualified to influence, by her seductive practices, the inconsistent and disorganized mind of Henry. She had every qualification that, in his thoughtless hours, could fascinate, allure—seduce! that could rouse and sport with his voluptuous passions, and, playing upon these, could conduct him, from step to step, and from purpose to purpose, till all the master keys of his heart were in her power, and his captive reason became, as it were, the obsequious vassal of her smiles.

Henry, accordingly, was completely dazzled and enthralled. Melinda! Melinda—the gay, the splendid, fascinating Melinda was the subject of his nocturnal and his waking dreams.

Once to have possessed her person (as Edmunds very pertinently suggested) would have been to have dissolved the charm: for she had certainly very little of that about her which interests the more delicate feelings, or constitutes the sentimental part of the tender passion—even if the all-surpassing tenderness and amiable qualifications of Seraphina had left any vacancy in the heart of Henry for impressions of that description.

There was no danger, however, or, as Edmunds would have said, no *hope*, of the permanency of this new passion being prematurely brought to such a test: not that Melinda seems to have been cast in that Vestal[1] mould in which the demi-divinities of poets and novelists are so frequently stamped, or fashioned of an ore so genuine, as never to have been mingled with the alloy of passion.

If the reports of the tea-table may be quoted as authorities in our high court of history, her heart had not always been inexorable, nor the palm of her dressing-woman always unconscious of a bribe.

It is true, indeed, there were circumstances that tended to impeach the credibility of these tales; for the heroes of them happened to be *married men, and the husbands of her particular friends.*

These insinuations, however, whether true or false, were not unknown to Melinda; neither were they objects of any very serious anxiety: for her morals were as fashionable as her manners. She had been early initiated (as has been already hinted) in all the *mysteries* of *the ton.* She knew very well that, in these higher altitudes, prudence (like every other virtue) rests upon the basis of a very different set of maxims and *precautions*, from those that assume a similar denomination in the lower and middling classes. She did not, therefore, believe that her reputation could be materially injured by the tattling of antiquated tabbies,[2] who could neither impeach her discretion, as choosing gallants among those who might have purchased a more subservient title by the offer of advantageous establish-

---

1 A poetic term for a woman of spotless chastity (with allusion to the mythological Vestal Virgins, six priestesses who tended the sacred fire in the temple of Vesta, the virgin goddess of the hearth, in Rome).

2 Elderly gossipy spinsters.

ments, nor accuse her of being so wanting to herself and to *decorum*, as to have been in the way of becoming an unmarried mother!

In the present amour she even derived some advantage from the reputation of these gallantries.

Had Henry regarded her from the first dawn of his infatuation, as one who was clearly and decidedly unassailable in any other way than that of marriage, it is probable that he would still have had so much virtue, and so much remaining sense of what was due to the generosity and confiding innocence of Seraphina, as to have avoided entangling himself in this affair. But the whisper was soon buzzed in his ear; and what the promptitude of malevolence suggested, his interested passions as readily believed.

The prospect was inviting. A mistress such as Melinda seemed all that was requisite to complete the enviable felicity of his present situation. He thought it not quite impossible that Lewson himself might not be very averse to such a connection—(for Henry was very capable of being preyed upon by a parasite whose character he, at the same time, despised;) and as to the lady herself, he supposed it, at any rate, not very improbable that the lover who had prevailed over the enlarged capacity and philosophic purity of Seraphina, might be equally successful with the flirting levity of the dissipated Melinda. Nay, she herself, when he first began to make his advances, did not seem to be very fastidiously delicate as to the kind of hopes her deportment might encourage him to form.

But this was only a part of that profound system of politics upon which she acted. She perceived very plainly that it was upon infatuating the passions of Henry that she was to depend; not upon any chance of inspiring a more tender and respectful sentiment. And indeed the former, not the latter, was her particular forte. She understood, also, from her brother (who since Woodhouse's anonymous letter had taken care to worm himself into all the particulars of that affair) the kind of connection in which Henry was already involved, the peculiar character of the rival she was to endeavour to supplant in his affections, and the designs he meditated with respect to the fulfilment of that prior engagement.

It was necessary, therefore, that Henry should not, in the first instance, have too distinct a view of the nature and tendency of the new connection he was forming—that his feet should be entangled in the labyrinth, before he discovered the object to which it was to lead him; and his senses bewildered in the mists of passion, before the means should be even suggested by which that passion was alone to be gratified.

It was a part, therefore, rather than an impeachment of her prudence, that the lures which she sometimes spread were such as might not have been entirely out of character with a Laïs or a Phryne;[1] or that the freedoms which she sometimes tolerated were somewhat

---

1 See p. 245, note 1.

"More

Than *a chaste Roman Virgin* would dare to own."[1]

But the first part of her project had no sooner succeeded—the infatuation no sooner appeared to be complete, than her line of conduct was immediately varied. It was then high time to mark "the distinction between that playful freedom—that innocent unsuspecting vivacity which flows from the mere ebullition of youthful spirits, and those indelicate freedoms that speak the unguarded wantonness of the heart."

The frown that chills was now thought as necessary as the smile that encourages, or the glance that warms. Her conduct began to say, in a thousand different ways, that her unsuspecting vivacity seemed to have been misapprehended. In short, she began from the Laïs to play the Lucretia;[2] and even to trust herself less frequently in *the too presumptuous society of her aspiring lover:* practically, as it were, threatening a return to her recent domestication and seclusion.

This part of the plot, however, was not to be carried too far. It was easy to perceive that it might be a very dangerous experiment to give Henry time for deliberate reflection; or to suffer his desires to cool for want of their accustomed stimuli.

His was not the sort of passion that was to be increased by absence, or to be inflamed by perpetual coyness and reserve. Melinda, accordingly, had full occasion for all her management, and all the versatility of her talents. It was necessary, indeed, on the one hand, to convince him that his desires could only be gratified through the medium of marriage; but it was necessary, on the other, that those desires should be perpetually fed with the fuel of fresh excitement.

His visits to her toilet,[3] therefore, were not actually forbidden; nor the opportunities of meeting with her, at other places, very studiously precluded. Neither was it thought advisable to preserve a very uniform coldness, or a modesty over-severe, in her deportment towards this ambiguous lover.

Sometimes her vivacity would break out, as if it were unawares, and display itself in all its fascinating varieties—at others, the eye would languish as with some involuntary emotion; or the bosom, heaving with the half-stifled sigh, would yield to the watchful gaze of the lover a transient view of its swelling symmetry and transparent whiteness; while, perhaps, at the same time, the pressure of her soft hand, not quite permitted nor obstinately withdrawn, was suffered to assist the progress of the sweet contagion through his veins.

---

1 Untraced.

2 In Roman legend, Lucretia, the virtuous wife of the nobleman Lucius Tarquinius Collatinus, was raped by Sextus Tarquinius. She stabbed herself after exacting from her father and husband an oath of vengeance against the Tarquins.

3 Dressing room; in the eighteenth century it was fashionable for ladies to receive visitors during the last stages of their dressing or grooming.

In this manner were the passions of Henry urged and goaded by the most refined coquetry during his residence at Brighthelmstone; where distance from the object of his more virtuous attachment gave leisure and opportunity to this meretricious rival to spread her bewitching snares, and twine her silken fetters: so that, by the time he was returning to London, his mind had become so harassed and enfeebled, by a perpetual ague and fever of jealousy and desire, that he was no longer master of his own thoughts and determinations.

At this crisis a more than ordinary degree of management was deemed requisite; lest, on the renewal of his intercourse with Seraphina, his mind should suddenly revolt from the idea of that indissoluble kind of connection with another, into which it was the purpose of Melinda to draw him. Her conduct, therefore, just at this time, and during the journey in particular, was to be somewhat more free and ambiguous; so as rather to revive his hopes of prevailing upon her affections on those more easy terms that might not appear totally inconsistent with his virtuous engagements.

This deportment had the desired effect. Henry, not quite despairing of obtaining Melinda as his mistress, considered that, as he should still be at liberty to take Seraphina as his wife, he might persevere in this amour without any aberration from the laws of honour and morality, beyond what his fortune and rank in society might excuse.

The first operation, therefore, of this affair, as far as related to our heroine, was merely that his attentions to her became less assiduous; and that a temporary adjournment (for such only he then intended it should be) of the subject of marriage took place:—the publicity of such an event not agreeing very well with an intrigue of this description, in which he seemed on the very eve of embarking.

But these hopes were gradually suppressed as the purpose for which they were inspired seemed to be accomplished. The conduct of Melinda soon began to make it again apparent, that marriage was the lowest price at which the possession of her person would be disposed of: while, at the same time, every blandishment was employed that could inflame the desire for that possession to the pitch almost of phrensy.

The fickle mind of Henry soon began to pendulate. The proved affection, the intellect, and virtues of Seraphina, and the voluptuous gaiety, the elegant accomplishments, and obtrusive beauties of Melinda (that soft bosom he had never reposed upon—those charms he had never enjoyed!) seemed alternately to preponderate in the balance, as the former or the latter had the advantage of more recent impression.

But, in such a contest, how great were the advantages of the meretricious coquet over the lovely disciple of simplicity and virtue! Melinda was perfectly aware whom she had to contend with, and what were the arts that were requisite for such a contention. Seraphina had no arts. She knew not that contention was necessary; and, if she had, she would have disdained to contend. Seraphina, it is true, when the occasions presented themselves that called forth her powers, could not fail of a victorious impression. But those occasions were such as appealed to the powerful sympathies and moral energies of the soul, and could not, therefore, be of daily occurrence, or be produced at all hours and seasons by premeditation and design—even if such had been the attributes of Seraphina. The fascinations of Melinda, on the contrary, were of a more familiar nature; they consisted in arts and blandishments that were always at command—in specious exteriors, which she could never be at a loss to display.

In short, her preponderancy[1] soon began to be conspicuous. Infrequency of attention to Seraphina grew in time almost to a suspension of intercourse. A transient inclination spread into a restless desire. Voluptuous passion supplanted sentiment. Virtue and Seraphina seemed to be forgotten; and Sensuality and Melinda triumphed.

Not that Henry ever dreamed of absolutely relinquishing Seraphina, or questioned the superior permanency of the passion he entertained for her. The thought of such a separation, even while his soul was dissolved in luxury, in the lap of this new *Armida*,[2] would at all times have been sufficient to have roused him from his voluptuous trance. The fact was, that he could not bring himself to the resolution of relinquishing either of these rival beauties; and, if the laws of the community had tolerated polygamy, both would undoubtedly have been exalted to distinguished places in his haram.[3] But, as it was, one only could be his wife; and, as Melinda could not be possessed as a mistress, he seemed disposed to purchase the gratification of his desires upon the terms she propounded, since he appeared to be already secure of Seraphina upon his own.

Infatuated man! blind, as ungenerous, in this degrading passion! As if the exalted mind of Seraphina could stoop to such co-partnership!—or that she who, in the hour of tenderness and unbounded confidence, had yielded the possession of her person to one of whose heart she felt herself secure in the permanent and undivided possession, would therefore, of necessity, submit to hold a subordinate rank in his perverted affections—to "keep a corner in the heart she loved,"[4] and, lost alike in the estimation of the world and of herself, accept the stolen endearment of a lover who could no longer consider her as the equal partner of a virtuous passion, but the instrument of sensual gratifications—who took his affection upon alms, and banqueted upon the offal from another's table.

Lewson and his sister perceived, from a thousand indications, how the matter stood. They considered the crisis as arrived; and believed that

---

1 Superiority in power or influence.
2 An enchantress in Torquato Tasso's epic poem *Gerusalemme Liberata* (1581; translated as *Jerusalem Delivered*).
3 "[T]he wives and concubines collectively of a Turk, Persian, or Indian Muslim" (*OED*).
4 Possibly an allusion to John Crowne, *The Ambitious Statesman; or, The Loyal Favourite* (1679), 2.74-75.

nothing more was necessary than to seize the first fortunate coincident, to bring the business to the conclusion they desired.

Fortune seemed to favour their designs—as she pretty frequently does, indeed, the designs of those who are always upon the watch to receive her.

An Emigrant Count, who happened to have had the good fortune to save a considerable proportion of his property, as well as his life, from the revolutionary wreck, and who had it, accordingly, in his power to preserve the appearances and the gaiety of his rank,[1] had fallen accidentally into the society of Melinda; and, fascinated by the more than English gaiety of her manners, had paid her some particular attentions.

This was a circumstance not to be passed by unimproved. It was resolved to bring Henry and him together, the first opportunity, where their rival attentions to Melinda might be the object of some publicity, and furnish a pretence for forcing Henry to an immediate explanation.

A grand public Gala,[2] with entertainments of song and dance and banqueting, to which the world of fashion and dissipation were invited by certain *Arbitri Elegantiarum*,[3] at the Pantheon,[4] was considered as likely to furnish a fit occasion for the execution of their design.

The conspiracy was profoundly laid. Melinda was to make a party for the Gala, in which neither Henry nor the Count was to be included, that their rencounter,[5] and whatever effects might be produced from it, might appear to be mere accidental concurrences. The Count, however, was to receive private intimation of her intention, in a circuitous way: and this they trusted would be sufficient inducement to him to keep himself disengaged, that he might give her the meeting there. Henry, in the mean time, was to be previously engaged to a drinking party at some other place.

This latter engagement, however, was to be only a sort of feint; it not being intended that his evening should be there consumed. On the contrary, Lewson himself was to have it in charge so to manage with him, as to bring him to the spot, in proper time, and in a proper state of mind for their designs.

Things being thus arranged, the appointed evening being arrived, Melinda and her party being dismissed to the Gala, and a proper agent sent to crack a jolly bottle with the Count at the St. James's coffee-

---

1   During the French Revolution many royalists and members of the privileged classes sought refuge in England.

2   A festive occasion, typically one for which guests wear their finest attire.

3   Latin for arbiters of elegance. An allusion to the Roman nobleman Gaius Petronius Arbiter, aka Titus Petronius Niger (d. 66 CE), who served as the emperor Nero's "director of elegance" (*arbiter elegantiae*) and passed judgment on all matters of taste. The epithet "Arbiter" thus became attached to Petronius's name.

4   Large building in Oxford Street, London, opened in 1772 as a place of public entertainment. In 1791 the Pantheon was converted into a theatre for Italian opera and was frequented by people of rank and fashion. It burned down the following year and was rebuilt as a theatre in 1795.

5   A hostile meeting to fight or duel.

house,[1] and detain him till he was in a proper state of animal spirits for the adventure, Lewson repaired to the accustomed place of rendezvous, to keep (though somewhat tardily) his appointment with Henry.

The party had been drinking for some time; as Lewson expected them to have been: and, as it was part of his plan that he should be thought intoxicated, and that the rest should, in some degree, be really so, he began immediately to assume the tone and action of one who had already taken more than enough; and (having coined, in his fabling brain, an adventure to account for the phenomenon) he let out as decent a collection of oaths as any gentleman commoner in the nation could have wished to string together: and, d——g "their adulterated tavern burgundy, for turning a man's brains bottom upwards at such a rate," proceeded to apologize for having been detained so long——

"But d— the sons of b——s of parsons," continued he, "with their sanctified faces! When they are once snugly seated in a sly corner of a b—y house, there is no getting away from them, though their wenches are beckoning from behind the curtain, with less than a sixth bottle."

"What, fix a piece? That's right," says Mordant, "and orthodox: for then, between you, you might be *apostolically drunk*—that is to say—*infallibly*."

"For the wit of which commentary," said Henry, "we must refer to the Book of Numbers."

M. "Yes, yes, my wit, to be sure, is very numerous. The book that should record it must be a book of numbers."

"Or rather beyond enumeration," added Falkland, "*for numbers would never find it.*"

H. "Come, come, gentlemen, your wit is a little husky, I perceive— Nothing but puns and quibbles—the very chaff of the floor. As we grow so dull, we may as well return to our devotions.

"Come, fill! fill!—Bumpers!—Bumpers, if you please. I shall put your faith to the inquisition. It is

"*Our holy mother the Church!*

"And now, if you please, we will have Lewson's story of the drunken parson; *et cætera! et cætera!*"

"With all our hearts," said Falkland—"but, first, why should we not drink the State also?"—filling his glass by way of example.

It was instantly followed.

"Aye, *states! states!*" vociferated Mordant—"Let us all drink our states. We may do it with EES, if we have the Church to help us—especially when the wine is so good, and the glasses are so large."

"O, most execrable punster!" exclaimed Henry—"Why, this is crambo[2] itself outcramboed! However, if puns and conundrums are to be the order of the day,

---

1 See p. 266, note 1.

2 A game in which one player gives a word or line of verse to which the others have to find rhymes.

> *"Lay on, Macduff!*
> *And Hell take him who first cries—Hold! enough!*[1]

"So charge your glasses if you please, and let us drink another bumper——

"*A quick conception and a happy delivery to the next worse pun!* And let the midwife who brings it forth be rewarded with a half-pint rummer.[2] *Who can do worst?* in this way, is a more laughable, and therefore a better, game than *Who can do best?* Let us luxuriate therefore in

"*Ænigmas that had drove the Theban mad,*
And puns, then best when exquisitely bad.[3]

"But first, if you please, let us have Lewson's story of the parson, the six bottles of Burgundy, and the peep behind the curtain!"——

Such is the wit of bacchanals. And yet these were young men of talent, when the madness of wine was not in them.

Lewson's tale was in the same decent style: as *decent* as it was *true*. But *truth and decency!* what were they to him? It was matter substantial enough for inebriate laughter to feed upon; and that was more in point. It answered the purpose, also, of keeping the glass and the animal spirits in heedless circulation; till the latter should be wound up to the pitch that was requisite; and it kept the web of his design out of sight, till the proper time should arrive for the unravelling of it.

That time arrived. Henry appeared sufficiently flushed; and Lewson, who, in the midst of his apparent drunkenness, took care to be most soberly watchful that it should not go too far, seized the opportunity of somebody happening to mention the Gala, to blab it out, as if unpremeditatedly, that his sister was gone there with a large party.

"But, pho! p—x! d—n it!" continued he, as if recollecting himself; and hiccuping at the same time—"it was all to have been mum; mum as the grave with a vengeance.

"But women and wine, they say, (with a plague upon them!) keep no secrets."

Henry was as chagrined as he was intended to be: and Lewson, shortly after, took the opportunity, *when he saw the eyes of Henry were fixed upon him*, to endeavour *privately* to withdraw. But he was stopped, as he intended, by an impatient interrogatory, of whither he was going?

---

1 *Macbeth* 5.8.33-34.

2 A large glass for alcoholic drinks.

3 Here and in the earlier reference to the game of crambo Thelwall seems to have in mind a letter of 31 December 1796, in which Coleridge expressed a longing to meet him. Coleridge concluded the letter by quoting a passage from his "Lines to Thomas Poole" that describes a scene of fireside mirth which he hoped to relive with Thelwall:

> How many tales we told! What jokes we made!
> Conundrum, Crambo, Rebus, or Charade;
> Ænigmas, that had driven the Theban mad,
> And Puns then best when exquisitely bad[.] (*Collected Letters* 1: 295)

Thus *taken by surprise*—he confessed he was under promise to join the party at the Gala; and that it was already past the hour.

Henry immediately proposed, and it was seconded by acclamation, that they should all go in a body.

The coaches were called, and away they went; all of them a little mellow—Lewson alone excepted, who pretended to be the mellowest of them all.

CHAP. II.

The Progress of the Conspiracy between Lewson and Melinda—
the Time of Action—Part of a Night of Dissipation,
and a Portion of the ensuing Day.

The Gale.—Woes of wounded Delicacy.—Symptoms of Indecision.— The definitive Appeal.—Hesitations, and obtrusive Remembrances.

OUR Bacchanalian group arrived full of glee and vivacity at the Pantheon. The laughter of Henry, indeed, was a little hysteric:—a spasm of the muscles, rather than an expression of the heart.

The emigrant Count had arrived some time before, and made advances to attach himself to the previous party. He, also, was a little mellow, and had been very assiduous in his attentions to Melinda; who, on her part, had not been sparing of encouragement.

But no sooner had Henry and his party made their appearance in the Rotunda,[1] than her deportment was conspicuously altered.

All then was coldness and reserve.

This the Count considered only as a piece of coquetry; and, presuming upon the encouragement she had so lately given to his advances, he repeated his attentions with so much the more freedom and vivacity.

Melinda pretended embarrassment.

Henry, in whose brain the dæmon[2] of Jealousy began to conspire with the dæmon of Claret,[3] flew to her assistance.

His hasty temper and the wine he had been drinking hurried him into a thousand indecorums: the Frenchman resented his interference. Cards were angrily exchanged; and the terrified Melinda fainted in the arms of Henry; who carried her away to his own carriage; while the whole company were thrown into confusion by the event.

Thus far all was as it ought to be. The lady came to herself in due time. She found herself in the coach—in the arms, of Montfort—

---

1 A circular hall or room, often having a domed ceiling (in this case one in the London Pantheon).

2 A ministering or indwelling spirit.

3 A type of red wine.

"Good heaven! where were they?—Whither was she going? Where was her brother? Why was she torn from him?—the protector of her innocence!—of her honour!

"In Mr. Montfort's coach!—Heaven and earth! what would the world say?—What could he mean?—Did he presume upon her partial——upon that state of temporary insensibility into which she had been thrown by her fears for——by—by the—the conduct of that odious Frenchman?

"Distracting recollection! And what may be the consequences of your interference?

"O! Mr. Montfort!!!"

This last was quite in piano. But wilder notes were to be renewed.

"But take me—take me home; for heaven's sake! Restore me to my brother—to my friends——

"O! Mr. Montfort! how could you—"

Words had done their part; and now was the cue for tears:

"And tears began to flow!"[1]

Nor did they cease to flow (though Henry, in spite of her gentle repulsion, repeatedly kissed them away) till she was assured that the carriage had stopped at her own door. And then she recollected, for the first time, the state of the flambeaux; and the tears flowed again.

"All the world would know that she had come home in Mr. Montfort's coach; and that he had accompanied her.

"What would her brother say?—What would every body say?"

And then she fell into hysterics again: so that Henry of course was obliged to carry her into the house in his arms.

He seated her on a sopha. He seated himself by her side. He called for proper assistants. He chaffed her hands—her temples—He invited the zephyrs with her fan.[2] The fan disturbed the drapery from her bosom. He drank inebriation at every glance; and his heart throbbed at once with pity and desire.

At length she opened her eyes. She fixed them upon him. They scorched like lightning. She drew them away in bashful confusion, and heaved a deep sigh. The sigh was as scorching as the glance.

By this time Lewson himself arrived; having disentangled himself, as he said, with great difficulty, from the angry Count; whom he had in vain endeavoured to pacify.

He inquired with great impatience for his sister.

She was up stairs; and Mr. Montfort with her.

"*Mr. Montfort!!!*"

He rushed up stairs.—

---

1   The line appears in several eighteenth-century poems including Thomas Chatterton, *Bristowe Tragedie*, l. 104; Samuel Jackson Pratt, "The Family of Time," l. 132; Oliver Goldsmith, "The Hermit, or, Edwin and Angelina" (from *The Vicar of Wakefield*), l. 60; and Dryden, *Alexander's Feast*, ll. 88 and 92.

2   Fans and zephyrs figure throughout Thelwall's poetry as erotic metaphors.

"O! Mr. Montfort! what have you done?—Was ever any thing so unfortunate?

"I will not believe you intended—No: you are too generous—

"But let me beg of you to leave my poor distracted sister to herself. Let me entreat you to leave me to my pillow, till reflection has sobered me; that I may think what is to be said, and to be done: for, indeed, I am almost out of my mind."

"Faith, dear Will!" replied Henry, "I am exceedingly sorry. I believe I was too precipitate. But, could I stand by and see your sister ill-used?"

L. "I know not how it arose, Montfort: for I believe we were none of us sober. But this I know, that the whole company are against us: even Mordant himself confesses you were wrong: and very distressing things are said on the subject of your behaviour.

"The gentlemen who were of the party, also feel themselves very indignant: and one of them took the liberty of saying, the world must think there was something very particular between you and my sister, that should make you intrude yourself in such a way, when they, under whose protection she had placed herself, did not think it necessary to interfere.

"And then your tearing her away from me, in that manner, and carrying her off to your coach——

"I knew indeed, that you were a man of honour. I knew I should find my sister here. But what will the world say? What will not they find in so many ambiguous and indecorous circumstances?"

The young lady of course was extremely agitated during this conversation. She wept, and sighed, by turns; and blushed and wept again; and threw herself upon the sopha, in graceful woe.

The eye of Henry dwelt almost incessantly upon her form. Every look added fresh fuel to his passion. The very virtues of his nature rose in arms against him; and that keen and throbbing sympathy, which formed so prominent a trait in his character, prompted him almost every instant to throw himself at her feet, and offer his hand, his heart, his fortune, in atonement of his indiscretion.

The words were several times at the very tip of his tongue. But, somehow or other, the thought of Seraphina, or some untoward reflection, darted across his mind, and his tongue was palsied.

At length, however, bending over the sopha where she lay, he took her tenderly by the hand, and, in a voice of the gentlest sympathy, endeavoured to raise and console her.

"No—no!" exclaimed she, with a tone and look of the most melting melancholy—"Ah! no, Mr. Montfort!—Leave me—leave me to my sorrows—to the malice of my evil destiny—leave me—leave me, I pray, that I may endeavour to compose my afflicted spirits, and regain the calm of reason: if that calm, indeed, is ever to be mine again."

Lewson, perceiving no probability of pushing the affair any further at this interview, joined in the request: and Henry pressing her soft hand to his lips, and, with a sort of hesitating ambiguity, professing his anxiety to make every atonement that man could make for his indiscretion, yielded to their joint solicitations, and retired.

Lewson and Melinda were both a little chagrined that this pathetic scene, every part of which had gone off with such eclat,[1] should, nevertheless, not have brought on the actual catastrophe[2] they desired.

They determined, however, to follow up their design, without delay; that the impressions that had been made might not have time to be counteracted, or reflection to regain her empire. In short, they believed that the citadel was never likely to be in a better disposition to surrender, and they resolved therefore to insist upon an immediate ultimatum.

Henry in the mean time retired to a sleepless couch. The wine in his head, and the form and apparent affliction of Melinda floating before his eye, and sometimes the intruding image of Seraphina, he endeavoured to collect the confused impressions of the last night's adventure, and bring himself to some consistent resolution. But all was chaos: a chaos in which a variety of crude and contradictory ideas were successively floating on the surface; but from which nothing could be drawn into likelihood or form.

He tossed about. He changed the position of his pillow. He turned it, and turned it again and again: but all to no purpose. Sleep was not there.

He endeavoured to think. Thought was not there either. His faculties were all confused. There was lethargy enough both of mind and body; but yet there was no repose.

About twelve o'clock in the day, he was roused, from his benumbing torpor, by the receipt of the following letter from Lewson; which was brought to his bedside:

"Dear Montfort,

"You will readily imagine, in part at least, how much my sister and myself have suffered from the unhappy affair of last night. Indeed I feel myself exceedingly alarmed for the consequences to poor Melinda's health.

"Perhaps I ought not to acknowledge it, but there is a circumstance (I allude of course to what might have taken place in consequence of this affair, between the count and yourself) that seems to have afflicted her much more than even those well grounded apprehensions of disadvantageous reports that may be circulated to her discredit.

"It was more than my sympathy could support, to witness the hysterics, the tears, the frantic apprehensions in which she has consumed the night. You must pardon me, therefore, for having taken a step which your courage and your high sense of honour, I am aware, will not approve; but which, I hope, will not appear too great a sacrifice to the tears of my afflicted sister.

---

1 Brilliancy, conspicuous success.
2 In the sense of a final event or conclusion that changes the order of things.

"In short, I have contrived to get the count arrested under the alien act,[1] and, from circumstances that I know can be well attested, it is pretty certain that he will not be in the country eight-and-forty hours. If there is any thing improper in this transaction, it must lie at my door. I have taken care you should know nothing about it till it was irremediable: and, for my own part, I shall be perfectly satisfied with balancing against any censure that may attend upon my conduct in this respect, the proud reflection of having preserved from the hazard of an irrational contest, the invaluable life of Henry Montfort.

"As to what remains to be mentioned, I am sure you would not think me justified as a brother, if I did not request from you a candid and explicit declaration of the object of those very particular attentions, with which you have, for some time, thought fit to flatter the humble merits of the otherwise unfortunate Melinda.

"If you have honoured her, in your serious thoughts, with those sentiments and feelings which alone can justify such persevering attentions, perhaps you may be of opinion, with me, that the events of last night may seem to render it indispensable to the honour of all parties, that those sentiments should no longer remain a secret. But should I have flattered myself too lightly with a hope so gratifying to all the feelings of the brother and the friend, your candour, I am sure, will excuse the anxiety that dictates an appeal, whose consequences must be to dissolve in my mind the charm of a pleasing but dangerous illusion, and to preserve a beloved sister from the possibility of cherishing expectations that may be destructive to her peace, or from pursuing a line of conduct that might bar all other prospects of an eligible and happy establishment.

"At any rate, the eyes of the world having been drawn upon Melinda in so particular and extraordinary a manner, it must evidently appear to you that (except for the purposes of any explanation this letter may render requisite) it is an indispensable duty, incumbent upon me, to preclude all further acquaintance between you and her, till the honourableness of your views and intentions shall have become of equal notoriety, with the circumstances that have caused so much unhappiness, both to her and to

"Your sincere friend

"and obliged humble servant,

"W. LEWSON."

P.S. "If no engagement of more importance to your happiness, than this business must evidently be of to mine, should call you to any other quarter, I should be happy in the pleasure of your company to a family dinner, at four o'clock, or any other hour that may be more agreeable."

Baker-street, &c.

Henry read this letter with considerable emotion. He read it a second time. His mind was not more composed.

---

1 The 1793 Aliens Act regulated the growing numbers of refugees arriving from revolutionary France.

The arrest of the count (which by the way was a part of Lewson's plan from the first, to preclude explanations, and prevent the possibility of a catastrophe that would have marred the plot) filled his mind with the most revolting sensations. But these were presently confounded by the more distracting impressions the ensuing paragraphs produced.

"Cursed accident!" exclaimed he, striking his forehead, and throwing himself backwards in his bed—"And yet, some time or other it must have come to this crisis.

"What then is to be done?—Lovely afflicted girl!

"Desert her?—leave her in this distressing situation?"

"Madam Seraphina, sir"—said William, who was still in waiting—though Henry seems to have forgotten him.

Henry shrunk as from an electric shock.

Seraphina!—The name rang like a larum bell[1] through his heart; and a thousand passions and sensations rushed in tumultuous confusion to the call.

He raged—he melted—he was abashed; and the transitions of his voice and gesture were as abrupt as his feelings.

"Dolt!—Scoundrel!—Seraphina!—Who gave you leave to talk? What of——of——?" He endeavoured to avoid the repetition of the name. There was a charm in it, whose influence he dared not again encounter.

W. "Sir—sir—I beg your pardon, sir—only, sir, that madam Seraphina—"

H. "Seraphina again!—Well—well—what of her?"

W. "Only, sir, that madam Seraphina is walking in the shrubbery, in the square, sir; very thoughtfully: and that Nanny is with her, sir. Nanny says that she takes her out very often to talk about our good lady your mother, sir, that is now no more!"

(Henry bit his lips, and pursed up the lower lids of his eyes, as struggling to keep in the tears.)

"I do really think, sir, that had madam lived, she would"——he would have added—she would have been very fond of this good young lady. But Henry seems to have had some presentiment of what he would have said, and to have determined to spare himself the confusion of hearing.

"Scoundrel!" exclaimed he, sharply, and with a loud voice, cutting him short in the very middle of a word—"Edmunds has taught you this lesson. It is he who has instructed you to talk to me in this way. Begone from my sight this instant!"

Henry's conscience began to be troublesome; and he very gladly escaped into a passion from its importunities.

"Shall I be played upon by this boy, thus, at second hand?—Shall I be governed by the intrigues of my own servants? I will decide immediately. I am decided." (He rung the bell as he spoke.) "Here, fellow: tell the

---

1 Or alarum-bell, rung as a signal of danger.

servant that brought this letter, I will wait upon his master at the appointed hour."

The decree went forth; and Henry had no time to reconsider it: for, before he was properly dressed, Mordant and Falkland called upon him, to rally him on the adventure of the preceding night, and take him along with them to the tennis-court; where the time, of course, was dissipated, till the hour of appointment arrived.

CHAP. III.

A long Chapter, embracing, exclusive of Retrospects, only the short Space of a few Hours; but in the course of which the Reasons of a very mysterious Attachment will be explained.

Moral Distinctions.—Poignant Reflections.—The Rencounter à-propos.—More profound Politics.—Ambiguous Appearances.— Important Coincidences.—Ambiguities explained.—Love and Eloquence.—The Repulse.—The Dismission.[1]—The Climax of Delirium.

THE incident at the Pantheon took place but a little while after Edmunds's angry communication of his discoveries to the old duenna. That little while, however, had not passed idly away. Edmunds and Morton had both been very busy. The former (little suspecting the arts that would be employed to bring the business to so speedy a conclusion) had fallen upon a scent, by means of which he hoped to bring some matters to light that would place the character of Melinda in such a point of view as would effectually prevent the match. The latter had directed her inquiry entirely to the mind of Seraphina.

She had still a firm faith in the power of her ward to reclaim the lost affections of Henry, if she would but follow her admonitions and advice. It was a favourite plan of hers that Seraphina should, of a sudden, launch into the gaieties and splendour of high life—should renounce her pedantic retirement, and, turning her taste to the decorations of fashion, and her accomplishments into lures of public admiration, should endeavour to foil her rival at her own arts, and with her own weapons.

But this advice Seraphina had perseveringly rejected with disdain.

There were terms upon which even the heart of Henry would not be acceptable. She could not consent to degrade herself in her own eyes. From the hour when she first met the ardours of his passion with reciprocal tenderness, to the present time, she had lived to him with the pure integrity of a wife; she should not now assume the meretricious air of a courtezan.

"If Henry wished for her society in the gayer scenes of life, so far as that gaiety was innocent, and consistent with the dignity of a moral and intel-

---

1 Or dismissal.

lectual agent, he knew how to obtain it. He must place her upon such a footing that she might mingle with the respectable part of her sex, in his own rank of life: for with such only would she ever mingle.

"She must associate upon a footing of equality with the man she loved, or relinquish his society altogether.

"Had she fixed her affections on a peasant swain, she could have contented herself with his homely cottage and his scanty fare—could have shared his rude society, and have entered into his rustic friendships. Whatever he was obliged to submit to, had been good enough for her. She would have been the partner of his fortunes, as of his heart.

"Nay, she could dwell in obscurity, while the man she loved was dazzling the circles of splendour, so long as his welfare seemed to require it.— She could even descend from the rank of moral respectability (so far, at least, as that rank was dependant on public estimation) rather than blight his prospects and endanger his essential interests. But when these were no longer at stake, all temporising was at an end: she must be acknowledged and respected as the equal partner of his destinies; whether they had placed him in a hovel, or on a throne.

"Since the death of his father there had been but two possible relationships that could exist between her and Henry—that of the wife, or of the simple *friend*. The ambiguous character of the mistress terminated on the publicity of that event. The part of a friend she had since performed with anxious solicitude, so long as his endangered health required it: and she had reposed, with ample confidence, upon his intentions of attaching her by the more endearing tie. If these intentions were laid aside, the deportment prescribed by Morton was little calculated to recall them to his mind."

Not more favourable were the reception she gave to the second proposition, of seeking an interview and explanation with Henry; of trying the force of endearment and expostulation, and then, "seizing the minute of returning love," to urge the final fulfilment of his engagements.

"No—no, Morton," said she, "neither shall my heart be tributary to his compassion. When you attempt to persuade me to appeal to such resources, you in fact convince me that nothing worthy of an appeal is left.

"I am sunk—I am fallen in his eyes. Or rather Henry is sunk and fallen in mine. It is no more the Henry I have once so reverenced—the Henry of Limbé and of Margot. Falkland and Lewson have made another Henry of a very different character. Of materials the most dissimilar they have compounded a thing of vice and weakness, and dressed it in his alluring form.

"Why clings my heart thus to the phantom, when the substance is no more? Reason should rejoice that our compact is not indissoluble; that I am not bound by legal obligation, to be a participator in the sordid pleasures to which he is attached, or to lend my society and countenance to such companions as seem to infest his table.

"No, Morton! torture your brain no more for expedients that suit not with my views and character. My expedient is fixed upon already. I will fly, Morton. I will fly from this forbidden roof, where I have ceased to look for a legitimate home. I will fly far away to solitudes and sequestrations—to some such privacy as I once meditated in my virgin days—and think no more of this mansion of reproachful splendour.

"Fond fool that I was, I thought it the land of my promise. But the oracle was misunderstood. No such promised land is mine. The bondswoman Hagar must flee and wander; and the sandy desert of the world is before her.[1] A desert indeed!!! No tree to shelter! No flowering shrub throws forth its fragrance to regale my sense! No friend! no relative! no sweet endearing fond connection, to twine round the sad heart, and link my soul to life!

"But that is my consolation!" continued she wildly—"that is my consolation!—I have no duties to fetter me to my burthen. I am at liberty to lay it down!"

She paced about the room, in great agitation. Morton was petrified with horror.

After a pause, resuming a degree of tranquility, "O! Morton!" she proceeded, "what a destiny is mine!—I look forward, and all is gloom and anguish—I look around me, and all is desertion and disappointment. Backwards I turn, in hopes of consolation from the careless hours of infancy. Alas! no consolation is even there. No recollected, retrospective joys gild the sad dawn of memory. Some few short hours indeed—O sweet retreat of Limbé! O Parkinson!—O Amanda!—some few brief hours—(How closed!!!—how closed!!!)—gilded by them, just proved that in this wilderness of woes there is *some* bliss—though like a summer flower it does but bloom to wither. But what else can memory recall of which it may be said—*For this, it was worth while to have been?*

"Brothers, sisters, relatives, I never knew!
>   No mother's care
>   Shelter'd my helpless infancy with pray'r![2]
No father's love taught me to lisp, at the protecting knee, the cheerful notes of gratitude.

"Mysterious workings of an eternally existing necessity![3] how have ye engendered in this bosom the ardours with which it glows?—How has this heart become thus formed to all the social passions?—Oh! formed in vain. This heart may thirst for them—but shall never taste.

"Farewell, all ye fond flattering hopes of social tenderness!—the constant companion! the faithful partner!—endearing babes, whose sweet reflective faces catch all the varying passions as they rise, and instruct

---

1   A bondswoman is a female slave. In the Bible, Hagar is the Egyptian servant of Sarah, who persuades her husband Abraham to send Hagar and her son Ishmael into the desert for fear that Ishmael may become a rival heir to Sarah's son Isaac.

2   Joseph Cottle, "Written, (1793) with a Pencil, on the Wall of the Room in Bristol Newgate, where Savage Died," ll. 9-10.

3   An allusion to Godwin's doctrine of necessity (see p. 223, note 3).

while they receive instruction!—farewell to all!—these joys are not for me. My lot is nought but bitterness!

"O! guilty parents! why did ye give me existence?—O! guilty parents! why did ye plant what ye would never train?—why leave my tender shoots, unfenced, unpropped, to the rude spoil of adversity, without the neighbourhood of one kindred spray, to which, in the raging storms of affliction, my soul might sometimes cling for support?"

Morton was agitated, almost to delirium. She smote her breast. She lifted up her eyes to heaven. She covered them with her hands, and, shrinking with her head upon her knees, with half-stifled sobs, and sighs that cleaved the heart, rocked herself from side to side, as if endeavouring, by corporeal agitation, to shake off the heavy load of anguish.

Seraphina was too much absorbed to notice her.

"Isolated!" exclaimed she, meditating—"Isolated!—

"My situation points out my remedy. I will fly from this room, where I can no longer remain without dishonour. I will bury myself in seclusion, I will leave to Henry the liberty he wishes for—of forming a heartless union with this daughter of dissipation, whose wanton witchery has ensnared his soul. I will leave him to those prodigal pleasures he so much prefers to the society, to the love, to the peace of Seraphina.—And as for myself—if I find it impossible to forget, I at least can die.[1] If I cannot lull my soul to the soft slumbers of tranquility, the deep—the eternal sleep of oblivion is always at command."

The anguish of Morton burst silence at this conclusion. She started from her seat; threw her arms round the neck of Seraphina, and with a thousand tears, and a thousand expressions of endearment, entreated her not to talk so wildly; not to cherish such desperate meditations—to have compassion upon herself, to have compassion upon her—"who live only for thee," she continued, "my Seraphina! only for thee—Guilty wretch as I am! for thy dear sake alone do I support the stings of conscience, and the burthen of a joyless existence!"

Seraphina endeavoured to soothe her. She appeared to be somewhat consoled, by the effort to give consolation. She became indeed more calm; for she had formed her project; and occupied with the means of accompanying it, the poignancy of her affliction was suspended by new impressions.

Morton, who understood not the cause, rejoiced in the effect. There was also one part of what had fallen from Seraphina, in the torrent of her emotions, that, upon recollection, gave her some comfort—her determination to dissolve the connection with Henry. This she seems to have mistaken for a symptom of the alienation of her affections; and, as she now began to consider him as lost; or, in her own language, "no longer worth troubling themselves about," she thought it desirable that Seraphina,

---

1 An allusion to Wollstonecraft's suicide attempts in 1795 after being spurned by her lover Gilbert Imlay.

whose youth was but little worn, and whose charms were not diminished, should be at liberty to seize whatever opportunities might arise of forming some better connection; a plan which she thought it would be easy to persuade her to adopt, when once Henry and she were fairly separated.

When we are in the right humour to be tempted, the devil is seldom far off.

While Morton, full of these meditations, was upon the scent of inquiry (more with a view of collecting materials to urge on the final separation, than from any hope of restoring the wandering affections of Henry) she happened (most opportunely and happily as she imagined) to meet with her old favourite suitor and employer, Moroon.

Hope darted across her mind. She determined to accost him. She revived the subject of his unfortunate addresses to Seraphina. She found his passion rather smothered than extinguished. She hinted hopes. His inclinations caught fire. He requested, and she promised an opportunity of further conversation on the subject.

An appointment was made. It was punctually attended to, by both parties. An eclaircissement took place. Moroon was equally liberal in promises, and in earnests of his sincerity, to the good duenna. He repeated his offers of marriage in the same unrestricted way as formerly; and Morton promised him an opportunity of declaring his passion in person: for the intercourse with the fashionable world which the fortune of our sub-hero had procured him, had worn away some portion of that *amiable modesty* which the reader will remember as a trait of his former character.

These interviews, of course, were to be perfectly accidental. Morton was to take care that he should be enabled, by mere chance, to cross the way of our heroine, in some of those walks in which she daily indulged herself. And, to further the design, our duenna thought it most advisable to preserve an entire silence with respect to him, till she had marked the effect which she expected his improved address and deportment could not fail to produce: for we have already observed, that the person of Moroon was far from being exceptionable; and, now that he had learned to imitate, in some sort, the manners and accomplishments of the circles in which he had been moving, during his residence in the gay metropolis of France and Britain, she imagined it not very probable that any young lady of taste should regard him with aversion.

The very first, however, of these perfectly natural and accidental interviews (if it did not produce the impression that was desired) gave Seraphina some suspicion of the plot that had been contrived. The conversation of Morton gave strength to this suspicion. It was a perpetual panegyric on the alteration that had taken place in the deportment and appearance of Moroon—the ease and polish that a little time had given to his manners, and the more matured graces of his person.

Seraphina heard, and was silent.

A second rencounter determined her to change her accustomed walk. Still, however, in a day or two, Moroon happened to meet her again.

She took no pains to conceal from Morton that she saw through the contrivance; but, as she showed no marks of anger, Morton was rather encouraged than abashed: and began to unfold her design, by dwelling upon the merits and constancy of Moroon, and the generosity of his unaltered attachment.

Seraphina made no reply: and, encouraged by her silence, the duenna proceeded to avow the conversations that had passed between her and Moroon—to state that she had found him to be still as anxious as ever to lay his fortune at the feet of Seraphina; and that it remained therefore only for her not to have the imprudence to reject his addresses, and she might still be placed even in a more eligible situation of life, than that to which the fidelity of Henry Montfort could have raised her.

Seraphina heard her to the end; and still preserved her silence. The next day, however, when she went out, for her accustomed walk, Nanny accompanied her, and Morton was left behind. But as, to soften the mortification, she had taken care to employ her upon some business which she pretended it was requisite not to delay, the sage duenna was not entirely put out of heart; but determined to proceed with her machinations, and even to give Moroon, who grew very importunate, an early and ample opportunity of making whatever proposals he should think fit: and it so happened that she had absolutely engaged to introduce him into the house on the afternoon of that same important day, at which our history is now standing still—the day on which the final eclaircissement was to take place between Henry and the artful Melinda, and in which some other important events were also ripening for disclosure, with which the reader will in due course be made acquainted.

In the mean time, that no misconstruction may be put upon the somewhat mysterious conduct of Seraphina, it may not be amiss to notice, that Morton had for some time been very rapidly declining in her regard and confidence; and that, considering her as a very improper and very dangerous companion, in the new mode of life she was about to enter upon, she had begun very seriously to meditate the design of breaking off all further connection. This design was at once confirmed and hastened forwards towards the execution, by the discovery of the fresh intrigues the duenna had entered into with Moroon.

It was for this reason that she had not thought it necessary to expostulate on the subject: for it was not in the heart of Seraphina to be forgetful of past services; and she was desirous that the separation, which, in a moral point of view, appeared to be so necessary, should not be attended with any circumstances that might be construed into sudden anger or resentment.

In the mean time she had discovered in the humble, the uneducated, but sympathizing Nanny, a character and disposition more congenial to her views and wishes. To her she had disclosed the secret of her intended departure from Grosvenor-square; and her, upon earnest entreaty, she had consented to make the companion of her flight; and her future attendant in the humble privacy to which she had determined to retire.

It was upon the execution of this plan that (without the least knowledge of the transactions of the preceding evening) they were talking together, in the shrubbery of the square, when honest William, with such designing simplicity, intruded the name of our heroine upon the meditations of his master, after the receipt of Lewson's letter.

The subject of course was interesting. Many details were to be entered into, and many preliminaries were to be adjusted; for the better arrangement of which they had extended their walk from the square to the neighbouring fields, and protracted it through a considerable portion of what is fashionably called the morning. In vulgar English, it was between three and four o'clock in the afternoon before they returned.

But what was the surprise of Seraphina, when, on entering the antichamber of the little study, where she usually sat, she found herself immediately accosted by the profound bow, and "Madam, your most obedient servant," of the splendid and amorous Moroon!

"Start not, adorable lady!" said he, attempting to take her by the hand—"you have nothing to fear from the most constant, the most ardent, the most tender, the most inexhaustible of lovers—whose passion is like mount Ætna,[1] as eternised and as fervid; and who is ready to pour out the whole volcano of his wealth into your most adorable lap. Yes, O! divinest, most beautiful, and three times most angelic creature!—fairer than the moon in the transparent nights of Barbadoes, and graceful as the tallest sugar cane on my vast plantations!—I am come *to lay* my heart, *my hand*, my fortune *at your feet*—Aye, madam—all the wealth I am master of. And I have a vast deal of property, madam—a vast deal of property, I assure you—a vast deal in Barbadoes, in plantations, in buildings, in sweets, in rums and spirits, in horses, mules, negroes, and oxen!—a vast deal on the high-seas, both in vessels and in goods; in the coasting trade, and the African trade; in the ports of Liverpool, of Bristol, of London—a vast deal in the British and in the American funds. I have a splendid establishment, also, madam, in Portland place—A mansion of decoration, most adorable effulgence! fitted up by Siddols[2] himself in the last style of elegantness[3] and fashion; with a coach, a chariot, a curricle, a *vis-à-vis*, and a landau[4] (to say nothing of horses, servants, hammer-cloths,[5] and splendid liveries!); and I wait, O! most adorable effulgence! only for the discriminative decidence of your directing and discerning taste, in the coin-

---

1 Or Etna, a volcano in Sicily.

2 Unidentified.

3 The first of a string of coinages with which Moroon attempts to speak what he imagines to be the elevated language of suitors.

4 All varieties of carriage. A coach is a large four-wheeled carriage with seats inside and out; a chariot is a light four-wheeled carriage with only back seats; a curricle is a light two-wheeled carriage usually drawn by two horses abreast; a vis-à-vis is a light carriage for two persons sitting face-to-face; and a landau is a four-wheeled carriage with a top in two parts that can be closed or open.

5 Cloths that cover the driver's seat in a state or family coach.

cidences of site and vicinage, to form another establishment of equal splendency in any picturesque department of the more provincialised parts of the country; where your most adorable effulgence may poeticalise in all the luxurancy of your resplendent imagination; may cultivate the Muses and invoke the Graces and the Arts; cull the flowers of the cataracts, listen to the tumbling of the groves, and delineate the harmony of the feathered songsters of the—the—the vale. In—in—in short, most adorable effulgence! consent but to the consummation of the nuptial tie with Lucius Moroon, *esquire*, of Portland-place London, and the island of Barbadoes, and you shall have reason to rejoice in the base ingratitude and vile inconstancy of that most insensible and insensate—"

"Hold, sir!" said Seraphina, suddenly interrupting him.

It will be obvious to the reader that several of the *ideas* in this most elaborate and most eloquent harangue must have been supplied by the suggestions of Morton; who perhaps imagined that, of all the splendour Moroon could offer, the most alluring to the romantic taste of Seraphina would be a splendid retreat. By what accomplished master of the incomparable, incomprehensible, and super-anglicised style of newspapers, and magazines,[1] the language and the arrangement were supplied, or how much of it was attributable to his own most effulgent pen (for it was evidently a production of the composite order), may be difficult to decide. Certain, however, it is that (with the exception only of two or three highly ornamented passages, into which the precipitancy of his delivery, or some other cause, introduced some of those striking inversions of epithet that constitute the distinguishing beauties of the Asiatic style[2]) he had committed it so faithfully to memory, and poured it out in so uninterrupted a torrent of emphasis and fervour, that Seraphina was actually overwhelmed; and had neither strength nor resolution to oppose it; till perceiving in what direction that torrent was at length about to flow, her heart, which would not yet permit her to be even a tacit accessory to aught of injurious tendency in that quarter, prompted her to a sudden effort.

"Hold, sir!" said she with great firmness, stretching out her hand, at the same time, to the bell, and ringing it with such earnestness as was likely to insure immediate attention—"Hold, sir! you shall be answered."

William almost instantly appeared.

"Send Morton to me; and let Edmunds know that I should be glad to speak with him, without delay."

W. "Morton has been gone out for some time, madam; and we thought this gentleman had gone with her."

---

1   Thelwall had a keen ironic eye and ear for the styles and follies of popular print culture, which he satirized in the "Epic Poem" chapter of *The Peripatetic* and in his unfinished poem *Musalogia, or the Paths of Poesy* (1827).

2   Possibly an allusion to the "eastern style" that Sir William Jones popularized through his translations from Arabic, Persian, and Hindu, and published in a journal called *Asiatic Researches* throughout the 1790s.

S. "And Edmunds?"

W. "He is out, also, madam. He snatched up his hat, in great haste, as soon as the postman was gone from the door, and, putting the letters in his pocket, hurried out of the house. We thought the postman had made some mistake, and that he was running after him; but he has not since returned."

S. "That is unlucky. You, then, William, must be my witness. Call up your fellow-servants. They shall be witnesses too."

Moroon stood trembling and confounded; not knowing what to make of all this preparation.

Seraphina walked about the room in considerable agitation, till the servants arrived; when turning round to her astonished suitor—

"Sir," said she, with as much composure as she was mistress of, "under other circumstances, I might have been desirous to spare you the confusion of this public address. Modest rejection and private rebuke would have been more accordant to my feelings, as well as less painful, I presume, to yours. But there are circumstances that render it, at this time in particular, an imperious duty to take care that my conduct be not misunderstood—and that it should be evident to all, that there is no possible connection between the circumstance of your unexpected and unauthorised visit, and the event that is so shortly to take place.

"Hear then, sir, in the presence of these people, what answer I have to make to your long, profuse, and eloquent harangue.

"So long as you confined yourself to the real business of your intrusive visit, I listened, though not without reluctance, with respectful silence, to the splendid proposals with which you thought fit to honour me. But when, violating the laws of hospitality, you proceeded to asperse and calumniate a gentleman into whose house (by what degrading arts and dishonourable connivances you yourself best know) you had presumed to insinuate yourself, I thought it a duty to him—to you, and to myself, not even to be tacitly accessary to your further degradation.

"Beware, therefore, sir, how, in the presence of my friend of Henry Montfort, you presume to take liberties with his name, for which you would fear to answer.

"With respect, sir, to your vast opulence, and your very flattering and very extraordinary proposals of laying it at my feet, I can only reply that I have neither a hand nor a heart to bestow in exchange for such sacrifices;— that I am already, in the eye of nature, of justice, of morality—and, what is more, in every sentiment and feeling of the heart, the wife of another; to whom, to the last hour of my existence, I shall endeavour to preserve inviolate, that unrepining fidelity that constitutes (in my estimation) the essence and the glory of that character. It is not therefore in the mockery of laws and institutions, even if my own inclinations could run in such a channel, to place me in that relationship towards Lucius Moroon.

"If I have in any respect misrepresented your meaning, sir, you are at liberty to explain yourself. If not, these servants will so far obey my instructions as to conduct you, in the most respectful way, out of the house, with whose master if you should happen to encounter, you will be obliged to me for concealing the liberties you have taken with his name."

This last hint roused the gaping lover from the torpor of astonishment, in which his faculties had hitherto been confounded.

"Ma—madam!" said he, with the hesitation of precipitancy, "I pro—protest I never intended, madam—never in—in—intended, madam, to insult Mr. Montfort, madam!—I protest, madam—I am—I am your most humble servant, madam."

Morton met the discarded lover on the stairs.

His looks were a sort of telegraphic dispatch[1] of the main outline of what had taken place: and the duenna had as little inclination to inquire, as he had leisure to explain, the details of his misadventure.

She perceived very plainly that she had made a false step; and she felt, from a variety of indications, that the ground upon which she at present stood was not such that a false step ought to have been hazarded.

She dreaded to meet the eye of Seraphina: and, retiring to her own room, with a heavy heart, would have avoided the interview for the present. But William having announced her return, and our heroine, according to the arrangements she had made, having but little time to lose, she was immediately summoned before her.

"Mrs. Morton," said Seraphina, as she entered, "pray be seated; and you, Nanny, leave us to ourselves—We must have a few words in private before we part."

Nanny curtsied and obeyed.

"Part!" exclaimed Morton, in agony and astonishment—"Part! my Seraphina?—Part?"

S. "Be calm, and listen to me, Morton. I am not in anger; but to that which is indispensable we must all submit.

"I am not insensible, Morton, of the many obligations I owe to you. I shall endeavour to show, as far as my humble means will suffer me, that I have not forgotten them.

"You have attended me, with devoted and unrewarded attachment, in the dingle of Limbé, in the perils of flight, in the sequestration (to you how irreconcilable!) of the cottage at Somers-town. You have preserved my life, you have ministered to me, in all the trying situations I have been placed in, all the comforts and consolations which you had the means of ministering. You have devoted your life to my service—And I will do you the justice to add, that I believe you have never been actuated by any other motive than your *apprehensions* of the means of promoting my welfare.

---

1 Telegraphic devices had been in use from ancient times, but according to the *OED*, "the name was first applied to that invented by Chappe in France in 1792, consisting of an upright post with movable arms, the signals being made by various positions of the arms according to a pre-arranged code."

"If this were the only side of the account that were to be reckoned upon, hard were, indeed, my heart, if, under any circumstances, I could suffer you to be involuntarily separated from my side.

"But obligations are dissolved, when superior obligations oppose them. It is the business of a moral agent to weigh the adverse claims of irreconcilable duties; and to hold the balance with a steady hand.[1] This painful obligation I now am called upon to fulfil; and, in the discharge of this, that I may not be misapprehended, I must recapitulate some things that are past, and explain to you the prospect of my future destinies.

"Morton! Morton! perhaps one of the most inexplicable mysteries of the labyrinth of the human heart, is the circumstance of your devoted attachment. There is between us, no single sympathy either of sentiment or of morals. Our tastes are as wide as the opposite winds of heaven—our pursuits are in diametrical hostility, and our conceptions of almost all possible things and situations are as adverse as our propensities.

"And yet you have loved without any assignable reason, and I loved because I was conscious of being beloved.

"Did this dissimilarity merely produce a difference of opinion, did it merely prevent the participation of pleasures, and the reciprocations of that social communion for which my heart is formed, I should lament, indeed, our infelicity in this respect, but it should never be a cause of our separation."—

"Separation, again!" interrupted Morton, throwing herself in an agony at her feet—"O talk not of separation!"

"Rise, Morton," resumed Seraphina; "and hear me to the end.

"I would not, I say, for any dissimilarities of character, and consequent privations of happiness, dismiss from my side a person whom, during so many years, (and some of them years of great trial and sharp affliction) I have always considered less as a servant than a friend. Nay, I would not, for all the positive misery your misconduct and crooked machinations have entailed upon me—even for reputation betrayed and Henry lost, I would not thus have exiled you from my heart. I would have said, it was the error of your judgment: it was the fault of those false and contracted views which it had been your misfortune to adopt. That, to me at least, your heart was upright: and though you had rendered me most miserable, you had intended my prosperity and welfare."

"Miserable! miserable!" exclaimed Morton, wringing her hands, "most miserable! And have I—I made you miserable?"

S. "Yes, Morton! you have—transcendently miserable! By robbing me of the esteem, you have divorced me from the heart, of Henry. By betraying my virgin innocence to those advances, which but for your suggestions he never would have made, you have weakened my influence over his dissipated affections, and given an unbalanceable advantage to a rival, who upon no other foundation could have disputed with me, for an hour, the

---

1 Seraphina's assertions throughout this scene are strongly Godwinian.

possession of his heart—a rival whom, when once this distinction is removed, he will hate with all the bitterness of execration (my proud, sad heart knows that he so will hate her) for having placed a barrier of separation between us, that must render it impossible for Seraphina ever to behold him more.

"Deny it not, Morton,—deny it not. You know it was your contrivance.

"O fatal harbour of Fonchiale! O disastrous interview!—O treacherous and well-guarded seclusion! Thou knowest, Morton! thou knowest too well, that all was of thy plotting—That having worked with every artifice, upon the tenderest sympathies of my unsuspecting soul—that having urged his impetuous, but till then respectful passions to their bent, you seized the opportunity of the absence of honest Edmunds—that you dictated the interview, that you secured the privacy—that you meditated that which followed.

"I saw the flickering smile upon your lip, when at last you entered. I saw that you had wilfully betrayed me. And though such was the devotion of my soul to Henry that I could not then repent me—(no never till now have I indeed repented) yet could not I but ask my heart whether I ought not to hate you.

"Tell me not, Morton, that you thought what you were doing was for the best—that it was my interest—my happiness that you alone pursued. I know it was so. Experience has at length unfolded to me (that master one alone excepted that attaches you to me) all the springs and movements of your soul. I perceive the chain of reasoning upon which you acted—upon which you still continue to act—upon which alone you are capable of acting—and my soul revolts from it with horror. Interest— sordid interest—my interest in the most sordid point of view—that sort of interest (strange inconsistency!) which in your own attachment to me, I believe, you have never consulted—My sordid—my *supposed* interest— (for you insult the frame and faculties of my soul when you suppose it capable of an interest to which that epithet belongs)—this is the sole motive of all that you have done—of all that, if I prevent not, you will still continue to do.

"For this you would have had me desert the sick bed of Henry, when his life was in danger from his exertions for the preservation both of yours and mine—For this you betrayed to him my maiden innocence—for this you would have persuaded me to become his acknowledged concubine, and to have assumed all the profligate manners of an abandoned prostitution—For this you would, again, have persuaded me to neglect the restoration of his health and the preserving of his life, till I had made a bargain of his infirmity; and turned his weakness to my personal account. And you still blame me—your eye, at this very instant, seems to reproach me for not having been so persuaded—as if the sufferings of generosity ought to have taught me that it is disgraceful to be generous!—For this you have dared to introduce, even beneath his roof, the rival—alas! I can no longer say of his love—but of his honour; and have conspired to seduce me, in violation of every principle of virtue and every feeling of affection, to become the legalized prostitute of that worse than pirate and murderer—the assassin and slave-merchant, Moroon.

"This brings me to my point, Morton.—It is not the misery you have heaped upon me. No: insupportable as it is, I yet can pardon that. But our connection is an insuperable bar to the moral agency of my soul. It destroys my utilities, and counteracts my reason. Part of those utilities are for ever gone: for they depend on the estimation of the world. Something, however, as yet, remains; and of that I am determined to be more chary.

"As a moral agent, I have a right, I have a duty, in the free exercise of my understanding—in the choice of my own motives—in my preference of moral action. This you have assumed to yourself a right of abridging and counteracting. It is inherent in your very nature that you should so assume.

"It is in vain that you would protest—Neither promises nor oaths—neither superstition nor reason can subdue the inveterate habit.

"Neither peace nor duty, therefore, admits of any alternative. We must part. I will no longer endure about my person one who presumes to abridge my freedom of moral action, and counterworks the feelings of my soul.

"I will be mistress of my own conduct; as far as human reason can command. As far as the imperfections of my own nature will admit, I will be the being I think I ought to be; and that which I am I will appear.

"This resolution is so much the more necessary, on account of another that I have taken.

"I sleep no more beneath the roof of Henry Montfort. I see his face no more, from this day. Pomps, and indulgences, and the seducing luxuries of opulence, and you, ye dearer hopes, that once flattered this fond heart—ye dreams of love and constancy—ye visions of social and intellectual happiness—ye all in one, my Henry! fare ye well. No more the soul of Seraphina reposes in you;—no more seeks for felicity in a world that (for her at least) has nought but woes. Tranquility and forgetfulness are all that she now desires: and all that she would preserve from oblivion is the sense of those few duties she can still perform.

"The hour is arrived, Morton, that I have fixed for my departure. The humble retreat is provided, and Nanny is the sole confidante and companion of my sequestration.

"With the plan of life I have determined to adopt, your attendance is not consistent. With the system of morals I am determined to preserve, your presence is altogether irreconcilable. I am determined to respect myself as the *deserted* but *unimpeachable wife* of Henry Montfort. I will not be degraded to the level of a discarded courtezan; nor insulted with overtures that would assimilate me to that class of beings.

"Farewell, then, Morton!—farewell!

"I pronounce it with firmness that tears cannot shake—but I pronounce it without anger or resentment.

"For all the errors you have committed, and all the misery they have cost me, take with you my most hearty forgiveness:—if forgiveness, in reality, be an admissible term, where resentment has been never harboured. For all your kindness and solicitudes, and all the intentional benefits you have heaped upon me, take my unceasing thanks; for while life remains they shall not cease to survive in my remembrance. And for your long services," continued she, taking a little book from her pocket—"(it is but a poor remuneration—more proportioned to my means than your deserts) take this; and may its contents contribute to make the calm evening of your days as comfortable, as the rayless noontide of mine is forlorn and wretched!"

"O! do not kill me, my Seraphina!" exclaimed Morton, throwing herself again upon her knees, in still wilder agonies—"O! do not kill me! We must not part.—Talk not of services: I will never leave you. Wherever your destiny may lead you, I will follow while I live. I will follow you upon my knees—I will melt your obdurate bosom with my tears."

S. "Peace, Morton, peace—You cannot shake my determination. I have prepared myself against these assaults. My resolution is unalterable. Take this, and leave me."

M. "I will not take it, Seraphina! I will not take it. My services are not to be paid by pecuniary returns. I have not served for this—they were the services of the heart—the services of an affection that cannot be rooted out—that is entwined with the fibres of my existence; and identified with my vital being. I live but in Seraphina; and but in Seraphina can consent to live. Wherever you hide yourself, my solicitude shall discover your retreat—Wherever you attempt to fly, I will overtake you with my cries; I will arrest you with my expiring groans. I can die, Seraphina—Seraphina, I can die, but I can never leave you!"

S. "Forbear, Morton—forbear these vehement exclamations. They shake my bosom with anguish, but my resolution they cannot move.— There," continued she, throwing it upon the floor, "in that little book is contained (as far as my circumstances permit) what I think it my duty to give you. You may take it up at your better leisure. In the mean while, and for the last time, farewell!"

"Hold!" exclaimed Morton, with more frantic gesture—seizing her, at the same time, and clinging, with convulsive earnestness, to her knees— "Hold!—hold!—you cannot leave me!—No!—no!—you CANNOT!!!" repeated she, with increased emphasis, half rising from the ground, and still grappling to her; while her eye-balls rolled, and her whole frame shook, as with an ague, from head to foot—"You CANNOT!!!"

Seraphina was thrilled with horror. The tone—the gesture—the countenance—the grasp—the agitation—all were supernatural.

"*Cannot!*——Mysterious woman!——Cannot?——What shall withhold me?"

M. "God and nature shall withhold thee.——These hands shall withhold thee, that to the last ebb of life, still grasping with convulsive energy, shall link thee to me, and, as the life retires from these extremities, shall yet retain their hold, fixed—fixed as now, while my heart throbs and mine eyes glare upon thee!"

"Poor phrenetic!" exclaimed Seraphina, endeavouring to recollect her fortitude, "my soul pities thee—wondering it pities. But it can do no more. My resolution is fixed, and the imperious convictions of moral duty forbid me to reverse the decision."

M. "What duty—what moral obligation can ever release the claims *I* have upon your heart?

"Do you not feel them? Do they not cling and twine around your soul? Do they not swell and struggle in your bosom?—as in spite of oaths and dreaded imprecations they struggle now in mine; bursting their forbidden way.

"Do you not hear them—feel them, Seraphina?"

S. "I feel it my duty to pursue my course. Loose me, and let me go."

M. "Why, then there is no God. Nature is nothing—There are no ties between the child and mother. 'Tis all romance we have been frighted with, and I may break my vows. Thou art——thou art—"

S. "Heaven and earth! thou terrifiest me. What am I?—What dost thou mean?—Why dost thou shake so?—What oaths, what imprecations dost thou rave about?—Speak out!—speak out!—What art thou?"

M. (after a pause of delirious agitation)—"Thy mother!—It is past!—It is past!—Visit me not, ye dreaded imprecations! I am thy mother, Seraphina! My child! my child!—I am—thy guilty mother!"

S. "My mother, Morton!—Heaven and earth! my mother!"

The strong emotions of nature came rushing over their souls. They oppressed—they overwhelmed them.

They fell in each other's arms—They sunk down together on the floor.

Poor Nanny, who had been alarmed by the vehemence of the concluding part of the dialogue, came rushing into the room.

She found them seated together in a state of insensibility; supported only by interfolding arms, that still locked them in convulsive embrace.

BOOK IX.

=========

CHAP. I.

Containing the Space of a few Weeks from the Return of old Montfort, to the double Conspiracy against the Fortune and Life of Henry.

Brief Explanations.—Fresh Discoveries.—Paternal Projects.—An extraordinary Rencounter.—A Matrimonial Bargain.—The Reporter chagrined.—The Eclaircissement interrupted.—Paternal Moderation.— Filial Obedience.—Consistent Generosity.—Old Friends with new Faces.—Expanding Prospects, and growing Resentments.—Amorous Mysticism.—A Text of Love.—A Clerical Commentary.

THE feelings and attachment of Morton towards our heroine are now no longer mysterious. It remains only to explain the circumstance of her having thus become, during so considerable a space of time, the unknown attendant of her own daughter.

To remove all difficulties, with respect to which, it is only necessary to observe, that Robertson, when he first adopted Seraphina, observing that this Morton (then passing by the name of Newcomb[1]) notwithstanding the immorality of her life, was very deeply impressed with notions and terrors of superstition, the more effectually to bar her from all intrusion into his family, had administered to her a very formal and tremendous oath, binding her to relinquish all claim and authority over the child, and never again, on any pretence whatever, to challenge, or own her as her daughter:—That trusting to this oath, he had thought it of very little importance, to what part of the world she were sent, so she were but out of the way of such perpetual temptations as might some time happen to overpower her resolution and terrors. He shipped her off, therefore, in one of those contraband traders that make a practice, as has been already noticed, of visiting the ports of the several islands.

Parkinson's information, however, was so far correct, that she never reached the island of Barbadoes, to which the vessel was ultimately bound. Anguish for her separation from the little Seraphina, and horror of the oath she had taken, having driven her to the frequent sallies of insanity, in one of these, while the vessel was lying off one of the intermediate islands, for the purposes of its illicit traffic, she seized her remaining child in her arms, and exclaiming, "We will swim back to her—we will swim back to her," threw him overboard into the sea, and plunged immediately after him.

---

1   Among the principled and hospitable names to which Thelwall pays tribute in "On Leaving the Bottoms of Gloucestershire" is one Newcomb, probably Thomas Newcombe, a mill-owner of Stroud, who resided in Bowbridge House.

It was during the calm of a moon-shiny night. The child, she supposed, perished; and she would have perished also, but for a large Newfoundland dog, belonging to a person of the island then trading on board.

By this animal she was carried to the shore, not quite in a state of insensibility: the vessel pursuing its voyage early in the morning, here she was left, and here she remained for some years, struggling for a livelihood, in a state of misery that might look with envy upon non-existence.

At length, an opportunity presenting itself, she determined to revisit the island of Jamaica: that she might hear, at least, of her Seraphina, and sometimes perhaps, behold, though she might never own her.

On her arrival she found that Robertson was no more: that his family were about to depart for England: but that the object of her inquiry had found another friend; having been adopted into the family of the Parkinsons.

It were needless to repeat all the inquiries a mother so situated would feel herself impelled to make; or all the precautions she appealed to, that she might preclude suspicion. Suffice it to say, that every thing she heard tended alike to gratify maternal pride, and inspire maternal longings.

She burned to see her lovely child—her accomplished Seraphina. She hovered about the neighbourhood. She watched her opportunities. She did see her. Her eyes were entranced, and her heart yearned more than ever. After meeting her some two or three times, she ventured to speak to her. Had she been really the stranger she pretended, she could not but have been charmed with the sweetness of our blooming heroine. What must have been the feelings of the mother! During this time, she had taken up her residence, as a lodger, in the neighbourhood, and maintained herself by industry and frugality, with such decorum as to obtain some degree of credit and esteem among those around her: and an old servant the Parkinsons had brought with them from England (the nurse of the former Seraphina) happening to die, Morton (for it was then that she had assumed that name) made application to supply her place. She had the good fortune to succeed in that application.

What followed is already known.

Seraphina was not the only inhabitant of our little world who was doomed to regain a parent on this day.

It is high time to inform the reader, that the supposed death of Montfort was a mere fabrication of the reverend Emanuel Woodhouse.

That goodly clerk, as has been evident from a variety of circumstances, had long entertained a settled design of ruining entirely the wayward Henry in the affections of the old gentleman; where, indeed, it was palpable that he sat but lightly. By this notable exploit he made no doubt of securing to himself the inheritance of, at least, a considerable portion of the alienated property.

Much towards this design he seemed already to have effected; and nothing more he thought was necessary towards its completion, than to hurry him into an immediate marriage with Seraphina—an offence which, as it would be irremediable, he was confident, in his own mind, the father would never pardon.

Taking advantage, therefore, of the death of a person of the same name, a resident also of the same part of the island (the neighbourhood of Kingston)—but who had been an established planter there many years before our Montfort had first visited the West Indies, he procured an article, of his own drawing up, to be inserted in one of the daily prints (from which, of course, it was copied into all the rest,) mentioning the event in such ambiguous terms as could not fail to be mistaken by the connections of the Montfort of our tale: and to confirm the fraud, he forged, also, on the blank side of the cover of a packet he had just received from the West Indies, a short letter announcing the same event; which he caused to be communicated to Henry.

How far this fabrication succeeded, the reader has seen; and by what means the most material part of this plot was frustrated. In the mean time, however, he was by no means backward in communicating to Montfort the effects that the rumour of his death had produced on the moral conduct of his son—neither did he fail to add such colouring and heightening touches, or such obscurities of outline, as might tend to give to the career of dissipation, some appearance of a triumph; anticipating, at the same time, the marriage which he supposed would immediately have taken place.

These communications decided Montfort upon the plan he had for some time meditated, of returning to England, to prevent, if not too late, this disgraceful union; to chastise the prodigal spendthrift by some severe exertion of his authority; and prevent the future hazard of all improper connections, by compelling him to marry some person or other that his paternal discretion might select as an eligible and adequate match.

If this threefold project did not succeed, he determined to keep no further terms; to cut off immediately the entail of his estates, to discard Henry totally from all grace and favour, and disinherit him without further demur.

To this voyage, and these resolutions, he was still further moved by the gathering gloom of internal dissatisfaction—by certain stings and perturbations within, that, rendering himself dissatisfied with all that was around him, induced him, at once, to seek for ease and consolation from exterior change, and to vent, in wrath and vengeance upon others, the torments of his own sullen mind.

With these motives and these dispositions, he embarked in the next packet; and, by a short and prosperous voyage, arrived off the coast of England at this busy and critical period to which we have now brought our history.

The ill state of his health rendered him desirous of quitting the vessel as soon as possible. He was accordingly put on shore on the southern coast of the Isle of Wight;[1] the weather for the season being mild and temperate; and took up his temporary abode at Steephill. His intention was to proceed the next day to Newport; where he would sleep again: for he expected some benefit from the salubrious air of the island; and then to cross the Solent, to Southampton; that he might avoid the bustle of Portsmouth. He would afterwards, he thought, proceed post to London, and take Henry by surprise, in the midst of all his prodigalities.

This plan of proceeding, however, was very considerably altered in consequence of a very unexpected reencounter—a rencounter that will be as unexpected to the reader as it was to himself; and which formed another of those extraordinary coincidents that seemed at this time conspiring to bring our history to some sort of crisis. In short, at the Inn at Newport, he met with his old friend and companion Lewson: the father of that Lewson and Melinda of whom such frequent and honourable mention has been made in the present volume.

This gentleman, at the period of his disappearance already marked, had embarked for the East Indies, with all possible secrecy; and he had there the perhaps unprecedented good fortune to acquire, in a very short time, an immense property, without sullying his conscience with an iniquitous and cruel action.

He had an aged relation in that country, who had spent his life in the accustomed modes of Asiatic accumulation; and to whom, on his arrival, he had applied, to be introduced, in his turn, to some of the gainful mysteries of the country.

The relationship was not very near: but there was no rival interest in the vicinage. The old nabob had, till his arrival, neither namesake nor relative in the country, nor any human being about him, (his bosom slaves, or native mistresses, alone excepted) to whom he had any attachment. The name therefore of Lewson, and the appellation of cousin, were sources of immediate gratification; and as the adventurer was a man of a pleasant, and in some respects an amiable, turn of mind, and had the talents and resources for conversation, he soon rendered himself so agreeable, and even necessary to his superannuated relative and patron, that the latter would not suffer him to embark in any project or connection that should rob him of his society, but detained him under his roof by a bond so forcible as the actual adoption of him for his heir.

Of this adoption it was not long before Lewson was put in possession of the full advantages: for the old nabob, who had not become much of a Bramin by his residence in the country of the Hindoos, but on the contrary, like a true European Orientalist, loved to stew his lampreys in a

---

1   Thelwall knew the Isle of Wight well, having retreated there for his health during the summer of 1795, and written there "A Patriot's Feeling. On Leaving the Isle of Wight," which initiated his poetic conversation with Coleridge.

silver saucepan, took a surfeit, at one of his public dinners, which being succeeded by a dangerous fever, carried him off in a few days.

Lewson delayed not, even for the final adjustment of his affairs, his return to England; but, leaving them in the hands of agents that he imagined he could trust, embarked the first opportunity, and had arrived only a few days before his old bottle companion and crony, Montfort, at the Isle of Wight; where his ill health had also occasioned him to be put on shore; and where the same cause had hitherto detained him, under the care of a physician of that place.

He had sent no intimation of his arrival to his son and daughter; for, as he expected to be able to travel again in a few days, he was determined to come upon them by surprise, that he might the better become acquainted with the manner in which they had husbanded the little property and the advice he had left behind him, at the period of his sudden and mysterious departure: though to this he was instigated more by humour and curiosity than any thing else; his mind being infected by none of the moroseness or meditated resentments that tormented the soul of Montfort.

The rencounter of these two voyagers was, of course, productive of a multiplicity of agreeable sensations; and, were it our business to dwell upon the garrulities of age, we might easily fill up our volume with the comparisons of their respective adventures, and the recapitulations of their former frolics and exploits. But we pass these over, till we have an opportunity of meeting the parties and the reader together, at some coffee-house or tea-table; having, at present, other matters to record.

Suffice to say that the story of Lewson's sudden acquisition, immediately suggested to Montfort the idea that nothing in the world could be more eligible or desirable than a matrimonial alliance between two families whose friendship had been of such intimacy and old-standing. He accordingly proposed, and Lewson agreed, that immediately on their arrival in London (if the rashness of Henry had not already precluded it) a contract of marriage should be celebrated between the only son of the one and the daughter of the other.

This bargain once agreed upon, Montfort began to see the conduct of Henry, or at least to be desirous of seeing it, in a more favourable point of view. He was willing to shut his eyes to all his faults; and avoid the opportunities of detecting them, for the sake of this new project.

But, of all things, he thought it necessary, in the first instance, to ascertain whether the dreaded marriage with Seraphina had taken place. For this purpose, as the health of his friend did not yet permit him to travel, and as he was desirous of not leaving him till every thing was concluded, he sent an express to Woodhouse, desiring that goodly divine to meet him at Southampton; to which place it was thought proper, for the sake of further advice, that Lewson should be removed.

Woodhouse brushed up his memory and invention together, and obeyed the summons with alacrity; believing himself excellently furnished for making *a good report*: for, though he could neither state the completion, nor, under present circumstances, the probability, of the desired obnoxious marriage, yet he thought he could make out such a tale about young Lewson and Melinda, and the connection between Henry and that extravagant dissolute *demirep*, (for as such he thought he had documents to represent her) as, in combination with all his prodigalities and excesses, could not fail of doing the business pretty nearly as well.

But what was the astonishment and confusion of our pious *reporter*, when he found that Montfort (instead of testifying his gratitude for the *diligence* with which the conduct of the young reprobate had been scrutinised, and the *fidelity* with which it had been reported) turned a deaf ear to every malicious tale? that his mind seemed fruitful of excuses and favourable constructions? that the censures heaped upon the characters of young Lewson and Melinda, and even of Henry himself, were silenced with impatient rebuke? and, in short, that (gratified with the intelligence of the connection with Seraphina seeming in so fair a way to be broken off) every thing else appeared to be as it should be; or, at worst, so venial, that all might be brushed away with a slight apprehension, as follies and irregularities of youth.

It was in this humour, finding his friend still unfit to be removed any further, that Montfort wrote from Southampton the letter, the delivery of which had caused the abrupt disappearance of Edmunds; which the reader will remember to have been related by William in the preceding book: for Edmunds knew the hand-writing on the direction; and, from the post-mark, and the recentness of the ink, he laboured under no small degree of apprehension that the writer was not merely risen from the dead, but actually ready to manifest himself among them, and call the terrified Henry to an immediate and unprepared account—

"And then what was to become of Seraphina?"

This was, above all, the thought that, "adding new wings to his amazement,"[1] hurried him away in quest of Henry. Accordingly, with the letter in his pocket, he ran from coffee-house to coffee-house, and from haunt to haunt: wherever he thought there was a chance that he should be found. But he ran and inquired for a long time to little purpose; till at last he stumbled upon the tennis-court. Here indeed he met not with Henry; but he met with Falkland and Mordant, who had just parted company with him, and who, upon understanding the reason of his earnest inquiry, ventured to suggest their suspicions (for they were not absolutely in the secret) that he was gone to dine with Lewson.

Edmunds posted, immediately upon this information, to Baker-street; and being informed that Henry was actually there, rushed, without further ceremony, into the room, where Melinda, (adorned in all her arts and witcheries, and accompanied by her no less artful brother) was

---

1   No source has been found for this exact quotation. The "adding new wings" usage is common.

spreading her snares for the final explanations and anticipated proposals of the infatuated renegade.

The abrupt intrusion of Edmunds, of course, threw the whole party into confusion. Melinda shrunk. Lewson looked stern. Henry was alarmed—was terrified.

"Edmunds there! What could have happened?"

He began to feel the real state of his heart. The transient passions fled: they were scattered; they were dissipated. The more permanent sympathies rose in arms.

The indecorous precipitancy of the messenger—the wildness of his gesture—his embarrassment—his speechless agitation, all seemed to forebode something that was dreadful.

"And what that was dreadful could have happened except to one beloved—one injured individual?—

"Perhaps she had heard of his purposed falsehood!—perhaps her noble but too susceptible mind—driven to desperation by the intelligence"—

The thought was too terrible to be pursued.—Decorum was forgotten, and apprehension burst silence—"Seraphina!" he exclaimed, incoherently, "where, what! Edmunds!—speak!"

E. "Seraphina, sir, is where you left her, I believe; and as you left her; better in health than in heart. But where she may be to-morrow this letter, it is probable, may decide,—In short, sir, not to be more abrupt than the circumstances of the case compel—your father"—he watched the eye of Henry, "is not dead.—Your father"—he paused again, "is returned to England.—Your father—(for any information the post-mark of this letter contains to the contrary) may be home before you."

Henry snatched the letter with great agitation. He tore it open with a trembling hand. He read it hastily over. Unconscious what he was doing, he even read it aloud. It was as follows—

Southampton, &c.

"Henry Montfort—

"If I were not in a very indulgent humour I might think myself justified in writing to you with great severity. I am acquainted with the undutifulness of your deportment on the report of my death. I am acquainted with your wasteful extravagance, and all your prodigal courses. I am acquainted with the disgraceful connection you formed in St. Domingo, and to which you have ever since continued to be a slave. But I am acquainted also with the attentions you have lately paid to the daughter of my old and very esteemed friend Cromer Lewson; and for that one indiscretion I am disposed to become blind to all the rest; and, changing my original plan of taking you by surprise in the midst of all your follies, I give you this opportunity of preparing yourself to meet me in a dutiful and decorous manner: for, to let you into so much of the secret as is at this time necessary or convenient, I have determined that Melinda and Melinda alone"—

Henry began to recollect where he was, and what he was doing. His heart died within him. His voice died away also. He perused the rest in silence.

—"I have determined that Melinda, and Melinda alone, shall be the future companions of your life."—

Henry glanced his eye from the paper, as he read these words, towards the proffered bride. But her charms were faded—her fascinations were gone. What an Aethiop to Seraphina!

"Never!" he sighed out—"never!"

"Upon these two conditions, then, and upon these alone, I am willing to cancel the long account I have to settle against you—That you take immediate measures for shipping your wanton Creole back to the plantations—and for securing the consent of Melinda to *the union I have contracted* between you.

"These two preliminaries fulfilled, I am ready to sign a treaty of oblivion for past offences, and to judge of you by no other part of your conduct than that which I may myself henceforward observe:—Upon no other terms whatever must you expect me to subscribe myself again

Your affectionate father,

PERCIVAL MONTFORT."

It would be impossible to describe the multitude of powerful and contending passions that agitated the heart of Henry. Those that related to the lovely heroine of our tale were, however, the most prevalent: and, as persons by sudden and violent contusions of the sensorium are said to have lost the remembrance of a more recently acquired language, and to have been restored to the involuntary use of that which had been long forgotten; so by this sudden shock and concussion of unexpected intelligence, the some-time relaxed fibres, that used to vibrate alone with the pure love of Seraphina, were once more tuned and braced, while those that of late had thrilled with lascivious wantonness of the dissipated Melinda, were jarred and rendered tuneless.[1]

"Seraphina! Seraphina!" he exclaimed, and rushed out of the house.

Edmunds followed.

He ran like a lunatic through the streets, never stopping till he had arrived at the square. The impatient knocker seemed to burst the door; it flew open so immediately. There was a sort of wildness and agitation in every countenance, that did little to compose his mind.

"Seraphina!" he exclaimed again, "Seraphina!"

"O! such a discovery, sir!"—

He paused not to hear the tale; but flying upstairs he rushed into the apartment of the lovely Creole.

---

1   Thelwall's musical metaphors of mind reflect both his medical training and his reading in the associationist theories of David Hume and, especially, David Hartley, who studied connections between physiological and psychological processes, and suggested that sensation is caused by vibrations in the nerves. These ideas are a fundamental part of Thelwall's later elocutionary theory and therapy.

What a scene was presented?—Seraphina and Morton (pale and almost delirious with agitation) mingling their embraces and their tears. Nanny and her assistant maidens, by whose attentions they had been recently recovered from the state of insensibility in which we left them, some with hartshorn, some with water, and all with anxious faces, imprinted with amazement and terror.

"Seraphina!—Seraphina!" ejaculated Henry a third time; his former anguish mingled with new astonishment.

This was a fresh shock that the nerves of Seraphina were not prepared to sustain.

"Henry here?" she exclaimed—"O Henry!"

She fainted again in the arms of Morton.

"My child! My love! My daughter! Seraphina!" exclaimed Morton, supporting her.

Nanny ran again to her assistance, with the hartshorn and water.

"Daughter?—What can all this mean?" said Henry. "My life! my love! my wife! my Seraphina Montfort! my Seraphina!" continued he, snatching her from Morton and Nanny, and ministering the drops himself.

"O Henry! Henry!" said she, faintly—just recovering. "Why art thou come, Henry?—Why art thou come?—We must part, Henry.—We must part."

H. "O say not so, my Seraphina! O say not so! He shall not part us. Not all the fathers in the world shall part us."

S. "Fathers! fathers!"

H. "Let him reprobate me. Let him disinherit me. He shall never part us."

S. "He part us!—Fathers?—Disinherit?—What does this mean? Hast thou another father? Does the grave give up its dead for thee, also?"

H. "It does—it does!—Oh! Why has he a heart so hard, my Seraphina! To make me grieve, it does? I would fain be a son. I would cherish the feelings of nature. But that which links my heart to Seraphina, is not that Nature too?"

S. "Oh! Henry!—Henry," said Seraphina—the severity of her glance tempered with a starting tear.

H. "Oh! Look not so my Seraphina!—look not so. Pardon and pity, Seraphina. Pity me, and pardon.—See here, my love! See here!" continued he, giving her the letter.—"But he shall never part us."

Seraphina read with considerable emotion.

S. "He does but order, Henry, what you have wished; and what, in all essential particulars I have resolved. He shall be obeyed. I'll be no bar to Henry's wishes, or to Henry's fortune. I meant, indeed, to have concealed myself in an obscurity not so remote. But there is still, it seems, one sacrifice in my power, and I will make it as freely, Henry, as I have made all others.

"Nay, it is not much; it is nothing. For what is space?—What are disjointed continents, or separating seas?—When hearts are alienated, the neighbouring cottage or the remotest isle make equal distances. In the furthest of the distant Antilles, I cannot be more exiled from Henry Montfort, than I have been beneath this roof.

"Hasten, then, Henry; obey your father! Inquire out some vessel that may convey me back. Restore me to the fatal shore where first it was your misfortune to behold me (me and my new-found mother!) It is more peaceful now; and there, perhaps, I may still find some sad employment that suits *the mournful tenor of my soul*[1]—I may collect in their urn the bones of brave Mozambo; or, wandering by the rapid fatal stream, learn where the floating forms of Parkinson and Amanda were washed at last on shore, and build the empty tomb to their remembrance."

H. "O! Talk not thus, my Seraphina! Drive me not quite to madness. I cannot lose you—will not survive your loss. By heaven and earth I will not.

"I am unworthy, Seraphina—I am unworthy of you. But I cannot live without you. By heaven, I cannot! I will not, Seraphina. Fool! fool! fool! that cannot know the worth of my heart's treasure but when I am like to lose it. But save me, Seraphina: pardon and save me. Let us put our destiny beyond the reach of future danger—beyond the temptations of folly—beyond the tyranny of an obdurate father. Swear, swear, swear with me, my Seraphina, that we will never be separated—Hasten with me to the altar, and swear it there. Edmunds shall give thee to me. We will summon all the neighbourhood—all the town to witness it. We will publish it to all the world. Never shall he part us. He may disinherit—he may banish—he may kill me—but he shall never part us. He is no father that would seek to part us. I abjure—I renounce the tie."

We need scarcely record the readiness with which our heroine complied with so much of this rhapsody as related to forgiveness and pity—How willingly she received her repentant prodigal to her arms—to her heart!—how tenderly she endeavoured to soothe his distraction—how sincerely she plighted to him her reiterated promise, never to surrender to any but to Henry, her hand, her affections, or her person.

With the proposition of an immediate marriage, however, she was very far from complying. The reasons against this appeared now to be more strong than ever; considering the footing on which Henry stood with his father, and the overwhelming embarrassments into which his return, in case of an absolute rupture, must inevitably plunge the circumstances of our hero.

"Palliatives and compromises," she said, "at least ought first to be tried." Perhaps his father might be so far softened, by his entreaties, as to be content with the negative obedience of not marrying without his consent, "and we must rest satisfied with that, my Henry—satisfied with

---

1 Alluding to one of Thelwall's favorites among Charlotte Smith's *Elegiac Sonnets*, Sonnet 12, "Written on the Sea Shore": "suits the mournful temper of my soul" (l. 8).

the confidence, which, forgetting all that is past, I will still renew, and which surely, on his part, Henry could never want, of fixed and unalterable affection, till time, or some fortunate occurrence may prove more favourable to our union. The positive and open disobedience of such a prohibition as this, what could it produce but immediate and irretrievable ruin.

"I must retire, Henry; for the present I must retire to the privacy I contemplated. Not as I once intended, indeed, to seclude myself from your knowledge or from your correspondence: but from your society; from the anger of your father, and the observation of the world."

We shall not enter into the tender altercations these opposite propositions produced. A throng of important incidents, rushing upon us, prohibits the pathetic detail. Suffice it to say that Henry, at length yielding his reluctant consent to this pleaded reason, it was agreed that (till a more eligible situation could be procured) Seraphina and her mother (for as such during the course of the present scene she was introduced to the knowledge of Henry) and poor Nanny (who had been terribly afraid that these discoveries should displace her from her new service) should that very evening depart for the cottage, to which our heroine had previously determined to retire. Henry at the same time was to prepare to meet his father with the best grace he could, and contrive the best means of delaying, without coming to an immediate rupture with the old gentleman, the marriage upon which he seemed so strangely and so suddenly to have resolved.

Upon this score, indeed, Edmunds gave them some shrewd hints that they might set their hearts perfectly at ease, since he believed it would very shortly be in his power to put an effectual stop to that business. In short, he was, at this time, in the train for some very important discoveries with respect to that young lady; which, though from tenderness to her sex they ought not without absolute necessity be divulged, yet, in case of such necessity, he had little doubt he could bring very clearly home, by testimony no less indubitable than that of a certain accessary to the facts. In the mean time it was agreed that the epistolary correspondence and other communications between the lovers should be carried on by the means of Edmunds and Nanny—both of whom had zeal, and the former ability enough to let slip no opportunity that could conduce to their happiness or consolation.

These arrangements once made, the plan was immediately put in execution. Seraphina and her little suite departed for the sequestered cottage; and Henry, torn by a thousand anxious apprehensions, and agitated by a thousand conflicting passions, waited for the arrival of his father.

The whole of the ensuing day, and part of a second, passed in this suspense. At length, though Montfort arrived not, there arrived from him a letter: but this was not very consolatory.

It was an order that he should immediately repair to Southampton, in company with Melinda and young Lewson; who had also received their order; for the malady of old Lewson gaining daily ground, and the physicians beginning to apprehend him to be in danger, it was thought necessary to change his plan of procedure, and at once announce his arrival to his children, and desire their attendance upon his sick bed.

It was, therefore, concerted between the two fathers that the three young ones should be instructed to come down together, in the carriage of Montfort: instructions which, from what they had heard, it was imagined would be very cheerfully obeyed.

As matters now stood, however, they were not a little embarrassing to all parties. Melinda, of course, had not forgotten the conduct of Henry at their last interview—her slighted charms—his avowed preference and devotion for her rival—his look of contempt and repulsion, when he read the proposal of his father—

The apparent failure of this project made Lewson also feel the degradation of his conduct; and as for Henry, the new state of his feelings may pretty well be conjectured from what has so lately passed.

But there was no alternative. The order must be obeyed; and he determined to do it with the best grace he could; to preserve at least the decorums of politeness, and even to pay some attentions to Melinda; to make a sort of procrastinated courtship; and when things could no longer be prevented from coming to a crisis, trust to the evidence Edmunds had collected for breaking off the match; or perhaps to her apprehensions of the publicity of such testimony, to influence her to put a resolute and apparently voluntary negative upon it.

It had been happy for him if he could have persevered in that prudent resolution. What there was of duplicity in it perhaps the occasion might have excused; and certainly much misfortune and misery might have been prevented by it. But, alas! Henry was the slave of humour; and in the present state of his feelings he had not self-command enough to execute his project. He waited, indeed, in person upon the brother and sister in Baker-street, very punctually, at the appointed hour. He presented his hand to the lady. He handed her into the coach. He seated himself facing her, and endeavoured to enter into discourse upon the ordinary topics of the day. But disgust was preponderant over every other impression. From infatuation he ran into the opposite stream of aversion. His eyes, his taste, his apprehension—not a faculty about him could do her common justice. He wondered how he could even have regarded her as either beautiful or elegant; and his mind was filled with the horror of the situation in which he should feel himself if chained to such a woman for life.

The converse of the picture rushed immediately upon his mind; and comparing all her meretricious airs and degrading artifices to the generous virtues and dignified simplicity of Seraphina, he exclaimed to himself, in the language of Shakespeare, (but in the bitterness of a heart-felt application.)

"Could I on that fair mountain cease to feed,

To batten on this moor!"[1]

In short, nothing could have been more dull than the journey to Southampton, or more opposite to those conversations in which the same parties had so frequently been engaged together.

Melinda, indeed, seemed by no means anxious to regain her fugitive influence over his heart. The truth is, that she, also, began to see with other eyes.

Old Lewson, indeed, had not thought it necessary to explain all at once to his son and daughter the extent of those acquisitions he had so fortunately made; but he did not conceal that they might have to congratulate themselves on a favourable reverse of fortune; and indeed, they concluded that, after so abrupt and mysterious a departure, and after having left behind him so many unsatisfied demands, nothing but such a reverse would have brought him back to England. They knew also pretty well the selfish and grasping character of old Montfort; and did not suppose it very likely that he should be so desirous of such an alliance as was now in agitation, on the mere score of old standing familiarity and bottle association.

In short, she thought it very conspicuous that her future reign of splendour and elegant delight depended no longer on the solitary attachment of Henry Montfort—that his passion was no longer a necessary torch to display her taste and accomplishments to the world, and illuminate the paths of her triumph: but that, on the contrary, she could shine at birthday balls, and set the fashions at the opera, although he should never more be seen in her train.

These reflections disposed her not to pass over without a very marked resentment the indignities that had been put upon her. Neither was her resentment unaccompanied with contempt: nor did either the one or the other preclude the subtle spirit of revenge. And as, upon her arrival at Southampton, her prospects began still further to unfold themselves, she began also to display, in a more imperious manner (at least in her deportment towards Henry, when neither of their fathers happened to be present,) the pride and intoxicated vanity of her heart: while counting on the boundless opulence (for so to her it appeared) of her dying parent, she began to look forward, through crapes and scarfs, to titles and coronets, and all the splendour of rank as well as fortune.

In short, it is evident that, if Henry had but played his cards so well as not to have seemed averse to the match before the old gentlemen, and to have soothed so far her wounded pride, by his attentions, as to have prevented her from harbouring the designs of revenge and enmity, he might easily have saved appearances with his father, by obtaining her resolute, but at the same time civil refusal. Neither was her father so unconscious

---

1 *Hamlet* 3.4.67.

of what his fortune might command, nor so infatuatedly bent upon the match, as to have forced his daughter upon a reluctant lover; nor, had Henry been at once respectful to his daughter and candid to him, would he, perhaps, have been backward, in extricating him from the embarrassment in which the commands of his father and his own prior engagements had entangled him.

But dejection, and impatience, and that imperious humour which was apt, at times, to get the better of his discretion, threw away not only these advantages, but even those that might have served him as a dernier ressort,[1] the important discoveries of Edmunds: for Melinda, determined to do him all the injury in her power, so played upon his temper, and so effectually, in the presence of the two fathers, guarded her own, that although the elder Lewson, before his death (which took place in less than a month after their arrival at Southampton), withdrew his concurrence from the purposed match, he did in a manner that so completely threw all the blame upon young Montfort, and marked so indignant a resentment of his conduct, that it placed him upon as bad terms with the old gentleman, as if he had himself refused, in the most positive way, to comply with his favourite proposition.

Within less than a week after the death of the elder Lewson, while Montfort was yet waiting to do the last honours to the remains of his friend (who, notwithstanding his displeasure against the son, had left the father executor to his children, with a very handsome legacy,) our hero was much surprised by the appearance of the enthusiast Edmunds.

Nothing could have been less expected; and his heart misgave him that some fresh disaster must have happened; for it had been the fate of poor Edmunds to be the frequent messenger of ill tidings. He fixed his eyes, therefore, with much anxiety on his countenance. But there was nothing very alarming there.

His heart revived—it danced—it fluttered. Perhaps it might be a more welcome errand.

His inquiry grew warm and impatient: for he had been indulging his passion in the riot of imagination; dwelling with impatient longings on the lovely form of his Seraphina; and, expatiating on those delights from which he had been so long estranged, had wrought himself almost into a resolution of breaking at once all terms of compromise with his father, hastening to her arms, and by the vehemence and ardour of his passion overpowering all her objections to an immediate union.

"Who knows," said he to himself, "but that my Seraphina may have sympathised with me in these feelings?—but that some spirit unseen, that presides over the emotions of united hearts, may awaken them at the same instant to correspondent wishes, and govern them by an intermediate communion?"

---

1 Last resort (French).

This amorous Swedenborgianism[1] seemed verified by the event. The business, indeed, was a little mysterious. But what is mystery to minds in a certain temperament?

Edmunds had brought a letter. It was the hand-writing of Seraphina. But he had come by it in so very extraordinary a way, that he knew not what to make of it.

Nanny had not been at the place of rendezvous for two or three days, and Edmunds (though contrary to the preconcerted arrangement) had determined to go himself to the retreat, to learn whether all was well: for he had promised Henry to take special care that he should not be unacquainted with the slightest circumstance that might threaten the tranquillity of Seraphina. But, as he was going out in the evening, for the purpose of this inquiry, he perceived a letter, that seemed to have been recently thrust through the crevice under the door.

It was directed to him. It was the hand-writing of Seraphina. He opened it; and found that it enclosed another, directed to H. Montfort, esq. junior. This, also, though not her accustomed *form* of direction, was in the character of Seraphina. On the case was written in the same hand,

"Good Edmunds,

"Deliver this, *without delay*, into the hands of your master, my Henry, wheresoever he be. But deliver it yourself, that you may be sure he has it: and you had best take a post-chaise, or a horse, or something—and go off immediately as it comes to hand, for fear of accidents.

"I am obliged to send this in a strange way, because Nanny is ill in bed."

Edmunds, staggered as he was by the strangeness of the composition, yet convinced that it was the writing of Seraphina, thought it his duty, at any rate, to obey; and, taking the enclosed letter with him, had travelled all night, that he might deliver it as soon as possible.

The enclosed letter was not less extraordinary.

Henry burst it open, with a trembling hand, and read as follows:

"My dearest Henry,

"Hasten to me, my love! My delight of consolation; my soul languishes for thee; and my health declines, because I cannot bear you to be so long absent from my arms. Besides, indeed, I must leave this place, I am not safe here; nor comfortable: the people trouble me so!

"Come to me directly as you receive this sweet melody. But come in the dark of the night, and *all alone*; when every thing is quiet; that our loves may be very private.

---

1   Thelwall had both celebrated and satirized a similar amorous metaphysics drawn from the Swedish mystic Emanuel Swedenborg (1688-1772) in "The Platonic Fair" chapter of *The Peripatetic*. Henry's Swedenborgianism here seems to complement the theory of correspondent vibrations of body and mind introduced above.

——————— "O come to me
With thy wakeful Diligence, whose brooding wing
Shelves off the brooding tempest as it falls,
And tames the wint'ry dew.

"From your true love,   "SERAPHINA"
Cottage, Walcot Place, Feb. &c.[1]

The reader, without doubt, will immediately perceive that, whosoever the *hand* might be, this was not the style of Seraphina—the verses excepted; which Henry immediately recognized.

They were part of a sonnet (for so Seraphina chose to call her little plaintive poems, though they were neither limited to the exact number of fourteen lines, nor hampered with the crambo of rhyme)[2] which she had written some months before by the side of his sick bed.

Henry immediately recalled the whole strain to his mind: and perhaps the reader may have no objection to hearing him repeat it. It was thus—

Daughter of Song! If thee my soul invokes,
O! come in softest numbers—such as trill
From Philomela's throat, when thro' the groves
(Charming her nurslings with her matron song)
Steals the sweet melody: or rather such
As in my native land, at evening hour,
Courting the cooling sea-breeze, I have heard
Poured from the Triton's shell, when all around
Was tranquil, and along the murmuring beach
Sighed the slow wave retiring. Such soft strains
As woo propitious dreams, when Matron Love
Her holiest vigils o'er the cradled sleep
Tunes anxious—sole companions of her watch
The frugal Toil, that stays invading woe,
And wakeful Diligence, whose brooding wing
Shelves off the brooding tempest as it falls,
And tames the wint'ry dew. Such strains I ask—
Care-soothing strains! For o'er my Henry's couch
I'd woo the balmy Slumber; on whose wing,
Dull tho' it be and heavy, she, the nymph
Of soul-enlivening freshness, blest Hygeia
Waits with her rosiest smile.

---

1   Seraphina's "sequestered cottage" retreat is given the same address as the Thelwall family cottage, which is also described in "The Retreat" chapter of *The Peripatetic*.

2   Seraphina shares Thelwall's eccentric ideas regarding sonnet form, expressed in "The Sonnet" chapter of *The Peripatetic*, in his 1792 "Essay on the English Sonnet," and in a letter of Coleridge: "being a freeborn Briton, who shall prevent you from calling twenty-five blank verse lines a sonnet, if you have taken a bloody resolution so to do" (CLSTC I: 351).

> Daughter of Song!
> If thou hast any spell of magic power
> To charm these sweet associates, breathe it now,
> And with thy welcome influence fill my soul!

Henry dwelt upon this association with delight. As for the letter itself, the reader may very well believe that he did not peruse it with all that intellectual rapture which every paragraph he had hitherto seen in that hand-writing was wont to inspire. Perhaps, in any other state of mind, notwithstanding the form of the letters and the quoted verses, he might have questioned its authenticity. But his impetuous passions were too eager for the interview to scrutinize the language of the invitation.

Without further consideration; and without so much as seeing his father, or leaving behind any *voluntary* intimation of his return to London, he ordered a post-chaise; and, accompanied by Edmunds, set off to obey the summons.

But his carelessness was equal to his other imprudence. Whether it was that the un-Seraphina-like style (if we may be permitted such a coinage) of this brief epistle occasioned him not to feel that delightful solicitude, with which he had heretofore, by an action almost spontaneous, carefully enclosed in the inner folds of the pocket-book every thrice perused effusion from the pen of our heroine; or whether the flutter of certain thoughts and passions around his heart, prevented him from considering what he was about; certain it was that his hand went not to his pocket-book, and consequently the letter was not enclosed in its inner folds. On the contrary, it was committed carelessly to the pocket, as though it were no part of Seraphina, and from thence was, very naturally, whisked out again with the handkerchief the very next time that it was used.

Had the letter only been lost, it had been matter of no great consequence. The Seraphiniana, whenever they shall come to be collected, might very well afford to spare it. But unfortunately it was also found; and found by the very person most disposed to make a malicious use of it—to wit, the reverend Emanuel Woodhouse.

It was to him, indeed, a precious *bonne-bouche*[1]—a prize beyond expectation. With equal malignity and much deeper interest he had entered into all the resentments and plans of Melinda for the completion of the ruin of Henry; and had never failed to insinuate that, notwithstanding the pretended separation between him and Seraphina, that connection was evidently the real and only assignable cause of all the affronts that had been put upon Melinda, and the indignities that had disturbed the last hours of the departed, the generous and worthy friend of *his good patron* Mr. Montfort.

What before was conjecture, this letter brought into proof: nay, it did more: it seemed to prove against Seraphina, and thence by inference

---

1 A delicious morsel; literally, good mouth (French).

against Henry himself, what even the malice of Woodhouse himself had hitherto not even ventured to insinuate. It would place him therefore in the light of an over candid and favourable reporter; since, in the worst of his representations, he had never presumed to impeach either the accomplishments of our heroine's mind, or the decorum of her manners. But he had now a fair opportunity, as it seemed, of making her place herself in a very different point of view.

"I am sorry, sir," said he, as they were sitting down to dinner, "that our apprehensions are all confirmed. Mr. Henry, sir, is no where to be found. I concluded as much from a document that has fallen in my hand. But God forbid, sir, that a minister of peace should be the first to put an ill construction upon a single ambiguous fact; or, when the moral estimation of a fellow-creature is at stake, consider a mere presumption as a proof! I thought it more consistent therefore, sir, with my duty and my conscience, and that candour of judgment which (as frail beings, sir,) we all owe to one another, to conceal this instrument of crimination" (producing the letter from his pocket) "till other circumstances should either invalidate or confirm it. Heaven above knows, sir, how penetrated I am with grief that the latter should be the predicament."

"How, how!" exclaimed Montfort when he had read the letter—"and is this the creature? And he is gone, is he—galloped away to his fine Creole! His accomplished Seraphina? Hey! Woodhouse?"

W. "So it seems, sir. His convenient go-between—his *librarian!* Edmunds—the mutual friend and confident of this *sentimental* pair! brought the letter; and they set off in a post-chaise together. They are alone enough when Edmunds is with them, sir. He is a sentimentalist also—an intellectual being! and has always a book in his pocket to improve his mind while he is guarding the door.—

"Oh! The profligacy, sir—the profligacy of this age! This comes of their free-thinking and their infidelity. There is no hope of the rising generation. But for this, sir, they might live to repent in their old age, and be forgiven."

Montfort lifted up his eyes towards heaven, at this concluding sentence, as though he felt it comfortable to his smarting conscience. But he turned them again immediately to the letter. His piety was awakened: but it was the piety of a gloomy mind: his zeal was vindictive rage, and moral intolerance his contrition.

"Let him go—let him go!" exclaimed he, "I have done with him—he is disinherited. I see his face no more."

W. "Heaven forbid, sir! Let me be a peace-maker, sir, as becomes my holy profession. You will think of it again, I hope. Let us hope even yet that he is not absolutely marked with the seal of reprobation. Though to be sure it must be confessed, sir, the vulgar harlotry of this wanton epistle places the affair in a much more serious point of view, even than we have hitherto considered it.

"What depravity!—what infatuation!

"Should he really think of profaning the altars of God, by the mockery of a marriage with such a creature!—Alas! I shudder to think of it.

"And then, in the eye of the world too, what disgrace! How my heart bleeds when I think of the scorn and public derision that must fall upon the name and family of my generous patron when this boasted paragon shall come to be acknowledged as his daughter—this Aspasia;[1] who, after all the fuss that has been made about her dignified virtues, (for in these days of liberality it seems we are to talk of the virtues of harlots!) her refinements and exalted intellect, plays upon the passions of her tardy lover with lascivious billets-doux that, for style and composition, would disgrace the common chambermaid of an inn![2]

"But infidelity, sir—infidelity, in this enlightened age, is of itself both intellect and virtue; and he or she who does but profess the faith of Atheism shall have credit for every thing besides."

If this grace before meat did not much whet the appetite of Montfort for his dinner, it stimulated to some purpose an appetite of another kind. In short, he determined, without further remonstrance or deliberation, to disinherit our ill-starred hero from all future share in his fortune or regard. Melinda seemed secure of her revenge, and Woodhouse of his share of the estate.

CHAP. II.

The Conspiracy of Moroon for the Assassination of Henry, and the Rape of Seraphina.

Old Connections revived.—The fatal Compliance.—Authority and Reason.—Desperate Resolutions.—The Cottage.—The Pirate.—The Plot Developed.—Further Developments.—The Daw in borrowed Plumes.—The Assassination.

WHILE the conspiracy at Southampton was thus triumphantly advancing to the accomplishment of its object, another, of a still more atrocious nature, of which the fatal letter, so successfully commented upon by Woodhouse, was in reality only an instrument, was beginning to unfold itself into action, in another place.

But before we enter upon the particulars of this conspiracy (so atrocious in design! so important in its consequences!) It is necessary that we

---

1 Mistress of Pericles. See p. 77, note 2.

2 In Woodhouse's hypocritical condemnation of Seraphina, Thelwall echoes the vitriol poured on Mary Wollstonecraft after her death and the publication of Godwin's *Memoirs of the Author of A Vindication of the Rights of Woman*, especially by the *Anti-Jacobin*, which accused her of being a "concubine." Aspasia, the companion of the Athenian statesman Pericles, was likewise accused by his enemies of being a prostitute.

state some preliminary circumstances that, however undesignedly, paved the way for all the horrors that ensued.

From the time that Morton had avowed herself to be the mother of Seraphina, and had been acknowledged as such, she began gradually to assume a much larger degree of authority and influence; and it was natural enough that Seraphina should, in the first instance, give way to this assumption. In short, she felt herself what she had never felt before—a daughter, and the impression was an awful one.

If Morton could have used that authority with discretion, it might have been permanent, and have secured to her a sort of deference which, if not absolutely constituted of respect and love, might have stood in the place of those feelings, and been mistaken for them by the world, and even, perhaps, by herself. But the habits of her mind, as Seraphina had heretofore very justly observed, were inveterate: and now that she found herself invested with the title of mother, she began to think of extending the prerogatives of maternal power, according to the maxims and practices of the old school, to the enforcement of such schemes of life and conduct as the parent may believe best calculated to promote the happiness of the child.

Past experience had little influence in deterring her from fresh experiments. For circumstances were now altered; and she made no sort of doubt that the mother would prevail where the duenna failed. And as for the result, if her exertions at last succeeded, she had no doubt they would be as conducive to the happiness as to the interests of her daughter.

In her younger days, her days of beauty and of splendour, she had known several romantic creatures, who, if left to their own visionary nonsense, would have remained most obstinately insensible to all the overtures of fortune and of pleasure, who, nevertheless, when the authority of some experienced friend had put them in the way of making a right use of their charms, entered very heartily into all the enjoyments the exercise of their power secured them: and she persuaded herself that, by whatever means her daughter might be put into possession of an eligible establishment, when once she came to taste what such possession was, she would soon find herself disposed to be thankful for the happy change.

Considering, therefore, the circumstances of Henry as absolutely desperate, she began once more to cast her eyes upon the still solicitous, still infatuated Moroon.

She took care, accordingly, to inform him of the new claims of influence which she had acquired, the effects those claims had in many instances so conspicuously produced in rendering much more docile the mind of Seraphina, and the new turn that things had taken in disfavour of his rival.

The invitation with which this address concluded was very acceptable to Moroon, whose passions had been inflamed rather than extinguished by repulses, and whose gloomy mind, blending the thirst of revenge with the fever of desire, had been for some time brooding over strange thoughts and projects for the gratifications of this double appetite.

He embraced, accordingly, with great eagerness the proposals of renewing his address; which if not more successful, he thought, in the way of persuasion, might yet be assistant in paving the way for more efficacious methods of address.

But he remembered, to his confusion, the ridiculous incoherencies into which his embarrassment had betrayed him towards the conclusion of his recent harangue. He determined, therefore, that his next appeal to the passions of his beloved, should be made, not in the way of *oral*, but of *written* eloquence. And, as he supposed that Henry must be certainly possessed of some peculiar grace of composition, or be particularly initiated into the secret of writing love letters, to which his power over the affections of Seraphina was to be attributed, he flattered himself that, if he could but get possession, by any means, of some of his favourite epistles, he might be able, by the assistance of the same eloquent journalist that penned the most shining paragraphs in the aforementioned oration, to produce something of equal power and efficacy, and accordingly triumph in his turn.

Morton, to whom he suggested this idea, thought it not entirely an ill expedient: for she was very well convinced that, notwithstanding the polish given to his manners by the gay circles of Paris and London, he was still somewhat deficient in certain little graces, particularly of sentiment and delicacy, that might be very acceptable to such a woman as Seraphina. She procured him, therefore, without delay, one of Henry's letters, which Seraphina, who had been re-perusing it, with particular attention, had left, unintentionally and unconsciously, upon her writing table; and that she might render him still further acquainted with the particular tastes, and with the talents and accomplishments of her daughter, she accompanied the present with two or three copies of verses, which at different times had been purloined and treasured with an equal portion of maternal stealth and vanity; and with one of which the reader has, by these means, so recently become acquainted.

Thus furnished, he summoned his faithful journalist to his side, and, producing his models, desired him to manufacture something for him in the same style. The faithful journalist obeyed, while he drank his claret, and a splendid imitation of the tender original was struck off in a heat; which, in the opinion both of the writer and the employer, could not fail of melting the icy heart of any fair lady in the universe who should be destined to peruse it: and, as the pen of Moroon was a more faithful copyist than his tongue, it was retraced with great accuracy on the ensuing day, and dismissed, by a proper messenger, with no other imperfections on its head than a little newspaper common place, and magazine bombast, together with about a score of gallicisms, and a like proportion of new coinages, and new constructions, that constituted *the distinguishing originality of our* imitator's style.[1]

---

1 From his "ready-made" imitation of Della Cruscanism in *The Peripatetic* (1793) to his mockery of "poetical advertisements" in an unpublished satire on "the Poesy of the Age" in the 1820s, Thelwall was acutely conscious of the manufacture and commodification of romantic language.

These beauties, however, were all thrown away on the incurious insensibility of our heroine, who no sooner perceived the name of Moroon at the bottom of the letter, than, throwing it aside unread, "How is this madam?" said she, turning round to her mother, with a very grave, and very suspicious look—"How is this?—Moroon, of all people in the world, is acquainted with the place of my retreat. He is tormenting me again with his addresses."

M. "Well, my dear! And who, of all people in the world, so likely to give himself the trouble to find you out? Do pray let us hear what he has to say for himself. I protest, my dear, that I am very glad his passion is so permanent and so industrious; for I am afraid it will not be long before we are in want of such a friend."

S. "But do you not yet know, madam, that the time will never come when I shall accept of such a one?"

M. "Come, come, child! Lay these airs of unbecoming gravity aside. I do not wish to exert the *authority* of a mother." (This was a sense in which Seraphina had never heard the word before; and she shrunk from the novelty of the impression.) "But you ought to consider, my dear," continued Morton, "and pay a little attention to those who have a right to direct you."

S. "A right to direct, Madam! What but reason can have any right to direct the moral conduct of a rational being?"[1]

M. "Fie! fie! Seraphina! I desire I may hear no more of this nonsense. It might do very well to silence the admonitions of Morton the tiring-woman; but you now know who it is that advises you."

S. "Pardon me, madam! I hope I do know, I hope I shall never, by want of kindness or affection, give you reason to suppose that I have forgotten that knowledge. But this also I know, that *the nature of the advice is not changed by the character of the adviser.* I may listen indeed with a more respectful silence: but adoption and rejection will still, as heretofore, be the mere result of my own sense of moral propriety.

"Let me add also, madam, that the *sensation* with which I may listen to such advice may happen to be somewhat different. What from the lips of Morton I should have heard with indignation, might thrill me now with horror."

M. "Seraphina! Seraphina! Is this the language of a child!!?"

S. "It is the language, madam, presume, of a rational being: and children may aspire to be such; while parents cannot pretend to be more.

"But I perceive, madam, what this would lead to. It is necessary for me, therefore, to be explicit; that, where differences would be so painful, we may avoid the grounds upon which we cannot fail to differ.

"You are my mother, madam: as such I will love and serve you. The labour of my hands, the efforts of my mind, the exertions of my best diligence and solicitude, whether in sickness or in sorrow,—these, madam,

---

1 One of Seraphina's most Wollstonecraftian statements, and scenes.

you shall command at your need: and if there is aught beside of kindness or endearment that may tend to your ease or consolation, I will pay it as a debt that grows as it is discharged, because the payment itself is a pleasure.

"This, madam, is my duty, feebly perhaps expressed; but assuredly not feebly felt. But there are services that duty cannot claim. The conscience—the conscience owns no subordination. In itself it is independent and supreme. In this respect our relationship is not altered. For vice and virtue—rectitude and error are neither child nor parent. In this respect experience and reflection are my sole progenitors, and I must therefore be the thing my reason bids me be, or I am guilty of the parricide of mind.

"If, therefore, I should ever have occasion (which I trust I shall not) to address you again upon the same subjects that led to the awful avowal of our endearing relationship, I should endeavour indeed to find words of greater tenderness in which I might express my sentiments; but those sentiments would be precisely the same:—the duty, madam—the resolution—(however painful!)—the resolution would be the same.

"Whatever was then a motive of separation, would now, if persevered in with maternal authority, divorce me from the maternal side. If the intrigues and importunities of a mistaken mother should obstruct the virtue of the daughter, keen indeed would be the pang that must rend the conflicting heart! but the daughter must again be motherless.

"Weepest thou, my mother—at the prospect of such an event? I too should weep—and my tears would be tears of blood. Weepest thou still, my mother?—I will wipe away thy tears," continued she—and she pulled out her handkerchief, and wiped them, with looks of overflowing sympathy—"I will mingle mine. I will kiss them with holy tenderness from thy cheek; and my heart shall let fall drop for drop. For I can sympathise; though I must not retract. If, even in the assertion of conscious rectitude and moral independence, I should sometimes be too harsh; pardon the cruel necessity. I will use my endeavours to abate the edge of the instrument, though its temper must not be allayed."

The mingled benignity and fortitude with which this was delivered, silenced the assumption of authority; and though Morton knew not how to reconcile it with her notions of filial duty; and, perhaps, felt in some degree

"How sharper than a serpent's tooth it is
To have a thankless child";[1]

yet the tone—the look—the action were so many drops of balm that mitigated the wound; and she was soothed.

But the warning in the concluding sentences sunk deepest in her mind. Convinced that she must set narrower limits to her authority than she had lately begun to imagine; and must either leave her daughter to her own

---

1 *King Lear* 1.4.288-89.

elective course, or lose the consolation of her society, her election was presently made. She took, therefore, an early opportunity of informing Moroon that she could interfere in his amour no further; and that, therefore, if he was determined upon perseverence, he must depend entirely upon time and his own resources.

Morton little imagined the uses that would be made of this hint.

The gloomy and malignant mind of Moroon was immediately set to work; and the expedients his resources pointed at were of no less horror than the rape of Seraphina, and the assassination of Henry.

To the latter of these he was instigated as much by a principle of fear, as of jealousy and revenge: though these latter passions burned in his bosom with a degree of fury which, happily for this country, a mere Englishman can scarcely comprehend.

The preference that had been given to our hero, during the voyage from St. Domingo, the awful distance at which *he* had been kept, and, above all, the terror with which *he* had been impressed by the eye of his rival, and his own gloomy apprehensions, were so many unpardonable injuries, for which he had never ceased to meditate a severe retaliation.

Seraphina had unwittingly added to this terrible account, during the interview in Grosvenor-square, by the fear she had inflicted of his encountering Henry on the stairs. Her hint, distant as it was, had occasioned him to hurry down (as fast as his tottering knees would permit) with a haggard eye and palpitating heart: and every thump of that dastardly organ against his ribs was a new item in the long arrear of wrongs and injuries which was some time or other to be settled.

"Fears any man the thing he does not hate?
Hates any man the thing he would not kill?"[1]

This is a process of practical reasoning by which such a mind as Moroon's (which with all its defects, had energies—terrible energies when the master-springs were once touched) is easily wrought up to the climax of assassination: and to work him the more completely to this bent (the project of the rape once determined upon), this counterpart of the plot seemed absolutely necessary to his own future safety: for he had conceived an idea almost supernaturally terrible of the courage and enthusiastic perseverance of our hero: and though the sullen impetuosity of his passions, and the prospect of approaching gratification, prevented him from looking beyond the boundaries of the land he trod upon for any probable operations of established justice, and from anticipating the possibility that the vindictive arm of British law should attack him in the midst of his *vast property* in Barbadoes; yet his imagination was haunted, as by a phantom, with the supposed omnipresence of Henry, whose vengeance he seemed to apprehend would be certain to pursue and overtake him wheresoever he should fly for safety.

---

1 *The Merchant of Venice* 4.1.66-67.

There was but one way to prevent:—A cowardly heart and a confused intellect never blunder upon any other:—the way of brutal violence.

There are situations, also, as Shakespeare expresses it, that "put toys of desperation in the brain";[1] and the way to the retreat was of that description.

It was a humble but decent mansion, built of wood, and in the cottage style, with a garden around it, a small brook on one side, and a row of poplars on the other. It stood in the midst of some large callico-grounds,[2] just out of the Vauxhall road, and in the neighbourhood of St. George's fields.

Though now surrounded almost by buildings, and retaining little of rural similitude but the loneliness, the situation had been once sufficiently pastoral; for flocks and herds used to be seen grazing all around.

In such state it was when the cottage was first built, as a sleeping place and Sunday's retreat, by a thriving but valetudinarian tradesman. It was now, in its state of revolution, a place of refuge for the misfortunes of his lame and aged widow; whom the sympathy of the neighbourhood called *the old Lady of the Garden*. Its customary inhabitants were herself only, and her son; an eccentric youth who at this time happened, as was his frequent wont, to be wandering about the country, marking the varieties of men and manners and the phaenomena of the wintry year.[3]

The way to this lonely and unprotected retreat, was by a long irregular avenue that connected it with the road—partly inclosed with paling, and in part by shrubs; and the open fields behind presented the ample means of escape.

"If one did but know how to meet with Henry Montfort in this avenue," said he to himself, as he was surveying the ground. "And what more easy? This way he must come to his stolen joys—to revel in those delights that are so scornfully forbidden to me. It is but way-laying him.[4] But how long must one way-lay? Could not one bring him at the hour one wanted? I can—I can. Morton! mother! I thank thee. I can trap them both. Love and revenge! I have them!"

---

1 An allusion to Horatio's observation on the cliffs in *Hamlet* 1.4.75.
2 The fields around a mill where calico cloth was made and printed, often used for drying the cloth.
3 As noted in the previous chapter (p. 355, note 1), Seraphina's cottage is based on the Thelwall family home at Walcot Place. Thus, the old Lady of the Garden is Thelwall's mother and he himself makes a cameo appearance as her son; in the "eccentric" wanderings referred to here Thelwall conflates the excursions of 1792 on which *The Peripatetic* is based and the wanderings around Llyswen that are recorded in his essay on "The Phenomena of the Wye, during the winter of 1797-98."
4 Moroon's plot is a fictionalized version of the incident recalled in Mrs. Thelwall's biography (15), in which a young Thelwall was waylaid and robbed on the dark footpath leading to Walcot Place.

This twofold atrocity thus resolved upon, and a maternal project for the final execution devised; Moroon proceeded immediately to the adjustment of all the detail of his plot: the ground-work and first principle of which was his immediate return to his vast plantations in Barbadoes.

This part of his plan had, indeed, been determined upon, ever since his disgraceful repulse in Grosvenor-square: for there was now no longer any impediment to the security of such return.

The dreaded vengeance of his swarthy Medea was effectually charmed to sleep. She had drunk of Lethé[1]—not of the river but the cask. In other words, deserted by the seducer, who had plundered her both of her virtue and her wealth, and stung by the remembrance of her atrocious crimes, she had drowned her reflections in such liberal draughts of ardent spirits, as had put an end both to those reflections, and her life. Of this he had received due information: and as neither the climate nor the manners of England suited very well with his constitution and habits, he determined to return to that more congenial clime.

For this purpose, he had actually disposed, by private contract, of his splendid establishment in Portland-place—mansion of decoration, furniture of elegancy, carriages, horses, hammer-cloths and splendid liveries, all together; and had resolved to embark in the first packet or merchant-man that should be ready to depart for the destined island.

But the plan of compelling Seraphina to be the reluctant companion of his flight, being once determined upon, neither packet nor merchant-ship would any longer be suitable to his purpose. A new expedient was to be sought for; and chance, conspiring with his diligence, threw in his way a hero of the true ancient school, endowed with all the requisite qualifications for an associate and assistant in the perilous adventures which our amorous Creole had determined to undertake: a hero who had at once the means and the courage to *act* what his instigator had only the genius to *design*.

This hero, by name and addition captain Roberts,[2] was one of those erudite geniuses who seem to be actuated by a profound veneration for every thing that is of classical record in the way of their profession; who regard with noble disdain the mockery of pretended barter, and the whole train of sneaking subterfuges that mark the compromising spirit of the chartered combinations and merchant-adventurers of the age: and who, setting before their eyes the more splendid examples of the nautical heroes of the elder world, exert their laudable efforts to bring back the degenerated commercio-heroic system to its simple original and elementary principles.

---

1 In Greek myth, Medea was the vengeful wife and murderer of the Argonaut hero Jason, and Lethe the underground river of forgetfulness in Hell.

2 Captain Roberts is based on a real captain of that name, who led the press-gang mob that attacked Thelwall's lectures in Yarmouth in August 1796, as outlined in Thelwall's sensational "An Appeal to Popular Opinion."

Knowing, undoubtedly, very well, that neither Jason, nor Hercules, nor Castor and Pollux, nor any of those famous Argonauts or merchant-adventurers of old, whose oracular ship and voyage from Greece to Colchis still makes such a racket in the learned world,[1] ever thought of making a beggarly pretence of purchasing that invaluable commodity, the golden fleece, with half a dozen brass buttons, and two or three ounces of glass beads; but that, on the contrary, with most heroical virtue and plain dealing, they seized upon the said commodity, sword in hand, and, throwing it over their shoulders, bore it (willy nilly) to their ship, together with the son and daughter of the original proprietor.—Knowing, I say, most undoubtedly, all this, and much more of the same kind, that is recorded in the pages of ancient history, whether sacred or profane, of the heroic and primitive merchant-adventurers of those better times, the said captain Roberts had collected together a band of Argonauts, not indeed from the palaces of surrounding princes, but from those (externally at least) not less sumptuous edifices, the town and country gaols of this well-furnished land, with whose assistance, he had long continued to carry on the antient and honourable calling of a merchant-adventurer, in the true primitive way. In base and degenerate language, this redoubted hero had, for many years, been captain of a gang of pirates; so called at least in times of peace; for when the potentates of the earth chose to take up that calling, and dignify it with another name, he generally, being an enterprising fellow, found means to procure a commission from one or other of them, and his Argo became a privateer.[2]

Such a hero had, of course, no silly prejudices to revolt at the truly classical ideas of rape and assassination. On the contrary, there is reason to believe that he had been already serviceable to some great and opulent personages, in more countries than one, by whom he had been employed in carrying off dangerous or troublesome individuals from the coasts; and the rocks of St. Kilda,[3] and the deserts of Siberia, are perhaps indebted to this gallant adventurer for some part of their present population. The subordinate heroes were of a character not unworthy of their chief; having

---

1 Jason led the Argonauts in search of the Golden Fleece, which he found at Colchis (on the Eastern coast of the Black Sea), whose tribes he fought; Hercules, a mortal son of Jupiter, was famed for his superhuman strength; twins Castor and Pollux fought among the Argonauts.

2 The Argo (hence Argonauts), Jason's ship. A similar satiric conjunction of capitalist imperialism and classical antiquarianism is found in Thelwall's ballad of 1805, "Sawney's Pocket-Knife."

3 See the History of the Insulation of Lady Grange, p. 144. Buchanan's Western Hebrides. *Robinsons*, 1793. [Thelwall's note]. St. Kilda is one of the remote Outer Hebrides, off the north-west coast of Scotland, famed as the residence of Lady Grange, who was imprisoned there by her husband for seventeen years in the mid eighteenth century. In his "An Appeal to Popular Opinion" Thelwall speculates that the intention of Captain Roberts was either to murder him or transport him to Siberia (19).

been trained to deeds of hardihood, in the first instances, in press-gangs, in the smuggling trade, and in offices of police; and having since passed through all the gradations of heroism from solitary house-breaking to their present gregarious employment on the high seas.

Having formed this honourable alliance, the nature and terms of which were settled with great accuracy; and a considerable portion of the stipulated subsidy being advanced, in order to encourage the confederates to bring their forces into immediate action; and captain Roberts having pointed out a convenient creek, upon the coast of Sussex, where his Argo might be concealed, as well as certain other contiguous stations, where the land-forces might rendezvous till the critical hour of final cooperation should arrive; nothing remained for the hero of the cabinet but to devise some stratagem by means of which the antagonist parties might be taken at unawares, and their resistance rendered impotent, if not destroyed.

For the accomplishment of this, as has been suggested, an expedient was already provided.

This was no other than the simple forgery of a letter to each of the respective parties, and in their reciprocal names: an expedient for which Moroon himself (already furnished with documents by the fatal intrigues of Morton) was excellently qualified by the habits of his former life.

Practised in the dexterous use of the pen, during the life time of his mulatto predecessor, he had found a thousand conveniences in the aptitude of imitating the hand-writing of others: an art which he presently acquired; and which had become so familiar to him, that his own ordinary writing was only to be identified by the mixture and confusion of so many different hands as left to his letters no distinct or characteristic form.

Possessing, therefore, the writings of both the parties, the forgery was easy; and, from the enthusiasm of their attachment, he had no doubt of the promptitude with which each of them would obey the respective call.

His principal difficulties, were only so to time the respective movements, that Seraphina might be off the ground before Henry made his appearance, and to get Edmunds out of the way, before he set his grand machine in motion, lest his officious visits might happen to mar the design. It was for the latter purpose that the particular instructions were penned that accompanied the inclosed letter to Henry.

The person that thrust it under the door waited to see its effects, and, having dogged the honest enthusiast to an inn, brought intelligence to his employer, that he had seen him fairly off upon his journey.

Nothing now was requisite but to put the finishing stroke to the business. Every thing seemed propitious. The illness of Nanny, and the absence of the old lady's son, removed the probabilities of obstruction; and whatever was wanted of skill and foresight in the design, seemed to be supplied by chance.

Accordingly, having made the necessary arrangements for the tragic counterpart of his plot, and having purchased a travelling chaise, dressed up one of the banditti, who had been heretofore a post-boy at an inn, in the livery of his old employ, and provided another of them with a proper disguise, a horse, a pair of dirty boots, and a travelling coat, he sent the following letter, thus attended, to the cottage, a little before twilight, on the ensuing evening.

"My dearest Seraphina!

"Come to me *my angel of consolation*! by the bearer. He brings a post-chaise along with him for you, to bring you to Southampton.

"There will be *healing on thy wings*!

"My father is going to be reconciled: at least I hope as much.

"Come, that your *medicinal solicitudes may heal* his mind; *for it is that alone can heal him.*

"If I was not afraid that my father would go back again, while I was away, *I would, myself, have hastened to conduct you—not as Seraphina Parkinson, but Mrs. Montfort*: but fate defers *this completion of my happiness* till your coming.

"*Come then, my love! With thy looks of love and forgiveness charm away the reluctance of my father, which is now the only bar to our indissoluble union. Come, and receive the fond breath, of,*

Thine, to the last ebb of life,

HENRY MONTFORT

"P.S. Edmunds is gone another way, or he should have attended upon you."

The reader will immediately recollect, that this is not the first time he has met with several of these expressions; otherwise, and if he did not call to mind the anecdote of the purloined letter, he might, perhaps, comparing them with the apparent intellectual attainments of the writer, exclaim—"Fine words! I wonder where he stole them!"

Seraphina recollected, also, the phrases in question. But though she wondered not a little at the repetition, and still more at the confused and incoherent style in which the sentences were put together, yet, as it never once occurred, that any person, but herself and Henry, could have seen the letter in which they were originally used, this species of imitation (awkward as it was) conspired with the exact resemblance of the handwriting to preclude all suspicions of imposture.

The idea was never started. All was referred to that hurry of animal spirits into which she supposed that Henry might have been thrown, by some sudden and favourable turn in the disposition of his father; and she hastened with Morton, as unsuspecting as herself, to obey the welcome summons.

Unfortunately Seraphina did not read the letter aloud. It was natural she should not. She had not the pride in reading it to herself, which she had heretofore almost uniformly felt in perusing the epistles of Henry. She had contented herself, therefore, with merely stating to her mother the invitation it contained, and the flattering prospects it seemed to hold out; otherwise, in all probability, her recollection must have furnished her with circumstances by which the forgery, and the quarter it proceeded from, would have been suggested; though even in that case, as it is not very likely that she should have suspected any thing like the full extent and profligacy of the plan, it may be somewhat doubtful, whether she would have exposed herself to the confusion of a confession, to prevent what she might have hoped would terminate according to her wishes.

But, however this might have been, certain it is that her virtue was not put to the test; but that, thoughtless and unsuspecting, with a joyous heart bounding at the prospect that her daughter was about to be advanced to all the consequence and felicity she had wished her, and in the manner she herself had desired, she assisted to make her ready with all possible expedition; and, accompanying her to the chaise, was hurried away with her to the coast of Sussex, in the manner that will be hereafter described.

Seraphina being thus effectually ensnared and the shades of night gathering fast around—the selected assassin, the boldest and most profligate of the gang, hastened to his appointed stand:—and, meditating present plunder and future reward, waited impatiently for the arrival of Henry.

His waiting was not long. Henry had not, indeed, found the post-boys uniformly in as much hurry as he could have wished them; nor the horses always ready harnessed at the inns: but, as he had the day before him when he set out, these delays had only precluded him from his intended prior visit to Grosvenor-square—a matter that was of little importance, especially as he had taken the Guildford road. From Kingston, therefore, he had ordered the driver to keep all the way upon the Surry side; and, accordingly, he was driven directly to the cottage.[1]

The chaise was stopped at the entrance of the long avenue. Henry alighted. Edmunds would have alighted too, but Henry stopped him.

"Drive home!—drive home!" said he, with an ardour that betrayed what was passing in his mind—"she has ordered me to come in darkness, and alone!"

"In darkness and alone!" said Edmunds musing, almost as soon as the chaise was in motion again.—"And why *alone*? Is this the language of Seraphina?

"What if it should be a forgery? The note to me is certainly not her style: nor the direction!

"What if it should be a trick?—

"The situation is horribly convenient."

His blood thrilled at the thought. He wondered it had not occurred before. He called to the post-boy to stop. He leaped out of the chaise. He darted up the avenue with the wings of terror.

It was as he apprehended. A transient glimpse of the misty moon, just breaking between the fissures of a denser cloud, revealed all the horrors of the scene. He saw the grim assassin rushing from his concealment—he

---

1 Although Henry's point of departure, Southampton, is to the southwest of London, his route via Guildford and Kingston keeps him south of the Thames, and makes Lambeth more accessible.

saw the gleaming dirk struck violently into the side of Henry—he saw the arm uplifted to repeat the blow. He shrieked, as he rushed forward, with horror.

The cry of assistance disarmed the ruffian of his force. The repeated blow fell powerless; he leaped the fence of the avenue, and darted across the grounds; and, favoured by returning darkness, was presently out of sight.

Indeed, the attention of Edmunds was too much engrossed by the unfortunate victim, to mark the course of the fugitive.

His well known voice, and vehement calls for assistance, roused poor Nanny from her sick bed: and the old Lady of the Garden, hurrying on her night-gown, and taking her crutch-stick in her hand, came hobbling out to their assistance.[1]

Henry, faint and all covered with blood, was helped into the cottage; and Edmunds flew, like lightning, to the house of the nearest surgeon, for assistance.

CHAP. III.

Further Particulars of the desperate Attempt of Moroon
upon the Person of Seraphina.

Morning Prospects.—The deserted Mansion.—Injurious Suspicions.—
Menaces, and ostentatious Overtures.—The Petrifying Repulse.—Delirious Agitations.—Overwhelming Terrors.

IN the mean time Seraphina and Morton were hurried rapidly along, without suspicion of whither they were going. Neither of them being at all acquainted with the Southampton road, the deviations would have caused no alarm, even if the darkness of the night had suffered them to discriminate the objects in their way.

They were somewhat surprised, indeed, at the badness of the road during the last long stage, and thought it a strange approach to a town of such population and importance. But even this excited no apprehensions, till at last the morning began to break, and the delusion, of course, to vanish.

They were within a few miles of the seashore.—No appearance of a turnpike road was to be seen—no town—no village spire—no house,—

---

1   Autobiographical details in this scene include the darkness, the attacker rising up out of concealment (in a ditch, according to Mrs. Thelwall's biography), and the old lady's crutch-stick (a gift from Thelwall, according to his "Lines presented by the Author, to his Mother, together with a crutch stick," one of the pieces reprinted in *Poems Chiefly Written in Retirement*, but originally dating from 1791).

except one lonely, half-ruined, ivy-mantled, and desolate building,[1] just upon the boundary of the rock, to which the chaise appeared to be driving.

"Good God!" exclaimed Morton—"where can they be driving us?"

"Whither, indeed?" said Seraphina—"This can never be the road to Southampton."

They gazed in each other's faces. The reciprocal gaze spread the contagion of reciprocal terror.

"Stop! Stop!" exclaimed Seraphina, thrusting her head through the window towards the postillion. "Stop!—where are you driving us?"

The postillion lashed on the horses more furiously than ever. The horseman who had brought the letter rode up to the chaise. There was another with him of not very horsemanlike appearance; the sight of whom thrilled her with increasing terror. It was the assassin of Henry. The fact, indeed, was unknown; but the triumphant ghastliness of his looks was truly horrible.

"Sit still, miss," said the former of these, in a tone of voice not very engaging. "You need not be frightened. Nobody means to hurt you."

This ambiguous sort of consolation rather aggravated than allayed their terrors.

They began to rend the air with their cries. But their cries fell upon no friendly ear. They were only signals to the banditti to rush from the lonely house to which the chaise was galloping like fury, to seize upon and conduct their prey.

The forlornness of the situation, and the desolation of the mansion, increased the wildness of their terror.

The building was spacious. It had the marks about it of something like former elegance and splendour. But, though the architecture was modern, desertion, and the ravages of seasons, in so exposed a situation, and those of pillage also, had given it the appearance of a ruin.

To let the reader into a piece of secret history, it had been heretofore the country-house, as it was called, of one of those worthy gentlemen (or, to speak more truly, a sort of receiving-house to a grand combination of those worthy gentlemen) who were carrying on the respectable trade of defrauding his majesty of his revenues.

Its situation upon the cliff so conveniently opposite to the coast of France, had rendered it a station of considerable importance in this point of view: and, for several years, the principal occupant had maintained an establishment here, which, for splendour and liberality, rivalled, or outshone, all that was to be seen in that part of the country. But cross accidents, revenue officers, and heavy confiscations, at length destroyed the

---

1   The setting is conventionally gothic, but its desolation and especially the stark repetition of negative syntax used to describe it, recall Wordsworth's Salisbury Plain poems, to which Thelwall also alludes in his "Pedestrian Excursion," published at around this time.

fabric of this prosperity; and the mansion partook of the evil destiny of its master.[1] Its movables were sold by public auction; and the house itself put up for sale. But such a mansion, in such a situation, nobody was disposed to purchase; and it had remained ever since untenanted: for, although the person to whom the confiscated property had been transferred, had made several attempts to keep it from falling into absolute decay, by placing persons in it with fire-boot and liberty of free habitation,[2] on condition of keeping it aired; yet the report, in which all the successive inhabitants agreed, of its being haunted with spirits and strange noises, frustrated this intention, and it was consigned over without further resource to the ravages of accident and time.

Such was the habitation which Moroon, under the direction of his gallant ally, captain Roberts, had chosen for the place of rendezvous and temporary seclusion: some such place being absolutely necessary, on account of the particular situation of the coast. For it was only at high water (which at this time happened to be at about 12 o'clock) that they could get out of the creek, and bring the vessel (which, when the tide was out, lay actually upon dry land) round to the coast, to receive its purposed freight; nor could they have carried the reluctant partners of their flight to the creek itself, without passing through parts of the country sufficiently populous to render the experiment exceedingly hazardous. It was necessary, therefore, as the execution of every part of their enterprise required the darkness and secrecy of night, that Seraphina and her mother should, somewhere or other, be kept in seclusion and security till the return of the night tide, when the vessel might be brought round, for their reception, to the untenanted part of the coast.

For this and every other part of the conspiracy, the mansion in question was excellently accommodated: and a large room, upon the ground, or rather under, floor, that had been heretofore used as a private store-house, and, on that account, was well provided with strong bolts and bars, was furnished for the reception of the prisoners, with whatever could be requisite (as far as the situation would permit) for their temporary accommodation and comfort.

The chaise had no sooner stopped, than Moroon himself appeared at the door of the mansion, ready to receive his prisoners: and Seraphina no sooner beheld him, than, from a natural association of ideas, she began to

---

1 The coast of East Sussex between Beachy Head and Dover, where the sheltered mouths of low-lying streams alternate with white chalk cliffs, was well known as a haven for smugglers, operating in well-established gangs with prosperous leaders such as the one alluded to here, whose mansion becomes a measure of the rise and fall of capitalist empire, in the same manner that it does so frequently in Thelwall's The Peripatetic.

2 According to the OED, "fire-boot" is an obsolete legal term denoting "fuel (granted by the landlord to the tenant)" and "the right of a tenant to take fire-wood from off the landlord's estate."

suspect that her mother was at the bottom of the plot; and that her terrors had been the counterfeitings of art. These suspicions, indeed, appeared to be confirmed by the deportment of Morton, whose agitation rather subsided than was increased by discovering into whose power they had fallen:—her suspicions hitherto having dwelt entirely upon old Montfort's proposal of retransportation to that island of horrors, St. Domingo; with which she supposed that Henry might, by some means or other, have been induced, or compelled, to comply.

But there was now no time for explanations. Moroon offered his hand, to conduct our heroine; but she indignantly refusing, and, at the same time, rending the air with renewed shrieks and exclamations, she was delivered over to his myrmidons,[1] who dragged her, by main force, into the fortified apartment: whither Morton followed, with a mixture of solicitude and terror.

At the far end of this room were two small windows, near the top; but they were so obscured, by cobwebs, and thick bushes, and ivy, as to admit scarcely a single ray of light. This deficiency, however, was doubly supplied by the flare of a wood-fire upon the capacious hearth, and two large candles that were burning in a pair of silver candle-sticks upon a little table.

The assistant banditti were no sooner removed, than Moroon, in his usual style of ostentation, began to boast of the preparations he had made for the temporary accommodation of his adorable and angelical mistress; who should never want any thing that his vast property could procure.

"The apartment to be sure was unworthy her excellency; and his fortune. But that was mere necessity; and it was only for a single day. They should go on board at night; and though the little cabbin, to be sure, was small, the furniture was in a style of elegance, he flattered himself, not quite unworthy of that vast deal of property he was going to make her mistress of."

He then proceeded again to the most pompous display of this property; and his means of perpetual increase, by his coasting trade, and his African trade, and his trade in rums and sugars. Neither did he neglect to inform her, with the swelling consciousness of rank, that his vast plantations were all canes—that he was no planter of coffees and cottons.—No: sugars and rums were the only commodities a man of his vast opulence would condescend to produce.

"And all this, adorable mistress!" continued he, with much stammering and hesitation "I will lay at your angelic feet. I will lay it there, immediately. For I am no shilly shally, like your Henry Montforts—and I have no father, thank God! To say me nay, and put his claws upon my estates and plantations and ships and warehouses, for marrying where I like. And we will be mar—married immediately. I know where—to have—have a

---

1 The myrmidons were a warlike tribe mentioned in Homer's *Iliad*; the term was commonly used to signify a gang of henchmen.

parson in half an hour, if your adorable beauties will but consent to be my—my angel of my consolation. He shall mar—marry us on board: and we will be married again in Barbadoes, if—if—if my adorable wishes it: for all my ambition, adorable angel! Is to—to make you—make you mistress of all my vast property; and nothing but the violence of my passion and your cruel scorn could have driven me to these courses.

"But Oh! adorable angel of consolation!" continued he, throwing himself at her feet, and waxing eloquent (after his sort) with the fury of his passion, "consent to make me blest in this way; and (although you are in my power, and all the people here will do whatever I bid them—) I will not proceed to force your person. I would rather revel in those adorable beauties with your consent than without it. I will not attempt to force your most angelic and desirable charms (although it is in my power whenever I please) unless your cruel refusal should force me to it.

"Consent, then, without forcing me to force you, most angelic Seraphina! Make me blest, and be blest yourself, by being the wife of Lucius Moroon, esq., the first—the greatest—the opulentest sugar-planter in the whole island of Barbadoes!"

The impression of terror gave way to indignation, and indignation to contempt, as Seraphina listened to his harangue.

She fixed her eyes upon him, for some time, with so mingled an expression of severity and scorn as made him shrink almost into annihilation.

At length, rising from her seat, and still looking down upon him, as though the conscious dignity of virtue had elevated her to some higher sphere—

"Despicable ruffian!" exclaimed she, with the utmost coolness and composure—"and dost thou really think it is in *thy* power (by threats or violence) to subjugate the soul of Seraphina? Dost thou think I am a being to be thus trampled into degradation?—or made a wanton spoil to the sordid appetites of a reptile whom I can petrify by the bending of a brow?

"How little dost thou know me!—How little know thyself!

"Force!!!—force my person?—Yes, to *death* you may force it: for your instruments are around you, and murder is your proper trade: but never to pollution: never to pollution:—No. Seraphina can be feared, where it would be hateful to be desired; and your fears are my sufficient guard."

She paced about the room several times, when she had uttered this—while conscious worth and glowing indignation wrestled with the anguish of her soul.

Moroon perceived plainly enough that "she fabled not. He felt that he did fear."[1]

At length, however, he recovered just so much command over his muscles as enabled him to rise. But his eyes were still rooted to the ground, and his tongue remained completely palsied.

---

1 *Othello* 5.2.39: "Guiltiness I know not; but yet feel I fear."

"Force me to Barbadoes"—resumed she, in a higher tone. "Drag me across your ruthless seas. You drag but your own chastisement.

"Not mine shall be the terror, guilty wretch! but thine!—the sufferance not mine but thy own! I will haunt thee with apprehensions: I will rack thee with alarms: I will make thy conscience *a common larum bell*:[1] and thy couch I will stuff with thorns. These beauties thou talkest of revelling in shall be basilisks to strike thee dead: and while thou holdest in thy hand the power of life and death, thou shalt tremble to meet my eyes.

"Thy days shall be worn with useless plottings, and thy nights with fear: and when harrassed and disappointed, thou wouldst wish to shake me off, my insulted honour shall still fasten upon thee for vengeance. Seas shall not protect thee, nor thy boasted property preserve. I will drag thee to the public eye of scorn. I will trample thee by the confiscations of vindictive justice. I will hurl thee to the chastising arm of Henry Montfort."

A ghastly grin relieved the blank confusion of his countenance, as she uttered this.—He hazarded one exulting, sidelong glance: and, muttering inarticulate congratulations between his teeth, hurried out of the room.

"Hold!—hold!—What meanest thou?" exclaimed she, terrified by his significant gestures. "Return! return!—Ah! hold!"

But the heavy hinge creaked; the bars fell; and the huge bolts shot into their sockets in his rear; and Seraphina sunk down, in hideous apprehension, upon the chair.

"Horror on horror!" exclaimed she, wringing her hands, "what has my imperious phrensy done?

"Henry Montfort! Henry Montfort!

"He will set his blood-hounds to murder him. What he dares not in person, he will do by proxy. His hangmen are gone forth; and the warrant of execution is signed by me."

She flung herself down upon the dank foul floor. She ploughed it with her throbbing breast.

Morton endeavoured to raise her, and, with maternal solicitude, administer the consolations of hope.

M. "Be comforted my child! My child, be comforted. He cannot be such a monster."

S. "Monster!—a parricide!! And why not a monster, when mothers themselves are monstrous? Nature engenders naught but horrors.

"Thou—thou art in the plot," continued she, springing from the earth, and seizing her deliriously by the arm. "Thou—thou are in this league of massacre and rape—thou cause at once of my being, in its curse! Thou—thou are the machinator—the contriver of all his schemes; and Moroon is but the instrument of thy crimes.

"Didst thou give me existence, like a creating demon, only to doom me to this hell of horrors? and does thy presiding providence still hover over my head to prevent me from escaping thy decree?"

---

1 *2 Henry 4* 3.1.17.

"Oh! No: no: no: my child!" exclaimed Morton, falling on her knees—"by HIM WHO CREATED ALL THINGS! No.

"I knew not of this plot. I am guiltless of this rape. I assisted not in this scene of horrors!

"By the heaven I fain would hope for!—by the hell I fear! I am innocent of this design.

"Oh! believe me, my child!—for heaven's sake believe me.—To the child the mother kneels!"

S. "It may be so Morton! It may be so.—

"But the *letter*!—No: no: the letter!

The very hand of Henry.—Yet *that* he might have seen without your conniving guilt. But the very words of Henry—the dear, fond words—disjointed indeed and marred.

"Fool that I was, not to see through the shallow fraud!—to be cheated by words alone!—not to perceive that some tutored starling had stolen the accents of my beloved, and repeated them without the mind!"

The countenance of Morton fell. Her heart died within her.

"Words!—the *very words*!—O! heaven!—What words?"

S. "Oh! it is too palpable, Morton!—It is too palpable. The very—very words of that dear, fond, sad invitation, he wrote to me from his sick bed, on the report of his father's death!

"O, such a letter! so marred! and for such ends!"

Recollection, like a bolt of thunder, struck the confounded faculties of Morton.

"Then I, indeed, am guilty!" said she, tremulously; and shrunk with her face upon the earth.

Seraphina walked to and fro with a hasty step, half musing to herself, and half raving.

"I had missed it for some time. I thought it had been mislaid. Little—little did I think upon what shelf it had been placed:—for what purpose it had been so carefully treasured.

"It was an important document. In some projects that I have contemplated, I thought to have made use of it to melt the heart of an obdurate father:—thou hast used it to murder the son—

"You?—no!—no!—It is I!—It is I that murder him. I have sent the assassin forth—I have sent him forth to murder Henry!

"But I will follow"—she exclaimed, with shriller emphasis—"Through bolts, and bars, and walls of stone, I'll follow.

"Mountains have moved, it is said," continued she, grappling the door with supernatural earnestness, "and rocks themselves melted for human sufferance. If fabling Superstition may be believed, walls have fallen prostrate, and the earth unclosed on weaker argument than mine. Be realised, ye dreams of holy dotage!" continued she, redoubling her efforts, "and make my heart a proselyte."

The wainscotting began to shake, as she spoke this. A hoarse and rumbling noise was heard, as from hollow vaults below. The pannel yawned; and a chasm appeared in the wall.

Morton shrieked with delirious amazement.

Seraphina approached the opening. She examined it with a steady eye.

"It is done! it is done!" she ejaculated, with aweful exultation—"Henry, or oblivion is mine!"

She sprang into the chasm, and almost instantly disappeared.

"My Henry! my Henry! my Henry!" was reverberated every time less and less distinctly, as she descended, till the hollow sound was lost in articulate murmurs.

"My child! my child!" exclaimed Morton, as the last accents died upon her ear; and she rushed to the chasm to follow.

But a whir—r—ring noise was heard from below; and instantly the pannel closed.

"God of heaven and earth!" exclaimed she.

Her tongue cleaved to her mouth. Her lips refused to approach. Her eyes moved not; nor her breath perceptibly heaved. She was fixed a living statue.

Moroon, in the mean time, who had not been in bed during the preceding night, had retired to a hammock in an adjoining room, in the hopes of a few hours sleep, and to devise fresh plans for the seduction of Morton, and the subduing of the proud virtue of Seraphina. But the shrieks and unusual noises that assailed his ear, almost the instant that he had laid himself down, shook him with undefinable terrors.

He rushed again to the mysterious apartment. The bolts flew back, the bars were hurled down; and, with haggard eyes and hairs all standing on end, he flew through the door, with nothing on him but his trowsers and his shirt.

"What is the matter?" exclaimed he, staring around—"What is the matter?—In the name of hell and all its devils! what is the matter?"

"There!———There!" ejaculated Morton, without moving;—Her eyes still fixed upon the pannel.

"There?—where is Seraphina?" exclaimed he, looking still more wildly about the room—"Where is Seraphina?"

He searched every corner; every closet; every nook and crevice. All was close; but no Seraphina was to be seen.

"Where—where is she?" repeated he, coming up to the motionless Morton—the blood forsaking his cheeks, and his eyes rolling in frantic vacancy—"Where is she?"

"There———There!" repeated Morton, pointing with one finger and slowly waving her head towards the pannel.—"There!"

Moroon fixed his eyes also upon the spot. He could see nothing. But his frame was convulsed with horror.

"There—there—she disappeared," added Morton, at last, scarcely articulate—"There I saw her vanish!"

"Vanish!!!"—

The faculties of Moroon were completely overpowered. He fell down backwards in a swoon; and, oversetting the table, on which the candles were standing, in his fall, involved the room in darkness—"Darkness visible!"[1] for the embers on the hearth, half expiring and involved in smoke, and the few imperfect rays that stole through the thick drapery of filth and foliage by which the loop-hole windows were invested, rather begloomed than illuminated the scene of horrors.

Morton shrieked again more loudly than ever—a long,—a death awakening shriek! such as might have emptied charnel-houses and unpeopled graves.

The fearful trampling of feet was heard; and the faint buz of discordant voices, that died in inarticulate whispers.

All was silent again. Silent, and dark, and fearful. Moroon did not breathe, nor Morton move.

---

1 Milton, *Paradise Lost* I.63. Thelwall mocks Milton's epic and parodies gothic conventions here, as throughout this scene.

VOLUME IV

BOOK X.
=========
CHAP. I.

Containing the Conclusion of the Adventures of the Haunted House.

Torches and Torch-bearers.—The Picture.—Testimony of the Senses.—
The Picture.—The Chasm—The Descent.—The Cave.—Horrors of
Isolation.—Apprehensions and new Alarms.—Confessions and further
Discoveries.—The Chasm. Prudent Precautions.—The Magistrate.—
Benevolent Attentions.—Tender Solicitudes.—The Document restored.
—The Conspirators.

THE darkness and horrid silence that concluded the preceding volume
were not of long duration. A flaring light burst from the antichamber; and
the trampling, and the voices returned.

The heart-thrilling shrieks of Morton had reached the ears of such of
the banditti as were about the premises. They had rushed to the place
from which the noise proceeded; but, terrified by the gloomy horror in
which the apartment was involved, and still more so by the phantom or
winding-sheet (for such to them appeared the only object that was
visible,) that lay stretched along the ground, they had fled again more
hastily than they approached.[1]

They fled, however, but for their torches; and having lighted three or
four of these, they came rushing again to the spot.

The scene was still terrific.

Moroon, whose shirt and white trowsers had formed the ghost and
winding-sheet of their former terrors, still continued, without apparent
motion, in his swoon.

Morton was standing in the very posture into which she had started as
she heard him fall.

A deadly paleness sat upon her cheek. Her feet were still pointed to the
pannel; her body was turned half around; her hands were clasped
together; and her neck declined over the breathless length that lay
stretched upon the earth beneath her.

The attitude was critical. The dress, or rather undress, in which he had
hurried into the room, was critical also. Fresh discoveries were yet to be
made; and discoveries of the first importance often depend upon such
minutiae.

---

1 In its over-the-top gothicism, this chapter reflects Thelwall's ambition to
"outmonk Monk Lewis" in his interrelated writings of 1798-1801, as recalled in
his 1820 essay "On Human Automatonism."

The light of the torches fell on his naked bosom. There lay a small picture there. Distracted as was the mind of Morton, she could not but observe it. It was a source of new distractions.

"God of Heaven!" exclaimed she, stooping, and seizing it in her hand—"What new miracle?—Woodville!—the Picture of Woodville!"

Moroon began to revive. The sailors gathered around, and some of them attempted to assist him.

"Whose picture is this?" demanded Morton; with impatient wildness—"How came you by this picture?"

"Vanished!" exclaimed Moroon, rising partly from the earth, and turning his eyes again to the panel—"Vanished there!"

The sailors stared at each other with open mouths. Their countenances became more ghastly than ever.

Morton turned round, also, with a ghastly gaze: but she still kept the picture in her grasp. The string broke.

"Woodville's picture!" repeated she.

She gazed upon it. She gazed upon the face of Moroon. She gazed upon the pannel: and then upon the picture, and upon Moroon again—with a divided—a distracted attention.

"Woodville's picture!—How cam'st *thou* by this?"

"I know not," replied he, in a slow, sepulchral tone; his eyes still fixed; and scarcely attending to what he said.—"I do not remember the time when I had it not.—

"Vanished!—Seraphina vanished!"

"Vanished!—vanished!" repeated the banditti—the consternation increasing as the exclamation travelled from tongue to tongue—"Vanished!!!"

When they first missed Seraphina, on their entrance into the room with the torches, some of them indeed were stricken with those supernatural terrors which every thing around had such a tendency to encourage. But others, with more probability on their side, concluded that she had taken advantage of the darkness and confusion that prevailed, to make her escape. Nay, one or two of them very confidently affirmed that they had seen her rush by them, in her white gown, as they were huddling in and out of the room the first time, in so much consternation. But the exclamations of Moroon changed immediately the very record and evidence of their senses. All were now convinced that they had seen something or other of the supernatural disappearance; though, as to the detail of the phenomena, they could by no means bring each other to agree. One had seen her mount into the air, without doors, when they heard the clap of thunder. Another had met her in the antichamber, surrounded with a blue flame, as they were blundering along in the dark. A third saw her fly through the ceiling, on a curling smoke, just as they were entering with their torches; and the assassin, who had just been glorying and blaspheming over his exploit, swore, with peculiar earnestness and horror, that, "it was not Moroon, stretched along the floor, they had seen upon their first entrance, but Henry in his winding sheet, who had come from the dead, like a true *lovier*, to save his sweetheart from being ravished.

"You may say what you will," added he, staring about still more wildly, as if he expected to see the phantom again—"but I will take my Bible oath I saw the very wound in his side I made with this dagger, as he was flying away with her in his arms."

A horrible confirmation of this tale appeared to all their senses. The blood was yet to be seen upon the floor.

To them, at least, it appeared to be such; though it was nothing, in reality, but the remains of a bottle of port, with which Moroon had been keeping up his spirits, previous to the arrival of his prisoners; and which had been overset, together with the candles, by his fall.

This idle jargon struck not on the ears of Morton or Moroon. Their faculties were otherwise absorbed.

The eye of Morton rolled from the pannel to the picture; and from the picture to the pannel;—and from vacancy to the moveless countenance of Moroon.

"You were not born in Barbadoes then?"

"No—no!" (Replied he, still in the same tone and attitude,)—"in Jamai"—

"Vanished!"

Mort. "And how preserved from the waves into which I plunged you?"

"Vanished?—vanished!!" exclaimed Moroon, his horror still rising at every repetition. "Vanished!!!"

Morton's eye travelled again to the pannel—It returned.

"Nay, answer me—but answer me!" continued she, with frantic earnestness, fastening upon his arms, and endeavouring to shake him from his trance: "You must answer me.

"Did not your guilty mother hurl you into the sea?"

"Aye!—aye!" he replied still immovable. "But the waves would not swallow me.—The measure of my reprobation was not full.—A mulatto woman—

"Vanished!!!"

Mort. "What! the poor Victorine?—*She* plunged and saved thee?"

Mo. "And died—and *another Mulatto woman*—Hell and its torments!" continued he, starting at length from the ground, and beating his breast and forehead, as he hurried up and down the room—"the other!—I feel— I feel them here! Memory itself is hell—All thought is hell!"

Then returning to the pannel (upon which Morton was still poring) and gazing with still wilder look—"

"Vanished!" repeated he—"O earth! O hell! it is wonderful!—Vanished!!!"

Mort. "Aye, vanished. Heaven would not look on incest. Walls *have* fallen prostrate, and the earth *has* yawned to prevent such horrors.

"She was thy sister.—Thou wouldst have ravished thy sister!"

Mo. "Sister!—The vanished Seraphina?—Sister!"

Mort. "Yes, thy sister. The vanished Seraphina was thy sister. I am thy guilty mother. This is the picture of your common father."

"Sister!—S-is-ter!" ejaculated he, with a climax of tone and emphasis.

"Heaven and earth! thou art mad, my son—thou art mad!" exclaimed Morton, shrieking, and clinging to him. "Thy frame is convulsed;—thy eye-balls burst their sockets.

"Oh! Run not mad! Oh! Run not mad!—thou hast not done the deed. Thy soul *is not stained* with incest. Heaven has interposed. Heaven has preserved thee."

Mo. "Preserved from *Incest*! and why not from murder?—why not from murder?—Cares Heaven for nothing but for incest?

"Murder!—adulterous murder! Fratricidal murder!—The husband of my sister!—My own foster father!—

"Is incest worse than parricide!—or does that jealous and avenging power (whom in my cups I have so often laughed at while I trembled,) decree me just scope enough for crimes to damn me; but nothing to delight?

"Seraphina!—sister!—That had been, indeed a sin, had given me something to balance against damnation!—But for the thought only! or for a stale Mulatto!"—

"Oh! My son! My son!" said Morton, still clinging to him with aggravated horror;—"this is madness, my son! and not repentance. Down on thy knees—down on thy knees and pray."

"Pray!—I cannot pray," replied he, shaking her off. "Let those who practise, and have nothing to fear, say prayers: for me, I have only belief enough to blaspheme.

"To ship! To ship!

"Pray thou thyself—if, indeed, thou canst think of any thing that is worth a prayer.

"Pray Montfort's spirit back to his mangled side! pray together again the dry bones and scattered dust of my murdered foster-father! Pray into second life and innocence the rank adultress! And teach her to undrug again the fatal bowl!—Or—one great prayer for all—Pray me back again into the polluted womb; and crush me there, unborn!—This were perhaps worth praying for.

"To ship I say, to ship! Confederate villains; let us hasten to our ship. The wretch who supposes he can slay here and not be hanged, may remain behind and pray. I will cheat hell a while."

So saying, he rushed out of the house like a madman; with the whole affrighted crew brandishing their torches at his heels, like so many pursuing furies: and Morton again, was left alone in all the horrors of darkness.

She could not follow; her feet were spellbound. The raving phrensy of Moroon aggravated the horror, but did not divide the interest.

Seraphina! Seraphina! Every thought—every feeling was absorbed in Seraphina: and, impressed with all the delirious emotions her supernatural disappearance was calculated to inspire, renewed and urged as they were to still more wild extravagance by the absolute solitude in which she was now left, and the palpable gloom that every where surrounded her, *her* brain also began to turn, and her tongue to arraign Omnipotence.

She threw herself upon the earth. She groped her way to the mysterious pannel;—she sat there for a few moments. The daemon of phrensy rose high.

"Why not to me?—why not to me?" exclaimed she, striking her head with reiterated fury against the wall—"Why not entomb me also?"

A noise was again heard. The pannel yielded again: it shattered into a heap of fragments; and the chasm once more appeared.

"God of Heaven!" she cried—"for me also! Are thy miracles renewed?—*thine*, or *the devouring fiend's*?"

She ventured to look down.

New wonders presented themselves to confound her bewildered senses. She beheld a wavering light below—Deep—deep below: a light at once faint and tremulous; not unlike the dim reflection of the mist enveloped moon, when it breaks through the dancing foliage of the aspen or the ash on the mossy fragments of some ancient tower. But it was still more obscure and tremulous.

"Whence could this proceed?—Light!—subterranean light!" A thousand visionary horrors thronged into her mind.

The depth appeared immeasurable.

"Did it open to the flaming centre of the earth? And were these, seen through smoke and intermediate mists, the eternal, and unquenchable fires?

"But could that gulf have opened for the purity of Seraphina?

"Guilty wretch that I am!—Are not the sins of the parent visited upon the child?

"I must follow!—I must follow!—My child! my Seraphina!—I must follow."

She thrust her head once more into the chasm. She paused in a dreadful meditation.

A confused and mournful murmur arose from below.

"Was it the plaint of anguish from the deep?—Was it the far distant groans?"

Reason tottered. Her head began to swim.

But while she lay in this state of desperate meditation—her body half incumbent over the chasm, her eyes accustomed to darkness, began to distinguish the more approximating objects; and to discriminate its form.

It had the appearance of a large shaft or upright tunnel, rudely cut into the rock; not unlike to those that are frequently to be seen descending into coal-pits or mines. Some pegs, driven into the fissures, and successive projections of the rock, seemed to have been constructed for the purpose of descent.

The terrors of superstition began to subside. The situation of the mansion suggested the purposes for which it had been constructed; and the mystery was in part explained. A large rope that hung in the middle of the chasm seemed to remove all doubt.

She seized the end of this as a means of helping her to the steps: but her weight was no sooner trusted to it than it began rapidly to descend.

Horror and consternation resumed their empire; but they resumed it in a different shape.

The murmur and the tremulous light became more and more distinct, as she descended. They were mysterious, indeed, no more. But were they less tremendous? It was the sea that was underneath her. The tide was still driving upwards, and she was descending to meet the swell.

Terror and a giddy brain almost compelled her to relinquish her hold.

At length, however, the rope stopped. The descent was completed. She had alighted on a shelving prominence of the rock: but her terrors had overpowered her faculties; and she sunk backwards into a state of insensibility.

But the pause of sensation was of slight continuance. She awakened to fresh terrors.

She found herself now, from a perpendicular, transported into a horizontal tunnel; still more rudely fashioned; yet apparently the work of art: to the sea-chaffed mouth of which a narrow, and, to her unaccustomed feet, an apparently dangerous path, seemed to conduct, a little above the highest mark of the waves.

Along this (for she had no alternative) she ventured to proceed; till it brought her, not, as she expected, to the open channel, but to one of those natural and spacious excavations, formed by the perpetual dashing of the sea, in the chalky cliffs of this bold and dangerous coast.

Here her further retreat seemed effectually to be cut off: for the path abruptly terminated as the cave expanded, and before her raged the rising sea.

"Seraphina! Seraphina!" she exclaimed—"Alas! if the heedless foot of Seraphina should have slipped from this dangerous path!"

A deep sigh struck upon her ear, stealing in whispered echo, through the chalky cavern, in the pause of the ebbing wave.

She turned suddenly round. It was the sigh of Seraphina.

She was sitting on a low and insulated bank, towards the further extremity of the cave. Her hands were folded in her lap, and her neck was bending forward; as, in composed despondency, she pored over the invading element; and marked the half-retiring ebb, and the still encroaching flood that threatened every moment to overwhelm her.

While the sea was yet low, she had made her way to this little island (a mere temporary bank of shells and beach, thrown up by the action of the waves) in hopes of escaping out of the cavern, and finding some sort of path, by which she might ascend the cliffs. But she had found it impossible to proceed any further: and while, between despair and meditation, she stood debating with herself what was to be done, the unheeded sea kept rapidly advancing, wave rising above wave, till the bank was surrounded; and it became as impracticable to retire, as to proceed.

She had set herself down, therefore, in patient resignation, to await her approaching destiny.

That destiny appeared inevitable; for sea after sea, still advancing with bolder encroachment, roared up the bank, uprooting its foundations, as it were, and lessening its contracted bounds; till the white foam played over her shrinking feet, and the looser folds of her garment floated upon the wave.

"Seraphina! my child! My child! my Seraphina!" cried Morton in the wildest anguish of her soul.

"Peace, mother!" returned Seraphina, without lifting up her head—"Peace!—peace!—It will soon be over."[1]

M. "O God! O God!—What shall I do to save her?"

S. "Nothing. Nothing. It is past. Even your fatal fondness can no longer forbid my soul repose.

"It is well;—It is well!—The sea has only done what Nature had done before.

"Isolated! Isolated!—I am still but isolated!

"I have been, from my cradle upwards, a solitary being standing on a little island of my own, with a dark prospect bounded all around, save only where the flood of my misfortunes came pouring in."

Morton beat her breast, and tore her hair, in the fury of distraction. But in vain. To get to her was impossible: still more impossible, if the case admitted of comparatives, if with her, to lend her any assistance.

All that remained to the wretched mother was to sit down on the end of the over-hanging path, till the victim was overwhelmed, and then to share her fate.

Mean time the chacing waves continued their ruthless course:—that ruthless course how marked by the eye of Morton! How throbbed her heart as it followed the partial ebb!—how died as it retired before the increasing swell!

And now the wave came on, foaming and splashing in its threatening rage, that seemed destined, at once, to swallow its devoted victim; and Morton hung bending over, with arms outstretched, and with breathless apprehension, ready to accompany its fatal retreat. But again it broke short of its mark.

Another came—But it burst not further than the former.

A third—a fourth—Morton flattered herself they were somewhat short. She was not deceived.

Fortunately it was but a neap tide; and the wind blowing *from* the shore, even this did not swell to its accustomed height.

---

1 An allusion to the last words of Mary Wollstonecraft's mother, to which she frequently referred in her work: "a little patience, and all will be over."

The waves retired. The insulated bank expanded. The sea continued ebbing from the cave; till the bank at length was insulated no more: and the delighted mother rushed forward, with a bound, to clasp in her eager arms the daughter she had regarded as lost.

As the first terrible apprehensions of Morton retired with the ebbing tide; a new anxiety arose. It was then that she first began to be conscious of those damp and shivering sensations which (mild and open as the weather was for the season, for it was about the latter end of February) could not fail to be produced in such a situation, at such a time of the year. What then might be the consequences to the health of Seraphina, who had been so much longer exposed, and in so much worse a situation, not only to the cold and misty air, but to the spray, and the dashing waves!

Cold, and wet, and agitated as she must have been, notwithstanding her apparent composure, how was she now to be comforted—sustained—preserved? Where was fire—where was repose—where was social—or where medical assistance to be had?

In this distressed situation the only expedient Morton could devise was to attempt, difficult as it must be, to reascend by the tunnel, into the deserted house. There, though no other assistance was to be had, they would, at least, find bed and firing; and probably provisions; and wine or cordials of some description, which under their present circumstances might undoubtedly be very useful.

It was in vain to advise this measure, or indeed any other, without endeavouring to regain the confidence of her daughter by explaining the business of the letter; and also, entering in some degree into the history of what had taken place above; so far, at least, as related to the terror and flight of Moroon; for as to the discovery of affinity that had preceded that event, she thought it no time to oppress the wearied spirits of the unhappy sufferer with the emotions that might be awakened by such disclosure.

Her precautions however were vain: new alarms and new agitations forced the fearful secret from her unconscious lips.

A growing noise, as of a multitude of voices, came murmuring upon their ears; and a sudden flare of light burst from the innermost recesses of the cavern.

They turned suddenly round; and discovered, through the reeking and curling vapour, a throng of terrific countenances reflecting the red blaze of torches and flambeaux, and hurrying, as it seemed, towards them.

Seraphina shrieked. "He comes! Murder and rape come for me. Deceitful mother!—treacherous and inhuman! But I can die. I have yet power to die!"

She rushed towards the retiring sea. But Morton caught her in her arms.

"Who comes, my Seraphina?—Hold! hold! what is it you fear?"

"Your brother is flown. Heaven would not suffer incest: Your distracted brother is flown—flown in delirious phrensy. That vessel there—Do you not see it crouding all its sail before the wind?—That vessel wafts him upon his way to Barbadoes."

S. "Brother! Brother! What new mystery—or what new fraud?—I have no brother. It is the monster Moroon—the murderer—the ravisher Moroon I fear. Unhand me!—Inhuman mother! Loose me and let me die."

M. "Alas! Alas! my child!—that ravisher is thy brother. Moroon is thy brother:—and he is flown—flown in that little bark."

By this time the throng that had occasioned the alarm were gathering around them; and the terrors of Seraphina subsided.

It was not the banditti, but a mingled group of the country people and others of different classes and descriptions, led on by one of the magistrates of the neighbourhood, and the other officers of police, who were come to make search, and inquiry into this extraordinary affair.

The assassin who had way-laid Henry, terrified by the supernatural interpositions (the evidence of which appeared so indubitable to all his senses) by which Seraphina had been snatched away; and feeling all the consequent horrors of an afflicted conscience, had stolen out of the room while his companions were too busy with their own particular terrors to notice his escape; and running immediately to the nearest town, had surrendered himself to the constable, confessed the murder, and been conveyed for examination before the magistrates—who happened to be then assembled.

Much of this tale was of course so wild and incoherent, that some of the justices were doubtful whether they should pay any other attention to it, than merely securing the informant as a lunatic. There was one, however, of this sagacious body, who (knowing very well of what stuff the superstitions of the vulgar are composed; and how little dependence is to be placed upon the accuracy of their senses when any of their passions, particularly their fears, are strongly stimulated) dissented from the general opinion. To him it appeared, notwithstanding the extravagance of all the stuff about yawning earth, and claps of thunder, and ghosts and winding-sheets flying away with ravished virgins through the ceiling, that there was, at least, a clear and consistent story, as to the actual assassination and the meditated rape; and that all the rest might be easily accounted for from the perturbations of an imagination distempered by the hauntings of a guilty conscience; and perhaps by some yet unexplored mysteries of Smuggler's Hall, as it was now come to be generally denominated—several strange recesses in which had been heretofore discovered.

Upon his persuasion therefore it was determined, at least, to search the place in question: and his suggestions conspiring with the strange tale and wild deportment of the informant to provoke a very considerable degree of curiosity, some of the magistrates, attended by the constables, and a throng of people, still gathering as they went along, proceeded to the place in question.

The chaise concealed in one of the tumbling out-houses, and the horses that yet remained in another, confirmed the reality of the conspiracy; and, when conducted by the assassin into the room where all the supernatural events had been reported to have taken place, the sagacious magistrate immediately perceived how well his suggestions had been founded.

The chasm in the wall was standing wide open: for the pannel had not merely slid down, it will be remembered, in the second instance: an event which, at first, had taken place in consequence of the vehemence of Seraphina having displaced some loose stones, that struck the outward spring in their fall. It had yielded in a very different way to the phrensy of Morton; whose violence had not displaced the spring, but absolutely shattered the pannel into fragments. The cavity in the wainscot, therefore, had not closed again as heretofore upon the reascent of the rope; and the mechanism that had so frequently eluded the jealous diligence of the Custom-house officers, and police research, was at length revealed and destroyed.

The lighted torches with which the magistrates had thought fit to be provided; and of which, indeed, the premises furnished them with a supply, were no sooner applied to this mysterious recess than the whole arcana[1] were revealed.

The bolt, with its internal and external spring was detected. A chain of intricate cellars, or excavations, was found to communicate with the warehouse; the curious construction of whose sliding pannel might at once facilitate escape, by precluding the possibility of suspicion or pursuit, and stop all further inquisition beyond this apparent depôt;[2] even in cases of partial detection.

Though the first projectors and principal conductors of this ingenious system of contraband had been dispersed and ruined, part of the secret appeared still to be in the possession of some of the subordinate instruments, who had escaped: for several smuggled articles were still found in the subterranean recess, that had very little appearance of having lain there neglected ever since the desertion of the house; a circumstance that very well accounted for the reports of apparitions and strange noises that had been bruited about the country; and which, also, conspiring with the example of the horrid uses to which such a building might be converted, suggested the necessity of a resolution, afterwards to put effectually into practice, of erasing the whole mansion to its very foundations, and filling up the entrance to those subterranean recesses, for the prevention of future frauds and enormities.

Nature cooperated with the judicious diligence of the magistracy, in this respect: for during the storms and severe frosts of a succeeding winter, part of the cliff cracked and fell suddenly in; so that little is now

---

1   Secret systems or hidden mysteries.
2   Warehouse or stopping-place (French).

to be traced of this scene of so many extraordinary adventures, but the natural cave, at the mouth of which we left our unfortunate heroine, to pursue the mazes of this digression.

But no traces either of the vanished lady; or of any of the conspirators being visible in these recesses; it was thought fit to divide the troop into several bodies; that, at one and the same time, the other parts of the premises, the surrounding country, and the yet unexplored tunnel might be effectually searched.

The department of the tunnel was chosen by the worthy magistrate whom we have already particularised: and who will be found, throughout the whole of this business, "bearing his faculties"[1] with a degree of diligence, humanity and politeness equally honourable to his office, to his rank (for he was allied to the first families of the country), and, what is still more, to the name and upright form of man.

He had chosen this department from motives that speak the generous feelings of his heart. He thought it inevitable, that, unless she had unfortunately perished in her endeavour to escape, the lady, whose alarming situation had been the chief object of his anxiety, must be still in some cavern or other, with which this tunnel would be found to communicate, and he was not willing to depute to any other the duty of those attentions her calamitous situation might require. Having on further examination observed sufficient appearances of a communication between this rocky shaft and the sea, he gave orders (previous to his descent) for his own chariot to drive to the nearest practical declivity: that, as soon as the tide was low enough, it might meet him upon the beach; and if the persecuted lady were yet to be found, he might take her under his own protection.

His benevolent precautions were not in vain. Our heroine was found, in the situation already described. She was soothed, and in some degree, consoled, by his polite attentions; and the chariot not long afterwards arriving, she was conveyed in it, thus accompanied and protected, along the beach to New Haven;[2] and from thence to his elegant mansion in that neighbourhood: where the worthy baronet, introducing her, and her tragical story, to the care and kindness of his lady, every attention was assiduously bestowed upon her, that the circumstances of her situation could require.

One part of this story, however, was for the present very carefully suppressed: for Morton found means to hint to their conductor that Seraphina was as yet unacquainted with the circumstances of the assassination, of which the ravings of Moroon had suggested some idea: and the propriety of concealing from her every thing that might relate to that part

---

1 *Macbeth* 1.7.17.

2 Newhaven, slightly west of the cliffs of Beachy Head (where Thelwall appears to have set his "haunted house") sits at the mouth of the Ouse River, and is still an important channel port.

of the tragedy, till further information could be obtained, was too obvious to require animadversion.

But, though by this precaution she was kept in ignorance of the disaster that had befallen her Henry, she was not without apprehensions of the consequences that might arise from the anguish and desperation of his mind when he should hear the ambiguous circumstances of her disappearance: and notwithstanding the polite attentions she received, and the cold, the wet, the exhaustion and fatigue that threatened such serious consequences to her health, and the exotic delicacy of her frame, she would fain have hurried back again without delay, that the cause of these anxieties might be removed.

But the worthy baronet and Morton were as anxious to keep her away from the cottage at present, as she was to return to it. The former therefore joined his felicitations with those of his lady and the latter, to prevail upon her to take not only some refreshment, but some repose; and to permit them to send for a neighbouring physician, that the necessary precautions might be taken for preventing the ill consequences that might arise from what she had already endured. In support of this advice he thought it not improper to add an argument of a more official nature— namely, that her presence might perhaps be necessary, as that of her mother most assuredly would, in the prosecution of those examinations and legal inquiries into which it was absolutely necessary to persevere with respect to this atrocious affair.

But the argument that more than all had weight in reconciling her mind to this delay, was the assurance of this worthy magistrate that neither messengers nor horses should be wanting to convey any intelligence she desired to her friends, in whatever direction; and which would be sure to reach them some hours earlier than she herself could possibly arrive. Seraphina also recollecting that Henry, especially if he had not heard of her elopement, would in all probability be still at Southampton, yielded very contentedly to these solicitudes: and, two messengers being procured, she dispatched by one of them a short note to poor Nanny at the cottage, and a second to Edmunds at Grosvenor-square, while the other was hastened towards Southampton with the following letter to Henry.—

"My dearest Henry,

"It is probable that before the arrival of this you may have heard of my mysterious disappearance from the cottage. If the forgery by which I was decoyed into this horrible snare should have fallen into your hands, it will at least have relieved your mind from the painful apprehensions of infidelity or voluntary desertion on my part. What I am now writing, will I hope come timely enough to prevent you from experiencing, on my behalf, those long and heart-rending sensations which I have been doomed to sustain on yours.

"I am well, my dearest Henry. I am safe. I have passed through many horrors, of which subterraneous dungeons and surrounding seas have been the very least. I have escaped from the impending dangers of violation—of brutal rape and incest!—

"O Henry! What a discovery!—Moroon, the meditated ravisher, is proved by the most unequivocal evidence, to be my brother! But I have no time for details. The messenger is waiting. Suffice it to say that I am here under the very flattering protection of the lady of Sir Herbert Elmsley: the worthy magistrate to whose solicitudes and exertions have more obligations than I have words to express.

"Were I at liberty to follow the impatient dictates of my heart—or were my Henry at liberty to open his arms to receive me, I would myself be the bearer of these tidings, that I might soothe, with the endearments of an unalterable affection, the perturbations of that bosom, whose sufferings throughout the whole of this sharp trial have been the bitterest sources of my own. But I am detained here in a sort of generous captivity, under a variety of pretences; the whole of which, I can very plainly perceive, are only so many subterfuges to disguise what appears to this amiable family a necessary caution, but which I cannot but regard as a superfluous solicitude, for the preservation of my health: and, even if these impediments were removed, the prejudices of a father, who does not, and who will not know the soul of Seraphina, would forbid me the consolation I desire.

"I shall return to the cottage to-morrow. In the mean time I remain, my dearest Henry, in perfect health and security, and in the purity and fervour of an unalterable affection,

Yours

most sincerely

SERAPHINA."

Elmsley Hall, Sussex,
    Feb. 1795.[1]

While Seraphina was dispatching the messengers in question (the former of whom had, of course, his particular instructions also from Sir Herbert) the other magistrates, &c. who had been left to complete the search for the conspirators, returned, as had been appointed, to the mansion of our worthy baronet.

Conspirators they had found none; but they had found among other things the portmanteau of Moroon, which being broken open, the purloined letter of Henry was found, among several other papers; and being claimed by Seraphina with great eagerness, it was very politely restored to her without inspection; Sir Herbert simply putting his signature upon the direction, that in case it should hereafter be necessary to call for it in the progress of legal inquiry, it might be, thereby, in his power to identify it.

---

1 Although the places and names are fictional, they are probably based on acquaintances of Thelwall in the area. To this day there is an Elmsley Cottage in a village near Rye, East Sussex. Elmsley was the name of a well-known bookseller in London; his son Peter, a classical scholar, was a friend of Robert Southey.

Seraphina having thus regained what she considered as so valuable a document, as well as so dear a pledge of affection, retired, with so much the more composure, to that slumber, which the physician, who by this time was arrived, thought absolutely indispensable to allay the febrile symptoms that began to appear.

In the mean time, means were not neglected for pursuing the conspirators. But, as they had slipt their cable, and, by the help of a favourable wind, got out of the creek into the open channel, immediately as they arrived on board, nothing was to be done without the assistance of Revenue cutters[1] to give them chace on the open sea.

Proper applications were now made for these, and they were accordingly dispatched, with as much expedition as possible, from New Haven. But to no effect. The privateer was an excellent sailor; and having wind, and sea-room, and apprehension to boot, was presently out of hazard of being overtaken.

In fact, when it came to be discovered who was missing in their muster, the cause of his disappearance was easily conjectured; and Moroon (the latent energies of whose character seem to have been called forth by the terrors and horrors into which this adventure had involved him) had the address to persuade, or rather intimidate, his associates into an effectual method of disappointing all pursuit, by changing their original destination; and, instead of making for Barbadoes, mounting the tri-coloured flag and running into the port of Cherbourg.

In this manoevre, he might not quite so readily have succeeded, had the noble commander himself been present.—For captain Roberts was not one of those whose morality is so etymological as to perceive any incongruity in being, at the same time, very *loyal* and very *lawless*; and, though he would have made no sort of scruple of plundering his majesty's subjects on the high seas, or kidnapping them from the coasts, to give them an *airing at Kamtschatka,* or a *bathing in the Atlantic,* he would nevertheless, with great zeal and fervency, have d—d the Jacobin eyes of the French, all together in a lump; and, swearing that he was for King George, for ever, would have clapped a torch to the powder-room, rather than they should have had so much as his very cock-boat.[2]

But captain Roberts was not in all respects so like that Jason of old, whom we have supposed to be the classical model of his heroic imitation, as to be foremost himself in the grand exploit of danger while his subor-

---

1 Light boats employed by the customs authorities for the prevention of smuggling.

2 Here again Thelwall draws on personal experience to criticize the strategies of press-gangs, who were authorized to kidnap men they found at sea (the crew of merchant vessels) or on land (in coastal villages like Yarmouth, where Thelwall narrowly escaped from a press-gang). Once pressed, sailors might be "bathed in the Atlantic" by accident or as punishment (by being keelhauled, or dragged beneath the ship) or stranded in remote places like Kamchatka (in Siberia, where Captain Roberts threatened to transport Thelwall).

dinate Argonauts were reposing upon their oars.[1] On the contrary, approving in that respect the ameliorated system of modern heroism, he satisfied himself, on the present occasion at least, with delivering his very particular instructions after which, not expecting that the vessel would sail before the ensuing evening, he had retired, whether in pursuit of business or of pleasure, from the scene of action; and thus escaped the formidable alternative to which his loyalty might have happened to be driven.

By some means or other, also, (to pursue his history to the conclusion, before we dismiss him) he contrived to escape the vigilance of justice, and to get into the privateering trade again. But dabbling once more in the coasting business, or, as it is vulgarly called, the trade of kidnapping, he got himself into such a predicament, that his *new employers*, to prevent the inconvenience of a legal inquiry, made interest to procure him the command of a ship of war, and got him sent on the West India station; where he had his share of "the yellow harvest"; for he caught the fever and died.[2]

In the mean time, the subordinate banditti having disposed of their vessel, entered themselves into the service of the enemy; and Moroon who was looked upon, very properly, as the real author of this piece of service, easily made interest to be conveyed to the island of St. Domingo; where he might, at least, enjoy the pleasures of a climate and state of society more congenial to his tastes, and have an eye to the conduct of certain branches of his lucrative concerns; and where, perhaps, he might some how or other find opportunities of learning how far it might be safe for him to return to his vast plantations.

Having thus finally disposed of these conspirators, it is high time to return to the more interesting concerns of our heroine.

CHAP. II.

The return of Seraphina to the cottage; and her conduct under the new circumstances in which she finds herself to be placed.

Elmsley Hall;—Family Sketches.—The Paragraph.—Departure from Elmsley Hall.—Persevering Attentions.—The Journey;—Intelligence by the Way;—Maternal Cautions.—The Arrival.—Physic for the Heart.— Altered Circumstances, or new Maxims from old Principles.—The Disherison.—More Eccentricity.—Operations of Sincerity.

THE arrangements that had been made to quiet the mind of Seraphina, seemed to have answered the purpose to the full expectations both of Sir Herbert and Morton; and the precautions with regard to her health

---

1 See p. 365, note 1.
2 Here Thelwall fires a final satiric broadside and takes revenge on the Captain Roberts who assaulted him at Yarmouth.

were not less efficacious. These latter owed, perhaps, some part of their operation to the benign attentions of lady Elmsley; who was a female of very excellent understanding as well as of a most amiable disposition; and whose conversation, accordingly, as well as her solicitudes, imparted that kind of pleasure to our heroine which, since the melancholy fate of Amanda, it had never been her lot to experience from female society.

Nor was the daughter of Sir Herbert (a fine attractive girl of seventeen, with a charming mixture of tenderness and vivacity in her deportment) less interesting in the eyes of Seraphina; who saw realised in this amiable family one of those pictures of domestic felicity with the coinage of which she had so often delighted her imagination.

All these circumstances cooperating together, restored, in a considerable degree, the calmness and complacency of her mind. She seemed the next morning to be almost entirely recovered from the fatigue and agitation which she had endured; and, seeing this happy and benevolent family assembled around her at the breakfast table, renewing their enquiries and attentions for her accommodation and comfort, her heart expanded with new sympathies, and she even began to assume some degree of that interesting vivacity, with which, when her mind was at ease, few people were more happily blest. So that it appeared from her deportment, altogether, that she was waiting, with great composure, the return of her messengers.

But how quickly was all reversed.

The worthy baronet, with disastrous politeness, having put his newspaper (The Evening Mail) into her hands, without having previously read it himself, her eye unfortunately fell, almost immediately on the following paragraph.—

"ASSASSINATION.—Yesterday evening, at between eight and nine o'clock, Henry Montfort, Esq. of Grosvenor-square, was way-laid in the neighbourhood of Walcot-place, by a rough sailor-looking fellow, who gave him several deep wounds with a dirk, or dagger, in various parts of his body, and left him on the ground for dead. At the time when this atrocity was perpetrated, he appears to have been going upon a clandestine visit to a young lady who has *private apartments* in one of the *avenues* of the neighbourhood; and from whom he had received *a tender invitation*. The Young lady however, *together with her mamma*, had thought fit to decamp, a few hours before, under the protection of a more favoured lover; and was thus most critically out of the way of all suspicion at the time when the *accident* took place."

If the distance between Southampton and London, and the time when the paper must have been printed, did not seem to throw a grand impediment in the way of such conjectures, the reader might, perhaps, conceive it not very difficult to discover the writer of this very decent paragraph. He will have no difficulty in concluding what effect the perusal of it had upon our slandered heroine.

Poor Seraphina!—the sharpness of the intelligence needed not the poison of such base insinuations to aggravate the wound it inflicted on her heart.

She dropped the paper from her hand with a shriek.

She fell in a swoon upon the floor.

Lady Elmsley, and the gentle Caroline, and the anxious Morton, flew to her assistance.

The worthy baronet, suspecting the substance of what must have occurred, took up the newspaper and read.

"Detestable villains!" he exclaimed: "Worse assassins than the ruffians whose atrocity they record!"—for Sir Herbert was one of those with whom newspaper testimony was not evidence of very high authority—and with whom, indeed, testimony of any kind against the evidence of his senses was no testimony at all. He had found frequent occasions to observe, in his magisterial capacity, that the silent evidence of deportment, and the expressions of a benign and intelligent countenance, were more to be confided in than a crowd of vulgar witnesses; and, after what he had read in the demeanour and looks of Seraphina, it would have required better testimony than might have satisfied the *deliberate caution* of the Court of Chancery, to persuade him to give credit to any report that was to her disadvantage.

"Let me fly! Let me fly!" exclaimed Seraphina, as she recovered—"Alive or dead, let me fly to him this instant!

"Oh Lady Elmsley! Oh, Sir Herbert!—what a wretch have you harboured if these tales be true!

"My Henry! Oh, my Henry!—He too has been imposed upon. Fraud and forgery have visited him also.

"Those verses! ah, those verses!"—continued she, turning to Morton with a look that had a thousand daggers in it.

"This—this was the counter-part of this unnatural plot.

"Murder and rape!—incest and fratricide!

"These are the endearments—these are the consolations that relative affection keeps in store for me.

"My Henry! Oh, my Henry!"

Why should we describe her delirious agitations?—Why attempt what words can never paint? Why dwell upon the unavailing solicitudes of her generous protectors; or the confusion and repentant horror that oppressed the soul of Morton.

Suffice it to say, that, unappeasable by friendly entreaty or endearing remonstrance, she refused even to stay for the return of that messenger whom Sir Herbert now informed her, he had particularly instructed to enquire into the extent to which this part of the developed plot had, in reality, been executed; and to hasten back, with all possible expedition, with whatever intelligence could be collected respecting the unfortunate gentleman.

In two or three hours, at furthest, this messenger was expected to return. But hours were ages in the distracted state of Seraphina's mind.

If Henry were yet alive, she concluded from the paragraph that he might still be at the cottage. To the cottage therefore she determined to fly; and every proposition of delay did but irritate the frantic anguish of her soul.

Sir Herbert, therefore, was obliged to yield to her importunities. Accordingly, at once desirous of seeing her beyond the reach of further danger, and of obtaining all the intelligence that could be collected concerning this most atrocious conspiracy, he ordered the horses to his own carriage, in which he conveyed our heroine and her mother as far as Lewis.[1] There, procuring a post-chaise and four, he accompanied them, with the expedition to which bribes and entreaties could conduce, to the retreat at Walcot-place.

They had not proceeded far upon their journey, when they met the expected messenger on his return, spurring his horse with all the zeal and impatience the urgency of this business seemed to require.

The servant that accompanied the chaise first recognised, and rode forward to meet him.

The chaise stopped; and he approached the window.

He had brought a letter for the young lady.

"He is dead!—he is dead!" she shrieked out in an agony of apprehension. "It is not Henry that writes, but Edmunds!"

"No, madam—he is not dead," answered the messenger; "I have seen the surgeon myself, madam: and he says the wound is not mortal."

S. "But you did not see him!—you did not see him!—No, no! you did not see *him*!"

Mes. "The letter, madam, I believe will inform you why I did not."

She burst it open with great agitation. It was as follows:

"Dearest Madam,

"The happy arrival of your letter has been a matter of great consolation, and will, I hope, be productive of the most salutary effects.

"I perceive you are not yet acquainted with all the circumstances of this horrible plot. Your messenger will inform you what has happened. I have only to add, that my poor master was decoyed by the same kind of artifice that seems so successfully to have been practised upon you; and to boast (as, with no small degree of exultation, I do) that my fortunate suspicions alone prevented the effectual perpetration of this part of the enormity.

"The wound, madam, is not mortal: and but for the agitation into which his mind was thrown, and has ever since continued, by the circumstances of your mysterious disappearance, there would not, in all probability, have been the smallest danger of any serious consequences.

"But it is not to be disguised that this agitation has produced an alarming degree of fever, which has occasioned both the surgeon and Dr. Pen-

---

1 Lewes is a town in East Sussex, about 10 miles inland from Sir Herbert's home in Newhaven, on the road to London.

garron to order him to be kept as quiet as possible; and which not only renders it totally improper for him to answer your welcome note, but also would prevent his immediate removal from the cottage, even if Mr. Wood-house had not arrived at Grosvenor-square in the forenoon of yesterday, with positive instructions from old Mr. Montfort to suffer neither him nor myself to enter there any more.

"If I have thought it necessary to practise some finesse to prevent him from the imprudence, which it would otherwise have been impossible to restrain, of using pen and ink on this occasion; I have, therefore, only just informed him, that intelligence has been received that you are safe and well; that you have escaped out of the hands of the ruffians, and are taking measures for your immediate return: but I shall not as yet either commu-nicate the letter with which you have honoured me, or give him to under-stand that any direct messenger from you has arrived.

"Let not these circumstances, madam, agitate, too much, the noble sensibility of your nature. But rest yourself assured, that there are no alarming symptoms in the present distemper, but what the consciousness of your safety will abate, and your presence effectually remove.

"Such I do assure you is the confident hope of,

"Madam,

"Your obliged and devoted servant,

ARION EDMUNDS."[1]

The concluding paragraph of this letter, if it did not remove, at least mitigated, in some degree, the apprehensions of Seraphina; while, at the same time, her impatience was rather urged than allayed.

Sir Herbert sympthised with her feelings, and neglected no means of expediting their pace.

In the mean time Morton, who had been highly gratified by the atten-tions that had been paid to her daughter by this worthy baronet and his family, and who had never before known what it was to taste of the *respect* of persons of their condition, began to feel herself very jealous of every circumstance that might tend to diminish that respect; and to entertain great anxiety for the removal or prevention of those ambiguous impres-sions which the situation of the cottage, the presence of Henry there, and a variety of probable occurrences, conspiring with the malicious insinua-tions in "The Evening Mail," might have a tendency to produce.

She thought it not amiss, therefore, to give Sir Herbert to understand so much of the history of her daughter as might seem to place her con-nection with Henry in the most honourable point of view: and entering somewhat at large into the adventures at St. Domingo—the disappoint-

---

1 Arion, a Greek devotee of Dionysius, invented the dithyramb, an impassioned form of choral lyric. This, as well as the myth of his being captured by pirates and rescued by dolphins, resonates with the lyric enthusiasm and nautical adventur-ousness of Edmunds, as well as of Thelwall, who wrote a dramatic shipwreck scene for *The Hope of Albion* at about this time.

ments and uncertainties of Seraphina as to the property of Parkinson—the obduracy of old Montfort—the intended marriage upon the false report of his death—his return and determined opposition to the match—the consequent seclusion of Seraphina; and, in short, every circumstance of this interesting amour (those only excepted that might suggest the most distant idea of the consequences of a certain tender scene in the Bay of Fonchiale). She contrived to make out such a tale as she imagined (not unwisely) would at the same time anticipate all censorious conclusions, and increase the sympathy and interest which the worthy magistrate had hitherto displayed.

Had Seraphina been at leisure to attend to this proceeding, the reader may very well be assured that she would have been far from being pleased with this artifice. She would have felt herself in a very awkward predicament.

To tell, designedly, *part only of the truth*, was, according to her principles, to tell a *falsehood*: and silently to listen to such a tale was to be a partner in the fraud: yet, as Morton had managed it, this co-partnership was not to have been avoided but by the voluntary correction of omissions which it must have been even more indelicate than imprudent to supply. She would have been precluded accordingly from the only species of sincerity that the nature of the case admitted, (that of leaving circumstances to speak for themselves, and conclusion to take its course,) and would have been compelled to submit to the uneasy consciousness of a tacit connivance in deception.

But the soul of Seraphina was too much absorbed to listen to the loquacity of Morton. The name of Henry indeed, sometimes roused her from her reverie, and some few incoherent impressions were made of the subject of the discourse: but she was incapable of attention to any other subject than the letter she had received, and her impatience to arrive at the cottage.

Her impatience was at length gratified: She did arrive at the cottage. She flew to the bedside of her Henry. The servant had been posted on before-hand to announce her approach, and prepare the respiring lover for the flood of happiness that was about to pour upon him; and which, if it had rushed too suddenly, his enfeebled nerves might not have had the fortitude to hear.

Why should we attempt to describe the interview. It cannot be described. Lovers can alone conceive it. Such lovers alone can feel.

Suffice it to say, that Henry once more experienced the more than Esculapian[1] skill of his fair physician. Dr. Pengarron could only prescribe to the symptoms of the disorder; and the surgeon could only dress the exterior wound. But Seraphina, from the precious lymbics[2] of her eyes,

---

1 Medical; related to doctors, from the name of the ancient Greek physician. See p. 292, note 1.
2 Poeticization of "alembic," a vessel used in chemistry for distillation.

distilled the healing drops that went radically to the inmost causes, and stopped the threatened gangrene of the heart.

Dr. Pengarron himself acknowledged the superior efficacy of her prescriptions. He did more. He freely acknowledged that her title to success was scientific and not empirical—the results of her merit, not of chance.

In short, Dr. Pengarron soon began to view this connection in a very different light from that in which it had formerly been exhibited: a circumstance, indeed, which not uncommonly happens when a man takes the resolution or the opportunity of seeing with his own eyes.

Not that it was Dr. Pengarron's fault that he had not seen so before. The means were not presented.

Under the circumstances that existed during her residence in Grosvenor-square, Seraphina, of course, regarded it as a point of decorum to be as retired as possible. It was neither the wish of herself, nor of Henry, that she should appear in the light of a *mistress*; and in what other light could she appear at the side of his sick-bed. She had, accordingly, always shunned the room, when either the gentlemen of the faculty, or other necessary visitants, were there.

But circumstances were now altered.

The events that had produced the present illness of Henry must give inevitable publicity to the connection; and so scrupulously to shrink from observation would, therefore, look like acknowledging a shame she did not feel—would be confessing depravity where she was conscious of nothing but virtue.

Henry was stretched on the bed of pain and sickness notoriously in her apartment. Did sympathy, affection, duty, all conspire to bid her, under these circumstances, retain him as her guest? and was she to blush, under such circumstances, at appearing in the character of his hostess? should she shrink from the acknowledgment of those feelings that alone could have produced, or could justify, their present situation?

Besides, with their present contracted bounds, and still more contracted establishment, her attendance could not properly be dispensed with. Morton, of course, had too little of the confidence either of her daughter or of Henry to be a very acceptable attendant on his sick couch: they could neither of them forget, that to her violation of that confidence, all the horrors of the recent conspiracy, and all the consequences that resulted and might yet result from it, were, in the first instance to be attributed. Edmunds must frequently be away; for they had nobody else who could be entrusted to transact their concerns without. Nancy was still confined to her bed; and *the old lady of the garden*, who possessed, indeed, in an eminent degree, all the virtues of a nurse, and a sympathy that prompted her very readily to extend her assistance to all that might stand in need of it, was nevertheless, by means of her lameness, somewhat disqualified for the task; and, from decay of memory, not the fittest person in the world to be made the depository of such verbal instructions as, from time to time, physicians and surgeons might think it necessary to leave.

In short all circumstances seemed to conspire to call for the constant attentions and solicitudes of *the wife*: and, though Seraphina disdained to assume *a name* which till the ceremony had been performed would imply a falsehood; yet she determined from thence forward to sustain *the character* of a relationship, whose *duties* she was called upon to fulfil.

Every thing indeed, conspired to prompt her to this resolution.

The time was arrived, the event had taken place, which she had always looked forward to as the criterion of her conduct in this respect. The crisis, the catastrophe of old Montfort's indignation, was no longer suspended. The decree of reprobation was sealed; and Henry was formally banished from his presence and his inheritance for ever.

Henry, indeed, had not seen the decree. It had been sent inclosed in a long letter of insulting reproof and pious exhortation from the Reverend Emanuel Woodhouse, before the intelligence arrived from Seraphina. But as Edmunds had some intimation of its probable contents from the bearer, honest William, and as the gentlemen of the faculty had given particular orders that every thing should be kept out of the way, and from the knowledge of the patient, that could disturb or agitate his mind, he had taken the liberty (there being no other person at hand who could perform that confidential duty) to open the seal; and having made him self master of the contents, he resolved to take the still further liberty of keeping both the sermon and text from the knowledge of his master till the recovery of his health might enable him to sustain the shock: precautions, for which, as soon as she arrived, he received the very hearty thanks of Seraphina; as he had before the blunt but entire approbation of Dr. Pengarron.

From the instant in which Henry announced the return of his father, Seraphina had always looked forward to the probability of this event: and (although she had not thought fit to suggest so much to Henry, lest, from the vehemence of his passions, he might relax in his endeavours to avert that misfortune) she had from that very instant decided in her mind, that whenever it should actually and irretrievably take place, from that day forward all compromises with the smiles or frowns of fortune—all subterfuges and expedients were at an end; she would be Henry's as publicly as she was wholly and entirely—his friend, his mistress, his *wife*.—That instead of repelling his importunities, she would claim his promise; and share his poverty with greater triumph, than ever she would have felt in the participation of his affluence.

She had therefore another powerful motive for the alteration of her conduct already noticed.

The fiat was passed. New scenes and prospects of life were opening before them: and she determined that the decree of his father and her own decision should be announced together as soon as the health of Henry should render such disclosures safe and proper. In the mean time she determined to let it be seen to all, by every part of her conduct, that her determination was taken to be separated no more from the side—from the bosom of the man she loved.

The openness, or, as *she* called it, the indiscretion, of this conduct, was not very pleasing to Morton. It seemed to mar all the inferences of her fine spun tale; and she feared that, in defiance of all the pains she had taken to prevent such a calamity, Sir Herbert (who, while he was promoting official inquiry into the atrocious plot, made three or four very friendly calls at the cottage) should carry a tale back with him that might induce Lady Elmsley to believe that Seraphina was, after all, *nothing better than a sort of a kept mistress to young Montfort.*

The fact is, that Sir Herbert *did* carry home a true statement of the case, in all its shades and peculiarities; and it will be seen in the sequel, to the honour of both the worthy baronet and his lady, that neither of them entertained on that account a whit the less esteem and sympathy for our persecuted heroine.

Dr. Pengarron was another person upon whom this frankness of deportment, and the matron-like solicitudes of our heroine had, as we have already noticed, made no unfavourable impression. Its operation, in fact, had been the very reverse.

To behold the countenance and witness the conduct of Seraphina, was at once to be dispossessed of that legion of false impressions that had been conjured into his breast by the spells and mutterings of that subtile cabalist William Lewson. And our good physician had not been above two or three times in her company before he found himself possessed with a very different sort of spirit, that in despite of the cynical turn of his character, and the roughness of his habits, prompted him to a sort of humorous but respectful politeness towards her; and urged him not only to seek and to obtain her confidence, (which was, indeed, no very difficult matter) but produced, also, some other inward workings and cogitations, with whose effects the reader may, perhaps, hereafter become acquainted.

CHAP. III.

The Recovery of Henry; and the Eclaircissement with Seraphina.

Trials of the Heart—The Preamble.—The Prospect.—Revolting Suggestions.—Cordial Recollections.—Decisive Struggles.—Triumphs of the Heart.—The Disclosure.—Reciprocation, or the Logic of Affection.—Definitive Concessions.—Effusions of Social Gaiety.

IN the mean time the health of Henry being sufficiently restored, it became necessary to inform him of the revolution that had taken place in Grosvenor-square: and Seraphina determined to be herself the first to announce the unpropitious event.

As her views, however, went somewhat beyond the mere communication of the intelligence, so, also, she had her peculiar way in which she wished to communicate it. She accordingly developed her plan, in the first instance, to Edmunds and Dr. Pengarron; the latter of whom had become so much attached to her, that, by a sort of transition not uncommon with old gentlemen of his humorous and peculiar character, he was now to the full as anxious for promoting the union between her and Henry, as he had been heretofore to prevent it by his interference: these both of them approving of the whole detail, the Doctor was invited to spend a cheerful evening with them on the recovery of his patient.

The Doctor accepted the invitation, and Henry, Seraphina, and this benevolent oddity, together with Morton and Edmunds, being assembled together in the old lady's best parlour, Seraphina, with a glowing cheek and an eye conscious of the generosity of her feelings, began as follows:

S. "Henry! I am going to put your heart and your affections to the proof. It is time that I should know, Henry, and that the world should know, whether you have really all that romantic affection for me which you have sometimes professed; and for which the few persons who are acquainted with our attachment seem to give you credit."

H. "Do you doubt it, my Seraphina?—do you doubt it?"

S. "Nay, that shall be seen in the sequel. You have given me many proofs, Henry—you have offered me still more; which I have hitherto rejected. But I have now to require of you a still stronger proof than all that you have either given or offered."

"Aye!" said Dr. Pengarron, bluntly—"and I am come here as a witness, to bind you to your promise."

Henry was astonished. His mind was somewhat wounded.

"Does my Seraphina remember the errors that are past so jealously as to think such precautions necessary.

"Humph!—aye!—aye!" says Pengarron, jocularly,—"we believe you to be but a slippery sort of a fellow, young gentleman!—But hear her to the end."

"No!—no!" said Seraphina, pressing his hand, and looking into his eyes with an expression of the utmost tenderness—"I remember them not at all."

The heart of Henry was appeased.

S. "Why I have chosen that this last explanation should be thus public, as it were, you shall know before we separate; and my Henry shall not accuse me of unkindness."

H. "*Last* explanation, Seraphina!"

S. "Yes, Henry—the last. Our arrangements must now be final. I can no longer endure this state of agitation and suspense. I can no longer endure those racking emotions, and that eternal succession of embarrassments and calamities to which our unsettled and unauthorised connection is perpetually giving birth. An end must be put to these. Separation itself, my Henry—however poignant may be the thought—separation itself, once settled and assured, were preferable to this feverish dream of an unstable union; which every accident may interrupt, and the moody caprice of others may destroy."

H. "Separation, Seraphina!—You would not leave me—you would not leave me, Seraphina!"

S. "I would do that, or whatever else the steady convictions of my Henry's heart might dictate. But something must be done."

Peng. (*bantering*) "Hem!—aye!—aye! and quickly too, Master Henry: for I have half a moon's mind to the young lady myself."

H. "My heart—my hand—my dearest Seraphina!—Have I not offered—"

S. "Hold! Henry—hold! I know you have offered—often offered; and I as often have refused. But pause and consider what you are offering now.

"The case is altered.

"I have said, my Henry, that I am now to require a still stronger proof of your affection than any that you have yet given or proposed to give: and it is true.

"You have shown how heroically you could *die* for me. I have now to ask you to *live* in outcast poverty for my sake:—to be an exile from your father's house—a disinherited reprobate:—to give up all the golden expectations of opulence and splendour, in which from your very infancy you have been nurtured:—to take me and beggary to your arms together:—to relinquish all your habits—all your connections—all your views:—to lay aside at once the trappings of fashion and the pride of birth; and consent to eat with me the daily bread of solicitude and toil!

"This is my dowery, Henry. These are the terms on which I claim the execution of your promise. Or, if they seem too hard, take back the vows you have so often made me. My soul shall not reproach you. With one sad kiss of peace we will part for ever. My heart may break: but my tongue shall not repine."

"And is this all, my Seraphina?" exclaimed Henry, clasping her in his arms, with a mingled expression of delight and anguish—"Is this all?—Cruel Seraphina! to suggest a doubt."

S. "No, Henry; this is not all. That is to say, in consequence and particular enumeration, it is not all. It is but the mere outline—the sum total of the account put in a few figures upon paper. To understand the amount you should have it counted out before you.

"Consider well, Henry. You have often offered—not knowing what you offered, to run the hazard of all this: but it is now no longer a hazard. Remember, it is certain. Remember too, that the little property your mother left you is already dissipated—that her jointure, so long as your father lives, you cannot touch—and that of the trifling independence I am entitled to by the will of my lamented foster father, we have as yet neither intelligence nor hopes.

"The sacrifice is more, my Henry, than heretofore you have offered: it is, now, the sacrifice of *all* that remains. Poverty, the scanty meal, the homely apartment, and the threadbare coat, and the necessities of sordid labour might then, with oeconomy, have been avoided. They now can be avoided no more.

"Henry, who has been heretofore waited upon by obsequious throngs, must learn to wait upon himself—nay, upon others. He must open his

own door to the single rap of the petty tradesman, who brings his commodity—or his bill. He must bend his proud spirit to a thousand weary-
ing offices which opulence enjoys without ever recollecting that they have
been performed. He must imitate the example which so many of the
unfortunate noblesse of France are setting before your eyes; must employ,
like them, in the sordid cares of parsimony, those faculties he used to exercise only in the discriminations of taste and the selection of elegant pleasures: like them too he must make the distinctions of his pride a traffic; and
the accomplishments he acquired from the vanity of rank and station, he
must impart again to others, with whom formerly he would scarcely have
conversed, for the hire of a scanty subsistence.

"In other words, he must become the laborious husband of a laborious
wife, and maintain the independency of himself and his little ones by parsimonious abstinence and inglorious toil.

"This canst thou do, my Henry?—for I will never be wedded to
dependent baseness—nor call that man my husband who sells himself to
faction, or cringes at the heels of greatness for patronage and support.

"Thus endowed, canst thou take Seraphina for thy wife?—Canst thou
cease to be the expectant heir of all the vast possessions of Montfort, and
become the unreproaching, unrepining husband of an ill-starred orphan,
whose disastrous love blasts all the budding prospects of thy ambition,
and hurls thee down to the abasements of penury and toil?"

Henry rose from his seat. He walked about the room in great agitation.
The description had brought the whole picture, with all its series of connections and associations, to his mind,

It was a serious question. He had never considered it in so awful a
point of view.

"Friends!—Relatives!—Connections!"—said he to himself.

"Sneering companions of my former affluence!

"The ribald jest!—

"The cold disavowal!—

"The averted eye!—

"The pointed finger of derision!—

"The still more degrading profession of pity and commiseration!—

"The dejected brow!—

"The proffered charity!—

"Death and all its furies!!!—"

His pace quickened—His eye rolled wildly.—His bosom laboured—
His whole frame was agitated: almost convulsed.

Seraphina sympathised in all his agitations. She felt the pangs of compassion—the awfulness of suspense. Her bosom laboured, also; and her
heart fluttered and trembled, as the bird that is falling from its perch.

Even Pengarron betrayed some emotion.

Edmunds trembled. Had he been a Quaker, he would certainly have
believed that *the spirit moved him* to fortify the staggering virtue of our
hero with the eloquence of exhortation. He did almost believe it as it was:

for his mind ran over in an instant all the heads of a splendid harrangue; and the energies of language—"thoughts that breathe and words that burn"[1]—were pregnant in his brain:—upon his tongue.

"And what is all," he could have said, "in comparison with what *she* has sacrificed for you?" a text upon which he could have commented by the hour; had not Seraphina previously imposed the seal of her absolute injunction; and stipulated, when she first suggested her plan, that the heart of Henry should be left entirely to the operation of its own unprompted feelings.

As for Morton (who neither liked the picture, nor the prospect in any of its shapes,) she cherished the silent hope that for once her established creed of the infatuated folly of our sex would fail of illustration; and that Henry would have the common sense, as she called it, to decline.

But Henry turned his eyes upon Seraphina. They met with hers, moist with the expression of a generous sympathy. He gazed for some seconds upon her face. He surveyed her all over: traversing again and again each particular excellency of form, and tint, and texture, with a still growing ecstacy. His heart beat softer. His eye lost its wildness.

"And such a mind too!" continued he, pursuing the chain of exclamation aloud, in which his soul had been silently indulging—

"And such a mind!"

The tears gushed as he spoke—

"Such matchless virtue!—So dignified, yet so amiable!—So awful, yet so lovely!"

Seraphina blushed. The modest curtains dropped over the eyes that had inspired this rhapsody; and nothing but the stealing tear was to be seen. The sun was veiled; but the dew drops were glittering beneath.

The heart of Edmunds began to leap about in his bosom.

Pengarron could not think what it was that made his eyes water so.

As for Morton, she looked somewhat blank.

"Is she not all," continued Henry to himself, "that the soul can pant for?—Friends! relatives! society! respect, and wealth, and dignity, and honour?—an intellectual universe?—a concentrated world?

"Did she not seem so in the bower of Margot, when not the very tythe of her excellence was known?—when the beauteous casket alone had been examined, and my soul was yet unconscious of the inestimable value of the gems within!

"The bower of Margot!" said he aloud—"the bower of Margot!"

A thousand tender associations rushed upon his mind:—a thousand generous recollections.

Yet "still the *world* prevailed, and its dread laugh!"[2] and his frame began once more to be agitated.

---

1 Thomas Gray, "The Progress of Poesy" (1757), l. 110.
2 James Thomson, *Autumn* (1730), l. 233.

"The world!—the world!!" repeated he, communing within himself—"How many of those petty circles we call *worlds* are there upon this little sphere?"

The thought struck him like electricity.

His doubts were ended. He rushed to his Seraphina. He seized her in his arms; and straining her throbbing heart to his—

"Yes—yes, I can"; he exclaimed, while he kissed away the falling tears—"my wife!—my all!—my Seraphina!—Yes, I can:—but not in England. No, not in England, Seraphina!"

"No: not in England"; answered Seraphina, returning all his tenderness. "That were, I know, impossible.

"And canst thou then consent to become a vagrant exile for my sake?"

H. "There is no exile but from Seraphina!"

"No, no, sir," echoed Edmunds, sobbing and leaping about for joy, at his conclusion—"No—no, there is not; and I'll go with you, wherever you go, to the furthest extremity of the world—to the deserts of Siberia—to the unexplored regions of Africa:—any—any where:—but to the West Indies, sir,—to fight against the poor blacks."

"Well, Henry, I shall put you to the test," said Seraphina, recollecting herself.

"You call yourself the son and heir of Percival Montfort. You know the opulence to which, as such, you have looked forward. You know what it is to indulge, to the full extent, in all the luxuries and enjoyments that wealth can secure.

"Here I stand, a poor unfortunate orphan. You know my dowery, Henry; and you know, also, that my unthrifty generosity has conspired with my misfortunes, and has left me *nothing* to bestow. But I am weary of the life I lead—weary of expectation—weary of the world's scorn—and still more weary of the persecutions that result from the uncertain state. I know that your father is fixed against me. You, also, know how immoveable he has always been. You cannot be at once my husband and his son.

"Think of it well then, Henry. Such, and so friendless, as I am, will you, for my sake, renounce the prospects you were born to?—will you take me with all this dowery of misfortunes, and, by making me your immediate wife, shut the doors of your father for ever against you?"

H. "I will, by heaven! Fix but the day, and dearest Seraphina—an early day. Let that day be to-morrow."

S. "No, not so hastily, Henry—not so hastily. Is there no possible circumstance, thinkest thou, Henry," added she with an air of mystery, "that may have happened since you received that forged—that fatal letter, that might urge you to retract the promise? Are you ready to pledge yourself to that?"

The soul of Henry was thrilled with horror. As the sort of circumstance she alluded to never entered into his brain, another of a much more horrible description did.

"Since that fatal letter!" repeated he, trembling, and looking wildly—"the horrid ruffians!—sure it is not possible—Oh, Seraphina!"

Seraphina shuddered at the idea she had evidently, though unintentionally, suggested. She was about to undeceive him. But he prevented her—

"No, no—not even that, my Seraphina!—not even that"—exclaimed he, snatching her to his agitated bosom—"Misfortune, however terrible, is not guilt—nor sufferance pollution!"

"Generous, beyond the trial I meant to make of thee!" exclaimed Seraphina, in an agony of delightful emotion—"I meant not that, my love!—I meant not that. Thy Seraphina stands above the reach of pollution.—That could never happen."

Then, after a pause—

"But it is time, Henry, to reveal the cause of this mysterious conduct:—to tell you why I have drawn from you this solemn promise: why I have called you, thus, before witnesses, that should bear testimony to the troth you have pledged.

"It is because when the altered circumstances shall be stated to you—when that one event to which I alluded, and which you so widely misapprehend, shall be made known to you, as now it must—these, these who have heard the unexampled generosity of your resolutions, should sit in judgment between us, should you endeavour to evade the little (little indeed it is) that may appear like generosity in me.

"Oh Henry, Henry! with what proud delight have I heard the generous offers of the sacrifices you were ready to make!—With how proud a delight (for misfortune thus becomes delightful) can I now pronounce, that *you have no such sacrifices to make*—that you are already no more the heir of Percival Montfort—that you are banished already from his roof!

"Here are the letters, Henry, that contain the decree. Here are the letters that authorise me without delay to consent to what my heart desires."

She gave them to him—the brief note of Montfort, and the malignant homily of Woodhouse; and while he was reading these, she continued walking about the room, calming the agitations of her heart.

"You see, my Henry," resumed she, "the cause why I am changed;—why I compromise with fortune no more. There is nothing now to compromise about. It was not my wish to share the affluence of Henry that made me repel the propositions by which that affluence might have been endangered. No, no—it was for his sake, and for his alone, that I advised him to steer the middle course of prudence. If, in defiance of that prudence, the event should happen, which now has taken place, it was my meditated resolution to do as I have done; because then I might be, at once, both blest and guiltless:—blest with my Henry; guiltless of his ruin!

"I am *the cause* indeed, my Henry!" continued she, taking him by the hand, while her eyes were full of tears—"*the fatal cause*: I warned you from the first that I should be so:—but, fatal as I am, I am innocent! The blow that was aimed at thy heart has reached thy *fortune*: through me it was aimed, it is true: but it was aimed at my heart also."

"Why, let it go," said Henry, clearing his brow, and assuming the better heroism of philosophy—"let it go, my Seraphina,—the worst of it only is that it has robbed me of the power of making that sacrifice, which it seems you never would have suffered me to make."

S. "No, never, my dearest Henry—most assuredly never. This act of persecuting fortune had forced us upon one of those bold leaps, by which I feel myself confident we may reach the shore of felicity, but which it would have been madness voluntarily to take.

S. "Yes, Henry, we may still be happy. I am confident,—thanks to the fostering care of the ever-honoured Parkinson—I am confident I have the resources within me; by which (in whatever quarter of the world we may think fit to settle) a humble, but reputable subsistence may be obtained. I am conscious, also, that it is upon my resources, almost exclusively, that we must depend.—Your habits—your feelings—the very texture of your constitution and your mind, forbid you to accommodate yourself to many exertions, which to me will be recreation and pleasure.

"On these, then, we must depend. These must be my trade; my calling. For we must subsist, Henry; we and our little ones—if with little ones we are blest; and effort can alone subsist us. Henry we must therefore consent that the attainments I owe to the diligent instructions of fostering love, should be converted into the means of our emolument and support;—that the accomplishments, in which his flattering commendations have taught me so much to pride myself, should be put up to sale and barter, that he, and that I, and the little pledges of our mutual loves may derive from them the vulgar accommodations of food and raiment.

"I see, my Henry, what is struggling in your mind. I see that my precautions were not vain. I see the daemon of false pride is rising in your heart: but we have a spell to charm him down.

"Would Henry have made all the sacrifices he has offered?—Let us consider them then as made. Nay, he did make them. All that is essential in the morality of human action, he has essentially performed:—for

"The intent and not the deed is in our power:
And therefore who dares nobly—nobly does."[1]

"The act of the mind is thine, my Henry—the resolve; the effort; the soul; the substance of virtuous achievement:—Fortune robbed thee only of the empty form of action.

"Well, then; Henry has made a voluntary sacrifice to love and Seraphina of fortune, of country, of friends. Henry has thrown himself a friendless outcast on the world for her; and Seraphina, as it happens, has a little property—an inherent property of acquisition and of mind. Shall Henry refuse to share a part with her for whom he has given all? Shall her

---

1 Misquoted from *Barbarossa*, a popular 1754 tragedy by John Brown (1715-66): "who dares greatly / Does greatly."

sacrifices be refused, because it is so poor a mite? Was she worthy the price that Henry paid for her in these offers? and is she, at the same time, so unworthy, and so base, that it is degradation to receive kindnesses from her?

"For shame,—for shame, Henry!—Did you insult me with offers from the revenues of dirty acres, and are you ashamed to share with me the revenues (if smaller, yet more noble) that may spring from my inheritance of mind?

"I call for judgment—Is Henry at liberty to retract? Is Henry at liberty to refuse participation in the earnings of that industry, which the ruin that has overwhelmed him, through his disinterested love for me, has rendered necessary for his support?

"Henry loves not Seraphina, if his pride revolts from this proposition?—Henry loves not Seraphina as Seraphina can alone endure to be beloved, if he is not capable of that entire and absolute union of soul, which in all considerations of this kind annihilates individuality; and, without balancing, in the nice scale of traffic, the reciprocations of mutual aid, considers the blended stock of both, whether of accumulated production or productive power, as the common property of each.

"Whatever is either mine *or* yours, is both yours *and* mine. When the knot of indissoluble union once is tied—nay, when hearts are once actually united, the pronouns *my* and *thy* are, in this sense, obliterated and expunged—it is *our* efforts, *our* earnings, *our* necessities from that day:— *our* hopes, *our* fears; *our* solicitudes, *our* happiness, or *our* woes!

"These are the only possible conditions upon which, under any circumstances, an union could subsist between Henry and Seraphina: and under the present circumstances these he shall not refuse.

"Friends, fortune, country, he could sacrifice for me; for without his Seraphina Henry could not live. But I am insatiable of sacrifices. He has given up nothing till he has given up all. To me also, his *false pride* must be sacrificed: for Seraphina cannot live without her Henry."

"Transcendent excellence!" said Henry, clasping her to his bosom— "thou more than man in dignity and firmness—in every alluring softness more than woman!

"But when, my Seraphina, when shall I be completely blest? When shall my soul identify itself with thine, and, losing its own worthless individuality in indissoluble union with thy nobler qualities, be authorised, in the honest pride of regeneration, to boast of our magnanimity, our fortitude!—our transcendent generosity, that the malice of fortune cannot limit!—our confiding constancy, that no wrongs can shake!—our purity, that neither temptation can seduce, example contaminate, nor lawless violence defile!—our virtues exalted above the limits of morality! our boundless expansion of intellect and of heart!"

"Fie! fie!" answered Seraphina, blending rebuke with a blush and a smile, "if you talk thus it must *never* be, lest *our vanity* should spoil every thing."

"Troth, thou art a noble wench!" said Pengarron, jumping up and kissing her (for he was no longer able to restrain his ecstacy)—"If women had been made after this fashion when I was young, I would never have remained an old bachelor to these days.

"There never was but one: never, but one: and a dissipated prodigal had snapt her up before me, to help that young reprobate there into the world, as dissipated and as prodigal as himself. But look you, young sir, keep your mother's example before your eyes for the future; and think it your duty to forget your father as completely as he can forget you: for, if ever you should take it into your crazy brain, or your rotten heart, to run into your old courses again, you had best never be sick upon it—or at least not call me to prescribe for you if you are so; for I'll give arsenic for your physic, you young rascal—arsenic, as sure as you are born. I'll poison him, like a rat, for thy sake, chick," concluded he, offering to kiss her again.

"Nay, nay, doctor," said Seraphina, "that is a contract we shall never seal, I assure you. Besides, doctor," continued she archly, "I will answer for him; upon condition that you and Lewson do not send him again to Brighthelmstone, to cure a rheum, and catch *the Melinda*."

Pen. "Umph!—Umph!—Aye! Plague confound it! this comes of us old fellows (bags of rattling bones without marrow!) interfering in young folks' matters—Plague upon it! We must leave the young devils to themselves, I believe.

"That old rascal, Percival, there too—with his methodistical tricks and his surly humours!—Gout and stone and gravel upon him!—Or apoplexy—aye, apoplexy (if he has not made his will yet), a good thorough apoplexy would be best of all. *He* must be led by the nose too by that canting rascally priest Woodhouse, and have no bowels for the follies of youth, because they have a little more principle than his own.

"Plague upon him! If he could but have heard her now—it would have made a better convert of him than a conventicle sermon!

"A murrain[1] o' this head—a murrain!—If I had but a memory now, to carry away these things—or if I had thought of bringing one of our parliamentary reporters with me, and clapped him with his ear against the shutter there, to take it down in short hand—[2]

"But come, when is it to be?—when is it to be?—when are we to go to church?

"You see what pain I take for you—you young reprobate! You shall name the first boy Pengarron—The first shall be a Pengarron."

---

1 See p. 293, note 1.

2 Thelwall employed a man to take shorthand notes of his lectures, in case charges of sedition were laid. The ear to the keyhole motif is used effectively in one of his most famous lectures, "On the Moral Tendency of a System of Spies and Informers" (1794).

H. "I hope not, doctor—for my Seraphina and I have agreed to adopt no names from contemporary worthies till death has put the seal of consistency upon them."

P. "Humph! No?—But suppose I should be inclined to adopt him, and make him heir of what I have?—Won't that alter the question?—'Tis my own earning—all my own—and if I have a mind to play a bachelor's trick, what's that to the whole rascally legion of second and third cousins that have been gaping open-mouthed like so many carrion crows, for my death, these ten or twenty years, in hopes that each may have a mouthful of my carcase? And my carcase they may take, if they will—for they shall have none of my estate—A plague upon all cousins and cousinings! I say—What affinity can there be between me and a parcel of hungry legacy-hunters?—I'll have an heir of my own—So, when are we to go to church? That you may set to work, and get me one as soon as you can."[1]

S. "Fie! fie, doctor!—I declare I must run away from you, if you talk at this rate.

"You know we cannot answer that question yet. I have an important visit to make to-morrow."

H. "Visit, Seraphina! what visit?"

P. "Umph!—To-morrow!—No—no—'t must not be to-morrow. He'll be engaged to-morrow—it must not be to-morrow."

S. "Engaged!"

P. "What now?—What, you're impatient too, are you?—you sly vixen!—A day, to be sure, makes a great difference!—Lover's days!—"

S. "Fie! fie upon you, doctor!—what constructions!"

P. "Well, well, I tell you it cannot be to-morrow. I know he will be engaged to-morrow. So, can't you do as I bid you, without more words, and put it off till the next day?"

S. "Well, doctor! it shall be just as you wish."

P. "Well said, now—well said—that's as it should be. I'll lay a month's fees you don't answer your husband so prettily six months hence. But I suppose wishing is to go by *we* and *our* too. *I* and *you* and *your* and *my*, and so forth, are to be entirely out of the question."

S. "We will endeavour to make them so, doctor."

H. "But what is all this about, Seraphina?—Whom are you going to visit?"

S. "Hold your tongue, Henry: *Can't you do as I bid you, without any more words?* You see I can be as absolute as the doctor himself. And prithee let me be so: for my power, it seems, is to be of short duration. By and bye, Henry (perhaps in three or four days) it shall be *our* projects, and *our* appointments: but, for the present, I am determined to enjoy at once the

---

1 In the delightful Dr. Pengarron, Thelwall combined a familiar character of stage comedy and of Smollett's novels with several "kind doctors" of his acquaintance, as well as his grandfather Walter, a naval surgeon, to create a vivid proto-Dickensian "character" (indeed several details here seem to foreshadow *Great Expectations*).

privileges of liberty and individuality, and cling to those dear—delightful pronouns (ah! poor departing friends! that must so soon be buried!)—*me*, and *my*, and *mine*!"[1]

---

1 The play on pronouns here reflects Thelwall's interest in both John Horne Tooke's revolutionary politics of language and etymology in the late eighteenth century, and Wollstonecraft's equally revolutionary questioning of the law of man and woman as one after marriage.

BOOK XI.
=========
CHAP. I.

Schemes of Dr. Pengarron to reconcile Old Montfort to Henry, and the purposed Marriage.

The Project.—The Atonement.—Prescriptions for Hypochondria.—
Traits of Penetration and Character.—The detection.—Specious Evasions.—The detection.—Confronting Facts.—Diamond cut Diamond.—
Religious Distinctions; or, A Layman's Faith.—The Atonement.—
Crotchets of Benevolence.—The Confidant exchanged; Symptoms of
intellectual Imbecility.—The Conference.—Overtures and Apologies.—
Discords and Unisons.—Vibrations of Conscience.—Symptoms of
Conciliation.—Scruples and Agitations.—Struggles of Remorse.—
Repentance and Reparation.

IF the reader be one of those who has hitherto considered our heroine as
having somewhat of the romantic in her sentiments and conduct, he may
not perhaps be very much inclined to alter that opinion, when he is
informed that the meditated important visit, alluded to at the conclusion of
the preceding book, was to no other person than the father of our hero, Percival Montfort, Esq. Of Grosvenor-square: and it may be thought, perhaps,
an equal proof of her presumption, and her enthusiasm, when it is acknowledged that she was not entirely without hopes of operating some change in
his mind, and inducing him to relax in his hostility, both to Henry and to
the determined nuptials; or, if she could not absolutely persuade him to
restore to his favour a repudiated son, and acknowledge as his daughter that
only partner with whom that son could have felicity or peace, she hoped, at
least, so far to mitigate his obduracy, that the embarrassments of Henry
might not, by swallowing up entirely the little property bequeathed him by
his mother, and the reversionary expectancy of her jointure, leave them
absolutely destitute upon the world; or give the appearance of a disgraceful
flight from the claims of injured creditors, to the voluntary exile which their
circumstances occasioned them to meditate.

When the bases, however, of her reasoning upon this subject are understood, the project may not appear quite so extravagant.

It was evident that the indignation that had produced the final reprobation of Henry (for as *final* at least it was denounced), whatever foundations it might have in the evil humours of the old man, or the indiscretions
and irregularities of the young one, was principally rested by Montfort
himself upon two pretences or assumptions which not only were completely false, but with respect to both of which, it was fortunately very
practicable to give the clearest demonstrations of their falsehood.

The undutiful conduct charged upon Henry on the report of his
father's death, in the first letter from Southampton, and the terms in

which our heroine herself was alluded to, both in the enclosed and enclosing letter in which the reprobation was announced, made it evident that the characters of both were materially misunderstood: and Seraphina, at any rate, resolved, that, disinherited or not disinherited—acknowledged as children or exiled as strangers, at least they would be known for what they were. The morning therefore having arrived on which, according to the final arrangement with Dr. Pengarron, the grand attack was to be made, she put into her pocket the letter written by Henry at the time when his feelings were represented to have been so undutiful, and, without disclosing her intentions either to her mother or to Henry, took the former with her, and set off in a hackney coach to pay another visit to her some time residence in Grosvenor-square.

At Grosvenor-square she arrived; and her reception there, in the first instance, was so very different from any thing she had reason to expect, that, before we announce it to the reader, it may be necessary, by way of preparation, to enter into those preceding circumstances that led to this extraordinary change.

The fact is, that Dr. Pengarron had been labouring very hard, ever since the arrival of Montfort from Southampton (and more and more in proportion as he became better acquainted with the real character of our heroine), to make a noble atonement for the injurious suspicions and conduct into which he had been betrayed by the plots and artifices of Lewson.

The state of Montfort's health—or rather his mind (for there the disease principally lay)—gave all the opportunities that could be desired. For he had no sooner arrived in Grosvenor-square (which he did the very day after the Rev. Emanuel Woodhouse, and on the very day that our heroine returned to the cottage) than he sent for Dr. Pengarron, in whom he had that sort of confidence the most important in such a state as his: the confidence of habit—the impression that he had always done well in his hands—and the sort of tacit inference that, therefore, well he must always do. In the whole class of hypochondria and disorders of the mind, this sort of confidence is undoubtedly more important than all the science of the medical profession; though in this respect also our humorous and benevolent doctor was very eminently endowed.

Pengarron soon discovered that this was one of those cases, by no means the first that had fallen within the course of his practice, in which it was his duty to take his daily fee for sitting half an hour by the side of his patient, and talking him into a good humour with himself and others.[1]

This was a task, indeed, for which he was peculiarly gifted. Familiar in his manners; in his humour, at once cynical and benevolent; and, in con-

---

1 Pengarron's remarkably modern, holistic approach to medicine in this scene also reflects Thelwall's own methods, as outlined in his *Letter to Cline*, in which he recognizes that "physical and moral phaenomena run a circle, and become alternately cause and effect."

versation, not less intellectual and vivacious than he was garrulous and *outré*; he abounded at the same time in those tales and anecdotes of former days that are so delightful to the prejudices of that season of life in which such diseases are mostly prevalent. And as he knew very well that in such cases the prescription is only amusement, and the amusement is the real physic, his qualifications and his management seldom failed to give him considerable influence over patients of this class: an influence he had used to the best of purposes; for, as it generally happens among such that there is something or other, in the texture or temporary dispositions of the heart, that, in a moral and social point of view, is not exactly right, he had found many opportunities of exerting that influence in restoring the violated peace of families, and rendering this species of professional friendship conducive to the best interests of private morality and individual happiness.

The first look of Montfort, and the first word he spoke, convinced him of the nature of his disease: and the first thought that occurred to him was, that the chaplain, as he called Woodhouse, was one of the designing, as himself had, in some respect, been one of the unintentional, causes of the aggravation of this complaint.

A little conversation soon confirmed this suspicion. It was very evident that though there were some latent causes of despondency and remorse (and the doctor perhaps imagined he could guess at some of them,) yet, at present at least, the symptoms most predominant were fanaticism and paternal irritation.

Dr. Pengarron had, at this time, been once in company with Seraphina: (for he had visited Henry in the morning, and was called to old Montfort in the afternoon:) and the interview had made some impression. He had, also, seen the epistolary homily of the holy chaplain; and, what is more, he had seen the face of the holy chaplain himself: and the doctor, if not *by science*, was so much of a physiognomist *by sensation*, that he could see at once certain traits at least at gun-shot off, as for example, whether a face was naked in simplicity, or had a mask of hypocrisy an inch thick upon it.[1] He had therefore seen enough to be aware that poor Henry must have a special game played against him, with the glass upon the one side and the false dice upon the other; and that he himself had made a pretty mess of it, by throwing the cards into the hands of these sharpers, and "lending his beak, to be sure, to these rascally rooks, and croaking carrion crows, to strip a pair of cooing pigeons that had never picked the mortar from his house.—A murrain to it!"

Sympathy therefore, in part, and partly conscience and his impressions of religion, (which though not very fanatical were very sincere, and some-

---

1 Thelwall's interest in physiognomy, the study of facial features and bodily gestures as an indication of character, is evident throughout his career, from the early essays on Lavater (1741-1801); one of the most influential theorists of this ancient "science," he wrote for the *Biographical and Imperial Magazine*.

times very fervent) irresistibly impelled him to endeavour, as has already been observed, to make some recompense for the injury he had committed.

Every interview with our heroine increased the force of this propensity; so that he became every day more and more enthusiastical in the prosecution of the plan he had already begun to act upon, not only for the restoration of Henry to the good graces of his father, but, also, for drawing him, by hook or by crook, into a concurrence with so desirable a match.

His first care was so to manage with the old man, that, without appearing to be the advocate of the offending son, he might lay open all the artifices that had been made use of for his seduction (as far, at least, as he was acquainted with them,) and the characters and designs of those by whom he had been seduced. In the execution of this part of his project, our good doctor was not at all sparing in the exposure either of the fair Melinda, or her no less crafty brother. Both of these, indeed, he took care to lay out in such colours, bringing at the same time such circumstances of proof against them, that, notwithstanding all the wealth of the deceased nabob, Montfort (whose pride was not extinguished by his rapacity) began to consider the disappointment of his views, with respect to the projected marriage, as a sort of lucky escape: and Pengarron had even the art, while he yet appeared to be falling in with the general sentiment of Montfort's paternal reprobation, to throw in such particulars of the character and history of the heroine of our tale, as made her seduction appear the most reprehensible part of Henry's conduct. And indeed, independent of the policy of this, it was becoming every day more and more the preponderating feeling in the doctor's mind. The reconciliation grew to be an object of less importance than the marriage; and the happiness of Henry (at first the main purport of his anxiety) to be principally regarded only as an essential to the felicity of Seraphina.

When the mind of Montfort was thus predisposed for the reception of more favourable impressions, our worthy doctor took care to introduce the subject of the sickness and deportment of Henry "upon the forged process of his father's death":[1] the filial emotions, the altered habits, the reflection and symptoms of returning virtue that ensued;—the solicitudes of Seraphina (which he had since learned from the servants, and which he called upon the servants to prove) to retain him in those habits; and above all the villainous schemes of Lewson to drag him back again to the paths of licentious prodigality, that he might trepan him into a marriage with his no less licentious and still more prodigal sister.

This narrative, so different in many essential particulars from the reports of Woodhouse, made some impressions upon the mind of Montfort, notwithstanding the hold that pious gentleman had taken upon his irritable, rather than tender *conscience*: impressions that were not a little

---

1 *Hamlet* 1.5.37.

strengthened when the pretended West India letter (by which the reader will remember that the intelligence of Montfort's death was conveyed to Henry) happened to fall, among Henry's other papers, into the old gentleman's hand.

The ink within tallied not very well in colour with the ink without; and the hand, though somewhat disguised, had yet, upon examination, the characteristic marks of the writing of the person to whom it was directed, rather than of the direction itself. Besides, it was signed with the name of a person who, it was clear and palpable, could never have fallen into the mistake that it contained.

The assurance and policy of Woodhouse, however, seemed to help him through this awkward business in a most notable way: for the suspicion was no sooner suggested, than, with admirable effrontery and presence of mind, he avowed the forgery.

"He had such good reasons to suspect that the heart of the unrepentant prodigal had entirely fallen away from the reverence due to the fifth commandment (assuredly the most sacred and inviolable of the whole Decalogue, in which it has pleased Almighty God to reveal his moral will to blind and sinful mortals,)[1] that he had deemed it a sacred duty to his conscience, to his generous patron, and to the inquisitorial functions of an office, instituted by the Lord himself, for the searching and trying of the hearts of men, not indeed like a papal inquisitor, with the rude hand of violence, to tear away the mask of hypocrisy, but, in a way more consistent with the pure spirit of meekness, to give the hypocrite an opportunity of laying itself aside; and throwing his undutifulness in all its naked deformity."

"And are you sure, Mr. Woodhouse," said Montfort, "that he did discover this deformity? Were your visits frequent?—Did you see his apparent exultations, his dissipations—his enormities, with your own eyes?"

"Heaven forbid!" replied Woodhouse—"Was it consistent with the known severity of my morals—with the sacredness of my holy character, that I should mingle with these sons of Belial! that I should participate in these profane orgies and abominations? Was I for the service of my earthly patron (my good and generous, yet still but earthly, patron!) to offend that most awful Patron that is on high, by partaking, or but seeming to partake, in these fleshly lusts and vanities? Could I have done this, sir, how could I have expected those helps and lights of the divine grace that have enabled me to be a ministering vessel of repentance, of hope and consolation to your afflicted mind?"

But although this holy jargon silenced, for awhile, the suspicions of the devotee, the confession was productive of consequences little expected. It happened that Dr. Pengarron, to whom Montfort had shown the letter, was immediately stricken "with a sort of confused impression, that he had seen something like the same sort of hand-writing before; and under some

---

1 The fifth commandment is "Honour thy father and mother."

sort of a villainous association or another: but rheums and catarrhs upon his stupid head if he could remember a word about the where, or the how!"

The suspicion was natural enough, in the state of the Doctor's mind, even if there had been nothing in it:—for it was, in fact, constantly on that stretch of watchful jealousy which results from the joint conviction of the hypocrisy of a despised object, and the importance of his detection to some favourite project or pursuit. In such a state of mind the faintest traces of similitude are easily revived in the sensorium, and memory will often challenge as her own, even the mere impressions of fancy.

In the present instance, however, the recollection, though faint, was real; and at length, after battering his brains about for a whole night to no purpose, the accidental circumstance of seeing the name of Lewson on the plate of the door as he rode through Baker-street to visit a patient, brought to his remembrance the anonymous letters that junior impostor had produced, in support of his calumnies against Seraphina.

The suspicion suggested the idea of a fine train of discoveries. If it could but be made to appear, as now seemed very likely, that Woodhouse had fabricated the report of Montfort's death, for the express purpose of hurrying on that very marriage of which he had constantly expressed such abhorrence; and that he had been in the habit of making the most profligate of Henry's associates instruments of his designs for drawing that unwary youth into such measures as might effectually ruin him with his father; he should at least strip the wolf of his sheep's clothing, and spoil the chaplain's preferment, if he did not even restore an injured son to the pardon and good graces of his father.

But how to get at these documents? In friendship to Henry they would never be produced. Might they not be extorted from enmity?

Lewson was too conscious how completely all his despicable artifices must have been exposed, and how contemptible a figure he must make in the eye of Henry, and of every person to whom Henry might repeat the tale, not to be desirous completely to crush, and exile him from all those circles of society in which otherwise they might happen to encounter. And as everything that could depreciate the character of Seraphina might easily enough be represented as involving the more assured disgrace and reprobation of her lover (or, as he might be called by a designed anticipation, her husband,) Pengarron made up a plausible tale of a discovery of the scribe she had employed in composing those artful documents; and, having taught the lesson to a proper agent, sent him to Lewson to persuade him to produce the documents themselves, which were now, it was pretended, all that were requisite to complete a disgrace and exposure, the prospect of which it was foreseen would be so gratifying to his malevolence.

Lewson fell into the snare. He even outstripped the expectations of the Doctor: for he enclosed them in a malignant and triumphant letter to old Montfort, that betrayed his exultation over the ruin of a friend, whom, it was by this time evident, his parasitical and seductive artifices, rather than his own natural propensities, had conspired to ruin.

Pengarron exulted, in his turn, in having outwitted his deceiver, and taken his revenge upon him in his own coin. He exulted still more, when, on comparing the anonymous letters with the pretended communications from the West Indies, Montfort admitted them to be indisputably the same.

"Umph! And what do you think now of your Man of God?" said Pengarron. "A murrain upon these canting, praying, eye-lifting hypocrites! A murrain upon them! I never knew any of these over-godly fellows good for any thing in my life. While they are canting about another world, they are always playing one rascally trick or another to feather their nests in this: and when they lift up their right hand in prayer to heaven, take care they are not picking your pocket with the left.

"Gout, stone, and gravel upon them! and an empty pocket, that they may die without a physician to help them out of the world, or a draught of opium to quiet their consciences in their last moments!

"Not that I am an enemy to religion, friend Montfort—No, no. I can't fall into these newfangled notions neither. I reverence religion; and its ministers, when they are its ministers indeed; and do the work of their Master, by making peace between man and man. I had a mind to have been a parson myself once; only I don't like tests:[1] and I am not stiff enough for a Presbyterian. I love a dash of waggery, or so, that don't suit with a cloak and band. But I trust I've religion enough to help a layman to heaven as it is. I pray sometimes; and I believe always: and now and then I practise a little, without making a fuss about it. If I meet with a misfortune I take it as a chastisement, and bear it without repining: and if good luck falls in my way, why, I thank God for it; and that makes me enjoy it so much the more. But that which of all things I thank God for most fervently, is, that I am neither fanatic, hypocritical, nor intolerant. I can bear with all sorts and sects; infidels and all;—your canting infidels excepted: a tribe of rascally Pharisees! whose mouths are always full of godliness, while their actions are a perpetual series of atheism. A plague upon them! I could be Catholic enough to hate them heartily, for God's sake, as well as my own; for they blaspheme him worse than the open Atheist; aye, and make a worse jest of him too: for a jest is never so ridiculous as when you put a grave face upon it.

"As for the rest, friend Montfort,—the repentance, and making peace with heaven, and so forth, that this fellow was always canting about—I'll tell you my rule in a few words; and I never knew it fail of comforting and consoling me. If I have done a man an injury, I make him amends: and if he has happened to slip out of my way, by death or any other accident, I

---

1 From 1673 until the repeal of the Test Act in 1828, British citizens were subject to a religious test, which excluded Catholics, Nonconformists, and Dissenters (e.g., Baptists, Unitarians etc.) from holding public office or attending university.

look out for somebody else that is in want, and make him amends in his place. And, as to the follies and vices of my youth, friend Montfort!— when I recollect these—why *I show my repentance by making allowance for those of others!*"[1]

The full development of this discovery took place the very morning preceding the eclarcissement between Henry and Seraphina. The doctor neglected not the opportunity of turning it to the purpose of the main design; and the success of these efforts was such as sent him to the fulfilment of his engagements with the lovers, in a frame of mind very well calculated to enjoy the tender scene that followed.

Neither Henry nor Seraphina, indeed, knew any thing of the attack he had been making upon the prejudices and feelings of Montfort. It was not till the latter communicated to him the projects she was meditating, that he so much as informed either of them that he had, at present, any intercourse whatever with him. For the doctor had his oddities even in his benevolence. Nothing in nature was good with him without its joke, verbal or practical; and part of the relish of this adventure was derived from the whim, or, as he called it to himself, his deep stroke of policy, in playing the mediator and go-between to bring the parties together; and making them all happy, without either of them knowing that he had any communion with the other.

The frankness of Seraphina, therefore, rather disconcerted him. It put secrecy out of countenance. He contrived, however, still to keep his own counsel as to the main. And, finding that their schemes chimed in very well together, he just promised her a lift in his way, as a peace-offering for the past; but in reality set all his engines to work, and pushed on the attack with so much the more vigour to prepare the old gentleman for her reception.

This he now supposed to be pretty well done.

Woodhouse was to all appearance effectually disgraced. His frauds and impositions were brought to light; a sense of the unfair play that had been given to Henry was impressed upon the mind of his father; and Pengarron had not been wanting in doing whatever could be done, without avowing acquaintance with her (which would have spoiled the finesse of the thing,) to place the character of our heroine in a very different point of view from that which had resulted from the clerical commentary on Moroon's factitious specimen of her works: a task for which the genuine specimen that had fallen into the hands of Montfort, just before his departure from Southampton, had done some thing to pave the way: as well as

---

1 Pengarron's religious philosophy matches Thelwall's own. Like Pengarron, Thelwall was as a young man a religious enthusiast and "complete church-and-king man" (*Life* 22), and while later he became (and was criticized as) an "infidel," he always advocated ecumenical tolerance, admired Quakers for their principled benevolence and good works, and supported Catholic emancipation (his second wife was Catholic).

some other effusions of her pen, which, as they were found among Henry's papers, Montfort was still too much of a father not to think himself at liberty to peruse.

Pengarron had, therefore, told Seraphina privately, on his first arrival at the cottage, that he had been sounding the old gentleman; that every thing was ready; and that the sooner she made her final assault the better.

But the scene that followed had struck him with such delight and admiration, and so raised the character of Seraphina in his esteem, that by a sudden quirk of the brain, to which he was a little subject, he changed, at once, his whole plan of operation: determined to make another and more open attack himself upon the prejudices of the old gentleman; to declare openly, all he had seen, all he had learned, and all he believed and felt concerning her: to relate, so far as he was acquainted with them, (which, indeed, was somewhat more imperfectly than he was himself aware) all the circumstances of her interesting story; and to give him such a picture of the excellence of her understanding and her heart, as must, he thought, if there were any thing like human sympathy in the soul of Montfort, dispose him to give her at least an indulgent hearing. And if that were once obtained, he had no doubt that Seraphina herself would be certain to secure all the rest.

It was thus that his parting tale came to disagree with his meeting salutation: a disagreement, as has been seen, that had occasioned our heroine to be so much surprised at his proposal for deferring her purposed visit. She had no doubt, however, that he had some crotchet or other in his head more likely to make harmony than discord in the tune she was about to play; and, therefore, very contentedly acquiesced.

Our benevolent doctor lost no time in the verification of this conjecture. He went to Grosvenor-square the following day, somewhat later, indeed, than usual: but it was only because he was determined to have time to extend his visit as the necessity of the case should require; and had, accordingly, hurried through all his other engagements before he entered upon this.

He could not possibly have found his patient in a better humour for the furtherance of his design. To speak professionally, the state of his pulse indicated a predisposition in the constitution of the exhibition of the purposed menstruum.[1]

The chaplain had been disgraced and dismissed. The impressions his artful malignity had made to the discredit of Henry, began, in some degree, to operate by inversion; and the fraud and falsehood that had been practised in one important instance being rendered so apparent, the whole began to be considered as, in some degree, false and fraudulent.

But this was not all. During the few weeks that Woodhouse had been domesticated with old Montfort, he had wormed himself into his confi-

---

1 In medical terms, a nutritive or formative medium, especially the menstrual blood in which the embryo is formed.

dence, and, by assuming the tone of fanaticism that accorded with the state of his mind, at once so depraved and so despondent, had obtained an entire ascendancy over his conduct and his conscience.

This sort of spiritual dominion, Montfort had found to be a kind of stay and consolation to his mind. It saved him, in a considerable degree, from the trouble, and from the torment of thought. Confession and contrition, indeed, became more frequent upon his lips; but they became also mere acts of mechanical obedience, following rather the suggestions of his spiritual pastor, than springing from the volitions of a penitent mind. In short, they were certainly a very comfortable exchange for those silent terrors and inward agitations, with which, heretofore, he had been so incessantly racked.

Having once enjoyed this species of consolation, Montfort soon became incapable of supporting himself without it. The short interval (little more than four-and-twenty hours) from the departure of his spiritual confessor to the arrival of Dr. Pengarron, had been a period of restless anarchy; during which the disorganizing terrors of conscience had tossed and torn his feelings with perpetual commotion. His thoughts were all at sea again, as it were, in a tempest of apprehensions; and his eye rolled around, in vain, in quest of harbour or anchorage. The arrival of our worthy doctor, therefore, was as welcome as it was opportune.

"I am glad you are come, doctor—glad you are come," said he, rising from his arm-chair, and seizing him by the hand, as soon as he entered—"I was afraid you had forgotten me: and I have been so agitated!—so haunted!—so harassed!—so sleepless all night!—such thoughts and dreams!—What can you give me to compose me?"

"Umph! Sit down, Mr. Montfort, sit down," said the doctor, placing his hand upon his pulse, as he seated himself by his side, "let us talk a little while; and I will write for you by and bye. I think I know what will do you good. I suppose the chaplain has been disturbing you with his farewell sermon. A plague upon him! If you would confide in me now, I'd venture my reputation in the world I gave you more comfort and consolation (ghostly and bodily!) in one half hour, than ever he administered to you in his life."

"Will you!—will you, indeed?" said Montfort emphatically; lifting up his head, at the same time, as if partially relieved from the dejection under which he laboured—"Well, well! I know you will: and it is only you that can console me. I will lay my heart naked to you in confidence—a broken and a contrite heart. You shall pray with me. You shall be the physician of my soul, as well as my body—my comforter—my consolation—my friend."

This disposition was one of the consequences Pengarron had calculated upon from the full detection of the villainy of Woodhouse. He had very plainly perceived, that the mind of Montfort had neither rest nor confidence in itself; and that, in the midst of those morose and melancholic humours, which were partly the result of constitutional temperament, and partly of the inward workings of remorse, a confidential counsellor—or, more properly speaking, a sort of intellectual dictator, had become absolutely essential to his comfort, almost to his existence. He perceived also, that notwithstanding the gloom and fanaticism of his patient, and his own very opposite complexion, he had, nevertheless, a degree of influence over him; that, if the spiritual corrupter were once removed, could not fail to mature into a complete ascendency.

He seized, therefore, the expected opportunity to plead, with such blunt pathos as he was master of, the cause of Henry; and to point out to him the injustice done to that young man, and the hard thoughts that had been so cruelly put into the head of a credulous father, as effective causes of the depression and agitations of his mind.—

"For the heart of man, friend Montfort," continued he—"though I am an old bachelor who say so—the heart of man wants the softening, and comfort, and support of family connections and kindnesses. Brothers and sisters, and sons and daughters—these are the things that humanise us, and prevent our hearts from becoming crabbed as we grow old.

"I never had them, to be sure, and that's the reason that I am such a half-licked bear as you see me. My profession, indeed, which makes one a sort of brother to all one's fellow-creatures, does something to cheer me up; or I should be as melancholy as you are.

"But what is all this to nature?—to flesh and blood, man?—one's own flesh and blood?

"But then to live in enmity with it!—enmity with one's own flesh and blood!—Pho! pho!—and for a little folly, and extravagance, and dissipation?—A plague o' such nonsense! Grave faces, and angry letters, and disinheritings, and a p-x to them for such nonsense?—Tut! tut! If I had such a boy, he should run through half my estate, and oblige me to mortgage the other, before I'd live at daggers drawn at this rate, with my own bowels."

M. "Well! well! It is wrong, doctor—I own that I may have been wrong in all this. But then his disobedience, doctor—His violation of God's holy commandment, *Honour thy father*—His neglect of all my admonitions, all my orders! You would not countenance his disobedience!"

P. "Disobedience! A fico[1] for such disobedience! You did not go the way to be obeyed. You commanded, where you ought to have reasoned. You ordered like a tyrant, when you ought to have advised like a friend. You spoke to him as if you were more jealous of your own power than his welfare.

"Does the Father of all speak to his children in this manner? No. He *would gather his children together as a hen gathers her chickens under her wing.*[2] You would beat and cuff them into obedience, as vultures and carrion crows cuff the prey they are about to devour.

---

1 Fig (Italian).
2 Luke 13:34 and Matthew 23:37.

"Imitate *that* Father, and he will be a better son than you have been. For he does honour you after all—he does love you. What!—Have I not given you proof?—And you shall have more—better proof!—Such a letter! Did he not fall sick?—Was he not ready to die, on the report of your death?

"Disobedience?—Tut—tut!—He obeyed your example instead of your precept—*a chip o' the old block*. If he had done as you told him, you might have doubted whether he were your own.—Come, come, you said I should pray with you—So I will—Let us lift up our hearts together to Him whom we have so often disobeyed, and repeat my favourite clause of my favourite prayer—

"AND FORGIVE US OUR TRESPASSES AS WE FORGIVE THEM THAT TRESPASS AGAINST US!!!"[1]

"And now think with bitterness of these things again, if you can."

M. "Well—well! I will not think with bitterness."

P. "That's right—that's right—Tut! tut! I tell you they are not worth tormenting yourself about. More than half is not true; and the other half is not half so bad as it has been represented; and what remains he was trapped into, *willy nilly, as the devil goes to mass,* by the very Judas who accuses him.

"What, man! have we not proof—proof positive? Have we not unfleeced the wolf?—shown Mr. Chaplain in his fangs, and filed the edge of them?—Have we not caught him out in his vile predestinarian tricks?— causing the offence that he might punish the offender!—A murrain upon him, a sour-faced hypocrite!—a murrain!"—

(This concluding sneer of our good doctor was somewhat unfortunate. It jarred the feelings—it shocked the principles of the penitent. An apparent gloom gathered upon his brow.

Pengarron perceived his error. He endeavoured to retrieve it—to soften the impression, if not to wipe it away.)

"Which certainly," added he, "is not admissible in the actions of that short-sighted and limited being, man. *He* must not do evil that good may come of it."

Montfort's returning composure indicated that he accepted the explanation.

"Well—well! Dr. Pengarron," said he, "I admit all this. I have been misled—I have gone too far. Yet Henry has had his vices."

P. "Vices!—Psh! mere tricks of youth. Perhaps he may have gambled a little; that's the worst of them: but I'll be bound for him for the future— he shall have a better game to play than meddling with cards and dice:— and drank a little—a beastly vice, that—a beastly vice! but I have a charm to keep his drunken companions aloof, I'll warrant; and then there is nothing to be feared on that score:—and wenching, too, I suppose—a

---

1 Its ideal of reciprocity makes this an appropriate text at the heart of Thelwall's social gospel.

little wenching may lie at his door: and this too is bad enough, I confess, but, marry him to his liking—to a woman of beauty, of soul, of sentiment, and he will leave this off.

"What, shrinking and shuddering?—Tut! tut, man! As if you and I had never tripped a little, in this way, when we were young.

(Montfort turned up his eyes and groaned.)

"Psha! psha!—a plague o'such nonsense!" If he had seduced an innocent young creature now—a creature of intellect, of feeling, of virtue—had betrayed her, under the specious show of honourable intentions; and then for some dirty consideration of interest, refused to marry her—or had married another—or if he had left the poor little helpless consequences of his amours, unfriended and unprotected, to bear all the earthly penalty of his guilt—"

(Montfort groaned still deeper. He rose from his seat, and walked about the room in great agitation.

Pengarron observed him well. His intention had been merely to awaken such sympathies as might be favourable to the cause of Seraphina: but he perceived, that, in the execution of this he had touched some string of powerful passion that might chime in unison with his design. He determined therefore to try which it was, and to strike a deeper note.)[1]

"Umph!—Aye, aye, friend Montfort! deliberately to seduce a woman of character and virtue"—He paused—"and then, from motives of paltry interest, to desert her—"

(He paused again: but the string did not vibrate. It was not that. He proceeded to the other.)

"Or to leave one's little pledges of love—the little guiltless consequences of one's irregular passions"—He paused—the vibration was as evident—"unprotected!"—The string vibrated again.—"Unprovided for!—perhaps to perish!"

(This chord vibrated indeed. All the echoes of the heart rung with the larum that it made.)

"Well!—what of that" exclaimed Montfort wildly, drawing his breath very deep, between each articulation—"what of that?—what of that?"

(Pengarron turned his penetrating eye upon him. He looked him through.)

"Why *that*, friend Montfort!" said he, with deliberate emphasis—"*that* were an offence which might call for serious reprehension—aye, and for atonement too. And if I had a son who had been guilty of such an offence, I would disinherit him on earth, as God must do from heaven—*if*—"

"If what?—If what?" exclaimed Montfort, aspirating from the very bottom of his lungs—"if what?"

P. "If he did not make instant reparation."

---

1 Thelwall frequently uses metaphors of music and sound to explain both bodily and mental foundations and operation of his moral philosophy.

M. "But suppose *they* were not, to whom the reparation should be made?—Suppose no search could find them?"

P. "Why, then, the only way to make his peace, either with heaven or with me—would be to find out some amiable and injured orphan, whose misfortunes had been similar, and make, by proxy (you know my maxim, sir), that atonement he could not make in person.

"But tut!—tut! friend Montfort," said he resuming his humourous vivacity.—"Henry has nothing of this sort to answer for that ever I heard of. The only injustice he ever committed in the way of youthful frailty he is ready to repair."

The proposed atonement sunk into the heart of Montfort, like balm into a rankling wound. It opened new prospects of hope and consolation. His brow expanded. His eye became irradiated. He looked upon Pengarron with a complacency almost like worship. The doctor affected not to mark him.—He continued to ramble—but he kept the road in view.

"But come, come—you shall be reconciled—I say you shall be reconciled. Odds my heart! he's a fine lad—a very fine lad!—with his graceful person, and his accomplishments, and his understanding! And then so like you!—the very model of you!—Odd's my conscience! 'twill make your old heart young again to throw your arms round his neck, and recollect all his pretty childish tricks!—"

(Montfort listened with a pleasing attention. Memory filled up the picture, which Pengarron had but sketched.)

And then to gaze upon him, and listen to him kindly, and indulgently, with all the father in your soul, and see how the flower of early promise has expanded.—A plague o' your Osborns and all the crabbed old fellows who write against Love and Matrimony![1] why may not I have my share of such pleasures, as well as you, to cheer up my old age?"

(Montfort laid his hand upon his arm.)

"Well—well! you shall be reconciled—I say you shall be reconciled immediately. Your heart shall be at ease; and I will have one good deed the more (a deed of peace and love, friend Montfort!) To balance against the vices of my youth: and that's better than canting, friend Montfort?—canting and making mischief, like that murrain of a chaplain."

(Montfort slid his hand along the arm of Pengarron till both hands met. A sort of familiar pressure seemed to say, *Well, do so—do so!* The doctor proceeded.)[2]

"I'll bring you together, I say—I'll bring you together to-morrow; and he shall bring Seraphina with him; or she shall come by herself."

M. "Seraphina!"

---

1 Possibly a reference to a character named Osborn in Thomas Holcroft's moral comedy *Duplicity* (1781), who saves his friend from the evils of gaming by pretending to be a villain.

2 The attention to body language, like that given to breathing earlier, reflects the materialist basis of Thelwall's moral philosophy.

P. "Aye; Seraphina. You shall be reconciled to her too. At least, you shall see her and hear her; and then refuse it if you can.

"O 'tis a noble wench!—such a Seraphina!—Why it makes the blood dance in one's veins again, like the may-tide of youth, to look at her.

"But looking is nothing to hearing. Such sentiments!—such language!—such feelings!—so noble! so generous! so amiable! so magnificent! So disinterested! so divine!

"Odd's my life! had you heard her last night!—I only wished you could have been there—Such a scene!—If you would not have kissed her in an ecstasy, as I did—If you would not have asked yourself, in astonishment, How the devil you could deserve such an angel of a woman for your daughter? why, drive me to Rumford to see a patient, and send me back again without my fee."[1]

Montfort was stunned and confounded by this unexpected panegyric—"Last night!—heard her!—scene!—kissed!—Why surely, doctor, you are not—"

P. "*Are not?* Yes, friend Montfort, but I am. Why, she is my pride—my paragon—my adopted daughter—Heiress of all I have, and all I may have. I'll be party to the marriage settlement, I'm determined.

"If you resolve (in defiance of all the precepts of Christianity) like a Jew, a Turk, an Infidel, to harden your heart against all grace and forgiveness, and disinherit the poor lad for this act of wisdom, of honour, of moral and religious duty, why the first boy shall be a Pengarron, and my fortune shall be settled upon him.—If you think wiser of it, and feel the pride you ought to feel in such a daughter, why I would wait a year the longer for an heir, and it shall be settled upon the second."

This case was put somewhat too strongly to be immediately assented to by Montfort.

"Wisdom and honour! doctor Pengarron," repeated he, with revolting astonishment—"Moral and religious duty?"

P. "Aye, moral and religious! What man—is it not a moral duty to repair an injury—to fulfil a solemn engagement? Is it not a religious duty to obey the commandments of revelation. *He that findeth a virgin, and humbleth her*—What must I be quoting Scripture to you for every thing?[2]—Can you remember nothing of it for yourself?—Or has that cunning false prophet of a chaplain stuffed your head with the belief that religion consists in the repeating the jargon of its ministers, and rejecting the precepts of its Author."

M. "Well, well, doctor!—but honour and wisdom?—What can you say to that?"

"Why, more than to the other," replied he, with pointed gravity, and deep emphasis, "unless, indeed, it ceases to be wise and honourable to unite oneself to every excellence of virtue and understanding, because the

---

1 Possibly an eccentric idiom. Rumford is a village in Cornwall, therefore remote.
2 *Exodus* 22:16.

unfortunate possessor happens to have had a scoundrel for her father, who deserted her in her infancy, and left her, from her most helpless years, the prey and sport of all the malice of persecuting fortune."

(Montfort's agitation rose higher than ever. The doctor marked him and proceeded—)

"Poor flower! scattered by the way side, for every passenger to tread on! and yet how sweet it has blossomed! Wild woodbine of the hedge, which the clown has so often hacked and bruised! yet how beautiful in colour and in fragrance![1]

"And these, friend Montfort! these are the little germs of promise, which the licentious barbarian man, after giving them existence, for the gratification of his unlawful appetites, can desert—can neglect—can leave, without remorse, to perish.—Perdition on such villains!"

"Hold, hold!" exclaimed Montfort, seizing upon his arm, in delirious agitation—"hold!—do not curse!"

P. "Not curse, friend Montfort! I must curse.—They are cursed already. It is not whining canting repentance that can redeem them. It is not groaning in a corner, or turning up the whites of their eyes with a hypocritical rascal of a chaplain—*Atonement*, I say—they must make atonement—*grand atonement*, or perdition is their inevitable lot."

M. "What atonement!—what atonement can I make?—Tell me!—tell me!—Comfort my shuddering, my sinking soul."

P. "You make?" said Pengarron, with affected astonishment—"Your soul!—What do you mean, friend Montfort?—What do you mean?"

M. "I—I am one of the licentious barbarians—the villains—the monsters, against whom you have pronounced perdition! *I had a daughter!*—an unlawful daughter—*I* left her; and she *has* perished!"

P. "A daughter?—You a daughter!—an unlawful daughter?"

M. "Aye—aye—a daughter!—Not a Seraphina, indeed, but a little Anna!"

P. "And what has become of her?"

M. "Perished, I tell thee!—perished!—My poor little scattered blossom has been trampled!—my neglected woodbine bruised and hacked—hacked to the very root—Never to blossom—never to emit its fragrance.

"This it is, that, for upwards of twelve years, has torn my afflicted conscience; that awakened my tardy repentance—that urged me to inquiry when inquiry was too late—to solicitude, when solicitude was vain. My Anna!—my little Anna."

P. "And what did your canting chaplain prescribe for you in this case? Prayer, and a good benefice to him, I suppose, while you lived; and when you died, half the estate out of which he had swindled your injured son.

---

1 Fundamental to Thelwall's poetry and his philosophy throughout his life, the language of flowers that is used for Seraphina here compares with "The Woodbine," in the *Poems, Chiefly Written in Retirement*, in which his daughter is compared to the same flower.

"If you have faith in such consolations let me call him to you again. The faith of a simple layman, cannot administer absolution at so cheap a rate. If you ask *me* the price of pardon—I shall tell you, that neither fasting nor prayer can purchase it—nor hospitals for monks, nor benefices to methodists. Reparation—reparation can alone redeem you!"

M. "What reparation!—Tell me—tell me what reparation can I make?"

This was the very question the doctor wished. It was the point he drove at: the object of all his management. From the instant that his random bolt had struck the tender part of Montfort's conscience, and discovered to him the original source of his remorse and agitation, the parity of the cases occurred to him as a fortunate coincidence: and he doubted not but that, by a little finesse, he might make the Original Sin of the penitent the source of his ultimate virtue. The present inquiry, therefore, led him immediately to his predetermined appeal.—

"*Seraphina!*—*Seraphina!*" replied he emphatically—"The cases are parallel enough to be substituted for each other. Differences there may be in fact, but there are none in principle. Begin with her. She, also, has been abandoned—deserted—thrown friendless on the wide common of the world, not always, indeed, unpitying, but rude and thorny. Adopt her, then, for your daughter, in place of the daughter you have suffered to be lost. Make her your daughter, indeed, (and such a daughter!) by marrying her to your son. Thus shall you repair the injury you have done to him, and, in the person of Seraphina Parkinson, atone for the irreparable wrongs of Anna Montfort. This were a beginning as happy as it were noble: and if this is not sufficient (as it is not) cast your eyes around you, and you shall find similar instances enough, to whom (in some way or other) the arrears of this long account may be paid."

M. "Well, well!—Something must be done: something shall. But Seraphina my daughter?—married to Henry Montfort?—Would you have me marry my son to his kept mistress!"

P. "*Kept mistress!* Death and fire. Percival! Do you talk of Seraphina in such terms? Are we to be led by the nose by cant names, that may arise from the performance, or the omission of a ceremony, useful, indeed, to restrain the villainy of our own sex; but which can make no difference in the essential purity of the other. A murrain o' your nick-names—I tell you, I know her: and not even that excellent woman, whose memory I shall ever revere—and of whom (notwithstanding the Tenth Commandment[1]) I could never help envying you the possession: for I knew you were unworthy of her—Not even she was more pure, or more exalted, in every matron-like virtue—more removed from the dispositions and deportment of the concubine.

"And then, in every noble quality of mind, and accomplishment—I tell you, Percival, she has no paragon—no equal: nor ever had. And as for the connection between Henry and her, though the peculiarity of their situa-

---

1 "Thou shalt not covet any thing that is thy neighbour's" (*Exodus* 20:17).

tion, and the feelings of nature and affection may have betrayed them in some unguarded hour; I tell you that I know—that I can discover, by a thousand circumstances, that their cohabitation, upon the main, has been regulated by such principles of Platonism, as such debauched and vitiated old rascals as you and I have been, can scarcely comprehend.

"But you shall see her—Odd's my life! you shall see her, and hear her, and know her, as I have: and then, if your old heart do not leap and bound at the prospect of the atonement I have propounded to you, the devils of pride and avarice have gotten possession of your heart, and to their management I resign you."

M. "Well—well, doctor, I will see her—I will see her. At least, I will *see* her. Perhaps, I will do all that you wish me. I confess there is a mystery about her that awakens my curiosity; that much has come already to my knowledge that corresponds with what you wish me to believe. And something must be done—Atonement must be made. The torments of reproaching conscience must be appeased.

"But how came you acquainted with this Seraphina?"

P. "Umph! What, that must out—must it? Why, by the side of the sick bed of Henry."

M. "Sick bed! What sick bed!"

P. "Why, the sick bed upon which he has been lying ever since he received that dreadful wound."

M. "Wound!—What wound?—What do you mean?"

P. "What now, I warrant you have not heard a word about the assassination and the rape, and I know not what all, that some of the chaplain's seconds—I don't know indeed, that he was confederated with them—though he is bad enough for any thing—"

M. "Assassination!"

P. "Umph! Umph! Here's a pretty fellow for a father now, not to know whether his son is dead or alive, killed or buried; though the whole town is ringing about him.

"What you were never permitted so much as to see a newspaper with your own eyes, I suppose—nor hear a common report with your own ears! Faith, the chaplain cooped you up prettily; and while he was paragraphing the newspapers with malicious accounts of this terrible affair, your paternal feelings were guarded against the shock; lest your compassion should interfere to prevent your only son from perishing in the little miserable hut where he lies.

"Faith, it is lucky that you happened to fancy yourself ill in time, and send for me to cure you of the megrims; or you might have lived, perhaps, in this holy keeping, *till you had made your will*; and then have died, as you deserved, without either being seen or heard of by kin or kindred.

"But come, let me just write you a prescription, to complete your agitated faculties; and then I will tell you the whole story; and indeed the whole history (so far as I am acquainted with it) of this amour: and then, if you are not interested for its happy conclusion, the nerve of sympathy is dead within you; and your last offence is worse than all the rest."

CHAP. II.

The Visit of Seraphina to Old Montfort.

The unexpected Reception.—Poignant Remembrances.—The Picture—a Disclosure of Horrors—Recriminations and Self-reproaches.—Suggestions of Phrensy.—Difficulties explained.

THE narrative of Pengarron, imperfect as it was, scarcely was less interesting to the feelings of Montfort than his appeal had been forcible to his conscience. It was a parallel case, indeed. Change but the island described as the scene of action, and the names given to the earlier actors in the drama, and the heroine might have seemed to a less credulous father, the lost, the lamented Anna. How powerfully these associations would operate upon such a state of mind as Montfort was worked into, may be readily suggested. In short, every thing proceeded as our worthy doctor desired; and he left his patient in the best predisposition that could be imagined for the operation that was to take place the following day.

That day arrived; Seraphina, as we have seen, accompanied by her mother, repaired to the scene of action; where her reception, as has been already suggested, was such as the preparation seemed to augur.

Unconscious of what had passed, she was perfectly astonished at the apparent complacency with which her first greeting was immediately returned.

But the astonishment of the mother surpassed even that of the daughter.

"My name, sir," said Seraphina, with some hesitation, as soon as she was ushered into the breakfast parlour, where he was sitting—"My name is Seraphina Parkinson—And—and—"

Montfort arose from his seat. He placed a chair by the side of his own; and taking her gently by the hand—

"Pray be seated, Miss Parkinson," said he, surveying her with a look very far removed from forbidding severity.—"I beg you will be seated."

S. "This posture, sir, is better suited to a petitioner."

(He laid his hand upon her arm, and pressed her into the chair. Morton seated herself at the far end of the room; and fixed her eyes upon them with great agitation.)

S. "I am a bold intruder, sir, thus uninvited, to break upon your privacy. But I have an important cause to plead, in which the happiness of future human beings is involved:—my Henry's sir,—your's sir,—and my own—"

M. "You are welcome, miss Parkinson. There needs no apology—That form," continued he, still gazing upon her, and musing to himself, in a

sort of half-articulate exclamation—"who could blame him?—So interesting!—So like a ministering messenger of peace.—Outwardly at least,
she is all that Pengarron has said about her—

"O God! O God! and if it be thy will, that she should heal this heart."

Seraphina was more embarrassed than ever.—"Sir!—Sir, I—I, Sir,—I
fear—"

M. "Fear nothing, Miss Parkinson—You are welcome! It has pleased
God to send you to me—to heal—to save me: and I am happy to see
you—"

Then falling to his musing again—"That form," continued he, in the
same half-articulating reverie, "those years!—Had I been more fortunate—Wretch! wretch! disguise not thy offences from the All-seeing
Eye—If I had been less vicious, I might have been the father of such a
daughter, without my son's assistance."

Nature swelled into his eyes, as he uttered this. The tears stole down
his cheeks; and all the rugged features of his face were softened.

"But I beg your pardon, miss Parkinson. You have something to say.
What is it, miss Parkinson? You shall be heard with attention—with something more. After what I have learned concerning you, I cannot but be disposed to listen. My ears, my heart, are open to you—Pray proceed."

"O! no, Sir. I cannot proceed. You have disarmed me of all utterance,"
exclaimed she, bursting into tears. "I came not prepared for such a reception. Is this the rugged father—the man of obdurate and unfeeling heart,
that I expected to have encountered?"

S. "O! sir—if you, indeed, are cruel enough (which I hope you are
not) to mean to mock and baffle me—you have found out a most effectual means: for my heart is so swoln with the first belief of your kindness, that my tongue fails me. I have forgotten every thing that I meant
to say."

M. "No, no—miss Parkinson, I do not mean to mock you. My heart is
too sad for mockery. I have a great—a terrible account to settle, Miss
Parkinson; and you must help me to make it up.

"*I had a daughter once, Miss Parkinson.*"

"A daughter!!! Mr. Montfort,"—exclaimed Seraphina, in astonishment—"*A son,* you mean—*a son!* Oh, have one still. Let me not be the
fatal cause of division between son and father.

"Oh! take him again, Sir, to your heart. If there be any means by which
Henry can be rendered happy, without his Seraphina, point them out to
him, and I will bear my wretchedness without repining.

"I came to plead the cause of our mutual loves—I came to vindicate
the claims of nature, stamped and imprinted in the feelings of our united
hearts—I came to combat, with the arms of reason, the unfeeling arro-
gance of parental tyranny: and I thought that I had arguments of sufficient
cogency and appeals sufficiently forcible to compel reluctant attention,
and triumph over the obstinacy of inveterate prejudice. But your forbearance, sir, defeats my resolution, and frustrates all my endeavours. I was

not prepared to meet with this urbanity:—to contend with gentleness; and confront the tearful eye of sympathy.

"You have prevailed. I will not plead for any thing in which I am myself concerned. I will only plead for Henry and for you. Let me be forgotten. I will only say, live for each other again, and *in* each other; as father and son should live.—I will only say, take again to your heart, sir, your generous, your affectionate, your slandered son—I will only bid you to read that letter, and see how much he has been slandered; and then, sir, I will conclude, as I began, let me not be the fatal cause of division between so blest a father and such a son."

Montfort took the letter she presented—The reader will remember which it was—But he read it not. His mind was otherwise engaged. He held it, without opening, in his hand; and, gazing still upon her with rising admiration and wonder—

"It must be so!" exclaimed he. "God has sent her to me, in pity to my afflicted heart, to heal and save me—to show me the loveliness of personified virtue, and guide my steps to Heaven.

"Afflict not yourself, miss Parkinson," continued he, addressing himself to her, with great emotion—"you shall cause no division. It has pleased God that *by you our division shall be healed*: that by you the wounds that lacerate my afflicted heart shall be healed also.

"I had once a daughter, miss Parkinson—I mean a *daughter*. She is no more. She perished. By my neglect she perished:—miserable that I am!—by my neglect!!—

"What's past, miss Parkinson, cannot be recalled. Can tears and self-reproaches unlock the grave? Can a father's anguish recall the long lost child? Can he weep back the spirit to her clay-cold breast; or, with broken lamentations, recall again the times that are past, and revise with maturer judgment the recorded actions of his life, like the fictions of some written tale?

"It cannot be. Groans heave this breast in vain, and tears as vainly fall.

"Well!—well!—What cannot be recalled, miss Parkinson, I would replace. Dr. Pengarron has made me sensible of your worth. He has told me your interesting story. I have disclosed to him all the secrets, and all the anguish of my heart; and it has pleased God to make him a minister of grace and mercy, to find the remedy.

"It is this—You must supply the place of the daughter I have lost. Henry must be restored to my affections and his inheritance; and you must share them with him.

"Art thou appeased, my conscience?" said he to himself, and walking up and down the room, after he had thus pronounced—"Art thou appeased?—Shall consolation and peace again be mine?"

Seraphina, overpowered by surprise and emotion, could neither speak nor stir—but her eye followed him to and fro, with a gaze of vacant wonder. At length, coming up to her again, and taking her by the hand,

"Yes, miss Parkinson," resumed he, "all that you meant to ask, I grant without your asking. Go, and be yourself the most welcome messenger of good tidings to your Henry—to mine. Bring him hither yourself. Tell him that I am his father again. Doubly his father; and that I wait with impatience for the consolation that the Almighty will pour into my heart, while I present him, in one hand, with the pardon I hope he will merit, and, in the other, with the bride he has so long desired."

"My father! my father!" exclaimed Seraphina, throwing herself at his feet, "and may I call you by that name? Is that endearing relationship again to be renewed; Is it to be realised, indeed,—and is Henry to be a partaker in my felicity?

"O, sir!—I cannot thank you. I am poor in thanks; yet I have a heart that is not poor in feeling.

"But let me fly to my Henry! He shall thank you, sir—better than I can do it. He shall thank you; and shall thank our generous advocate;—my heart shall thank you both in silence; and our mutual happiness shall thank you best of all."

So saying, she rushed impatiently out of the room.

Montfort followed her with his eyes. His heart approved what he had done; and he strode about the room, in conscious satisfaction, anticipating his approaching happiness.

In the midst of these meditations, while he was still walking about, his eye alternately rolling to heaven, and alternately poring upon the earth, with unconscious gaze, he was struck with the appearance of a little frame—the back of which lay towards him. At first, indeed, he did not much regard it; but kicked it with his foot, as though its lying there had been a matter of course. But it presented itself again; and, his mind being somewhat more at leisure, he stooped and picked it up.

He turned the face of it towards him. It was his own miniature.

"God of heaven!—how came this picture here?—Not a soul has set a foot in this room but Seraphina."—(Morton was forgotten, who had remained but a few minutes, an agitated spectator of the scene.)—"If she should have dropped it, who must this Seraphina be?—this bedded wife of the disastrous Henry!"

The thought had scorpions in it.

"Richard! William! Thomas!" he exclaimed in a breath.—"Miss Parkinson!—Seraphina!—Seraphina!"

He was about to lay his frantic hand upon the bolt, and follow her; when the door flew open; and, pale as the shrouded corpse, with lips convulsed, and eyes starting from her head with horror, Morton appeared before him.

"Peace!—monster!—peace!" exclaimed she, in a sort of aspirated whisper—"Father of Incest, peace!—Drive not thy child to madness—Peace!—peace!—peace!"

Then following him into the room, as he shrunk before her, and closing the door in her rear—

"*I* dropped that picture, *Woodville*! It was I that dropped it."

"Thou—thou!"—returned he, thrilled to the soul with horror, as he recollected rather her voice than her person—"and who art thou?"

"Newcomb!" replied she—Anna Newcomb! the mother of that miserable daughter—the daughter of the false—the savage Woodville!—That daughter who, deserted by him, and worse betrayed by me, has lived in unconscious incest with her brother!

"Horror of horrors!" continued she, with more obstreperous phrensy—"It was I that seduced them to this hideous consummation, I shut the door of privacy upon them. I spread the couch for their unnatural joys; and trapped them to perdition!"

M. "Didst thou?—accursed!—didst thou?—detested woman! Siren of lust!—bawd of abominations! Why opens not hell to swallow thee?"

N. "Why not to swallow you?—savage!—barbarian!—wretch!—My crime was an unconscious one—but yours was planned.—Mine was anxiety for the welfare of my child. Yours, base and vile unnatural desertion.

"Why did you impose upon me with a fictitious name? Why leave the helpless offspring of our guilty pleasures destitute of a father's aid; and suffer the children of the proud and wealthy Montfort to depend for their support on the precarious wages of my prostitution?

"Rapacious, ruthless, avaricious monster!

"You pretended, indeed, to question whether Lucius was your own. You could not forge a doubt of little Anna. Why was she left, then, to the terrible alternative of perishing with want before my eyes, or being torn from my maternal arms by a strange adoption, whose capricious benevolence obliterated, by the extinction and exchange of names, every memorial that might have led to timely discovery?

"Thou ruthless monster!—more ruthless than the beasts that prowl for prey! Behold the dreadful consequences of this desertion!

"Oh! hell! Oh! hell!—the living—the untimely hell that burn already in my tormented heart! what curses can I invent to equal your detestable and fatal meanness?

"Why spins not your brain to madness?—Why do you not curse your worse than brutal nature?—Why not grow wild as I do?

"Incest! Incest!—Hear you not, monster?—Incest! Your children have engendered with your children; and but that Heaven permitted not the offspring of such unnatural lusts to live, even now, your little grandchild might have joined me in this hideous yell, and lisped of Incest—Incest!!!"

Montfort, who, till now, had stood a motionless statue of dismay and horror, threw himself, with a heavy groan, into his chair.

"Is this my consolation?—Is this my peace?" said he—"Is this the messenger of comfort sent by the Almighty, in pity to my afflicted heart, to heal and save me?"

"Oh! Hideous anticipation of all the hell I merit! Seraphina Parkinson Anna Montfort! The bedded wife of my only son, proved to be my only daughter! And the partner of my guilt confronting me as my accuser!

"God of heaven!—But how dare I call upon that God?" continued he, starting up again, and whirling round the room, in desperate agitation— "The seal of reprobation is upon me!—the seal of reprobation! The bottomless gulf opens wide its flaming vortex to devour me; and my accumulated crimes drag me down headlong.

"Bowbridge!—Louisa!—and thou grief-strangled offspring of that disastrous union—(disastrous through my vices!)—ye shall be avenged!

"Ye groans of whip-galled Africans!—ye countless sufferings of a most miserable race, the guilty sources of my still accumulating wealth! ye shall have vengeance also!

"Eternity has space enough for the long arrear of retribution; and with giddy brain I am tottering upon its verge.

"The scale is uplifted. The red right arm is bared. The bolt of vengeance is alarmed at my predestinated head; and the thunder of Eternal wrath bellows out Incest!—Incest!"

He paused for a few seconds; whilst his eye turned suddenly inward, as if upon some new recollection of dismay and horror—

Perhaps they are renewing their crime, at this very instant. I have sent her forth, with the seal of paternal approbation upon her lips, and the promise of approaching nuptials in her eye, to fire his fraternal veins with new impetuosity, and rush upon renewed damnation!

"Hold! hold! incestuous pair! Forbear the polluted embrace! Those joys are prohibited—they are the joys of fiends. Your father, indeed—your guilty father has sanctioned them;—but that Father above, in whom there is no guilt, HE has prohibited: He calls upon me to revoke my decree, and to shriek out *Incest! Incest!!!*

"My voice shall reach them. I will find it wings." He stretched forth his hand towards the bell.

Morton understood his purpose. She rushed upon him, and withheld his arm—

"Wilt thou kill her?—wilt thou kill her with these tidings? Let her live innocent of this offence:—as innocent of memory as in heart. Ours is the guilt alone; let ours alone be the horror.

"I have taken care to delay their interview—I have kept out of her way, that she might not see the phrensy of my agitation: I have caused her to be sent to Pengarron's to wait for me. I have seen her (unobserved myself) driven towards his house. Let it be our care that they meet no more: and as for ourselves—our hell begins already. It matters not what shall become of us."

M. "Let it be so. Poor innocents! Let them remain unconscious. Why should they know their guilt?—*not theirs; but ours.*

"O! Newcomb! Newcomb! embitter not my anguish—fan not the devouring fire that consumes my brain with thy reproaches.

"We have been guilty both—guilty beyond hope of pardon; and avenging Heaven has struck us with its thunders. But why should we assist the wrath of Omnipotence? Is he not strong enough for our chastisement? Is not eternity duration enough for our unabating sufferance? Why then should we anticipate his consuming vengeance? and by mutual recriminations make that vengeance double?

"I have repented, Newcomb—enough repented (if the seal of reprobation had not been stamped upon my heart) to have saved me from these horrors. To you, at least, and to my hapless child, I have endeavoured to make reparation.

"Twelve long years of agitation and remorse I have spent in fruitless searches and inquiries—at first by letter, and afterwards in Jamaica itself; the guilty scene of our polluted and accursed loves—but all in vain. I am a vessel marked for perdition before the world yet was. I see it plainly. It was written in the heavens in characters of fire, and glares before my eyes. What else—what else, after such repentant effort, could have led to this consummation?

"I see—I feel that I am predestinated to wrath. It stares me in the face. It is plain and obvious. This last accomplishment is the primal cause of all. All the crimes and abominations of my guilty life are but the necessary links in this predetermined chain. To justify my condemnation. It is completed now!—It is complete. The measure of my crimes is full: and I have nothing to plead—nothing to sustain me: nothing to comfort me now.[1]

"Where is Pengarron?"

(He rung the bell with great violence. A servant immediately appeared.)

"Where is Dr. Pengarron? Has he been here? Why does he not come? Is it not past his hour? Did he say he should not come today? What has prevented him?"

"It wants almost an hour, sir, of his usual time," replied the servant, in astonishment.

M. "An hour?—an hour? Fly—hasten him—bid him come immediately—that I am frantic, that I am dying—that his cordial has proved my poison.—But where are you to seek him?—whither art you to fly?—Go! go! go!—Begone, I say. I am mad. I do not want you."

The servant stared, and shuddered, and withdrew.

"An hour? Almost an hour? Yet what can Pengarron do? What atonement can he talk of now? It was his atonement that brought to light these horrors. Seraphina and Morton were to be substitutes for Newcomb and my deserted Anna; and reparation was to be made in their names.

"Ah, who could have believed that they were indeed that mother and daughter whom I had sought in vain? That Morton was Newcomb, and Seraphina Anna?

---

1 Montfort's rhetoric of despair and predestination echoes that of Milton's Satan and a raft of gothic villains, and looks forward to the Byronic hero, but with a psychological acuity and element of social critique that reflects Thelwall's enlightenment rationalism.

"The cases were parallel, indeed, and the similitude soothed the anguish. But by what magic, or what mystery, could they become the same?

"He told me that Seraphina was a native of St. Domingo. He told me that her father's name was Parkinson. Something, indeed, he told me of a Woodley—an adopting father, who perished in that insurrection from which the disastrous virtue of Henry had rescued her.

"Disastrous virtue indeed! But all must be disastrous that springs from my accursed loins.—Virtue itself becomes abhorrent vice when connected with decreed perdition. The sins of the father have involved the children. The denunciations of the decalogue are completing.[1] On the second generation they have already fallen: I have involved it in the horrors of incest.

"Stop—stop their sources of fecundity, O! Almighty God! Let their generations proceed no further! Let the career of reprobation cease!"

It was thus that the time was passed (till the arrival of Pengarron) in frantic ejaculations; and in explanations almost as wild and incoherent.

From the latter of these, however, it appeared, that, shortly after the first return of Montfort from Jamaica, Newcomb (for so from henceforward we must call her) removed, in consequence of a new connection, from Kingston to Spanish Town. It was there that she was, almost immediately upon her arrival, attacked by the small-pox; which putting a final period to the reign of her attractions and her prosperity, occasioned her to be no longer an object of curiosity or conversation. She was accordingly very soon forgotten; and the circumstance of Robertson's adoption of the little Anna was scarcely known beyond the home of the single family whom he was visiting, when he chanced to hear her interesting tale.

As this family happened to have no acquaintance with any of the connections of Montfort, (or, as he was then denominated Woodville) and as Robertson took his little fosterling immediately with him to his living, near the western extremity of the island, while the unfortunate mother was immediately shipped away, the memory and record of the whole transaction quickly perished, as it were, in that part of Jamaica where the first events had taken place, and where the connections of Montfort lay; so that by that time when the stings of conscience had so far inflamed his bosom as to compel him to seek the allay of its restless agitations in inquiries into the fate of his deserted daughter, not the least intimation could be obtained by which the thread of her adventures might be traced.

When Newcomb afterwards returned to Jamaica, though Montfort, indeed, had returned to the new hemisphere, he was still in the island of St. Domingo, settling some concerns and negotiations there—the derangement of which was the ostensible, and indeed, one of the real causes of his second voyage to the West Indies. On that occasion, therefore, she had little opportunity of collecting any information concerning

---

1 The Decalogue is the Ten Commandments; Montfort alludes to Old Testament passages testifying to the sins of the fathers being visited upon children.

the pretended Woodville; even if the object of her more solicitous curiosity had not confined her to a remote corner of the island.

The space, indeed, was not very long between the time of his clandestine return, and her final departure, with the family of Parkinson, for St. Domingo. But it was long enough to have permitted her some time paramour to conclude his business in this island, and depart upon his anxious and unavailing inquiry to the scene of his former settlement and unfortunate connection.

And as, upon this second voyage, he had no longer any occasion for concealment or disguise, the name of Montfort that he left behind him furnished no sort of clue by which he could be identified to Morton.

There were still, indeed, some circumstances, connected with the protraction of this discovery, which the parties could not properly explain.

Part of these, arising from the mistakes and inversions of Dr. Pengarron, may be easily accounted for, from that sort of blundering untenacious memory which the reader will remember him to have ascribed to himself; and which, indeed, is very common with studious and professional men, in every thing not immediately connected with the subject of their profession. This, in the present instance, was so much the more natural, as this information must of course have been collected only by hasty snatches and unconnected conversations: and as the plan of entering at all upon the narrative part of the subject, was only, as has been seen, a sudden crotchet of his brain, hastily conceived and as hastily executed, without co-operation or intercourse, and consequently without necessary inquiry and preparation.

But there are other particulars of more apparent difficulty. The change of the name of our heroine from Anna to Seraphina was one of these.

Newcomb knew, indeed, that it was one of the caprices of Robertson to christen the child again, upon his adoption, and that Seraphina was the name that was then conferred: and this was enough to satisfy the distempered curiosity of the wretched father.

But our readers, who are acquainted with more particulars than he was then at leisure to inquire into, and who have heard the narrative of Parkinson, by which this child of misfortune was first introduced to notice and sympathy, will necessarily inquire, how it came that he should take no notice of this circumstance. It is necessary therefore to observe, that, in fact, he was not acquainted with it himself.

Robertson, who had known and remembered the former Seraphina, and who had felt in common with all who knew her, a powerful interest and admiration for that short-lived example of human excellence, had been struck, in the first instance, with that resemblance which had afterwards, as we have seen, so powerful an influence on the heart of the venerable Parkinson. He had adopted the name, therefore, from this circumstance; and this second coincidence, which hitherto, perhaps, may have appeared somewhat extraordinary, was, in fact, only a result of the first.

It happened that Parkinson (who was fond of a sort of rambling life, and not very constant in his residence upon his cure) was not in the way of seeing this new fosterling for the better part of a twelvemonth after her adoption, when the new name had become confirmed by uniform habit, and the old one was, of course, almost obliterated from the remembrance of so young a child.

It had been no part of the original plan of Robertson to conceal the circumstance of this change of name from his friend: but when he saw the powerful effect, in the first interview, which these united associations had upon the heart of that childless father, he was unwilling, for obvious reasons, to weaken their force, by divulging the original and actual name. Accordingly the appellation of Anna remained to him unknown: while in the mind of Seraphina the impression of it died and faded away; or at most remained there in that state of oblivious inertion from which the recurrence of some powerful association might perhaps have recalled it; but from which it had not sufficient energy to revive of itself.

The ignorance of Henry of the assumed name of Woodville, which is now the only difficulty that remains, may be easily explained from a circumstance, which of itself will be rendered more accountable before this history is concluded; we mean the reluctance entertained by Amelia against entering into any explanations or conversations with our hero, upon the subject of those adventures, which had occasioned her husband to adopt the temporary disguise of the misnomer.

CHAP. III.

Containing the Space of about three Months; from the fatal discovery to the death of Morton.

The Dilemma.—The Separation.—Doubts and Difficulties.—Stolen Interviews.—Invocation.—The death of Morton.

THE intelligence of his discovery was, of course, an afflicting stroke to Dr. Pengarron. He had been feasting his benevolent imagination with the prospect of the happy reconciliation, which he concluded by this time had effectually taken place; and was anticipating the happiness of the lovers. But the very countenance of Montfort dashed all his hopes, as soon as he entered the room; and the incoherent tale that was poured immediately upon his ear overwhelmed him with keen affliction.

Could he have trod back the steps he had so officiously taken, and married the unfortunate pair in happy ignorance, he would most cheerfully have transported himself with them to any quarter of the world where the discovery might never have reached them.

"And why not now?" said he to himself, pondering as he walked about the room—"why not banish them in love and happy ignorance? What worse can happen than has already happened? The crime, if crime can be where the heart is unconscious, is already completed. And what must be the horror if the mystery should be explained?—the misery, if they are torn asunder? They will die—they will die in anguish, and in phrensy— Poor miserable couple, they will die! Can I suffer them thus to perish?

"And where is the guilt?—where is the relationship, in any rational point of view? Have they been reared and nurtured together in those reciprocations that constitute the essential bonds of fraternity?—How is the son of Amelia Montfort brother to this woman's daughter?—this wanton! who, perhaps, can scarcely tell who the father of her children are!

"Tut! tut! It will not stand the test of reason.

"And yet, if that could be undone which has been done already, consciously to lead them to it, in the first instance—Nature, I confess, would revolt at the idea. Nature would shudder!

"But it has been done. The union has been consummated already— consummated in perfect innocence. How barbarous to transform into guilt an action, after it has passed, that in the acting was mere simplicity and innocence! But how is this to be voided if they are to be torn asunder? or, if this could be avoided—to what harassing precautions and tormenting mysteries must we appeal?—How much better would the anguish of so mysterious a separation be, than all the horrors of the dreadful disclosure?—Would not the affliction differ more in character than in degree?— What rending—what tearing of their tender and affectionate hearts! What a life of misery!—Perhaps, what a miserable death!

"And after all—Is it from Nature, or from institution, that these ideas of crime and abhorrence have originated?

"The turtle, whom we deem the emblem of conjugal purity, was she not hatched in the same nest with her bridal dove?—twin offspring of the same fraternal pair!

"Who was the wife of Abel—or of Seth?

"But that was necessity. There was no other family.

"But if it had been vicious, would God have created such a necessity?— Would he have decreed all population from a single stock—from the inevitable marriages of sisters and of brothers?

"Nay was not this a necessity, also? The necessity of unconsciousness, and of sympathy! And is it not *now* a necessity to preserve this brace of turtles from a heart-breaking separation?—to snatch two such minds as Henry's and as Seraphina's from the ravages of phrensy and desperation?

"My logic may perhaps be weak," continued he, still debating only with himself, "but human sympathy cannot support the prospect of that misery that is inevitable upon their separation.

"But hold: do I not remember something of such a case?—Secker!— good archbishop Secker!—had he not a familiar dilemma once put to him?—A worse!—much worse! An incestuous mother—whose unconsciously incestuous son, married unconsciously to *his* incestuous, *her* incestuous daughter—at once a husband, father, and a brother! And what did pious Secker!—Who doubts of Secker's piety?—What did he advise this demon of a mother to do? Why, to give herself up for lost, and leave the innocent couple to themselves, in unconscious happiness—innocent, as he conceived, because unconscious!—Can I be wrong, if I advise what pious Secker would have advised?—At least," concluded he, "if the case were my own, I know what I would do. I would have the grace to slip out of the world at once, with the secret in my own keeping; let the devil take his own; and leave the guiltless couple in ignorance and bliss.[1]

"But what is to be done with these people?" said he, casting his eyes upon Montfort and Newcomb, who, dumb with horror and expectation, were gazing upon his silent agitation—"What hope from them—a brace of miserable fanatics, with whom dogmas and creeds are devotion—and prayers are the only ethics?

"It is in vain to attempt to reason on such a case with them. Palliatives—palliatives are the only things that are practicable; and temporary separation is the only palliative—This will give one time at least to think—"

Having decided upon this point, he endeavoured, in some degree to calm and compose the distracted parents; and recommending the separation for which they were already so eager, he proposed that Henry should be sent away immediately to the West Indies; and that he should be induced to undertake this voyage, by its being made the sole and absolute condition of his pardon; and by the ambiguous promise that Seraphina should be immediately taken under the roof and protection of Montfort, as his intended daughter, and as the only person ever meant to be proposed or adopted in that character.

"When they are once separated," said the doctor, "expedients perhaps may easily be found to perpetuate their separation without disclosing the dreadful circumstance that renders the separation necessary. At any rate, we shall have gained time; and if the secret must out at last, it will come upon them less abruptly than at present; while the hopes of union and happiness are just fresh and glowing upon their minds."

This proposal was immediately approved both by Montfort and Newcomb: and, for the immediate execution of it, Pengarron was to return to his own house, where he was given to understand that Seraphina was then waiting; and under the appearance of some mysterious and eccentric project of his own, he was to take her into the country to the house of a particular and familiar friend of his, while Henry could be sent for to Grosvenor-square, and prevailed upon to embark on board the famous West India convoy, which at that time was waiting at Portsmouth for the opportunity of a favourable wind.

---

1   Among numerous writings by Thomas Secker (1693-1768), archbishop of Canterbury, is a pamphlet on incest to which Thelwall is here referring. The rationalist arguments put forward here by Pengarron reflect the "ongoing narrative tradition" in Enlightenment epistemology regarding incest surveyed by Pollak. See p. 27, note 1.

This plan, in one of its parts at least, was much easier of execution than at first blush might have been expected. Seraphina had already experienced so much advantage from a sort of passive obedience to the whims of Pengarron, that she readily persuaded herself that he had some new project of benevolence on foot, that he could only pursue in his own odd and mysterious way; and therefore, after writing to Henry a brief account of her successful visit to his father, she suffered herself, very contentedly, to be conveyed to Hammersmith, where she was introduced to a family almost as agreeable as that at Elmsley Hall; and had at least, the advantage of forming a new and eligible connection.

Henry indeed was not quite so tractable. Notwithstanding his satisfaction at the prospect of an apparently sincere and hearty reconciliation with his father, and the caution with which all ambiguity with respect to the promise about Seraphina was concealed, the idea of any separation, however temporary, appeared so insupportable; and the request itself, and the pretended important business that called for his presence in the West Indies, coupled with the prohibition of seeing Seraphina before his departure, had altogether an air of such suspicious mystery, that at first he absolutely refused to accept of pardon or reconciliation upon such terms, and declared that he would never consent to set his foot on board the vessel, till his marriage should first be consummated.

This declaration threw old Montfort into a paroxysm of phrensy. His horror rose with the terrific ideas it recalled to his distempered mind; and the dreadful secret was ready to burst from his lips.

Pengarron had contrived to return from Hammersmith time enough to be present at this interview. He saw the precipice down which the afflicted father was about to leap, and removed the temptation by taking Henry aside.

He had been harping again upon that string of casuistry which the reader has heard him touching at the opening of the chapter; and the alternative notes, with which it perpetually vibrated, were the authority of Secker, and the frantic misery that must inevitably attend upon the final separation of the lovers. At the very idea of this his heart bled at every pore. He determined that, if he could prevent it, at least, they should not so be separated.

Having once brought himself to regard the affair steadily in this point of view, he began to derive some consolation from the state of mind into which both Montfort and Newcomb had fallen upon this discovery; and the consequences that must inevitably result to their health. In short he cherished a sort of secret hope that it could not be long before they must both of them sink, under the weight of their afflictions, into the oblivious gulph; where it was his fervent prayer that the secret might perish with them. In which case (under the whole of the existing circumstances) he saw no great impropriety in leaving the young people to the workings of nature and their own hearts, and suffering them to come together again to perpetuate, in the unconsciousness of their relative affinity, that connection which in the like unconsciousness they had already formed.

With the arguments, under these impressions, he thought himself at liberty to use, he did not find it impracticable to prevail over the reluctance of Henry.

"There were some crotchets," he said; "at present in the disordered brain of Montfort, which, if rashly opposed, would be productive of consequences that must render the wished for union utterly and for ever impossible; yet, if the present delay was yielded to with a good grace, he pledged himself in the most solemn manner, upon his veracity and honour, that he would not suffer any thing to be done (and he thought his influence over the father sufficient to prevent it) to interrupt their future, nay their speedy union. In his present state of mind and health," continued he, "the old gentleman cannot live many months. When he is gone, you may unite, and be happy. But, I repeat it, should you irritate him now by your perverse refusal, you will find impediments thrown in your way that will divorce you from each other for ever. You know me. I would not deceive you."

Henry was so far pacified by these assurances, that, to the no small satisfaction both of Montfort and of Morton, he consented to the purposed voyage; and suffered himself to be hurried on board one of the vessels of the convoy that was daily expected to sail.

In less than four-and-twenty hours after the arrival of Henry the convoy weighed anchor; and, Montfort believing that all further danger of the dreadful interview was now past, Seraphina was conducted back to Grosvenor-square, to take up her permanent abode with her acknowledged mother and her unknown father, in that splendid mansion in which she had already been a temporary resident.

Here for the prevention as far as possible, of all suspicions, the letter that Henry had left behind him was put into her hands, and a specious account was given of the causes and necessities of his sudden voyage.

Seraphina, however, knew not what to make of all this mystery. Nothing but the part that Pengarron had evidently born in the conduct of it, could have reconciled it to her mind; but the high opinion she entertained of his integrity and friendship, inclined her to believe that, notwithstanding so many suspicious appearances, all must be right at bottom.

In the mean time these appearances became more and more mysterious. The conduct and deportment of Montfort and Morton (for such was still her name to Seraphina)—their deep dejection, and starts of occasional wildness—the mingled passion with which they so frequently fixed their eyes upon her, and particularly that growing infatuation of fondness, in the former (as strange in its character as its growth—for he could neither bear her to be out of his sight, nor look on her without conspicuous anguish), were so many Sphinx's riddles that she could devise no possible means of solving. But the consternation into which they were evidently thrown by the circumstance of the wind changing about, and compelling the fleet to return to St. Helen's, was a circumstance she thought of a less ambiguous nature: especially when this was followed up by the palpable precautions that ensued to prevent, as far as possible, any sort of intercourse, even by the way of letters, during the long interval in which the convoy was detained, by a variety of disasters and accidents, in that situation.

That week after week should thus roll away; and even moon succeed to moon, and yet Henry never be permitted to return to London to visit his father—to visit her, from whom it was pretended that sudden emergency had torn him so abruptly and that his very letters should not come to her unless when conveyed by stealth, nor her own be received by him unless transferred in the same way—these were so many circumstances as amounted to a demonstration, in her mind, that, how specious soever other appearances might be, there was a settled design, both on the part of Montfort and her mother, for their complete and perpetual separation.

The account that Henry had given her, in one of these clandestine letters, of his conversation with Dr. Pengarron, previously to his consenting to the voyage, checked her suspicions with respect to him. But still he had grown cautious and reserved; and, fearful perhaps, of being driven to explanations, avoided as much as possible all opportunities of conversation with her. This was, at least, a very ambiguous circumstance.

In short, every thing conspired to produce impressions of mystery and suspense, that were perfectly incompatible with her feelings.

She would have remonstrated openly with her mother, and have demanded an explanation; but the rapid decline of the health of that wretched woman, and the evident agitation into which she was thrown by every attempt to lead the conversation to that subject, compelled her to relinquish this design.

In the mean time Edmunds was as indefatigable to bring the lovers together, as their miserable parents were to keep them asunder. Though he knew not what to suspect, the opinion he entertained of Morton put it out of doubt with him, that the old Devil, as he called her, had formed some villainous project or other against the happiness of Seraphina and his master; and he determined to counteract her if possible.

The reader needs scarcely be informed that it was by his means that the private correspondence had been carried on; the simplicity and attachment of William, rendering him a willing instrument, within doors, for the immediate conveyance of the letters to the hand of Seraphina, and of her answers either to Edmunds again, or to the post.

Neither did Henry, however watched, neglect the opportunities, which long delay afforded him, of paying repeated visits to the metropolis; nor Seraphina, situated as they were, and surrounded by so many ambiguous and suspicious circumstances, refuse to listen to his tender invitations and overtures of private interview.

These meetings were of a very different character from any thing they had ever experienced before. They were meetings of doubt, of agitation, of alarm. Their confidence in each other, indeed, was not shaken. But there was nothing else around them in which they could confide. They were involved in the thickest shades of mystery: and conjecture was in vain let loose to suggest what was the nature of the evil they had to apprehend. Evil there must be, of some sort: serious and malignant evil—or why these suspicious precautions—these artifices—these concealments.

These doubts and difficulties racked them when separate, and obscured their happiness when together; and the ardours of love were mingled with the gloom of scepticism.

Of these interviews Edmunds was the only confidant. He was indeed the only counsellor, in whom, under their present circumstances they could possibly confide: and they made him accordingly, a partner in their deliberations.

The advice he gave was at once consistent with the enthusiasm of his character, and with the feelings and wishes of their hearts. It was no other, than that they should appeal to the very obvious expedient of making sure against all cross accidents, and all the intrigues and villainous conspiracies that might be entered into for the purpose of their final separation, by a legal, though private, marriage.

It is evident that the arguments formerly urged against this expedient by Seraphina, would not, in the present instance, apply.

The question was not now what rank or estimation their connection should hold in the world? or whether the essential purity and virtue of that connection could be altered by a compliance with established forms and ceremonies? but, whether there was not sufficient evidence of the existence of some mysterious cabal and conspiracy for tearing them asunder, and disappointing all their hopes of that union, without which it was sufficiently evident happiness could be enjoyed by neither?—and if so, whether the marriage proposed was not, in fact, the only expedient by which this conspiracy could be effectually counteracted?

Both these questions our lovers (assuredly upon no very slight suggestions) answered in the affirmative; and as no finger of Providence wrote the word *Incest*, in characters of fire, upon that azure canopy, beneath which the proposal was made and acceded to, nor warning spirit from the dead, nor vision of the night, revealed the tale of horror, the marriage was, accordingly, celebrated (by banns) at the parish church of St. Mary's, Lambeth; and consummated beneath the veil of artificial night, at the humble cottage, where their former apartment had been prudentially retained by Edmunds: and where he still continued to reside.[1]

This was an event, with the apprehension of which the tedious and notorious detention of the famous West Indian convoy,[2] kept the minds

---

1 For a different, though equally Wollstonecraftian, perspective on private marriage and the effect of secrecy on romantic love, see Eliza Fenwick's *Secresy* (1795).
   Like the cottage, the church of St. Mary, Lambeth would have been well known to Thelwall.

2 Storms and various disasters delayed the West India convoys in autumn 1795, and this prevented the British from mounting an offensive against the French at that time.

both of Montfort and Newcomb in a state of perpetual horror and alarm: and it will undoubtedly be considered as very unfortunate, that among all their various precautions for preventing the interviews and correspondence of the lovers, no measures should have been taken to prevent the accomplishment of the dreaded design, in a way so probable and so obvious.

The fact, however, is—that every thing was finally accomplished before Montfort had conceived the slightest suggestion of the stolen visits of Henry, and consequent interviews with Seraphina: for, as Henry never ceased to importune him for permission to make a temporary return, and continued to write, by the post, such letters to Seraphina as he knew would be intercepted, he contrived effectually to prevent the suspicions of the old gentleman, till the event had taken place. Soon after it had taken place, indeed, he began somewhat to relax in his precautions, and to become almost desirous that the suspicion should not only be cherished but confirmed.

In short, love and Seraphina triumphed over every other consideration. He had familiarised himself so much, in contemplations, to the picture of humble industry and independent poverty, that the lovely partner of his heart had drawn, upon a former occasion, that he almost wished to realise it. And when he looked backwards upon the uses himself had made of wealth, and considered the degree of happiness which it seemed to have conferred upon his father, he regarded it with contempt—almost abhorrence, and could not help asking himself "What is there in the West Indies that can be worth my voyage?—What can my father deprive us of that we cannot spare?"

In these feelings the reader may be well assured that Seraphina was not far from sympathising.

The task of disguise which she had undertaken, was so inconsistent with her nature; and the fraud and privacy of their stolen interviews so revolting to her feelings, that she soon began to repent her of the subterfuge to which they had submitted; to look back with regret upon her former project of publicity, poverty, and independence; and to believe that every consequence that could possibly result from the disclosure of their marriage, was preferable to the degradation of its concealment.

It was in this state of mind, after returning from one of these scenes of clandestine tenderness, that she wrote the following:

INVOCATION

Nymph of unfaltering step, whose parting locks
Give to the fronted light the unveil'd brow
Expansive—thou thro' whose unshrinking eye,
Clear as the alpine rill, the inward mind
Beams on the gazer's sight, why should my soul
Forego thy sweet communion?—for my heart,

Even from the earliest dawn of infant thought,
Hath lov'd thee, fair Sincerity! and still,
As thro' life's varying path, with ambling tread,
Or frolic bound, or the more stately pace
Of ripening woman-hood, my feet have trod,
Painful or pleas'd, thou, constant at my side,
Hast own'd me for thy sister. Wherefore then
Am I divorc'd thy converse? Why forbad
To sound my quiver in thy sportive train,
Or share thy sylvan toils? Have I with crimes
Of covert fraud, that ill can bear thy glance,
Defil'd my once pure essence? Has this hand
Leagu'd with the legion fiends that fill the world
With cries of wretchedness?—this tongue conspir'd
With envious Slander?—or this bosom, stain'd
With some unhallow'd passion, learn'd to heave
For joys that virtue owns not?—Well thou know'st,
Maid of expansive brow! full well thou know'st
My soul of these unconscious: now as erst.
   I have but lov'd, and with a flame so true!
The vestal lamp nor purer!—Lov'd, alone,
As the steel loves the pole star, turning still,
With undiverg'd affection, to that point,
And that alone, whether the lustrous ray
Beam'd thro' the azure cope, or, hid in clouds,
Mourn'd his shorn glories. Wherefore fly'st thou, then,
Shunning my footsteps. If such love be crime,
Nature is criminal—the mystic law
That tunes the circling spheres itself is crime,
And entity is guilt. Come, then, return,
Belov'd Sincerity! and, as thy hand
Oft for my virgin brow hath cull'd the wreath
Of purest fragrance, and with simple braid
Bound up mine artless hairs, with equal love
Adorn the nuptial couch: in Hymen's fane
Lift, with propitious hand, the flaming torch,
And be the Matron's, as the Virgin's pride!

Morton (as we are about to relate) escaped the renewed horror of that full disclosure to which the feelings both of Henry and Seraphina seemed to be thus impelling them. She did not however escape the bitterness of the suspicion. The frequent morning rides and vernal walks of Seraphina; and the length of time to which they were protracted, filled her mind with repeated apprehensions that, notwithstanding all the boasted precautions of Montfort, Henry contrived, at times at least, to hover about the skirts of the metropolis; and that something like unto what had taken place, was in meditation if not accomplished. She thought, also, that she saw sufficient evidence of the secret conveyance of letters to and fro; and several other circumstances tended to increase her suspicions.

But, confined to her room as she was, and indeed almost constantly to her bed, how was she to satisfy these apprehensions, or to prevent their fulfilment, without entering upon a strain that might lead to the divulging of that secret, the horrors of which she was so anxious to conceal? And yet if she did not satisfy them, if some effort were not made to prevent their accomplishment, the event she apprehended was inevitable.

This was a dilemma she knew not how to get through, or to evade; and the agitation into which it threw her mind, enflaming the fever, which, ever since the former discovery, had been preying, with accumulating strength upon her vitals, threw her, at last, into a delirium, in the paroxysm of which she died.

It was fortunate (if fortunate any thing could be considered under the existing circumstances of our tale) that Seraphina (though a pretty constant attendant on the sick bed of her mother) was not at that time at home; or the incoherent ravings that gave terror to the last hours of that miserable woman, could not but have revealed the dreadful secret with which she laboured: for certain it is, that to the less perceptive faculties of one, at least, of the servants that hovered round the bed, the idea was suggested; and so strongly, that she could not afterwards, without shuddering, either look upon our heroine, or hear the name of Henry.

But Seraphina, who, though not without occasional apprehensions of the impending catastrophe, had never expected it to be so near, had left her that morning, as she supposed, considerably better than she had been for many days; and had flown to the cottage, according to appointment, to meet her beloved Henry: who had just arrived from St. Helen's.

She had made use of less precaution, for the prevention of suspicion, than ever: and the interview was, also, much more protracted.

The fact is, they were deliberating upon the subject of the future concealment or avowal of their nuptials. The advantages and disadvantages of publicity and disguise were alternately weighed; and the balance seemed to preponderate in favour of the former.

In short, they had determined to make a secret of their loves no longer: a determination to which they were the more impelled, as Seraphina began to suspect that their intercourse had already been productive of consequences that, in a few months, might render all further concealment impracticable; and perhaps necessitate her to a disclosure at a time when the absence of Henry might render the consequences of such disclosure particularly irksome.

Full of this determination, her mind expanding with the reviving consciousness of frankness and sincerity, and repeating to herself the Invocation we have so recently quoted, she returned impatiently home.

She bounded up the steps; for her mind was gay—

"Her bosom's lord sat lightly on its throne";[1]
and she suspected not the heaviness that waited for her within. The countenances, the condolences of the servants presently informed her.

A sensation of horror ran through her veins. She flew to the apartment of the deceased; and, setting herself down by the bedside, watered with filial tears the maternal corpse.

---

1 *Romeo and Juliet* 5.1.3.

BOOK XII.
CHAP. I.

In which our History advances only a few Days, in point of Time, from the Death of Newcomb to the Disclosure of the Private Marriage.

Perplexing Ambiguities.—Tormenting Apprehensions and Dilemmas.—The Awful Disclosure.—The Intrusive Visit.—The Sudden Transition.

IF Seraphina knew not what to make of the deportment of Montfort and her mother, during the life of the latter, still less could she pretend to account for the evident anxiety of the former upon the recent event of her death; or the ostentation (for so to the simple feelings of Seraphina it appeared) with which the ceremony of her interment was performed.

"If this expensive profusion, in particular, were not meant as a mark of respectful attention to herself, what could it mean?

"And yet, why should he be so solicitous about attentions and respect to one, all relative connection with whom, in the only way in which relationship could ever exist, he was evidently so solicitous to avoid?

"But if this were a mystery; was not every other part of his conduct and deportment equally mysterious?

"Why did his voice always soften, and his eye become alternately tearful and complacent, whenever he addressed her?—Why all that anxious solicitude about every thing that concerned her?—that evident attention to the very anticipation of her wishes—that profusion of preparation for her accommodation, her amusement, her comfort?—as if opulence itself (of which, in other respects, he appeared sufficiently tenacious) were held but in stewardship for the gratification of her tastes and her desires!

"Why those starts of anguish?—those gleams of delight?—those glances always followed by a sigh?—And why did his tongue so frequently falter when he pronounced the adoptive name of Daughter?

"Is it possible that he should himself have conceived the wish of becoming the rival of his Son?"

This idea was dismissed almost as soon as suggested. "The affection which he displayed had none of the characteristics that might justify such a suspicion. There was a chastened sadness in every look—in every word—in every accent: and if his fondness, in a considerable degree, was stamped with the marks of dotage, it was of such dotage as an aged father might feel for a daughter indeed!"

A chilly tremor ran through her veins as this was passing across her mind. Not that she had really any distinct apprehensions of the fact; but that fancy had suggested a circumstance the realizing of which would be horror. The thought too was instinctively, as it were, accompanied with the sort of look with which Montfort was accustomed to regard her; and this reflected association seems to have awakened the very feelings from which, in the original, they resulted.

The impression, however, was but transient: at least in its distinctness it was so; for it passed away, and left no definite trace behind it. There was a sort of inward sinking or depression of the animal spirits, indeed; but even fancy itself did not dwell upon any thing in the form of a suspicion. Indeed, how should it have done so? All that she had ever heard of a daughter was that she had perished. Montfort and Morton had found sufficient reason to avoid the development of all further circumstance. And how could actual affinity have been suspected as the motive of an adoption that was announced before any such affinity was supposed, and consequently before its symptoms were in the least apparent?

The mystery, however, altogether rendered her very uneasy; and she determined to have the peace of certitude.—

The peace of certitude!—Alas! poor innocent! How little did she think to what a precipice of horror she was rushing!

While Seraphina was bewildering herself in the maze of this inextricable mystery, Montfort himself was tormented with wilder agitations.

The death of Newcomb was a species of memento of the probable approach of his own. And, independently of the horrors he felt, under his present impressions, as the idea of dissolution, and of the terror with which he "peer'd beyond the grave,"[1] the fatal secret with which he laboured, and the predicament in which Henry and Seraphina would be left, if that secret were not disclosed, drove him to the very verge of distraction.

Pengarron was constantly exerting all his influence (and all his influence was necessary) to prevent the horrible disclosure. But even Pengarron could not restrain the bewildered wanderings of his imagination; and our at least kind-hearted, if mistaken, casuist was under perpetual apprehension that, short lived as he considered his patient likely to be, he might live long enough to rush into all the mischief that he dreaded.

Indeed, there were many circumstances consequent upon the death of Newcomb to aggravate the feelings of Montfort. The difficulty was considerably increased, so long as the fleet remained at St. Helen's, of preventing those private interviews of the lovers, which, by this time, he was beginning to suspect. The residence also of Seraphina under his roof, always perhaps an ambiguous circumstance, might now become (as in reality it did) irksome to her feelings, and indecorous in her estimation.

To what resolutions—to what explanations might this lead?

But this was not all—nor the worst—

"Thus bad begins, but worse remains behind."[2]

---

1   Bertie Greatheed, *The Regent: A Tragedy* (1788): "But who, lynx-ey'd, has peer'd beyond the grave, / And view'd that phoenix Immortality" (1.1)
2   *Hamlet* 3.4.182.

It was evident to his jealous apprehension that the servants (the old house-keeper in particular) had picked up something or other from the incoherent ravings of the deceased mother, that had suggested the idea of that real affinity towards him, and consequently towards Henry, in which Seraphina stood.

If this were the case, it was easy to foresee that, under the present arrangements, the secret would not be long concealed from Seraphina herself; and the probability was that it would be bolted out in some blunt and inconsiderate way, that might render it the more terrible and afflicting.

"What was to be done?

"To impose silence on the suspected discoverers was only to confirm the discovery, and to enflame them, so much the more, with a burning desire for the disclosure!

"To dismiss the whole household was to goad them, by the resentful feelings, to make the neighbourhood ring with their suspicions, and infect whomsoever should supply their places with aggravated accounts of the circumstances upon which those suspicions rested."

In this dilemma, he advised, as was usual with him in all his difficulties, with our benevolent physician, Pengarron.

"It was a case of difficulty. It admitted of but one resource. As it was not prudent to turn his servants away from him, he must turn himself away from his servants."

In other words, Pengarron advised him to withdraw, as speedily as he could, from London; and, taking Seraphina with him, to fix his residence, for a time at least, at his long neglected family mansion of Ridgmont in the North of England.

This advice was in every shape perfectly agreeable to Montfort.

Like the generality of persons who are restless and dissatisfied with what is passing within, he was willing to snatch at the flitting shadow of relief by variegating the scene without. But, what was of still more importance, he flattered himself that, besides the advantage immediately proposed, a more effectual bar would be erected to prevent the possibility of those clandestine interviews he dreaded.

The journey to the North was determined upon accordingly. A proper messenger was dispatched to Ridgmont without delay, to prepare the necessary apartments for their reception: and the necessary arrangements were made for travelling with hired carriages; and without any of the servants of the town establishment: all of whom were to be left in their respective stations behind; while the new group, hired in the neighbourhood of this provincial residence, or sent down by Pengarron, without intercourse or knowledge of any of the parties in Grosvenor-square, were effectually prevented from receiving the slightest intimation of their disastrous suspicions.

The resolution being taken, and every thing ready for its execution, Montfort proceeded to the intimation of his design.

"Seraphina," said he to her one morning, while they were yet sitting together at the breakfast-table—as soon as the servants were all withdrawn, "I have something to propose to you, my child; which, by the will of God, I hope may be for our mutual comfort."

S. "I shall be happy, sir, if any thing you can propose may enable me to give comfort to you."

M. "That is kindly said, my child! that is kindly said. But thy soul is full of gracious kindness.

"You see the state of my health; and how hastily I am journeying to that country where, sooner or later, the final destination of all must be settled.—That destination!"

His eyes rolled in wildness. He heaved a deep groan.

S. "Nay, sir! be comforted. If these melancholy impressions were removed, there might yet be many years in store for you, of happiness and of health.

"Would, sir, that I might administer to your comfort! There is a way, sir—"

M. "Yes—there is—there is. Dr. Pengarron has pointed one out to me. He is of opinion that change of scene, and change of air, and a little travelling about (if it please the almighty dispenser of sickness and of health,) might furnish me some relief."

S. "I dare say it might, sir. I wish you would try it. And if Henry were to accompany you—"

M. "Henry!—Henry!—What talk you of Henry?—No—no—no! Henry must to the West Indies.—Henry must to the West Indies.—Disastrous winds!—Eternal, ominous delay!"

Then, after some pause, calming his agitation—

"Well, well, Seraphina!—I have an old family mansion, not visited for many years: a monument of ancestral grandeur, in furniture as well as architecture; venerable with time, but still I believe in tenantable repair. It is situated, indeed, in a very distant part of the kingdom; but in the midst of a country every part of which must be full of charms for one of your taste and turn of mind.

"It stands in one of the hollows of that romantic ridge of mountains that bounds the northern extremity of Yorkshire:—in that very scope through which the precipitous Swale hurries along to the fearful cataract and ancient Roman city of Caturactonium.[1] In its neighbourhood rise the gigantic mountains of Bowfell, Ingleborough, and Wharnside, and

---

1   The Roman fortress of Cataractonium became the town of Catterick, North Yorkshire. The area was hospitable to reformers; Thelwall had friends nearby whom he visited while criss-crossing Yorkshire giving elocution lectures 1801-06. Its proximity to "the fine hills and lakes of Westmorland and Cumberland" would already have been attractive in 1800, when he proposed an "expedition" to the Lake District to visit Coleridge, similar to the one referred to here.

the distance is not great to the fine hills and lakes of Westmorland and Cumberland.

"I mention these things, my child, not from my own delight in them—(Would that my delights had been of such a nature!)—but to show you that while endeavouring (by divine permission) to find out the means of prolonging my own wretched existence, I am not forgetful of the sources of your happiness."

S. "Your kindness, sir, in these particulars, wants no further proof. It is engraven in a thousand interesting remembrances, upon this heart.—One only thing—"

M. "Well,—well, my child! I have persuaded myself that a summer's residence in this romantic retirement, diversified, as it might be, by accompanying you to those scenes and objects of natural and artificial curiosity that will be always within our reach, might be a means, through your attentions and the grace and goodness of heaven, to divert my afflicted mind, and restore, in some degree, my shattered health. I have therefore occasioned preparations to be made for our immediate reception."

"Immediate reception, sir!" repeated Seraphina, with surprise and agitation.

M. "Yes, my dear child! Dr. Pengarron has been kind enough to provide a proper companion for you: and you can confide in his choice. She will be introduced to you this afternoon, and, with God's grace and permission, we will set off to-morrow."

S. "To-morrow, sir?—And what will my Henry—"

M. "Your Henry!—Your Henry!"

S. "Yes, sir! My Henry! By your sanction and authority mine. What would he say to my abrupt departure!"

Montfort was strongly agitated. He rose from his chair. He endeavoured, in vain, to bridle his emotions.

"Pardon me, sir!"—continued Seraphina, "if I feel myself necessitated to introduce a subject you seem so anxiously and so mysteriously to avoid. But my peace—my honour, and the sense of derogated worth forbid me to be longer silent."

Montfort's agitation rose still higher and higher.

"Forbear! Seraphina, forbear!" he exclaimed, in a tone of frantic wildness; "by all your hopes of comfort and of peace I conjure you to forbear! Touch not that dreadful string!"

S. "Dreadful?—You astonish me, sir!—Dreadful?"

Montfort perceived the precipice to which his frantic terrors were impelling him. He endeavoured to collect himself. "May not he, who adopts the cares of a father, expect the submission of a child? May he not look for obedience?"—

S. "Obedience! Pardon me, sir! He who was best entitled to the character of father—the guardian—the tutor of my infant years!—to whom I owe every thing that I am in intellect and in moral rectitude—he taught me no submission but to reason; no obedience but to justice and honour.[1] The homage I paid to him (I were unjust if I did more) I will transfer to you—the ardours of gratitude!—the consolations (if you will suffer me to administer them) of an unfeigned sympathy!"

M. "Well, be it sympathy, then; be it sympathy. Will not even this induce you, Seraphina, to administer to the consolation of an expiring old man—outcast from hope, and scourged by Heaven?"

S. "O, yes, I will administer to you, most cheerfully, whatever is morally in my power. I will administer to you more than you desire. I will point out your remedy. I will bring him to you. My Henry shall join his efforts; and we will unite to make you happy."

M. "Your Henry, again!—Unite?—Your Henry?"

S. "Heaven and earth! Mr. Montfort!—what can be the meaning of this delirious agitation? Why should the name of Henry and of union produce this mysterious phrensy?

"What but such a union can justify my accompanying you in the excursion you propose?

"In what character shall I be regarded as participating in your retirement?"

M. "Character, Seraphina! Will that character be altered by the change of place? Will not the character of our connection be the same at Ridgmont as it is here?"

S. "Most assuredly, sir! And it is a character so ambiguous, that neither here nor there can I think of sustaining it any longer: and therefore it was, sir, that, before I had any intimation of this journey, I had decided on the necessity of an immediate explanation."

M. "Explanation!—Explanation!!!

"Distraction! Whither would you drive me? Whither would you rush yourself?

"Alas! you know not. But let the phrensy of my anguish warn—let me—What would I say?—

"—May not he who is daughterless in nature, comfort his declining years by taking to his bosom a daughter of adoption? Or does Seraphina disdain to be that daughter?"

S. "Disdain, sir?—It is the point of my ambition. But there is only one way in which that ambition can be gratified.

"I cannot be adopted, and Henry be abjured. I cannot remain an inmate of your house, while Henry is doomed to exile.

---

1   In echoing here the parental philosophy of Wollstonecraft and Godwin, Seraphina becomes the imaginative stand-in not only for Wollstonecraft, and the dead Maria Thelwall, but for the infant Mary Godwin, and for Manon Thelwall, born in March 1799. Wollstonecraft herself did something similar with the unnamed daughter of Maria in *The Wrongs of Woman*, which Thelwall read as he was writing his novel, taking its alternative title (*Maria, a Fragment*) for the title of one of his elegies for his daughter Maria.

"It is as the wife of Henry Montfort alone, that Seraphina Woodville ever can be adopted as your daughter."

M. "Seraphina Woodville, wife of Henry Montfort!—Furies and fiends?—Hell! Hell!—insufferable hell!

"Why do you thus torment me?—why drive me thus to madness?—Seraphina Woodville wife of Henry Montfort. Distraction! phrensy! fiends!"

S. "Phrensy, indeed!—What am I to make of this, Mr. Montfort?—Why do you shake so? Why repel this proposition with such bewildering rage?—Why are you thus changed?

"Think of your own words, sir. I shall never forget them: nor the cheering—the unexpected light of benignity and happiness that beamed from your countenance while you so emphatically pronounced them!

"Did you not say that it had pleased God that I should be the instrument of comfort and reconciliation?—that Henry should be restored to your affections and his inheritance, and that I should share them with him?"

M. "I did—I did—But then I did not know—Horror of horrors!—What?"—

A loud knocking was heard at the street-door. Montfort started. His eye became wild and haggard. His limbs shook under him. Reason tottered.

"Are they here?—Are they here? Do they knock so loud, and so importunate?

"Shield! shield me, heaven! They snatch me!—tear!"

S. "Who snatch—who tear you, sir? Be calm! be comforted, sir. There is nothing to harm you. It is only your son, sir, I dare to say."

M. "Son!—Son!"

S. "Your only son, sir! My Henry! My husband! He is coming according to our mutual agreement, to acknowledge and to—claim—"

"Husband?" vociferated Montfort, more wild than ever—"Husband!—Husband! Husband!"

Then seizing her by the hand, and assuming a look of dreadful tranquility—"And hast thou married him, Seraphina?—hast thou married him?—Hast thou outstripped my caution, and renewed—"

S. "Why should you make me tremble, sir, to answer you? Why, with mysterious agitation, make me wish undone that which was done in innocence and purity?—

"Your looks terrify me, sir! They infect me with distraction.

"Why do you shake so?—For what new horrors am I reserved?"

M. "Art thou—art thou married?"

S. "I cannot descend to falsehood, sir—strongly as your passion moves me. Or, if I could, Nature would tell the tale!"

M. "Nature!—Nature tell the tale?"

S. "I am the wife of Henry Montfort, sir."

M. "And Nature!—Nature!—What of Nature? Nature!

"She has given you assurances that you shall be a mother?"

S. "She has, sir."

M. "And I—

"The maledictions of heaven shall be complete!—

"And I!—

"This—only this, was wanting to my damnation!—

"And I—shall see all Nature's abominations thickening round me!—a sea of chaos of unnatural lusts—All order mingled—all connections jarred—all ties, and all affinities confounded—with uncle fathers, and with sister wives.

"I hear the universal shout of hell peel out my crime!—

"And you shall curse me!—Henry shall curse me!—The first accents of the yet unborn babe shall curse me!—He too, mincing his grandsire's name, *shall join the hideous yell! And lisp of Incest!—Incest!*"

S. "Incest?—Incest?"

A servant opened the door. Seraphina had been mistaken in the conjecture that had produced this final paroxysm. It was not Henry, but the reverend Mr. Woodhouse that was announced.

"Woodhouse! Woodhouse!" exclaimed Montfort—"I have no ears for Woodhouse. They are torn enough already. Would he too join the yell?—Agent of fiends!—would he too join the shriek, and yelp of Incest? Incest!

"Bid him depart!—Depart yourself!—Begone."

The poor domestic was petrified with horror. He closed the door in trepidation, and hastened back to Woodhouse.

"Alas, sir! Mr. Montfort!" said Seraphina, trembling—"what can this mean? What can have thus distempered your imagination?"

M. "Distemper!—distemper!—Would that it were distemper!—The thought of madness, and not madness from the thought!—Would that it were phrensy indeed—the dream of bewildering passion!—that Montfort were not Woodville, nor Woodville Montfort.

"But your guilty mother bursts again from the grave to curse me. Again she shrieks in my affrighted ears—Thy children have engendered with thy children! and thy little grandchild, clinging to thy knees, shall lisp of Incest! Incest!"

Another servant appeared at the door.

"Mr. Woodhouse says he must see you, sir. Some papers of the late Mrs. Montfort's have fallen into his hands, that are of the utmost importance; and he can deliver them to nobody but yourself.

"Fiends! fiends!' exclaimed Montfort, "why do you torment me with Woodhouse? There is hell enough here already.—Begone! begone!"

The second messenger was as terrified as the first. He also closed the door with precipitancy: but it was suddenly burst open again; and Henry came rushing into the room.

"For God's sake! what is the matter?" exclaimed he—"What is the meaning of the shrugs, the whisperings, the affrighted looks of the servants?—the scowling insolence of that fellow below?—these countenances of affliction and horror?

"God of heaven! My Seraphina! My Seraphina!"

He caught her in his arms, as, pale and breathless, she was sinking into the earth.

"Fiends! fiends!" cried Montfort, with a shriek that thrilled their souls; rushing between them, and hurling them asunder. "Incestuous fiends! be separated thus for ever!

"For me—for me!"—continued he, rushing out of the room, "Hell is prepared for me!"

Silence and horror succeeded to this burst of phrensy. Seraphina threw herself into a chair; and Henry, rooted on the spot, to which the frantic violence of his father had hurled him, stood gazing upon her, with hands clasped about his breast, and eyes rolling in delirium.

At length, after a fearful pause—

"Have I escaped one incest," said Seraphina, "only to rush into another?"

"Incest!—Incest!" repeated Henry with a groan, "God of heaven!—Incest?" He started from stupor into phrensy.

"Incest!—Incest!—Incest!" continued he, pacing about the room, as distracted as Montfort himself—"God of heaven! Is it possible?—Incest!"

"Oh! Henry! my Henry!" exclaimed Seraphina. "Is Woodville Montfort? And is Montfort Woodville?

"Oh! speak to me, my Henry!—speak to me. Pace not thus around in silent agony.—My husband!—brother!—Henry!

"We are innocent, my love!—WE are innocent!—My soul acknowledges not transgression.—Unconsciousness cannot be guilt."

H. "It is all that guilt is known by—Punishment!—eternal punishment!—the punishment of eternal exile from Love and from Seraphina!

"Lost! lost! to heaven above! to happiness below!

"What demon has proclaimed it?—Why slept not the secret in eternal mystery?—Why perished it not in oblivious night?

"If unconsciousness is innocence, why were we not suffered to be unconscious still? that still we might have loved!—still sighed and mingled our enraptured souls; and here, at least, had blessedness!

"The heavings of that soft bosom—the gentle throbbings of that responsive heart, had never whispered *Incest!* The swimming eye had never suggested it! The sigh had never breathed it! Thought never had conceived!—This world, at any rate, had not been lost!

"But now!—

"Can Nature support the recollection—Or, if conscience could be appeased for what is past, is it possible, for the future, to exist without Seraphina?

"O! which way shall I turn my distracted thoughts?—How hope to escape from madness? Terror behind, and dreariness before, and incest and separation upon either hand!—

"The babe, too!—the babe!—the poor unconscious embryon!—What shall be its fate?—Pain and Affliction shall welcome it into life! Loathing shall be its nurse, and its preceptor Horror!"

"Ah! torment not your soul with such reflections, Henry," said Seraphina,—"torment not mine. We are innocent, my Henry!—We are innocent—The babe will be innocent too. It shall not lose the privilege of innocence. It shall have a mother's love!"

H. "But not a father's,—not a father's!—No; wretched orphan of a living parent! Infamy and desertion is its lot.

"You say that we are innocent. How shall we be innocent now?—By separation—by misery—by worse than death.

"O! would that it were not worse? Would that I might die indeed!—that the grave might be oblivious!—that I might think no more."

While Henry was thus indulging his imagination in aggravating the horrors of his fate, the voice of Pengarron—the eager, happy voice of delighted benevolence, was heard upon the stairs.

He rushed into the room, skipping and capriolling about, with a sort of delirious rapture.

"Huzza! huzza!" shouted he, throwing up his hat, and kicking it with his foot as it descended—"Huzza! Where is old Percival? Where is the old boy? I'll warm the cockles of his heart, I'll warrant you.

"Huzza! huzza! Let me buss[1] you, girl? Let me hug you, boy! Such news, my boy! Such news!

"Where's dad? Pho! pho! Dad?—Old Montfort I mean—the old boy!

"Where is your dad, girl? Where's your dad?" repeated he, turning round to Seraphina—"Such news!"

"What news, doctor?" said Henry—"What news?"

"*What news?*" repeated Pengarron, drily—"What I shall tell you first, I'll be bound. Umph! Umph!—Why, the fleet has sailed without you:— there's news for you, you young rakehell!—There's news."

"Is that all?" said Henry, dejectedly—"Is that all! Would it had not."

P. "Ho! Ho!—Is the wind in that corner?—Why, then, it has not sailed; and you may get aboard as fast as you please.

"Umph! Umph! Why, what the devil's the matter with you both?— What, pale as ashes? and trembling and snivelling? Why, sure the old fool hasn't—

"But no matter!—No matter!—Where is the old boy?"

William entered the room.

"My master is upon the bed, sir—He desires to see you immediately. We are afraid he is out of his mind, sir; and going to die."

P. "So bad?—so bad?—Why, then, the old fool has—But no matter!— No matter!—I have a cordial for him, I'll warrant."

W. "Aye, sir—and so you need; and a strait waistcoat to boot: for I'm sure he's out of his mind, sir—for he raves! and groans! and looks so wildly! and talks about the devil, sir!"

---

1 Kiss.

P. "Never fear, boy!—Never fear. We'll lay the devil presently. We'll lay him. He shall have no chop amongst us this bout, I'll promise him!

"Cheerly, boy—I tell you, cheerly—The fleet has not sailed yet. But slip its cables when it will, I'll lay a month's fees it sails without you."

So saying, he hurried up to old Montfort; leaving the lovers astonished and confounded; bewildered in a sort of twilight hope—Hope amidst despair; for they could suggest to themselves no possible means by which they were to be extricated from this labyrinth of afflictions.

CHAP. II.

The amour of Woodhouse, and Nerissa; an essential Episode.

Brief Retrospect.—The eventful Procrastination.—The Breach of Confidence.—The Clerical Amour.—The Discovery.—Fresh Perplexities. The Discovery confirmed.

BEFORE we inform the reader of the immediate cause of that paroxysm of delight in which our worthy doctor has been displaying so many juvenile antics, it is absolutely necessary to enter into some retrospective views, and trace the remoter causes of the intrusive visit of the reverend Emanuel Woodhouse.

It cannot be forgotten, that, at the beginning of our first volume, and again towards the conclusion, a young lady was introduced, by the name of Nerissa, who was announced, in the first instance, as a personage of some importance in our history.

On the further of these occasions it will be remembered, that, among other traits of an equally excusable nature, we noticed the habitual and cherished propensity she entertained of insinuating herself into the confidence of those who favoured her with their friendship and protection. It will be remembered, that foresight and a sense of interest, rather than tattling loquacity, were the motives of this curiosity; and it will be remembered, also, that it was the intention even of the penetrating Amelia (encouraged by the apparent prudence of her character in this respect) to have made her the depositary of some awful secret with which the bosom of that amiable woman very evidently laboured; and that she even began the purposed narrative, and had almost proceeded to the unlimited disclosure of the mystery, when the arrival of Montfort suddenly interrupted the discourse, at the very instant when the passions and curiosity of the confidant were worked up to the highest pitch of expectation.

It followed, of course, that, immediately upon the return of Montfort, the new arrangements and new circumstances that arose out of that event, would leave Amelia but little liberty, and still less inclination, to renew a subject evidently so agitating to all her feelings; and it has been already suggested that the deportment of that gentleman soon occasioned it to be considered as prudent, at least, if not necessary, to remove this young woman out of the way of those temptations which he might probably have spread before her.

This was a bitter mortification to Nerissa. The circumstances of the imperfect narrative had made a deep impression upon her mind; and she burned with the eager desire of becoming acquainted with the mysterious something that still remained untold.

The second departure of Montfort for the West Indies, as it restored her to familiarity and domestication with her generous patroness, revived her hopes of obtaining possession of the remaining secret. But the reader has been already informed that she did not, upon this occasion, recover all the confidence she had formerly possessed: the progressive changes of her character having occasioned Amelia to regard her in a somewhat less interesting point of view.

The tale of mysteries therefore never was renewed; and the secret, so devoutly desired, remained locked up in the uncommunicative guardianship of that writing-desk upon which the longing eyes of Nerissa were so often fixed in vain.

Independently of the altered estimation in which Amelia now held the character of this young woman, there was also another reason why, by this time, she should have become more reluctant to communicate the story to her ear.

She was beginning to look forward to the season when Henry himself should become a fit depositary for that secret, with which, upon the whole, it was better, perhaps, that nobody should be acquainted but himself. She determined therefore to lock it up in silence in her own bosom, until he should be of proper age to keep a secret of so much importance; and, in the mean time, to avoid all conversations even with him, that might have any tendency to betray her into a premature disclosure.

It was once her intention, to have put the papers into his hand that contained the aweful narrative—those papers which the reader remembers her to have mentioned to Nerissa, and which Nanny has described her as so frequently perusing, with emotion, previous to his departure for St. Domingo. But the dread lest he should imprudently indulge himself in allusions to the facts in his correspondence, and that his letters (by some perverse accident) should fall into other hands, restrained her from executing this design.

Upon his return from that island, she meditated this disclosure with greater earnestness. But secrecy, upon this point, had now become so settled a habit; and the disclosure itself would necessarily be so painful and agitating to her feelings, that day after day, and week after week, were suffered to pass away in saying, upon this occasion it shall be done, or upon that, till procrastination itself became also habitual, and perpetuated its adjournments by larger and still larger strides.

In the midst of these delays, Amelia was surprised, though not without some warnings, yet the reader has seen how unexpectedly, by the evident approaches of dissolution.

Then, indeed, recollecting that the important disclosure had never been made, she caused herself to be hurried home, and called for her dear Henry, that she might pour the important secret into his ear. But it has been seen by what accidents he was prevented from arriving time enough to receive it from her lips.

Thus circumstanced, finding that the moment of dissolution was at hand, Amelia had no resource but to entrust to Nerissa the key of her writing-desk, where the papers that contained the narrative and respective documents were to be found; and to conjure her to apprise her Henry of the circumstances as soon as he should arrive.

But the curiosity of Nerissa was now too powerfully excited to admit of the faithful discharge of this duty. Seventeen years had elapsed since the imperfect narrative of her agitated patroness had so strongly awakened that passion in her breast, and time, that weakens so many impressions, had given additional force to this.

The eyes of Amelia, therefore, were no sooner closed by the last sad office of attendant friendship, than Nerissa, seeing herself in possession of the means of satisfying her inveterate propensity, hastened, as has been already seen, and opened the cabinet of interdicted knowledge.

But now a fresh impediment presented itself. The packet of papers, indeed, was found; but it had been recently sealed: and the only alternative that presented itself, was to remain, with this additional excitement and mortification upon her mind, in the same state of painful ignorance in which she had so long continued; or to gratify her passion, with the certainty of detection before her eyes.

Had Henry been as sensible to her attractions as she had endeavoured to make him, this latter might have been a consideration of slight importance. But ten years, on the wrong side, was something in the estimation of Henry, even in a mistress; and, although art conspired with nature to prolong the softness and the bloom of youth, to her at least, he was as cold and chaste as even the sermons of Emanuel Woodhouse could have made him.

To do Henry justice, he had moral feelings that revolted from the idea of such a connection. The orphan ward of his mother stood in a degree of moral affinity towards him that precluded the possibility of an illicit intercourse.

Nerissa, who had made love to the secret, as much as to the person of Henry, though to this she was not indifferent, felt the cruelty of her dilemma so much the more insupportable on this account. Sighs and blandishments would not, on the one hand, excuse the clandestine gratification of her curiosity, nor, on the other, procure the open development she so much desired.

Should it be found that she had broken open the packet, she should be overwhelmed with inevitable confusion and disgrace. But on the other hand, the secret—Could that be resisted?

At length another expedient suggested itself, which she thought might be appealed to with impunity.

It was evident, from the dying words of Amelia, that Henry, as yet, had not the slightest intimation that any such packet was in existence. Thus far, at least, the secret was hers; and it was hers alone. All that was wished therefore was in her power. She could take away the packet entirely, and make herself mistress of the contents at leisure. If the secret was of that importance which its mysterious concealment seemed to augur, it might be in her power to stipulate for pardon—perhaps for something more. If not, she had still the refuge of sheltering herself from indignation by a protracted—an unlimited concealment.

While she was yet balancing in her mind the inducements and the objections to this mode of procedure, the arrival of Henry necessitated her to an immediate decision. Honour fled in the panic; and curiosity prevailed. She locked the desk; hurried the packet into her pocket; and hastened, with that embarrassment that has been already noticed, to meet him as he was proceeding to the chamber of the deceased Amelia.

It was thus that the secret, which was upon the very verge of discovery at the commencement of our history, remained so long undeveloped. It was thus that the revival of the subject of these papers, by the affecting loquacity of Nanny, conducted to no traces of discovery.

In short, thus has the catastrophe of our history been delayed by the series of calamities and horrors, in which it has lately been involved; and the passions and feelings of the principal parties have been brought to that climax of agitation from which little could be anticipated but final distraction and separation.

In the mean time Nerissa, thus possessed of the important secret, had entered upon new scenes of life; she had become, in many respects, a new character.

When the reader first became acquainted with her, she had, at least, all the innocence and tenderness of youth to interest his feelings in her behalf. Time and dependence operated alike upon the foibles and better dispositions of her nature. Affection became insinuation, and affectation art. The susceptibility of tender impression was exchanged, or rather associated with the ensnaring wiles of meretricious coquetry; till disappointed in her repeated efforts to allure some youth of fortune or expectations into the chains of matrimony, she had begun (some time before the event of which we are now speaking) to cast her eyes about for some eligible connection of another kind; and to repent her, not a little, of the inflexible virtue with which she had heretofore rejected some advantageous offers of that description.

To this change of sentiment, for which the growing depravity of nature had begun to prepare her, she was indeed the more powerfully stimulated from the consideration that Amelia (the only friend whose kindness she had not already exhausted) was, at that time, drawing, very evidently and rapidly, towards the fatal period of her days.

Disappointed in her advances to the passions of Henry, she descended to lower game; and fortune threw in her way, at last, a *friend* and *protector* more sensible of the attraction of her charms.

This was, in fact, no other person than the reverend Emanuel Woodhouse. This pious gentleman, sufficiently solicitous, as we have seen, to collect every information respecting the conduct and irregularities of Henry, had suspected, not unwisely, that it must be in the power of this young lady to furnish him with many interesting particulars; if he could but have the good fortune to get her into the proper humour.

In this he supposed there could be little difficulty. "The tattling loquacity of woman was sufficient inducement." He took, therefore, an early opportunity, after the death of Amelia, and the consequent departure of Nerissa from Grosvenor-square, to wait upon the fair confidante at her lodgings: and, without any other ceremony or preparation than a few common-place compliments, he introduced, somewhat covertly indeed, but in such terms as easily were understood, the subject of his inquiry.

But Nerissa, who (as it has been already seen) was no walking gazette of anecdote and scandal, evaded his enquiries with a coldness that not a little confounded him.

In other respects, however, her coldness could not be complained of. The visits of the reverend gentleman were very politely and very cordially encouraged. She took, also, especial care to be dressed up in all her attractions, whenever he was expected: and if he had his designs, it was soon apparent that she had also hers.

Nor were her lures displayed, or her springes set, in vain.

Woodhouse, though sufficiently attentive to the decorums of his cloth, was not without the frailties of man. And as Nerissa (who was only two or three years upon the wrong side of thirty) was still, altogether, a woman of some attractions; and as, moreover, the connection appeared somewhat promising for the furtherance of his main design—(from the likelihood of its conducing to that confidence which he could not otherwise obtain,) he was easily induced to prefer a suit which he foresaw could not be rejected. In short, a friendly intimacy took place, which had continued (though with the most decent privacy—and, of course, the utmost exactness of Platonic purity) to the very time of which we are at this instant writing.[1]

To this time, however, Nerissa had never communicated the contents of the purloined packet; nor, indeed, suggested the most distant hint that any such packet was in her possession: for an over promptitude of confidence was not one of the foibles of this lady; and the mistress was scarcely more communicative than the mere acquaintance.

---

1   Thelwall's satire on "Platonic" amours here is comparable to that of the chapter "The Platonic Fair" in *The Peripatetic*, whose protagonist Beatissa is similar to Nerissa.

In truth, there were more reasons than one for the secrecy of Nerissa, in this respect. She knew very well, by this time, the designs of Woodhouse; and the uses that would be made, by that reverend gentleman, of the discovery, if once it were in his power; and she had, even yet, no inclination to be assistant in the ruin of Henry; which, as she supposed, must have been the inevitable consequence of Montfort being made acquainted with the content of the mysterious packet. She imagined, also, that circumstances might naturally enough arise that would tender the secret she had so clandestinely obtained, a source of no small advantage to the possessor: and her attachment to Woodhouse was not of so romantic a character as to induce her to be more solicitous of his welfare than her own. On the contrary, indeed, she regarded the connection she had formed somewhat in the same point of view that it would have been considered by another more experienced matron, who has so lately made her final exit from our scene.

Thus it happened that the reverend and sagacious gentleman, who had so often made tools and instruments of his own sex, for the prosecution of his nefarious designs, found himself foiled and baffled in the like attempts upon a person, certainly by no means of the first rate capacity, of the other.

If Woodhouse, however, was disappointed, Nerissa was not. If he could not insinuate himself into her confidence, she had contrived to worm herself, most effectually, into his heart; and she continued to maintain an unshaken ascendency over his affections: an ascendency, however, not very conducive to his happiness. His sullen and disingenuous mind was perpetually tormented by the demon of Jealousy: a passion which it was a part of her nefarious policy rather occasionally to encourage than to allay; from the imagination that the less secure a being of so depraved an appetite might feel himself of her affections, the greater security she would have of the permanency of his attachment.

It was in one of the jealous fits that resulted from these dispositions and this management, that the discovery we are now about to record came so critically to light.

Woodhouse had become possessed of the idea that she was in correspondence with some rival; and she, aware of his suspicions, had tantalized him with the appearance of mysterious concealment, about a letter of no real importance whatever, that happened to be delivered while he was there.

A quarrel ensued—one of those jealous quarrels which, as yet, she had never failed to turn to her advantage; and, that she might aggravate him still further, she contrived to be away from home when he repeated his visit, as she expected, the ensuing evening, with a heart full of contrition and repentance.

Woodhouse waited for some time, with considerable impatience, for her return; his reviving jealousy rising still higher and higher, in proportion to the tediousness of the delay: yet no Nerissa appeared.

His suspicions rose to a paroxysm—

"She was gone to meet his rival; and that d— letter was the messenger of assignation!"

His eye happened to fall, as he was uttering this, upon the drawer, into which he had seen her convey the letter in question, and lock it up with such mysterious care.

"Death and fire! he would know the bottom of it!"

He had no sooner vented the ejaculation, than he fell to the execution of the threat implied.

He forced open the drawer. A letter presented itself. He opened and read it—

"Psha! that could never be it! Trash and nonsense! She had hid it deeper."

He proceeded to empty all the papers upon the floor, till, at the bottom of the drawer, he found a small packet of manuscripts, wrapped up with particular care; and which evidently had been, heretofore, no less carefully sealed—

"Sealed?—Aye, and with the arms of Montfort!"

In short, as the reader, of course, will be ready to apprehend, it was the very packet that Nerissa had purloined, as has been heretofore stated, from the writing-desk of her departed patroness.

Woodhouse, indeed, could form no idea either of the contents, or the manner in which a packet, so sealed and directed (for it was addressed to Henry), could have fallen into the possession of his mistress. With respect to the former of these points, however, he determined to be satisfied without delay: for his jealousy, violent as it was, finding no proper food to sustain it, had given way to another passion.

The contents were a treasure indeed. Much of the manuscript enclosed (enough for his purpose) was in the hand-writing of Amelia herself—the remaining parts were documents, evidently authentic, by which the narrative was substantiated and explained.

He did not stop, however, to peruse the whole. Having seen enough to satisfy himself of the general importance of the papers he folded them up again and, putting them very carefully into his pocket, hurried back to his chambers; leaving the shattered drawer, and the remainder of its rifled contents, scattered about the floor, to apprise Nerissa, upon her return, of the discovery that had been made in her absence.

This misfortune could never have happened to Nerissa at a season when its importance would have been more critically felt. She had lost her treasure, just at the very time when it was in the way of becoming to her a treasure indeed. She had gone, in the first instance, upon a visit of no importance, merely that she might be out of the way when Woodhouse came to visit her: but her return had been procrastinated by much more powerful motives.

She had, all along, for obvious reasons, kept an eye upon the family of Montfort, and had, indeed, maintained a sort of acquaintance with the old housekeeper, that she might know what was going on with respect both to Henry and the old gentleman.

From her and from Woodhouse together, she had learned, pretty accurately, the history of those transactions that had taken place previous to the disgrace of that reverend gentleman; and from her alone she had since heard the much more extraordinary circumstance of Seraphina's being received into the house of Montfort, while Henry was sent into a sort of banishment on board the West India fleet.

She could not help regarding this as a very mysterious sort of business; and now that she was out, and in a sort of rambling inquisitive humour, she determined to make some effort to worm herself into the mazes of this secret.

She went, therefore, to the house of a common acquaintance (a tradesman in the neighbourhood of the square) where she and the old housekeeper had often met; and from thence sent a private intimation of her desire to see her. Her desire was immediately complied with.

Now it so happened that this was the very person, who (as we have already hinted) had collected the fatal secret from the incoherent ravings of the dying Newcomb.

What does the reader think was the consequence? Had the old housekeeper, also, the continence of tongue for which we have celebrated Nerissa?

Assuredly she had not; and the discovery was accordingly imparted with the customary injunctions of secrecy.

Nerissa immediately perceived in this tale of apparent horrors one of those opportunities, which, through some medium or other, she had expected might arise, of turning her former breach of confidence to some advantage. She had accordingly returned home, full of the contemplation of that discovery she thought it in her power to make, to draw the important packet from its concealment.

Judge of her disappointment—of her vexation—her rage, when she saw what had taken place in her absence.

Furious with the sense of injury—that injury which, with so little scruple, she had herself committed upon another, she flew, the next morning, before she thought it possible for him to be out, to the interdicted chambers of Woodhouse. But this was an attack for which the artful spoiler was prepared. He knew very well that, in such a case, the decent prohibition (which hitherto, from regard to her own character as well as his, she had implicitly obeyed) against visiting him at his acknowledged residence, would be but of little avail. He had arisen therefore, in the morning, from his sleepless couch, before the laundress arrived to light his fire; that he might take care himself that the outer door should be closed after her to and fro; and that closed it should be kept, as though he were not at home, till he were really and bona fide out.

It was in vain, therefore, that the enraged Nerissa assailed the dumb planks of this unresponsive barrier. Those who are acquainted with inns of court, know very well that the closing of this is as effectual a "*not at home*" to all intruders, and visitors at unwelcome hours, as ever was brazed upon the countenance of any liveried varlet from Temple Bar to Pimlico and Tyburn turnpike.[1]

Nerissa, however, persevered in her attack. She saw through the artifice: and she determined to practise equal artifice in her return. She pretended to withdraw—but she took care not to lose sight of the sortie of the staircase; and after having walked half a dozen of times or so, to and fro, she returned again to reconnoitre the garrison. She repeated the stratagem again and again. But all to no effect.

Woodhouse was prepared for this also; and here he had, likewise, the advantage. He was upon his own ground. He knew the proper station of ambush; and his faithful laundress procured him a no less faithful spy, to watch the ambiguous motions of the enemy.

All the effect, therefore, of this visit was only to keep the reverend discoverer a sort of prisoner for some hours later than he intended, and to prevent him from hastening to Grosvenor-square with his discovery, till his scout could bring him intelligence that the besieging party, worn out of all patience, had turned her tedious blockade into an actual retreat, and left the plain open for his escape.

It was with this packet then, thus obtained, that the reverend Emanuel Woodhouse had repaired to the house of Montfort, and it was for the purpose of disclosing its contents that he was so importunate for an interview with the old gentleman: for the documents were too important, he thought, to be entrusted to any intermediate hand; and he was not without hopes, that this important service (much more important, indeed, than he expected or desired) would do something, with the assistance of a little canting and moralizing, towards restoring him to grace and favour.

Unsubdued, therefore, by denial and repulse, he determined to remain in the hall, and to reiterate his messages, with such additional circumstances as might be likely to awaken interest and curiosity, till he should obtain the desired interview.

While he was thus waiting, Pengarron alighted from his carriage, and was brushing by him.

Two greater antipathies, perhaps, could scarcely exist in nature: yet necessity brought them a while into contact.

Woodhouse immediately accosted him. "Good morning to you, Dr. Pengarron! I hope I have the happiness to see you well."

---

1 The mock-heroic battles of strategy and subterfuge that follow between Nerissa and Woodhouse, as well as (rhetorically) between Woodhouse and Pengarron, no doubt draw upon Thelwall's experience as a legal apprentice, as well as his own trial, with the same satire of law that is also present in *The Peripatetic*, and his 1804 *Letter to Jeffray* [sic] and ballads. Temple Bar, home to the legal profession, was a traditional boundary of the City of London, Pimlico an area of West-End just becoming fashionable at this time, and Tyburn, near present-day Marble Arch, a longtime site of public execution, to which prisoners would travel from Newgate prison, beyond Temple Bar. In drawing this map, Thelwall connects fashion with felony.

P. "Umph! Mr. Chaplain! No great happiness to see you here again, sir, I assure you. What, you have been giving ghostly comfort to my patient, I suppose? With a murrain to you!"

W. "I have not yet been able to get sight of him, sir. I must beg for you, sir, to be kind enough to introduce me—"

P. "Introduce you?—Yes, with a vengeance! To the gallows, Mr. Chaplain; or to the devil, if I had any interest that way, I would introduce you and welcome, Mr. Chaplain! but never to my patient, I assure you. So, good morning, Mr. Chaplain!"

W. "But, sir! I have news of the utmost importance to communicate."

P. "Hum!—News! What, you have learned that Henry ventured ashore, I suppose, without permission, and are come to inform the old gentleman, under whose window his son spent the night."

W. "I am come to inform him, sir, that he has no son at all."

P. "How? Hey? What? Dead?—Henry Montfort dead!"

W. "Dead enough, sir, as Montfort, though Henry may be yet alive. Mr. Montfort has been imposed upon, sir—Henry is not his son."

P. "Not his son? Hey! How, scoundrel!—My Lucretia![1]—

"And yet, egad," said he, recollecting himself, and rubbing his hands— "If it should be so! if it should be so!"

W. "Perhaps, sir, you may know this hand"—showing the papers.

P. "Hand! Let me see, let me see. I believe I do. It is the writing of Amelia Montfort. I could swear to it."

W. "Here then, sir, is a full disclosure of the facts in the lady's own hand-writing. Henry Montfort, as you call him, sir, is an impostor—a spurious child—and neither the son of Mr. nor of Mrs. Montfort."

CHAPTER THE LAST.

Containing in the Space of a few Weeks, a Funeral, a Resurrection, and a Wedding;
equally conducing to the happy Catastrophe of our Drama.

Fresh Perplexities.—The Death Bed.—The Testament.—The Adoption.—Final Adjustments.—A pathetic Catastrophe.—News from St. Domingo.—The Packet.—The Family at Elmsley; a concluding Incident.

SUCH was the news that had sent Pengarron skipping into the breakfast-room, as described at the conclusion of the first chapter of the present book.

---

1 Most likely a poignant allusion to the wronged wife in Shakespeare's *The Rape of Lucrece*, who became an icon of political liberty after her violation and suicide led to the founding of the Roman republic; there may be an ironic allusion to Lucretia Borgia, famous for ruthless sexual and religious corruption and manipulation, but that does not fit Pengarron's sympathy for Amelia.

Woodhouse, indeed, had refused to put the papers into his hand. He would deliver them to nobody but Montfort himself: but he had given him such proofs as were sufficient to satisfy his mind, and to send him, full-charged with rapture, in quest of the unnecessarily afflicted father.

Montfort received the intelligence with an overwhelming delight. He desired that Woodhouse might be immediately admitted, that the papers he was in possession of might be produced.

But Woodhouse had hurried out of the house, while the doctor was capering about in the breakfast-room, and had taken the papers with him.

This circumstance threw every thing into confusion again. Pengarron was astonished; and Montfort began to doubt—to despair.

The fact is, that the raptures of Pengarron, so unexpected, at the intelligence, had occasioned Woodhouse to make inquiries among the servants, who soon (for the supposed relationship between Henry and Seraphina was now no longer a secret) gave him so many hints as convinced him that, instead of ruining Henry, as he expected, he was come to snatch him from that ruin, which, but for his officiousness, would apparently have been inevitable: and that the property that had been upon the eve (by the probable death or distraction of the intervening parties) of falling into the lap of himself, and the other secondary heirs of Montfort, would now, by his busy, meddling testimony, only be snatched from a suppositious son, to be conferred upon a real daughter, who, together with herself, would restore it to the long-imagined heir.

Impressed with these convictions, he execrated himself for all he had done; cursed his jealous curiosity for the discovery to which it had led him; and (determining, if he could not recall the secret he had developed, at least to conceal the proofs, and throw every thing into doubt and difficulty) had retired, as has been already stated. Indeed, he was not entirely without hopes, though those hopes were feeble, of retrieving his error. Nerissa and himself were the only depositaries of the secret. If he could but persuade the former, by any promises of reward or views of interest, to declare the whole to have been a forgery of her own, he had nothing to do but to throw the yet unproduced documents into the fire; and all would at least be reduced again into a state of ambiguity that might answer all his purpose. And as for the confidence of Pengarron about Amelia's hand-writing, he thought the recent forgeries of Moroon that had imposed even upon the lovers themselves, notwithstanding their frequent correspondence, was a sufficient answer to that.

He hurried, therefore, to the apartments of Nerissa, to see how far she could be worked upon to his purpose.

But Nerissa was not at home.

She was gone indeed (for now it appeared her only course) to the house of Montfort, to disclose the whole of the facts respecting the purloined papers, and the important secret which they contained.

Her arrival at Grosvenor-square, and the avowal of the object of her visit, restored the smile of hope to every countenance.

The horrors of Montfort subsided—the consternation of Pengarron, and the pendulous apprehensions of the lovers.

She could not, indeed, produce the papers. She could only reveal the manner in which they came first into her possession, and afterwards into that of Woodhouse. But she could vouch the contents: for she had perused them again and again, and treasured them up in her remembrance.

The particulars of these contents she immediately recounted: and, from her narrative, all that had been stated by Woodhouse was amply confirmed, with the addition of other particulars, in a general point of view, scarcely less interesting or important.

Henry was not the son of Montfort and Amelia, but of that disastrous couple, Bowbridge and Louisa.

The reader will remember, how nearly at the same time the two amiable and unfortunate women, whose friendship was the subject of one of our earliest episodes, were delivered of those respective children, the tender anticipations of whose birth had been interrupted by the catastrophe of horrors produced by the adventure at Vauxhall. It will be remembered also, that, in the pangs of child-birth, or, at least, shortly after her delivery, the unfortunate Louisa expired; leaving behind her "an affecting testament," by which some legacy or other (the nature of which has never yet been stated) was bequeathed to her surviving friend, Amelia.

The contents of this testament, and the fate of the respective children, brought into the world under these calamitous circumstances, Amelia was then prevented from disclosing in the recorded conversation. It remains, therefore, to be recorded now—It remains now to be stated, that the legacy in question was no other than the new-born Henry; that "*the affecting testament of the ever to be lamented, loved Louisa,*" was no other than an exhortation to Amelia, written by the dying hand of maternal anxiety; and conjuring her, by every memorial of their former friendship—by every afflicting remembrance that could arise from events more recent, to be a mother to her orphan babe, and let her fostering virtues make some atonement for the dreadful catastrophe, by which *she*, and all that was dear to her, were overwhelmed.

Amelia performed her injunction—the reader has seen how well. Accident furnished her with the opportunity of performing it better than Louisa could have expected—better than even Amelia, herself, could, at that time, have wished: an accident, however, that rendered the charge thus committed to her doubly welcome and endearing; and which, in time, occasioned her even almost to rejoice (or at least, at times, to persuade herself that she ought to do so) in a loss that would otherwise have been irreparable.

In short, the child of Amelia had just expired, in sudden convulsions, when the trusty old woman, to whom the babe and the letter of Louisa had been entrusted, entered the room.

She had been instructed, by her dying mistress, to speak to Amelia alone: and alone she had spoken to her, and presented the sleeping Henry.

The circumstances, the situation, sympathy, and a sense of moral duty, all conspired to suggest, upon the very instant, the line of conduct that was to be pursued.

"He lives!—he lives again!—my child revives!" said she, seizing the little Henry, in an agony of mingled passions, "in *thee* he is again restored. O Louisa! Louisa! my lost, my murdered Louisa! you shall be obeyed. I will be a mother indeed!"

She ordered the trusty messenger to strip the lifeless infant; to dress up in his apparel the little Henry (for so it had been the request of Louisa that he should be named;) to lay corpse with corpse, and leave the living infant at the breast of a living mother; and, with gifts and promises securing the secrecy of this only agent and confidante of the exchange, she imposed upon the servants with the pious fraud that her infant was not dead; that he had revived; and, by her maternal solicitude, was again restored.

She thought it necessary, however, to take precautions to prevent the changeling from being seen by the woman who had nursed her. Pretending dissatisfaction, therefore, at her having so lightly given up the infant as dead, she made her a very handsome present for her attendance; dismissed her from the house; and took the faithful attendant and messenger of the departed Louisa in her place.

In short, the child of Amelia was buried in the same coffin with Louisa; and the son of Louisa was nurtured in Amelia's lap.

This, affecting as it was in many of its parts, was a tale of rapture to Montfort, to the lovers, and to Pengarron, in the presence of all of whom it was repeated.

Henry and Seraphina rushed to each other's arms. Montfort lifted up his hands and eyes, with blessings, and with prayers; and Pengarron fell to capering about the room and kissing Nerissa, not for real love, as he said, for she had been a sad jade, but as a messenger of good tidings!

"And are you mine then, my Seraphina?" said Henry, as soon as he could find breath enough to speak—"May you be mine for ever?"

"Yes! yes! my Henry!" replied Seraphina, with equal transport— "Woodville is Montfort—and Montfort is Woodville—but Henry is not Montfort."

"It is realised!—it is realised!" exclaimed Montfort, sympathizing in their delight. "It was the voice of Heaven that I heard when I first beheld her—It was the voice of Heaven that whispered to my heart—*She is my messenger of love—I have sent her to heal and to save!* It has pleased God to realise his promise! It has pleased God to realise it!

"Be happy, my children! be happy. Your trials are ended. It was my guilt alone that brought them upon you: and my sins are now atoned. The son of Bowbridge shall be the heir of Montfort—the wrongs of the father shall be repaired in the person of the child. God accepts of the atonement. I see the finger of His Providence in these events; and the crimes of Montfort and Woodville are at once atoned."[1]

"And I shall have an heir too," said Pengarron—"I shall have an heir. But it shall not be the first. No—the second shall be the Pengarron. The first will have enough without me."

"He shall have no more, doctor," said Seraphina, "than all the rest—at least if I can help it."

"Or I either," continued Henry—"We will have none of the Gothic savagery by which the bonds of affinity are cracked asunder—by which the first born is rendered a lordly tyrant, and the rest dependent slaves."

P. "Well! well! as you like—as many of your new crotchets as you like. Though, 'faith, I know not how to enter into them—Family! family! Building up a family."

S. "They build a family indeed, good doctor, who bring them up in social equality and reciprocal love."

P. "Umph! Well! well! as many of your crotchets, I tell you, as you please. But that's a vile word—Equality!—a vile word, if it had come from any other quarter. But which is to be the Pengarron, then?—which is to be the Pengarron?"

H. "The first, good doctor!—the first; if it be a boy."

P. "But what says mamma to this?—What says mamma? Is it *our* will that it should be so? Or only *my*?"

S. "*Our*—good doctor!—I assure you. Ours entirely. If ever we are happy enough to have a son, he shall inherit the name of Pengarron; and it will be the first with all our hearts, that he should inherit also his virtues. But not his fortune—Situated as we now are, most assuredly not his fortune. We have enough for all.

"Let those poor carrion crows, doctor, of whom you spoke I am afraid with rather too much of the bitterness of contempt, share that between them. Or, if they are really unworthy of it, seek out some proper objects—some hapless group of intellect, of virtue, and of woe (there are groups enough of this description to be found, doctor!) and divide it among them."

P. "What, then, you reject me—you disdain my humble mite. The heiress of the opulent Montfort is too proud to accept the humble earnings of a mere mender of crazy carcases."[2]

S. "No, doctor. Never can property be more honourably procured. If moral dispensation be an attribute of that eternal necessity by which the system of the existing universe is governed, never could property be accompanied with greater blessings to its possessor. But if the heirs of

---

1 Along with the reversal of primogeniture that follows, the ethos of reciprocity, displacement, and surrogacy articulated here is an appropriate climax both formally and thematically.

2 Through the same logic of surrogacy, Thelwall here validates and celebrates his own inheritance, as his grandfather Walter was a naval surgeon (*Life* 2).

Montfort are not too proud, they will endeavour to be too just, to accumulate every thing to a few, and leave the many wretched."

P. "Umph!—Well, well—This is another of your crotchets, now—another of your new crotchets. But hold your tongue, you, vixen! I say—hold your tongue. I'll have none of your new philosophy! So name the boy Pengarron, and leave me to do as I like.—That's my philosophy, you vixen!—To do as I like—The old philosophy! and the best."

S. "Well, well, doctor! I have no objection to that philosophy in you: for it is only to show you what is good and amiable, and you will like to do precisely the thing you ought."

P. "What, coaxing! coaxing! Here's another crotchet now. A pretty sort of mother, truly—Coaxing an old man *not* to leave his money to her children. But I suppose this is the new philosophy too; and the universe is to be *our* family!"

S. "That is a height of abstraction, I am afraid, doctor, at which we shall never have virtue enough to arrive in practice. We will endeavour, however, to keep it in view, that, by straining towards this highest peak of excellence, we may at least attain some of those subordinate eminences of liberality and social virtue, which, without the assistance of such efforts, we might have failed to reach. In the mean time, doctor, be not afraid, we will not forget what duties we have to perform, on the smooth lawn of friendship, and the lowly vale of relative attachment."

Seraphina turned round to her father, as she uttered this. He was reclining on the bed; and his face was covered with his hand.

"How do you do, sir? You do not join in the vivacity which our change of fortune has produced. How are you, sir?"

M. "Ill enough, my child! ill enough: and yet well. I am at peace, and happy. I feel the blessed seal of forgiveness upon my heart. I feel it in your felicity. I have many sins to answer for—many sins—but I feel that they are forgiven. Had I been marked as a vessel of reprobation, the Almighty had not suffered me to live to be a witness of the blessedness of this day. But mine eyes have seen salvation, and I depart in peace."

"Depart! depart!" exclaimed Seraphina and Henry at the same time, "talk not of departing, sir—we must not lose you!"

Doctor Pengarron looked earnestly in his countenance. He marked his laboured respiration. He felt his pulse.

"Retire, retire, my children," said the doctor, "and compose yourselves. Your emotion is more than he can bear. He must be left to himself awhile: to solitude and tranquility. It is the only hope. You must leave him to me, I tell you.—You must leave him to me. Send up one of the servants—two of them—that I may dispatch them immediately for what is requisite."

So saying, he put them out of this room: and then turning to Montfort—"I will not deceive you, sir," said he—"the trials of this day have been more than your enfeebled nature could bear. Your end approaches. Has this discovery made no changes requisite in your will?

"Shall I send these men for a lawyer and proper witnesses?"—"Yes, yes," answered Montfort—(Pengarron gave them instructions).

"Though much is not necessary," continued the dying man, "I cut the entail, at the instigation of Woodhouse, when I was about to disinherit Henry. It is well I did so: or that worthless hypocrite would now have been one of the joint heirs of my real property. Since I discovered Seraphina to be my daughter, I have made a will, in which I have divided the bulk of my property between her and Henry. It is only necessary to remove, by a codicil, certain obstructions and prohibitions, and confirm to the son of Bowbridge what I had bequeathed while I thought him to be my own."[1]

Montfort lived, in the full possession of his faculties, long enough for the accomplishment of his design. It was the last act of his life; unless the prayers and confessions in which he spent his remaining hours, with the patient and benevolent pastor who at that time did the duties of the cure, may be considered as acts.

He died, in the course of the following day, with great composure, in the arms of Seraphina and Henry: and in the presence of Pengarron and the benevolent divine, whose attentions we have already noticed; and his obsequies were performed, in a manner suitable to his fortune and situation in life, with a reverential attention to all the wishes and peculiarities he had himself suggested.

Henry and Seraphina wept over his grave (for he had desired their attendance). Yet perhaps his death was fortunate both to himself and others. He died as yet unconscious of the peculiar sentiments of Seraphina upon a very delicate point; which, if once he had come to comprehend them, could not have failed to be productive of much misery to one of his religious views and sentiments. And, perhaps, it would be difficult to conceive how, with such a father (from whom, in his declining years and declining health, duty would have prohibited them to separate) two such beings as Seraphina and Henry could either have enjoyed or imparted, for any duration of time, the comforts of social communion.

It will be readily believed that, after these events, Edmunds was not left to the solitary seclusion of the little cottage. He was sent for again to Grosvenor-square: but not to fill the place of librarian. Neither Henry nor Seraphina would suffer him any longer to remain in any situation of dependence and servitude. He was sent for, as a friend, to share their happiness, and receive the reward of his fidelity and attachment.

Edmunds, however, cannot be said to have obeyed the summons with alacrity: for, in fact, he had anticipated it. He had received a letter for Seraphina, and had hastened to deliver it, when the messenger arrived at Walcot-place.

"A foreign letter!—a West India letter?" said Seraphina, as she received it—"a letter from St. Domingo. It must be from the planter Rabeau."—

---

1   These somewhat specialized instructions reflect Thelwall's legal training.

(For she had found means to write to him since the return of Montfort from Jamaica.)

"Well, Edmunds, if it should contain news of that little property, you shall take the contents for postage. Would that which was enough for the philosophic Parkinson in St. Domingo, be sufficient for the philosophic Edmunds in Britain?"

E. "The consciousness of having administered to your happiness, madam, and that of my master, is itself enough. I ask no other reward."

"Friend Edmunds!" said Henry, stretching out his hand, "there is one word in this modest answer of yours, that you must never let us hear again. The profession I made in you in the glen of Limbé at length is realised. I ought to have realised it before: You are no longer my servant. I am no more your master. Call me friend—call me patron—call me Henry Montfort: any thing your independent affection may prompt you to: for independent you are; and, some how or other, you shall have the means of supporting that independence."

Edmunds was overcome by his feelings. He bowed, and was silent.

"But come," said Seraphina, opening the letter, "let us see, Edmunds, what fortune may have done for you here."

Rabeau—No, it was not from Rabeau: but the outer case, at least, for there was another inclosed, was from her fugitive brother, Moroon: whom the reader will remember to have repaired from France to St. Domingo, after the horrors and discoveries that took place in the deserted mansion.

It was of course, a curious epistle—but part of it, at least, we believe, will not be thought uninteresting. We will quote it at length, and let the reader judge for himself.

"Dear sister,

"You hav'n't been used to be very much pleased with receiving letters from me—and, indeed, I must own I have been very wicked.—But I flatter myself you will be glad of this that I am writing of now—because I have two things to write about that will please you very much—especially as I am very glad to find, by the English newspapers that I saw before I left France, about the murder, that my wicked attempt upon my brother Montfort did'n't take place.

"But in the first place, as I was going to say you will be very glad to hear, that I have found the grace to repent of all my wickedness. I have met with a Moravian minister here, who is one of the missioners, who are going to make all the blacks christians; which, they say, will make 'em work a good deal better: and they are to make all the blacks upon the coast christians too; and he has poured the light of grace and comfort into my heart; and I have subscribed a hundred pound towards the good work; and he prays with me every Sunday, and three times a week beside; and so I hope God will pardon me; and you too—[1]

---

1 Moravian missionaries worked extensively with slave populations in the West
   Indies, seeming to accept the plantation system yet working from *(continued)*

"And I suppose you will be almost as glad to hear about your good old foster father—But he tells me that I must'n't tell you, all at once, that he is alive: because that's the reason that he encloses his letter in mine, without any direction at all, from

"Your repentant brother, with permission of God's grace,

"LUCIUS MOROON WOODVILLE"

"Alive!—Encloses his letter!" exclaimed Seraphina—Near as she was to the end of this scroll, she could read no further; but snatching up the undirected paper—"He lives! he lives!" exclaimed she—"He lives!—he lives!—he lives!"

She threw herself in a chair, and clasped the unopened letter to her bosom.

"Lives!" said Henry—astonished at the wildness of her agitation—"Who lives?"

S. "My foster father lives!—Parkinson lives!—the beloved—the honoured—venerable Parkinson. Here is a letter from him. When shall I have strength to open it?"

Henry took it from her trembling hand; and opened it for her. He read it. The reader may guess how different it was from the former. He may guess, also, the sensations that accompanied the perusal. How high the tide of rapture swelled in the bosom of Seraphina, of Henry, of Edmunds, when they learned that not Parkinson only, but Amanda, also, and "the babe with bloody hands" were all alive.

That the reader, however, may perceive that, extraordinary as it may appear, there was no absolute miracle in it, it is necessary to inform him, that Parkinson had been, in his youth, a very expert and powerful swimmer—that it had been one of his eccentric pleasures to buffet the rough waves of the ocean, when the sea ran so high that few would have ventured, even in cases of the last emergency, to encounter its fury.

He had been out of the practice of this important art, indeed, for some time before the formidable adventure of the Rapids of Margot. But still he had confidence; and that confidence, saved them. It was a confidence, indeed, sad and afflicting: for he knew that he could save but one; that Amanda or Seraphina must, as he concluded, perish.

It was this conviction which dictated that look of agonised affection, already noticed in Seraphina's tale of woes,—when (to use his own expression) "compelled to make an election between the two objects in the universe dearest to his throbbing heart, he clung to the trembling faithful partner of his heart (who for five and thirty years had shared in all its joys and all its sorrows,) and left the darling child of his adoption—his beloved—his Seraphina, as he imagined, irretrievably to perish.

---

within it to promote and prepare for emancipation (Furley). Thelwall's attitude to them appears equally ambivalent, judging from this satiric description; he may have been personally acquainted with their work through connections in Mirfield, where there was a well-known Moravian community.

"But she has not perished!" continued he—"Stronger sympathies, to me unknown, were hovering over for her protection: and again I shall clasp to my aged bosom,—my Amanda again shall clasp to hers, our beloved, our adopted Seraphina!"

But to resume the narrative. The force of the torrent swept them, of course, a considerable way down the river. But the weight of waters that roared round the insulated ridge being considerably greater from the one side than the other, the ascendancy of the stream bore them towards the nearest bank; and Parkinson still maintaining his buoyancy, and his presence of mind, his exertions co-operated with this tendency, and they were thrown at last upon a shelving part of the shore, upon the opposite side (as will be evident upon comparing the different descriptions of the river and the connected events) from that where they originally embarked; and to which Seraphina and her mother were reconducted by the unfortunate Mozambo.

Amanda was almost senseless; but the babe (almost perished, also) was locked in unconscious embraces in her arms: and as that side of the river was less infested by the insurgents than the other, the requisite assistance had easily been obtained to restore them to health—though not to comfort.

Comfort was indeed a word they expected to have heard no more. For though, upon the pacification of the country, they returned to the sequestered valley, and found that their little cottage had escaped, by its obscurity and seclusion, the ravages of insurrection, yet she (she grace and ornament of that retreat) was no more; and their parental checks were drenched with incessant tears.[1]

The letter to Rabeau was, therefore, a reprieve from something worse than death. Seraphina was alive—she was in England. They determined therefore to take the first possible opportunity of hastening to her. The advantage was taken of a flag of truce to make the circumstances known to the commander of the English troops in the island, and passports and permissions were applied for, to enable them to embark on board the first vessel that might sail directly for England.

During these preparations Moroon arrived at St. Domingo. His acquaintance with Rabeau had been already noticed. Further intelligence was of course communicated by him, with which Parkinson and Amanda could not but be deeply interested: and they soothed the anxiety of delay, during the time that applications were reiterated upon all hands for the requisite passports, by writing through two different channels (Amanda enclosing her letter in the answer of Rabeau, and Parkinson his as has

---

1 Another reference to the death of Thelwall's daughter Maria, even as the tale of survival of the flood through a combination of strength, persistence, and buoyancy mirrors the imagery used by Thelwall to describe his own miraculous exile and revival; the climactic survival and reunion of father and daughter is therefore the climax of the logic of adoption.

been seen, in the curious epistle of Moroon) to apprise her of their existence, and their intention.

While Henry and Seraphina, and the enthusiast Edmunds, were indulging themselves in that delight which bathes itself in tears, Pengarron arrived, to share in their felicity, and contribute his mite to its increase.

He had been at the chambers of Woodhouse for the papers and documents that reverend gentleman had purloined; and which hitherto he had thought proper to withhold. But, as he found that the parties were already in ample possession of the whole proveable contents, and that, if he persisted in his refusal to deliver them up, he had no other alternative than either to undergo a commitment and prosecution for the robbery, or to answer before the magistrates (with an immediate visit to whom he was threatened,) that the apartments in which Nerissa resided were his own apartments, and consequently to disclose the illicit connection his reverence had with that lady, he thought proper (for the sake of his character and his cloth) to comply with the present demand.

Pengarron, however, as soon as he had put the important document safely in his pocket, swore, with a big oath, profane enough to have frightened any parson in the land, that "the reverend Mr. Whoremaster should not escape so easily, with a murrain to him! but that he should either marry his punk, yet, and make an honest woman of her again; or have his gown stripped over his ears by the ordinary": and so left him to weigh the alternative.

The recovery of the papers was not the only piece of intelligence the opportunity of communicating which had elated the spirits of Pengarron.

He had written to Elmsley-hall, to inform the worthy Baronet and his lady of the leading facts of the discoveries and other incidents that had recently taken place; and, in the character of a trustee and guardian to Seraphina (for so he had been appointed by Montfort's will) to announce to them, that the young couple, already privately married, were, according to the request of their deceased father, and from other motives of prudence and decorum to be married again, on an approaching day (which he thought fit, of his own head, to appoint for them) by the names which these events had shown of reality to belong to them; and with a degree of publicity more suited to their fortune and the situation they were henceforward to fill in life.

His letter was concluded with an intimation of his conviction, how much the presence of Sir Herbert and his lady and their amiable daughter would contribute to the happiness of that day; and to render propitious the prospects of an union whose full confirmation had been so long and so disastrously delayed.

The invitation had been cheerfully accepted. The worthy baronet, in the name of himself, of lady Elmsley, and of Caroline, returned for answer, "that they would do themselves the happiness to attend, and that Caroline, in particular, would be a candidate for the honour of attending the bride to the altar."

This answer was eminently gratifying to Dr. Pengarron. The reader may easily conjecture how transcendently it would have been so to Seraphina, had not this lesser planet (if we may so express ourselves) in the now clear horizon of her fortunes, been obscured and swallowed up by the approximating and more powerful rays of that day-star of felicity that was beaming upon her heart.

But why should we pursue any further the thread of our history? The catastrophe is already obvious. The arrival of Parkinson and Amanda; their presence at the nuptials (delayed only for their return,) the congratulations of Sir Herbert and lady Elmsley; the dawning friendship of the interesting Caroline; the liberal reward of Edmunds; the enjoyments of splendour, corrected by taste, and of opulence rendered amiable by benevolence, these and more, the imagination of the reader will realise without our descriptions: and we have only to add, that Dr. Pengarron, upon the stipulated condition that the first boy of the new happy couple, should nevertheless be called after his name, consented to adopt as his heir the babe with bloody hands, and to educate this little interesting orphan as his own.

These arrangements completed, the whole of this happy party set off for the antiquated and romantic mansion of Ridgmont, to spend the remainder of the summer in visiting the lakes and mountains, and other beauties of nature, and the monuments of antiquity, with which the surrounding country every where abounds.[1]

THE END

---

1   Given the location of Ridgmont (see pp. 453-54, note 1), this prospective finale seems to predict Thelwall's proposal for an expedition to the Lakes, made in a letter to Coleridge in spring 1801.

Appendix A: Biographical Documents

1. From John Thelwall, "Prefatory Memoir," *Poems, Chiefly Written in Retirement.* Hereford, 1801

[Some months after *The Daughter,* Thelwall published—again through Richard Phillips—*Poems, Chiefly Written in Retirement,* a collection that comprises his Arthurian romance *The Fairy of the Lake,* fragments of his epic poem *The Hope of Albion,* selections from his juvenilia, and, at the centre of it all, a series of twenty-two "Effusions of Social and Relative Affection" composed between 1796 and 1801, during Thelwall's quest for a quiet retreat and subsequent relocation to Wales. Aware that the political notoriety that had forced him into "retirement" might hinder sales of the collection and bar his return to public life, Thelwall included a forty-eight-page "Prefatory Memoir" that narrates his life from childhood to the conclusion of his "ill-starred experiment" as a farmer and poet in Wales. As Michael Scrivener has shown, the memoir is a carefully composed narrative of thwarted literary ambition designed to palliate the suspicions of a hostile middle-class readership.[1] The following selections shed light on the sources for and composition of *The Daughter of Adoption.*]

The Creolean Character

[Thelwall is describing his social sphere around 1791, when he began attending medical lectures at Guy's and St. Thomas's hospitals in London. He suggests that his acquaintance at this time with several West-Indian Creoles was the basis for his depiction of Creole characters in *The Daughter* a decade later.]

Among the professional youth with whom he now associated, were several West Indians: and if their conversation and manners did not give him a very favourable impression of the Creolean character, his observation of that effeminate, or rather childish vivacity, that unfeeling and tyrannical vehemence, and that sort of hoggish voluptuousness, so frequently predominated amongst them, produced those Delineations of West Indian Manners, which, in a late anonymous publication, were considered as the sketches of an author, "evidently acquainted with other countries and with other scenes."[2]

The Abolition Debate

[In the early 1780s Thelwall began attending the debating societies then popular in London, particularly Coachmaker's Hall. He was until that point, in his own words, a "zealous ministerialist."]

---

1 See Scrivener, "The Rhetoric and Context of John Thelwall's 'Memoir,'" *Spirits of Fire: English Romantic Writers and Contemporary Historical Methods,* ed. G.A. Rosso and Daniel P. Watkins (Rutherford, NJ: Fairleigh Dickinson UP, 1990), 112-30.
2 See the excerpt from the *Critical Review* in Appendix C1.

The discussions on the subject of the Slave Trade, into which he entered with an almost diseased enthusiasm, led the way to very considerable changes in his political sentiments; as they did, also, in those of many others: and, in the new field of enquiry, which was opened by the events of the French Revolution, he proceeded, step by step, to those sentiments, his active exertions in the diffusion of which are matters of such public notoriety.

The Retreat at Llyswen

[By 1797 the combined force of the Two Acts and of violent loyalist mobs had effectively prohibited Thelwall from continuing his public lectures, and forced him to seek a quiet retreat with his family. The farm in Wales to which they retired inspired some of the settings of *The Daughter*, as discussed in the Introduction, pp. 11-12.]

The assistance of a few friends enabled him to stock a little farm, of about five-and-thirty acres, in the obscure and romantic village of *Llys-Wen*, in Brecknockshire; a scene once famous in Cambrian story, as one of the residences of Roderick the Great; from whose *White Palace* it derives its name.[1]

In the election of this spot, so far as it might be considered elective (for he had already devoted four months to a pedestrian excursion, in unavailing search for an eligible retreat:[2]) Thelwall was principally influenced by the wild and picturesque scenery of the neighbourhood. For the village (embowered with orchards, and over-shadowed by grotesque mountains) is sweetly situated upon the banks of the Wye, at one of the most beautiful, tho least visited, parts of that unrivalled river; and the cottage itself, thro the branches of the surrounding fruit trees, catches a *glympse*——while its alcove (elevated on the remains of an old sepulchral tumulus) commands the *full view*, of one of the characteristic and more-than-crescent curves of that ever-varying stream; with its glassy pool sleeping beneath the reflected bank, its rapids above, and roaring cataracts below, bordered with plantations and pendant woods, and diversified with rocks and pastures.

---

1   The ninth-century Welsh chieftain Roderick the Great (Rhodi Mawr) is reputed to have had his court at Llyswen (literally llys wen, or White Court). See Judith Thompson, "Citizen Juan Thelwall: In the Footsteps of a Free-Range Radical," *Studies in Romanticism* 48 (2009): 69-75.

2   Thelwall had initially hoped to settle in Somerset near Coleridge and Wordsworth. On the poets' unease at having the notorious radical join their circle, see Nicholas Roe, "Coleridge and John Thelwall: The Road to Nether Stowey," in *The Coleridge Connection: Essays for Thomas McFarland*, ed. Richard Gravil and Molly Lefebure (Basingstoke: Macmillan, 1990), 60-80.

The Death of Maria Thelwall

[Thelwall relates the sudden death of his young daughter Maria at Llyswen in December 1799. She died of the croup, an inflammatory disease of the larynx and trachea.[1]]

Disastrous as had been every other part of his destiny, in his family he had been, hitherto, particularly happy: and it was the frequent boast of his heart, That Nature, in this respect, had made atonement for the malice of Fortune. But, above all, his hopes (and indeed the expectations of all who, from her earliest infancy, had known her) were concentrated in his eldest child—a daughter of most premature attractions, endeared to both her parents by all the associations that can give new force to the affections of nature, and all the dispositions that can render the innocency of childhood thrice amiable. But this child (who, while every other part of the family seemed sinking under the influence of the ungenial season, appeared, alone, all health and bloom, and loveliness) was suddenly snatched away. Her danger was not perceived till it was too late; and before *distant* assistance could be procured, all assistance was vain. She died on the 28th of December, a few days after she had completed her sixth year—and left her unfortunate parents, amid the horrors of solitude, in a state of mind which souls of keenest sensibility alone can conceive; which Stoicism may condemn, and Apathy might, perhaps, deride.

Composition and Sale of The Daughter of Adoption

[Thelwall attributes the failure of his Llyswen farm to various hardships culminating in the "calamitous harvest of 1799," which left the family in financial distress.]

It was under a stimulus of this kind, that he put into his pocket the first chapter (all that was then written) of "The Daughter of Adoption"; and *walked* up to London to dispose of it, in that state, to some bookseller. In that state, Phillips, of St. Paul's Church Yard, had the confidence to purchase it—and what was still more he had the liberality to advance the sum demanded for it, on the spur of the occasion; and Thelwall returned to the Vale of the Wye to cultivate his farm with the mortgage of his brain.

---

1 Notice of Maria's death appeared in the *Monthly Magazine* 9 (February 1800): 98. Judith Thompson notes that Maria is not listed in Llyswen church records and may have been denied a consecrated burial ("Citizen Juan Thelwall" 70).

2. **From John Thelwall to Susan Thelwall ("Stella"), 18 July 1797. The Pierpont Morgan Library, New York, MA 77 (17). Reprinted in Damian Walford Davies, *Presences that Disturb: Models of Romantic Identity in the Literature and Culture of the 1790s* (Cardiff: U of Wales P, 2002), 294-97**

"A delightful ramble ... among the plantations"

[Thelwall writes to his wife from "the Enchanting retreat (the Academus of Stowey)" in Somerset, where he visited Coleridge and Wordsworth in July 1797 as he looked for a retreat of his own. The scene he describes bears comparison with the site of Henry and Edmunds's exchange about treason in St. Domingue, as discussed in the Introduction, pp. 12-13.]

We have been having a delightful ramble to day among the plantations & along [word deleted] a wild romantic dell in these grounds [of Alfoxden] thro which a foaming, murmuring, rushing torrent of water winds its long artless course—There have we sometime sitting on a tree—sometimes wading boot-top deep thro the stream ~~sometime~~ & again stretched on some mossy stone or root of a decayed tree, a [word deleted] literary & political triumvirate [word deleted] passed sentence on the productions and characters of the age—burst forth in poetical flights of enthusiasm—& philosophised our minds into a state of tranquility which the leaders of nations might envy and the residents of Cities can never know.

3. **From John Thelwall to Dr. Peter Crompton, 3 March 1798. The Houghton Library, Harvard University, Lobby VIII. 4. 22, fMS Eng. 947. 2 (21). Reprinted in Davies, *Presences*, 298-305**

"Maria ... grows a very stout and vigorous girl"

[Thelwall writes from his farm at Llyswen to his friend and benefactor Peter Crompton, a physician and philanthropist from Derby who stood unsuccessfully as an independent candidate in the Nottingham election of 1796. Thelwall's description of his daughter Maria in the bloom of health makes a poignant contrast with his account of her death less than two years later (Appendix A1). The brook and cascade alongside which his son Algernon Sidney liked to sit is, like the whole of Llyswen farm, a source of inspiration for the description of Parkinson's retreat in *The Daughter*.]

With respect to ourselves & our concerns—We are all very well & highly delighted with our situation. Maria in particular grows a very stout and vigorous girl, much taller also than we expected. We have daily & hourly proofs of the advantages of the stile of dress we have adopted—for she bounds along in her trowsers in all the romping vivacity of independence, runs up the mount, clambers among the rocks, & by her perpetual activity takes health by storm as it were. Sidney continues still the same fantastic unmanageable & unaccountable boy he was at Derby. [...] Across one end of our orchard flows a pretty little brook buddling & babbling ~~over many~~ thro a [word deleted] small romantic dingle to empty itself into the wye; in which with hobbyhorsical industry I have built a cascade of 8 or 9 feet height & am making a rude hermitage (a sequestered summer study) in the dingle beneath. The boy has found out this place & is as delighted with it as myself—for he will sit whole hours listening to the rush of the water & "pouring on the brook that bubbles by"[1]—a perfect "Il Penseroso"[2]—his whole countenance harmonises to a most soothing melancholy. The old women say he will be drowned—I say he will be philosophised— [...]

[...] I am writing for the M. Mag[3]—but a guinea or two P[er] Month is all that can be expected from that quarter. Phillips[4] seems also disposed to treat either for the Novel or the Memoirs, or both.[5] I am getting a specemin of the latter ready to send to him—& I am therefore at present almost a little of a farmer as when in Beauf. B^gs.[6]

4. From John Thelwall, *A Letter to Francis Jeffray* [sic], *Esq. On Certain Calumnies and Misrepresentations in the Edinburgh Review*. Edinburgh, 1804

[The following excerpt is from a portion of Thelwall's *Letter* in which he answers the *Edinburgh Review*'s caustic remarks on his *Poems, Chiefly Written in Retirement* (1801). As evidence of the *Edinburgh*'s vicious principles he cites in a footnote a reviewer's attack elsewhere on West-Indian slaves as "Jacobins" and "domestic enem[ies]," adding the following remark.]

Poor Negroes of the West Indies! do *I* strike at you because you are hopeless? No—I leave you, indeed, to your destiny. Miseries enough have already bowed me down in consequence of that enthusiasm which your sufferings first inspired. I have no more sacrifices to make. My own little ones, and the faithful partner of my own afflictions claim all my heart, and challenge *all* my efforts:—and they shall have them. But I leave you, at least, as I found you, I do not swell the tide of your distress. My name is not enrolled in the list of your enemies; nor ever shall.

---

1 Thomas Gray, *Elegy Written in a Country Churchyard* (1751), 1.104.

2 Milton, *Il Penseroso* (c. 1631).

3 The *Monthly Magazine*.

4 The London publisher Richard Phillips, who purchased *The Daughter* (see Appendix A1 and the Introduction, p. 10).

5 *The Daughter of Adoption* and the "Prefatory Memoir," which was published as part of Thelwall's *Poems, Chiefly Written in Retirement*. Phillips also published a version of the "Prefatory Memoir" in *Public Characters of 1800-1801*, vol. 3 (London, 1801), 202-19.

6 Beaufort Buildings, in the Strand, London, where Thelwall lived and lectured in the mid-1790s.

5. **From Samuel Taylor Coleridge, *Specimens of the Table Talk of the Late Samuel Taylor Coleridge*. Ed. Henry Nelson Coleridge. 2 vols. London, 1835**

[These anecdotes, from the volumes posthumously compiled by the poet's nephew, offer circumspect reminiscences of his relationship with Thelwall that mask the intensity of their Jacobin fellow-feeling, but capture their witty opposition. The first is Coleridge's version of the conversation at Alfoxden, also recalled by Wordsworth, that Thelwall dramatized in the exchange between Henry and Edmunds at Limbé. The second offers a clever comment upon Thelwall's pedagogical philosophy.]

From Vol. I—Recollections of Thelwall

John Thelwall had something very good about him. We were once sitting in a beautiful recess in the Quantocks,[1] when I said to him—"Citizen John! this is a fine place to talk treason in!"—"Nay! Citizen Samuel," replied he, "it is a place to make a man forget that there is any necessity for treason!"

———————

Thelwall thought it very unfair to influence a child's mind by inculcating any opinions before it should have come to years of discretion, and be able to choose for itself. I showed him my garden, and told him it was my botanical garden. "How so?" said he, "it is covered with weeds."—"O," I replied, "*that* is only because it has not yet come to its age of discretion and choice. The weeds, you see, have taken the liberty to grow, and I thought it unfair in me to prejudice the soil towards roses and strawberries."

6. **From William Wordsworth to Henrietta Cecil Thelwall, 16 November 1838. Berg Collection, New York Public Library. K (—). LY ii. 959 (—). Reprinted in *The Letters of William and Dorothy Wordsworth: The Later Years*, ed. Ernest De Selincourt, rev. Alan G. Hill, 2nd ed., 4 vols. (Oxford: Clarendon, 1982) 3: 639-41**

[On November 12, 1838, Thelwall's widow had written to Wordsworth asking for reminiscences of her late husband that might inform the second volume of her *Life of John Thelwall*, the first volume of which had been published the previous year. (The second volume was never published.) Wordsworth's reply consisted chiefly of the following anecdote.]

Circumstances were not favourable to much intercourse between your late Husband and myself: I became acquainted with him during a visit which he made to Mr Coleridge, who was then residing at Nether Stowey; and I was not a little pleased with the natural eloquence of his conversation, and his enthusi-

———

1 A range of hills above the homes of Coleridge in Nether Stowey and Wordsworth at Alfoxden, in Somersetshire.

astic attachment to Poetry. He was likewise very sensible to the beauty of Rural Nature; one instance of this in particular I remember. Having led him and Mr C to a favorite Spot, near the house in the grounds of Alfoxden—(where I then lived, in the neighbourhood of Nether Stowey) a little Hollow in a wood down which the brook ran making a Waterfall, finely overarched with trees,—Mr C. observed that it was a place to soften one's remembrances of the strife and turmoil of the world—"Nay," said Mr Thilwall [sic] "to make one forget the world altogether." Your impression is correct that I, in company with my Sister and Mr Coleridge, visited him at his pleasant abode on the banks of the Wye.[1] Mr Southey was not of the party, as you suppose.

7. From William Wordsworth, Notes Dictated to Isabella Fenwick, first published as Notes in the *Poetical Works*. 6 vols. London, 1857

[In his note on "Anecdote for Fathers" Wordsworth explains that the name of "Liswyn Farm" was taken from Thelwall's farm in Wales, which Wordsworth visited with Coleridge and Dorothy in August 1798. This is Wordsworth's version of their conversation there about retirement. For Coleridge's recollection, see Appendix A5.]

I remember once, when Coleridge, he [Thelwall], and I were seated together upon the turf, on the brink of a stream in the most beautiful part of the most beautiful glen of Alfoxden, Coleridge exclaimed, "This is a place to reconcile one to all the jarrings and conflicts of the wide world." "Nay," said Thelwall, "to make one forget them altogether."

---

1 In early August 1798.

Appendix B: Contextual Documents

1. Literature and Education

a. From Henry Fielding, *The History of Tom Jones, a Foundling*. London, 1749

[A noted writer and magistrate, Henry Fielding (1707-54) is known as a father of both the British novel and the modern justice system (as a legal reformer and founder of the Bow Street Runners). Of his numerous plays, novels, and satires, all distinguished by their earthy humour, vivid theatricality, and active humanitarianism, *Tom Jones* (1749) is considered the greatest; Coleridge proclaimed its plot one of the three most perfect ever written, and contrasted its wholesome and expansive good nature with the hothouse hypocrisy of the Richardsonian sentimental novel. It is this, along with his dual identity as literary satirist and social activist, that made him a model for Thelwall, who adapted *Tom Jones* first in *The Peripatetic*'s narrative of Belmour and Sophia, and then in the Farmer Wilson episode of *The Daughter*, as seen in the extract below, which also shows how the hypocrisy of Blifil and Thwackum are rechannelled in the character of Woodhouse.]

Book III Chapter 2: The Hero of This Great History Appears with Very Bad Omens. A Little Tale of so Low a Kind That Some May Think It Not Worth Their Notice. A Word or Two Concerning a Squire, and More Relating to a Gamekeeper and a Schoolmaster.

As we determined, when we first sat down to write this history, to flatter no man, but to guide our pen throughout by the directions of truth, we are obliged to bring our hero on the stage in a much more disadvantageous manner than we could wish; and to declare honestly, even at his first appearance, that it was the universal opinion of all Mr. Allworthy's family that he was certainly born to be hanged.

Indeed, I am sorry to say there was too much reason for this conjecture; the lad having from his earliest years discovered a propensity to many vices, and especially to one which hath as direct a tendency as any other to that fate which we have just now observed to have been prophetically denounced against him: he had been already convicted of three robberies, viz., of robbing an orchard, of stealing a duck out of a farmer's yard, and of picking Master Blifil's pocket of a ball.

The vices of this young man were, moreover, heightened by the disadvantageous light in which they appeared when opposed to the virtues of Master Blifil, his companion; a youth of so different a cast from little Jones, that not only the family but all the neighbourhood resounded his praises. He was, indeed, a lad of a remarkable disposition; sober, discreet, and pious beyond his age; qualities which gained him the love of every one who knew him: while Tom Jones was universally disliked; and many expressed their wonder that Mr. Allworthy would suffer such a lad to be educated with his nephew, lest the morals of the latter should be corrupted by his example.

An incident which happened about this time will set the characters of these two lads more fairly before the discerning reader than is in the power of the longest dissertation.

Tom Jones, who, bad as he is, must serve for the hero of this history, had only one friend among all the servants of the family; for as to Mrs. Wilkins, she had long since given him up, and was perfectly reconciled to her mistress. This friend was the gamekeeper, a fellow of a loose kind of disposition, and who was thought not to entertain much stricter notions concerning the difference of *meum* and *tuum* than the young gentleman himself. And hence this friendship gave occasion to many sarcastical remarks among the domestics, most of which were either proverbs before, or at least are become so now; and, indeed, the wit of them all may be comprised in that short Latin proverb, "*Noscitur a socio*"; which, I think, is thus expressed in English, "You may know him by the company he keeps."

To say the truth, some of that atrocious wickedness in Jones, of which we have just mentioned three examples, might perhaps be derived from the encouragement he had received from this fellow, who, in two or three instances, had been what the law calls an accessary after the fact: for the whole duck, and great part of the apples, were converted to the use of the gamekeeper and his family; though, as Jones alone was discovered, the poor lad bore not only the whole smart, but the whole blame; both which fell again to his lot on the following occasion.

Contiguous to Mr. Allworthy's estate was the manor of one of those gentlemen who are called preservers of the game [...] Little Jones went one day a shooting with the gamekeeper; when happening to spring a covey of partridges near the border of that manor over which Fortune, to fulfil the wise purposes of Nature, had planted one of the game consumers, the birds flew into it, and were marked (as it is called) by the two sportsmen, in some furze bushes, about two or three hundred paces beyond Mr. Allworthy's dominions.

Mr. Allworthy had given the fellow strict orders, on pain of forfeiting his place, never to trespass on any of his neighbours; no more on those who were less rigid in this matter than on the lord of this manor. With regard to others, indeed, these orders had not been always very scrupulously kept; but as the disposition of the gentleman with whom the partridges had taken sanctuary was well known, the gamekeeper had never yet attempted to invade his territories. Nor had he done it now, had not the younger sportsman, who was excessively eager to pursue the flying game, overpersuaded him; but Jones being very importunate, the other, who was himself keen enough after the sport, yielded to his persuasions, entered the manor, and shot one of the partridges.

The gentleman himself was at that time on horseback, at a little distance from them; and hearing the gun go off, he immediately made towards the place, and discovered poor Tom; for the gamekeeper had leapt into the thickest part of the furze-brake, where he had happily concealed himself.

The gentleman having searched the lad, and found the partridge upon him, denounced great vengeance, swearing he would acquaint Mr. Allworthy. He was as good as his word: for he rode immediately to his house, and complained of the trespass on his manor in as high terms and as bitter language as if his house had been broken open, and the most valuable furniture stole out of it. He added, that some other person was in his company, though he could not discover him; for that two guns had been discharged almost in the same instant. And, says he, "We have found only this partridge, but the Lord knows what mischief they have done."

At his return home, Tom was presently convened before Mr. Allworthy. He owned the fact, and alledged no other excuse but what was really true, viz., that the covey was originally sprung in Mr. Alworthy's own manor.

Tom was then interrogated who was with him, which Mr. Allworthy declared he was resolved to know, acquainting the culprit with the circumstance of the two guns, which had been deposed by the squire and both his servants; but Tom stoutly persisted in asserting that he was alone; yet, to say the truth, he hesitated a little at first, which would have confirmed Mr. Allworthy's belief, had what the squire and his servants said wanted any further confirmation.

The gamekeeper, being a suspected person, was now sent for, and the question put to him; but he, relying on the promise which Tom had made him, to take all upon himself, very resolutely denied being in company with the young gentleman, or indeed having seen him the whole afternoon.

Mr. Allworthy then turned towards Tom, with more than usual anger in his countenance, and advised him to confess who was with him; repeating, that he was resolved to know. The lad, however, still maintained his resolution, and was dismissed with much wrath by Mr. Allworthy, who told him he should have to the next morning to consider of it, when he should be questioned by another person, and in another manner.

Poor Jones spent a very melancholy night; and the more so, as he was without his usual companion; for Master Blifil was gone abroad on a visit with his mother. Fear of the punishment he was to suffer was on this occasion his least evil: his chief anxiety being, lest his constancy should fail him, and he should be brought to betray the gamekeeper, whose ruin he knew must now be the consequence.

Nor did the gamekeeper pass his time much better. He had the same apprehensions with the youth; for whose honour he had likewise a much tenderer regard than for his skin.

In the morning, when Tom attended the reverend Mr. Thwackum, the person to whom Mr. Allworthy had committed the instruction of the two boys, he had the same questions put to him by that gentleman which he had been asked the evening before, to which he returned the same answers. The consequence of this was, so severe a whipping, that it possibly fell little short of the torture with which confessions are in some countries extorted from criminals.

Tom bore his punishment with great resolution; and though his master asked him, between every stroke, whether he would not confess, he was contented to be flead rather than betray his friend, or break the promise he had made.

The gamekeeper was now relieved from his anxiety, and Mr. Allworthy himself began to be concerned at Tom's sufferings: for besides that Mr. Thwackum, being highly enraged that he was not able to make the boy say what he himself pleased, had carried his severity much beyond the good man's intention, this latter began now to suspect that the squire had been mistaken; which his extreme eagerness and anger seemed to make probable; and as for what the servants had said in confirmation of their master's account, he laid no great stress upon that. Now, as cruelty and injustice were two ideas of which Mr. Allworthy could by no means support the consciousness a single moment, he sent for Tom, and after many kind and friendly exhortations, said, "I am convinced, my dear child, that my suspicions have wronged you; I am sorry that you have been so severely punished on this account." And at last gave him a little horse to make him amends; again repeating his sorrow for what had past.

Tom's guilt now flew in his face more than any severity could make it. He could more easily bear the lashes of Thwackum, than the generosity of Allworthy. The tears burst from his eyes, and he fell upon his knees, crying, "Oh, sir, you are too good to me. Indeed you are. Indeed I don't deserve it." And at that very instant, from the fulness of his heart, had almost betrayed the secret; but the good genius of the gamekeeper suggested to him what might be the consequence to the poor fellow, and this consideration sealed his lips.

Thwackum did all he could to persuade Allworthy from showing any compassion or kindness to the boy, saying, "He had persisted in an untruth"; and gave some hints, that a second whipping might probably bring the matter to light.

But Mr. Allworthy absolutely refused to consent to the experiment. He said, the boy had suffered enough already for concealing the truth, even if he was guilty, seeing that he could have no motive but a mistaken point of honour for so doing.

"Honour!" cried Thwackum, with some warmth, "mere stubbornness and obstinacy! Can honour teach any one to tell a lie, or can any honour exist independent of religion?"

b. From Thomas Day, *The History of Sandford and Merton*. 3 vols. London, 1783-89

[Thomas Day (1748-89) was an abolitionist, philanthropist, political essayist, and children's writer. His hugely popular *History of Sandford and Merton* was one of the first books written for children, and his equally influential "The Dying Negro" (1773) was one of the first poems to attack slavery. Closely connected with the Edgeworth family and a friend of Erasmus Darwin, he was an early admirer of Rousseau, and an educational reformer who adopted two girls and tried to train them according to Rousseauvian methods (and failed miserably). Something of this is reflected (and critiqued) in Parkinson's story of first Robertson's, and then his own, adoption of Seraphina. Day's *Sandford and Merton* leaves its mark on Henry's adventures with Farmer Wilson, and the overall analysis of the influence of slavery upon methods of education in the novel.]

From Chapter 1

In the western part of England lived, many years ago, a gentleman of great fortune, whose name was Merton. He had a large estate in the Island of Jamaica, where he had passed the greater part of his life, and was master of many servants, who cultivated sugar and other valuable things for his advantage. He had only one son, of whom he was excessively fond; and to educate his child properly was the reason of his determining to stay some years in England. Tommy Merton, who, at the time he came from Jamaica, was only six years old, was naturally a very good-tempered boy, but unfortunately had been spoiled by too much indulgence. While he lived in Jamaica, he had several black servants to wait upon him, who were forbidden upon any account to contradict him. If he walked, there always went two negroes with him; one of whom carried a large umbrella to keep the sun from him, and the other was to carry him in his arms whenever he was tired. Besides this, he was always dressed in silk or laced clothes, and had a fine gilded carriage, which was borne upon men's shoulders, in which he made visits to his playfellows. His mother was so excessively fond of him, that she gave him everything he cried for, and would never let him learn to read because he complained that it made his head ache.

The consequence of this was, that, though Master Merton had everything he wanted, he became very fretful and unhappy. Sometimes he ate sweetmeats till he made himself ill, and then he suffered a great deal of pain, because he would not take bitter physic to make him well. Sometimes he cried for things that it was impossible to give him, and then, as he had never been used to be contradicted, it was many hours before he could be pacified. When any company came to dine at the house, he was always helped first, and to have the most delicate parts of the meat, otherwise he would make such a noise as disturbed the whole company. When his father and mother were sitting at the tea-table with their friends, instead of waiting till they were at leisure to attend to him, he would scramble upon the table, seize the cake and bread and butter, and frequently upset the tea-cups. By these pranks he not only made himself disagreeable to everybody else, but often met with very dangerous accidents. Frequently he cut himself with knives, at other times threw heavy things upon his head, and once he narrowly escaped being scalded to death by a kettle of boiling water. He was also so delicately brought up, that he was perpetually ill: the least wind or rain gave him a cold, and the least sun was sure to throw him into a fever. Instead of playing about, and jumping, and running, like other children, he was taught to sit still for fear of spoiling his clothes, and to stay in the house for fear of injuring his complexion. By this kind of education, when Master Merton came over to England he could neither write nor read nor cipher; he could use none of his limbs with ease, nor bear any degree of fatigue; but he was very proud, fretful, and impatient.

Very near to Mr. Merton's seat lived a plain, honest farmer, whose name was Sandford. This man had, like Mr. Merton, an only son, not much older than Master Merton, whose name was Harry. Harry, as he had been always accustomed to run about in the fields, to follow the labourers while they were ploughing, and to drive the sheep to their pastures, was active, strong, hardy, and fresh-coloured. He was neither so fair nor so delicately shaped as Master Merton; but he had an honest good-natured countenance, which made everybody love him, was never out of humour, and took the greatest pleasure in obliging everybody. If little Harry saw a poor wretch who wanted victuals while he was eating his dinner, he was sure to give him half, and sometimes the whole; nay, so very good-natured was he to everything, that he would never go into the fields to take the eggs of poor birds, or their young ones, nor practise any other kind of sport which gave pain to poor animals, who are as capable of feeling as we ourselves, though they have no words to express their sufferings. Once, indeed, Harry was caught twirling a cockchafer round, which he had fastened by a crooked pin to a long piece of thread; but, then, this was through ignorance and want of thought; for, as soon as his father told him that the poor helpless insect felt as much or more than he would do, were a knife thrust through his hand, he burst into tears, and took the poor cockchafer home, where he fed him during a fortnight upon fresh leaves; and when he was perfectly recovered, turned him out to enjoy liberty and fresh air. [...]

These sentiments made little Harry a great favourite with everybody; particularly with the clergyman of the parish, who became so fond of him that he taught him to read and write, and had him almost always with him. Indeed, it was not surprising that Mr. Barlow showed so particular an affection for him; for besides learning with the greatest readiness everything that was taught him, little Harry was the most honest, obliging creature in the world. He was never discontented, nor did he ever grumble, whatever he was desired to do. And then you might believe Harry in everything he said; for though he could have gained a plum cake by telling an untruth, and was sure that speaking the truth would expose him to a severe whipping, he never hesitated in declaring it. [...]

The day after Tommy came to Mr. Barlow's, as soon as breakfast was over, he took him and Harry into the garden: when he was there, he took a spade into his own hand, and giving Harry a hoe, they both began to work with great eagerness.

"Everybody that eats," said Mr. Barlow, "ought to assist in procuring food; and therefore little Harry and I begin our daily work. This is my bed, and that other is his; we work upon it every day, and he that raises the most out of it will deserve to fare the best. Now, Tommy, if you choose to join us, I will mark you out a piece of ground, which you shall have to yourself, and all the produce shall be your own."

"No, indeed," said Tommy, very sulkily, "I am a gentleman, and don't choose to slave like a plough-boy."

"Just as you please, Mr. Gentleman," said Mr. Barlow; "but Harry and I, who are not above being useful, will mind our work."

In about two hours, Mr. Barlow said it was time to leave off; and taking Harry by the hand, he led him into a very pleasant summer-house, where they sat down; and Mr. Barlow, taking out a plate of very fine ripe cherries, divided them between Harry and himself.

Tommy, who had followed, and expected his share, when he saw them both eating without taking any notice of him, could no longer restrain his passion, but burst into a violent fit of sobbing and crying.

"What is the matter?" said Mr. Barlow very coolly to him.

Tommy looked upon him very sulkily, but returned no answer.

"Oh! sir, if you don't choose to give me an answer, you may be silent; nobody is obliged to speak here."

Tommy became still more disconcerted at this, and, being unable to conceal his anger, ran out of the summer-house, and wandered very disconsolately about the garden, equally surprised and vexed to find that he was now in a place where nobody felt any concern whether he was pleased or the contrary.

From Chapter 2

The next day Mr. Barlow desired Harry, when they were all together in the arbour, to read the following story of ANDROCLES AND THE LION.

There was a certain slave named Androcles, who was so ill treated by his master that his life became insupportable. Finding no remedy for what he suffered, he at length said to himself, "It is better to die than to continue to live in such hardships and misery as I am obliged to suffer. I am determined, therefore, to run away from my master. If I am taken again, I know that I shall be punished with a cruel death; but it is better to die at once than to live in misery. If I escape, I must betake myself to deserts and woods, inhabited only by beasts; but they cannot use me more cruelly than I have been used by my fellow-creatures; therefore I will rather trust myself with them, than continue to be a miserable slave." Having formed this resolution, he took an opportunity of leaving his master's house, and hid himself in a thick, forest, which was at some miles distance from the city. But here the unhappy man found that he had only escaped from one kind of misery to experience another. He wandered about all day through a vast and trackless wood, where his flesh was continually torn by thorns and brambles: he grew hungry, but could find no food in this dreary solitude! At length he was ready to die with fatigue, and lay down in despair in a large cavern which he found by accident.

"Poor man!" said Harry, whose little heart could scarcely contain itself at this mournful recital, "I wish I could have met with him; I would have given him all my dinner, and he should have had my bed. But pray, sir, tell me why does one man behave so cruelly to another, and why should one person be the servant of another, and bear so much ill treatment?"

"As to that," said Tommy, "some folks are born gentlemen, and then they must command others; and some are born servants, and then they must do as they are bid. I remember, before I came hither, that there were a great many black men and women, that my mother said were only born to wait upon me; and I used to beat them, and kick them, and throw things at them whenever I was angry; and they never dared strike me again, because they were slaves."

"And pray, young man," said Mr. Barlow, "how came these people to be slaves?"

Tommy. Because my father bought them with his money.

Mr. Barlow. So, then, people that are bought with money are slaves, are they?

Tommy. Yes.

Mr. Barlow. And those that buy them have a right to kick them, and beat them, and do as they please with them?

Tommy. Yes.

Mr. Barlow. Then if I was to take and sell you to Farmer Sandford, he would have a right to do what he pleased with you.

"No, sir," said Tommy, somewhat warmly; "but you would have no right to sell me, nor he to buy me."

Mr. Barlow. Then it is not a person's being bought or sold that gives another a right to use him ill, but one person's having a right to sell another, and the man who buys having a right to purchase?

Tommy. Yes, sir.

Mr. Barlow. And what right have the people who sold the poor negroes to your father to sell them, or what right had your father to buy them?

Here Tommy seemed to be a good deal puzzled, but at length he said, "They are brought from a country that is a great way off, in ships, and so they become slaves."

"Then," said Mr. Barlow, "if I take you to another country in a ship, I shall have a right to sell you?"

Tommy. No, but you won't, sir, because I was born a gentleman.

Mr. Barlow. What do you mean by that, Tommy?

"Why," said Tommy, a little confounded, "to have a fine house and fine clothes, and a coach and a great deal of money, as my papa has."

Mr. Barlow. Then if you were no longer to have a fine house, nor fine clothes, nor a great deal of money, somebody that had all these things might make you a slave, and use you ill, and beat you, and insult you, and do whatever he liked with you?

Tommy. No, sir, that would not be right neither, that anybody should use me ill.

Mr. Barlow. Then one person should not use another ill?

Tommy. No, sir.

Mr. Barlow. To make a slave of anybody is to use him ill, is it not?

Tommy. I think so.

Mr. Barlow. Then no one ought to make a slave of you?

Tommy. No, indeed, sir.

Mr. Barlow. But if no one should use another ill, and making a slave is using him ill, neither ought you to make a slave of any one else.

Tommy. Indeed, sir, I think not; and for the future I never will use our black William ill, nor pinch him, nor kick him, as I used to do.

Mr. Barlow. Then you will be a very good boy. But let us now continue our story.

c. From John Thelwall, *The Peripatetic; or, Sketches of the Heart, of Nature and Society; in a Series of Politico-Sentimental Journals, in Verse and Prose, of the Eccentric Excursions of Sylvanus Theophrastus, Supposed to Be Written by Himself.* 3 vols. London, 1793

[Thelwall's *The Peripatetic* is an eccentric miscellany of verse and prose, whose publication in 1793 coincided with his rise to prominence as a radical activist and orator. Its "politico-sentimental" excursions, journals, reflections, effusions, digressions, anecdotes, conversations, and essays register the impact of Romanticism and the New Philosophy on inherited narrative forms and conventions, and address almost every significant idea or subject of the age, including the themes of education addressed here.]

The Vernal Shower

"It was in the midst of this charming association of vernal phenomena," said I, "that I felt one of the earliest inspirations of the Muse.

"I was walking solitarily across the fields towards Dulwich, upon one of those honorable embassies, the qualifications for which constitute a considerable part of the education of those who are intended for a certain liberal profession, so much concerned in establishing the claims of justice between man and man, and composing the disputes and differences of litigious neighbours.

[...]

"But that which particularly riveted my attention, was the wild shrill strain of an aspiring lark, who higher than the ken could pierce, and perhaps above the misty cloud that was sprinkling its refreshing coolness around me, trilled forth so long, and so sweet a succession of variegated notes, as I think I have never heard, either before or since, from this frequent inspirer of my lyric Muse.

"I slackened my pace, I turned, again and again, to every point of the compass, that I might catch every charm of the surrounding landscape. Then straying slowly and unwillingly, with many a pause, listening, with sweet enthusiasm, to the high-poised songster, I arrived at length at the place of my designation, time enough to learn that the poor unfortunate old man, to whom my unwelcome embassy was addressed, had just departed from his home.

"This was the third journey I had made, to no purpose, upon a trifling affair, which a man of parts in his professions would have had address—to wit, dissimulation, enough to have executed with ease upon the first: for so totally unsuspicious were the family of the poor debtor at my first appearance, that they pressed me, with all the generous ardour of hospitality, to set down with them to the breakfast table, alleging, that they knew he would be at home again in half an hour. So that I had nothing to do but to eat of the poor man's bread, and to drink of his cup, and enjoy, with hypocritical countenance, the friendly conversation of his dearest attachments, and I might have secured the opportunity of making such a return of gratitude, as ninety-nine out of an hundred of all the attornies in England would have thought worthy of the highest commendation.

"But, inconceivable as it may appear to gentlemen of this description, my heart smote me at the bare idea: the whole system of intellectual nature seemed to revolt within me: and though half the attractions of the little blooming maiden, who with all the unsuspicious innocence of youth, placed me a chair, and repeated the invitations of her mother, would have been sufficient, on any other occasion, to rivet me on the spot, I made an awkward apology, told them I would call again, and retreated with a degree of confusion, which nothing less than the consciousness of perpetrated guilt could possibly have increased.

"Good, artless, hospitable family! said I, as I hurried back to the fields to indulge in privacy the starting tear—Ye little, smiling, unsuspecting cherubs! and thou sweet blossom of expanding beauty (for the interesting form of Anna had touched my heart) how little do ye suspect the ruin that is perhaps impending!"

But, my embarrassment had roused suspicion. The husband, when I returned, had departed for the day; the deportment of the wife was become distant and abrupt; and even the charming little Anna, lovely in the midst of her confusion, seemed to blush as much with anger, as with modesty.—Yet my heart was innocent of offence; nor would I have blighted with the dews of sorrow the unfolding rose of her simple loveliness, for all that the spoils of legal oppression could furnish.

A Digression for Parents and Preceptors

Of the power of such lessons over the infant mind, I had once a very striking example. A little orphan, who was formerly an object of my frequent attention, while amusing herself, one summer's day, in my garden, having caught a lady bird and put it into a bottle with some grass, came running up to me, with the innocent vivacity of one unconscious of a fault, that I might sympathize in the pleasure of her attainment. I did not express my disapprobation immediately; (for perhaps there is nothing in which it is more necessary to proceed with caution than in the management of the infant mind:) but when next the little fondling came playfully to my side, I took her tenderly upon my knee, and with a tone and countenance of affection, told her I would relate her a pretty story.

"We are informed," said I, "my dear! In a book that you will read, perhaps, before it is long, that at one time there were *Giants* in the world: great tall men, a vast deal larger than we are, and strong enough to do as they liked with such little folks as you or I. One of these, I am informed, while he was young and thoughtless, and did not know that we little people could feel, and love liberty and walking about in the gardens, and playing together, as well as himself, had used to catch little boys and girls, which he carried home and shut up in cages and caves for his pastime and amusement; and in this unhappy situation he used to keep them till they died for want of air and food. Was not this," added I, assuming a voice and look of greater seriousness, "a naughty thoughtless giant? And do you think that you or any body ought to love him?"

The tale had precisely the effect I intended. My pretty little pupil hung down her blushing head, slid silently from my knee, and withdrew. Presently, however, she returned with a brightened countenance, to tell me that she had set her lady bird at liberty; informing me, at the same time, that she never had intended to starve it to death, for that she had put some grass into the bottle for it to eat.

"Pretty little innocent," said I to myself, gazing on the tender generous tear that was swimming in her eyes, as I folded her in my arms and kissed her, "what pity would it not have been that the embers of sensibility so kindly provided by Nature to warm this infant bosom, should have been smothered and neglected till the spark had at last expired! Let me fan it—let me rouse it with my kindest breath, till the spreading fire shall give warmth to all around it, and attractive animation to these little budding beauties!"—But my little Felicia must be benefited by my instructions no more; and whether I ever again shall behold her, to see the ripened produce of my culture, is matter of considerable doubt. Sometimes, however, I please myself with the flattering prospect that my instructions have not been bestowed in vain; and that to the latest of her days she will be a better member of society for this kiss and this harmless fiction. Those who can agree with me in the expectation will not consider this an impertinent digression; but will readily excuse me for descending from the character of the poet, or the topographer, to relate a little childish anecdote, and repeat the fable that fixed the sportive attention of an infant's mind.

But these early cruelties are so far from shocking the unfeeling mass of mankind, that they are rather cultivated than discouraged: and I have even known a lady, whose delicate *sensibility* was shocked by every "rude gale of heaven that visited her check too roughly," *take the trouble of rising from her chair*, to catch flies, and pull their wings off, for her little boy; that he might play with them and torture them at pleasure.

The School

[...] Strange infatuation! That in an enlightened age and country the education of youth should be so shamefully and so notoriously neglected!—that no proof of qualification whatever should be expected from those who undertake the important duties of tuition; but that beings, disqualified even for the most ordinary situations of society, should be permitted to riot at large upon the indolent credulity of parents, and cramp and fetter the infant minds it is their profession to cultivate and enlarge.

But hold: before I take my farewell of this spot, let me do an act of gratitude and justice to one mental benefactor, whose name deserves to be rescued from oblivion. [...]

During the short space of two months there was an usher at this school (a young unbeneficed clergyman, of gay and familiar manners, intelligent mind, and engaging conversation) from whom I certainly derived more than from all the other tutors who ever had any share in my education. The good nature with which he regarded all the innocent, and some of the little mischievous tricks of youth, and the familiarity with which he endeavoured to draw them into more serious pleasures, quickly endeared him to all the most valuable members of the juvenile community; and the art he had of discovering, and encouraging the particular bias of every genius, rendered him not less useful than respected among us. It is true, the particular part of the school where he presided, and where all the more intelligent boys generally assembled, whenever the master was out of the way, had used to bear more resemblance to an amicable *Conversatione*, than to the timid circle that usually surrounds the desk of a pedagogue. But the little conferences that frequently diversified our exercises, were generally so instructive and decorous, as to be much more useful than all the rigours of scholastic discipline.

The practise of modern times, it is true, does not give much countenance to this colloquial mode of instruction, and this is, perhaps, a principal reason why so few of the English excel in the talent of conversation, and why all modern nations fall so far behind the ancient Greeks in the vivid energies of eloquence and imagination. The tutors of the present day, instead of exciting to emulation by instructive discourse, and calling forth the powers of the infant mind by familiar interrogation, sit retired in haughty silence, like sullen and imperious bashaws,[1] singling, with cowering look, the unhappy objects of chastisement, who, (fettered to one unhealthy attitude, for a tedious and unreasonable period, their imaginations blunted, and their vivacity suppressed), are doomed to acquire many things from the tedious drudgery of reiterated perusal, which, did the ear but occasionally relieve the fatigue of the eye, would be accomplished in a third part of the time.

d. From Richard and Maria Edgeworth, *Practical Education*. 2nd ed. 3 vols. London, 1801

[Maria Edgeworth (1768-1849) was a leading Irish novelist, educational theorist, and writer for children, whose progressive, cosmopolitan views on property, politics, economics, child-raising, women's rights, nationalism, and religious toleration harmonized with those of Thelwall, who probably visited her while touring Ireland in 1817. She shared his interest in speech idioms and theatricality, as shown in her 1800 *Castle Rackrent*, widely acclaimed as a groundbreaking regional tale, historical novel, and Anglo-Irish Big-House saga; later

---

1 A Turkish nobleman; hence haughty and autocratic.

novels such as *Belinda* (1801) and *Harrington* (1817) showcased controversial ideas on marriage and racial tolerance. She collaborated with her father on *Practical Education* in 1798, and published several books of tales and lessons for children, renowned for both their charming realism and moral didacticism.]

From Chapter 8. On Truth

When children have formed *habits* of speaking truth, and when we see that these habits are grown quite easy to them, we may venture to question them about their thoughts and feelings; this must, however, be done with great caution, but without the appearance of anxiety or suspicion. Children are alarmed if they see that you are very anxious and impatient for their answer; they think that they hazard much by their reply; they hesitate and look eagerly in your face, to discover by your countenance what they ought to think and feel, and what sort of answer you expect. All who are governed by any species of fear are disposed to equivocation. Amongst the lower class of Irish labourers, and *under-tenants*, a class of people who are much oppressed, you can scarcely meet with any man who will give you a direct answer to the most indifferent question; their whole ingenuity, and they have a great deal of ingenuity, is upon the *qui vive* with you the instant you begin to speak; they either pretend not to hear, that they may gain time to think, whilst you repeat your question, or they reply to you with a fresh question, to draw out your remote meaning. [...]

It is curious to observe how regularly the same moral causes produce the same temper and character; we talk of climate, and frequently attribute to climate the different dispositions of different nations: the climate of Ireland, and that of the West Indies, are not precisely similar, yet the following description, which Mr. Edwards, in his history of the West Indies, gives of the propensity to falsehood amongst the negro slaves, might stand word for word for a character of that class of the Irish people who, till very lately, actually, not metaphorically, called themselves *slaves*.

"If a negro is asked even an indifferent question by his master, he seldom gives an immediate reply; but affecting not to understand what is said, compels a repetition of the question, that he may have time to consider, not what is the true answer, but what is the most politic one for him to give."

Mr. Edwards assures us, that many of these unfortunate negroes learn cowardice and falsehood after they become slaves; when they first come from Africa many of them shew "a frank and fearless temper"; but all distinctions of character amongst the native Africans is soon lost under the leveling influence of slavery. Oppression and terror necessarily produce meanness and deceit in all climates, and in all ages; and wherever fear is the governing motive in education, we must expect to find in children a propensity to dissimulation, if not confirmed habits of falsehood. [...] Where individuals are oppressed, or where they believe that they are oppressed, they combine against their oppressors, and oppose cunning and falsehood to power and force; they think themselves released from the compact of truth with their masters, and bind themselves in a strict league with each other; thus schoolboys hold no faith with their schoolmaster, though they would think it shameful to be dishonourable amongst one another. We do not think that these maxims are the particular growth of schools; in private families the same feelings are to be found under the same species of culture: if preceptors or parents are unjust or tyrannical, their pupils will contrive to conceal from them their actions and their thoughts. On the contrary, in families where sincerity has been encouraged by the voice of praise and affection, a generous freedom of conversation and countenance appears, and the young people talk to each other, and to their parents, without distinction or reserve; without any distinction but such as superior esteem and respect dictate: these are feelings totally distinct from servile fear, these feelings inspire the love of truth, the ambition to acquire and to preserve character.

From Chapter 9. Rewards and Punishments

A child distinguishes between anger and indignation very exactly; the one commands his respect, the other raises his contempt as soon as his fears subside. Dr. Priestley seems to think, that "it is not possible to express displeasure with sufficient *force*, especially to a child, when a man is perfectly cool." May we not reply to this, that it is scarcely possible to express displeasure with sufficient *propriety*, especially to a child, when a man is in a passion. The propriety is in this case of at least as much consequence as the force of the reprimand. The effect which the preceptor's displeasure will produce must be in some proportion to the esteem which his pupils feels for him. If he cannot command his irascible passions, his pupil cannot continue to esteem him, and there is an end of all that fear of his disapprobation, which was founded upon esteem, and which can never be founded upon a stronger or a better basis. [...]

As young people grow up, and perceive the consequences of their own actions, and the advantages of credit and character, they become extremely solicitous to preserve the good opinion of those whom they love and esteem. They are now capable of taking the future into their view as well as the present; and at this period of their education the hand of authority should never be hastily used; the voice of reason will never fail to make herself heard, especially if reason speak with the tone of affection. [...] Those who reflect are more influenced by the idea of the duration, than of the intensity of any mental pain. In those calculations which are constantly made before we determined upon action or forbearance, some tempers estimate any evil which is likely to be but of short duration, infinitely below its real importance. Young men of sanguine and courageous dispositions hence frequently act imprudently; the consequences of their temerity will, they think, soon be over, and they feel that they are able to support evil for a short time, however great it may be. Anger, they know, is a short-lived passion, and they do not scruple running the hazard of exciting anger in the hearts of those whom they love the best in the world. The experience of lasting, sober disapprobation, is intolerably irksome to them; any inconvenience which continues for a length of time wearies them excessively. After they have endured, as the consequence of any actions, this species of punishment, they will long remember their sufferings, and will carefully avoid incurring in future similar penalties.

From Chapter 11. Vanity, Pride and Ambition

The ambition to rise in the world usually implies a mean sordid desire of riches, or what are called honours, to be obtained by the common arts of political intrigue, by cabal to win popular favour, or by address to conciliate the patronage of the great. [...] There is a more noble ambition, by which the enthusiastic youth, perfect in the theory of all the virtues, and warm with yet unextinguished benevolence, is apt to be seized; his heart beats with the hope of immortalizing himself by noble actions; he forms extensive plans for the improvement and the happiness of his fellow-creatures; he feels the want of power to carry these into effect; power becomes the object of his wishes. In the pursuit of this object, how are his feelings changed? [...] Examples from romance can never have such a powerful effect upon the mind as those which are taken from real life; but in proportion to the just and lively representation of situations, and passions resembling reality, fictions may convey useful moral lessons. [...] If we fairly place facts before young people, who have been habituated to reason, and who have not yet been inspired with the passion, or enslaved by the habits of vulgar ambition, it is probable, that they will not be easily effaced from the memory, and that they will influence the conduct through life.

It sometimes happens to men of a sound understanding, and a philosophic turn of mind, that their ambition decreases with their experience. They begin perhaps with some ardour an ambitious pursuit; but by degrees they find the pleasure of the occupation sufficient without the fame, which was their original object. This is the same process which we have observed in the minds of children with respect to the pleasures of literature, and the taste of sugar-plums.

Happy the child who can be taught to improve himself without the stimulus of sweetmeats! Happy the man who can preserve activity without the excitements of ambition!

From Chapter 24. Prudence and Economy

Most parents think that their sons are more disposed to extravagance than their daughters; the sons are usually exposed to greater temptations. Young men excite one another to expence, and to a certain carelessness of economy, which assumes the name of spirit, while it often forfeits all pretensions to justice. A prudent father will never, from any false notions of forming his son early to *good* company, introduce him to associates whose only merit is their rank or their fortune. Such companions will lead a weak young man into every species of extravagance, and then desert and ridicule him in the hour of distress. [...] The intermediate state between that of a schoolboy and a man is the dangerous period, in which taste of expence is often acquired, before the means of gratifying it are obtained. [...] During this boyish state parents should be particularly attentive to the company which their sons keep; and they should frequently in conversation with sensible, but not with morose or old-fashioned people, lead to the subject of economy, and openly discuss and settle the most essential points. [...]

Before a young man goes into the world, it will be a great advantage to him to have some share in the management of his father's affairs; by laying out money for another person he will acquire habits of care, which will be useful to him afterwards in his own affairs. [...]

It is scarcely possible, that the mean passion of avarice should exist in the mind of any young person who has been tolerably well educated; but too much pains cannot be taken to preserve that domestic felicity, which arises from entire confidence and satisfaction amongst the individuals of a family with regard to property. Exactness in accounts and in business relative to property, far from being unnecessary amongst friends and relations, are, we think, peculiarly agreeable, and essential to the continuance of frank intimacy. We should, whilst our pupils are young, teach them a love for exactness about property; a respect for the rights of others, rather than a tenacious anxiety about their own. When young people are of a proper age to manage money and property of their own, let them know precisely what they can annually spend; in whatever form they receive an income, let that income be certain. [...] All persons who have a fluctuating revenue are disposed to be imprudent and extravagant. It is remarkable, that the West Indian planters, whose property is a kind of lottery, are extravagantly disposed to speculation; in the hopes of a favourable season they live from year to year in unbounded profusion. It is curious to observe, that the propensity to extravagance exists in those who enjoy the greatest affluence, and in those who have felt the greatest distress. Those who have little to lose are reckless about that little; and any uncertainty as to the tenure of property, or as to the rewards of industry, immediately operates, not only to depress activity, but to destroy prudence. "Prudence," says Mr. Edwards, "is a term that has no place in the negro vocabulary; instead of trusting to what are called the *ground provisions*, which are safe from the hurricanes, the negroes, in the cultivation of their own lands, trust more to plantain-groves, corn, and other vegetables that are liable to be destroyed by storms. When they earn a little money, they immediately gratify their palate with salted meats and other provisions, which are to them delicacies. The idea of accumulating, and of being economic in order to accumulate, is unknown to these poor slaves, who hold their lands by the most uncertain of all tenures." We are told, that the *provision ground*, the creation of the negro's industry, and the hope of his life, is sold by public auction to pay his master's debts. Is it wonderful that the term prudence should be unknown in the negro vocabulary?

e. From John Thelwall, *Introductory Discourse on the Nature and Objects of Elocutionary Science*. Pontefract, 1805

[Thelwall's *Introductory Discourse* was a digest of and guide to the theories he developed and expounded in his elocutionary lectures, beginning in 1801; it was appended to some of the many variant versions of *Selections and Outlines* that he produced and sold to order at the door of lecture rooms through the midlands and north of England, before taking a more regular format when he settled into his Institute in London in 1806. This extract illustrates the continuity between Thelwall's moral, political, and pedagogical philosophies, as it emphasizes "discourse" as the foundation of morality, begins with a popular animal fable and details the "expansive virtue" that is also embodied in the structure and the theme of his novel.]

Each Lecture will generally be divided into three distinct Parts.

   I.   Of these, the priority will generally be given to the Didactic Discourse [...]
   II. The second place will usually be occupied by Illustrations [...] Readings and Recitations
   III. To these will be added,—some specimen of spontaneous Elocution

[...]

Part III. ORATORICAL DISSERTATION—*On the Importance of Elocution, in a Moral and Intellectual Point of View*; as evidenced by the facts of Natural History, the exclusive Improvability of the Human Race, and the comparative condition of Man in the Savage, and in the Civilized state of Society.

OUTLINE.—Object of the Lectures—Popular attraction to the most important of all Sciences: FACULTY OF DISCOURSE, the sole discriminating attribute of Man—"Destitute of this Power, Reason would be a Solitary and, in some degree, an unavailing principle"—BLAIR'S LECT [...]

EXTRACT.—"But Science and Refinement are not the only advantages we derive from this exclusive faculty of discourse. By this it is that we are enabled to attain—VIRTUE! *the god-like attribute of Man!—and of Man alone.*

"I am well aware that to this position there are some who have their objections ready: that there are Cynical and Misanthropical Philosophers in the world, who would shew their zeal for morality, by degrading their species, and exalting the inferior animals. By such we are sent, for examples of every virtue, not to the circles of social intellect; but—Among the beastial herds to range.

"Among the most favourite themes of these satyrical fabulists, are the *Gratitude and Fidelity of Dogs.* But let us examine these pompous epithets, by which the brute is exalted, for the degradation of the human being. In what does the gratitude and fidelity of these inferior beings consist?

"You feed your Dog,—you shelter, and you caress him:—and you do well; for he protects your house from the midnight robber, and guards your steps in the walks of obscurity and peril. But if his daily sop had been ministered by the Assassin, would he not have guarded the Assassin also?—Would not the midnight depredator, the perjurer, or the calumniator be an object as dear to his *grateful Fidelity*, as the Benefactor of the sentient universe? Would he not guard the cavern of the Banditti, (if that *Banditti* were his feeders) with as fierce a courage, against the officers of justice,—as he guards the mansion of the *honest proprietor*, against the assaults of depredation? Is he not, universally, the enemy of the *needy Mendicant*, as much as of the *sanguinary Ruffian*?—and exists there among the teachable tribes of these inferior beings, a single animal (if trained and pampered with individual gratification) whom this pretended gratitude and fidelity, will not render the traitor and destroyer, even of his own particular species?

"Is this the principle which, in the *human being*, we should dignify with the name of virtue? Is the *gratitude* we admire—is the fidelity we commend, a mere attachment for reward—a mere barter, or return, for selfish gratification? Is the sympathy of selfishness, the only genuine virtue?

"Some men there are, it cannot be denied, who act upon no better principle. I wish there were not some, who (*like all other animals*) too frequently act upon a worse. But these are not the beings we distinguish as the virtuous: nor can Virtue be so defined.

"*Virtue* is, in reality, an expansive principle—that acts not alone upon individual impression; but soars to generalization, and takes the universe in its fold. With passion for its goad, and reason for its rein, it looks beyond itself, (not only *behind*, but *before*;) and, even in the reciprocation of kindness, or the pursuits of individual gratification, it forgets not the general welfare. Its gratitude is not confined to the personal benefactor; it is extended to the benefactors of mankind. And he who is truly virtuous, will deplore and restrain the errors even of a father; will counteract the injustice, even of a benefactor, or a friend; and acknowledge, with veneration, the benevolence that dispenses blessings upon his species,—altho' it should happen (as, by accident or mistake, it may)—that such general benefactor, to him is personally hostile.

"Such is *Virtue*—if I comprehend the term. It has its source, indeed, in individual *feeling*—(for till we have *felt* we cannot know); but its indispensable constituents are comparison and generalization; which can only proceed from discourse. Hence, from the central throb of individual impulse, the feeling expands to the immediate circle of relative connections;—from relatives, to friends and intimate associates; from intimate association, to the neighbourhood where we reside—to the country for which we would bleed!—from the patriot community to civilized society—to the human race—to posterity—to the sentient universe: and wherever the throb of sensation can exist, the Virtuous find a motive for the regulation of their actions.

"Such are the expanding undulations of virtuous sympathy—Such are its objects: and in the comparison and practical adjustment of the *various claims* of these—(which but for discourse could never be comprehended or perceived) does Virtue, in reality, consist."

f. From John Thelwall, "The Historical and Oratorical Society," *A Letter to Henry Cline, Esq. on Imperfect Development of the Faculties, Mental and Moral, as well as Constitutional and Organic; and on the Treatment of Impediments of Speech.* London, 1810

[Thelwall's *A Letter to Henry Cline* is one of several book-length essays written at the height of his fame as an elocutionist and healer of speech impediments. It explains and defends his "Science and Practice of Elocution" to a specialist audience, in this case Dr. Cline, one of his early friends and teachers at Guy's

Hospital, and a founder of the Royal College of Surgeons. Among the miscellaneous case studies, letters, autobiographical anecdotes, and reminiscences that comprise the *Letter* is this description of key feature of his Institute, which also gives us some insight into his teaching methods. Founded upon the same principles as the debating societies that were so important to Thelwall's political education, the aims and methods of this Society also inform the structure and philosophy of his novel, emphasizing the moral development of character through dialogue, debate, and enquiry. It is worth noting, too, the inclusiveness and equality of Thelwall's educational program, in which the "privilege of nature" is extended to the disabled, according to the same principles by which racial and gender differences are interrogated and overturned in *The Daughter of Adoption*.]

Fully persuaded that the tardiness, the imperfect manifestation, and the premature decline of oratorical phaenomena, in a country, whose language, if properly wrought, is an exhaustless mine of oratorical capability, could only be attributed to the want of a proper system of oratorical education, it became an object of my ambition to supply this defect; and tho an institution, expressly established for the education of the orator, might have been too bold a singularity, yet the studies and habits of my life, having been almost entirely oratorical, it seemed not quite presumptuous to hope,—that by blending together (what indeed ought never to have been separated) the profession of the rhetorician with that of the teacher of elocution, and by making my institution, at the same time, a seminary for the study of history, and the graces of literary composition, something might be done towards the accomplishment of this great national desideratum; without relinquishing, or in any way detracting from, the principal and ostensible object—the removal of those troublesome defects of utterance, that deprive so many of our species of the noblest privilege of their nature. Nay, [...] the hope might fairly and rationally be entertained,—that, even from among the pupils of this description, might start forth some new Demosthenes, to enlighten and to energize the rising generation.

[...]

The following are, at present, the principal regulations of the society [...] That every member of the society open, in his turn, with a written dissertation, the question previously proposed for discussion; and every member be prepared to deliver his sentiments, in his turn, if called upon, during the further discussion of such question; and that it be expected, with the exception of the opening dissertation, that the members shall deliver their sentiments extemporary. [...]

The most essential objects of study, in the formation of the mental character of the orator, are, 1. For the substance and manner of his discourses, History, (including the progress of opinion, jurisprudence, political oeconomy, and constitutional law;) 2. For induction and sentiment, Moral Philosophy (including the study and regulation of the passions, those parts of Logic that are not merely technical, and so much of Metaphysics as relates to the perceptions and definable operations of the human mind, and does not pretend to subtilties and abstractions beyond the reach of ordinary comprehension;)—and thirdly, Poetry, for the depth of pathos, the excitement of the imaginative or inventive faculty, and the improvement of the energies of impressive diction.

[...]

At the discussion of these questions, I have regularly presided, to point out the sources of information, to interrogate the speakers as to the authorities for disputed facts, to rectify their mistakes, assist them in appreciating the value of historical evidence, and religiously to enforce the observance, even in the ardour of debate, of the undeviating language of decorum and urbanity. [...] To spread the facts of history before them, to guide them to the attainment of a thorough knowledge of the institutions of their country; to store my shelves, impartially, for their edification, with every respectable authority, *pro* and *con*, for every period or event of disputed record; to form their taste for the more elegant departments of literature, and to inspire, at once, a thirst for knowledge and for eloquence, and an emulation of utility and distinction in their generation, (whatever may be their class, their party, or their professional destination)—these are the views with which, in the next session of the historical and oratorical society, I shall proceed to direct the attention of my pupils. [...]

2. The West Indies and the Abolition Debate

a. From John Thelwall, "The Connection between the Calamities of the Present Reign, and the System of Borough-Mongering Corruption—Lecture the Third.—The Connection between Parliamentary Corruption and Commercial Monopoly: with Strictures on the West-India Subscription, &c. Delivered Wednesday Oct. 14. 1795." *The Tribune, a Periodical Publication, Consisting Chiefly of the Political Lectures of J. Thelwall.* 3 vols. London, 1795-96. 3: 47-62

[In 1795-96 Thelwall published as the *Tribune* the political lectures that he delivered weekly in London. The following excerpt refers to the recent defeat in Parliament of a bill to abolish the slave trade.]

[T]hus, Citizens, what with this fine management, and the finesse of that great politician *Henry Dundas*, the English nation, after having expressed its almost unanimous wish for the abolition, was compelled to continue this abominable traffic. But France abolished it, though we would not; for abolished in effect, it is:—more than abolished:—premature emancipation is rushing upon the kidnapped sons of Africa. What the scenes may be, through which these unfortunate islands have yet to pass—what the calamities of this struggle of emancipation, I cannot pretend to divine: and fain would I draw a veil over the melancholy prospect. But with respect to West-India slavery, it is abolished: its final doom is fixed. It may, perhaps, keep up a struggling, feeble existence, for a little time; but the period cannot be distant, when the West-India islands will be cultivated by slaves no more—when the West-India shores will be no more dependent upon any European power: and for my own part, Citizens, I own that I cannot very much lament the prospect of this separation. [...] Every country having a right to independency—every country having a right to chuse its own government, I should be led, in the first instance, to suppose it for the happiness and welfare of the whole, that these rights should be exercised and enjoyed. [...] [F]or if this independence should ever take place, Trade must be open! Traffic must be free! and every individual and every country, must have a fair and equal opportunity of struggling for a share of this general commerce. [...]

But your monopolists would be injured; and therefore a fresh armament is to be equipped for the *West-Indies*, with the vain and hopeless expectation of preventing a catastrophe which is inevitable: which may be delayed, perhaps, for a few years, but which never can be permanently prevented. The principle is broad awake; and no drug, in all the shops of all the political quack doctors, who have so long been dosing us with their potions and their pills, can send it to sleep again. But still we are to struggle with Despair: like men who, in their sleep, dream they are running, and though their feet are clogged with the bed-clothes, endeavor to kick and sprawl about; so in our dream of conquering the *West-India* islands, we send our fleets, with the best blood of the country, stored with necessaries for which our poor at home are starving, to flounder and sprawl, and buffet the adverse elements, till, faint and exhausted, we wake from the delirious slumber, and find that we have toiled in vain.

b. From John Thelwall, *Rights of Nature, against the Usurpations of Establishments.* London, 1796

[Framed as a response to Edmund Burke's *Letters on a Regicide Peace* (1796), Thelwall's *Rights of Nature* contains the most comprehensive articulation of his political and economic thought. His attack on Burke's arguments about nature, reform, and political representation in the following passages resonates throughout *The Daughter*.]

Slavery and Burke's Definition of "Nature"

[...] Mr. B[urke]'s *Nature* and mine are widely different. With him every thing is natural that has the hoar of ancient prejudice upon it; and novelty is the test of crime. In my humble estimate, nothing is natural, but what is fit and true, and can endure the test of reason. With him the feudal system, and all its barbarous, tyrannical, and superstitious appendages, is natural. With him, all the gaudy, cumbrous fustian of "the old Germanic, or Gothic customary" is natural; and all the idolatrous foppery and degrading superstition of the church of Rome are natural, also. Nay, with him, that detestable traffic in blood and murder—that barter of groans, and tortures, and long lingering deaths, the *Slave Trade*, is also natural!!! Nor do I doubt, that, with equal facility, and upon the very same principles, as he maintains the masters and employers of this country to be the natural representatives of the workmen they employ, he could prove, also, those very humane, and very, very respectable beings, who, as they walk upon two legs, I shall continue to call men, by *courtesy*, (I mean the West

India planters, and their Negro drivers) to be the natural representatives of those poor, harassed, half-starved, whip-galled, miserable slaves, whom they, also, *employ* in their farms and factories.

In short, this champion of the privileged orders adopts, most unequivocally, the principles of this similitude. Having assigned the exclusive privilege of opinion to the favoured four hundred thousand[1]—a mixed herd of nobles and gentles, placemen, pensioners and court-expectants, of bankers and merchants, manufacturers, lawyers, parsons and physicians, warehousemen and shop-keepers, pimps and king's messengers, fiddlers and auctioneers, with the included "twenty thousand" petticoat allies—ladies of the court, and ladies of the town!—having secured this motley group (the favoured progeny of Means and Leisure) in the exclusive, and unquestioned enjoyment of the rights of information and discussion, he proceeds to observe, that "the rest, when feeble, are the *objects* of protection!"—Objects of protection!—so are my lady's lap-dog and the Negro slave. It is easy to determine, which, of the two, *polished sensibility* will shelter with the most anxious care!—Ye murky walls, and foul, straw-littered floors of the plantation hospital! Yet full-crammed, noxious workhouses of Britain—vile dens of tyrannic penury and putrescence![2] speak—Ye roofs and floors of wretchedness! speak ye (for that part of nature which should be loud and eloquent, is spell-bound in panic apathy)—What is the *protection* which the feeble labourer, or the sick Negro finds? and then refer, for comparison, to the down pillow of yon pampered, snarling cur; or the commodious chambers of the canine palace at *Godwood*.[3]—But to return to the description.—"The rest, when feeble, are the objects of protection—when *strong*, they are the MEANS of force."[4] So is the dray-horse; and the poor ass that drudges day and night in the sand-cart! So are the bludgeon, and the pistol, with which, under *existing circumstances*, every man (at least, every obnoxious[5] man) will do well to be provided, as preservatives against assassination.[6] But foul befall the govern-

---

1 In *Letters on the Prospect of a Regicide Peace* Burke had proposed that public debate be restricted to an educated and leisured elite of some 400,000 (Burke, *WS* 9:224).

2 There are some few, and but few exceptions, to this general description. At any rate, however, a workhouse is but a gaol; and, therefore, a fit receptacle only for those paupers, whose infirmities make confinement necessary to their preservation. [Thelwall's note]

3 A splendid edifice, erected by the D.[uke] of Richmond for his dogs, with commodious kitchens, parlours, dining-rooms, bed-rooms, lying-in-rooms, pleasure-ground for the morning sun, pleasure-ground for the evening sun, baths, &c, &c.—N.B. It is a strict rule at Godwood, that no servant be permitted to give a morsel of broken victuals either to mendicant traveller, or neighbouring peasant. Poor women, who presume to pick up withered sticks from under the trees in the park, are taught, by a "severe and awful" administration of "justice," to respect the sacred rights of property. [Thelwall's note]

4 Letters, p. 67. [Thelwall's note]

5 Meaning, here, objectionable (as Thelwall was to the government at this time).

6 See "An Appeal to Popular Opinion Against Kidnapping and Murder: Including a Narrative of the Atrocious Outrages at Yarmouth, Lynn, and Wisbeach"; and the motion made by Mr. Erskine, in the Court of King's Bench, on Saturday the 19th instant, on the subject of these flagitious aristocratic violations of law and order. [Thelwall's note, referring to his pamphlet of 1796]

ment, that considers the great mass of the people as brute machines; mere instruments of physical force; deprived of all *power*, and destitute of all *right* of information; and doomed, like the dray-horse, or the musquet, to perform, mechanically, whatever task of drudgery, or murder, a few "counselors and deliberators" may command! And yet, Mr. B. tells us, that "they who *affect* to consider that part of us" (to wit, nine-tenths of the adult population of the country) "in any other point of view, *insult us while they cajole us!*"

Revenge and Rebellion

But beware, Mr. Burke, and you, his hypocritical employers, how *ye* cajole and insult *us* too far. Abuses, when discovered, inspire the sober wish of peaceful and rational reform: but when wrong is added to wrong, and coercion to coercion; when remonstrance is answered by the goad and the yoke, and insult is heaped upon oppression, reason may be overpowered, and madness may succeed; and the philanthropic few, who admonish in vain, may deplore the destiny from which they cannot preserve you. In vain do you shudder at the cannibals[1] of Paris—in vain do ye colour, with exaggerated horrors, the "tribunals of Maroon and Negro slaves, covered with the blood of their masters"; if, obstinately vicious, instead of being warned, ye are irritated by the example.

I deplore, as ye do, the "robberies and murders," committed by these poor wretches—the blind instruments of instinctive vengeance. But, I cannot, like you, forget by whom those lessons of murderous rapacity were taught. I cannot forget, that slavery itself is robbery and murder; and, that the master who falls by the bondsman's hand, is the victim of his own barbarity.

I am no apologist for the horrible massacres of revenge; whether perpetrated by negroes, by monarchs, or by mobs. I abhor revenge. Vengeance, Mr. Burke, with me is crime. All retrospective principle is crime; and to its criminality adds folly. In your own sort of language I should say—we were *made* with our eyes in our foreheads, that we might look onward to the future, not linger upon that which is gone by, and cannot be recalled. [...] But we are not to expect whole nations (whether of Maroon negroes, or of feudal vassals) to become of a sudden so entirely speculative. Revenge, it cannot be concealed, is a rude instinct, common to all animated being, which nothing but deep reflection, and well digested principles can eradicate. [...] It is a wild growth of nature, it is true: but it is fatally cherished by authoritative example: and if tyrants will teach bloody lessons, it is unreasonable in them to complain of the aptitude of

---

1 The reader will, of course, give me credit, for using this word in a figurative sense. Mr. B. in the very dotage of credulity, applies it literally. "By cannibalism, I mean their devouring, as a nutriment of their ferocity, some part of the bodies of those they have murdered; their drinking the blood of their victims, and forcing the victims themselves to drink the blood of their kindred, slaughtered before their faces." *Let.* p. 105. Can Bedlam surpass the madness that could write, can idiotcy match the credulity that should *believe*, this trash? There is another passage, in the same page, still more hideous. Mr. B. is a *romance writer* of the German school: If he can but excite horror, no matter how incredible the tale. But surely there are scenes too terrible to amuse a benevolent mind, even in *fictions and poetic legends*! [Thelwall's note, quoting Burke's *Regicide Peace*]

their scholars. [...] Had the Maroons and negroes never been most wickedly enslaved, their masters had never been murdered. Had the chains of France been less galling, they had never fallen so heavy on the heads of French oppressors. To avoid their fate, let governors avoid their crimes. To render sanguinary *revolutions* impossible, let them yield to temperate *reforms*. To avert a dreaded vengeance, let the provocations of injustice be instantly removed; and the padlock from the mouth of an injured people, be transferred to the lips of pensioned indolence!

On Primogeniture and Bastardy

The very principles of property are violated by this law [of Primogeniture]; for, if there is such a thing as a principle of descent, growing out of the nature and foundations of property, it is this—that *the property acquired by the industry of the parents, should descend to those whom the passions of such parents have brought into an appropriated world.* If all, then, are, alike, the children of their parents, all, are, alike, their heirs:[1] and if this consanguinity ought not to dictate the descent of property, then is not property at all descendable; but ought either to depend entirely on the bequest of the proprietor, or return into the bosom of the state, for the general benefit of the community. I am, however, for the relative feelings and the regular descent of property.

c. From Baron de Wimpffen, *A Voyage to Saint Domingo, in the Years 1788, 1789, and 1790.* Trans. J. Wright. London, 1797

[Alexandre-Stanislas, Baron de Wimpffen (1748-1819), was a captain under Count Rochambeau in 1781-82. Two of his brothers were generals, and he himself worked for Napoleon from 1804 to 1814. His *Voyage*, an important source for Books III and IV of *The Daughter*, is a mixture of Enlightenment liberalism, planter prejudice, and counter-revolutionary passion.]

On Race Prejudice

As it seems necessary that a certain number of absurd prejudices should imprint the mark of folly on every thing which relates to the human species; it is here the colour of the skin, which, in its different degrees of shade, from black to white, takes place of the distinctions of rank, of merit, of birth, of honours, and even of fortune. So that a negro, although he proved his descent in a right line from the Magi who came to adore our Saviour, although he

---

1   I would add, "However begotten—whether in marriage, or out," but Mr. B. and the priests would call me an encourager of licentiousness, of bastardy and prostitution. O words! words! how are things abused by you. But man is man, and nature nature, and parent is parent, and child is child, whether a conjuror in a black gown mutter his spells or not. [Thelwall's note]

joined to the genius of a celestial intelligence, all the gold "which the profound earth hides," would never be any thing in the eyes of the poorest, the most paltry, the most stupid, the most contemptible of the whites, but the dregs of the human race, a worthless slave, a *black*!

"He has relations on the coast!" Such, Sir, is the expression by which they manifest their contempt, on the slightest suspicion that a single drop of African blood has found its way into the veins of a white. And such is the force of prejudice, that it requires an effort of reason and courage to enable you to contract with such an unfortunate being, that kind of familiarity, which a state of equality pre-supposes and demands.

You see then that the chaos of claims and pretensions so perplexed and confounded *elsewhere* by the diversity of ranks, is *here* easily reduced to method. In Europe the knowledge of the different degrees of regard, of consideration, of esteem more or less *felt*, of respect more or less profound, is a science which requires a particular study: and as the exterior does not always correspond with the title, a discernment of the nicest kind, a long acquaintance with the great world, is necessary to enable us to distinguish the patrician from the plebeian, the noble from the vassal. Here on the contrary, it is only necessary to have eyes, to be able to place every individual in the class to which he belongs.

Discipline of Slaves

A walk of an hour served to dissipate the chagrin of this gloomy awaking. I came back in time to see a troop of male and female negroes lying against the wall, or squatting upon their heels, and waiting, amidst a universal yawn, for the master's giving the signal of going to work, by loud cracks of the Arceau [which he explains in a note is "A kind of short-handled whip, so called in the colonies"], on their back and shoulders—for, you will hardly conceive, and indeed it cost six months observation to convince me of the truth of it, there are negroes who must absolutely be beaten before they can be put in motion. The arceau is the true key of this species of watch—If I had chosen to take the word of the masters for it, I should have looked no farther for the cause of this singular disposition of the slaves, than to their natural sloth and inactivity: but on considering the matter a little more narrowly, I fancied I could see that these dispositions were marvelously seconded by the inactivity and sloth of their masters, who, for the greater part, too ignorant and too unindulgent to comprehend that the vices of education can only be subdued by time and patience, find the plan of beating more practicable than that of instructing! The natural consequence of which is, that the negro, once accustomed to this mode of treatment, can only be wrought on by rigour and severity. I have persisted, month after month, in lavishing on those who attended me, nothing but patience, gentleness, and good offices of every kind——all were in vain: the bent was taken, and nothing was left me, after all my endeavours, but the alternative of waiting on myself, or of having recourse to the *arceau*.

Of these dances, which may be truly styled characteristic, the *Gragement* and the *Chicca* are the most esteemed: never did voluptuousness in motion spread a more seducing snare for the eager and insupportable love of pleasure:—— Hence, *to dance the chicca*, is considered as the supreme good; and I confess, with no little confusion, that the austerity of my principles never prevailed so far as to interdict me from the enjoyment of this singular spectacle, as often as it was in my power.

The orchestra is composed of one or two fiddlers, much superior for the talents which their occupation requires, to the majority of our European scrapers. They have still another advantage over them; that of never being the passive instruments of the pleasure of others, for they enter so deeply into the spirit of the entertainment, that the part of their body which is seated, moves in perfect unison with the foot that beats the measure, and the hand that conducts the bow.

These female mulattoes, who dance so exquisitely, and who have been painted to you in such seducing colours, are the most fervent priestesses of the American Venus. They have reduced voluptuousness to a kind of mechanical art, which they have carried to the highest point of perfection. In their seminaries Aretine[1] himself would be a simple and modest scholar!

They are, generally speaking, above the middle size, perfectly well formed, and so extremely supple in their limbs, that they appear as if they had a swinging in their gait. They join the inflamability of nitre,[2] a petulance of desire, which, in despite of every consideration, incessantly urges them to pursue, seize, and devour pleasure, as the flame devours its aliment; while, on every other occasion, these furious Bacchantes who would madly rush on the palpitating remains of the wretched Orpheus [a note: "See the conclusion of the Fourth Book of the Georgics"][3] scarcely seem to have strength enough to drag along their limbs, or articulate their words.

It is from these women that the housekeepers are usually taken; that is to say, the acknowledged mistresses of the greatest part of the unmarried whites. They have some skill in the management of a family, sufficient honesty to attach themselves invariably to one man, and great goodness of heart. More than one European, abandoned by his selfish brethren, has found in them all the solicitude of the most tender, the most constant, the most generous humanity, without being indebted for it to any other sentiment than benevolence.

d. From Bryan Edwards, *An Historical Survey of the French Colony in the Island of St. Domingo: Comprehending an Account of the Revolt of the Negroes in the Year 1791, and A Detail of the Military Transactions of the British Army*

---

1 Pietro Aretino (1492-1557), Italian libertine writer, known for his elegant pornography.
2 Gunpowder.
3 Virgil, *Georgics*, 4:453-527, the story of Orpheus and Eurydice, including Orpheus's death at the hands of the enraged Bacchantes, female followers of Bacchus.

in that Island, in the Years 1793 & 1794. Vol. 3, The History, Civil and Commercial, of the British West Indies. With A Continuation to the Present Time. 1798. 5th ed. 5 vols. London, 1819

[A West Indian merchant, Jamaican plantation owner, opponent of slave-trade abolition, and MP for Grampound (1796-1800), Bryan Edwards (1743-1800) published the most influential West-Indian history in the English-speaking world, and his account of the St. Domingue rebellion was considered authoritative in the early nineteenth century. "He visited St. Domingo," according to the *DNB*, "shortly after the revolt of the negroes in 1791" (16:112). Thelwall uses Edwards's account of the rebellion for eyewitness accuracy—as it was then assumed—and ideological subversion of racism and slavery.]

1. Cause of the Rebellion

All therefore that I can hope and expect is, that my narrative, if it cannot delight, may at least *instruct*. On the sober and considerate, on those who are open to conviction, this assemblage of horrors will have its effect. It will expose the lamentable ignorance of some, and the monstrous wickedness of others, among the reformers of the present day, who, urging onwards schemes of perfection, and projects of amendment in the condition of human life, faster than nature allows, are lighting up a consuming fire between the different classes of mankind, which nothing but human blood can extinguish. To tell such men that great and beneficial modifications in the established orders of society, can only be effected by a progressive improvement in the situation of the lower ranks of the people, is to preach to the winds. In their hands reformation, with a scythe more destructive than that of Time, mows down every thing, and plants nothing. Moderation and caution they consider as rank cowardice. Force and violence are the ready, and, in their opinion, the only proper application for the cure of early and habitual prejudice. Their practice, like that of other mountebanks, is bold and compendious; their motto is, *cure or kill*.

[...]

It was not the strong and irresistible impulse of human nature, groaning under oppression, that excited either of those classes [Negroes and mulattoes] to plunge their daggers into the bosoms of unoffending women and helpless infants. They were driven into those excesses—reluctantly driven—by the vile machinations of men calling themselves philosophers (the proselytes and imitators in France, of the Old Jewry associates in London[1]) whose pretences to philanthropy were as gross a mockery of human reason, as their conduct was an outrage on all the feelings of our nature, and the ties which hold society together!

---

1   Edmund Burke's *Reflections on the Revolution in France* caricatured and harshly criticized Richard Price, Dissenting clergyman, and liberal reformer, whose chapel was in Old Jewry, London. See Burke, *WS* 5:61-66.

[...]

Thus did the national assembly [in the 15 May 1791 decree granting political rights to propertied men of colour] sweep away in a moment all the laws, usages, prejudices, and opinions concerning these people [of colour], which had existed in the French colonies from their earliest settlement, and tear up by the roots the first principle of a free constitution [for the colonial whites]:— a principle founded on the clearest dictates of reasons and justice, and expressly confirmed to the inhabitants of the French West Indies by the national decree of the 8th of March, 1790; I mean, the sole and exclusive right of passing laws for their local and interior regulation and government.

[...]

Concerning the enslaved negroes, however, it does not appear that the conduct of the whites towards them was in general reprehensible. I believe, on the whole, it was as lenient and indulgent as was consistent with their own safety. It was the mulatto people themselves who were the hard-hearted task-masters to the negroes. The same indignities which they received from the whites, they directed without scruple towards the blacks; exercising over the latter every species of that oppression which they loudly and justly complained of, when exercised on themselves;—and this is a true picture of human nature.

2. Race and Racial laws

On racial hierarchy

To contend, as some philosophers have idly contended, that no natural superiority can justly belong to any one race of people over another, to Europeans over Africans, merely from a difference of colour, is to waste words to no purpose, and to combat with air. Among the inhabitants of every island in the West Indies, it is the colour, with some few exceptions, that distinguishes freedom from slavery: so long therefore as freedom shall be enjoyed exclusively by one race of people, and slavery be the condition of another, contempt and degradation will attach to the colour by which that condition is generally recognized, and follow it, in some degree, through its varieties and affinities.

On the legal disabilities of the mulattos

A mulatto could not be a priest, nor a lawyer, nor a physician, nor a surgeon, nor an apothecary, nor a schoolmaster. He could not even assume the surname of the white man to whom he owed his being. Neither did the distinction of colour terminate, as in the British West Indies, with the third generation. The privileges of a white person were not allowed to any descendant from an African, however remote the origin. The taint in the blood was incurable, and spread to the latest posterity. Hence no white, who had the smallest pretensions to characters, would ever think of marriage with a negro or mulatto woman: such a step would immediately have terminated in his disgrace and ruin.

On abolitionist whites in St. Domingue

Against such of the whites as had taken any part in these disturbances [by mulattos in 1789], in favour of the people of colour, the rage of the [white] populace knew no limits. *Mons. Dubois*, deputy *procureur general*, had not only declared himself an advocate for the mulattoes, but, with a degree of imprudence which indicated insanity, sought occasions to declaim publicly against the slavery of the negroes. The Northern assembly arrested his person, and very probably intended to proceed to greater extremities; but the governor interposed in his behalf, obtained his release, and sent him from the country.

3. Rebellion of 1791

Initial actions

The rebellion broke out on a plantation called Noé, in the parish of Acul, nine miles only from the city. Twelve or fourteen of the ring-leaders, about the middle of the night, proceeded to the refinery, or sugar-house, and seized on a young man, the refiner's apprentice, dragged him to the front of the dwelling-house, and there hewed him into pieces with their cutlasses: his screams brought out the overseer, whom they instantly shot. The rebels now found their way to the apartment of the refiner, and massacred him in his bed. A young man lying sick in a neighbouring chamber, was left apparently dead of the wounds inflicted by their cutlasses: he had strength enough however to crawl to the next plantation, and relate the horrors he had witnessed. He reported, that all the whites of the estate which he had left were murdered, except only the surgeon, whom the rebels had compelled to accompany them, on the idea that they might stand in need of his professional assistance.

Sexual violence

At this juncture, the negroes on the plantation of M. Flaville, a few miles distant, likewise rose and murdered five white persons, one of whom [...] had a wife and three daughters. These unfortunate women, while imploring for mercy of the savages on their knees, beheld their husband and father murdered before their faces. For themselves, they were devoted to a more horrid fate, and were carried away captives by the assassins.

[...]

On some few estates, indeed, the lives of the women were spared, but they were reserved only to gratify the brutal appetites of the ruffians; and it is shocking to relate, that many of them suffered violation on the dead bodies of their husbands and fathers!

THE DAUGHTER OF ADOPTION   519

[...]

In the parish of Limbé, at a place called the Great Ravine [where Thelwall's Edmunds and Henry experience their profound communion with nature and history], a venerable planter, the father of two beautiful young ladies was tied down by a savage ringleader of a band, who ravished the eldest daughter in his presence, and delivered over the youngest to one of his followers: Their passion being satisfied, they slaughtered both the father and the daughters.

[...]

In the neighbourhood of *Jeremie* a body of [mulattos] attacked the house of M. Séjourné, and secured the persons both of him and his wife. This unfortunate woman (my hand trembles while I write!) was far advanced in her pregnancy. The monsters whose prisoner she was, having first murdered her husband in her presence ripped her up alive, and threw the infant to the hogs. They then (how shall I relate it!) sewed up the head of the murdered husband in—!!!—Such are thy triumphs, philanthropy!

"Faithful Negro" model for Thelwall's Mozambo

Amidst these scenes of horror, one instance however occurs of such fidelity and attachment in a negro, as is equally unexpected and affecting. Mons. and Madame Baillon, their daughter and son-in-law, and two white servants, residing on a mountain plantation about thirty miles from Cape François, were apprised of the revolt by one of their own slaves, who was himself in the conspiracy, but promised, if possible, to save the lives of his master and his family. Having no immediate means of providing for their escape, he conducted them into an adjacent wood; after which he went and joined the revolters. The following night, he found an opportunity of bringing them provisions from the rebel camp. The second night he returned again, with a further supply of provisions; but declared that it would be out of his power to give them any further assistance. After this, they saw nothing of the negro for three days; but at the end of that time he came again; and directed the family how to make their way to a river which led to Port Margot, assuring them they would find a canoe on a part of the river which he described. They followed his directions, found the canoe, and got safely into it; but were overset by the rapidity of the current, and after a narrow escape, thought it best to return to their retreat in the mountains. The negro, anxious for their safety, again found them out, and directed them to a broader part of the river, but said it was the last effort he could make to save them. They went accordingly, but not finding the boat, gave themselves up for lost, when the faithful negro again appeared like their guardian angel. He brought with him pigeons, poultry and bread; and conducted the family, by slow marches in the night, along the banks of the river, until they were within sight of the wharf at Port Margot; when telling them they were entirely out of danger, he took his leave for ever, and went to join the rebels. The family were in the woods nineteen nights.

It was computed that, within two months after the revolt first began, upwards of two thousand white persons, of all conditions and ages, had been massacred;—that one hundred and eighty sugar plantations, and about nine hundred coffee, cotton, and indigo settlements had been destroyed (the buildings thereon being consumed by fire), and one thousand two hundred Christian families reduced from opulence to such a state of misery, as to depend altogether for their clothing and sustenance on public and private charity. Of the insurgents, it was reckoned that upwards of ten thousand had perished by the sword or by famine; and some hundreds by the hands of the executioner;—many of them, I am sorry to say, under the torture of the wheel;—a system of revenge and retaliation, which no enormities of savage life could justify or excuse.

e. From John Thelwall, "The Negro's Prayer," *Monthly Magazine* 23
   (April 1807): 252-53

[Commemorating the passage of Britain's slave trade abolition, first published in Richard Phillips's periodical, the *Monthly Magazine* (Phillips published *The Daughter of Adoption*), this poem was reprinted several times, usually with the addition of a final stanza depicting Britain as a leader in the abolitionist cause: Thelwall's *The Vestibule of Eloquence* (1810), 75-77; *Poetical Register* (1814), 350-51. A modern edition is included in Marcus Wood's *The Poetry of Slavery: An Anglo-American Anthology, 1764-1865* (Oxford: Oxford UP, 2003), 239-41.]

O SPIRIT! that rid'st in the whirlwind and storm,
    Whose voice in the thunder is heard,
If ever from man, the poor indigent worm,
    The prayer of affliction was heard;
If black man, as white, is the work of thy hand—
    (And who could create him but Thee?)
      Oh give thy command—
      Let it spread thro' each land,
That Afric's sad sons shall be free!

If, erst when the man-stealer's treacherous guile
    Entrap'd me, all thoughtless of wrong,
From my Niciou's dear love, from the infantile smile
    Of my Aboo, to drag me along;—
If then, the wild anguish that pierced thro' my heart,
    Was seen in its horrors by thee,
      O ease my long smart,
      And thy sanction impart,
That Afric, at last, may be free!—

If while in the slave-ship, with many a groan,
      I wept o'er my sufferings in vain;
While hundreds around me reply'd to my moan,
      And the clanking of many a chain:—
If then thou but deign'st, with a pitying eye,
      Thy poor shackled creature to see,
          Oh thy mercy apply,
          Afric's sorrows to dry,
      And bid the poor Negro be free!

If here, as I faint in the vertical sun,
      And the scourge goads me on to my toil,
No hope faintly soothing, when labour is done,
      Of one joy my lorn heart to beguile;—
If thou view'st me, Great Spirit! as one thou hast made,
      And my fate as dependent on thee,
          O impart thou thy aid,
          That the scourge may be stay'd,
And the Black Man, at last, may be free.

3. The Revolution Debate

a. From Mary Wollstonecraft, *A Vindication of the Rights of Woman*. London, 1792

[*A Vindication of the Rights of Woman* was the second contribution of the radical feminist writer Mary Wollstonecraft (1759-97) to 1790s' debates about rights and revolution, following by two years her anonymous *Vindication of the Rights of Men*, a response to Burke's *Reflections on the Revolution in France*. Wollstonecraft's proposals for the improved education of women, whose condition she compared with that of plantation slaves, established her as the foremost advocate of women's rights in Britain, and also made her a favourite target of the anti-Jacobin press. The greatest blow to Wollstonecraft's ideas and moral character came with the publication of William Godwin's *Memoirs of the Author of a Vindication of the Rights of Woman* (1798), which candidly detailed her love affairs with various men including Godwin (whom she married in 1797), her failed suicide attempts, and her death in 1797 shortly after giving birth to their daughter Mary. As noted in the Introduction (pp. 30-32), Thelwall's *Daughter* is in many respects a tribute to Wollstonecraft's ideas and an attempt to give them new life.]

From Chapter 2. The Prevailing Opinion of a Sexual Character Discussed

By individual education, I mean, for the sense of the word is not precisely defined, such an attention to a child as will slowly sharpen the senses, form the temper, regulate the passions, as they begin to ferment, and set the understanding to work before the body arrives at maturity; so that the man may only have to proceed, not to begin, the important task of learning to think and reason.

To prevent any misconstruction, I must add, that I do not believe that a private education can work the wonders which some sanguine writers have attributed to it. Men and women must be educated, in a great degree, by the opinions and manners of the society they live in. In every age there has been a stream of popular opinion that has carried all before it, and given a family character, as it were, to the century. It may then fairly be inferred, that, till society be differently constituted, much cannot be expected from education. It is, however, sufficient for my present purpose to assert, that whatever effect circumstances have on the abilities, every being may become virtuous by the exercise of its own reason. [...]

Consequently, the most perfect education, in my opinion, is such an exercise of the understanding as is best calculated to strengthen the body and form the heart. Or, in other words, to enable the individual to attain such habits of virtue as will render it independent. In fact, it is a farce to call any being virtuous whose virtues do not result from the exercise of its own reason. This was Rousseau's opinion respecting men. I extend it to women, and confidently assert that they have been drawn out of their sphere by false refinement, and not by an endeavour to acquire masculine qualities. Still the regal homage which they receive is so intoxicating, that till the manners of the times are changed, and formed on more reasonable principles, it may be impossible to convince them that the illegitimate power which they obtain, by degrading themselves, is a curse, and that they must return to nature and equality, if they wish to secure the placid satisfaction that unsophisticated affections impart. But for this epoch we must wait—wait, perhaps, till kings and nobles, enlightened by reason, and, preferring the real dignity of man to childish state, throw off their gaudy hereditary trappings. [...]

I love man as my fellow; but his scepter, real, or usurped, extends not to me, unless the reason of an individual demands my homage; and even then the submission is to reason, and not to man. In fact, the conduct of an accountable being must be regulated by the operations of its own reason; or on what foundation rests the throne of God?

It appears to me necessary to dwell on these obvious truths, because females have been insulated, as it were; and, while they have been stripped of the virtues that should clothe humanity, they have been decked with artificial graces that enable them to exercise a short-lived tyranny. Love, in their bosoms, taking place of every nobler passion, their sole ambition is to be fair, to raise emotion instead of inspiring respect; and this ignoble desire, like the servility in absolute monarchies, destroys all strength of character. Liberty is the mother of virtue, and if women are, by their very constitution, slaves, and not allowed to breathe the sharp invigorating air of freedom, they must ever languish like exotics, and be reckoned beautiful flaws in nature [...].

From Chapter 3. The Same Subject Continued

The baneful consequences which flow from inattention to health during infancy, and youth, extend further than is supposed—dependence of body naturally produces dependence of mind; and how can she be a good wife or mother, the greater part of whose time is employed to guard against or endure sickness? Nor can it be expected that a woman will resolutely endeavour to strengthen her constitution and abstain from enervating indulgencies, if artificial notions of beauty, and false descriptions of sensibility, have been early entangled with her motives of action. Most men are sometimes obliged to bear with bodily inconveniences, and to endure, occasionally, the inclemency of the elements; but genteel women are, literally speaking, slaves to their bodies [...].

Educated in slavish dependence, and enervated by luxury and sloth, where shall we find men who will stand forth to assert the rights of man;—or claim the privilege of moral beings, who should have but one road to excellence? Slavery to monarchs and ministers, which the world will be long in freeing itself from, and whose deadly grasp stop the progress of the human mind, is not yet abolished.

Let not men then in the pride of power, use the same arguments that tyrannic kings and venal ministers have used, and fallaciously assert that woman ought to be subjected because she has always been so.—But, when man, governed by reasonable laws, enjoys his natural freedom, let him despise woman, if she do not share it with him [...].

It is time to effect a revolution in female manners—time to restore to them their lost dignity—and make them, as a part of the human species, labour by reforming themselves to reform the world.

[S]upposing a woman, trained up to obedience, be married to a sensible man, who directs her judgment without making her feel the servility of her subjection, to act with as much propriety by this reflected light as can be expected when reason is taken at second hand, yet she cannot ensure the life of her protector; he may die and leave her with a large family.

A double duty devolves on her; to educate them in the character of both father and mother; to form their principles and secure their property. But, alas! she has never thought, much less acted for herself. She has only learned to please men, to depend gracefully on them; yet, encumbered with children, how is she to obtain another protector—a husband to supply the place of reason? A rational man, for we are not treading on romantic ground, though he may think her a pleasing docile creature, will not choose to marry a *family* for love, when the world contains many more pretty creatures. What is then to become of her? She either falls an easy prey to some mean fortune-hunter, who defrauds her children of their paternal inheritance, and renders her miserable; or becomes the victim of discontent and blind indulgence [...].

But supposing no very improbable conjecture, that a being only taught to please must still find her happiness in pleasing;—what an example of folly, not to say vice, will she be to her innocent daughters! The mother will be lost in the coquette, and instead of making friends of her daughters, view them with eyes askance, for they are rivals—rivals more cruel than any other, because they invite a comparison, and drive her from the throne of beauty, who has never thought of a seat on the bench of reason.

From Chapter 4. The State of Degradation to which Woman Is Reduced

[I]f love be the supreme good, let woman be only educated to inspire it, and let every charm be polished to intoxicate the senses; but, if they are moral beings, let them have a chance to become intelligent; and let love to man be only a part of that glowing flame of universal love, which, after encircling humanity, mounts in grateful incense to God. [...]

Friendship is a serious affection; the most sublime of all affections, because it is founded on principle, and cemented by time. The very reverse may be said of love. In a great degree, love and friendship cannot subsist in the same bosom; even when inspired by different objects they weaken or destroy each other, and for the same object can only be felt in succession. The vain fears and fond jealousies, the winds which fan the flame of love, when judiciously or artfully tempered, are both incompatible with the tender confidence and sincere respect of friendship.

Love, such as the glowing pen of genius has traced, exists not on earth, or only resides in those exalted, fervid imaginations that have sketched such dangerous pictures. Dangerous, because they not only afford a plausible excuse, to the voluptuary who disguises sheer sensuality under a sentimental veil; but as they spread affectation, and take from the dignity of virtue. [...] [I]t is not against strong, persevering passions; but romantic wavering feelings that I wish to guard the female heart by exercising the understanding.

From Chapter 7. Modesty, Comprehensively Considered, and Not as a Sexual Virtue

To render chastity the virtue from which unsophisticated modesty will naturally flow, the attention should be called away from employments which only exercise the sensibility; and the heart made to beat time to humanity, rather than to throb with love. The woman who has dedicated a considerable portion of her time to pursuits purely intellectual, and whose affections have been exercised by humane plans of usefulness, must have more purity of mind, as a natural consequence, than the ignorant beings whose time and thoughts have been occupied by gay pleasures or schemes to conquer hearts. The regulation of the behaviour is not modesty, though those who study rules of decorum are, in general, termed modest women. Make the heart clean, let it expand and feel for all that is human, instead of being narrowed by selfish passions; and let the mind frequently contemplate subjects that exercise the understanding, without heating the imagination, and artless modesty will give the finishing touches to the picture.

From Chapter 8. Morality Undermined by Sexual Notions of the Importance of a Good Reputation

[A]dvice respecting behaviour, and all the various modes of preserving a good reputation, which have been so strenuously inculcated on the female world, were specious poisons, that incrusting morality eat away the substance ... it is reputation, not chastity and all its fair train, that they are employed to keep free from spot, not as a virtue, but to preserve their station in the world.

[...] If an innocent girl become a prey to love, she is degraded forever, though her mind was not polluted by the arts which married women, under the convenient cloak of marriage, practise; nor has she violated any duty—but the duty of respecting herself. The married woman, on the contrary, breaks a most sacred engagement, and becomes a cruel mother when she is a false and faithless wife. [...] I have known a number of women who, if they did not love their husbands, loved nobody else, give themselves entirely up to vanity and dissipation, neglecting every domestic duty; nay, even squandering away all the money which should have been saved for their helpless younger children, yet have plumed themselves on their unsullied reputation, as if the whole compass of their duty as wives and mothers was only to preserve it. [...]

This regard for reputation, independent of its being one of the natural rewards of virtue, however, took its rise from a cause that I have already deplored as the grand source of female depravity, the impossibility of regaining respectability by a return to virtue, though men preserve theirs during the indulgence of vice. [...]

Mrs. Macaulay has justly observed, that "there is but one fault which a woman of honour may not commit with impunity." She then justly, and humanely adds—"This has given rise to the trite and foolish observation, that the first fault against chastity in woman has a radical power to deprave the character. But no such frail beings come out of the hands of nature. The human mind is built of nobler materials than to be so easily corrupted; and with all their disadvantages of situation and education, women seldom become entirely abandoned till they are thrown into a state of desperation, by the venomous rancour of their own sex."

From Chapter 9. Of the Pernicious Effects which Arise from the Unnatural Distinctions Established in Society

[L]et me return to the more specious slavery which chains the very soul of woman, keeping her for ever under the bondage of ignorance.

The preposterous distinctions of rank, which render civilization a curse, by dividing the world between voluptuous tyrants, and cunning envious dependents, corrupt, almost equally, every class of people, because respectability is not attached to the discharge of the relative duties of life, but to the station, and when the duties are not fulfilled the affections cannot gain sufficient strength to fortify the virtue of which they are the natural reward. Still there are some loop-holes out of which a man may creep, and dare to think and act for himself; but for a woman it is an herculean task, because she has difficulties peculiar to her sex to overcome, which require almost super-human powers.

A truly benevolent legislator always endeavours to make it the interest of each individual to be virtuous; and thus private virtue becoming the cement of public happiness, an orderly whole is consolidated by the tendency of all the parts towards a common centre. But, the private or public virtue of woman is very problematical; for Rousseau, and a numerous list of male writers, insist that she should all her life be subjected to a severe restraint, that of propriety. Why subject her to propriety—blind propriety, if she be capable of acting from a nobler spring, if she be an heir of immortality? Is sugar always to be produced by vital blood? Is one half of the human species, like the poor African slaves, to be subject to prejudices that brutalize them, when principles would be a surer guard, only to sweeten the cup of man? Is not this indirectly to deny woman reason? [...]

[I]s not that government then very defective, and very unmindful of the happiness of one half of its members, that does not provide for honest, independent women, by encouraging them to fill respectable stations? [...] [T]he most respectable women are the most oppressed; and, unless they have understandings far superiour to the common run of understandings, taking in both sexes, they must, from being treated like contemptible beings, become contemptible. How many women thus waste life away the prey of discontent, who might have practised as physicians, regulated a farm, managed a shop, and stood erect, supported by their own industry, instead of hanging their heads surcharged with the dew of sensibility, that consumes the beauty to which it at first gave lustre. [...] How much more respectable is the woman who earns her own bread by fulfilling any duty, than the most accomplished beauty!—beauty did I say!—so sensible am I of the beauty of moral loveliness, or the harmonious propriety that attunes the passions of a well-regulated mind, that I blush at making the comparison.

From Chapter 11. Duty to Parents

The parent who sedulously endeavours to form the heart and enlarge the understanding of his child, has given that dignity to the discharge of a duty, common to the whole animal world, that only reason can give. This is the parental affection of humanity, and leaves instinctive natural affection far behind. Such a parent acquires all the rights of the most sacred friendship, and his advice, even when his child is advanced in life, demands serious consideration.

b. From William Godwin, *An Enquiry Concerning Political Justice, and Its Influence on Morals and Happiness.* 3rd ed. London, 1798

[First published in 1793, *Political Justice* was the major work of the political theorist and novelist William Godwin (1756-1836), a friend and mentor of Thelwall, but also a stern critic of his outspoken, interventionist approach to reform. Their difference of opinion about the means of achieving political justice finds fictional expression at several points in *The Daughter*, notably the debate about abolition between Henry, Edmunds, and Parkinson, and Seraphina's eventual reassessment of her radical principles, both discussed in the Introduction.]

From Book IV, Chapter II, "Of Revolutions"

Revolution is engendered by an indignation against tyranny, yet is itself ever more pregnant with tyranny. The tyranny which excites its indignation can scarcely be without its partisans; and, the greater is the indignation excited, and the more sudden and vast the fall of the oppressors, the deeper will be the resentment which fills the mind of the losing party. What more unavoidable than that men should entertain some discontent at being violently stripped of their wealth and their privileges? [...]

Revolution is instigated by a horror against tyranny, yet its own tyranny is not without peculiar aggravations. There is no period more at war with the existence of liberty. The unrestrained communication of opinions has always been subjected to mischievous counteraction, but upon such occasions it is trebly fettered. At other times men are not so much alarmed for its effects. But in a moment of revolution, when everything is in crisis, the influence even of a word is dreaded, and the consequent slavery is complete. Where was there a revolution in which a strong vindication of what it was intended to abolish was permitted, or indeed almost any species of writing or argument, that was not, for the most part, in harmony with the opinions which happened to prevail? An attempt to scrutinize men's thoughts, and punish their opinions, is of all kinds of despotism the most odious; yet this attempt is peculiarly characteristic of a period of revolution. [...]

Perhaps no important revolution was ever bloodless. It may be useful in this place to recollect in what the mischief of shedding blood consists. The abuses which at present exist in political society are so enormous, the oppressions which are exercised so intolerable, the ignorance and vice they entail so dreadful, that possibly a dispassionate enquirer might decide that, if their annihilation could be purchased by an instant sweeping of every human being now arrived at years of maturity from the face of the earth, the purchase would not be too dear. [...] The case is altogether different when man falls by the hand of his neighbour. Here a thousand ill passions are generated. The perpetrators, and the witnesses of murders, become obdurate, unrelenting and inhuman. Those who sustain the loss of relations or friends by a catastrophe of this sort are filled with indignation and revenge. Distrust is propagated from man to man, and the dearest ties of human society are dissolved. It is impossible to devise a temper more inauspicious to the cultivation of justice and the diffusion of benevolence.

To the remark that revolutions can scarcely be unaccompanied with the shedding of blood, it may be added that they are necessarily crude and premature. Politics is a science. The general features of the nature of man are capable of being understood, and a mode may be delineated which, in itself considered, is best adapted to the condition of man in society. [...] Now it is clearly the nature of science to be progressive in its advances. [...] Political knowledge is, no doubt, in its infancy; and, as it is an affair of life and action, will, in proportion as it gathers vigour, manifest a more uniform and less precarious influence upon the concerns of human society. [...]

The only method according to which social improvements can be carried on, with sufficient prospect of an auspicious event, is when the improvement of our institutions advances in a just proportion to the illumination of the public understanding. [...] Imperfect institutions [...] cannot long support themselves when they are generally disapproved of, and their effects truly understood. There is a period at which they may be expected to decline and expire, almost without an effort. Reform, under this meaning of the term, can scarcely be considered as of the nature of action. Men feel their situation; and the restraints that shackled them before vanish like a deception. When such a crisis has arrived, not a sword will need to be drawn, not a finger to be lifted up in purposes of violence. The adversaries will be too few and too feeble to be able to entertain a serious thought of resistance against the universal sense of mankind.

Under this view of the subject then it appears that revolutions, instead of being truly beneficial to mankind, answer no other purpose than that of marring the salutary and uninterrupted progress which might be expected to attend upon political truth and social improvement. They disturb the harmony of intellectual nature. They propose to give us something for which we are not prepared, and which we cannot effectually use. They suspend the wholesome advancement of science, and confound the process of nature and reason. [...]

[...] The duty therefore of the true politician is to postpone revolution if he cannot entirely prevent it. It is reasonable to believe that the later it occurs, and the more generally ideas of political good and evil are previously understood, the shorter, and the less deplorable, will be the mischiefs attendant on revolution.

From Book VIII, Chapter VIII, "Objections to This System [of Equality] from the Inflexibility of Its Restrictions"—Appendix, "Of Co-Operation, Cohabitation and Marriage"

It is a curious subject to enquire into the due medium between individuality and concert. On the one hand, it is to be observed that human beings are formed for society. Without society, we shall probably be deprived of the most eminent enjoyments of which our nature is susceptible. [...]

On the other hand, individuality is of the very essence of intellectual excellence. He that resigns himself wholly to sympathy and imitation can possess little of mental strength or accuracy. [...]

From these principles it appears that everything that is usually understood by the term co-operation is, in some degree, an evil. [...]

[...] We ought to be able to do without one another. He is the most perfect man to whom society is not a necessary of life, but a luxury, innocent and enviable, in which he joyfully indulges. Such a man will not fly to society, as something requisite for the consuming of his time, or the refuge of his weakness. In society he will find pleasure; the temper of his mind will prepare him for friendship and for love. But he will resort with a scarcely inferior eagerness to solitude; and will find in it the highest complacence and the purest delight.

Another article which belongs to the subject of co-operation is cohabitation. The evils attendant on this practice are obvious. In order to the human understanding's being successfully cultivated, it is necessary that the intellectual operations of men should be independent of each other.[1] We should avoid such

---

1   Vol. I, Book IV, Chap. III, p. 288. [Godwin's note, referring to his chapter "Of Political Associations," not reproduced here]

practices as are calculated to melt our opinions into a common mould. Cohabitation is also hostile to that fortitude which should accustom a man, in his actions, as well as in his opinions, to judge for himself, and feel competent to the discharge of his own duties. Add to this, that it is absurd to expect the inclinations and wishes of two human beings to coincide, through any long period of time. To oblige them to act and to live together is to subject them to some inevitable portion of thwarting, bickering and unhappiness. [...]

The subject of cohabitation is particularly interesting as it includes in it the subject of marriage. It will therefore be proper to pursue the enquiry in greater detail. The evil of marriage, as it is practised in European countries, extends further than we have yet described. The method is for a thoughtless and romantic youth of each sex to come together, to see each other, for a few times and under circumstances full of delusion, and then to vow eternal attachment. What is the consequence of this? In almost every instance they find themselves deceived. They are reduced to make the best of an irretrievable mistake. They are left to conceive it their wisest policy to shut their eyes upon realities, happy, if, by any perversion of intellect, they can persuade themselves that they were right in their first crude opinion of each other. Thus the institution of marriage is made a system of fraud; and men who carefully mislead their judgments in the daily affair of their life must be expected to have a crippled judgment in every other concern.

Add to this that marriage, as now understood, is a monopoly, and the worst of monopolies. So long as two human beings are forbidden, by positive institution, to follow the dictates of their own mind, prejudice will be alive and vigorous. So long as I seek, by despotic and artificial means, to maintain possession of a woman, I am guilty of the most odious selfishness. Over this imaginary prize, men watch with perpetual jealousy; and one man finds his desire, and his capacity to circumvent, as much excited as the other is excited to traverse his projects, and frustrate his hopes. As long as this state of society continues, philanthropy will be crossed and checked in a thousand ways, and the still augmenting stream of abuse will continue to flow.

The abolition of the present system of marriage appears to involve no evils. We are apt to represent that abolition to ourselves as the harbinger of brutal lust and depravity. But it really happens, in this, as in other cases, that the positive laws which are made to restrain our vices irritate and multiply them. Not to say that the same sentiments of justice and happiness which, in a state of equality, would destroy our relish for expensive gratifications might be expected to decrease our inordinate appetites of every kind, and to lead us universally to prefer the pleasures of intellect to the pleasures of sense.

It is a question of some moment whether the intercourse of the sexes, in a reasonable state of society, would be promiscuous, or whether each man would select for himself a partner to whom he will adhere as long as that adherence shall continue to be the choice of both parties. Probability seems to be greatly in favour of the latter. Perhaps this side of the alternative is most favourable to population. Perhaps it would suggest itself in preference to the man who would wish to maintain the several propensities of his frame, in the order due to their relative importance, and to prevent a merely sensual appetite from engrossing excessive attention. It is scarcely to be imagined that this commerce, in any state of society, will be stripped of its adjuncts, and that men will as willingly hold it with a woman whose personal and mental qualities they disapprove as with one of a different description. But it is the nature of the human mind to persist, for a certain length of time, in its opinion or choice. The parties therefore, having acted upon selection, are not likely to forget this selection when the interview is over. Friendship, if by friendship we understand that affection for an individual which is measured singly by what we know of his worth, is one of the most exquisite gratifications, perhaps one of the most improving exercises, of a rational mind. Friendship therefore may be expected to come in aid of the sexual intercourse, to refine its grossness, and increase its delight. All these arguments are calculated to determine our judgment in favour of marriage as a salutary and respectable institution, but not of that species of marriage in which there is no room for repentance and to which liberty and hope are equally strangers.

Admitting these principles therefore as the basis of the sexual commerce, what opinion ought we to form respecting infidelity to this attachment? Certainly no ties ought to be imposed upon either party, preventing them from quitting the attachment, whenever their judgment directs them to quit it.

Appendix C: *Reviews of* The Daughter of Adoption

[We reproduce four known reviews of the novel. The *Critical Review* (1756-1817), which had been originally slanted in a Tory direction and edited by Tobias Smollett, took a more moderate and liberal turn from 1791. The Whiggish *Monthly Review* (1749-1845) was still a major intellectual journal in 1801, while the *Monthly Magazine*—established in 1796 by Richard Phillips, *The Daughter*'s publisher—was the most culturally innovative periodical at the time aiming for a professional, Dissenting readership. The fourth review appeared in the *Annals of Philosophy*, a short-lived periodical (1801-04) whose initial editor was the physician and scientist Thomas Garnett (1766-1802).]

1. *Critical Review* n.s. 31 (February 1801): 234-35

These volumes are greatly superior to those ephemera which, under the appellation of novels, buz for a short period, and then are heard no more. They display no inconsiderable knowledge of human nature, and an acquaintance with other countries and different scenes; while the varied and often uncommon events firmly arrest the attention and soften the heart.

We will, however, first speak of the faults of these volumes, which are not unfrequent; yet nevertheless such as an inferior author would have avoided. The whole is much too long, and it is expanded with little professional judgement; for the mind is often diverted from interesting scenery and events to minute details of circumstances, the substance of which might have been told in three lines. The character of Edmund[s] "no vulgar boy," is somewhat improbable: a moralist, an "acute discerner of men's deeds" with accurate judgement and ready resource, under the age of twenty, is a phænomenon a little too extraordinary. The conclusion, moreover, is needlessly enveloped, and, at last, the mystery is explained in a trite hackneyed manner. Why was not Sterne's day-tall critic[1] at hand, to give to Seraphina the key of Mrs. Montfort's writing-desk? Except that it would have curtailed the bulk of the work.

To turn, however, to a more pleasing task.—The introduction is admirably conducted, and the chief event kept from even the eye of suspicion. Though it be one which has been too often employed, it is nevertheless involved with so much care that its triteness does not injure the effect. The story of Mrs. Montfort to her confident is dexterously broken off; and the detail of the youthful years of Henry skilfully managed, to account for the extravagant inconsiderate conduct of his life. The West-Indian adventures are well told; the heroine is interestingly introduced, and Mrs. Morton brought and kept on the stage with much art. Yet we wish the bosom of Seraphina had not been so tender, or her conduct so weak; it injures the moral of the story; and her errors are only nec-

---

1   Laurence Sterne, *Tristram Shandy* (1759), ch. XIII.

essary for some of the circumstances of the fourth volume, which we would rather had been suppressed.

One great political object of Dr. Beaufort seems to have been to detail and expose the miseries of the slave trade. This is a subject which cannot be introduced in this place; but we may add that the author, in his account of the cruelties of the slaves during the ebullition of their insurrection, has sufficiently answered his own arguments. This may be styled a momentary ebullition, but experience has not shown that, when power has been retained, it has been exercised with either mercy or discretion.

On the whole, we discover in these volumes talents which may be more successfully employed in a future work, when experience in this style of writing, if our author chuse to pursue it, shall add to his abilities a more intimate knowledge of that necessary arrangement, which, like the soil of a diamond, will display their luster to greater advantage.

2. *Monthly Magazine* Supplement 11 (20 July 1801): 606

Dr. Beaufort's "Daughter of Adoption," is a Novel of more than ordinary excellence: the characters are well drawn, the incidents striking and natural, the language correct, and the moral good: the author shews a knowledge of the human heart, and if he cultivates this mode of writing, will, in all probability, produce something still superior to the present work.

3. *Monthly Review* n.s. 35 (August 1801): 356-61

This novel is certainly not one of that negative class of insipid and senseless productions, which we see frequently issuing from the press merely to swell the catalogues of circulating libraries. The story is interesting, though singular and improbable; the plot is conducted with considerable skill; the descriptions are animated; the characters, in general, are well supported; and the composition possesses force and vivacity, though in many instances it borders on inflation. The work is evidently the production of a mind of no common powers, and an imagination of no vulgar cast: but its morality is, in our opinion, very exceptionable. Scenes of debauchery and libertinism, in which the hero acts a principal character, are too frequently brought to our view, and described in language too impassioned and prurient.

Seraphina, the heroine, in whose behalf our feelings are excited by all that can interest in suffering beauty and excellence, falls under the dominion of unguarded passion, and becomes the unrepenting mistress of the man whom she loves. It is perhaps less difficult to discover that the author is a Godwinian in principle, and that he is an advocate for the doctrine that individuality of affection and possession constitutes a sacred bond in the sexual union, independently of legal forms and social compacts; than it is to reconcile the conduct of his heroine with the profession of such a principle: since, after a long and steady resistance to the earnest and repeated solicitations of her Henry, she at last consents to be made his wife. Though the modern philosopher, in his own case and practice, might think it necessary to sacrifice a cock to Esculapius,[1] the fictitious heroine of a romance might surely have maintained a consistency of conduct and principle!—Be the intended moral of this novel, however, what it may, we cannot but condemn a work which represents the loss of female chastity as a matter of light concern, and only to be regretted because it incurs the loss of social respectability; and which tends to lessen the dread of vice by exhibiting a picture of its impunity, and by endowing the frail and guilty with every other quality that can command the love, esteem, and admiration of mankind. We think, also, that the palliating arguments respecting incest, which occur towards the close of the last volume, might as well have been omitted; because, though they are put into the mouth of an excentric Being [Dr. Pengarron], and are not made influential in the conduct of the story, yet, as the person who adopts them is an amiable character, and as they stand unopposed, they have too much the appearance of possessing some degree of weight with the author, and too strongly excite the idea that he wishes them to make some impression on the reader.

In the following extracts, will be found two good traits, characteristic of the English sailor: [long extract from IV.I describing the torture and execution of a rebellious slave, Aboan, whose torments are finally ended by the action of a British sailor. The two good traits are apparently the sailor's moral sense and his plain-speaking nationalism. Edmunds quarrels with his racist comments.]

The succeeding quotation, by affording a sample of the heroine's character, and a specimen of her reasoning on the subject of her marriage, will tend to justify some of our succeeding observations: [long extract from VII.I, where Seraphina sets the terms by which she will marry Henry; the terms are anti-aristocratic, feminist in a Wollstonecraftian sense, and classically republican.]

We shall add no farther remark than that we should be pleased to see talents, such as this writer possesses, more unexceptionably employed than in the present instance; and directed in such a manner that, while his abilities are readily acknowledged, the tendency of his labours may be equally applauded.

4. *Annals of Philosophy* 1 (1801): 285

Of this little work, we cannot refrain from speaking, as it is far superior to the common run of this kind of publication. It does great credit to the author in a moral point of view, as it tends to expose the miseries of the execrable slave trade.

5. Thelwall's Reply to the Reviews, from "Prefatory Memoir," *Poems, Chiefly Written in Retirement*. Hereford, 1801

[Thelwall, in his "Prefatory Memoir" to *Poems, Chiefly Written in Retirement* (1801), responded to the two major reviews of his novel by the *Critical Review* and *Monthly Review*. While generally pleased with the reviews, he also clarified an area that was criticized, namely, the sexual morality of the novel.]

---

1 Proverbial expression; Esculapius, Greek god of healing and medicine.

The moral tendency of the Work, indeed, has been somewhat questioned: and it is confessed, that the situation and sentiments of the heroine are marked with some peculiarities. The abstract moral of the tale, however, is simply this:——— "That the purity of the sexual intercourse consists, exclusively, in the inviolable singleness of attachment; but that, nevertheless, whatever be our theoretical opinion of the ceremonial part of the institution, it is an absolute moral duty, in the present state of society, to conform with the established usage." If this maxim be erroneous, it is an error in the Author's judgment of so long standing, that he cannot recollect the time when he did not err. But, be this as it may, he trusts there are passages enough in his Book to make ample atonement for an individual heresy; and, that no one will rise from the perusal of his pages, with a heart less disposed to the moral duties and social charities of life. To promote those charities (in their most extensive acceptation) has been the object he has perpetually had in view; and, if, in this respect, he has not failed, he is little solicitous about the cavils that may be raised upon disputable points of doctrine.

Works Cited and Recommended Reading

Primary

Anon. *A Particular Account of the Commencement and Progress of the Insurrection of the Negroes in St. Domingo.* 2nd ed. London, 1792.

Burke, Edmund. *The Writings and Speeches of Edmund Burke.* Gen. ed. Paul Langford. 9 vols. Oxford: Clarendon, 1981-96.

Coleridge, Samuel Taylor. *The Collected Letters of Samuel Taylor Coleridge.* Ed. Earl Leslie Griggs. 6 vols. Oxford: Clarendon, 1956-71.

——. *Specimens of the Table Talk of Samuel Taylor Coleridge.* Ed. H.N. Coleridge. Oxford: Oxford UP, 1917.

Earle, William. *Obi; or, The History of Three-Fingered Jack.* Ed. Srivinas Aravamudan. Peterborough, ON: Broadview P, 2005.

Edwards, Bryan. *The History, Civil and Commercial, of the British West Indies. With a Continuation to the Present Time.* 5th ed. 5 vols. London, 1819.

Edgeworth, Maria. "The Grateful Negro." 1803. *Popular Tales.* London, 1804.

Equiano, Olaudah. *The Interesting Narrative of the Life of Olaudah Equiano.* Ed. Angelo Costanzo. Peterborough, ON: Broadview P, 2001.

Hume, David. "Essay XIX: Of Polygamy and Divorces." *Essays Moral, Political, Literary.* Ed. Eugene F. Miller. Rev. ed. Indianapolis: Liberty Fund, 1987.

Kitson, Peter, and Debbie Lee, eds. *Slavery, Abolition and Emancipation: Writings in the British Romantic Period.* 8 vols. London: Pickering and Chatto, 1999.

Sansay, Leonora. *Secret History; or, The Horrors of St. Domingo,* and *Laura.* Ed. Michael J. Drexler. Peterborough, ON: Broadview P, 2007.

Smith, Adam. *The Theory of Moral Sentiments.* 1759. Ed. D.D. Raphael and A.L. Macfie. Oxford: Clarendon P, 1976.

Stedman, John Gabriel. *Narrative of Five Years Expedition against the Revolted Negroes of Surinam.* London, 1796.

——. *Stedman's Surinam: A Life in an Eighteenth-Century Slave Society.* Ed. Richard Price and Sally Price. Baltimore: Johns Hopkins UP, 1992.

Thelwall, John. "A Pedestrian Excursion through Several Parts of England and Wales during the Summer of 1797," *Monthly Magazine* (1799-1801).

——. "An Unpublished Letter from John Thelwall to S.T. Coleridge." Ed. Warren E. Gibbs. *Modern Language Review* 25 (1930): 85-90.

——. *The Daughter of Adoption; A Tale of Modern Times.* 4 vols. London: Richard Phillips, 1801; 2 vols. Dublin: N. Kelly, 1801.

——. *Incle and Yarico and The Incas: Two Plays by John Thelwall.* Ed. Frank Felsenstein and Michael Scrivener. Madison/Teaneck: Fairleigh Dickinson UP, 2006.

——. "Introductory Essay on the Study of English Rhythmus." *Selections for the Illustration of a Course of Instructions on the Rhythmus and Utterance of the English Language.* London, 1812, i-lxxii.

——. "John Thelwall's Letters in the British Library." Ed. Michael Scrivener. *Romanticism* 16.2 (2010): 139-51.

——. *A Letter to Henry Cline, Esq., on Imperfect Development of the Faculties, Mental and Moral, as well as Constitutional and Organic; and on the Treatment of Impediments of Speech*. London, 1810.

——. "The Moral Tendency of a System of Spies and Informers." *Political Lectures. Volume the First, Part the First*. 4th ed. London, 1795. 1-31.

——. *The Panoramic Miscellany; or Monthly Magazine and Review*. Vol. 1 (1826).

——. *The Peripatetic*. 1793. Ed Judith Thompson. Detroit: Wayne State UP, 2001.

——. *Poems, Chiefly Written in Retirement*. 1801. Oxford: Woodstock, 1989.

——. *Poems, Chiefly Suggested by the Scenery of Nature*. (Derby manuscript.) Derby Central Library: Local Studies. MS 5868-5870.

——. *Poems Written in Close Confinement* 1795 Oxford: Woodstock Books, 2000.

——. *The Poetical Recreations of the Champion*. London, 1822.

——. *The Politics of English Jacobinism: Writings of John Thelwall*. Ed. Gregory Claeys. University Park: Penn State UP, 1995.

——. *Selected Political Writings of John Thelwall*. Ed. Robert Lamb and Corinna Wagner. 4 vols. London: Pickering and Chatto, 2009.

——. *The Tribune, a Periodical Publication, Consisting Chiefly of the Political Lectures of J. Thelwall*. 3 vols. London, 1795-96.

——. "'Yours, a True Sans Culotte': Letters of John Thelwall and Henrietta Cecil Thelwall, 1794-1838." *Presences that Disturb: Models of Romantic Identity in the Literature and Culture of the 1790s*. Ed. Damian Walford Davies. Cardiff: U of Wales P, 2002.

Thelwall, Mrs. [Henrietta Cecil Boyle]. *The Life of John Thelwall*. Vol. 1. London, 1837.

Wimpffen, Francis Alexander Stanislaus, Baron de. *A Voyage to Saint Domingo, in the Years 1788, 1789, and 1790*. Trans. J. Wright. London, 1797.

Wollstonecraft, Mary. *A Vindication of the Rights of Men* [1790] *and A Vindication of the Rights of Woman* [1792]. Ed. D.L. Macdonald and Kathleen Scherf. Peterborough, ON: Broadview P, 1997.

Secondary

Allen, Beverly Sprague. "William Godwin's Influence upon John Thelwall." *PMLA* 37 (1922): 679-81.

Aravamudan, Srivinas. *Tropicopolitans: Colonialism and Agency, 1688-1804*. Durham: Duke UP, 1999.

Buck-Morss, Susan. *Hegel, Haiti, and Universal History*. Pittsburgh: U of Pittsburgh P, 2009.

Corfield, Penelope. "Rhetoric, Radical Politics and Rainfall: John Thelwall in Breconshire, 1797-1800." *Brycheiniog* 40 (2008): 1-27.

Craton, Michael. *Testing the Chains: Resistance to Slavery in the British West Indies*. Ithaca: Cornell UP, 1982.

Davies, Damian Walford. *Presences that Disturb: Models of Romantic Identity in the Literature and Culture of the 1790s.* Cardiff: U Wales P, 2002.

——, ed. *Romanticism, History, Historicism: Essays on an Orthodoxy.* New York: Routledge, 2009.

Davis, David Brion. *Slavery and Human Progress.* New York: Oxford UP, 1984.

Felsenstein, Frank. *English Trader, Indian Maid: Representing Gender, Race, and Slavery in the New World: An Inkle and Yarico Reader.* Baltimore: Johns Hopkins UP, 1999.

Furley, Oliver W. "Moravian Missionaries and Slaves in the West Indies." *Caribbean Studies* 5 (1965): 3-16.

Holmes, Richard. *Coleridge: Darker Reflections.* London: Pantheon, 2000.

——. *Coleridge: Early Visions.* London: Hodder & Stoughton, 1989.

Hörmann, Raphael. "Thinking the 'Unthinkable'? Representations of the Haitian Revolution in British Discourse, 1791 to 1805." *Human Bondage in the Cultural Contact Zone: Transdisciplinary Perspectives on Slavery and Its Discourses.* Ed. Raphael Hörmann and Gesa Mackenthun. Münster: Waxmann, 2010.

James, C.L.R. *The Black Jacobins: Toussaint L'Ouverture and the San Domingo Revolution.* 1938. 2nd ed. New York: Vintage, 1963.

James, Felicity. *Charles Lamb, Coleridge and Wordsworth: Reading Friendship in the 1790s.* Houndmills: Palgrave Macmillan, 2008.

Kitson, Peter. "Coleridge's Anecdote of John Thelwall." *Notes and Queries*, ns 32:3 (September 1985): 345.

——. "Coleridge, the French Revolution and the 'Ancient Mariner': Collective Guilt and Individual Salvation." *Yearbook of English Studies* 19 (1989): 197-207.

——. "John Thelwall in Saint Domingue: Race, Slavery, and Revolution in *The Daughter of Adoption: A Tale of Modern Times* (1801)." *Romanticism* 16.2 (2010): 120-38.

Magnuson, Paul. *Reading Public Romanticism.* Princeton: Princeton UP, 1998.

Markley, Arnold A. *Conversion and Reform in the British Novel in the 1790s.* New York: Palgrave Macmillan, 2009.

Mee, Jon. *Romanticism, Enthusiasm, and Regulation: Poetics and the Policing of Culture in the Romantic Period.* Oxford: Oxford UP, 2005.

Poole, Steve, ed. *John Thelwall: Radical Romantic and Acquitted Felon.* London: Pickering and Chatto, 2009.

Popkin, Jeremy D. *A Concise History of the Haitian Revolution.* Malden: Wiley-Blackwell, 2012.

Richardson, Alan. *Literature, Education and Romanticism: Reading as Social Practice, 1780-1832.* Cambridge: Cambridge UP, 1994.

Roe, Nicholas. "Coleridge and John Thelwall: The Road to Nether Stowey." *The Coleridge Connection: Essays for Thomas McFarland.* Ed. Richard Gravil and Molly Lefebure. Houndmills: Macmillan, 1990.

——. *Wordsworth and Coleridge: The Radical Years.* Oxford: Clarendon P, 1988.

Scrivener, Michael. *The Cosmopolitan Ideal in the Age of Revolution and Reaction, 1776-1832.* London: Pickering and Chatto, 2007.

——. *Poetry and Reform: Periodical Verse from the English Democratic Press 1792-1834*. Detroit: Wayne State UP, 1992.

——. *Seditious Allegories: John Thelwall and Jacobin Writing*. University Park: Penn State UP, 2001.

Solomonescu, Yasmin. "Mute Records and Blank Legends: John Thelwall's 'Paternal Tears.'" *Romanticism* 16 (2010): 152-63.

——, ed. *John Thelwall: Critical Reassessments*. September 2011. Romantic Circles Praxis. 12 June 2012 <http://romantic.arhu.umd.edu/praxis/thelwall/index.html>.

Thompson, E.P. *The Romantics: England in a Revolutionary Age*. New York: New P, 1997.

Thompson, Judith. "Citizen Juan Thelwall: In the Footsteps of a Free-Range Radical." *Studies in Romanticism* 48 (2009): 67-100.

——. *John Thelwall in the Wordsworth Circle: The Silenced Partner*. New York: Palgrave Macmillan, 2012.

——. "Origins, Contexts, Transformations: Reviving *The Fairy of the Lake*." *John Thelwall in Performance: The Fairy of the Lake*. Ed. Judith Thompson. Romantic Circles Scholarly Resources. 2012.

——. "Resounding Romanticism: John Thelwall and the Science and Practice of Elocution." *Spheres of Action: Speech and Performance in Romantic Culture*. Ed. Alexander Dick and Angela Esterhammer. Toronto: U of Toronto P, 2009.

——. "The Prose of John Thelwall." *Blackwell Encyclopedia of Romantic Literature: Prose*. Oxford: Blackwell, 2011.

——. "Why Kendal? John Thelwall, Laker Poet?" *Wordsworth Circle* 40 (2009): 16-22.

Todd, Janet. *Mary Wollstonecraft: A Revolutionary Life*. London: Weidenfeld and Nicolson, 2000.

from the publisher

A name never says it all, but the word "broadview" expresses a good deal of the philosophy behind our company. We are open to a broad range of academic approaches and political viewpoints. We pay attention to the broad impact book publishing and book printing has in the wider world; we began using recycled stock more than a decade ago, and for some years now we have used 100% recycled paper for most titles. As a Canadian-based company we naturally publish a number of titles with a Canadian emphasis, but our publishing program overall is internationally oriented and broad-ranging. Our individual titles often appeal to a broad readership too; many are of interest as much to general readers as to academics and students.

Founded in 1985, Broadview remains a fully independent company owned by its shareholders—not an imprint or subsidiary of a larger multinational.

If you would like to find out more about Broadview and about the books we publish, please visit us at **www.broadviewpress.com**. And if you'd like to place an order through the site, we'd like to show our appreciation by extending a special discount to you: by entering the code below you will receive a 20% discount on purchases made through the Broadview website.

Discount code: **broadview20%**

Thank you for choosing Broadview.

Please note: this offer applies only to sales of bound books within the United States or Canada.

MIX
Paper from
responsible sources
FSC® C103567

LIST
of products used:

1,096 lb(s) of Rolland Opaque50
50% post-consumer

Generated by : www.cascades.com/calculator

Sources : Environmental Paper Network (EPN)
www.papercalculator.org

RESULTS
Based on the Cascades products you selected
compared to products in the industry made with
100% virgin fiber, your savings are:

 5 trees

 3,801 gal. US of water
41 days of water consumption

 963 lbs of waste
9 waste containers

 2,946 lbs CO2
5,587 miles driven

 14 MMBTU
70,663 60W light bulbs for one hour

 9 lbs NOx
emissions of one truck during 12
days